You've Got to Read This

You've Got to Read This

Contemporary American Writers Introduce Stories That Held Them in Awe

EDITED BY

RON HANSEN AND **JIM SHEPARD**

HARPER **PERENNIAL**

HARPER PERENNIAL

HarperCollins books may be purchased for educational, business, or sales promotional use. For information, please write: Special Markets Department, HarperCollins Publishers, Inc., 10 East 53rd Street, New York, NY 10022.

FIRST EDITION

Reprinted in Perennial 2000.

Designed by Alma Hochhauser Orenstein

Library of Congress Cataloging-in-Publication Data

You've got to read this: contemporary American writers introduce stories that held them in awe / edited by Ron Hansen and Jim Shepard. — 1st ed.

p. cm.

ISBN 0-06-055358-8—ISBN 0-06-098202-0 (pbk.) ISBN 978-0-06-098202-7

1. Short stories. 2. Short stories. I. Hansen, Ron, 1927–
II. Shepard, Jim.
PN6120.2.Y68 1994
813'.0108—dc20 94-14460

---

06 07 08 RRD 40 39 38 37 36

Contents

Introduction

We were far into the old have-you-ever-read? questions. We were sitting on the shaded second-floor porch of a house at the Bread Loaf Writers' Conference in Vermont, talking about great short stories, the kind that hold you spellbound, make your hair stand on end, that you finish with the feeling of being wrung out, transported, and far better off than you were when you began reading. We lobbed titles at Tim O'Brien, who lobbed a few of his own back. We mentioned "In Dreams Begin Responsibilities" by Delmore Schwartz, "A Distant Episode" by Paul Bowles, Jack London's "To Build a Fire," Shirley Jackson's "The Lottery." We were two fiction writers on staff at the conference, and university professors in English departments otherwise, so we had read a fair share of the short story masterpieces that find their way into anthologies, but there were so many others that were too little known. We'd both had the experience of having a friend say, "You've *got* to read this," as he or she handed us a story we'd never heard of, and on finishing it we'd often wondered how we'd felt complete without it. And countless times we and other writers we knew had been asked in question-and-answer sessions after fiction readings. What are *your* favorite stories? What do *you* recommend?

Wouldn't it be great, we thought, if there were an anthology based upon the stories that other writers feel passionate about?

Which is where this book began. We compiled a long list of our favorite writers and shortened it to a manageable size by confining it to American citizens. Then we wrote to ask if they'd introduce a story in English or English translation that left them breathless, held them in awe, or otherwise enthralled them when they first read it. We offered a wide latitude in these introductions: teacherly comments, reminiscences of that first encounter, anything that would provide an intriguing entrance into the story for the uninitiated. We approached some very famous and busy people so it was no surprise that a good many begged off, but a far greater number were pleased to have been asked and supplied us with a roster of one or three or six or nine stories they'd be happy to introduce.

We were then faced with hard choices, some of them frankly financial but others having to do with balance and variety and our own highly subjective judgment of which were the greater masterpieces. Often the decisions were painful. We could fill another anthology with the stories we had to reject or could not afford, but what we have here is just what we wanted. Look at the contents page and you'll find the familiar and the unfamiliar, the hundred-years-old and the just-yesterday, stories that are symphonies of emotion and stories that are the simplest of melodies, beautifully played.

You may want to hold off on reading an introduction if you have not read a particular story before, in case it includes those passages a first reader would most want hidden for the sake of surprise and suspense. Other stories may be well known to you. Then you may want to try a fresh reading with the introduction sitting helpfully beside you, like a friend. However you dip into this book, you'll be rewarded. There are riches everywhere. Wherever you wander you'll find an introducing author stepping forward with something he or she is passionate about, giving you the news about the way we live now, and saying to you: Here. Take it. You've *got* to read this.

RON HANSEN AND JIM SHEPARD

A Mother's Tale

by James Agee

Introduced by Annie Dillard

AGEE TELLS MOST OF THIS QUEER STORY IN THE SPOKEN VOICE OF A cow. You can scarcely believe anyone could read such a preposterous thing. When you finish, you can scarcely believe anyone could write such a grand thing.

What compels is Agee's probing. What compels is the sheer winning length of the narrative line. It keeps going; Agee pushes it. Agee pushes it from its worrisomely sentimental beginning ("Mama!") through its dangerously allegorical middle (The One Who Came Back "even invited them to examine his wounded heels") to its austere, murderously violent end ("*Kill the calves*").

At any point until that end, it could have been a bad story: a sermon, a tiresome allegory, or even, at very worst, a parable against meat-eating. It's a mined field, this cow's tale—it's risky, bold, and crazy—so you want to leap to your feet and cheer when Agee makes it through.

Two things break up the allegory that threatens to harden around the drama's players. Agee fully enlarges the figure of the broken-skulled steer who came back. His hide "was flung backward from his naked muscles by the wind of his running and now it lay around him in the dust like a ragged garment." His figural vividness finally replaces Christ's, for the moment, as Agee enters his own story at last and we join him there. And the allegory's simple equations open into interesting complexities. The steer's oracular commandments, in their controlled fury, urge resistance and murder. So the steer is like Christ, but he is not. The cattle are like people, but are people's victims. The Man With The Hammer is like God, like death, but is man. And man's life, too, is a dumb herding toward death. It's not Christian allegory, this story, it's good old-timey existentialism.

A Mother's Tale

James Agee

The calf ran up the little hill as fast as he could and stopped sharp. "Mama!" he cried, all out of breath. "What *is* it! What are they *doing!* Where are they *going!*"

Other spring calves came galloping too.

They all were looking up at her and awaiting her explanation, but she looked out over their excited eyes. As she watched the mysterious and majestic thing they had never seen before, her own eyes became even more than ordinarily still, and during the considerable moment before she answered, she scarcely heard their urgent questioning.

Far out along the autumn plain, beneath the sloping light, an immense drove of cattle moved eastward. They went at a walk, not very fast, but faster than they could imaginably enjoy. Those in front were compelled by those behind; those at the rear, with few exceptions, did their best to keep up; those who were locked within the herd could no more help moving than the particles inside a falling rock. Men on horses rode ahead, and alongside, and behind, or spurred their horses intensely back and forth, keeping the pace steady, and the herd in shape; and from man to man a dog sped back and forth incessantly as a shuttle, barking, incessantly, in a hysterical voice. Now and then one of the men shouted fiercely, and this like the shrieking of the dog was tinily audible above a low and awesome sound which seemed to come not from the multitude of hooves but from the center of the world, and above the sporadic bawlings and bellowings of the herd.

From the hillside this tumult was so distant that it only made more delicate the prodigious silence in which the earth and sky were held; and, from the hill, the sight was as modest as its sound. The herd was virtually hidden in the dust it raised, and could be known, in general, only by the horns, which pricked this flat sunlit dust like little briars. In one place a twist of the air revealed the trembling fabric of many backs; but it was only along the near edge of the mass that individual animals were discernible, small in a driven frieze, walking fast, stumbling and recovering, tossing their armed heads, or opening their skulls heavenward in one of those cries which reached the hillside long after the jaws were shut.

From where she watched, the mother could not be sure whether there were any she recognized. She knew that among them there must be a son of hers; she had not seen him since some previous spring, and she would not be seeing him again. Then the cries of the young ones impinged on her bemusement: "Where are they going?"

She looked into their ignorant eyes.

"Away," she said.

"Where?" they cried. "Where? Where?" her own son cried again.

She wondered what to say.

"On a long journey."

"But where *to?*" they shouted. "Yes, where *to?*" her son exclaimed, and she could see that he was losing his patience with her, as he always did when he felt she was evasive.

"I'm not sure," she said.

Their silence was so cold that she was unable to avoid their eyes for long.

"Well, not *really* sure. Because, you see," she said in her most reasonable tone, "I've never seen it with my own eyes, and that's the only way to *be* sure; isn't it."

They just kept looking at her. She could see no way out.

"But I've *heard* about it," she said with shallow cheerfulness, "from those who *have* seen it, and I don't suppose there's any good reason to doubt them."

She looked away over them again, and for all their interest in what she was about to tell them, her eyes so changed that they turned and looked, too.

The herd, which had been moving broadside to them, was being turned away, so slowly that like the turning of stars it could not quite be seen from one moment to the next; yet soon it was moving directly away from them, and even during the little while she spoke and they all watched after it, it steadily and very noticeably diminished, and the sounds of it as well.

"It happens always about this time of year," she said quietly while they watched. "Nearly all the men and horses leave, and go into the North and the West."

"Out on the range," her son said, and by his voice she knew what enchantment the idea already held for him.

"Yes," she said, "out on the range." And trying, impossibly, to imagine the range, they were touched by the breath of grandeur.

"And then before long," she continued, "everyone has been found, and brought into one place; and then . . . what you see, happens. All of them.

"Sometimes when the wind is right," she said more quietly, "you can hear them coming long before you can see them. It isn't even like a sound, at first. It's more as if something were moving far under the ground. It makes you uneasy. You wonder, why, what in the world can *that* be! Then you remember what it is and then you can really hear it. And then, finally, there they all are."

She could see this did not interest them at all.

"But where are they *going?*" one asked, a little impatiently.

"I'm coming to that," she said; and she let them wait. Then she spoke slowly but casually.

"They are on their way to a railroad."

There, she thought; that's for that look you all gave me when I said I wasn't sure. She waited for them to ask; they waited for her to explain.

"A railroad," she told them, "is great hard bars of metal lying side by side, or so they tell me, and they go on and on over the ground as far as the eye can see. And great wagons run on the metal bars on wheels, like wagon wheels but smaller, and these wheels are made of solid metal too. The wagons are much bigger than any wagon you've ever seen, as big as, big as sheds, they say, and they are pulled along on the iron bars by a terrible huge dark machine, with a loud scream."

"Big as *sheds?*" one of the calves said skeptically.

"Big *enough,* anyway," the mother said. "I told you I've never seen it myself. But those wagons are so big that several of us can get inside at once. And that's exactly what happens."

Suddenly she became very quiet, for she felt that somehow, she could not imagine just how, she had said altogether too much.

"Well, *what* happens," her son wanted to know. "What do you mean, *happens*."

She always tried hard to be a reasonably modern mother. It was probably better, she felt, to go on, than to leave them all full of imaginings and mystification. Besides, there was really nothing at all awful about what happened . . . if only one could know *why.*

"Well," she said, "it's nothing much, really. They just—why, when they all finally *get* there, why there are all the great cars waiting in a long line, and the big dark machine is up ahead . . . smoke comes out of it, they say . . . and . . . well, then, they just put us into the wagons, just as many as will fit in each wagon, and when everybody is in, why . . . " She hesitated, for again, though she couldn't be sure why, she was uneasy.

"Why then," her son said, "the train takes them away."

Hearing that word, she felt a flinching of the heart. Where had he picked it up, she wondered, and she gave him a shy and curious glance. Oh dear, she thought. I should never have even *begun* to explain. "Yes," she said, "when everybody is safely in, they slide the doors shut."

They were all silent for a little while. Then one of them asked thoughtfully, "Are they taking them somewhere they don't want to go?"

"Oh, I don't think so," the mother said. "I imagine it's very nice."

"*I* want to go," she heard her son say with ardor. "I want to go right now," he cried. "Can I, Mama? *Can* I? *Please?*" And looking into his eyes, she was overwhelmed by sadness.

"Silly thing," she said, "there'll be time enough for that when you're grown up. But what I very much hope," she went on, "is that instead of being chosen to go out on the range and to make the long journey, you will grow up to be very strong and bright so they will decide that you may stay here at home with Mother. And you, too," she added, speaking to the other little males; but she could not honestly wish this for any but her own, least of all for the eldest, strongest and most proud, for she knew how few are chosen.

She could see that what she said was not received with enthusiasm.

"But I want to go," her son said.

"Why?" she asked. "I don't think any of you realize that it's a great *honor* to be chosen to stay. A great privilege. Why, it's just the most ordinary ones are taken out onto the range. But only the very pick are chosen to stay here at home. If you want to go out on the range," she said in hurried and happy inspiration, "all you have to do is be ordinary and careless and silly. If you want to have even a chance to be chosen to stay, you have to try to be stronger and bigger and braver and brighter than anyone else, and that takes *hard work. Every day.* Do you see?" And she looked happily and hopefully from one to another. "Besides," she added, aware that they were not won over, "I'm told it's a very rough life out there, and the men are unkind.

"Don't you see," she said again; and she pretended to speak to all of them, but it was only to her son.

But he only looked at her. "Why do you want me to stay home?" he asked flatly; in their silence she knew the others were asking the same question.

"Because it's safe here," she said before she knew better, and realized she had put it in the most unfortunate way possible. "Not safe, not just that," she fumbled. "I mean . . . because here we *know* what happens, and what's going to happen, and there's never any doubt about it, never any reason to wonder, to worry. Don't you see? It's just *Home,*" and she put a smile on the word, "where we all know each other and are happy and well."

They were so merely quiet, looking back at her, that she felt they were neither won over nor alienated. Then she knew of her son that he, anyhow, was most certainly not persuaded, for he asked the question she most dreaded: "Where do they go on the train?" And hearing him, she knew that she would stop at nothing to bring that curiosity and eagerness, and that tendency toward skepticism, within safe bounds.

"Nobody knows," she said, and she added, in just the tone she knew would most sharply engage them, "Not for sure, anyway."

"What do you mean, *not for sure,*" her son cried. And the oldest, biggest calf repeated the question, his voice cracking.

The mother deliberately kept silence as she gazed out over the plain, and while she was silent they all heard the last they would ever hear of all those who were going away: one last great cry, as faint almost as a breath; the infinitesimal jabbing vituperation of the dog; the solemn muttering of the earth.

"Well," she said, after even this sound was entirely lost, "there was one who came back." Their instant, trustful eyes were too much for her. She added, "Or so they say."

They gathered a little more closely around her, for now she spoke very quietly.

"It was my great-grandmother who told me," she said. "She was told it by *her* great-grandmother, who claimed she saw it with her own eyes, though of course I can't vouch for that. Because of course I wasn't even dreamed of then; and Great-grandmother was so very, very old, you see, that you couldn't always be sure she knew quite *what* she was saying."

Now that she began to remember it more clearly, she was sorry she had committed herself to telling it.

"Yes," she said, "the story is, there was one, *just* one, who ever came back, and he told what happened on the train, and where the train went and what happened after. He told it all in a rush, they say, the last things first and every which way, but as it was finally sorted out and gotten into order by those who heard it and those they told it to, this is more or less what happened:

"He said that after the men had gotten just as many of us as they could into the car he was in, so that their sides pressed tightly together and nobody could lie down, they slid the door shut with a startling rattle and a bang, and then there was a sudden jerk, so strong they might have fallen except that they were packed so closely together, and the car began to move. But after it had moved only a little way, it stopped as suddenly as it had started, so that they all nearly fell down again. You see, they were just moving up the next car that was joined on behind, to put more of us into it. He could see it all between the boards of the car, because the boards were built a little apart from each other, to let in air."

Car, her son said again to himself. Now he would never forget the word.

"He said that then, for the first time in his life, he became very badly frightened, he didn't know why. But he was sure, at that moment, that there was something dreadfully to be afraid of. The others felt this same great fear. They called out loudly to those who were being put into the car behind, and the others called back, but it was no use; those who were getting aboard were between narrow white fences and then were walking up a narrow slope and the man kept jabbing them as they do when they are in an unkind humor, and there was no way to go but on into the car. There was no way to get out of the car, either: he tried, with all his might, and he was the one nearest the door.

"After the next car behind was full, and the door was shut, the train jerked forward again, and stopped again, and they put more of us into still another car, and so on, and on, until all the starting and stopping no longer frightened anybody; it was just something uncomfortable that was never going to stop, and they began instead to realize how hungry and thirsty they were. But there was no food and no water, so they just had to put up with this; and about the time they became resigned to going without their suppers (for by now it was almost dark), they heard a sudden and terrible scream which frightened them even more deeply than anything had frightened them before, and the train began to move again, and they braced their legs once more for the jolt when it would stop, but this time, instead of stopping, it began to go fast, and then even faster, so fast that the ground nearby slid past like a flooded creek and the whole country, he claimed, began to move too, turning slowly around a far mountain as if it were all one great wheel. And then there was a strange kind of disturbance inside the car, he said, or even inside his very bones. He felt as if everything in him was *falling,* as if he had been filled full of a heavy liquid that all wanted to flow one way, and all the others were leaning as he was leaning, away from this queer heaviness that was trying to pull them over, and then just as suddenly this leaning heaviness was gone and they nearly fell again before they could stop leaning against it. He could never understand what this was, but it too happened so many times that they all got used to it, just as they got used to seeing the country turn like a slow wheel, and just as they got used to the long cruel screams of the engine, and the steady iron noise beneath them which made the cold darkness so fearsome, and the hunger and the thirst and the continual standing up, and the moving on and on and on as if they would never stop."

"*Didn't* they ever stop?" one asked.

"Once in a great while," she replied. "Each time they did," she said, "he thought, Oh, now *at last! At last* we can get out and stretch our tired legs and lie down! *At last* we'll be given food and water! But they never let them out. And they never gave them food or water. They never even cleaned up under them. They had to stand in their manure and in the water they made."

"Why did the train stop?" her son asked; and with somber gratification she saw that he was taking all this very much to heart.

"He could never understand why," she said. "Sometimes men would walk up and down alongside the cars, and the more nervous and the more trustful of us would call out; but they were only looking around, they never seemed to do anything. Sometimes he could see many houses and bigger buildings together where people lived. Sometimes it was far out in the country and after they had stood still for a long time they would hear a little noise which quickly became louder, and then became suddenly a noise so loud it stopped their breathing, and during this noise something black would go by, very close, and so fast it couldn't be seen. And then it was gone as suddenly as it had appeared, and the noise became small, and then in the silence their train would start up again.

"Once, he tells us, something very strange happened. They were standing still, and cars of a very different kind began to move slowly past. These cars were not red, but black, with many glass windows like those in a house; and he says they were as full of human beings as the car he was in was full of our kind. And one of these people looked into his eyes and smiled, as if he liked him, or as if he knew only too well how hard the journey was.

"So by his account it happens to them, too," she said, with a certain pleased vindictiveness. "Only they were sitting down at their ease, not standing. And the one who smiled was eating."

She was still, trying to think of something; she couldn't quite grasp the thought.

"But didn't they *ever* let them out?" her son asked.

The oldest calf jeered. "Of *course* they did. He came back, didn't he? How would he ever come back if he didn't get out?"

"They didn't let them out," she said, "for a long, long time."

"How long?"

"So long, and he was so tired, he could never quite be sure. But he said that it turned from night to day and from day to night and back again several times over, with the train moving nearly all of this time, and that when it finally stopped, early one morning, they were all so tired and so discouraged that they hardly even noticed any longer, let alone felt any hope that anything would change for them, ever again; and then all of a sudden men came up and put up a wide walk and unbarred the door and slid it open, and it was the most wonderful and happy moment of his life when he saw the door open, and walked into the open air with all his joints trembling, and drank the water and ate the delicious food they had ready for him; it was worth the whole terrible journey."

Now that these scenes came clear before her, there was a faraway shining in her eyes, and her voice, too, had something in it of the faraway.

"When they had eaten and drunk all they could hold they lifted up their heads and looked around, and everything they saw made them happy. Even the trains made them cheerful now, for now they were no longer afraid of them. And though these trains were forever breaking to pieces and joining again with other broken pieces, with shufflings and clashings and rude cries, they hardly paid them attention any more, they were so pleased to be in their new home, and so surprised and delighted to find they were among thousands upon thousands of strangers of their own kind, all lifting up their voices in peacefulness and thanksgiving, and they were so wonderstruck by all they could see, it was so beautiful and so grand.

"For he has told us that now they lived among fences as white as bone, so many, and so spiderishly complicated, and shining so pure, that there's no use trying even to hint at the beauty and the splendor of it to anyone who knows only the pitiful little outfittings of a ranch. Beyond these mazy fences, through the dark and bright smoke which continually turned along the sunlight, dark buildings stood shoulder to shoulder in a wall as huge and proud as mountains. All through the air, all the time, there was an iron humming like the humming of the iron bar after it has been struck to tell the men it is time to eat, and in all the air, all the time, there was that same strange kind of iron strength which makes the silence before lightning so different from all other silence.

"Once for a little while the wind shifted and blew over them straight from the great buildings, and it brought a strange and very powerful smell which confused and disturbed them. He could never quite describe this smell, but he has told us it was unlike anything he had ever known before. It smelled like old fire, he said, and old blood and fear and darkness and sorrow and most terrible and brutal force and something else, something in it that made him want to run away. This sudden uneasiness and this wish to run away swept through every one of them, he tells us, so that they were all moved at once as restlessly as so many leaves in a wind, and there was great worry in their voices. But soon the leaders among them concluded that it was simply the way men must smell when there are a great many of them living together. Those dark buildings must be crowded very full of men, they decided, probably as many thousands of them, indoors, as there were of us, outdoors; so it was no wonder their smell was so strong and, to our kind, so unpleasant. Besides, it was so clear now in every other way that men were not as we had always supposed, but were doing everything they knew how to make us comfortable and happy, that we ought to just put up with their smell, which after all they couldn't help, any more than we could help our own. Very likely men didn't like the way we smelled, any more than we liked theirs. They passed along these ideas to the others, and soon everyone felt more calm, and then the wind changed again, and the fierce smell no longer came to them, and the smell of their own kind was back again, very strong of course, in such a crowd, but ever so homey and comforting, and everyone felt easy again.

"They were fed and watered so generously, and treated so well, and the majesty and the loveliness of this place where they had all come to rest was so far beyond anything they had ever known or dreamed of, that many of the simple and ignorant, whose memories were short, began to wonder whether that whole difficult journey, or even their whole lives up to now, had ever really been. Hadn't it all been just shadows, they murmured, just a bad dream?

"Even the sharp ones, who knew very well it had all really happened, began to figure that everything up to now had been made so full of pain only so that all they had come to now might seem all the sweeter and the more glorious. Some of the oldest and deepest were even of a mind that all the puzzle and tribulation of the journey had been sent us as a kind of harsh trying or proving of our worthiness; and that it was entirely fitting and proper that we could earn our way through to such rewards as these, only through suffering, and through being patient under pain which was beyond our understanding; and that now at the last, to those who had borne all things well, all things were made known: for the mystery of suffering stood revealed in joy. And now as they looked back over all that was past, all their sorrows and bewilderments seemed so little and so fleeting that, from the simplest among them even to the most wise, they could feel only the kind of amused pity we feel toward the very young when, with the first thing that hurts them or they are forbidden, they are sure there is nothing kind or fair in all creation, and carry on accordingly, raving and grieving as if their hearts would break."

She glanced among them with an indulgent smile, hoping the little lesson would sink home. They seemed interested but somewhat dazed. I'm talking way over their heads, she realized. But by now she herself was too deeply absorbed in her story to modify it much. *Let* it be, she thought, a little impatient; it's over *my* head, for that matter.

"They had hardly before this even wondered that they were alive," she went on, "and now all of a sudden they felt they understood *why* they were. This made them very happy, but they were still only beginning to enjoy this new wisdom when quite a new and different kind of restiveness ran among them. Before they quite knew it they were all moving once again, and now they realized that they were being moved, once more, by men, toward still some other place and purpose they could not know. But during these last hours they had been so well that now they felt no uneasiness, but all moved forward calm and sure toward better things still to come; he has told us that he no longer felt as if he were being driven, even as it became clear that they were going toward the shade of those great buildings; but guided.

"He was guided between fences which stood ever more and more narrowly near each other, among companions who were pressed ever more and more closely against one another; and now as he felt their warmth against him it was not uncomfortable, and his pleasure in it was not through any need to be close among others through anxiousness, but was a new kind of strong and gentle delight, at being so very close, so deeply of his own kind, that it seemed as if the very breath and heartbeat of each one were being exchanged through all that multitude, and each was another, and others were each, and each was a multitude, and the multitude was one. And quieted and made mild within this melting, they now entered the cold shadow cast by the buildings, and now with every step the smell of the buildings grew stronger, and in the darkening air the glittering of the fences was ever more queer.

"And now as they were pressed ever more intimately together he could see ahead of him a narrow gate, and he was strongly pressed upon from either side and from behind, and went in eagerly, and now he was between two fences so narrowly set that he brushed either fence with either flank, and walked alone, seeing just one other ahead of him, and knowing of just one other behind him, and for a moment the strange thought came to him, that the one ahead was his father, and that the one behind was the son he had never begotten.

"And now the light was so changed that he knew he must have come inside one of the gloomy and enormous buildings, and the smell was so much stronger that it seemed almost to burn his nostrils, and the smell and the somber new light blended together and became some other thing again, beyond his describing to us except to say that the whole air beat with it like one immense heart and it was as if the beating of this heart were pure violence infinitely manifolded upon violence: so that the uneasy feeling stirred in him again that it would be wise to turn around and run out of this place just as fast and as far as ever he could go. This he heard, as if he were telling it to himself at the top of his voice, but it came from somewhere so deep and so dark inside him that he could only hear the shouting of it as less than a whisper, as just a hot and chilling breath, and he scarcely heeded it, there was so much else to attend to.

"For as he walked along in this sudden and complete loneliness, he tells us, this wonderful knowledge of being one with all his race meant less and less to him, and in its place came something still more wonderful: he knew what it was to be himself alone, a creature separate and different from any other, who had never been before, and would never be again. He could feel this in his whole weight as he walked, and in each foot as he put it down and gave his weight to it and moved above it, and in every muscle as he moved, and it was a pride which lifted him up and made him feel large, and a pleasure which pierced him through. And as he began with such wondering delight to be aware of his own exact singleness in this world, he also began to understand (or so he thought) just why these fences were set so very narrow, and just why he was walking all by himself. It stole over him, he tells us, like the feeling of a slow cool wind, that he was being guided toward some still more wonderful reward or revealing, up ahead, which he could not of course imagine, but he was sure it was being held in store for him alone.

"Just then the one ahead of him fell down with a great sigh, and was so quickly taken out of the way that he did not even have to shift the order of his hooves as he walked on. The sudden fall and the sound of that sigh dismayed him, though, and something within him told him that it would be wise to look up: and there he saw Him.

"A little bridge ran crosswise above the fences. He stood on this bridge with His feet as wide apart as He could set them. He wore spattered trousers but from the belt up He was naked and as wet as rain. Both arms were raised high above His head and in both hands He held an enormous Hammer. With a grunt which was hardly like the voice of a human being, and with all His strength, He brought this Hammer down onto the forehead of our friend: who, in a blinding blazing, heard from his own mouth the beginning of a gasping sigh; then there was only darkness."

Oh, this is *enough!* it's *enough!* she cried out within herself, seeing their terrible young eyes. How *could* she have been so foolish as to tell so much!

"What happened then?" she heard, in the voice of the oldest calf, and she was horrified. This shining in their eyes: was it only excitement? no pity? no fear?

"What happened?" two others asked.

Very well, she said to herself. I've gone so far; now I'll go the rest of the way. She decided not to soften it, either. She'd teach them a lesson they wouldn't forget in a hurry.

"Very well," she was surprised to hear herself say aloud.

"How long he lay in this darkness he couldn't know, but when he began to come out of it, all he knew was the most unspeakably dreadful pain. He was upside down and very slowly swinging and turning, for he was hanging by the tendons of his heels from great frightful hooks, and he has told us that the feeling was as if his hide were being torn from him inch by inch, in one piece. And then as he became more clearly aware he found that this was exactly what was happening. Knives would sliver and slice along both flanks, between the hide and the living flesh; then there was a moment of most precious relief; then red hands seized his hide and there was a jerking of the hide and a tearing of tissue which it was almost as terrible to hear as to feel, turning his whole body and the poor head at the bottom of it; and then the knives again.

"It was so far beyond anything he had ever known unnatural and amazing that he hung there through several more such slicings and jerkings and tearings before he was fully able to take it all in: then, with a scream, and a supreme straining of all his strength, he tore himself from the hooks and collapsed sprawling to the floor and, scrambling right to his feet, charged the men with the knives. For just a moment they were so astonished and so terrified they could not move. Then they moved faster than he had ever known men could—and so did all the other men who chanced to be in his way. He ran down a glowing floor of blood and down endless corridors which were hung with the bleeding carcasses of our kind and with bleeding fragments of carcasses, among blood-clothed men who carried bleeding weapons, and out of that vast room into the open, and over and through one fence after another, shoving aside many an astounded stranger and shouting out warnings as he ran, and away up the railroad toward the West.

"How he ever managed to get away, and how he ever found his way home, we can only try to guess. It's told that he scarcely knew, himself, by the time he came to this part of his story. He was impatient with those who interrupted him to ask about that, he had so much more important things to tell them, and by then he was so exhausted and so far gone that he could say nothing very clear about the little he did know. But we can realize that he must have had really tremendous strength, otherwise he couldn't have outlived the Hammer; and that strength such as his—which we simply don't see these days, it's of the olden time—is capable of things our own strongest and bravest would sicken to dream of. But there was something even stronger than his strength. There was his righteous fury, which nothing could stand up against, which brought him out of that fearful place. And there was his high and burning and heroic purpose, to keep him safe along the way, and to guide him home, and to keep the breath of life in him until he could warn us. He did manage to tell us that he just followed the railroad, but how he chose one among the many which branched out from that place, he couldn't say. He told us, too, that from time to time he recognized shapes of mountains and other landmarks, from his journey by train, all reappearing backward and with a changed look and hard to see, too (for he was shrewd enough to travel mostly at night), but still recognizable. But that isn't enough to account for it. For he has told us, too, that he simply *knew* the way; that he didn't hesitate one moment in choosing the right line of railroad, or even think of it as choosing; and that the landmarks didn't really guide him, but just made him the more sure of what he was already sure of; and that whenever he *did* encounter human beings—and during the later stages of his journey, when he began to doubt he would live to tell us, he traveled day and night—they never so much as moved to make him trouble, but stopped dead in their tracks, and their jaws fell open.

"And surely we can't wonder that their jaws fell open. I'm sure yours would, if you had seen him as he arrived, and I'm very glad I wasn't there to see it, either, even though it is said to be the greatest and most momentous day of all the days that ever were or shall be. For we have the testimony of eyewitnesses, how he looked, and it is only too vivid, even to hear of. He came up out of the East as much staggering as galloping (for by now he was so worn out by pain and exertion and loss of blood that he could hardly stay upright), and his heels were so piteously torn by the hooks that his hooves doubled under more often than not, and in his broken forehead the mark of the Hammer was like the socket for a third eye.

"He came to the meadow where the great trees made shade over the water. 'Bring them all together!' he cried out, as soon as he could find breath. 'All!' Then he drank; and then he began to speak to those who were already there: for as soon as he saw himself in the water it was as clear to him as it was to those who watched him that there was no time left to send for the others. His hide was all gone from his head and his neck and his forelegs and his chest and most of one side and a part of the other side. It was flung backward from his naked muscles by the wind of his running and now it lay around him in the dust like a ragged garment. They say there is no imagining how terrible and in some way how grand the eyeball is when the skin has been taken entirely from around it: his eyes, which were bare in this way, also burned with pain, and with the final energies of his life, and with his desperate concern to warn us while he could: and he rolled his eyes wildly while he talked, or looked piercingly from one to another of the listeners, interrupting himself to cry out, '*Believe* me! Oh, *believe* me!' For it had evidently never occurred to him that he might not be believed, and must make this last great effort, in addition to all he had gone through for us, to *make* himself believed; so that he groaned with sorrow and with rage and railed at them without tact or mercy for their slowness to believe. He had scarcely what you could call a voice left, but with this relic of a voice he shouted and bellowed and bullied us and insulted us, in the agony of his concern. While he talked he bled from the mouth, and the mingled blood and saliva hung from his chin like the beard of a goat.

"Some say that with his naked face, and his savage eyes, and that beard and the hide lying off his bare shoulders like shabby clothing, he looked almost human. But others feel this is an irreverence even to think; and others, that it is a poor compliment to pay the one who told us, at such cost to himself, the true ultimate purpose of Man. Some did not believe he had ever come from our ranch in the first place, and of course he was so different from us in appearance and even in his voice, and so changed from what he might ever have looked or sounded like before, that nobody could recognize him for sure, though some were sure they did. Others suspected that he had been sent among us with his story for some mischievous and cruel purpose, and the fact that they could not imagine what this purpose might be, made them, naturally, all the more suspicious. Some believed he was actually a man, trying—and none too successfully, they said—to disguise himself as one of us; and again the fact that they could not imagine why a man would do this, made them all the more uneasy. There were quite a few who doubted that anyone who could get into such bad condition as he was in, was fit even to give reliable information, let alone advice, to those in good health. And some whispered, even while he spoke, that he had turned lunatic; and many came to believe this. It wasn't only that his story was so fantastic; there was good reason to wonder, many felt, whether anybody in his right mind would go to such trouble for others. But even those who did not believe him listened intently, out of curiosity to hear so wild a tale, and out of the respect it is only proper to show any creature who is in the last agony.

"What he told, was what I have just told you. But his purpose was away beyond just the telling. When they asked questions, no matter how curious or suspicious or idle or foolish, he learned, toward the last, to answer them with all the patience he could and in all the detail he could remember. He even invited them to examine his wounded heels and the pulsing wound in his head as closely as they pleased. He even begged them to, for he knew that before everything else, he must be believed. For unless we could believe him, wherever could we find any reason, or enough courage, to do the hard and dreadful things he told us we must do!

"It was only these things, he cared about. Only for these, he came back."

Now clearly remembering what these things were, she felt her whole being quail. She looked at the young ones quickly and as quickly looked away.

"While he talked," she went on, "and our ancestors listened, men came quietly among us; one of them shot him. Whether he was shot in kindness or to silence him is an endlessly disputed question which will probably never be settled. Whether, even, he died of the shot, or through his own great pain and weariness (for his eyes, they say, were glazing for some time before the men came), we will never be sure. Some suppose even that he may have died of his sorrow and his concern for us. Others feel that he had quite enough to die of, without that. All these things are tangled and lost in the disputes of those who love to theorize and to argue. There is no arguing about his dying words, though; they were very clearly remembered:

" *'Tell them! Believe!'* "

After a while her son asked, "What did he tell them to do?"

She avoided his eyes. "There's a great deal of disagreement about that, too," she said after a moment. "You see, he was so very tired."

They were silent.

"So tired," she said, "some think that toward the end, he really *must* have been out of his mind."

"Why?" asked her son.

"Because he was so tired out and so badly hurt."

They looked at her mistrustfully.

"And because of what he told us to do."

"What did he tell us to do?" her son asked again.

Her throat felt dry. "Just . . . things you can hardly bear even to think of. That's all."

They waited. "Well, *what?*" her son asked in a cold, accusing voice.

" *'Each one is himself,'* " she said shyly. " *'Not of the herd. Himself alone.'* That's one."

"What else?"

" *'Obey nobody. Depend on none.'* "

"What else?"

She found that she was moved. " *'Break down the fences,'* " she said less shyly. " *'Tell everybody, everywhere.'* "

"Where?"

"Everywhere. You see, he thought there must be ever so many more of us than we had ever known."

They were silent. "What else?" her son asked.

" *'For if even a few do not hear me, or disbelieve me, we are all betrayed.'* "

"Betrayed?"

"He meant, doing as men want us to. Not for ourselves, or the good of each other."

They were puzzled.

"Because, you see, he felt there was no other way." Again her voice altered: " *'All who are put on the range are put onto trains. All who are put onto trains meet The Man With The Hammer. All who stay home are kept there to breed others to go onto the range, and so betray themselves and their kind and their children forever.*

" *'We are brought into this life only to be victims; and there is no other way for us unless we save ourselves.'*

"Do you understand?"

Still they were puzzled, she saw; and no wonder, poor things. But now the ancient lines rang in her memory, terrible and brave. They made her somehow proud. She began actually to want to say them.

" 'Never be taken,' " she said. *" 'Never be driven. Let those who can, kill Man. Let those who cannot, avoid him.' "*

She looked around at them.

"What else?" her son asked, and in his voice there was a rising valor.

She looked straight into his eyes. *" 'Kill the yearlings,' "* she said very gently. *" 'Kill the calves.' "*

She saw the valor leave his eyes.

"Kill us?"

She nodded. *" 'So long as Man holds dominion over us,' "* she said. And in dread and amazement she heard herself add, *" 'Bear no young.' "*

With this they all looked at her at once in such a way that she loved her child, and all these others, as never before; and there dilated within her such a sorrowful and marveling grandeur that for a moment she saw nothing, and heard nothing except her own inward whisper, "Why, *I* am one alone. And of the herd, too. Both at once. All one."

Her son's voice brought her back: "Did they do what he told them to?"

The oldest one scoffed, "Would we be here, if they had?"

"They say some did," the mother replied. "Some tried. Not all."

"What did the men do to them?" another asked.

"I don't know," she said. "It was such a very long time ago."

"Do you believe it?" asked the oldest calf.

"There are some who believe it," she said.

"Do *you?*"

"I'm told that far back in the wildest corners of the range there are some of us, mostly very, very old ones, who have never been taken. It's said that they meet, every so often, to talk and just to think together about the heroism and the terror of two sublime Beings, The One Who Came Back, and The Man With The Hammer. Even here at home, some of the old ones, and some of us who are just old-fashioned, believe it, or parts of it anyway. I know there are some who say that a hollow at the center of the forehead—a sort of shadow of the Hammer's blow—is a sign of very special ability. And I remember how Great-grandmother used to sing an old, pious song, let's see now, yes, 'Be not like dumb-driven cattle, be a hero in the strife.' But there aren't many. Not any more."

"Do *you* believe it?" the oldest calf insisted; and now she was touched to realize that every one of them, from the oldest to the youngest, needed very badly to be sure about that.

"Of course not, silly," she said; and all at once she was overcome by a most curious shyness, for it occurred to her that in the course of time, this young thing might be bread to her. "It's just an old, old legend." With a tender little laugh she added, lightly, "We use it to frighten children with."

By now the light was long on the plain and the herd was only a fume of gold near the horizon. Behind it, dung steamed, and dust sank gently to the shattered ground. She looked far away for a moment, wondering. Something—it was like a forgotten word on the tip of the tongue. She felt the sudden chill of the late afternoon and she wondered what she had been wondering about. "Come, children," she said briskly, "it's high time for supper." And she turned away; they followed.

The trouble was, her son was thinking, you could never trust her. If she said a thing was so, she was probably just trying to get her way with you. If she said a thing wasn't so, it probably was so. But you never could be sure. Not without seeing for yourself. I'm going to go, he told himself; I don't care *what* she wants. And if it isn't so, why then I'll live on the range and make the great journey and find out what *is* so. And if what she told was true, why then I'll know ahead of time and the one I will charge is The Man With The Hammer. I'll put Him and His Hammer out of the way forever, and that will make me an even better hero than The One Who Came Back.

So, when his mother glanced at him in concern, not quite daring to ask her question, he gave her his most docile smile, and snuggled his head against her, and she was comforted.

The littlest and youngest of them was doing double skips in his efforts to keep up with her. Now that he wouldn't be interrupting her, and none of the big ones would hear and make fun of him, he shyly whispered his question, so warmly moistly ticklish that she felt as if he were licking her ear.

"What is it, darling?" she asked, bending down.

"What's a train?"

Guy de Maupassant

by Isaac Babel

Introduced by Francine Prose

IF MYSTERIES, BY DEFINITION, CANNOT BE EXPLAINED, THE NEXT BEST thing—or the better thing—is to re-create them.

Isaac Babel's "Guy de Maupassant" does precisely that. This brilliant story addresses the linked or parallel mysteries of art and of sex. By its shocking conclusion, readers will have experienced something beyond the cerebral, something visceral, inexpressible, the shivery mix of pure clarity and dizzying confusion that we feel in the presence of mystery, and that both art and sex can provide.

Penniless, gifted, dreamy, the story's young narrator is a perfect Babel hero: the world is denying and promising him everything at once. Housed with a struggling literature teacher in a "yellow, frozen, evil-smelling" quarter of St. Petersburg, he's hired to help a rich man's passionate, plump, somewhat dopey wife with her translation from the French of de Maupassant's work. Their literary labors are interrupted and augmented by the distractions of proximity, fantasy, and flesh. And after a night of wine, flirting, and translating one of the French writer's steamier stories, our hero goes home, opens a biography of de Maupassant, and has a moment in which Babel gives us one of the most meaningful, complicated, beautiful, troubling, and absolutely irreducible passages in all of literature.

But plot summary doesn't come close to touching a Babel story. Even among writers, Babel was a true fanatic, a tireless reviser who would do fifty versions of a phrase and whose ranting about paragraphing and word choice, as reported in Paustovsky's *Years of Hope,* should be embroidered on a sampler and hung over every desk. ("I go over each sentence, time and again. . . . You have to keep your eye on the job because words are very sly, the rubbishy ones go into hiding and you have to dig them out. . . . Only a genius can afford two adjectives to one noun.") "Guy de Maupassant," too, is full of writing advice—"No iron can stab the heart with such force as a period put just at the right place"—pronouncements in which we hear Babel boasting and scaring himself, at once.

Knowing that every word has been put on trial fifty times does make one stop and wonder why it was chosen, and so often spared. Having written that way, Babel rewards you for reading that way. "Guy de Maupassant" has amazing details, astonishing descriptions, and studying it detail by detail, word by word, does bring us closer to the inner workings that make the story tick, or at least closer than we get from plot summary.

But not even close reading will take us all the way to the heart of the story—to which there is no access, except through some understanding that surpasses not merely the literary but the rational as well.

That is why I started by talking about a mystery.

There is much to be said about "Guy de Maupassant," about art and sex, literature, death, complication, the dark side of art and sex and literature, knowledge, experience . . . etc. (Several times, I've seen writers start to hyperventilate before giving up on trying to explain why Babel was such a great writer.)

But finally there is nothing to say. We can only reread the story—as if this time, at last, we will seize and reduce what was huge and inchoate before.

"Guy de Maupassant" is great art and defies all explanation while teasing us with elusive hints of higher information. This story explodes the silly idea that there can be any limit on how much larger and deeper something can be than the sum of its separate parts.

Guy de Maupassant

Isaac Babel

In the winter of 1916 I found myself in St. Petersburg with a forged passport and not a cent to my name. Alexey Kazantsev, a teacher of Russian literature, took me into his house.

He lived on a yellow, frozen, evil-smelling street in the Peski district. The miserable salary he received was padded out a bit by doing translations from the Spanish. Blasco Ibáñez was just becoming famous at that time.

Kazantsev had never so much as passed through Spain, but his love for that country filled his whole being. He knew every castle, every garden, and every river in Spain. There were many other people huddling around Kazantsev, all of them, like myself, flung out of the round of ordinary life. We were half-starved. From time to time the yellow press would publish, in the smallest print, unimportant news-items we had written.

I spent my mornings hanging around the morgues and police stations.

Kazantsev was happier than any of us, for he had a country of his own—Spain.

In November I was given the chance to become a clerk at the Obukhov Mills. It was a rather good position, and would have exempted me from military service.

I refused to become a clerk.

Even in those days, when I was twenty years old, I had told myself: better starve, go to jail, or become a bum than spend ten hours every day behind a desk in an office.

There was nothing particularly laudable in my resolve, but I have never broken it and I never will. The wisdom of my ancestors was firmly lodged in my head: we are born to enjoy our work, our fights, and our love; we are born for that and for nothing else.

Listening to my bragging, Kazantsev ruffled the short yellow fluff on the top of his head. The horror in his stare was mixed with admiration.

At Christmastime we had luck. Bendersky the lawyer, who owned a publishing house called Halcyon, decided to publish a new edition of Maupassant's works. His wife Raïsa tried her hand at the translation, but nothing came of her lofty ambition.

Kazantsev, who was known as a translator of Spanish, had been asked whether he could recommend someone to assist Raïsa Mikhaylovna. He told them of me.

The next day, in someone else's coat, I made my way to the Benderskys'. They lived at the corner of the Nevsky and the Moyka, in a house of Finland granite adorned with pink columns, crenellations and coats-of-arms worked in stone.

Bankers without a history and catapulted out of nowhere, converted Jews who had grown rich selling materials to the army, they put up these pretentious mansions in St. Petersburg before the war.

There was a red carpet on the stairs. On the landings, upon their hind legs, stood plush bears. Crystal lamps burned in their open mouths.

The Benderskys lived on the second floor. A high-breasted maid with a white cap on her head opened the door. She led me into a drawing-room decorated in the old Slav style. Blue paintings by Roerich depicting prehistoric stones and monsters hung on the walls. On stands in the corners stood ancestral icons.

The high-breasted maid moved smoothly and majestically. She had an excellent figure, was nearsighted and rather haughty. In her open gray eyes one saw a petrified lewdness. She moved slowly. I thought: when she makes love she must move with unheard-of agility. The brocade portiere over the doorway suddenly swayed, and a black-haired woman with pink eyes and a wide bosom entered the room. It was easy to recognize in Raïsa Bendersky one of those charming Jewesses who have come to us from Kiev and Poltava, from the opulent steppe-towns full of chestnut trees and acacias. The money made by their clever husbands is transformed by these women into a pink layer of fat on the belly, the back of the neck, and the well-rounded shoulders. Their subtle sleepy smiles drive officers from the local garrisons crazy.

"Maupassant," Raïsa said to me, "is the only passion of my life."

Trying to keep the swaying of her great hips under control, she left the room and returned with a translation of "Miss Harriet." In her translation not even a trace was left of Maupassant's free-flowing sentences with their fragrance of passion. Raïsa Bendersky took pains to write correctly and precisely, and all that resulted was something loose and lifeless, the way Jews wrote Russian in the old days.

I took the manuscript with me, and in Kazantsev's attic, among my sleeping friends, spent the night cutting my way through the tangled undergrowth of her prose. It was not such dull work as it might seem. A phrase is born into the world both good and bad at the same time. The secret lies in a slight, an almost invisible twist. The lever should rest in your hand, getting warm, and you can only turn it once, not twice.

Next morning I took back the corrected manuscript. Raïsa wasn't lying when she told me that Maupassant was her sole passion. She sat motionless, her hands clasped, as I read it to her. Her satin hands drooped to the floor, her forehead paled, and the lace between her constricted breasts danced and heaved.

"How did you do it?"

I began to speak of style, of the army of words, of the army in which all kinds of weapons may come into play. No iron can stab the heart with such force as a period put just at the right place. She listened with her head down and her painted lips half open. In her hair, pressed smooth, divided by a parting and looking like patent leather, shone a dark gleam. Her legs in tight-fitting stockings, with their strong soft calves, were planted wide apart on the carpet.

The maid, glancing to the side with her petrified wanton eyes, brought in breakfast on a tray.

The glassy rays of the Petersburg sun lay on the pale and uneven carpet. Twenty-nine volumes of Maupassant stood on the shelf above the desk. The sun with its fingers of melting dissolution touched the morocco backs of the books—the magnificent grave of a human heart.

Coffee was served in blue cups, and we started translating "Idyl." Everyone remembers the story of the youthful, hungry carpenter who sucked the breast of the stout nursing-mother to relieve her of the milk with which she was overladen. It happened in a train going from Nice to Marseille, at noon on a very hot day, in the land of roses, the birthplace of roses, where beds of flowers flow down to the seashore.

I left the Benderskys with a twenty-five rouble advance. That night our crowd at Peski got as drunk as a flock of drugged geese. Between drinks we spooned up the best caviar, and then changed over to liver sausage. Half-soused, I began to berate Tolstoy.

"He turned yellow, your Count; he was afraid. His religion was all fear. He was frightened by the cold, by old age, by death; and he made himself a warm coat out of his faith."

"Go on, go on," Kazantsev urged, swaying his birdlike head.

We fell asleep on the floor beside our beds. I dreamed of Katya, a forty-year-old washerwoman who lived a floor below us. We went to her every morning for our hot water. I had never seen her face distinctly, but in my dream we did god-awful things together. We almost destroyed each other with kisses. The very next morning I couldn't restrain myself from going to her for hot water.

I saw a wan woman, a shawl across her chest, with ash-gray hair and labor-worn, withered hands.

From then on I took my breakfast at the Benderskys' every day. A new stove, herrings, and chocolate appeared in our attic. Twice Raïsa took me out in her carriage for drives to the islands. I couldn't prevent myself from telling her all about my childhood. To my amazement the story turned out to be very sordid. From under her moleskin cowl her gleaming, frightened eyes stared at me. The rusty fringe of her eyelashes quivered with pity.

I met Raïsa's husband, a yellow-faced Jew with a bald skull and a flat, powerful body that seemed always poised obliquely, ready for flight.

There were rumors about his being close to Rasputin. The enormous profits he made from war supplies drove him almost crazy, giving him the expression of a person with a fixed hallucination. His eyes never remained still: it seemed that reality was lost to him for ever. Raïsa was embarrassed whenever she had to introduce him to new acquaintances. Because of my youth I noticed this a full week later than I should have.

After the New Year Raïsa's two sisters arrived from Kiev. One day I took along the manuscript of "*L'Aveu*" and, not finding Raïsa at home, returned that evening. They were at dinner. Silvery, neighing laughter and excited male voices came from the dining-room. In rich houses without tradition dinners are always noisy. It was a Jewish noise, rolling and tripping and ending up on a melodious, singsong note. Raïsa came out to me in evening dress, her back bare. Her feet stepped awkwardly in wavering patent-leather slippers.

"I'm drunk, darling," she said, and held out her arms, loaded with chains of platinum and emerald stars.

Her body swayed like a snake's dancing to music. She tossed her marcelled hair about, and suddenly, with a tinkle of rings, slumped into a chair with ancient Russian carvings. Scars glowed on her powdered back.

Women's laughter again came from the dining-room. Raïsa's sisters, with delicate mustaches and as full-bosomed and round-bodied as Raïsa herself, entered the room. Their busts jutted out and their black hair fluttered. Both of them had their own Benderskys for husbands. The room was filled with disjointed, chaotic feminine merriment, the hilarity of ripe women. The husbands wrapped the sisters in their sealskins and Orenburg shawls and shod them in black boots. Beneath the snowy visors of their shawls only painted glowing cheeks, marble noses, and eyes with their myopic Jewish glitter could be seen. After making some more happy noise they left for the theater, where Chaliapin was singing *Judith*.

"I want to work," Raïsa lisped, stretching her bare arms to me, "we've skipped a whole week."

She brought a bottle and two glasses from the dining-room. Her breasts swung free beneath the sacklike gown, the nipples rose beneath the clinging silk.

"It's very valuable," said Raïsa, pouring out the wine. "Muscatel '83. My husband will kill me when he finds out."

I had never drunk Muscatel '83, and tossed off three glasses one after the other without thinking. They carried me swiftly away into alleys where an orange flame danced and sounds of music could be heard.

"I'm drunk, darling. What are we doing today?"

"Today it's '*L'Aveu.*' 'The Confession,' then. The sun is the hero of this story, *le soleil de France*. Molten drops of it pattering on the red-haired Céleste changed into freckles. The sun's direct rays and wine and apple-cider burnished the face of the coachman Polyte. Twice a week Céleste drove into town to sell cream, eggs and chickens. She gave Polyte ten sous for herself and four for her basket. And every time Polyte would wink at the red-haired Céleste and ask: 'When are we going to have some fun, *ma belle?*—'What do you mean, Monsieur Polyte?' Jogging up and down on the box, the coachman explained: 'To have some fun means . . . why, what the hell, to have some fun! A lad with a lass; no music necessary . . . '

" 'I do not care for such jokes, Monsieur Polyte,' replied Céleste, moving further away the skirts that hung over her mighty calves in red stockings.

"But that devil Polyte kept right on guffawing and coughing: 'Ah, but one day we shall have our bit of fun, *ma belle,*' while tears of delight rolled down a face the color of brick-red wine and blood."

I downed another glass of the rare muscatel. Raïsa touched glasses with me. The maid with the stony eyes crossed the room and disappeared.

"*Ce diable de Polyte* . . . In the course of two years Céleste had paid him forty-eight francs; that is, two francs short of fifty! At the end of the second year, when they were alone in the carriage, Polyte, who had some cider before setting out, asked her his usual question: 'What about having some fun today, Mamselle Céleste?' And she replied, lowering her eyes: 'I am at your disposal, Monsieur Polyte.' "

Raïsa flung herself down on the table, laughing. *"Ce diable de Polyte . . . "*

"A white spavined mare was harnessed to the carriage. The white hack, its lips pink with age, went forward at a walking pace. The gay sun of France poured down on the ancient coach, screened from the world by a weatherbeaten hood. A lad with a lass; no music necessary . . . "

Raïsa held out a glass to me. It was the fifth.

"*Mon vieux,* to Maupassant."

"And what about having some fun today, *ma belle?*"

I reached over to Raïsa and kissed her on the lips. They quivered and swelled.

"You're funny," she mumbled through her teeth, recoiling.

She pressed herself against the wall, stretching out her bare arms. Spots began to glow on her arms and shoulders. Of all the gods ever put on the crucifix, this was the most ravishing.

"Be so kind as to sit down, Monsieur Polyte."

She pointed to an oblique blue armchair done in Slavonic style. Its back was constructed of carved interlacing bands with colorful pendants. I groped my way to it, stumbling as I went.

Night had blocked the path of my famished youth with a bottle of Muscatel '83 and twenty-nine books, twenty-nine bombs stuffed with pity, genius and passion. I sprang up, knocking over the chair and banging against the shelf. The twenty-nine volumes crashed to the floor, their pages flew open, they fell on their edges . . . and the white mare of my fate went on at a walking pace.

"You are funny," growled Raïsa.

I left the granite house on the Moyka between eleven and twelve, before the sisters and the husband returned from the theater. I was sober and could have walked a chalk line, but it was pleasanter to stagger, so I swayed from side to side, singing in a language I had just invented. Through the tunnels of the streets bounded by lines of street lights the steamy fog billowed. Monsters roared behind the boiling walls. The roads amputated the legs of those walking on them.

Kazantsev was asleep when I got home. He slept sitting up, his thin legs extended in their felt boots. The canary fluff rose on his head. He had fallen asleep by the stove bending over a volume of *Don Quixote*, the edition of 1624. On the title-page of the book was a dedication to the Duc de Broglie. I got into bed quietly, so as not to wake Kazantsev; moved the lamp close to me and began to read a book by Edouard Maynial on Guy de Maupassant's life and work.

Kazantsev's lips moved; his head kept keeling over.

That night I learned from Edouard Maynial that Maupassant was born in 1850, the child of a Normandy gentleman and Laure Lepoiteven, Flaubert's cousin. He was twenty-five when he was first attacked by congenital syphilis. His productivity and *joie de vivre* withstood the onsets of the disease. At first he suffered from headaches and fits of hypochondria. Then the specter of blindness arose before him. His sight weakened. He became suspicious of everyone, unsociable and pettily quarrelsome. He struggled furiously, dashed about the Mediterranean in a yacht, fled to Tunis, Morocco, Central Africa . . . and wrote ceaselessly. He attained fame, and at forty years of age cut his throat; lost a great deal of blood, yet lived through it. He was then put away in a madhouse. There he crawled about on his hands and knees, devouring his own excrement. The last line in his hospital report read: *Monsieur de Maupassant va s'animaliser.* He died at the age of forty-two, his mother surviving him.

I read the book to the end and got out of bed. The fog came close to the window, the world was hidden from me. My heart contracted as the foreboding of some essential truth touched me with light fingers.

Sonny's Blues

by James Baldwin

Introduced by Kenneth A. McClane

SONNY'S BLUES" SAVED MY LIFE, AND I AM NOT BEING HYPERBOLIC. In 1982, my brother Paul killed himself. He was an alcoholic, a brilliant jazz drummer, a tough, truculent kid, and an inspiration to his older brother, who, although not always understanding *who* Paul was, knew who Paul was not—and that was someone who was scared, timid, or obsequious. Paul did not talk much. If anything, he hated where we lived in Harlem; more precisely, he hated *how* we lived; and no one, in all my memory, ever made my brother cower. Life would lead him to more and more improbable scenarios—at first he was a college student, then a drifter, and all too soon he was on to drugs and alcohol. And yet Paul was strangely gentle and circumspect: his many girlfriends loved his characteristic good cheer—they knew him to be in their corner, and he had that ability (which is always the provender of the outwardly giving) to love those outside his immediate environs while dismissing those at his feet. If Paul was remote to his family, we were similarly distant. And yet he loved us and we him: one could glimpse it in the messiness of our interactions, the buoyancy which too often became icy. I vividly recall the many times when he walked up to his room, closed the door, and played his drums into the next morning, finally descending to have a bowl of cereal, sometimes providing a slight nod to one of us—and then, always returning to *that* room and its privacy. Paul would go to his drums, as he would travel through Harlem, with a saucy, ragged coolness. Those of you who know Baldwin's Sonny know my brother Paul.

Two years Paul's senior, I was, in every way, his absolute opposite. Where he was fearless and an inveterate street-blood, I was cautious, frightened, and retiring. Sometimes, he would push me to go out and I would beg off, suggesting that I wanted to see a movie or read a book. It was a lie, and Paul knew it. As he once said, half jokingly, "You live by not living."

When I began to teach at Cornell, Paul would often call me. We rarely talked about anything serious: Paul would hold court; I would pretend to be more in touch with life than I really was; the whole thing was rather comical. Then, one Friday, I received a call from my father telling me that Paul was dying. It was a surreal conversation, my father understandably uncontrollable, his son lying in a coma, his older son, hardly believing the inevitable: *Your brother is going to die*. Paul was in a New York hospital. I had best come immediately.

As luck would have it, I had been teaching summer school, and a student had suggested that we read James Baldwin's "Sonny's Blues" for our next class. Needing something to do and feigning to be the dutiful teacher, I read Baldwin's story on the plane ride to the hospital. It was a gift. The story involves an older unnamed man and his younger brother, Sonny, who is a jazz pianist and a heroin addict. The older brother is *safe*—that is, he has a job and a wonderful wife and has, at least temporarily, made peace with his existence. He is not rich, nor has he been able to truly escape Harlem—where he lives and where "dangers loom everywhere"—but he is a teacher. The younger brother, however, is menaced by his need to make life bearable.

The story, of course, is about much more, including love and how human beings cannot protect anyone, the reality that "sorrow never gets stopped," and the inexorable fact that the best among us may not survive—that life, sadly, often takes those whose dreams are greatest, whose voices are most needed. As the mother tells the far too cocky older brother when he protests that she needn't worry about Sonny, "It ain't only the bad ones, nor yet the dumb ones that gets sucked under." The older brother, at this early narrative moment, does not understand his mother; he is too caught in his own needful simplicity; reality is simply too costly. Yet as the story reminds, life is not interested in one's comfort, and the darkness—the terrors inside and outside—loom just above one's head.

"Sonny's Blues" saved my life. When my brother died, I felt terribly guilty. To my thinking I had not done all I could: I hadn't listened with enough passion; I had been too self-concerned, too self-infested. And yet the story admonishes that there is no ultimate safety, that a brother or a loved one may die (no matter what one does), and that, in the mother's wondrous and provident words, "You may not be able to stop nothing from happening. But you got to let him know you's *there*."

However tentatively and inappropriately, I did try to be my brother's witness. That I ultimately failed is certainly true: Paul is dead. But I am, at this hour, at this writing, *listening* to Sonny. *Deep water and drowning are not the same thing*. And yet they can be. And one can fall even further, farther. Baldwin does not lie about the landscape of suffering. Baldwin, quite simply, does not lie.

Sonny's Blues

James Baldwin

I read about it in the paper, in the subway, on my way to work. I read it, and I couldn't believe it, and I read it again. Then perhaps I just stared at it, at the newsprint spelling out his name, spelling out the story. I stared at it in the swinging lights of the subway car, and in the faces and bodies of the people, and in my own face, trapped in the darkness which roared outside.

It was not to be believed and I kept telling myself that, as I walked from the subway station to the high school. And at the same time I couldn't doubt it. I was scared, scared for Sonny. He became real to me again. A great block of ice got settled in my belly and kept melting there slowly all day long, while I taught my classes algebra. It was a special kind of ice. It kept melting, sending trickles of ice water all up and down my veins, but it never got less. Sometimes it hardened and seemed to expand until I felt my guts were going to come spilling out or that I was going to choke or scream. This would always be at a moment when I was remembering some specific thing Sonny had once said or done.

When he was about as old as the boys in my classes his face had been bright and open, there was a lot of copper in it; and he'd had wonderfully direct brown eyes, and great gentleness and privacy. I wondered what he looked like now. He had been picked up, the evening before, in a raid on an apartment downtown, for peddling and using heroin.

I couldn't believe it: but what I mean by that is that I couldn't find any room for it anywhere inside me. I had kept it outside me for a long time. I hadn't wanted to know. I had had suspicions, but I didn't name them, I kept putting them away. I told myself that Sonny was wild, but he wasn't crazy. And he'd always been a good boy, he hadn't ever turned hard or evil or disrespectful, the way kids can, so quick, so quick, especially in Harlem. I didn't want to believe that I'd ever see my brother going down, coming to nothing, all that light in his face gone out, in the condition I'd already seen so many others. Yet it had happened and here I was, talking about algebra to a lot of boys who might, every one of them for all I knew, be popping off needles every time they went to the head. Maybe it did more for them than algebra could.

I was sure that the first time Sonny had ever had horse, he couldn't have been much older than these boys were now. These boys, now, were living as we'd been living then, they were growing up with a rush and their heads bumped abruptly against the low ceiling of their actual possibilities. They were filled with rage. All they really knew were two darknesses, the darkness of their lives, which was now closing in on them, and the darkness of the movies, which had blinded them to that other darkness, and in which they now, vindictively, dreamed, at once more together than they were at any other time, and more alone.

When the last bell rang, the last class ended, I let out my breath. It seemed I'd been holding it for all that time. My clothes were wet—I may have looked as though I'd been sitting in a steam bath, all dressed up, all afternoon. I sat alone in the classroom a long time. I listened to the boys outside, downstairs, shouting and cursing and laughing. Their laughter struck me for perhaps the first time. It was not the joyous laughter which—God knows why—one associates with children. It was mocking and insular, its intent to denigrate. It was disenchanted, and in this, also, lay the authority of their curses. Perhaps I was listening to them because I was thinking about my brother and in them I heard my brother. And myself.

One boy was whistling a tune, at once very complicated and very simple, it seemed to be pouring out of him as though he were a bird, and it sounded very cool and moving through all that harsh, bright air, only just holding its own through all those other sounds.

I stood up and walked over to the window and looked down into the courtyard. It was the beginning of the spring and the sap was rising in the boys. A teacher passed through them every now and again, quickly, as though he or she couldn't wait to get out of that courtyard, to get those boys out of their sight and off their minds. I started collecting my stuff. I thought I'd better get home and talk to Isabel.

The courtyard was almost deserted by the time I got downstairs. I saw this boy standing in the shadow of a doorway, looking just like Sonny. I almost called his name. Then I saw that it wasn't Sonny, but somebody we used to know, a boy from around our block. He'd been Sonny's friend. He'd never been mine, having been too young for me, and, anyway, I'd never liked him. And now, even though he was a grown-up man, he still hung around that block, still spent hours on the street corners, was always high and raggy. I used to run into him from time to time and he'd often work around to asking me for a quarter or fifty cents. He always had some real good excuse, too, and I always gave it to him, I don't know why.

But now, abruptly, I hated him. I couldn't stand the way he looked at me, partly like a dog, partly like a cunning child. I wanted to ask him what the hell he was doing in the school courtyard.

He sort of shuffled over to me, and he said, "I see you got the papers. So you already know about it."

"You mean about Sonny? Yes, I already know about it. How come they didn't get you?"

He grinned. It made him repulsive and it also brought to mind what he'd looked like as a kid. "I wasn't there. I stay away from them people."

"Good for you." I offered him a cigarette and I watched him through the smoke. "You come all the way down here just to tell me about Sonny?"

"That's right." He was sort of shaking his head and his eyes looked strange, as though they were about to cross. The bright sun deadened his damp dark brown skin and it made his eyes look yellow and showed up the dirt in his kinked hair. He smelled funky. I moved a little way from him and I said, "Well, thanks. But I already know about it and I got to get home."

"I'll walk you a little ways," he said. We started walking. There were a couple of kids still loitering in the courtyard and one of them said goodnight to me and looked strangely at the boy beside me.

"What're you going to do?" he asked me. "I mean, about Sonny?"

"Look. I haven't seen Sonny for over a year, I'm not sure I'm going to do anything. Anyway, what the hell *can* I do?"

"That's right," he said quickly, "ain't nothing you can do. Can't much help old Sonny no more, I guess."

It was what I was thinking and so it seemed to me he had no right to say it.

"I'm surprised at Sonny, though," he went on—he had a funny way of talking, he looked straight ahead as though he were talking to himself—"I thought Sonny was a smart boy, I thought he was too smart to get hung."

"I guess he thought so too," I said sharply, "and that's how he got hung. And how about you? You're pretty goddamn smart, I bet."

Then he looked directly at me, just for a minute. "I ain't smart," he said. "If I was smart, I'd have reached for a pistol a long time ago."

"Look. Don't tell *me* your sad story, if it was up to me, I'd give you one." Then I felt guilty—guilty, probably, for never having supposed that the poor bastard *had* a story of his own, much less a sad one, and I asked, quickly, "What's going to happen to him now?"

He didn't answer this. He was off by himself some place. "Funny thing," he said, and from his tone we might have been discussing the quickest way to get to Brooklyn, "when I saw the papers this morning, the first thing I asked myself was if I had anything to do with it. I felt sort of responsible."

I began to listen more carefully. The subway station was on the corner, just before us, and I stopped. He stopped, too. We were in front of a bar and he ducked slightly, peering in, but whoever he was looking for didn't seem to be there. The juke box was blasting away with something black and bouncy and I half watched the barmaid as she danced her way from the juke box to her place behind the bar. And I watched her face as she laughingly responded to something someone said to her, still keeping time to the music. When she smiled one saw the little girl, one sensed the doomed, still-struggling woman beneath the battered face of the semi-whore.

"I never *give* Sonny nothing," the boy said finally, "but a long time ago I come to school high and Sonny asked me how it felt." He paused, I couldn't bear to watch him, I watched the barmaid, and I listened to the music which seemed to be causing the pavement to shake. "I told him it felt great." The music stopped, the barmaid paused and watched the juke box until the music began again. "It did."

All this was carrying me some place I didn't want to go. I certainly didn't want to know how it felt. It filled everything, the people, the houses, the music, the dark, quicksilver barmaid, with menace; and this menace was their reality.

"What's going to happen to him now?" I asked again.

"They'll send him away some place and they'll try to cure him." He shook his head. "Maybe he'll even think he's kicked the habit. Then they'll let him loose"—he gestured, throwing his cigarette into the gutter. "That's all."

"What do you mean, that's *all?*"

But I knew what he meant.

"I *mean,* that's *all.*" He turned his head and looked at me, pulling down the corners of his mouth. "Don't you know what I mean?" he asked, softly.

"How the hell *would* I know what you mean?" I almost whispered it, I don't know why.

"That's right," he said to the air, "how would *he* know what I mean?" He turned toward me again, patient and calm, and yet I somehow felt him shaking, shaking as though he were going to fall apart. I felt that ice in my guts again, the dread I'd felt all afternoon; and again I watched the barmaid, moving about the bar, washing glasses, and singing. "Listen. They'll let him out and then it'll just start all over again. That's what I mean."

"You mean—they'll let him out. And then he'll just start working his way back in again. You mean he'll never kick the habit. Is that what you mean?"

"That's right," he said, cheerfully. "*You* see what I mean."

"Tell me," I said at last, "why does he want to die? He must want to die, he's killing himself, why does he want to die?"

He looked at me in surprise. He licked his lips. "He don't want to die. He wants to live. Don't nobody want to die, ever."

Then I wanted to ask him—too many things. He could not have answered, or if he had, I could not have borne the answers. I started walking. "Well, I guess it's none of my business."

"It's going to be rough on old Sonny," he said. We reached the subway station. "This is your station?" he asked. I nodded. I took one step down. "Damn!" he said, suddenly. I looked up at him. He grinned again. "Damn it if I didn't leave all my money home. You ain't got a dollar on you, have you? Just for a couple of days, is all."

All at once something inside gave and threatened to come pouring out of me. I didn't hate him any more. I felt that in another moment I'd start crying like a child.

"Sure," I said. "Don't sweat." I looked in my wallet and didn't have a dollar, I only had a five. "Here," I said. "That hold you?"

He didn't look at it—he didn't want to look at it. A terrible closed look came over his face, as though he were keeping the number on the bill a secret from him and me. "Thanks," he said, and now he was dying to see me go. "Don't worry about Sonny. Maybe I'll write him or something."

"Sure," I said. "You do that. So long."

"Be seeing you," he said. I went on down the steps.

And I didn't write Sonny or send him anything for a long time. When I finally did, it was just after my little girl died, he wrote me back a letter which made me feel like a bastard.

Here's what he said:

Dear brother,

You don't know how much I needed to hear from you. I wanted to write you many a time but I dug how much I must have hurt you and so I didn't write. But now I feel like a man who's been trying to climb up out of some deep, real deep and funky hole and just saw the sun up there, outside. I got to get outside.

I can't tell you much about how I got here. I mean I don't know how to tell you. I guess I was afraid of something or I was trying to escape from something and you know I have never been very strong in the head (smile). I'm glad Mama and Daddy are dead and can't see what's happened to their son and I swear if I'd known what I was doing I would never have hurt you so, you and a lot of other fine people who were nice to me and who believed in me.

I don't want you to think it had anything to do with me being a musician. It's more than that. Or maybe less than that. I can't get anything straight in my head down here and I try not to think about what's going to happen to me when I get outside again. Sometime I think I'm going to flip and *never* get outside and sometime I think I'll come straight back. I tell you one thing, though, I'd rather blow my brains out than go through this again. But that's what they all say, so they tell me. If I tell you when I'm coming to New York and if you could meet me, I sure would appreciate it. Give my love to Isabel and the kids and I was sure sorry to hear about little Gracie. I wish I could be like Mama and say the Lord's will be done, but I don't know it seems to me that trouble is the one thing that never does get stopped and I don't know what good it does to blame it on the Lord. But maybe it does some good if you believe it.

Your brother,
Sonny

Then I kept in constant touch with him and I sent him whatever I could and I went to meet him when he came back to New York. When I saw him many things I thought I had forgotten came flooding back to me. This was because I had begun, finally, to wonder about Sonny, about the life that Sonny lived inside. This life, whatever it was, had made him older and thinner and it had deepened the distant stillness in which he had always moved. He looked very unlike my baby brother. Yet, when he smiled, when we shook hands, the baby brother I'd never known looked out from the depths of his private life, like an animal waiting to be coaxed into the light.

"How you been keeping?" he asked me.

"All right. And you?"

"Just fine." He was smiling all over his face. "It's good to see you again."

"It's good to see you."

The seven years' difference in our ages lay between us like a chasm: I wondered if these years would ever operate between us as a bridge. I was remembering, and it made it hard to catch my breath, that I had been there when he was born; and I had heard the first word he had ever spoken. When he started to walk, he walked from our mother straight to me. I caught him just before he fell when he took the first steps he ever took in this world.

"How's Isabel?"

"Just fine. She's dying to see you."

"And the boys?"

"They're fine, too. They're anxious to see their uncle."

"Oh, come on. You know they don't remember me."

"Are you kidding? Of course they remember you."

He grinned again. We got into a taxi. We had a lot to say to each other, far too much to know how to begin.

As the taxi began to move, I asked, "You still want to go to India?"

He laughed. "You still remember that. Hell, no. This place is Indian enough for me."

"It used to belong to them," I said.

And he laughed again. "They damn sure knew what they were doing when they got rid of it."

Years ago, when he was around fourteen, he'd been all hipped on the idea of going to India. He read books about people sitting on rocks, naked, in all kinds of weather, but mostly bad, naturally, and walking barefoot through hot coals and arriving at wisdom. I used to say that it sounded to me as though they were getting away from wisdom as fast as they could. I think he sort of looked down on me for that.

"Do you mind," he asked, "if we have the driver drive alongside the park? On the west side—I haven't seen the city in so long."

"Of course not," I said. I was afraid that I might sound as though I were humoring him, but I hoped he wouldn't take it that way.

So we drove along, between the green of the park and the stony, lifeless elegance of hotels and apartment buildings, toward the vivid, killing streets of our childhood. These streets hadn't changed, though housing projects jutted up out of them now like rocks in the middle of a boiling sea. Most of the houses in which we had grown up had vanished, as had the stores from which we had stolen, the basements in which we had first tried sex, the rooftops from which we had hurled tin cans and bricks. But houses exactly like the houses of our past yet dominated the landscape, boys exactly like the boys we once had been found themselves smothering in these houses, came down into the streets for light and air and found themselves encircled by disaster. Some escaped the trap, most didn't. Those who got out always left something of themselves behind, as some animals amputate a leg and leave it in the trap. It might be said, perhaps, that I had escaped, after all, I was a school teacher; or that Sonny had, he hadn't lived in Harlem for years. Yet, as the cab moved uptown through streets which seemed, with a rush, to darken with dark people, and as I covertly studied Sonny's face, it came to me that what we both were seeking through our separate cab windows was that part of ourselves which had been left behind. It's always at the hour of trouble and confrontation that the missing member aches.

We hit 110th Street and started rolling up Lenox Avenue. And I'd known this avenue all my life, but it seemed to me again, as it had seemed on the day I'd first heard about Sonny's trouble, filled with a hidden menace which was its very breath of life.

"We almost there," said Sonny.

"Almost." We were both too nervous to say anything more.

We live in a housing project. It hasn't been up long. A few days after it was up it seemed uninhabitably new, now, of course, it's already rundown. It looks like a parody of the good, clean, faceless life—God knows the people who live in it do their best to make it a parody. The beat-looking grass lying around isn't enough to make their lives green, the hedges will never hold out the streets, and they know it. The big windows fool no one, they aren't big enough to make space out of no space. They don't bother with the windows, they watch the TV screen instead. The playground is most popular with the children who don't play at jacks, or skip rope, or roller skate, or swing, and they can be found in it after dark. We moved in partly because it's not too far from where I teach, and partly for the kids; but it's really just like the houses in which Sonny and I grew up. The same things happen, they'll have the same things to remember. The moment Sonny and I started into the house I had the feeling that I was simply bringing him back into the danger he had almost died trying to escape.

Sonny has never been talkative. So I don't know why I was sure he'd be dying to talk to me when supper was over the first night. Everything went fine, the oldest boy remembered him, and the youngest boy liked him, and Sonny had remembered to bring something for each of them; and Isabel, who is really much nicer than I am, more open and giving, had gone to a lot of trouble about dinner and was genuinely glad to see him. And she's always been able to tease Sonny in a way that I haven't. It was nice to see her face so vivid again and to hear her laugh and watch her make Sonny laugh. She wasn't, or, anyway, she didn't seem to be, at all uneasy or embarrassed. She chatted as though there were no subject which had to be avoided and she got Sonny past his first, faint stiffness. And thank God she was there, for I was filled with that icy dread again. Everything I did seemed awkward to me, and everything I said sounded freighted with hidden meaning. I was trying to remember everything I'd heard about dope addiction and I couldn't help watching Sonny for signs. I wasn't doing it out of malice. I was trying to find out something about my brother. I was dying to hear him tell me he was safe.

"Safe?" my father grunted, whenever Mama suggested trying to move to a neighborhood which might be safer for children. "Safe, hell! Ain't no place safe for kids, nor nobody."

He always went on like this, but he wasn't, ever, really as bad as he sounded, not even on weekends, when he got drunk. As a matter of fact, he was always on the lookout for "something a little better," but he died before he found it. He died suddenly, during a drunken weekend in the middle of the war, when Sonny was fifteen. He and Sonny hadn't ever got on too well. And this was partly because Sonny was the apple of his father's eye. It was because he loved Sonny so much and was frightened for him, that he was always fighting with him. It doesn't do any good to fight with Sonny. Sonny just moves back, inside himself, where he can't be reached. But the principal reason that they never hit it off is that they were so much alike. Daddy was big and rough and loud-talking, just the opposite of Sonny, but they both had—that same privacy.

Mama tried to tell me something about this, just after Daddy died. I was home on leave from the army.

This was the last time I ever saw my mother alive. Just the same, this picture gets all mixed up in my mind with pictures I had of her when she was younger. The way I always see her is the way she used to be on a Sunday afternoon, say, when the old folks were talking after the big Sunday dinner. I always see her wearing pale blue. She'd be sitting on the sofa. And my father would be sitting in the easy chair, not far from her. And the living room would be full of church folks and relatives. There they sit, in chairs all around the living room, and the night is creeping up outside, but nobody knows it yet. You can see the darkness growing against the windowpanes and you hear the street noises every now and again, or maybe the jangling beat of a tambourine from one of the churches close by, but it's real quiet in the room. For a moment nobody's talking, but every face looks darkening, like the sky outside. And my mother rocks a little from the waist, and my father's eyes are closed. Everyone is looking at something a child can't see. For a minute they've forgotten the children. Maybe a kid is lying on the rug, half asleep. Maybe somebody's got a kid in his lap and is absent-mindedly stroking the kid's head. Maybe there's a kid, quiet and big-eyed, curled up in a big chair in the corner. The silence, the darkness coming, and the darkness in the faces frightens the child obscurely. He hopes that the hand which strokes his forehead will never stop—will never die. He hopes that there will never come a time when the old folks won't be sitting around the living room, talking about where they've come from, and what they've seen, and what's happened to them and their kinfolk.

But something deep and watchful in the child knows that this is bound to end, is already ending. In a moment someone will get up and turn on the light. Then the old folks will remember the children and they won't talk any more that day. And when light fills the room, the child is filled with darkness. He knows that every time this happens he's moved just a little closer to that darkness outside. The darkness outside is what the old folks have been talking about. It's what they've come from. It's what they endure. The child knows that they won't talk any more because if he knows too much about what's happened to *them,* he'll know too much too soon, about what's going to happen to *him*.

The last time I talked to my mother, I remember I was restless. I wanted to get out and see Isabel. We weren't married then and we had a lot to straighten out between us.

There Mama sat, in black, by the window. She was humming an old church song, *Lord, you brought me from a long ways off*. Sonny was out somewhere. Mama kept watching the streets.

"I don't know," she said, "if I'll ever see you again, after you go off from here. But I hope you'll remember the things I tried to teach you."

"Don't talk like that," I said, and smiled. "You'll be here a long time yet."

She smiled, too, but she said nothing. She was quiet for a long time. And I said, "Mama, don't you worry about nothing. I'll be writing all the time, and you be getting the checks. . . ."

"I want to talk to you about your brother," she said, suddenly. "If anything happens to me he ain't going to have nobody to look out for him."

"Mama," I said, "ain't nothing going to happen to you *or* Sonny. Sonny's all right. He's a good boy and he's got good sense."

"It ain't a question of his being a good boy," Mama said, "nor of his having good sense. It ain't only the bad ones, nor yet the dumb ones that gets sucked under." She stopped, looking at me. "Your Daddy once had a brother," she said, and she smiled in a way that made me feel she was in pain. "You didn't never know that, did you?"

"No," I said, "I never knew that," and I watched her face.

"Oh, yes," she said, "your Daddy had a brother." She looked out the window again. "I know you never saw your Daddy cry. But *I* did—many a time, through all these years."

I asked her, "What happened to his brother? How come nobody's ever talked about him?"

This was the first time I ever saw my mother look old.

"His brother got killed," she said, "when he was just a little younger than you are now. I knew him. He was a fine boy. He was maybe a little full of the devil, but he didn't mean nobody no harm."

Then she stopped and the room was silent, exactly as it had sometimes been on those Sunday afternoons. Mama kept looking out into the streets.

"He used to have a job in the mill," she said, "and, like all young folks, he just liked to perform on Saturday nights. Saturday nights him and your father would drift around to different places, go to dances and things like that, or just sit around with people they knew, and your father's brother would sing, he had a fine voice, and play along with himself on his guitar. Well, this particular Saturday night, him and your father was coming home from some place, and they were both a little drunk and there was a moon that night, it was bright like day. Your father's brother was feeling kind of good, and he was whistling to himself, and he had his guitar slung over his shoulder. They was coming down a hill and beneath them was a road that turned off from the highway. Well, your father's brother, being always kind of frisky, decided to run down this hill, and he did, with that guitar banging and clanging behind him, and he ran across the road, and he was making water behind a tree. And your father was sort of amused at him and he was still coming down the hill, kind of slow. Then he heard a motor and that same minute his brother stepped from behind the tree, into the road, in the moonlight. And he started to cross the road. And your father started to run down the hill, he says he don't know why. This car was full of white men. They was all drunk, and when they seen your father's brother they let out a great whoop and holler and they aimed the car straight at him. They was having fun, they just wanted to scare him, the way they do sometimes, you know. But they was drunk. And I guess the boy, being drunk, too, and scared, kind of lost his head. By the time he jumped it was too late. Your father says he heard his brother scream when the car rolled over him, and he heard the wood of that guitar when it give, and heard them strings go flying, and he heard them white men shouting, and the car kept on a-going and it ain't stopped till this day. And, time your father got down the hill, his brother weren't nothing but blood and pulp."

Tears were gleaming on my mother's face. There wasn't anything I could say.

"He never mentioned it," she said, "because I never let him mention it before you children. Your Daddy was like a crazy man that night and for many a night thereafter. He says he never in his life seen anything as dark as that road after the lights of that car had gone away. Weren't nothing, weren't nobody on that road, just your Daddy and his brother and that busted guitar. Oh, yes. Your Daddy never did really get right again. Till the day he died he weren't sure but that every white man he saw was the man that killed his brother."

She stopped and took out her handkerchief and dried her eyes and looked at me.

"I ain't telling you all this," she said, "to make you scared or bitter or to make you hate nobody. I'm telling you this because you got a brother. And the world ain't changed."

I guess I didn't want to believe this. I guess she saw this in my face. She turned away from me, toward the window again, searching those streets.

"But I praise my Redeemer," she said at last, "that He called your Daddy home before me. I ain't saying it to throw no flowers at myself, but, I declare, it keeps me from feeling too cast down to know I helped your father get safely through this world. Your father always acted like he was the roughest, strongest man on earth. And everybody took him to be like that. But if he hadn't had *me* there—to see his tears!"

She was crying again. Still, I couldn't move. I said, "Lord, Lord, Mama, I didn't know it was like that."

"Oh, honey," she said, "there's a lot that you don't know. But you are going to find it out." She stood up from the window and came over to me. "You got to hold on to your brother," she said, "and don't let him fall, no matter what it looks like is happening to him and no matter how evil you gets with him. You going to be evil with him many a time. But don't you forget what I told you, you hear?"

"I won't forget," I said. "Don't you worry, I won't forget. I won't let nothing happen to Sonny."

My mother smiled as though she were amused at something she saw in my face. Then, "You may not be able to stop nothing from happening. But you got to let him know you's *there*."

Two days later I was married, and then I was gone. And I had a lot of things on my mind and I pretty well forgot my promise to Mama until I got shipped home on a special furlough for her funeral.

And, after the funeral, with just Sonny and me alone in the empty kitchen, I tried to find out something about him.

"What do you want to do?" I asked him.

"I'm going to be a musician," he said.

For he had graduated, in the time I had been away, from dancing to the juke box to finding out who was playing what, and what they were doing with it, and he had bought himself a set of drums.

"You mean, you want to be a drummer?" I somehow had the feeling that being a drummer might be all right for other people but not for my brother Sonny.

"I don't think," he said, looking at me very gravely, "that I'll ever be a good drummer. But I think I can play a piano."

I frowned. I'd never played the role of the older brother quite so seriously before, had scarcely ever, in fact, *asked* Sonny a damn thing. I sensed myself in the presence of something I didn't really know how to handle, didn't understand. So I made my frown a little deeper as I asked: "What kind of musician do you want to be?"

He grinned. "How many kinds do you think there are?"

"Be *serious,*" I said.

He laughed, throwing his head back, and then looked at me. "I *am* serious."

"Well, then, for Christ's sake, stop kidding around and answer a serious question. I mean, do you want to be a concert pianist, you want to play classical music and all that, or—or what?" Long before I finished he was laughing again. "For Christ's *sake,* Sonny!"

He sobered, but with difficulty. "I'm sorry. But you sound so—*scared!*" and he was off again.

"Well, you think it's funny now, baby, but it's not going to be so funny when you have to make your living at it, let me tell you *that.*" I was furious because I knew he was laughing at me and I didn't know why.

"No," he said, very sober now, and afraid, perhaps, that he'd hurt me, "I don't want to be a classical pianist. That isn't what interests me. I mean—" he paused, looking hard at me, as though his eyes would help me to understand, and then gestured helplessly, as though perhaps his hand would help—"I mean, I'll have a lot of studying to do, and I'll have to study *everything,* but, I mean, I want to play *with*—jazz musicians." He stopped. "I want to play jazz," he said.

Well, the word had never before sounded as heavy, as real, as it sounded that afternoon in Sonny's mouth. I just looked at him and I was probably frowning a real frown by this time. I simply couldn't see why on earth he'd want to spend his time hanging around nightclubs, clowning around on bandstands, while people pushed each other around a dance floor. It seemed—beneath him, somehow. I had never thought about it before, had never been forced to, but I suppose I had always put jazz musicians in a class with what Daddy called "good-time people."

"Are you *serious?*"

"Hell, *yes,* I'm serious."

He looked more helpless than ever, and annoyed, and deeply hurt.

I suggested, helpfully: "You mean—like Louis Armstrong?"

His face closed as though I'd struck him. "No. I'm not talking about none of that old-time, down home crap."

"Well, look, Sonny, I'm sorry, don't get mad. I just don't altogether get it, that's all. Name somebody—you know, a jazz musician you admire."

"Bird."

"Who?"

"Bird! Charlie Parker! Don't they teach you nothing in the goddamn army?"

I lit a cigarette. I was surprised and then a little amused to discover that I was trembling. "I've been out of touch," I said. "You'll have to be patient with me. Now. Who's this Parker character?"

"He's just one of the greatest jazz musicians alive," said Sonny, sullenly, his hands in his pockets, his back to me. "Maybe *the* greatest," he added, bitterly, "that's probably why *you* never heard of him."

"All right," I said, "I'm ignorant. I'm sorry. I'll go out and buy all the cat's records right away, all right?"

"It don't," said Sonny, with dignity, "make any difference to me. I don't care what you listen to. Don't do me no favors."

I was beginning to realize that I'd never seen him so upset before. With another part of my mind I was thinking that this would probably turn out to be one of those things kids go through and that I shouldn't make it seem important by pushing it too hard. Still, I didn't think it would do any harm to ask: "Doesn't all this take a lot of time? Can you make a living at it?"

He turned back to me and half leaned, half sat, on the kitchen table. "Everything takes time," he said, "and—well, yes, sure, I can make a living at it. But what I don't seem to be able to make you understand is that it's the only thing I want to do."

"Well, Sonny," I said, gently, "you know people can't always do exactly what they *want* to do—"

"*No,* I don't know that," said Sonny, surprising me. "I think people *ought* to do what they want to do, what else are they alive for?"

"You getting to be a big boy," I said desperately, "it's time you started thinking about your future."

"I'm thinking about my future," said Sonny, grimly. "I think about it all the time."

I gave up. I decided, if he didn't change his mind, that we could always talk about it later. "In the meantime," I said, "you got to finish school." We had already decided that he'd have to move in with Isabel and her folks. I knew this wasn't the ideal arrangement because Isabel's folks are inclined to be dicty and they hadn't especially wanted Isabel to marry me. But I didn't know what else to do. "And we have to get you fixed up at Isabel's."

There was a long silence. He moved from the kitchen table to the window. "That's a terrible idea. You know it yourself."

"Do you have a *better* idea?"

He just walked up and down the kitchen for a minute. He was as tall as I was. He had started to shave. I suddenly had the feeling that I didn't know him at all.

He stopped at the kitchen table and picked up my cigarettes. Looking at me with a kind of mocking, amused defiance, he put one between his lips. "You mind?"

"You smoking already?"

He lit the cigarette and nodded, watching me through the smoke. "I just wanted to see if I'd have the courage to smoke in front of you." He grinned and blew a great cloud of smoke to the ceiling. "It was easy." He looked at my face. "Come on, now. I bet you was smoking at my age, tell the truth."

I didn't say anything but the truth was on my face, and he laughed. But now there was something very strained in his laugh. "Sure. And I bet that ain't all you was doing."

He was frightening me a little. "Cut the crap," I said. "We already decided that you was going to go and live at Isabel's. Now what's got into you all of a sudden?"

"*You* decided it," he pointed out. "*I* didn't decide nothing." He stopped in front of me, leaning against the stove, arms loosely folded. "Look, brother.

I don't want to stay in Harlem no more, I really don't." He was very earnest. He looked at me, then over toward the kitchen window. There was something in his eyes I'd never seen before, some thoughtfulness, some worry all his own. He rubbed the muscle of one arm. "It's time I was getting out of here."

"Where do you want to *go,* Sonny?"

"I want to join the army. Or the navy, I don't care. If I say I'm old enough, they'll believe me."

Then I got mad. It was because I was so scared. "You must be crazy. You goddman fool, what the hell do you want to go and join the *army* for?"

"I just told you. To get out of Harlem."

"Sonny, you haven't even finished *school.* And if you really want to be a musician, how do you expect to study if you're in the *army?*"

He looked at me, trapped, and in anguish. "There's ways. I might be able to work out some kind of deal. Anyway, I'll have the G.I. bill when I come out."

"*If* you come out." We stared at each other. "Sonny, please. Be reasonable. I know the setup is far from perfect. But we got to do the best we can."

"I ain't learning nothing in school," he said. "Even when I go." He turned away from me and opened the window and threw his cigarette out into the narrow alley. I watched his back. "At least, I ain't learning nothing you'd want me to learn." He slammed the window so hard I thought the glass would fly out, and turned back to me. "And I'm sick of the stink of these garbage cans!"

"Sonny," I said, "I know how you feel. But if you don't finish school now, you're going to be sorry later that you didn't." I grabbed him by the shoulders. "And you only got another year. It ain't so bad. And I'll come back and I swear I'll help you do *whatever* you want to do. Just try to put up with it till I come back. Will you please do that? For me?"

He didn't answer and he wouldn't look at me.

"Sonny. You hear me?"

He pulled away. "I hear you. But you never hear anything *I* say."

I didn't know what to say to that. He looked out of the window and then back at me. "OK," he said, and sighed. "I'll try."

Then I said, trying to cheer him up a little, "They got a piano at Isabel's. You can practice on it."

And as a matter of fact, it did cheer him up for a minute. "That's right," he said to himself. "I forgot that." His face relaxed a little. But the worry, the thoughtfulness, played on it still, the way shadows play on a face which is staring into the fire.

But I thought I'd never hear the end of that piano. At first, Isabel would write me, saying how nice it was that Sonny was so serious about his music and how, as soon as he came in from school, or wherever he had been when he was supposed to be at school, he went straight to that piano and stayed there until suppertime. And, after supper, he went back to that piano and stayed there until everybody went to bed. He was at the piano all day Saturday and all day Sunday. Then he bought a record player and started playing records. He'd play one record over and over again, all day long sometimes, and he'd improvise along with it on the piano. Or he'd play one section of the record, one chord, one change, one progression, then he'd do it on the piano. Then back to the record. Then back to the piano.

Well, I really don't know how they stood it. Isabel finally confessed that it wasn't like living with a person at all, it was like living with sound. And the sound didn't make any sense to her, didn't make any sense to any of them—naturally. They began, in a way, to be afflicted by this presence that was living in their home. It was as though Sonny were some sort of god, or monster. He moved in an atmosphere which wasn't like theirs at all. They fed him and he ate, he washed himself, he walked in and out of their door; he certainly wasn't nasty or unpleasant or rude, Sonny isn't any of those things; but it was as though he were all wrapped up in some cloud, some fire, some vision all his own; and there wasn't any way to reach him.

At the same time, he wasn't really a man yet, he was still a child, and they had to watch out for him in all kinds of ways. They certainly couldn't throw him out. Neither did they dare to make a great scene about that piano because even they dimly sensed, as I sensed, from so many thousands of miles away, that Sonny was at that piano playing for his life.

But he hadn't been going to school. One day a letter came from the school board and Isabel's mother got it—there had, apparently, been other letters but Sonny had torn them up. This day, when Sonny came in, Isabel's mother showed him the letter and asked where he'd been spending his time. And she finally got it out of him that he'd been down in Greenwich Village, with musicians and other characters, in a white girl's apartment. And this scared her and she started to scream at him and what came up, once she began—though she denies it to this day—was what sacrifices they were making to give Sonny a decent home and how little he appreciated it.

Sonny didn't play the piano that day. By evening, Isabel's mother had calmed down but then there was the old man to deal with, and Isabel herself. Isabel says she did her best to be calm but she broke down and started crying. She says she just watched Sonny's face. She could tell, by watching him, what was happening with him. And what was happening was that they penetrated his cloud, they had reached him. Even if their fingers had been a thousand times more gentle than human fingers ever are, he could hardly help feeling that they had stripped him naked and were spitting on that nakedness. For he also had to see that his presence, that music, which was life or death to him, had been torture for them and that they had endured it, not at all for his sake, but only for mine. And Sonny couldn't take that. He can take it a little better today than he could then but he's still not very good at it and, frankly, I don't know anybody who is.

The silence of the next few days must have been louder than the sound of all the music ever played since time began. One morning, before she went to work, Isabel was in his room for something and she suddenly realized that all of his records were gone. And she knew for certain that he was gone. And he was. He went as far as the navy would carry him. He finally sent me a postcard from some place in Greece and that was the first I knew that Sonny was still alive. I didn't see him any more until we were both back in New York and the war had long been over.

He was a man by then, of course, but I wasn't willing to see it. He came by the house from time to time, but we fought almost every time we met. I didn't like the way he carried himself, loose and dreamlike all the time, and I didn't like his friends, and his music seemed to be merely an excuse for the life he led. It sounded just that weird and disordered.

Then we had a fight, a pretty awful fight, and I didn't see him for months. By and by I looked him up, where he was living, in a furnished room in the Village, and I tried to make it up. But there were lots of people in the room and Sonny just lay on his bed, and he wouldn't come downstairs with me, and he treated these other people as though they were his family and I weren't. So I got mad and then he got mad, and then I told him that he might just as well be dead as live the way he was living. Then he stood up and he told me not to worry about him any more in life, that he *was* dead as far as I was concerned. Then he pushed me to the door and the other people looked on as though nothing were happening, and he slammed the door behind me. I stood in the hallway, staring at the door. I heard somebody laugh in the room and then the tears came to my eyes. I started down the steps, whistling to keep from crying, I kept whistling to myself, *You going to need me, baby, one of these cold, rainy days*.

I read about Sonny's trouble in the spring. Little Grace died in the fall. She was a beautiful little girl. But she only lived a little over two years. She died of polio and she suffered. She had a slight fever for a couple of days, but it didn't seem like anything and we just kept her in bed. And we would certainly have called the doctor, but the fever dropped, she seemed to be all right. So we thought it had just been a cold. Then, one day, she was up, playing, Isabel was in the kitchen fixing lunch for the two boys when they'd come in from school, and she heard Grace fall down in the living room. When you have a lot of children you don't always start running when one of them falls, unless they start screaming or something. And, this time, Grace was quiet. Yet, Isabel says that when she heard that thump and then that silence, something happened in her to make her afraid. And she ran to the living room and there was little Grace on the floor, all twisted up, and the reason she hadn't screamed was that she couldn't get her breath. And when she did scream, it was the worst sound, Isabel says, that she'd ever heard in all her life, and she still hears it sometimes in her dreams. Isabel will sometimes wake me up with a low, moaning, strangled sound and I have to be quick to awaken her and hold her to me and where Isabel is weeping against me seems a mortal wound.

I think I may have written Sonny the very day that little Grace was buried. I was sitting in the living room in the dark, by myself, and I suddenly thought of Sonny. My trouble made his real.

One Saturday afternoon, when Sonny had been living with us, or, anyway, been in our house, for nearly two weeks, I found myself wandering aimlessly about the living room, drinking from a can of beer, and trying to work up the courage to search Sonny's room. He was out, he was usually out whenever I was home, and Isabel had taken the children to see their grandparents. Suddenly I was standing still in front of the living room window, watching Seventh Avenue. The idea of searching Sonny's room made me still. I scarcely dared to admit to myself what I'd be searching for. I didn't know what I'd do if I found it. Or if I didn't.

On the sidewalk across from me, near the entrance to a barbecue joint, some people were holding an old-fashioned revival meeting. The barbecue cook, wearing a dirty white apron, his conked hair reddish and metallic in the pale sun, and a cigarette between his lips, stood in the doorway, watching them. Kids and older people paused in their errands and stood there, along with some older men and a couple of very tough-looking women who watched everything that happened on the avenue, as though they owned it, or were maybe owned by it. Well, they were watching this, too. The revival was being carried on by three sisters in black, and a brother. All they had were their voices and their Bibles and a tambourine. The brother was testifying and while he testified two of the sisters stood together, seeming to say, amen, and the third sister walked around with the tambourine outstretched and a couple of people dropped coins into it. Then the brother's testimony ended and the sister who had been taking up the collection dumped the coins into her palm and transferred them to the pocket of her long black robe. Then she raised both hands, striking the tambourine against the air, and then against one hand, and she started to sing. And the two other sisters and the brother joined in.

It was strange, suddenly, to watch, though I had been seeing these street meetings all my life. So, of course, had everybody else down there. Yet, they paused and watched and listened and I stood still at the window. *"Tis the old ship of Zion,"* they sang, and the sister with the tambourine kept a steady, jangling beat, *"it has rescued many a thousand!"* Not a soul under the sound of their voices was hearing this song for the first time, not one of them had been rescued. Nor had they seen much in the way of rescue work being done around them. Neither did they especially believe in the holiness of the three sisters and the brother, they knew too much about them, knew where they lived, and how. The woman with the tambourine, whose voice dominated the air, whose face was bright with joy, was divided by very little from the woman who stood watching her, a cigarette between her heavy, chapped lips, her hair a cuckoo's nest, her face scarred and swollen from many beatings, and her black eyes glittering like coal. Perhaps they both knew this, which was why, when, as rarely, they addressed each other, they addressed each other as Sister. As the singing filled the air the watching, listening faces underwent a change, the eyes focusing on something within; the music seemed to soothe a poison out of them; and time seemed, nearly, to fall away from the sullen, belligerent, battered faces, as though they were fleeing back to their first condition, while dreaming of their last. The barbecue cook half shook his head and smiled, and dropped his cigarette and disappeared into his joint. A man fumbled in his pockets for change and stood holding it in his hand impatiently, as though he had just remembered a pressing appointment further up the avenue. He looked furious. Then I saw Sonny, standing on the edge of the crowd. He was carrying a wide, flat notebook with a green cover, and it made him look, from where I was standing, almost like a schoolboy. The coppery sun brought out the copper in his skin, he was very faintly smiling, standing very still. Then the singing stopped, the tambourine turned into a collection plate again. The furious man dropped in his coins and vanished, so did a couple of the women, and Sonny dropped some change in the plate, looking directly at the woman with a little smile. He started across the avenue, toward the house. He has a slow, loping walk, something like the way Harlem hipsters walk, only he's imposed on this his own half-beat. I had never really noticed it before.

I stayed at the window, both relieved and apprehensive. As Sonny disappeared from my sight, they began singing again. And they were still singing when his key turned in the lock.

"Hey," he said.

"Hey yourself. You want some beer?"

"No. Well, maybe." But he came up to the window and stood beside me, looking out. "What a warm voice," he said.

They were singing *If I could only hear my mother pray again!*

"Yes," I said, "and she can sure beat that tambourine."

"But what a terrible song," he said, and laughed. He dropped his notebook on the sofa and disappeared into the kitchen. "Where's Isabel and the kids?"

"I think they went to see their grandparents. You hungry?"

"No." He came back into the living room with his can of beer. "You want to come some place with me tonight?"

I sensed, I don't know how, that I couldn't possibly say no. "Sure. Where?"

He sat down on the sofa and picked up his notebook and started leafing through it. "I'm going to sit in with some fellows in a joint in the Village."

"You mean, you're going to play, tonight?"

"That's right." He took a swallow of his beer and moved back to the window. He gave me a sidelong look. "If you can stand it."

"I'll try," I said.

He smiled to himself and we both watched as the meeting across the way broke up. The three sisters and the brother, heads bowed, were singing *God be with you till we meet again*. The faces around them were very quiet. Then the song ended. The small crowd dispersed. We watched the three women and the lone man walk slowly up the avenue.

"When she was singing before," said Sonny, abruptly, "her voice reminded me for a minute of what heroin feels like sometimes—when it's in your veins. It makes you feel sort of warm and cool at the same time. And distant. And—and sure." He sipped his beer, very deliberately not looking at me. I watched his face. "It makes you feel—in control. Sometimes you've got to have that feeling."

"Do you?" I sat down slowly in the easy chair.

"Sometimes." He went to the sofa and picked up his notebook again. "Some people do."

"In order," I asked, "to play?" And my voice was very ugly, full of contempt and anger.

"Well"—he looked at me with great, troubled eyes, as though, in fact, he hoped his eyes would tell me things he could never otherwise say—"they *think* so. And *if* they think so—!"

"And what do *you* think?" I asked.

He sat on the sofa and put his can of beer on the floor. "I don't know," he said, and I couldn't be sure if he were answering my question or pursuing his thoughts. His face didn't tell me. "It's not so much to *play*. It's to *stand* it, to be able to make it at all. On any level." He frowned and smiled: "In order to keep from shaking to pieces."

"But these friends of yours," I said, "they seem to shake themselves to pieces pretty goddamn fast."

"Maybe." He played with the notebook. And something told me that I should curb my tongue, that Sonny was doing his best to talk, that I should listen. "But of course you only know the ones that've gone to pieces. Some don't—or at least they haven't *yet* and that's just about all *any* of us can say." He paused. "And then there are some who just live, really, in hell, and they know it and they see what's happening and they go right on. I don't know." He sighed, dropped the notebook, folded his arms. "Some guys, you can tell from the way they play, they are something *all* the time. And you can see that, well, it makes something real for them. But of course," he picked up his beer from the floor and sipped it and put the can down again, "they *want* to, too, you've got to see that. Even some of them that say they don't—*some,* not all."

"And what about you?" I asked—I couldn't help it. "What about you? Do *you* want to?"

He stood up and walked to the window and remained silent for a long time. Then he sighed. "Me," he said. Then: "While I was downstairs before, on my way here, listening to that woman sing, it struck me all of a sudden how much suffering she must have had to go through—to sing like that. It's *repulsive* to think you have to suffer that much."

I said: "But there's no way not to suffer—is there, Sonny?"

"I believe not," he said and smiled, "but that's never stopped anyone from trying." He looked at me. "Has it?" I realized, with this mocking look, that there stood between us, forever, beyond the power of time or forgiveness, the fact that I had held silence—so long!—when he had needed human speech to help him. He turned back to the window. "No, there's no way not to suffer. But you try all kinds of ways to keep from drowning in it, to keep on top of it, and to make it seem—well, like *you*. Like you did something, all right, and now you're suffering for it. You know?" I said nothing. "Well you know," he said, impatiently, "why *do* people suffer? Maybe it's better to do something to give it a reason, *any* reason."

"But we just agreed," I said, "that there's no way not to suffer. Isn't it better, then, just to—take it?"

"But nobody just takes it," Sonny cried. "That's what I'm telling you! *Everybody* tries not to. You're just hung up on the *way* some people try—it's not *your* way!"

The hair on my face began to itch, my face felt wet. "That's not true," I said, "that's not true. I don't give a damn what other people do, I don't even care how they suffer. I just care how *you* suffer." And he looked at me. "Please believe me," I said, "I don't want to see you—die—trying not to suffer."

"I won't," he said, flatly, "die trying not to suffer. At least, not any faster than anybody else."

"But there's no need," I said, trying to laugh, "is there? in killing yourself."

I wanted to say more, but I couldn't. I wanted to talk about will power and how life could be—well, beautiful. I wanted to say that it was all within; but was it? or, rather, wasn't that exactly the trouble? And I wanted to promise that I would never fail him again. But it would all have sounded—empty words and lies.

So I made the promise to myself and prayed that I would keep it.

"It's terrible sometimes, inside," he said, "that's what's the trouble. You walk these streets, black and funky and cold, and there's not really a living ass to talk to, and there's nothing shaking, and there's no way of getting it out—that storm inside. You can't talk it and you can't make love with it, and when you finally try to get with it and play it, you realize *nobody's* listening. So *you've* got to listen. You got to find a way to listen."

And then he walked away from the window and sat on the sofa again, as though all the wind had suddenly been knocked out of him. "Sometimes you'll do *anything* to play, even cut your mother's throat." He laughed and looked at me. "Or your brother's." Then he sobered. "Or your own." Then: "Don't worry. I'm all right now and I think I'll *be* all right. But I can't forget—where I've been. I don't mean just the physical place I've been, I mean where I've *been*. And *what* I've been."

"What have you been, Sonny?" I asked.

He smiled—but sat sideways on the sofa, his elbow resting on the back, his fingers playing with his mouth and chin, not looking at me. "I've been something I didn't recognize, didn't know I could be. Didn't know anybody could be." He stopped, looking inward, looking helplessly young, looking old. "I'm not talking about it now because I feel *guilty* or anything like that—maybe it would be better if I did, I don't know. Anyway, I can't really talk about it. Not to you, not to anybody," and now he turned and faced me. "Sometimes, you know, and it was actually when I was most *out* of the world, I felt that I was in it, that I was *with* it, really, and I could play or I didn't really have to *play,* it just came out of me, it was there. And I don't know how I played, thinking about it now, but I know I did awful things, those times, sometimes, to people. Or it wasn't that I *did* anything to them—it was that they weren't real." He picked up the beer can; it was empty; he rolled it between his palms: "And other times—well, I needed a fix, I needed to find a place to lean, I needed to clear a space to *listen*—and I couldn't find it, and I—went crazy, I did terrible things to *me,* I was terrible *for* me." He began pressing the beer can between his hands, I watched the metal begin to give. It glittered, as he played with it, like a knife, and I was afraid he would cut himself, but I said nothing. "Oh well. I can never tell you. I was all by myself at the bottom of something, stinking and sweating and crying and shaking, and I smelled it, you know? *my* stink, and I thought I'd die if I couldn't get away from it and yet, all the same, I knew that everything I was doing was just locking me in with it. And I didn't know, I still *don't* know, something kept telling me that maybe it was good to smell your own stink, but I didn't think that *that* was what I'd been trying to do—and—who can stand it?" and he abruptly dropped the ruined beer can, looking at me with a small, still smile, and then rose, walking to the window as though it were the lodestone rock. I watched his face, he watched the avenue. "I couldn't tell you when Mama died—but the reason I wanted to leave Harlem so bad was to get away from drugs. And then, when I ran away, that's what I was running from—really. When I came back, nothing had changed, *I* hadn't changed, I was just—older." And he stopped, drumming with his fingers on the windowpane. The sun had vanished, soon darkness would fall. I watched his face. "It can come again," he said, almost as though speaking to himself. Then he turned to me. "It can come again," he repeated. "I just want you to know that."

"All right," I said, at last. "So it can come again. All right."

He smiled, but the smile was sorrowful. "I had to try to tell you," he said.

"Yes," I said. "I understand that."

"You're my brother," he said, looking straight at me, and not smiling at all.

"Yes," I repeated, "yes. I understand that."

He turned back to the window, looking out. "All that hatred down there," he said, "all that hatred and misery and love. It's a wonder it doesn't blow the avenue apart."

* * *

We went to the only nightclub on a short, dark street, downtown. We squeezed through the narrow, chattering, jam-packed bar to the entrance of the big room, where the bandstand was. And we stood there for a moment, for the lights were very dim in this room and we couldn't see. Then, "Hello, boy," said a voice and an enormous black man, much older than Sonny or myself, erupted out of all that atmospheric lighting and put an arm around Sonny's shoulder. "I been sitting right here," he said, "waiting for you."

He had a big voice, too, and heads in the darkness turned toward us.

Sonny grinned and pulled a little away, and said, "Creole, this is my brother. I told you about him."

Creole shook my hand. "I'm glad to meet you, son," he said, and it was clear that he was glad to meet me *there,* for Sonny's sake. And he smiled, "You got a real musician in *your* family," and he took his arm from Sonny's shoulder and slapped him, lightly, affectionately, with the back of his hand.

"Well. Now I've heard it all," said a voice behind us. This was another musician, and a friend of Sonny's, a coal-black, cheerful-looking man, built close to the ground. He immediately began confiding to me, at the top of his lungs, the most terrible things about Sonny, his teeth gleaming like a lighthouse and his laugh coming up out of him like the beginning of an earthquake. And it turned out that everyone at the bar knew Sonny, or almost everyone; some were musicians, working there, or nearby, or not working, some were simply hangers-on, and some were there to hear Sonny play. I was introduced to all of them and they were all very polite to me. Yet, it was clear that, for them, I was only Sonny's brother. Here, I was in Sonny's world. Or, rather: his kingdom. Here, it was not even a question that his veins bore royal blood.

They were going to play soon and Creole installed me, by myself, at a table in a dark corner. Then I watched them, Creole, and the little black man, and Sonny, and the others, while they horsed around, standing just below the bandstand. The light from the bandstand spilled just a little short of them and, watching them laughing and gesturing and moving about, I had the feeling that they, nevertheless, were being most careful not to step into that circle of light too suddenly: that if they moved into the light too suddenly, without thinking, they would perish in flame. Then, while I watched, one of them, the small, black man, moved into the light and crossed the bandstand and started fooling around with his drums. Then—being funny and being, also, extremely ceremonious—Creole took Sonny by the arm and led him to the piano. A woman's voice called Sonny's name and a few hands started clapping. And Sonny, also being funny and being ceremonious, and so touched, I think, that he could have cried, but neither hiding it nor showing it, riding it like a man, grinned, and put both hands to his heart and bowed from the waist.

Creole then went to the bass fiddle and a lean, very bright-skinned brown man jumped up on the bandstand and picked up his horn. So there they were, and the atmosphere on the bandstand and in the room began to change and tighten. Someone stepped up to the microphone and announced them. Then there were all kinds of murmurs. Some people at the bar shushed others. The waitress ran around, frantically getting in the last orders, guys and chicks got closer to each other, and the lights on the bandstand, on the quartet, turned to a kind of indigo. Then they all looked different there. Creole looked about him for the last time, as though he were making certain that all his chickens were in the coop, and then he—jumped and struck the fiddle. And there they were.

All I know about music is that not many people ever really hear it. And even then, on the rare occasions when something opens within, and the music enters, what we mainly hear, or hear corroborated, are personal, private, vanishing evocations. But the man who creates the music is hearing something else, is dealing with the roar rising from the void and imposing order on it as it hits the air. What is evoked in him, then, is of another order, more terrible because it has no words, and triumphant, too, for that same reason. And his triumph, when he triumphs, is ours. I just watched Sonny's face. His face was troubled, he was working hard, but he wasn't with it. And I had the feeling that, in a way, everyone on the bandstand was waiting for him, both waiting for him and pushing him along. But as I began to watch Creole, I realized that it was Creole who held them all back. He had them on a short rein. Up there, keeping the beat with his whole body, wailing on the fiddle, with his eyes closed, he was listening to everything, but he was listening to Sonny. He was having a dialogue with Sonny. He wanted Sonny to leave the shoreline and strike out for the deep water. He was Sonny's witness that deep water and drowning were not the same thing—he had been there, and he knew. And he wanted Sonny to know. He was waiting for Sonny to do the things on the keys which would let Creole know that Sonny was in the water.

And, while Creole listened, Sonny moved, deep within, exactly like someone in torment. I had never before thought of how awful the relationship must be between the musician and his instrument. He has to fill it, this instrument, with the breath of life, his own. He has to make it do what he wants it to do. And a piano is just a piano. It's made out of so much wood and wires and little hammers and big ones, and ivory. While there's only so much you can do with it, the only way to find this out is to try; to try and make it do everything.

And Sonny hadn't been near a piano for over a year. And he wasn't on much better terms with his life, not the life that stretched before him now. He and the piano stammered, started one way, got scared, stopped; started another way, panicked, marked time, started again; then seemed to have found a direction, panicked again, got stuck. And the face I saw on Sonny I'd never seen before. Everything had been burned out of it, and, at the same time, things usually hidden were being burned in, by the fire and fury of the battle which was occurring in him up there.

Yet, watching Creole's face as they neared the end of the first set, I had the feeling that something had happened, something I hadn't heard. Then they finished, there was scattered applause, and then, without an instant's warning, Creole started into something else, it was almost sardonic, it was *Am I Blue*. And, as though he commanded, Sonny began to play. Something began to happen. And Creole let out the reins. The dry, low, black man said something awful on the drums. Creole answered, and the drums talked back. Then the horn insisted, sweet and high, slightly detached perhaps, and Creole listened, commenting now and then, dry, and driving, beautiful and calm and old. Then they all came together again, and Sonny was part of the family again. I could tell this from his face. He seemed to have found, right there beneath his fingers, a damn brand-new piano. It seemed that he couldn't get over it. Then, for a while, just being happy with Sonny, they seemed to be agreeing with him that brand-new pianos certainly were a gas.

Then Creole stepped forward to remind them that what they were playing was the blues. He hit something in all of them, he hit something in me, myself, and the music tightened and deepened, apprehension began to beat the air. Creole began to tell us what the blues were all about. They were not about anything very new. He and his boys up there were keeping it new, at the risk of ruin, destruction, madness, and death, in order to find new ways to make us listen. For, while the tale of how we suffer, and how we are delighted, and how we may triumph is never new, it always must be heard. There isn't any other tale to tell, it's the only light we've got in all this darkness.

And this tale, according to that face, that body, those strong hands on those strings, has another aspect in every country, and a new depth in every generation. Listen, Creole seemed to be saying, listen. Now these are Sonny's blues. He made the little black man on the drums know it, and the bright, brown man on the horn. Creole wasn't trying any longer to get Sonny in the water. He was wishing him Godspeed. Then he stepped back, very slowly, filling the air with the immense suggestion that Sonny speak for himself.

Then they all gathered around Sonny and Sonny played. Every now and again one of them seemed to say, amen. Sonny's fingers filled the air with life, his life. But that life contained so many others. And Sonny went all the way back, he really began with the spare, flat statement of the opening phrase of the song. Then he began to make it his. It was very beautiful because it wasn't hurried and it was no longer a lament. I seemed to hear with what burning he had made it his, with what burning we had yet to make it ours, how we could cease lamenting. Freedom lurked around us and I understood, at last, that he could help us to be free if we would listen, that he would never be free until we did. Yet, there was no battle in his face now. I heard what he had gone through, and would continue to go through until he came to rest in earth. He had made it his: that long line, of which we knew only Mama and Daddy. And he was giving it back, as everything must be given back, so that, passing through death, it can live forever. I saw my mother's face again, and felt, for the first time, how the stones of the road she had walked on must have bruised her feet. I saw the moonlit road where my father's brother died. And it brought something else back to me, and carried me past it. I saw my little girl again and felt Isabel's tears again, and I felt my own tears begin to rise. And I was yet aware that this was only a moment, that the world waited outside, as hungry as a tiger, and that trouble stretched above us, longer than the sky.

Then it was over. Creole and Sonny let out their breath, both soaking wet, and grinning. There was a lot of applause and some of it was real. In the dark, the girl came by and I asked her to take drinks to the bandstand. There was a long pause, while they talked up there in the indigo light and after a while I saw the girl put a Scotch and milk on top of the piano for Sonny. He didn't seem to notice it, but just before they started playing again, he sipped from it and looked toward me, and nodded. Then he put it back on top of the piano. For me, then, as they began to play again, it glowed and shook above my brother's head like the very cup of trembling.

The School

by Donald Barthelme

Introduced by T. Coraghessan Boyle

I FIRST CAME UPON DONALD BARTHELME DURING MY UNDERGRADUATE days, when I was beginning, in the brief lucid intervals between binges of life, to entertain notions of actually writing a story or two of my own one day. *Unspeakable Practices, Unnatural Acts* was the book I seized on, and it, along with Robert Coover's *Pricksongs and Descants,* transformed me. Stories like "The Balloon," "Game," "Robert Kennedy Saved from Drowning," and "The Indian Uprising" seemed written in a new idiom—witty, hip, erudite, and playful. I became an apostle.

I went back then to Barthelme's only other extant collection—*Come Back, Dr. Caligari*—and sucked the sweetness from stories like "Me and Miss Mandible" and "A Shower of Gold," and I went forward to embrace *Snow White* with a sense of awakening possibility. After which, I awaited eagerly (yes: and this is not just some PR drone's delusion) each successive collection. Somewhere in there—middle seventies, I guess—I heard Barthelme read at Iowa. He read well, with relish, gusto, and a droll killing zip. The stories were "The Zombies," "The King of Jazz," and "Cortés and Montezuma."

Of all his work, and in spite of wonderfully clever conceptual pieces like "Eugénie Grandet" or "Views of My Father Weeping," "The School" remains my favorite. It is one of Barthelme's most conventional pieces—a straightforward dramatic monologue—and while not as groundbreaking or representative perhaps as a piece like the much-anthologized "The Indian Uprising," it is nevertheless one of his funniest and bizarrely wrenching stories.

The question it poses is simple: What good is human knowledge (i.e., the lesson plan) in the face of the unknowable? The speaker, an elementary-school teacher, has, in following the rigid course laid out by the lesson plan, inadvertently taught his students not so much about the miracle of life as about its ineluctable conclusion. In large part, the comedy derives from the speaker's laid-back language and lack of awareness in describing the increasingly absurd and ironic string of fatalities that collides head on with his best intentions.

The technique here is of escalation—an evolutionary progression from trees to snakes to fish to mammals—and that escalation presents the author with his biggest aesthetic dilemma: how to get out. As in any concept-driven story, the author is in danger of painting himself into a corner: once we go from the death of the puppy to those of the grandparents, parents, and finally even two members of the class, where do we go next? I think Barthelme has resolved the issue neatly—quick on his feet, as always—and given the story a final droll punch that makes wonderfully absurd sense and sends it into a comic orbit all its own. I couldn't have asked for more.

The School

Donald Barthelme

Well, we had all these children out planting trees, see, because we figured that . . . that was part of their education, to see how, you know, the root systems . . . and also the sense of responsibility, taking care of things, being individually responsible. You know what I mean. And the trees all died. They were orange trees. I don't know why they died, they just died. Something wrong with the soil possibly or maybe the stuff we got from the nursery wasn't the best. We complained about it. So we've got thirty kids there, each kid had his or her own little tree to plant, and we've got these thirty dead trees. All these kids looking at these little brown sticks, it was depressing.

It wouldn't have been so bad except that just a couple of weeks before the thing with the trees, the snakes all died. But I think that the snakes—well, the reason that the snakes kicked off was that . . . you remember, the boiler was shut off for four days because of the strike, and that was explicable. It was something you could explain to the kids because of the strike. I mean, none of their parents would let them cross the picket line and they knew there was a strike going on and what it meant. So when things got started up again and we found the snakes they weren't too disturbed.

With the herb gardens it was probably a case of overwatering, and at least now they know not to overwater. The children were very conscientious with the herb gardens and some of them probably . . . you know, slipped them a little extra water when we weren't looking. Or maybe . . . well, I don't like to think about sabotage, although it did occur to us. I mean, it was something that crossed our minds. We were thinking that way probably because before that the gerbils had died, and the white mice had died, and the salamander . . . well, now they know not to carry them around in plastic bags.

Of course we *expected* the tropical fish to die, that was no surprise. Those numbers, you look at them crooked and they're belly-up on the surface. But the lesson plan called for a tropical-fish input at that point, there was nothing we could do, it happens every year, you just have to hurry past it.

We weren't even supposed to have a puppy.

We weren't even supposed to have one, it was just a puppy the Murdoch girl found under a Gristede's truck one day and she was afraid the truck would run over it when the driver had finished making his delivery, so she stuck it in her knapsack and brought it to school with her. So we had this puppy. As soon as I saw the puppy I thought, Oh Christ, I bet it will live for about two weeks and then . . . And that's what it did. It wasn't supposed to be in the classroom at all, there's some kind of regulation about it, but you can't tell them they can't have a puppy when the puppy is already there, right in front of them, running around on the floor and yap yap yapping. They named it Edgar—that is, they named it after me. They had a lot of fun running after it and yelling, "Here, Edgar! Nice Edgar!" Then they'd laugh like hell. They enjoyed the ambiguity. I enjoyed it myself. I don't mind being kidded. They made a little house for it in the supply closet and all that. I don't know what it died of. Distemper, I guess. It probably hadn't had any shots. I got it out of there before the kids got to school. I checked the supply closet each morning, routinely, because I knew what was going to happen. I gave it to the custodian.

And then there was this Korean orphan that the class adopted through the Help the Children program, all the kids brought in a quarter a month, that was the idea. It was an unfortunate thing, the kid's name was Kim and maybe we adopted him too late or something. The cause of death was not stated in the letter we got, they suggested we adopt another child instead and sent us some interesting case histories, but we didn't have the heart. The class took it pretty hard, they began (I think, nobody ever said anything to me directly) to feel that maybe there was something wrong with the school. But I don't think there's anything wrong with the school, particularly, I've seen better and I've seen worse. It was just a run of bad luck. We had an extraordinary number of parents passing away, for instance. There were I think two heart attacks and two suicides, one drowning, and four killed together in a car accident. One stroke. And we had the usual heavy mortality rate among the grandparents, or maybe it was heavier this year, it seemed so. And finally the tragedy.

The tragedy occurred when Matthew Wein and Tony Mavrogordo were playing over where they're excavating for the new federal office building. There were all these big wooden beams stacked, you know, at the edge of the excavation. There's a court case coming out of that, the parents are claiming that the beams were poorly stacked. I don't know what's true and what's not. It's been a strange year.

I forgot to mention Billy Brandt's father, who was knifed fatally when he grappled with a masked intruder in his home.

One day, we had a discussion in class. They asked me, where did they go? The trees, the salamander, the tropical fish, Edgar, the poppas and mommas, Matthew and Tony, where did they go? And I said, I don't know, I don't know. And they said, who knows? and I said, nobody knows. And they said, is death that which gives meaning to life? And I said, no, life is that which gives meaning to life. Then they said, but isn't death, considered as a fundamental datum, the means by which the taken-for-granted mundanity of the everyday may be transcended in the direction of—

I said, yes, maybe.

They said, we don't like it.

I said, that's sound.

They said, it's a bloody shame!

I said, it is.

They said, will you make love now with Helen (our teaching assistant) so that we can see how it is done? We know you like Helen.

I do like Helen but I said that I would not.

We've heard so much about it, they said, but we've never seen it.

I said I would be fired and that it was never, or almost never, done as a demonstration. Helen looked out of the window.

They said, please, please make love with Helen, we require an assertion of value, we are frightened.

I said that they shouldn't be frightened (although I am often frightened) and that there was value everywhere. Helen came and embraced me. I kissed her a few times on the brow. We held each other. The children were excited. Then there was a knock on the door, I opened the door, and the new gerbil walked in. The children cheered wildly.

The Aleph

by Jorge Luis Borges

Introduced by Oscar Hijuelos

I FIRST ENCOUNTERED "THE ALEPH" BY THE GREAT ARGENTINE WRITER Jorge Luis Borges one afternoon over twenty years ago, in 1973—I believe—when I was down on the Lower East Side visiting a friend, a young Armenian intellectual, such as one might meet at City College in those days. While he fiddled about in his kitchen (or walked his dog, or pleaded/conversed with his girlfriend on the telephone), I sat on his itchy, cat-haired, roach-egged couch, idly riffling through a pile of books that I had pulled from his shelves, among them a mildewed, jaundiced-looking, much-read-over pocketbook edition of *The Aleph and Other Stories* by Borges. Now, just a few days earlier I had been informed about the results of an aptitude test I had taken, the upshot being that I was apparently most suited for the profession of accounting. That well may have been my destiny, but I am happy (unhappy?) to report that the experience of reading "The Aleph" for the first of many times had a great effect upon me and my future; I have loved and will always love that story—and I will always be indebted to Borges for having written it—because, aside from its many wonderful qualities, it will always hold a special meaning for me: quite simply, "The Aleph" is the story that first inspired in me the desire to one day write.

As for the story itself, "The Aleph" is part love tale, told in a voice that is both obsessively introspective and delicately urbane; it has an undertone of near horror, like a ghost story—as in an Edgar Allan Poe tale the object of the narrator's love, Beatriz Viterbo, exerts a great power long after she has been dead; it has a quite visual, nearly cinematic, narrative that is a pleasure to read. Ironically, Borges, who suffered from a hereditary progressive blindness, had often spoken about the influence of film upon his writing. In the economy and vividness of its details, it is instructive to young writers—note how effortlessly Borges suggests the shifting universe by opening with a most introspective and bemused narrator noticing yet another new brand of American cigarette being advertised on the billboards of Constitution Plaza in Buenos Aires. And it is quite funny—especially to writers—when, for example, the narrator, Borges himself, muses over the critical success of a decidedly second-rate talent, Carlos Argentino Daneri, who to the narrator's chagrin has risen to the top of the poet's profession while the narrator has not.

For a final note; without betraying the essence of the story, which is the "Aleph" itself, nor this story's spectacular climax, I will leave the reader with my sense that in this work, as in certain others—"Funes, the Memorious," for example—Borges is really writing about and paying tribute to the writer's consciousness, which, through its command of and access to the imagination and language, can contain and replicate everything that has existed or will ever exist in this universe.

The Aleph

Jorge Luis Borges

Translated by Anthony Kerrigan

> O God, I could be bounded in a nutshell and count myself a King of infinite space.
>
> —*HAMLET,* II, 2

> But they will teach us that Eternity is the Standing still of the Present Time, a *Nunc-stans* (as the Schools call it); which neither they, nor any else understand, no more than they would a *Hic-stans* for an Infinite greatness of Place.
>
> —*LEVIATHAN,* IV, 46

On the incandescent February morning Beatriz Viterbo died, after a death agony so imperious it did not for a moment descend into sentimentalism or fear, I noticed that the iron billboards in the Plaza Constitución bore new advertisements for some brand or other of Virginia tobacco; I was saddened by this fact, for it made me realize that the incessant and vast universe was already moving away from her and that this change was the first in an infinite series. The universe would change but I would not, I thought with melancholy vanity; I knew that sometimes my vain devotion had exasperated her; now that she was dead, I could consecrate myself to her memory, without hope but also without humiliation. I thought of how the thirtieth of April was her birthday; to visit her house in Calle Garay on that day and pay my respects to her father and Carlos Argentino Daneri, her first cousin, would be an act of courtesy, irreproachable and perhaps even unavoidable. I would wait, once again, in the twilight of the overladen entrance hall; I would study, one more time, the particulars of her numerous portraits: Beatriz Viterbo in profile, in color; Beatriz wearing a mask, during the Carnival of 1921; Beatriz at her First Communion; Beatriz on the day of her wedding to Roberto Alessandri; Beatriz a little while after the divorce, at a dinner in the Club Hípico; Beatriz with Delia San Marco Porcel and Carlos Argentino; Beatriz with the Pekingese which had been a present from Villegas Haedo; Beatriz from the front and in a three-quarter view, smiling, her hand under her chin. . . . I would not be obliged, as on other occasions, to justify my presence with moderate-priced offerings of books, with books whose pages, finally, I learned to cut beforehand, so as to avoid finding, months later, that they were still uncut.

Beatriz Viterbo died in 1929. From that time on, I never let a thirtieth of April go by without a visit to her house. I used to arrive there around seven-fifteen and stay about twenty-five minutes. Every year I came a little later and stayed a little longer. In 1933 a torrential rain worked to my advantage: they were forced to invite me to dine. I did not fail to avail myself of this advantageous precedent. In 1934, I appeared, just after eight, with a honey nutcake from Santa Fe. With the greatest naturalness, I remained for supper. And thus, on these melancholy and vainly erotic anniversaries, Carlos Argentino Daneri began gradually to confide in me.

Beatriz was tall, fragile, lightly leaning forward: there was in her walk (if the oxymoron is acceptable) a kind of gracious torpor, the beginnings of an ecstasy. Carlos Argentino is rosy, important, gray-haired, find-featured. He holds some subordinate position or other in an illegible library in the south side suburbs. He is authoritarian, but also ineffective. Until very recently, he took advantage of nights and holidays to avoid going out of his house. At a remove of two generations, the Italian *s* and the copious gesticulation of the Italians survive in him. His mental activity is continuous, impassioned, versatile, and altogether insignificant. He abounds in useless analogies and fruitless scruples. He possesses (as did Beatriz) long, lovely, tapering hands. For several months he was obsessed with Paul Fort, less with his ballads than with the idea of irreproachable glory. "He is the Prince of the poets of France," he would repeat fatuously. "You will set yourself against him in vain; no, not even your most poisoned barb will reach him."

The thirtieth of April, 1941, I allowed myself to add to the gift of honey nutcake a bottle of Argentine cognac. Carlos Argentino tasted it, judged it "interesting," and, after a few glasses, launched on a vindication of modern man.

"I evoke him," he said with rather inexplicable animation, "in his studio-laboratory, in the city's watchtowers, so to say, supplied with telephones, telegraphs, phonographs, radiotelephone apparatus, cinematographic equipment, magic lanterns, glossaries, timetables, compendiums, bulletins. . . ."

He remarked that for a man of such faculties the act of travel was useless. Our twentieth century had transformed the fable of Mohammed and the mountain: the mountains, now, converged upon the modern Mohammed.

His ideas seemed so inept to me, their exposition so pompous and so vast, that I immediately related them to literature: I asked him why he did not write them down. Foreseeably he replied that he had already done so: these concepts, and others no less novel, figured in the Augural Canto, or more simply, the Prologue Canto, of a poem on which he had been working for many years, without publicity, without any deafening to-do, putting his entire reliance on those two props known as work and solitude. First, he opened the floodgates of the imagination; then he made use of a sharp file. The poem was titled *The Earth;* it consisted of a description of the planet, wherein, naturally, there was no lack of picturesque digression and elegant apostrophe.

I begged him to read me a passage, even though brief. He opened a drawer in his desk, took out a tall bundle of pages from a pad, each sheet stamped with the letterhead of the Juan Crisóstomo Lafinur Library, and, with sonorous satisfaction, read out:

I have seen, like the Greek, the cities of men and their fame,
Their labor, days of various light, hunger's shame;
I correct no event, falsify no name,
But the voyage *I narrate is* . . . autour de ma chambre.

"By all lights an interesting strophe," he opined. "The first line wins the applause of the professor, the academician, the Hellenist, if not of superficial pedants, who form, these last, a considerable sector of public opinion. The second passes from Homer to Hesiod (the entire verse an implicit homage, writ on the façade of the resplendent building, to the father of didactic poetry), not without rejuvenating a procedure whose lineage goes back to Scripture, that of enumeration, congeries of conglomeration. The third line—Baroquism? Decadentism? Purified and fanatical cult of form?—is composed of two twin hemistichs. The fourth, frankly bilingual, assures me the unconditional support of every spirit sensitive to the gay lure of graceful play. I say nothing of the rare rhyme, nor of the learning which permits me—without any pedantry!—to accumulate, in four lines, three erudite allusions encompassing thirty centuries of compressed literature: first to the *Odyssey,* second to *Works and Days,* third to the immortal bagatelle proffered us through the idling of the Savoyard's pen. . . . Once more I have understood that modern art requires the balsam of laughter, the *scherzo.* Decidedly, Goldoni has the floor!"

He read me many another stanza, each of which obtained his approbation and profuse commentary, too. There was nothing memorable in any of them. I did not even judge them very much worse than the first one. There had been a collaboration, in his writing, between application, resignation, and chance; the virtues which Daneri attributed to them were posterior. I realized that the poet's labor lay not with the poetry, but with the invention of reasons to make the poetry admirable; naturally, this ulterior and subsequent labor modified the work for him, but not for others. Daneri's oral style was extravagant; his metric heaviness hindered his transmitting that extravagance, except in a very few instances, to the poem.*

Only once in my life have I had occasion to examine the fifteen thousand dodecasyllabic verses of the *Poly-Olbion,* that topographic epic poem in which Michael Drayton recorded the flora, fauna, hydrography, orography, military and monastic history of England; I am sure that this considerable, but limited, production is less tedious than the vast congeneric enterprise of Carlos Argentino. The latter proposed to put into verse the entire face of the planet; in 1941, he had already dispatched several hectares of the State of Queensland, in addition to one kilometer of the course of the River Ob, a gasometer north of Veracruz, the main business houses in the parish of La Concepción, the villa owned by Mariana Cambaceres de Alvear on Eleventh of September street, in Belgrano, and an establishment devoted to Turkish baths not far from the famous Brighton Aquarium. He read me from his poem certain laborious passages concerning the Australian zone; these large and formless alexandrines lacked the relative agitation of the Preface. I copy one stanza:

Know ye. To the right hand of the routinary post
(Coming, of course, from the North-northwest)
One wearies out a skeleton—Color? White-celeste—
Which gives the sheep run an ossuary cast.

"Two audacious strokes," he cried out in exultation, "redeemed, I can hear you muttering, by success! I admit it, I admit it. One, the epithet *routinary,* which accurately proclaims, *en passant,* the inevitable tedium inherent in pastoral and farming chores, a tedium which neither georgic poetry nor our already laureled *Don Segundo* ever ventured to denounce in this way, in red-hot heat. The other, the energetic prosaicism of *one wearies out a skeleton,* a phrase which the prudish will want to excommunicate in horror, but which the critic with virile taste will appreciate more than his life. For the rest, the entire line is of high carat, the highest. The second hemistich engages the reader in the most animated converse; it anticipates his lively curiosity, places a question in his mouth and answers it . . . instantly. And

* I recall, nevertheless, the following lines from a satire in which he harshly fustigated bad poets:

This one gives his poem bellicose armorings
Of erudition; that one puts in pomp and jubilee.
Both in vain beat their ridiculous wings . . .
Forgetting, the wretches, the factor BEAUTY!

Only the fear of creating for himself an army of implacable and powerful foes dissuaded him (he told me) from fearlessly publishing this poem.

what do you tell me of that find of mine: *white-celeste?* This picturesque neologism insinuates the sky, which is a very important factor in the Australian landscape. Without this evocation, the colors of the sketch would be much too somber, and the reader would find himself compelled to close the book, wounded in the innermost part of his soul by a black and incurable melancholy."

Toward midnight, I took my leave.

Two Sundays later, Daneri called me on the telephone, for the first time in his life, I believe. He proposed that we meet at four o'clock, "to drink a glass of milk together, in the salon-bar next door, which the progressivism of Zunino and of Zungri—the proprietors of my house, you will recall—is causing to be inaugurated on the corner. Truly, a confectionery shop you will be interested in knowing about." I accepted, with more resignation than enthusiasm. There was no difficulty in finding a table; the "salon-bar," inexorably modern, was just slightly less atrocious than what I had foreseen; at the neighboring tables an excited public mentioned the sums which Zunino and Zungri had invested without batting an eye. Carlos Argentino feigned astonishment over some wonder or other in the lighting installations (which he doubtless already knew about), and he said to me, with a certain severity:

"You'll have to admit, no matter how grudgingly, that these premises vie successfully with the most renowned of Flores."

Then, he reread me four or five pages of his poem. He had made corrections in accordance with a depraved principle of verbal ostentation: where he had formerly written *azurish,* he now put *azuritic, azuritish,* and even *azury*. The word *lacteous* proved not ugly enough for him; in the course of an impetuous description of a wool washer, he preferred *lactary, lactinous, lactescent, lactiferous*. . . . He bitterly reviled the critics; later, in a more benign spirit, he compared them to persons "who dispose of no precious metals, nor steam presses, nor rolling presses, nor sulphuric acids for minting treasures, but who can *indicate* to *others* the *site* of a treasure." Next he censured *prologomania* "which the Prince of Talents, in the graceful prefacing of his *Don Quixote,* already ridiculed." He nevertheless admitted to me now that by way of frontispiece to the new work a showy prologue, an accolade signed by the feather pen of a bird of prey, of a man of weight, would be most convenient. He added that he planned to bring out the initial cantos of his poems. I understood, then, the singular telephonic invitation; the man was going to ask me to preface his pedantic farrago. My fears proved unfounded: Carlos Argentino observed, with rancorous admiration, that he did not misuse the epithet in denominating as *solid* the prestige achieved in all circles by Álvaro Melián Lafinur, man of letters, who would, if I insisted on it, delightfully prologue the poem. So as to avoid the most unpardonable of failures, I was to make myself spokesman for two undeniable merits: formal perfection and scientific rigor, "inasmuch as this vast garden of tropes, figures of speech, and elegance, allows no single detail which does not confirm the severe truth." He added that Beatriz had always enjoyed herself with Álvaro.

I assented, assented profusely. For greater conviction, I promised to speak to Álvaro on Thursday, rather than wait until the following Monday: we could meet at the small supper that usually climaxes every reunion of the Writers' Club. (There are no such suppers, but it is an irrefutable fact that the reunions do take place on Thursdays, a point which Carlos Argentino Daneri would find confirmed in the daily newspapers, and which lent a certain reality to the phrase.) Adopting an air halfway between divinatory and sagacious, I told him that before taking up the question of a prologue, I would delineate the curious plan of the book. We took our leave of each other. As I turned the corner into Calle Bernardo de Irigoyen, I impartially considered the alternatives before me: a) I could talk to Álvaro and tell him how that cousin of Beatriz' (this explicatory euphemism would allow me to say her name) had elaborated a poem which seemed to dilate to infinity the possibilities of cacophony and chaos; b) I could fail to speak to Álvaro altogether. I foresaw, lucidly, that my indolence would choose b.

From early Friday morning the telephone began to disquiet me. It made me indignant to think that this instrument, which in other days had produced the irrecoverable voice of Beatriz, could lower itself to being a receptacle for the useless and perhaps even choleric complaints of that deceived man Carlos Argentino Daneri. Luckily, nothing awful occurred—except the inevitable animosity inspired by that man, who had imposed on me a delicate mission and would later forget me altogether.

The telephone lost its terrors; but then toward the end of October, Carlos Argentino called me again. He was terribly agitated; at first I could not identify the voice. Sadly and yet wrathfully he stammered that the now uncurbed Zunino and Zungri, under the pretext of enlarging their outrageous confectionery, were going to demolish his house.

"The house of my fathers! My house, the inveterate house of the Calle Garay!" he went on repeating, perhaps forgetting his grief in the melody.

It was not difficult for me to share his grief. Once past forty, every change is a detestable symbol of the passage of time. Besides, at stake was a house that, for me, infinitely alluded to Beatriz. I wanted to bring out this most delicate point; my interlocutor did not hear me. He said that if Zunino and Zungri persisted in their absurd proposal, Doctor Zunni, his lawyer, would enter an action *ipso facto* for damages and would oblige them to pay one hundred thousand *pesos nacionales* in compensation.

I was impressed to hear the name of Zunni: his practice, out of his office at the corner of Caseros and Tacuarí, was of a proverbial and solemn reliability. I asked if Zunni had already taken charge of the matter. Daneri said he would speak to him that very afternoon. He hesitated, and then, in that level, impersonal voice to which we all have recourse for confiding something very intimate, he told me that in order to finish the poem the house was indispensable to him, for in one of the cellar corners there was an Aleph. He indicated that an Aleph is one of the points in space containing all points.

"It's in the dining-room cellar," he explained, his diction grown hasty from anxiety. "It's mine, it's mine; I discovered it in childhood, before I was of school age. The cellar stair is steep, and my aunt and uncle had forbidden me to go down it. But someone said that there was a world in the cellar. They were referring, I found out later, to a trunk, but I understood there was a world there. I descended secretly, went rolling down the forbidden stairs, fell off. When I opened my eyes I saw the Aleph."

"The Aleph?" I echoed.

"Yes, the place where, without any possible confusion, all the places in the world are found, seen from every angle. I revealed my discovery to no one, and I returned there. The child could not understand that this privilege was proffered him so that the man might chisel out the poem! Zunino and Zungri will not dislodge me, no, a thousand times no. With the code of laws in hand, Doctor Zunni will prove that my Aleph is *inalienable*."

I attempted to reason with him.

"But, isn't the cellar very dark?"

"Really, truth does not penetrate a rebellious understanding. If all the places on earth are in the Aleph, the Aleph must also contain all the illuminations, all the lights, all the sources of light."

"I will go and see it at once."

I hung up, before he could issue a prohibition. The knowledge of one fact is enough to allow one to perceive at once a whole series of confirming traits, previously unsuspected. I was astonished not to have understood until that moment that Carlos Argentino was a madman. All the Viterbos, for that matter . . . Beatriz (I often say so myself) was a woman, a girl, of an almost implacable clairvoyance, but there was about her a negligence, a distraction, a disdain, a real cruelty, which perhaps called for a pathological explanation. The madness of Carlos Argentino filled me with malicious felicity; in our innermost beings, we had always detested each other.

In Calle Garay, the serving woman asked me if I would be kind enough to wait. The child was, as always, in the cellar, developing photographs. Next to the flower vase without a single flower in it, atop the useless piano, there smiled (more timeless than anachronic) the great portrait of Beatriz, in dull colors. No one could see us; in an access of tender despair I went up close and told her:

"Beatriz, Beatriz Elena, Beatriz Elena Viterbo, beloved Beatriz, Beatriz lost forever, it's me, Borges."

A little later Carlos came in. He spoke with a certain dryness. I understood that he was incapable of thinking of anything but the loss of the Aleph.

"A glass of the pseudo-cognac," he ordered, "and then you can duck into the cellar. As you already know, the dorsal decubitus is imperative. And so are darkness, immobility, and a certain ocular accommodation. You lie down on the tile floor and fix your eyes on the nineteenth step of the pertinent stairs. I leave, lower the trap door, and you're alone. Quite likely—it should be easy!—some rodent will scare you! In a few minutes you will see the Aleph. The microcosm of alchemists and cabalists, our proverbial concrete friend, the *multum in parvo!*"

Once we were in the dining room he added:

"Of course if you don't see it, your incapacity in no way invalidates my testimony. . . . Now, down with you. Very shortly you will be able to engage in a dialogue with *all* of the images of Beatriz."

I rapidly descended, tired of his insubstantial words. The cellar, barely wider than the stairs, had much of a well about it. I gazed about in search of the trunk of which Carlos Argentino had spoken. Some cases with bottles in them and some canvas bags cluttered one corner. Carlos picked up one of the bags, folded it in half and placed it exactly in a precise spot.

"A humble pillow," he explained, "but if I raise it one centimeter, you won't see a thing, and you'll be left abashed and ashamed. Stretch your bulk out on the floor and count off nineteen steps."

I complied with his ridiculous requisites; and at last he went away. Carefully he closed the trap door; the darkness, despite a crevice which I discovered later, seemed total. And suddenly I realized the danger I ran: I had allowed myself to be buried by a madman, after having drunk some poison! Behind the transparent bravado of Carlos was the intimate terror that I would not see the prodigy; to defend his delirium, to avoid knowing that he was mad, Carlos *had to kill me*. A confused malaise swept over me; I attempted to attribute it to my rigid posture rather than to the operation of a narcotic. I closed my eyes; opened them. Then I saw the Aleph.

I arrive, now, at the ineffable center of my story. And here begins my despair as a writer. All language is an alphabet of symbols whose use presupposes a past shared by all the other interlocutors. How, then, transmit to others the infinite Aleph, which my fearful mind scarcely encompasses? The mystics, in similar situations, are lavish with emblems: to signify the divinity, a Persian speaks of a bird that in some way is all birds; Alanus de Insulis speaks of a sphere whose center is everywhere and whose circumference is nowhere; Ezekiel, of an angel with four faces who looks simultaneously to the Orient and the Occident, to the North and the South. (Not vainly do I recall these inconceivable analogies; they bear some relation to the Aleph.) Perhaps the gods would not be against my finding an equivalent image, but then this report would be contaminated with literature, with falsehood. For the rest, the central problem is unsolvable: the enumeration, even if only partial, of an infinite complex. In that gigantic instant I saw millions of delightful and atrocious acts; none astonished me more than the fact that all of them together occupied the same point, without superposition and without transparency. What my eyes saw was simultaneous: what I shall transcribe is successive, because language is successive. Nevertheless, I shall cull something of it all.

In the lower part of the step, toward the right, I saw a small iridescent sphere, of almost intolerable brilliance. At first I thought it rotary; then I understood that this movement was an illusion produced by the vertiginous sights it enclosed. The Aleph's diameter must have been about two or three centimeters, but Cosmic Space was in it, without diminution of size. Each object (the mirror's glass, for instance) was infinite objects, for I clearly saw it from all points in the universe. I saw the heavy-laden sea; I saw the dawn and the dusk; I saw the multitudes of America; I saw a silver-plated cobweb at the center of a black pyramid; I saw a tattered labyrinth (it was London); I saw interminable eyes nearby looking at me as if in a mirror; I saw all the mirrors in the planet and none reflected me; in an inner patio in the Calle Soler I saw the same paving tile I had seen thirty years before in the entranceway to a house in the town of Fray Bentos; I saw clusters of grapes, snow, tobacco, veins of metal, steam; I saw convex equatorial deserts and every grain of sand in them; I saw a woman at Inverness whom I shall not forget: I saw her violent switch of hair, her proud body, the cancer in her breast; I saw a circle of dry land on a sidewalk where formerly there had been a tree; I saw a villa in Adrogué; I saw a copy of the first English version of Pliny, by Philemon Holland, and saw simultaneously every letter on every page (as a boy I used to marvel that the letters in a closed book did not get mixed up and lost in the course of a night); I saw night and day contemporaneously; I saw a sunset in Querétaro which seemed to reflect the color of a rose in Bengal; I saw my bedroom with nobody in it; I saw in a study in Alkmaar a terraqueous globe between two mirrors which multiplied it without end; I saw horses with swirling manes on a beach by the Caspian Sea at dawn; I saw the delicate bone structure of a hand; I saw the survivors of a battle sending out post cards; I saw a deck of Spanish playing cards in a shopwindow in Mirzapur; I saw the oblique shadows of some ferns on the floor of a hothouse; I saw tigers, emboli, bison, ground swells, and armies; I saw all the ants on earth; I saw a Persian astrolabe; in a desk drawer I saw (the writing made me tremble) obscene, incredible, precise letters, which Beatriz had written Carlos Argentino; I saw an adored monument in La Chacarita cemetery; I saw the atrocious relic of what deliciously had been Beatriz Viterbo; I saw the circulation of my obscure blood; I saw the gearing of love and the modifications of death; I saw the Aleph from all points; I saw the earth in the Aleph and in the earth the Aleph once more and the earth in the Aleph; I saw my face and my viscera; I saw your face and felt vertigo and cried because my eyes had seen that conjectural and secret object whose name men usurp but which no man has gazed on: the inconceivable universe.

I felt infinite veneration, infinite compassion.

"You must be good and dizzy from peering into things that don't concern you," cried a hateful, jovial voice. "Even if you rack your brains, you won't be able to pay me back in a century for this revelation. What a formidable observatory, eh, Borges!"

Carlos Argentino's feet occupied the highest step. In the half-light I managed to get up and to stammer:

"Formidable, yes, formidable."

The indifference in the sound of my voice surprised me. Anxiously Carlos Argentino insisted:

"You saw it all, in colors?"

It was at that instant that I conceived my revenge. Benevolently, with obvious pity, nervous, evasive, I thanked Carlos Argentino for the hospitality of his cellar and urged him to take advantage of the demolition of his house to get far away from the pernicious capital, which is easy on no one, believe me, on no one! I refused, with suave energy, to discuss the Aleph; I embraced him on leaving, and repeated that the country and its quiet are two grand doctors.

In the street, on the Constitución stairs, in the subway, all the faces struck me as familiar. I feared that not a single thing was left to cause me surprise; I was afraid I would never be quit of the impression that I had "returned." Happily, at the end of a few nights of insomnia, forgetfulness worked in me again.

P.S. March 1, 1943

Six months after the demolition of the building in Calle Garay, Procusto Publishers did not take fright at the length of Argentino's considerable poem and launched upon the reading public a selection of "Argentino Extracts." It is almost needless to repeat what happened: Carlos Argentino Daneri received Second Prize, of the National Prizes for Literature.* First Prize was awarded to Doctor Aita; Third, to Doctor Mario Bonfanti; incredibly, my book *The Cards of the Cardsharp* did not get a single vote. Once again incomprehension and envy won the day! For a long time now I have not been able to see Daneri; the daily press says he will soon give us another volume. His fortunate pen (no longer benumbed by the Aleph) has been consecrated to versifying the epitomes of Doctor Acevedo Díaz.

I would like to add two further observations: one, on the nature of the Aleph; the other, on its name. As is well known, the latter is the name of the first letter of the alphabet of the sacred language. Its application to the cycle of my story does not appear mere chance. For the cabala, this letter signifies the En-Sof, the limitless and pure divinity; it has also been said that it has the form of a man who points out heaven and earth, to indicate that the inferior

* "I received your pained congratulations," he wrote me. "You huff and puff with envy, my lamentable friend, but you must confess—though you choke!—that this time I was able to crown my bonnet with the reddest of feathers, to put in my turban the *caliph* of rubies."

world is the mirror and map of the superior; for the *Mengenlehre,* it is the symbol of transfinite numbers, in which the whole is no greater than any of its parts. I wanted to know: Had Carlos Argentino chosen this name, or had he read it, *applied to another point where all points converge,* in some one of the innumerable texts revealed to him by the Aleph in his house? Incredible as it may seem, I believe there is (or was) another Aleph; I believe that the Aleph in the Calle Garay was a false Aleph.

Here are my reasons. Toward 1867, Captain Burton held the office of British Consul in Brazil. In July, 1942, Pedro Henríquez Ureña discovered, in a library at Santos, a manuscript by Burton dealing with the mirror which the Orient attributes to Iskandar Zu al-Karnayn, or Alexander Bicornis of Macedonia. In its glass the entire world was reflected. Burton mentions other artifices of like kind: the septuple goblet of Kai Josru; the mirror which Tarik Benzeyad found in a tower (*The Thousand and One Nights,* 272); the mirror which Lucian of Samosata was able to examine on the moon (*True History,* I, 26); the diaphanous spear which the first book of Capella's *Satyricon* attributes to Jupiter; the universal mirror of Merlin, "round and hollow . . . and seemed a world of glas" (*The Faerie Queene,* III, 2, 19). And he adds these curious words: "But the former (besides the defect of not existing) are mere instruments of optics. The Faithful who attend the Mosque of Amr, in Cairo, know very well that the universe is in the interior of one of the stone columns surrounding the central courtyard. . . . No one, of course, can see it, but those who put their ears to the surface claim to hear, within a short time, its workaday rumor. . . . The mosque dates from the seventh century; the columns come from other, pre-Islamic, temples, for as ibn-Khaldûn has written: *'In republics founded by nomads, the assistance of foreigners is indispensable in all that concerns masonry.'* "

Does that Aleph exist in the innermost recess of a stone? Did I see it when I saw all things, and have I forgotten it? Our minds are porous with forgetfulness; I myself am falsifying and losing, through the tragic erosion of the years, the features of Beatriz.

A Day in the Open

by Jane Bowles

Introduced by Joy Williams

JANE BOWLES WROTE TO PAUL BOWLES ABOUT HIS STORY "THE ECHO" that "it was all so terrible and exciting that I almost threw up." Her own stories do not have quite that ultimate effect. The reader feels vertigo, more likely: a delicious imbalance, a sense of fever, I think. She is a dizzyingly unnatural writer. She introduces characters woodenly, usually in terms of their nationality. She doesn't know how to get into her stories or how to end them. Her husband urged her to utilize the "hammer and nails" available to the fiction writer, the tricks and tools of narrative construction. But she had to make her own hammer and nails before she could begin. Each word is built, each step painful, each transition a rope bridge thrown over a chasm. She makes it look as hard as it is. She feared that she had no intellect, certainly that she suffered from an absence of ideas that could be expressed; she was frightened of the surrealists when they came to call; Eudora Welty took her story "Camp Cataract" home to read and months later returned it with a note saying she had "failed" on it but would like to try something else of hers someday. Writing distressed Jane Bowles terribly. Her writer's block was as palpable as her destructive, quite possibly murderous Moroccan maid and lover, Cherifa. "I have decided not to become hysterical," she wrote. "If I cannot write my book then I shall give up writing, that's all. Then either suicide or another life." But there was no other life. She suffered a stroke when she was forty, and words, any words at all, came with increasing difficulty for sixteen terrible years.

Reading Jane Bowles I am always enchanted and unnerved, a little sick, actually, with love for her gloomy waterfalls, her morbid gazebos, her ghastly picnics, her serious ladies and frail whores—her tortured, awkward, groping, uncompleted souls.

A Day in the Open

Jane Bowles

In the outskirts of the capital there was a low white house, very much like the other houses around it. The street on which it stood was not paved, as this was a poor section of the city. The door of this particular house, very new and studded with nails, was bolted inside and out. A large room, furnished with some modern chromium chairs, a bar, and an electric record machine, opened onto the empty patio. A fat little Indian boy was seated in one of the chairs, listening to the tune "Good Night, Sweetheart," which he had just chosen. It was playing at full volume and the little boy was staring very seriously ahead of him at the machine. This was one of the houses owned and run by Señor Kurten, who was half Spanish and half German.

It was a gray afternoon. In one of the bedrooms Julia and Inez had just awakened. Julia was small and monkey-like. She was appealing only because of her extraordinarily large and luminous eyes. Inez was tall and high-breasted. Her head was a bit too small for her body and her eyes were too close together. She wore her hair in stiff waves.

Julia was moaning on her bed.

"My stomach is worse today," she said to Inez. "Come over and feel it. The lump on the right side is bigger." She twisted her head on the pillow and sighed. Inez was staring sternly into space.

"No," she said to Julia. "I cannot bear to feel that lump. *Santa Maria!* With something like that inside me I should go wild." She made a wry face and shuddered.

"You must not feel it if you do not want to," said Julia drowsily. Inez poured herself some *guaro*. She was a heavy drinker but her vitality remained unimpaired, although her skin often broke out in pimples. She ate violet lozenges to cover the smell of liquor on her breath and often popped six or seven of them into her mouth at once. Being full of enterprise she often made more money outside the whorehouse than she did at her regular job.

Julia was Mexican and a great favorite with the men, who enjoyed feeling that they were endangering her very life by going to bed with her.

"Well," said Inez, "I think that this afternoon I will go to the movies, if you will lend me a pair of your stockings. You had better lie here in your bed. I would sit here with you but it makes me feel very strange now to stay in this room. It is peculiar because, you know, I am a very calm woman and have suffered a great deal since I was born. You should go to a doctor," she added.

"I cannot bear to be out in the street," said Julia. "The sun is too hot and the wind is too cold. The smell of the market makes me feel sick, although I have known it all my life. No sooner have I walked a few blocks than I must find some park to sit in, I am so tired. Then somebody comes and tries to sell me orchids and I buy them. I have been out three times this week and each time I have bought some flowers. Now you know I can't afford to do this, but I am so weak and ill that I am becoming more like my grandmother every day. She had a feeling that she was not wanted here on this earth, either by God or by other people, so she never felt that she could refuse anyone anything."

"Well, if you are going to become like your grandmother," said Inez, "it will be a sad mistake. I should forget this sort of thing. You'll get to the doctor. Meanwhile, sit in the sun more. I don't want to be unkind. . . ."

"No, no. You are not unkind," Julia protested.

"You sit in this dark room all day long even when there is sun and you do not feel so sick."

Julia was feeling more desperately lonely than she had ever felt before in her life. She patted her heart. Suddenly the door pushed open and Señor Kurten came into the room. He was a slight man with a low forehead and a long nose.

"Julia and Inez," he said. "Señor Ramirez just telephoned that he is coming over this afternoon with a friend. He is going to take you both out to the country on a picnic and you are to hurry up and be ready. Try to bring them back to the bar in the evening."

"Hans," said Julia. "I am sick. I can't see Señor Ramirez or anyone else."

"Well, you know I can't do anything if he wants to see you. If he was angry he could make too much trouble. I am sorry." Señor Kurten left the room, closing the door slowly behind him.

"He is so important," said Inez, rubbing some eau de cologne over Julia's forehead. "So important, poor child. You must go." Her hand was hard and dry.

"Inez—" Julia clutched at Inez's kimono just as she was walking away. She struggled out of bed and threw herself into the arms of her friend. Inez was obliged to brace herself against the foot of the bed to keep from being knocked over.

"Don't make yourself crazy," said Inez to Julia, but then Inez began to cry; the sound was high like the squeal of a pig.

"Inez," said Julia. "Get dressed and don't cry. I feel better, my little baby."

They went into the bar and sat down to await the arrival of Señor Ramirez and his friend. Julia's arm was flung over the side of the chair, and her purse was swinging from her hand on an unusually long strap. She had put a little red dot in the corner of each eye, and rouged her cheeks very highly.

"You don't look very good," said Inez. "I'm afraid in my heart for you."

Julia opened her eyes wide and stared fixedly ahead of her at the wall. The Indian boy was polishing a very large alarm clock with care.

Soon Señor Ramirez stuck his head through the doorway. He had a German face but there was something very Spanish in the angle of his slouched fedora hat. His mustaches were blond and abundant. He had just shaved, and the talcum powder was visible on his chin and on his cheeks. He wore a pink shirt and a light tweed jacket, and on the fourth finger of each hand a heavy gold ring studded with a jewel.

"Come on, daughters," he said. "The car is waiting outside, with my friend. Move along."

Señor Ramirez drove very quickly. Julia and Inez sat uncomfortably on the edge of the back seat, hanging onto the straps at the side.

"We are going on a picnic," shouted Señor Ramirez. "I've brought with me five bottles of champagne. They are in the back of the car and they were all packed in ice by my cook. There is no reason why we should not have everything we want with us. They are inside a basket in the back. She wrapped the ice in a towel. That way it doesn't melt so quickly, but still we have to get there in a pretty short time. I drink nothing but American whiskey, so I brought along a quart of it for myself. What do you think of that?"

"Oh, how nice," said Julia.

"I think we shall have a wonderful time," said Inez.

Señor Ramirez's friend Alfredo looked ill and disgruntled. He did not say anything himself, nor did the angle of his head indicate that he was listening to a word that anyone else was saying.

It was a cold day and the parasols under which the policemen stood were flapping in the wind. They passed a new yellow brick building, high at the top of six or seven flights of yellow brick steps.

"That is going to be a new museum," said Señor Ramirez. "When it opens we are all going to have a big dinner there together. Everyone there will be an old friend of mine. That's nothing. I can have dinner with fifty people every night of my life."

"A life of fiesta," put in Inez.

"Even more than that. They are more than just fiestas," he said, without quite knowing what he meant himself.

The sun was shining into Julia's lap. She felt lightheaded and feverish. Señor Ramirez turned the radio on as loud as he could. They were broadcasting *Madame Butterfly* as the car reached the outskirts of the city.

"I have three radios at home," said Señor Ramirez.

"Ah," said Inez. "One for the morning, one for the night and one for the afternoon." Julia listened to Inez with interest and wonder. They were on the edge of a deep ravine, going round a curve in the road. The mountainside across the ravine was in the shade, and some Indians were climbing toward the summit.

"Walk, walk, walk. . . " said Julia mournfully. "Oh, how tired it makes me feel to watch them."

Inez pinched her friend's arm. "Listen," she whispered to her. "You are not in your room. You daren't say things like that. You must not speak of being tired. It's no fun for them. They wouldn't like it."

"We'll be coming to that picnic spot in a minute," said Señor Ramirez. "Nobody knows where it is but me. I like to have a spot, you know, where all my friends won't come and disturb me. Alfredo," he added, "are you hungry?"

"I don't think this Alfredo is very nice, do you?" Inez asked very softly of Julia.

"Oh, yes," said Julia, for she was not quick to detect a mean nature in anybody, being altogether kind and charitable herself. At last, after driving through a path wide enough for only one car, they arrived at the picnic spot. It was a fair-sized clearing in a little forest. Not far from it, at the bottom of a hill, was a little river and a waterfall. They got out and listened to the noise of the water. Both of the women were delighted with the sound.

"Since it is so sunny out, ladies," said Señor Ramirez, "I am going to walk around in my underpants. I hope that my friend will do the same if he wants to."

"What a lucky thing for us," said Inez in a strident voice. "The day begins right." Señor Ramirez undressed and slipped on a pair of tennis shoes. His legs were very white and freckled.

"Now I will give you some champagne right away," he said to them, a little out of breath because he had struggled so quickly out of his clothes. He went over to where he had laid the basket and took from it a champagne bottle. On his way back he stumbled over a rock; the bottle fell from his hand and was smashed in many pieces. For a moment his face clouded over and he looked as though he were about to lose his temper; instead, seizing another bottle from the basket, he flung it high into the air, almost over the tops of the trees. He returned elated to his friends.

"A gentleman," he said, "always knows how to make fun. I am one of the richest businessmen in this country. I am also the craziest. Like an American. When I am out I always have a wonderful time, and so does everyone who is with me, because they know that while I am around there is always plenty. Plenty to eat, plenty to drink, and plenty of beautiful women to make love to. Once you have been out with me," he pointed his finger at Julia and Inez, "any other man will seem to you like an old-lady schoolteacher."

He turned to Alfredo. "Tell me, my friend, have you not had the time of your life with me?"

"Yes, I have," said Alfredo. He was thinking very noticeably of other things.

"His mind is always on business," Señor Ramirez explained to Julia. "He is also very clever. I have gotten him this job with a German concern. They are manufacturing planes." Alfredo said something to Señor Ramirez in German, and they spoke no longer on the subject. They spread out their picnic lunch and sat down to eat.

Señor Ramirez insisted on feeding Julia with his own fingers. This rather vexed Inez, so she devoted herself to eating copiously. Señor Ramirez drank quantities of whiskey out of a tin folding cup. At the end of fifteen or twenty minutes he was already quite drunk.

"Now, isn't it wonderful to be all together like this, friends? Alfredo, aren't these two women the finest, sweetest women in the world? I do not understand why in the eyes of God they should be condemned to the fires of hell for what they are. Do you?"

Julia moaned and rose to her feet.

"No, no!" she said, looking up helplessly at the branches overhead.

"Come on," said Señor Ramirez. "We're not going to worry about this today, are we?" He took hold of her wrist and pulled her down to the ground beside him. Julia hid her face in her hands and leaned her head against his shoulder. Soon she was smiling up at him and stroking his face.

"You won't leave me alone?" she asked, laughing a little in an effort to bring him to terms with her. If anyone were to be pitted successfully against the Divine, she thought, it would certainly be someone like Señor Ramirez. The presence of such men is often enough to dispel fear from the hearts of certain people for whom God is more of an enemy than a friend. Señor Ramirez's principal struggle in life was one of pride rather than of conscience; and because his successes were numerous each day, replenishing his energy and his taste for life, his strength was easily felt by those around him. Now that he was near her, Julia felt that she was safe from hell, and she was quite happy even though her side still hurt her very badly.

"Now," said Inez, "I think that we should all play a game, to chase gloomy thoughts out of this girl's head."

She rose to her feet and snatched Señor Ramirez's hat from where it lay beside him on the ground, placing it a few feet away upside down on the grass. Then she gathered some acorns in the picnic basket.

"Now," she said. "We will see who can throw these acorns into the hat. He will win."

"I think," said Señor Ramirez, "that the two women should be naked while we are playing this; otherwise it will be just a foolish children's game."

"And we are not children at all," said Inez, winking at him. The two women turned and looked at Alfredo questioningly.

"Oh, don't mind him," said Señor Ramirez. "He sees nothing but numbers in his head."

The two girls went behind some bushes and undressed. When they returned, Alfredo was bending over a ledger and trying to explain something to Señor Ramirez, who looked up, delighted that they had returned so quickly, so that he would not be obliged to listen.

"Ah," he said. "Now this looks much more like friends together, doesn't it, Alfredo?"

"Come on," said Inez. "We will all get into line here with this basket and each one will try to throw the acorn into the hat."

Señor Ramirez grew quite excited playing the game; then he began to get angry because he never managed to get the acorn into the hat. Inez screeched with laughter and threw her acorn wider and wider of the mark, each time purposely, in order to soothe, if possible, the hurt pride of Señor Ramirez. Alfredo refused to play at all.

"Games don't interest me," said Señor Ramirez suddenly. "I'd like to play longer with you, daughters, but I can't honestly keep my mind on the game."

"It is of no importance at all, really," said Inez, busily trying to think up something to do next.

"How are your wife and children?" Julia asked him.

Inez bit her lip and shook her head.

"They are well taken care of. I have sent them to a little town where they are staying in a pension. Quiet women—all three of them—the little girls and the mother. I am going to sleep." He stretched out under a tree and put his hat over his face. Alfredo was absorbed in his ledger. Inez and Julia sat side by side and waited.

"You have the brain of a baby chicken," Inez said to Julia. "I must think for both of us. If I had not had a great deal of practice when I had to keep count of all the hundreds of tortillas that I sold for my mother, I don't know where we would be."

"Dead, probably," said Julia. They began to feel cold.

"Come," said Inez. "Sing with me." They sang a song about leaving and never returning, four or five times through. When Señor Ramirez awakened he suggested to Julia that they go for a walk. She accepted sweetly, and so they started off through the woods. Soon they reached a good-sized field where Señor Ramirez suggested that they sit for a while.

"The first time I went to bed with a woman," he said, "it was in the country like this. The land belonged to my father. Three or four times a day we would come out into the fields and make love. She loved it, and would have come more often if I had asked her to. Some years later I went to her wedding and I had a terrible fight there. I don't even remember who the man was, but in the end he was badly hurt. I can tell you that."

"If you put your arms around me," said Julia, "I will feel less cold. You don't mind my asking you to do this, but I love you very much and I feel very contented with you."

"That's good," said Señor Ramirez, looking off at the mountains and shielding his eyes from the sun. He was listening to the sound of the waterfall, which was louder here. Julia was laughing and touching various parts of his body.

"Ah," she said. "I don't mind my side hurting me so badly if I can only be happy the way I am now with you. You are so sweet and so wonderful."

He gave her a quick loud kiss on the mouth and rose to his feet.

"Listen," he said. "Wouldn't you like to come into the water with me?"

"I am too sick a woman to go into the water, and I am a little bit afraid."

"In my arms you don't have to be afraid. I will carry you. The current would be too strong for you to manage anyway." Señor Ramirez was now as gay as a lark, although he had been bored but a moment before. He liked nothing better than performing little feats that were assured of success from the beginning. He carried her down to the river, singing at the top of his voice.

The noise of the falls was very loud here, and Julia clung tightly to her escort.

"Don't let go, now," she said. But her voice seemed to fly away behind her like a ribbon caught in the wind. They were in the water and Señor Ramirez began to walk in the direction of the falls.

"I will hold tight, all right," he said. "Because the water runs pretty swiftly near the falls." He seemed to enjoy stepping precariously from one stone to another with Julia in his arms.

"This is not so easy, you know. This is damned hard. The stones are slippery." Julia tightened her grip around his neck and kissed him quickly all over his face.

"If I let you go," he said, "the current would carry you along like a leaf over the falls, and then one of those big rocks would make a hole in your head. That would be the end, of course." Julia's eyes widened with horror, and she yelled with the suddenness of an animal just wounded.

"But why do you scream like that, Julia? I love you, sweetheart." He had had enough of struggling through the water, and so he turned around and started back.

"Are we going away from the waterfall?"

"Yes. It was wonderful, wasn't it?"

"Very nice," she said.

He grew increasingly careless as the current slackened, with the result that he miscalculated and his foot slipped between two stones. This threw him off his balance and he fell. He was unhurt, but the back of Julia's head had hit a stone. It started to bleed profusely. He struggled to his feet and carried her to the riverbank. She was not sure that she was not dying, and hugged him all the more closely. Pulling her along, he walked quickly up the hill and back through the woods to where Inez and Alfredo were still sitting.

"It will be all right, won't it?" she asked him a bit weakly.

"Those damn rocks were slippery," he growled. He was sulky, and eager to be on his way home.

"Oh, God of mine!" lamented Inez, when she saw what had happened. "What a sad ending for a walk! Terrible things always happen to Julia. She is a daughter of misfortune. It's a lucky thing that I am just the contrary."

Señor Ramirez was in such a hurry to leave the picnic spot that he did not even want to bother to collect the various baskets and plates he had brought with him. They dressed, and he yelled for them all to get into the car. Julia wrapped a shawl around her bleeding head. Inez went around snatching up all the things, like an enraged person.

"Can I have these things?" she asked her host. He nodded his head impatiently. Julia was by now crying rhythmically like a baby that has almost fallen asleep.

The two women sat huddled together in the back of the car. Inez explained to Julia that she was going to make presents of the plates and baskets to her family. She shed a tear or two herself. When they arrived at the house, Señor Ramirez handed some banknotes to Inez from where he was sitting.

"Adiós," he said. The two women got out of the car and stood in the street.

"Will you come back again?" Julia asked him tenderly, ceasing to cry for a moment.

"Yes, I'm coming back again," he said. *"Adiós."* He pressed his foot on the accelerator and drove off.

The bar was packed with men. Inez led Julia around through the patio to their room. When she had shut the door, she slipped the banknotes into her pocket and put the baskets on the floor.

"Do you want any of these baskets?" she asked.

Julia was sitting on the edge of her bed, looking into space. "No, thank you," she said. Inez looked at her, and saw that she was far away.

"Señor Ramirez gave me four drinking cups made out of plastic," said Inez. "Do you want one of them for yourself?"

Julia did not answer right away. Then she said: "Will he come back?"

"I don't know," Inez said. "I'm going to the movies. I'll come and see you afterwards, before I go into the bar."

"All right," said Julia. But Inez knew that she did not care. She shrugged her shoulders and went out through the door, closing it behind her.

A Distant Episode

by Paul Bowles

Introduced by John L'Heureux

A DISTANT EPISODE" IS SOMETHING VERY RARE IN CONTEMPORARY literature, a story that partakes of the visceral power and primal intelligence of legend and myth. Once you have read it, it will stay with you forever. It is, quite simply, unforgettable.

Most stories in this collection take place in a world we recognize. They are social stories, concerned with characters in a moral universe, and in large part they depend on and take their significance from moral and social underpinnings. They explore the human struggle with humanity or with nature or with self. And why not? What is more immediate to us than *us:* our lives, our world? What matters more than the human condition?

And yet "A Distant Episode," this odd and inexplicable story, depends on nothing we acknowledge about the human condition. It concerns itself with horrors that are scarcely imaginable. It speaks of human nature not in its humanity but in its nature, which here is anything but human. It has an authority that springs not from knowledge but from intuition. It is a cold hard story, haunting and pitiless.

In "A Distant Episode," as in all his work, Bowles creates his fictive world with an economy as effective as it is astonishing. By the end of the first paragraph we have moved from our own known, rational world to the peculiar isolated world of Bowles, a moral vacuum surrounded by desert, where the air smells of orange blossoms, pepper, excrement, and rotten fruit, and where the accouterments of civilization carried by the Professor—maps, sun lotions, medicines—are worse than useless, they are ridiculous. The land of intellect, in the person of the Professor, is about to encounter its primal past and, like it or not, he stands in for us, he takes us with him. He is a professor of linguistics, passionate for sound and meaning, but romantic, reckless, offering himself eagerly—like all of us—to the dark seductions of the forbidden. "Hassan Ramani," he repeats over and over, a password to this fierce ancient land where he will discover there are no languages, only dialects, and where he will lose his tongue, his language, his identity, his self.

"The Reguiba is a cloud across the face of the sun," the Professor knows, but, preposterously, he is determined to buy keepsake boxes made from camel udders and, willfully and at least half aware of the dangers he faces, he pays a *qaouaji* to lead him out to the edge of the desert where the Reguibat are camped. The trip to the desert is itself a warning and a token of what is to come. It is deep night, and they pass through a rift in the city wall and descend on a winding road between rocks where the sweet black odor of rotten meat hangs in the air. The Professor fears the *qaouaji* will cut his throat, but the *qaouaji* has a fate more exquisite in mind. He takes the

Professor's fifty francs and leaves him within sight of the Reguibat camp, free to go down or go back. A true professor, he ponders whether this is a situation or a predicament; an eager victim, he climbs down the side of the moonlit cliff and delivers himself to the inhabitants of the encampment. At once he is fallen upon by dogs, and then by the Reguibat themselves, who kick him into unconsciousness, rob him, bind him, and dump him in a sack. Later, an indifferent gesture, they cut out his tongue.

He is a fool by nature, they recognize, and with his cooperation they make him into a fool of their own devising. They dress him in rows and rows of garlands made from the bottoms of tin cans strung together until he is cloaked from head to foot in tinkling armor. And then they make him dance. In time he does it well, adding flourishes of his own: guttural shouts, grimaces, and the obscene gestures they have taught him. He becomes a valuable property indeed.

For a year and a half he acts out the role they have given him. He does not think, he cannot talk, he exists only. Not Kafka, not Sartre, not Beckett, not one of them has explored the horrors and the emptiness of language lost, of meaninglessness, of man at the mercy of a universe without purpose or design or justification, in quite the way Bowles explores it here. It is horrible and unforgettable. And still more so at the end when the Professor is sold as an entertainment. Transported from the desert to a house and bargained for as the unique prize he is, the Professor hears the sound of classical Arabic and begins to recognize language; he sees the days and dates of a calendar and begins to recognize time. Feeling returns to him, and thought, and intolerable pain. For an unspeakable moment he is called back to the world he has lost, the language he professed, the self he will never be again in this mad and pointless universe.

Bowles takes us through this hideous pilgrimage to nowhere in the cool, disengaged voice of a narrator whose diction is elegant, whose tone is indifferent. The cleanliness of the prose serves only to intensify our horror.

We know that what happens to the Professor could happen to any of us. Alone, at night, in a foreign place where the language is strange and we have lost our way, we fear it will. To some, of course, it *has,* but they have not returned to tell about it.

"A Distant Episode" taps into something in us that is primeval, irrational, barbarous, and terror-ridden. It is, in the most aweful sense, a true story.

A Distant Episode

Paul Bowles

The September sunsets were at their reddest the week the Professor decided to visit Aïn Tadouirt, which is in the warm country. He came down out of the high, flat region in the evening by bus, with two small overnight bags full of maps, sun lotions and medicines. Ten years ago he had been in the village for three days; long enough, however, to establish a fairly firm friendship with a café-keeper, who had written him several times during the first year after his visit, if never since. "Hassan Ramani," the Professor said over and over, as the bus bumped downward through ever warmer layers of air. Now facing the flaming sky in the west, and now facing the sharp mountains, the car followed the dusty trail down the canyons into air which began to smell of other things besides the endless ozone of the heights: orange blossoms, pepper, sun-baked excrement, burning olive oil, rotten fruit. He closed his eyes happily and lived for an instant in a purely olfactory world. The distant past returned—what part of it, he could not decide.

The chauffeur, whose seat the Professor shared, spoke to him without taking his eyes from the road. *"Vous êtes géologue?"*

"A geologist? Ah, no! I'm a linguist."

"There are no languages here. Only dialects."

"Exactly. I'm making a survey of variations on Moghrebi."

The chauffeur was scornful. "Keep on going south," he said. "You'll find some languages you never heard of before."

As they drove through the town gate, the usual swarm of urchins rose up out of the dust and ran screaming beside the bus. The Professor folded his dark glasses, put them in his pocket; and as soon as the vehicle had come to a standstill he jumped out, pushing his way through the indignant boys who clutched at his luggage in vain, and walked quickly into the Grand Hotel Saharien. Out of its eight rooms there were two available—one facing the market and the other, a smaller and cheaper one, giving onto a tiny yard full of refuse and barrels, where two gazelles wandered about. He took the smaller room, and pouring the entire pitcher of water into the tin basin, began to wash the grit from his face and ears. The afterglow was nearly gone from the sky, and the pinkness in objects was disappearing, almost as he watched. He lit the carbide lamp and winced at its odor.

After dinner the Professor walked slowly through the streets to Hassan

Ramani's café, whose back room hung hazardously out above the river. The entrance was very low, and he had to bend down slightly to get in. A man was tending the fire. There was one guest sipping tea. The *qaouaji* tried to make him take a seat at the other table in the front room, but the Professor walked airily ahead into the back room and sat down. The moon was shining through the reed latticework and there was not a sound outside but the occasional distant bark of a dog. He changed tables so he could see the river. It was dry, but there was a pool here and there that reflected the bright night sky. The *qaouaji* came in and wiped off the table.

"Does this café still belong to Hassan Ramani?" he asked him in the Moghrebi he had taken four years to learn.

The man replied in bad French: "He is deceased."

"Deceased?" repeated the Professor, without noticing the absurdity of the word. "Really? When?"

"I don't know," said the *qaouaji*. "One tea?"

"Yes. But I don't understand . . . "

The man was already out of the room, fanning the fire. The Professor sat still, feeling lonely, and arguing with himself that to do so was ridiculous. Soon the *qaouaji* returned with the tea. He paid him and gave him an enormous tip, for which he received a grave bow.

"Tell me," he said, as the other started away. "Can one still get those little boxes made from camel udders?"

The man looked angry. "Sometimes the Reguibat bring in those things. We do not buy them here." Then insolently, in Arabic: "And why a camel-udder box?"

"Because I like them," retorted the Professor. And then because he was feeling a little exalted, he added, "I like them so much I want to make a collection of them, and I will pay you ten francs for every one you can get me."

"Khamstache," said the *qaouaji*, opening his left hand rapidly three times in succession.

"Never. Ten."

"Not possible. But wait until later and come with me. You can give me what you like. And you will get camel-udder boxes if there are any."

He went out into the front room, leaving the Professor to drink his tea and listen to the growing chorus of dogs that barked and howled as the moon rose higher into the sky. A group of customers came into the front room and sat talking for an hour or so. When they had left, the *qaouaji* put out the fire and stood in the doorway putting on his burnous. "Come," he said.

Outside in the street there was very little movement. The booths were all closed and the only light came from the moon. An occasional pedestrian passed, and grunted a brief greeting to the *qaouaji*.

"Everyone knows you," said the Professor, to cut the silence between them.

"Yes."

"I wish everyone knew me," said the Professor, before he realized how infantile such a remark must sound.

"*No* one knows you," said his companion gruffly.

They had come to the other side of the town, on the promontory above the desert, and through a great rift in the wall the Professor saw the white endlessness, broken in the foreground by dark spots of oasis. They walked through the opening and followed a winding road between rocks, downward toward the nearest small forest of palms. The Professor thought: "He may cut my throat. But his café—he would surely be found out."

"Is it far?" he asked, casually.

"Are you tired?" countered the *qaouaji*.

"They are expecting me back at the Hotel Saharien," he lied.

"You can't be there and here," said the *qaouaji*.

The Professor laughed. He wondered if it sounded uneasy to the other.

"Have you owned Ramani's café long?"

"I work there for a friend." The reply made the Professor more unhappy than he had imagined it would.

"Oh. Will you work tomorrow?"

"That is impossible to say."

The Professor stumbled on a stone, and fell, scraping his hand. The *qaouaji* said: "Be careful."

The sweet black odor of rotten meat hung in the air suddenly.

"Agh!" said the Professor, choking. "What is it?"

The *qaouaji* had covered his face with his burnous and did not answer. Soon the stench had been left behind. They were on flat ground. Ahead the path was bordered on each side by a high mud wall. There was no breeze and the palms were quite still, but behind the walls was the sound of running water. Also, the odor of human excrement was almost constant as they walked between the walls.

The Professor waited until he thought it seemed logical for him to ask with a certain degree of annoyance: "But where are we going?"

"Soon," said the guide, pausing to gather some stones in the ditch.

"Pick up some stones," he advised. "Here are bad dogs."

"Where?" asked the Professor, but he stooped and got three large ones with pointed edges.

They continued very quietly. The walls came to an end and the bright desert lay ahead. Nearby was a ruined marabout, with its tiny dome only half standing, and the front wall entirely destroyed. Behind it were clumps of stunted, useless palms. A dog came running crazily toward them on three legs. Not until it got quite close did the Professor hear its steady low growl. The *qaouaji* let fly a large stone at it, striking it square in the muzzle. There was a strange snapping of jaws and the dog ran sideways in another direction, falling blindly against rocks and scrambling haphazardly about like an injured insect.

Turning off the road, they walked across the earth strewn with sharp stones, past the little ruin, through the trees, until they came to a place where the ground dropped abruptly away in front of them.

"It looks like a quarry," said the Professor, resorting to French for the word "quarry," whose Arabic equivalent he could not call to mind at the moment. The *qaouaji* did not answer. Instead he stood still and turned his head, as if listening. And indeed, from somewhere down below, but very far below, came the faint sound of a low flute. The *qaouaji* nodded his head slowly several times. Then he said: "The path begins here. You can see it well all the way. The rock is white and the moon is strong. So you can see well. I am going back now and sleep. It is late. You can give me what you like."

Standing there at the edge of the abyss which at each moment looked deeper, with the dark face of the *qaouaji* framed in its moonlit burnous close to his own face, the Professor asked himself exactly what he felt. Indignation, curiosity, fear, perhaps, but most of all relief and the hope that this was not a trick, the hope that the *qaouaji* would really leave him alone and turn back without him.

He stepped back a little from the edge, and fumbled in his pocket for a loose note, because he did not want to show his wallet. Fortunately there was a fifty-franc bill there, which he took out and handed to the man. He knew the *qaouaji* was pleased, and so he paid no attention when he heard him saying: "It is not enough. I have to walk a long way home and there are dogs. . . ."

"Thank you and good night," said the Professor, sitting down with his legs drawn up under him, and lighting a cigarette. He felt almost happy.

"Give me only one cigarette," pleaded the man.

"Of course," he said, a bit curtly, and he held up the pack.

The *qaouaji* squatted close beside him. His face was not pleasant to see. "What is it?" thought the Professor, terrified again, as he held out his lighted cigarette toward him.

The man's eyes were almost closed. It was the most obvious registering of concentrated scheming the Professor had ever seen. When the second cigarette was burning, he ventured to say to the still-squatting Arab: "What are you thinking about?"

The other drew on his cigarette deliberately, and seemed about to speak. Then his expression changed to one of satisfaction, but he did not speak. A cool wind had risen in the air, and the Professor shivered. The sound of the flute came up from the depths below at intervals, sometimes mingled with the scraping of nearby palm fronds one against the other. "These people are not primitives," the Professor found himself saying in his mind.

"Good," said the *qaouaji,* rising slowly. "Keep your money. Fifty francs is enough. It is an honor." Then he went back into French: *"Ti n'as qu'à discendre, to' droit."* He spat, chuckled (or was the Professor hysterical?), and strode away quickly.

The Professor was in a state of nerves. He lit another cigarette, and found his lips moving automatically. They were saying: "Is this a situation or a predicament? This is ridiculous." He sat very still for several minutes, waiting for a sense of reality to come to him. He stretched out on the hard, cold ground and looked up at the moon. It was almost like looking straight at the sun. If he shifted his gaze a little at a time, he could make a string of weaker moons across the sky. "Incredible," he whispered. Then he sat up quickly and looked about. There was no guarantee that the *qaouaji* really had gone back to town. He got to his feet and looked over the edge of the precipice. In the moonlight the bottom seemed miles away. And there was nothing to give it scale; not a tree, not a house, not a person. . . . He listened for the flute, and heard only the wind going by his ears. A sudden violent desire to run back to the road seized him, and he turned and looked in the direction the *qaouaji* had taken. At the same time he felt softly of his wallet in his breast pocket. Then he spat over the edge of the cliff. Then he made water over it, and listened intently, like a child. This gave him the impetus to start down the path into the abyss. Curiously enough, he was not dizzy. But prudently he kept from peering to his right, over the edge. It was a steady and steep downward climb. The monotony of it put him into a frame of mind not unlike that which had been induced by the bus ride. He was murmuring "Hassan Ramani" again, repeatedly and in rhythm. He stopped, furious with himself for the sinister overtones the name now suggested to him. He decided he was exhausted from the trip. "And the walk," he added.

He was now well down the gigantic cliff, but the moon, being directly overhead, gave as much light as ever. Only the wind was left behind, above, to wander among the trees, to blow through the dusty streets of Aïn Tadouirt, into the hall of the Grand Hotel Saharien, and under the door of his little room.

It occurred to him that he ought to ask himself why he was doing this irrational thing, but he was intelligent enough to know that since he was doing it, it was not so important to probe for explanations at that moment.

Suddenly the earth was flat beneath his feet. He had reached the bottom sooner than he had expected. He stepped ahead distrustfully still, as if he expected another treacherous drop. It was so hard to know in this uniform, dim brightness. Before he knew what had happened the dog was upon him, a heavy mass of fur trying to push him backwards, a sharp nail rubbing down his chest, a straining of muscles against him to get the teeth into his neck. The Professor thought: "I refuse to die this way." The dog fell back; it looked like an Eskimo dog. As it sprang again, he called out, very loud: "Ay!" It fell against him, there was a confusion of sensations and a pain somewhere. There was also the sound of voices very near to him, and he could not understand what they were saying. Something cold and metallic was pushed brutally against his spine as the dog still hung for a second by his teeth from a mass of clothing and perhaps flesh. The Professor knew it was a gun, and he raised his hands, shouting in Moghrebi: "Take away the dog!" But the gun merely pushed him forward, and since the dog, once it was back on the ground, did not leap again, he took a step ahead. The gun kept pushing; he kept taking steps. Again he heard voices, but the person directly behind him said nothing. People seemed to be running about; it sounded that way, at least. For his eyes, he discovered, were still shut tight against the dog's attack. He opened them. A group of men was advancing toward him. They were dressed in the black clothes of the Reguibat. "The Reguiba is a cloud across the face of the sun." "When the Reguiba appears the righteous man turns away." In how many shops and market-places he had heard these maxims uttered banteringly among friends. Never to a Reguiba, to be sure, for these men do not frequent towns. They send a representative in disguise, to arrange with shady elements there for the disposal of captured goods. "An opportunity," he thought quickly, "of testing the accuracy of such statements." He did not doubt for a moment that the adventure would prove to be a kind of warning against such foolishness on his part—a warning which in retrospect would be half sinister, half farcical.

Two snarling dogs came running from behind the oncoming men and threw themselves at his legs. He was scandalized to note that no one paid any attention to this breach of etiquette. The gun pushed him harder as he tried to sidestep the animals' noisy assault. Again he cried: "The dogs! Take them away!" The gun shoved him forward with great force and he fell, almost at the feet of the crowd of men facing him. The dogs were wrenching at his hands and arms. A boot kicked them aside, yelping, and then with increased vigor it kicked the Professor in the hip. Then came a chorus of kicks from different sides, and he was rolled violently about on the earth for a while. During this time he was conscious of hands reaching into his pockets and removing everything from them. He tried to say: "You have all my money; stop kicking me!" But his bruised facial muscles would not work; he felt himself pouting, and that was all. Someone dealt him a terrific blow on the head, and he thought: "Now at least I shall lose consciousness, thank Heaven." Still he went on being aware of the guttural voices he could not understand, and of being bound tightly about the ankles and chest. Then there was black silence that opened like a wound from time to time, to let in the soft, deep notes of the flute playing the same succession of notes again and again. Suddenly he felt excruciating pain everywhere—pain and cold. "So I have been unconscious, after all," he thought. In spite of that, the present seemed only like a direct continuation of what had gone before.

It was growing faintly light. There were camels near where he was lying; he could hear their gurgling and their heavy breathing. He could not bring himself to attempt opening his eyes, just in case it should turn out to be impossible. However, when he heard someone approaching, he found that he had no difficulty in seeing.

The man looked at him dispassionately in the gray morning light. With one hand he pinched together the Professor's nostrils. When the Professor opened his mouth to breathe, the man swiftly seized his tongue and pulled on it with all his might. The Professor was gagging and catching his breath; he did not see what was happening. He could not distinguish the pain of the brutal yanking from that of the sharp knife. Then there was an endless choking and spitting that went on automatically, as though he were scarcely a part of it. The word "operation" kept going through his mind; it calmed his terror somewhat as he sank back into darkness.

The caravan left sometime toward midmorning. The Professor, not unconscious, but in a state of utter stupor, still gagging and drooling blood, was dumped doubled-up into a sack and tied at one side of a camel. The lower end of the enormous amphitheater contained a natural gate in the rocks. The camels, swift *mehara,* were lightly laden on this trip. They passed through single file, and slowly mounted the gentle slope that led up into the beginning of the desert. That night, at a stop behind some low hills, the men took him out, still in a state which permitted no thought, and over the dusty rags that remained of his clothing they fastened a series of curious belts made of the bottoms of tin cans strung together. One after another of these bright girdles was wired about his torso, his arms and legs, even across his face, until he was entirely within a suit of armor that covered him with its circular metal scales. There was a good deal of merriment during this decking-out of the Professor. One man brought out a flute and a younger one did a not ungraceful caricature of an Ouled Naïl executing a cane dance. The Professor was no longer conscious; to be exact, he existed in the middle of the movements made by these other men. When they had finished dressing him the way they wished him to look, they stuffed some food under the tin bangles hanging over his face. Even though he chewed mechanically, most of it eventually fell out onto the ground. They put him back into the sack and left him there.

Two days later they arrived at one of their own encampments. There were women and children here in the tents, and the men had to drive away the snarling dogs they had left there to guard them. When they emptied the Professor out of his sack, there were screams of fright, and it took several hours to convince the last woman that he was harmless, although there had been no doubt from the start that he was a valuable possession. After a few days they began to move on again, taking everything with them, and traveling only at night as the terrain grew warmer.

Even when all his wounds had healed and he felt no more pain, the Professor did not begin to think again; he ate and defecated, and he danced when he was bidden, a senseless hopping up and down that delighted the children, principally because of the wonderful jangling racket it made. And he generally slept through the heat of the day, in among the camels.

Wending its way southeast, the caravan avoided all stationary civilization. In a few weeks they reached a new plateau, wholly wild and with a sparse vegetation. Here they pitched camp and remained, while the *mehara* were turned loose to graze. Everyone was happy here; the weather was cooler and there was a well only a few hours away on a seldom-frequented trail. It was here they conceived the idea of taking the Professor to Fogara and selling him to the Touareg.

It was a full year before they carried out this project. By this time the Professor was much better trained. He could do a handspring, make a series of fearful growling noises which had, nevertheless, a certain element of humor; and when the Reguibat removed the tin from his face they discovered he could grimace admirably while he danced. They also taught him a few basic obscene gestures which never failed to elicit delighted shrieks from the women. He was now brought forth only after especially abundant meals, when there was music and festivity. He easily fell in with their sense of ritual, and evolved an elementary sort of "program" to present when he was called for: dancing, rolling on the ground, imitating certain animals, and finally rushing toward the group in feigned anger, to see the resultant confusion and hilarity.

When three of the men set out for Fogara with him, they took four *mehara* with them, and he rode astride his quite naturally. No precautions were taken to guard him, save that he was kept among them, one man always staying at the rear of the party. They came within sight of the walls at dawn, and they waited among the rocks all day. At dusk the youngest started out, and in three hours he returned with a friend who carried a stout cane. They tried to put the Professor through his routine then and there, but the man from Fogara was in a hurry to get back to town, so they all set out on the *mehara*.

In the town they went directly to the villager's home, where they had coffee in the courtyard sitting among the camels. Here the Professor went into his act again, and this time there was prolonged merriment and much rubbing together of hands. An agreement was reached, a sum of money paid, and the Reguibat withdrew, leaving the Professor in the house of the man with the cane, who did not delay in locking him into a tiny enclosure off the courtyard.

The next day was an important one in the Professor's life, for it was then that pain began to stir again in his being. A group of men came to the house, among whom was a venerable gentleman, better clothed than those others who spent their time flattering him, setting fervent kisses upon his hands and the edges of his garments. This person made a point of going into classical Arabic from time to time, to impress the others, who had not learned a word of the Koran. Thus his conversation would run more or less as follows: "Perhaps at In Salah. The French there are stupid. Celestial vengeance is approaching. Let us not hasten it. Praise the highest and cast thine anathema against idols. With paint on his face. In case the police wish to look close." The others listened and agreed, nodding their heads slowly and solemnly. And the Professor in his stall beside them listened, too. That is, he was *conscious* of the sound of the old man's Arabic. The words penetrated for the first time in many months. Noises, then: "Celestial vengeance is approaching." Then: "It is an honor. Fifty francs is enough. Keep your money. Good." And the *qaouaji* squatting near him at the edge of the precipice. Then "anathema against idols" and more gibberish. He turned over panting on the sand and forgot about it. But the pain had begun. It operated in a kind of delirium, because he had begun to enter into consciousness again. When the man opened the door and prodded him with his cane, he cried out in a rage, and everyone laughed.

They got him onto his feet, but he would not dance. He stood before them, staring at the ground, stubbornly refusing to move. The owner was furious, and so annoyed by the laughter of the others that he felt obliged to send them away, saying that he would await a more propitious time for exhibiting his property, because he dared not show his anger before the elder. However, when they had left he dealt the Professor a violent blow on the shoulder with his cane, called him various obscene things, and went out into the street, slamming the gate behind him. He walked straight to the street of the Ouled Naïl, because he was sure of finding the Reguibat there among the girls, spending the money. And there in a tent he found one of them still abed, while an Ouled Naïl washed the tea glasses. He walked in and almost decapitated the man before the latter had even attempted to sit up. Then he threw his razor on the bed and ran out.

The Ouled Naïl saw the blood, screamed, ran out of her tent into the next, and soon emerged from that with four girls who rushed together into the coffee house and told the *qaouaji* who had killed the Reguiba. It was only a matter of an hour before the French military police had caught him at a friend's house, and dragged him off to the barracks. That night the Professor had nothing to eat, and the next afternoon, in the slow sharpening of his consciousness caused by increasing hunger, he walked aimlessly about the courtyard and the rooms that gave onto it. There was no one. In one room a calendar hung on the wall. The Professor watched nervously, like a dog watching a fly in front of its nose. On the white paper were black objects that made sounds in his head. He heard them: *"Grande Epicerie du Sahel. Juin. Lundi, Mardi, Mercredi. . . ."*

The tiny inkmarks of which a symphony consists may have been made long ago, but when they are fulfilled in sound they become imminent and mighty. So a kind of music of feeling began to play in the Professor's head, increasing in volume as he looked at the mud wall, and he had the feeling that he was performing what had been written for him long ago. He felt like weeping; he felt like roaring through the little house, upsetting and smashing the few breakable objects. His emotion got no further than this one overwhelming desire. So, bellowing as loud as he could, he attacked the house and its belongings. Then he attacked the door into the street, which resisted for a while and finally broke. He climbed through the opening made by the boards he had ripped apart, and still bellowing and shaking his arms in the air to make as loud a jangling as possible, he began to gallop along the quiet street toward the gateway of the town. A few people looked at him with great curiosity. As he passed the garage, the last building before the high mud archway that framed the desert beyond, a French soldier saw him. *"Tiens,"* he said to himself, "a holy maniac."

Again it was sunset time. The Professor ran beneath the arched gate, turned his face toward the red sky, and began to trot along the Piste d'In Salah, straight into the setting sun. Behind him, from the garage, the soldier took a pot shot at him for good luck. The bullet whistled dangerously near the Professor's head, and his yelling rose into an indignant lament as he waved his arms more wildly, and hopped high into the air at every few steps, in an access of terror.

The soldier watched a while, smiling, as the cavorting figure grew smaller in the oncoming evening darkness, and the rattling of the tin became a part of the great silence out there beyond the gate. The wall of the garage as he leaned against it still gave forth heat, left there by the sun, but even then the lunar chill was growing in the air.

The Star Café

by Mary Caponegro

Introduced by John Hawkes

THE STAR CAFÉ" IS A REMARKABLE WORK OF FICTION WHICH RETELLS the myth of Eros and Psyche and treats a powerful subject in a most delicate fashion. The psychic content of the story is large and serious, but its comic achievement depends on the author's ability to sustain the protagonist's (Carol's) consciousness during all the funhouse business she encounters once she enters the café—or rather to create her consciousness in a way that is "realistic," that reveals or conveys a marvelous sheen of shyness, innocence, tentative self-concern, self-doubt, yet all phrased as mind or analysis. The long elegant sentences of this lyric prose go far toward creating the story's superb tone; the tone *is* in fact the story, which is about the joining and unjoining of love/sex which, for the protagonist, is always a matter of herself, so that despite her "betrayal" or violation she becomes her own partner, or at least a sort of androgynous person. The woman previously made helpless by some male world is now transformed into herself, with a power that is malelike but still hers. Thus this story, which operates on many levels, implying past and future lives, gender transformations, and so on, can be seen on the single present-life surface level as the story of a violated and liberated woman completing a transformation the bar owner never could have imagined. The blend of lyric, comic, and erotic used to narrate this transformation is the story's genius.

The Star Café

Mary Caponegro

Carol heard a noise as she undressed for bed; it frightened her—she'd actually been half undressing for bed and half searching for the book she had intended to read in bed, but after she heard the noise she was only a third involved with each of these tasks and a third involved in trying to figure out where the noise had come from—though of course these things could not be measured like sugar or flour; in fact, it would be more than a third of trying to determine the source of the sound anyway, because there was fear attached to that fraction, and fear has a way of dispossessing its neighbors. Carol checked the living room, bathroom and kitchen, and found nothing out of order.

The sound seemed to have come from below her apartment; the more she thought about it the more right that seemed, and since she couldn't stop worrying about it, she went back into the bedroom and slipped into the skirt she'd just taken off, rebuttoned the blouse she'd never gotten around to removing, was thankful she hadn't yet taken off underwear, considered putting back on her shoes but rejected that idea, and walked into the living room again, toward the door.

As she was undoing the latch, she saw on the small table between door and sofa the book she'd been looking for; it must have been there all along. She picked it up so as not to misplace it again, and opened the door. On the landing she heard the noise a second time. Though she'd been expecting it, it startled her anew, so much so that she dropped the book, then watched it tumble to the second-to-last step.

The hallway was dark and the darkness had intensified the sound. It was dark because the light switch was located on the wall opposite the banister at the bottom of the stairs, and she hadn't gotten there yet because she'd been interrupted by the sound; she was still standing there at fearful attention, like a deer with a flashlight shining in its eyes, as if stillness were some kind of defense instead of vulnerability.

Carol wondered why there wasn't a switch at the top landing as well as at the bottom. Perhaps the architect was biased toward those ascending? Or would it be the electrician? She knew so little about these practical matters; she knew so little about this building she lived in. If she had to guess when it had been built, she might have erred in the region of decades rather than single years. What she did know was that there was far too little light for a building with so many windows, all located on its tree-blocked western exposure.

The noise had stopped but Carol couldn't get it out of her head. It seemed to become clearer rather than less clear in proportion to time elapsed since its occurrence. But how could someone really know if the hold she had on what had been heard or seen or felt was really becoming clearer, that is, truer, or more distorted? Was intensity a proper gauge? Wasn't it often the case that those who felt most enlightened were in fact most deluded?

Then she heard it again, not memory or imagination. It had to be coming from somewhere downstairs, and she had to go downstairs, if only to retrieve her book, so she slowly descended, thinking that it was really the simplest sound, so why so difficult to characterize? It only seemed eerie because she didn't know the source, she kept telling herself.

When she reached the bottom of the staircase, Carol stood a moment, then sat down on the penultimate step, next to her book, listening to the sound that still hadn't stopped—its duration was the longest of the three occurrences—trying to get up the courage to go open the door that led to the little restaurant she'd lived above for all these months but never entered. The mixture of curiosity and fright had led her this far, she could hardly give up now; the noise might stop again any second and then it would be harder to trace. She walked down the hall and stood against the door with her hand curled on the knob, as if she were holding a piece of fruit still attached to a branch.

She placed the sound the instant she opened the door. The first time she heard it she should have known what it was. Who would have thought an innocent little blender—well, not so little, really, larger, in fact, than any she'd ever seen; she guessed it could hold several gallons—but who would have thought it could make such a queer noise, an innocent if somewhat oversized blender, making what looked like banana daiquiris? She giggled, and suddenly realized she wasn't alone, that she was being scrutinized by a man—a waiter?—more likely the owner, an extremely handsome man in all the conventional ways: dark and tall, both noble and rugged. He switched off the mighty appliance, poured a fraction of its contents into a long-stemmed glass, held that out to her and smiled.

"Hello, Carol," he said.

She was so relieved by the release of all that tension that she suddenly wanted, urgently, to talk to him, though it could have been to anyone, any sympathetic ear into which she could expel what had been building up inside her. She found herself babbling about how pleased she was to have the mystery solved; she was glad it was only that. He listened attentively, but rarely responded. Perhaps she didn't give him much chance.

He was looking at her intently from behind the counter, and when she felt too uncomfortable to confront his gaze directly she stared at the travel posters that adorned the wall behind him. She must have imagined that his eyes were unusually bright; it was her weariness, it was the candlelight, but for some reason she felt compelled. She was telling him all these things about herself, all the silly thoughts, the things about the architect and the light fixture, how they'd been so long next door to each other and never known each other better, and really she'd never done anything like this before but she was letting him hold her; first he had held her hand and then suddenly she was in his arms, he was murmuring softly, "yes, yes," consoling her, reassuring her, stroking her hair, and then other parts of her, and before she knew it she found herself in bed with him, in the back room, which was not so sordid as it might sound. There was a bed and all the accouterments of civilized sexuality, of comfort; it wasn't after all a closet, but she wondered what he would do if a customer came in, and then she began to wonder why there weren't customers out there. There hadn't been any when she came in, nor all the time they'd been, or she'd been, talking; she'd run on so about up and down and stairs and light; she'd been overwhelmed, full of herself in a way quite foreign to her, though there was also the sense that she was acting out a role that came very naturally, almost as if she'd rehearsed it, and she wondered if all this was the thing people always meant by the term "attraction," "I'm so attracted to you," as if people were magnets, which would be at least somewhat specific, or if she was just needy because of the fright, and lonely, lonely for a long time now, which would be at least not entirely, merely physical.

In either case she wasn't proud of herself; it was strange to be in bed with a man she barely knew, though in those minutes of talking it seemed there was some intense acquaintanceship occurring. It was strange to be in bed with someone at all, she'd been alone so long, almost out of habit; the "with" of "in bed with" was the important part of the construction, to be in the presence of another human being, because the sex came naturally enough; the angels never really withheld that.

Awkwardness granted, the motions materialized, to such a degree, in fact, that she felt she was experiencing far more than just going through them. She couldn't remember such satisfying sex; was it just the novelty? But everything clicked. She felt that they'd held each other's bodies for years and every gesture had the right timbre and timing, but with none of the staleness that might characterize the context. It was perfect but also felt, not slick. She certainly felt, and it seemed the kind of feeling that could not exist except reciprocally. It was as if they were lovers reunited after a long separation, fitting easily into place again. What was passion if not this? She slept a blissful, sated sleep.

When she woke up, she was alone. Everywhere around her were mirrors. The way school buses have mirrors to cover every possible vantage, this room, from her position on the bed, allowed her to see her body from every angle. She was fascinated by this, and distracted for quite a while, but then began to be afraid. She couldn't find her way past the immediate space around her. It reminded her of fancy New York stores in which it is difficult to find one's way because the different departments are separated by walls of mirrors.

Suddenly he was there in the mirrors. She was extremely moved that he'd come to be with her there, to rescue her; for some reason she was certain that he wasn't trapped by the situation, but had purposefully navigated to it, to get to her. Her first impulse was to take his hand and run with him out of this world of reflection, but he didn't lead her out; instead, to her shock, he climbed on top of her—what could be less appropriate?—at least out of sequence; that came after the rescue, in the gratitude and relief stage, while here she was, still a captive of this reflective dragon. But as the weight of his body pressed against her, she decided she'd been wrong; it was completely appropriate. She was so tied to her sense of propriety. There was no need to leave the place right now; no exits would seal while he entered—which happened so quickly she was startled, but startled at how *un*startled her body was, unkindled but still receptive—he taught her so much by his body.

He was thrusting in her so energetically it should have hurt, but it didn't, or if it did, the hurt was subsumed in the intensity of pleasure and excitement she felt. She had an orgasm as intense as any she had ever experienced, and felt after as if she could never have another, intense or otherwise, but just as she was thinking that he turned her over onto her belly and came into her from behind, and she heard herself make sounds she had never heard from her own mouth, in response to this pleasure on the crest of saturation.

She made them all the way to her second orgasm, not a very long way, in fact, and then there were others; she'd always thought that a myth. Only as she was coming did she remember the erotic potential of this room or space she was in—she'd been so overwhelmed with sensations and feeling that it hadn't occurred to her to heighten the effect with the visual; she was angry at herself to have missed out on that; when would she ever have such an opportunity again.

She loved the idea of watching their bodies in conjunction with each other, of him pressing into her. She turned to look back over her shoulder so that she could see him disappearing into her, and then turned her head in order to be able to see without straining, in all the mirrors. Her orgasm, at its most intense point, was retracted. The cry that rose from her throat continued, though perhaps the pitch changed just slightly, or the quality of the sound; maybe only she could hear the difference, that it wasn't from pleasure or surfeit anymore but from shock and bewilderment, because in all the mirrors she was there writhing—she could see her breasts and belly and legs, all from underneath, as if there were no bed obstructing; she could also see herself from his vantage; she could see what someone opening a door, if there were a door, would see, from far away, with the head prominent and the hair draped over the bed; she could see her shoulders and back, but he was not depicted in any of these images. She lay on the bed without partner.

She felt humiliated and horrified, and guilty too, though she couldn't have said why.

She had no idea how to attack this problem with relation to the other person who might or might not be present. It was an extreme case of some kind of sexual etiquette. The problem was, she didn't know this man, the café owner, at all; she knew him no better than she'd know a blind date, and yet they were sharing, weren't they, this intimate circumstance. Everything had felt so natural before; she'd let the sensation absorb any uncomfortableness, but now she was too disturbed by his absence from the mirror to retrieve her passion, and she felt too silly or shy to inquire about it directly.

Would he think she was crazy, or was he somehow manipulating his own image for some sinister reasons she had no idea of? Oh, why did she ever with this perfect stranger, and hadn't he seemed it in both senses of the term, but now she would pay. What would her mother say, who'd always been so cautiously liberal . . . "Carol, if you don't know a man's last name, you don't know him well enough to . . . " Thus what had seemed the most natural thing in the world suddenly de-naturalized and was transformed into the most awkward. How could she carry on this charade, when she possessed private knowledge that her partner was missing? It was just ludicrous to continue and at the same time witness the bleak absurdity of her body making love to the atmosphere. The postures could be made to look ridiculous enough even with both parties attending, but then at least they were salvaged by familiarity. Maybe the act itself was unnatural, maybe this was some elaborate lesson for her. She could be alone the rest of her life; she knew how.

She couldn't ask him what he saw in the mirror; she wished she could be so direct, but they hadn't spoken since that initial conversation, which might as well have taken place in some other world. She could feel the motions going on in some removed physical dimension, but to a very different effect. She was numb now, throughout her body; she wondered if he'd notice; he must notice. Was he intending all this, and should she then try her best to play along to try to counter-trick—how appalling to have to think in terms of strategy in such circumstances—pretending she really did see him in the mirror? Or was this some entirely different conspiracy of the elements in which he was as innocent as she? But was she? How could she be in such a terrible predicament if she hadn't done something terribly wrong; yes, it was repression and all the rest, but really, this kind of thing didn't happen to the average person. Confront, evade, despair? She didn't know which to do.

She'd never in her life faked an orgasm, as women were supposed to be notorious for, and she hadn't had so many either; in fact these recent ones constituted more than a small percentage of the total, but to do precisely that suddenly seemed the best plan, to get it all over with, so that this beginning-to-be-very-oppressive weight would be removed, and she wouldn't have to continue doing this thing, performing these movements, which are by definition directed toward another, to no one. She even managed to make some noise; she was surprised at how convincing it sounded, having expected the artificiality to be glaring. The trouble was, he took no notice; she might have spared herself the trouble—he wasn't through. Then she realized that she hadn't noticed if he had yet had one to her many, how selfish of her; she'd been caught up in the intensity of her own pleasure. But he seemed insatiable. It felt so odd, and now it was the etiquette thing amplified thousands of times, because she wanted to say, "Excuse me, do you think you'll be through soon?" as if to someone at a pay phone, except she had made all her calls and just wanted to hear the receiver click.

As she looked at her body now, it was limp and tense at once, receiving the invisible—less absurd than what she'd seen in the heat of her solitary passion, but still pathetic. Maybe there was a device analogous to the one-way mirror: a half-mirror, in which only one party at a time was visible. Such a thing could exist. So now the big question was, did he see only himself, the same way she saw only herself? How simple it all was; she was immensely relieved for the second time in—how many hours had this been going on?—she had no idea, but was overjoyed to realize that the sum of their perceptions would yield a complete love-making couple; she thought she might cry with the relief of it. Suddenly it was as it had been back in the café; she had invented all the problems; she was ashamed at having suspected him. She wanted to tell him everything and have him say, "Silly thing," and stroke her, make it all better.

But he didn't say that and she was still trapped underneath him: this man she was not with despite his presence. It was happening to someone else; he was inside someone else, who only happened to be Carol. Who cared about sex? She'd give up sex forever; just get her out of here. She yearned for nothing so much as the removal of this corporeal hook whose eye she was. Oh, give her the pain; she'd rather that, to feel her body affirming the wrongness of what was being done to/in it, the participation that pain was, rather than this numbness, distance, this irrevocable breach with the action she was party to.

She was exhausted now. Maybe she could cry so much that her body would force itself to sleep and when she woke up it would be normal, because that was the way things had worked till now; why shouldn't it solve itself so simply? But how could it when the situation had changed so drastically? She had not chosen this. Everything was different; he wasn't the same he; she herself—oh, was she also different, not just in the sense of having learned something, but substantially altered? Could she not go home again even to the home of her being? Was it going to prove that large a crime she'd committed, to herself, or invited if not committed: some psychic leaving of the keys in the car, or the house unlocked? Take from me; violate me? But no, how could she have known that the locks would not only be changed by the time she got home, but in her impotent presence the lock, the whole house changed, the door, the windows, the stairs (how long ago it seemed she'd stood at the top of her stairway) all turned inside out and impossible to put back in order.

That's when he stopped. Vision was the only sense that informed her, because feeling had long since been used up. The point was that nothing was different after he stopped, the same way on a long trip you feel like you're driving even after you get out of the car. She wanted to know what it was that made that particular point the one he'd selected as enough. Maybe he'd climaxed. But she suspected he had a completely different kind of sexuality, not based on that system. Even if it was the same system it was different, because no man ever took that long to get to the point conventionally regarded as completion; no ordinary man. Or had she drawn it out in her mind because she was so uncomfortable? No, there couldn't be that much disparity.

He was leaving. He had dismounted and left the bed. It seemed that he didn't need any time to recover from his own experience. He was walking away and she was free, no longer oppressed by that weight, that invasion; she'd been granted just what she pleaded for. But what would she do, if he left her all alone in the room again, with no one and no way out and no way of knowing where? She was more afraid than ever.

"Oh please don't go," she said. "Don't leave me alone. I'm afraid to be alone here."

Her request wasn't on the order of begging the lover to linger a little longer, wanting to draw out his sweet company, not Juliet bemoaning the lark song; it was simply preferring any risk to the risk of solitude, the way someone you're suspicious of suddenly seems harmless when you see the real villain. But she was only half involved with this anxiety about his departure, probably more than half, that is, not entirely consumed by the fear, because she was partly caught up in watching him begin to dress, seeing his body for the first time from a distance, with perspective. And she was also ashamed at feeling renewed attraction for this man whom she'd minutes ago felt utterly victimized by. But she couldn't get over his beauty; at this moment she wasn't so much aroused by the sight of him naked as interested in his body aesthetically.

She dwelled upon the refined features: cheekbones, throat, his beautiful hands. Her own hands had felt the softness of his dark hair, from that of his head to the field that pooled below his navel. He was fuzzy and nice down there; she remembered the feeling of that against her. Before she had only seen him hard, now she found it just as appealing soft; she supposed he wouldn't appreciate that sentiment, he would surely not deviate from the norm in that respect. She also wondered if it was abnormal of her to feel as she did, not to prefer it hard.

They had been united by that organ; now it was just a part of him again; perhaps it had its own little memory, its own will, and was choosing now to disassociate itself from the warm surround she had provided. And how she had soared in the first stages of that providing. She'd never had such a strong sense of being with a man: that she was the feminine to his masculine. He elicited from her a quality of her own femaleness that she'd never before experienced on that physical plane—a response she realized might be hopelessly bound up in the conditioning of role, but was nonetheless immensely powerful. It was getting clear again, with the distance, with his going, the power of the sensation that had made her respond in a way she never had: totally. She'd come outside herself to meet him through the medium of body, through the act of letting him inside her, and yet never felt so fully in her body, in her self, as when she had.

He was working now toward his clothes: a neat pile contrasting with her own things, scattered around it. She didn't remember him taking off what he was now putting on; she thought they were the same clothes he'd been wearing when they first met and talked. It was a button-down shirt, that much she remembered, but the color looked a little different than it had in the candlelight: pale pink oxford cloth; it might look effeminate on most men but on him it was just right, perfect for his blend of beauty and masculinity, his refined masculinity.

As she was observing him in the act of dressing, deep in her own reflections, she felt quite spontaneously in her genitals the muscular contractions of orgasm. She'd been concentrating on the pinkness of the shirt, and watching him put his firm, muscular—first right, then left—legs into his gray flannel trousers in a business-like manner, when out of nowhere her body had produced this gratuitous release to no accumulated tension, in an instant of incredible intensity that left her completely drained, as if she'd been building up to it for some time. She'd often wished she could speed up that process but this was a most undesirable other extreme, this joyless, arbitrary orgasm; it was in no way satisfying. If anything, scary. This very strange ventriloquism made her furious. For the first time toward him she felt her emotions focus as unmitigated, almost violent anger. She felt used, much more so even than when he had been doing to her what technically could be considered rape. But to do this intimate thing from across the room! How cowardly of him; that's what it was, truly unmanly, that he wouldn't even face her with his body to manipulate her, though in a way it was honest, to be so blatant.

A marvelous thing indeed it would be if she could think her way to orgasm, or come just by watching him, but this was quite different, as removed a process as artificial insemination, this artificial climax for which she had been just the vehicle. She wanted to hit him but she was practically incapacitated as a result of her climax. She wanted to hit him because she felt stunned as if she had been struck; she had fallen back from an upright position, and as she'd fallen back, her peripheral vision had received the mirror's version of that moment. It contained two genders; a man's reflection had been for that instant there: a single thrust by all the reflected men in all the mirrors: multiple petals around her lonely, central, actual pistil, from which no bee sucked nectar. Why was she surprised, that they would contradict no matter what, turn appearances around as a matter of course? She should have the pattern down by now.

A few minutes later she had her strength back, but since immediacy would have been the point, there was no use in striking him now. It would probably only end up hurting her anyway. Alternatively she decided to maintain utter dignity, which was difficult because she needed to go to the bathroom and there wasn't a chance she'd be able to divine the whereabouts of the ladies' room. She got off the bed in as stately a manner as she could accomplish and walked slowly but deliberately to where he stood. She tried not to feel vulnerable despite the fact that she was naked and he now completely clothed.

"There's a matter of some urgency," she said.

He looked up at her. "If you want to leave," he said, "all you have to do is figure it out. No one will stop you. I certainly won't."

After she had held her breath a minute, determined not to start crying, she tried again: "That's not the matter I had in mind—something much more mundane. You see, I have to, I need to [he was no help] find a bathroom."

"There aren't any." He wasn't very gracious.

"Oh," she said, at a loss. Then she found courage.

"Look, you have to help me."

She was afraid he wouldn't answer, and was thankful when he finally said, as if he'd been thinking about it all the while rather than ignoring her as she'd thought, "In fact, there is something," and hastened to add, "but it's only meant to be decoration. It was part of the architect's design."

Since her urgency was not decreasing she couldn't afford to be choosy. Responding to her expectant look, he led her to an alcove she could have sworn had not existed, but then it was hard to tell because of all the reflection. In any case she hadn't noticed this place before. Somehow the mirrors masked the contours. It was hard to tell how far the room extended, hard to distinguish what was reflection from what was actual space.

"This is all I have," he said (what a funny salesman he'd make, she thought), gesturing toward two gleaming urinals, affixed to the wall at waist height, totally out of place though in another way consistent with the atmosphere.

"Are you going to watch?" she asked in an injured tone, and he accommodatingly turned to walk away, but then she called him back and asked him to give her a hand, being pragmatic rather than proud.

"Help me," she said, but it was a question rather than a statement because she didn't know exactly what she wanted him to do for her, or whether he would even know how to help her. She had in mind a position that would somehow enable her to put feminine function into masculine form. She stood on tiptoe and stepped backward, facing him—she did not want to have her back to him—until she straddled the fixture. It was difficult to do this, but not impossible because she, although not tall, had fairly long legs, and the thing itself was not all that high. The insides of her thighs made contact with the porcelain rim; it was cold, but she couldn't raise herself high enough to avoid it.

She was still looking at him for some kind of assistance, and he, regarding her now as if she were truly demented, approached her, reaching his hand out hesitantly, as if he felt obliged to offer it but didn't know quite where to touch her, how to hold or support her. Finally he squatted in front of her and the urinal, and grasped her legs just above the knee, as one might hold a ladder someone else is standing on, to make it secure. This was no help. It was so strange to have him touching her in this functional way; she realized she didn't want him to touch her at all. Certainly she didn't want him to witness her in the actual act of urinating, especially in this awkward posture, and she couldn't wait much longer. Perhaps realizing that he was making no contribution, he rose, but kept standing there, out of malice or ignorance she wasn't sure: his face was blank.

"Thanks for the help," she said, hoping he would take that as dismissal.

He looked mesmerized by her sustained acrobatic—an expression foreign to his face as she knew it: being in the power of something rather than being in power over something, someone. Then he snapped out of it, looked normal again, and said, "The needs of his guest are a host's first priority." Was he sneering, or was it her own distortion of his smile? Then he turned quickly away. They seemed far from anything sexual now, poles apart from each other's sexuality. It was as if her nakedness were the most ordinary thing in the world to him now. At least he was gone and she could urinate in peace, if not exactly comfort, since relief was thwarted by the awkwardness of posture. There was so little space between her and the fixture that she got splashed by little droplets. Well, it's sterile anyway, she thought. Of course there was nothing to wipe herself with; there were no accessories to this monstrosity. It vaguely resembled a baptismal font.

She eased herself off, gripping the sides for support; this time she didn't have to worry about looking dignified. Once on land again, dry, flat land, she spread her legs, planting her feet far apart, and waved her hand rapidly between her thighs to speed up the air-drying process, as she leaned against the cold porcelain, too cold to keep contact with for any longer than necessary. She was tired of being in discomfort. Hadn't she suffered enough? She stopped leaning and tried fanning with no support but found her legs still too unstable, so she compromised by kneeling, though that didn't leave much space in which to wave her hand. All her muscles ached now; she wanted to find the bed again and lie down, but she couldn't summon the energy. Fatigue overcame any squeamishness she had about lying on the floor near the urinals: he had said they were only used as decoration. She lay on her back, at first with her legs up, positioned like an open scissor, as in one of the exercises she did, to facilitate fanning, which her left hand had taken over. The absurdity of the whole endeavor suddenly struck her; she dropped her legs to the floor, exhaled, and closed her eyes, vowing she would allow herself the luxury for only a minute. It might have been several minutes, before she was seized by panic. Where had he gone when she'd sent him away? She forgot about her fatigue and ran into the main part of the room, trying not to bump into glass. He was nowhere. As she was about to call him she realized she had no name for him. Oh, what a fool she was, alone just as she'd feared, and all her own fault. How useless everything was.

But she wouldn't let herself cry—no more despair. It was time to be practical, at least to go through the motions of being practical, for her own sake, to try to create some sense, even a contrived one, of order, in this most peculiar, relentless universe. So she began to dress, even though there was no rational reason to do so, except to feel dignified, and what else was there to do? She looked fondly at her scattered clothes. She regarded them as a soldier might some article that had been with him through numerous battles. And who knew what battles were yet to come, she thought, almost saying it out loud to her faithful skirt and blouse, the ones she'd been in the process of removing when she left her bedroom to investigate, the thing that got her into this nightmare: her fear of the sound, followed by her—feeling—for the café owner.

On some level she knew she was an intuitive person, but she hadn't learned to trust herself, too cautious, as if there were a very strong force at work inside her all the time that wasn't allowed to come to expression, like all that sun missing her house, all this foliage in her head, that was so pretty and interesting and alive, but how much it got in the way. She suspected that her mind had evolved in some distorted fashion, different from the rest of the world. And now here she was, trapped in this stagnancy of glass, that had become by all its clarity a blur, itself a distortion. She couldn't forgive herself, though she supposed she'd suffered enough to be redeemed of any number of sins or crimes. She cursed her intuition, because she'd never have stayed with him if she'd weighed, considered, evaluated. On the other hand, she'd never do anything if she always weighed, considered, evaluated; that was precisely what so often kept her from doing any number of things, things she felt a genuine desire to do, but couldn't get over this habit or obsession of getting stuck, nothing resolving itself. She felt the irony of the whole thing as deeply, as physically, as a metallic taste in her mouth: that the only time she'd ever felt not removed from her body, when will and act had meshed, was with him; it had felt so right, but clearly had been wrong, as wrong as anything could be. She slid the tab of the zipper all the way up and fastened the button at the waistband of her skirt, then leaned against one of the mirrors as she dreamily repeated the motion of button through opening, gentle grasps and pulls all the way up her blouse. If only there were as simple a motion to secure her exit. He had said she had only to figure it out. And there had to be a door; somewhere there had to be. She thrust her weight hard against the mirror as she leaned, then moved forward to tuck in her blouse. Had the mirror seemed to give a little as she had pressed? She must be imagining it. Perhaps if she pushed against every mirror, one of them might yield.

In the café, he poured her a drink, yellow, creamy stuff from the blender into a large, stemmed glass. He held it high as he poured, the way waiters had poured milk for her in restaurants when she'd been young; she'd been impressed at how high they could go and still not spill. She fumbled in her pocket for change, feeling stupid, not knowing where she stood. He put his hands over hers and said, "On the house."

"Oh," she said softly. "Thank you."

She had no idea what role she was playing. Was she customer, or worse, had he been hers? It was so different, he was nice again. His demeanor toward her suggested that they were only now about to be lovers, romantic, but she knew they'd already been, and what had gone on had had little to do with romance. She wasn't making much progress with the daiquiri, taking occasional nervous gulps, clutching the glass.

"It's different now," she said with desperate bravery.

"Same ingredients as always," he replied. "Are you sure you've had one before?" The way he smiled made her nervous. This was more confusing than ever.

Too uncomfortable to look at him, she kept surveying the room and its contents: the candles, the fancy Breuer chairs, all the bottles and glasses lined along shelves on the mirrored wall of the bar, a large quilt that somehow fit in with the rest of the decor; the central part of its design was a large star—it took her a minute to realize it was there because of the name of the place: the Star Café. The quilt took up almost all of one wall; the other walls were decorated with posters, mostly from museum exhibits. There were the travel posters as well, one a sophisticated montage of tourists and countryside in Greece, each scene in a separate little box. On the bottom was Greek lettering. She had always wanted to go there; it seemed like such a magical place, not just in some superficial sense of island and sun (one of the little boxes showed tourists lying on a beach) though that was appealing, and not just in the sense of the magic of the past either, being surrounded by ancient history, her sense was of a magic that was also chthonic. That was the world of myth, of gods and goddesses, of honor and heroism, justice, revenge. That was a much larger world than her own, she felt, that company of furies and sirens in which choice was fate, and fate was really everything, but no matter what brutality caused by what whim of some god's arbitrary favoritism, reliable rosy-fingered dawn was always waiting in the wings to make it all into poetry. She was enamored of that civilization which was a celebration of the splendor of form. She thought of the perfection of body that lived in those white marble statues, the strength and grace which rhymed for her with his body, the body that had mingled with her own, but was now so distant. She needed to know that it had.

"Were you ever there?" she asked him, not even asking for understanding so much as simple information.

"Once, years ago," he said, "but it's too dirty and the food's too greasy. I like a more antiseptic atmosphere; Scandinavia's more to my taste."

Willfully or inadvertently he had taken her to be referring to the travel poster. She resented this glib distortion of her meaning. He had no right to be so evasive. Or had he just misunderstood? He had no right not to understand. Anger supplanted her nervousness so that now she had no trouble looking directly at him. But he wasn't looking at her; he was eyeing the blender, and before she could challenge him he was onto that as the new topic, as if his little remark had been an adequate response to her searching question, and no more need be said about it. What nearly disarmed her was the tenderness with which he said, when he looked back at her, "How sweet that you were afraid of my blender; silly thing."

That was just what she would have wanted to hear before, but not now that she'd been through what she'd been through, an experience of suffering so vivid that it created a landscape in her mind as powerful as the mythical one in which she had just been lost. In fact they became one for her at this moment; she could envision her own story painted across some urn, the woman whose lover wasn't there, in little scenes that reminded her of the travel poster, except that they weren't photographed and weren't in boxes, little red figures depicted on the urn: Carol in her apartment, then going downstairs, then in the bar, Carol in bed, then in the mirrored room, Carol looking in the mirrors, him there, him not there, but Carol crouching in the urinal was really too squalid for the likes of any Grecian urn, and now, with her imagination engrossed in this world that did not take passion lightly, that addressed mortality and immortality as real concerns rather than abstractions, and raised to the highest pitch the difference and link between the two—now, it was grossly inadequate, even pathetic.

"I'm not your silly thing," she blurted out, and he seemed taken aback by her anger.

"What's got into you?" he asked.

"Stop pretending you don't know," she said. "You know what I'm talking about. Tell me if you were there or not."

"I've already told you . . . " he began, but she cut him off. She was very worked up now.

"When I ask if you were there, I mean were you with me, in the room? I mean I know you were with me, but what I'm asking is . . . why are you trying to make me think I was imagining you?" This speech was delivered *crescendo ed accelerando*. "You owe it to me to tell me!" She was very excited and annoyed to realize she had to urinate again. She must have managed to get down more of that daiquiri than she thought.

"Yes," he said quietly.

"What do you mean yes? You can't say yes or no if I ask you, was it a, b, or c. I need a specific answer. Was it real or my imagination?"

"Yes!" This time it wasn't quiet.

He didn't look like someone playing games; he looked tortured himself, but she was sure he must be trying to get away with something.

"You're being cryptic again," she said. "You're trying to confuse me. And I need the ladies' room; does that ring a bell? I may as well tell you that it's illegal not to have one in a public eating place, so don't try to tell me there isn't any."

"You think you're so smart," he raised his voice to match hers. "I have something to tell you too. There is, technically speaking, no ladies' room. There is, however, one rest-room, androgynous, past the bar and to your right."

She began the journey immediately. When she'd taken only a few steps he called to her, by name, for the first time since that very first time.

"Carol!"

She turned around.

"We're through."

That was fine with her; she turned away again directly and continued on the prescribed route. Once through a corridor she found the door immediately to her right, marked simply "rest." She opened it, entered, and shut it behind her, pushing in the little circle in the middle of the knob to lock it, then tried to jiggle the knob to make sure. She realized how silly that was; who was she locking out? The man who had seen and known her body to the full extent of possibility between human beings? But locking it made her feel better. The interior was clean enough; she would have tried to hold out if it hadn't been. This bathroom was extremely clean, in fact, so she didn't feel the need to get in and out as quickly as possible. It was mirrored, of course, mirrored tiles on the walls and floor. Also the ceiling. The toilet and sink were ordinary. A fresh bar of soap lay in the dish on the arm of the sink—so much nicer than powdery stuff out of a dispenser, she thought. How good it would feel to have clean hands. She rubbed the soap between her palms for a long time, working up a rich lather with warm water from the faucet. She decided to wash her face as well; she hadn't had the opportunity in so long. She held her hair with one hand but couldn't completely avoid getting it wet. She didn't mind; she would happily have dunked her whole head into the basin for the feel of this welcome refreshment.

In fact, why stop there, she thought, and pulled her blouse off over her head. She felt sweaty and horrible; scrubbing some soap under her arms would make her feel a little better, since she couldn't shower. She unhooked the closure in front of her bra and slipped the straps down her arms one at a time with her wet hand. In the mirror she stared at her small breasts, and was pleased with them. Her nipples were hard. She rubbed the soap vigorously under her arms, then rinsed, trying to stand over the sink in such a way that the least water would spill on the floor.

She had forgotten to check for a towel before she started; there was none, so she dabbed herself dry with pieces of toilet paper. She'd almost forgotten about her urgency; she'd make some superficial attempt at washing of genitalia after. She pulled down her panties, stepped out of them and hung them on a hook she'd just noticed protruding from the door. She rescued her blouse from where it had fallen and hung that too. She gathered up her skirt with her right hand, intending to sit on the toilet, but was distracted by suddenly seeing herself in the mirrored wall, as if seeing another person. She looked at this person who held her skirt in her arms so that it draped her hips but revealed her belly, fur and thighs. Her breasts were still uncovered also, and just as she had found them adequate, satisfying, she now found this lower region of her body, in fact the whole body, cut off as it was at the waist—she found the entire image attractive.

She stood transfixed by this lovely landscape under canopy of skirt. Her flesh seemed firmer than she remembered, more muscle tone; maybe the exercises she'd been doing in the morning and before bedtime had finally paid off. It had been hard to motivate herself to do them, with no prospect of anyone to appreciate the results, since she'd had no way of knowing about the café owner. She couldn't have predicted that, though as it was happening, there had been, in the midst of all that anguish and terror and pleasure, a tiny seed of déjà vu; that was a common phenomenon, of course.

Well, it didn't make much difference in the end, did it? She knew that she often allowed herself to become the victim of her own speculations, reflections. Now it all seemed unimportant compared to the immediacy of the woman in the mirror, the urgency of that woman's sexuality or physicality. Strange to feel genuinely aroused by this image of herself. She amused herself with the idea that it was perfectly logical for her to associate her unaccompanied reflection with arousal, since that had been the consistent image during her definitive sexual experience.

Now the woman in the mirror was touching herself, sliding her palm up her thigh, transferring the skirt to the guardianship of the left hand. Then she left skin to approach her breasts. She caressed them fervently, then left skin again to return below the skirt, lingering for a long time when the hand met flesh again, languidly rubbing the soft pubic hair, just a shade darker than the honey-colored hair of her head, which fell away from her shoulders, skimming the floor as she bent low for the mirror.

The mirror-woman did a seductive dance, holding the skirt tight across her hips, swaying; she watched the curve of her calves as she gracefully inscribed the area of the bathroom floor, often lifting her leg so high that her lips were visible.

She was extremely aroused by this time, and not ashamed of it; she wanted to possess this beautiful moving image. She felt a fullness in her groin, decided it was her old need to urinate, which seemed less and less urgent; she couldn't be bothered with addressing that now—it was confusing how similar that feeling was with that of being sexually excited. She was rubbing herself, much more vigorously than was her habit; she let the skirt drop to have both hands. She tried to put one finger of her free hand inside herself but couldn't gain entry, despite the fact that she was very wet by now. It wasn't necessary anyway, and she was happy enough to have access to both hands for rubbing.

She was so tensed and excited that her vision was blurred; she'd lost the mirror's reflection, but it was firmly fixed in her mind; she dwelled on all the postures, the confronting gaze, the beauty and sensuality of that body. She needed some kind of support, weak from so much excitement. When leaning against the sink proved insufficient she quickly closed the lid of the toilet and sat there.

Under the skirt she rubbed so fast that her hand was tiring, so she supported the right with the left, cupped the two and stroked, leaning back against the tank. She recalled there must be semen in her still, if he had come, that is, but he must have come, at least once, and probably generously, he had to have, it just wasn't possible—she felt it coming out of her, not just dribbling but in spurts, as she herself climaxed. She cried out with the new pleasure of it, an intense, confined pleasure, as she felt suddenly claustrophobic; she needed air, even if it was just the air of the corridor. She rose and unlocked the door by turning the knob hard, opened it and stuck her head out, like a seasick traveler leaning out a porthole; she saw down the length of the corridor into the room with the bar, where it had all begun. Directly in the line of her vision was the poster of Greece; it was far away, and the contents of the little boxes were fuzzy, like the last letters of the eye-doctor's chart, but she could see rocks and white sand, and tall, white columns. She was drawn toward them, she wanted to see every box clearly; her nakedness did not inhibit her for some reason. He didn't matter so much anymore; she wouldn't let him keep her from exploring. There was nothing to be embarrassed about. No one was there.

Reflections

by Angela Carter

Introduced by Robert Coover

WHILE LIVING REMOTELY ON THE KENT COAST OF ENGLAND SOME twenty years ago, beavering away on that impossible project *The Public Burning,* I began, with a kind of fan letter to the then largely unknown British writer Angela Carter, an intense penpal relationship that was to last for two years before we could actually meet and then, as a personal friendship, for many years more, until death stole her breath away. Perhaps I should have written more such letters; my life might have been much more beautiful.

I'd been working very hard, writing at least twelve hours a day (my hero was at the time boarding the train to Sing Sing prison while, behind him, the crowds were gathering in Times Square, and he, it, they, and I were all very hot), I badly needed a couple of short stories one night just to cool off, and there on the top of my stack of unread books was Angela Carter's *Fireworks,* published that year in England, without fanfare, by Quartet Books. I lay back, expecting nothing, hoping in fact to be lulled to sleep, but as soon sat up, astonished, riveted, filled with delight: I had just discovered, I knew in a moment, one of my greatest living contemporaries.

Even so, I probably would have remained a secret admirer had I not just accepted, in spite of (or because of) my isolation, the temporary fiction editorship of *The Iowa Review,* so I was able to write to her (a mere cover—I *loved* this writer—but useful for one for whom such letters were no easy habit) as a would-be publisher of her writing. As it happened, I ended up devoting an entire issue to her work, the centerpiece of which was the disturbingly beautiful masterpiece of *Fireworks,* "Reflections," which had, as I told her in my letter, "left me breathless." She replied, "I am especially pleased you liked 'Reflections,' because it is one of the very few pieces that I made up as I went along. I usually work to a very tight schema, and I *still don't know what it means*. The imagery was in charge of me instead of vice versa."

This was true about her writing instincts; we shared this, structure over image, substance over style, but we also most admired in each other those moments when our best intentions were overwhelmed by the raw story stuff within. "Reflections" is a most mysterious tale: violent, magical, comic, menacing, seemingly transparent, but, like the mirror through which it displays itself, bewilderingly deceptive.

Reflections

Angela Carter

I was walking in a wood one late spring day of skimming cloud and shower-tarnished sunshine, the sky a lucid if intermittent blue—cool, bright, tremulous weather. A coloratura blackbird perched on a bough curded with greenish mayblossom let fall a flawed chain of audible pearl; I was alone in the spring-enchanted wood. I slashed the taller grasses with my stick and now and then surprised some woodland creature, rat or rabbit, that fled away from me through long grass where little daisies and spindly branches of buttercups were secreted among gleaming stems still moist at the roots from last night's rain that had washed and refreshed the entire wood, had dowered it the poignant transparency, the unique, inconsolable quality of rainy countries, as if all was glimpsed through tears.

The crisp air was perfumed with wet grass and fresh earth. The year was swinging on the numinous hinges of the solstice but I was ingenuous and sensed no imminence in the magic silence of the rustling wood.

Then I heard a young girl singing. Her voice performed a trajectory of sound far more ornate than that of the blackbird, who ceased at once to sing when he heard it for he could not compete with the richly crimson sinuosity of a voice that pierced the senses of the listener like an arrow in a dream. She sang; and her words thrilled through me, for they seemed filled with a meaning that had no relation to meaning as I understood it.

"Under the leaves," she sang, "and the leaves of life—" Then, in mid-flight, the song ceased and left me dazzled. My attention abstracted from my surroundings, all at once my foot turned on an object hidden in the grass and I tumbled to the ground. Though I fell on the soft, wet grass, I was shaken and winded. I forgot that luring music. Cursing my obstacle, I searched among the pale, earth-stained rootlets to find it and my fingers closed on, of all things, a shell. A shell so far from the sea! When I tried to grasp it in order to pick it up and examine it the better, I found the act unexpectedly difficult and my determination to lift it quickened although, at the same time, I felt a shiver of fear for it was so very, very heavy and its contours so chill that a shock like cold electricity darted up my arm from the shell, into my heart. I was seized with the most intense disquiet; I was mystified by the shell.

I thought it must be a shell from a tropic ocean, since it was far larger and more elaborately whorled than the shells I'd found on the shores of the

Atlantic. There was some indefinable strangeness in its shape I could not immediately define. It glimmered through the grass like a cone of trapped moonlight although it was so very cold and so heavy it seemed to me it might contain all the distilled heaviness of gravity itself within it. I grew very much afraid of the shell; I think I sobbed. Yet I was so determined to wrench it from the ground that I clenched my muscles and gritted my teeth and tugged and heaved. Up it came, at last, and I rolled over backwards when it freed itself. But now I held the prize in my hands, and I was, for the moment, satisfied.

When I looked at the shell more closely, I saw the nature of the teasing difference that had struck me when I first set eyes on it. The whorls of the shell went the wrong way. The spirals were reversed. It looked like the mirror image of a shell, and so it should not have been able to exist outside a mirror; in this world, it could not exist outside a mirror. But, all the same, I held it.

The shell was the size of my cupped hands and cold and heavy as death.

In spite of its fabulous weight, I decided to carry it through the wood for I thought I would take it to the little museum in the nearby town where they would inspect it and test it and tell me what it might be and how it could have arrived where I found it. But as I staggered along with it in my arms, it exerted such a pull downwards on me that, several times, I nearly fell to my knees, as if the shell were determined to drag me, not down to the earth but into the earth itself. And then, to complete my confusion, I heard that witching voice again.

"Under the leaves—"

But, this time, when a gasp stopped the song, the voice changed at once to the imperative.

"Sick 'im!" she urged. "Sick 'im!"

Before I had a chance to do more than glance in the direction of the voice, a bullet whirred over my head and buried itself in the trunk of an elm tree, releasing from their nests in the upward branches a whirring hurricane of crows. An enormous black dog bounded towards me from the undergrowth so suddenly I saw no more than his yawning scarlet maw and lolling tongue before I went down on my face beneath him. The fright nearly bereft me of my senses. The dog slavered wetly over me and, the next thing I knew, a hand seized my shoulder and roughly turned me over.

She had called the dog away and now it sat on its haunches, panting, watching me with a quick, red eye. It was black as coal, some kind of lurcher, with balls the size of grapefruit. Both the dog and the girl glanced at me without charity. She wore blue jeans and boots, a wide, vindictively buckled leather belt and a green sweater. Her tangled brown hair hung about her shoulders in a calculated disorder that was not wild. Her dark eyebrows were perfectly straight and gave her stern face a gravity as awful as that of the shell I held in my hand. Her blue eyes, the kind the Irish say have been put in with a sooty finger, held no comfort nor concern for me for they were the eyes that justice would have if she were not blind. She carried a sporting rifle slung across her shoulder and I knew at once this rifle had fired the shot. She might have been the gamekeeper's daughter but, no, she was too proud; she was a savage and severe wood-ranger.

Why I do not know, but every impulse told me to conceal my shell and I hugged it close to me, as if my life depended on keeping it, although it was so heavy and began to throb with a wild palpitation so that it seemed the shell had disordered my own heart, or else had become my own disordered heart. But my brusque captress poked at my hands with the barrel of her rifle so roughly my bruised fingers let the shell fall. She bent forward so that her necromantic hair brushed my face and picked up the shell with amazing ease.

She examined it for a moment and then, without a word or sign to me, tossed it to her lurcher, who seized it in his mouth ready to carry it for her. The dog began to wag his tail. The rhythmic swishing of his tail upon the grass was now the only sound in the clearing. Even the trees had ceased to murmur, as though a holy terror hushed them.

She gestured me to my feet and, when I was upright, she thrust the mouth of the gun in the small of my back and marched me through the wood at gunpoint, striding along behind me while the dog padded beside her with the shell in his mouth. All this took place in unadulterated silence, but for the raucous panting of the dog. The cabbage white butterflies flickered upon the still air as if nothing whatsoever were out of the ordinary, while delicious-looking apricot and violet colored clouds continued to chase one another across the sun according to the indifferent logic of the upper heavens, for the clouds were moved by a fierce wind that blew so high above the wood everything around me was as tranquil as water trapped in a lock, and mocked the inward perturbation that shook me.

Soon we reached an overgrown path that took us to a gate set in a garden wall where there was an old-fashioned bellpull and, dangling above it, a bell stained with moss and rust. The girl with the rifle rang this bell before she opened the gate as if to warn whoever was at home that visitors were arriving. The gate led into a graceful and dilapidated walled garden full of the herbaceous splendors of early summer, hollyhocks, wallflowers, roses. There was a mossed sundial and a little stone statue of a nude youth stretching his arms up out of a cuirass of ivy. But, though the bees hummed among the flower-bells, the grass was as long as it had been in the wood and just as full of buttercups and daisies. Dandelions expired in airy seed heads in the flower beds; ragged robin and ground elder conspired to oust the perennials from the borders and a bright sadness of neglect touched everything as though with dust, just as it did the ancient brick house, almost covered with creepers, that slept within the garden, an ancient, tumbledown place with a look of oracular blindness in windows that were stopped up with vines and flowers. The roof was lichened quite over, so that it seemed upholstered in sleek, green fur. Yet there was no peace in the disheveled loveliness of the place; the very plants that grew there seemed tensed in a curious expectancy, as though the garden were a waiting-room. There was a short, crumbling flight of steps that led to a weathered front door, ajar like the door of a witch's house.

Before the door, I involuntarily halted; a dreadful vertigo seized me, as if I stood on the edge of an abyss. My heart had been thumping far too hard and far too fast since I had picked up the shell and now it seemed about to burst from too much strain. Faintness and terror of death swept over me; but the girl prodded me cruelly in the buttocks with her rifle so I was forcibly marched into a country-house hall with dark stained floorboards, a Persian carpet and a Jacobean oak chest with an antique bowl on it, all complete yet all as if untouched for years, for decades. A maze of dust danced in the beam of sunshine that disturbed the choked indoor air when we broke into it. Every corner was softened by cobwebs while the industrious spiders had wound filaments of geometric lace this way and that between the crumbling furniture. A sweet, rank smell of damp and decay filled the house; it was cold inside, and dark. The door swung to behind us but did not close and we went up a staircase of worm-eaten oak, I first, she after and then the dog, whose claws clattered on the bare wood.

At first I thought the spiders had cast their nets on both sides of the stair but then I saw the workmanship that wound down the inner side of the staircase was not that of the spiders for, though it was the same color, this web had a determinate pattern that resembled nothing so much as open-work knitting, the kind of featherlike, floating stuff from which they make courtesans' bedjackets. This knitting was part of an interminable muffler that, as I watched it, crept, with vegetable slowness, little by little downstairs towards the hall. Yard upon yard of the muffler was coiled up in airy folds on the landing and there I could hear the clack, clack, clack of a pair of knitting needles ticking away monotonously near at hand. The muffler came out of a door that, like the front door, stood a little open; it edged through the gap like a tenuous serpent.

My captress motioned me aside with the muzzle of her rifle and knocked firmly on the door.

Inside the room, someone coughed dryly, then invited us: "Come in."

It was a soft, rustling, unemphatic, almost uninflected, faded, faintly perfumed voice, like very old lace handkerchiefs put away long ago in a drawer with potpourri and forgotten.

My captress thrust me through the door before her; when I was close to her, my nostrils quivered at the vicious odor of her skin. It was a large room, part drawing-room, part bedroom, for the being who lived in it was crippled. She, he, it—whoever, whatever my host or hostess may have been—lay in an old-fashioned wicker bathchair beside a cracked marble fireplace bossed with swags and cupids Her white hands finished in fingers so indecently long, so white and so translucent they raised lewd thoughts of candles and feminine self-gratification; those tapering fingers were the source of the bewildering muffler, for they held two bone needles and never ceased to move.

The volatile stichery they produced occupied all the carpetless area of the floor and, in places, was piled up as high as the crippled knees of its maker. There was yards and yards of it in the room, perhaps even miles and miles of it, and I stepped through and across it very carefully, nudging it out of the way with my toes, to arrive where the girl directed me with her gun, in the position of a suppliant before the bathchair. The crippled being who lay in it had the most regal cast of chin and mouth imaginable and the proud, sad air of the king of a rainy country. One of her profiles was that of a beautiful woman, the other that of a beautiful man. It is a defect in our language there is no term of reference for these indeterminate and undefinable beings; but, although she acknowledged no gender, I will call her "she" because she had put on a female garment, a loose negligé of spider-colored lace, unless she, like the spiders, spun and wove her own thread and so had become clothed, for her shadowy hair was also the color of the stuff she knitted and so evanescent in texture it seemed to move of its own accord on the air around her. Her eyelids and the cavernous sockets of her eyes were thickly stuck with silver sequins that glittered in the strange, subaqueous, drowned, drowning light that suffused the room, a light filtered through windows caked with grime and half covered by creeper, clairvoyant light reflected, with an enhanced strangeness, by the immense mirror in a chipped gilt frame hanging on the wall opposite the fireplace; it seemed the mirror, like the moon, was itself endowed with the light it gave back to us.

With a touching fidelity, the mirror duplicated the room and all it contained, the fireplace, the walls covered with a stained white paper stippled with fronds of greenery, every piece of neglected ormolu furniture. How pleased I was to see my experiences had not changed me! though my old tweed suit was stained with grass, my stick gone—left behind where I had dropped it in the wood. And so much dirt on my face. But I looked as if I were reflected in a forest pool rather than by silvered glass for the surface of the mirror looked like the surface of motionless water, or of mercury, as though it were a solid mass of liquid kept in place by some inversion of gravity that reminded me of the ghastly weight of the shell that now dropped at the androgyne's feet from the dog's mouth. She never stopped knitting for one moment as she nudged it with a beautiful toe painted with a rime of silver; woe gave her a purely female face.

"Only one little stitch! And I only dropped one little stitch!" she mourned. And she bowed her head over her work in an ecstasy of regret.

"At least it wasn't out long," said the girl. Her voice had a clanging resonance; mercy was a minor key that would never modify its martial music. "*He* found it!"

She gestured towards me with her gun. The androgyne directed upon me a pair of vague, too-large, stagnant eyes that did not shine.

"Do you know where this shell comes from?" she asked me with a grave courtesy.

I shook my head.

"It comes from the Sea of Fertility. Do you know where *that* is?"

"On the surface of the moon," I answered. My voice sounded coarse and rough to me.

"Ah," she said, "the moon, the source of polarized light. Yes and no to your reply. It is an equivalence. The sea of fertility is a reversed system, since everything there is as dead as this shell."

"He found it in the wood," said the girl.

"Put it back where it belongs, Anna," said the androgyne, who possessed a frail yet absolute air of authority. "Before any harm is done."

The girl bent and picked up the shell. She scrutinized the mirror and took aim at some spot within it that seemed to her a logical target for the shell. I saw her raise her arm to throw the shell into the mirror and I saw her mirrored arm raise the shell to throw it outside the mirror. Then she threw the duplicated shell. There was no sound in the room but the click of the knitting needles when she threw the shell into the mirror while her reflection threw the shell out of the mirror. The shell, when it met its own reflection, disappeared immediately.

The androgyne sighed with satisfaction.

"The name of my niece is Anna," she said to me, "because she can go both ways. As, indeed, I can myself, though I am not a simple palindrome."

She gave me an enigmatic smile and moved her shoulders so that the lace negligé she wore fell back from her soft, pale breasts that were, each one, tipped with nipples of deep, dark pink, with the whorled crenellations of raspberries, and then she shifted her loins a little to display, savage and barbaric in their rude, red-purple repose, the phallic insignia of maleness.

"She can," said Anna, "go both ways, although she cannot move at all. So her power is an exact equivalent of her impotence, since both are absolute."

But her aunt looked down at her soft weapon and said gently: "Not, my darling, *absolutely* absolute. Potency, impotence *in potentia,* hence relative. Only the intermediary, since indeterminate."

With that, she caressed her naked breasts with a stunted gesture of her forearms; she could not move her arms freely because she did not stop knitting. They looked at one another and laughed. Their laughter drove icicles of fear into my brain and I did not know which way to turn.

"You see, we must do away with you," said the androgyne. "You know too much."

Panic broke over me like a wave. I plunged across the room towards the door, careless of Anna's gun in my attempted flight. But my feet were snared by the knitting and once again I plunged downwards but this time my fall half stunned me. I lay dazed while their renewed laughter darted cruelly about the room.

"Oh," said Anna, "but we shan't kill you. We shall send you through the mirror. We shall send you where the shell went, since that is where you belong, now."

"But the shell vanished," I said.

"No," replied the androgyne. "It did not vanish in reality. That shell had no business in this world. I dropped a stitch, this morning; only one little stitch . . . and that confounded shell slipped through the hole the dropped stitch made, because those shells are all so very, very heavy, you see. When it met its reflection, it returned to its proper place. It cannot come back, now; and neither will you, after we have sent you through the mirror."

Her voice was so very gentle, yet she offered me a perpetual estrangement. I let out a cry. Anna turned to her aunt and placed her hand on her genitalia, so that the cock sprang up. It was of redoubtable size.

"Oh, auntie, don't scare him!" she said.

Then they tittered, the weird harpies, so that I was quite beside myself with fear and bewilderment.

"It is a system of equivalences," said the androgyne. "She carries the gun, you see; and I, too."

She displayed her towering erection with the air of a demonstrator in a laboratory.

"In my intermediary and cohesive logic, the equivalences reside beyond symbolism. The gun and the phallus are similar in their connection with life—that is, one gives it; and the other takes it away, so that both, in essence, are similar in that the negation freshly states the affirmed proposition."

I was more bewildered than ever.

"But do all the men in the mirror world have guns between their thighs?"

Anna exclaimed with irritation at my simplicity.

"That's no more likely than that I could impregnate you with this—" she said, pointing her gun at me, "here or in any other world."

"Embrace yourself in the mirror," said the androgyne, knitting, knitting, knitting away. "You must go, now. Now!"

Anna maintained her menace; there was nothing for it but to do as they bid. I went to the mirror and examined myself in its depths. A faint ripple ran over its surface; but when I touched it with my fingers, the surface was just as smooth and hard as it should have been. I saw that my reflection was cut off at the thighs by the gilt frame and Anna said: "Climb on a stool! Who'd want you truncated, here or there?"

She grinned in an appalling fashion and slipped back the safety catch on her rifle. So I pulled a little, cane-seated, gilt-backed chair to the mirror and clambered up. I gazed at myself in the mirror; there I was, complete from head to toe, and there they were, behind me, the androgyne weaving her ethereal coils and the armed young girl, who, now that she could kill me with one little flick of her finger, looked as beautiful as a Roman soldier plundering a North African city, with her rapist's eyes and her perfume of murder.

"Kiss yourself," commanded the androgyne in a swooning voice. "Kiss yourself in the mirror, the symbolic matrix of this and that, hither and thither, outside and inside."

Then I saw, even if I could no longer be astonished, that though she knitted in both the room and the mirror, there was, within the room, no ball of wool at all; her yarn emanated from inside the mirror and the ball of wool existed only in the medium of reflection. But I did not have time to wonder at this marvel for the rank stench of Anna's excitement filled the room and her hand trembled. Out of rage and desperation, I advanced my own lips to meet the familiar yet unknown lips that advanced towards mine in the silent world of the glass.

I thought these lips would be cold and lifeless; that I would touch them but they could not touch me. Yet, when the twinned lips met, they cleaved, for these mirrored lips of mine were warm and throbbed. This mouth was wet and contained a tongue, and teeth. It was too much for me. The profound sensuality of this unexpected caress crisped the roots of my sex and my eyes involuntarily closed while my arms clasped my own tweed shoulders. The pleasure of the embrace was intense; I swooned beneath it.

When my eyes opened, I had become my own reflection. I had passed through the mirror and now I stood on a little, cane-seated, gilt-backed chair with my mouth pressed to an impervious surface of glass I had misted with my own breath and moistened with my own saliva.

Anna cried: "Hurrah!" She dropped her rifle and clapped her hands while her aunt, continuing, all the time, to knit, gave me a peculiarly sultry smile.

"So," she said. "Welcome. This room is the halfway house between here and there, between this and that, because, you understand, I am so ambiguous. Stay in the field of force of the mirror for a while, until you are used to everything."

The first thing that struck me was, the light was black. My eyes took a little time to grow accustomed to this absolute darkness for, though the delicate apparatus of cornea and aqueous humor and crystalline lens and vitreous body and optic nerve and retina had all been reversed when I gave birth to my mirror self through the mediation of the looking-glass, yet my sensibility remained as it had been. So at first, through the glass, I saw darkly and all was confusion but for their faces, which were irradiated by familiarity. But, when the inside of my head could process the information my topsy-turvy senses retrieved for me, then my other or anti-eyes apprehended a world of phosphorescent color etched as with needles of variegated fire on a dimensionless opacity. The world was the same; yet absolutely altered. How can I describe it . . . almost as if this room was the color negative of the other room. Unless—for how could I ever be certain which was the primary world and which the secondary—the other room, the other house, the other wood that I saw, transposed yet still peeping through the window in the other mirror—all that had been the color negative of the room in which I now stood, where the exhalations of my breath were the same as the inhalations of my mirror-anti-twin who turned away from me as I turned away from him, into the distorted, or else really real, world of the mirror room, which, since it existed in this mirror in this room beyond the mirror, reflected all of this room's ambiguities and was no longer the room I had left. That endless muffler or web wound round the room, still, but now it wound round contrariwise and Anna's aunt was knitting from left to right, instead of from right to left, with hands, I realized, had they wished, could have pulled a right-hand glove over the left hand and vice versa, since she was truly ambidextrous.

But when I looked at Anna, I saw she was exactly the same as she had been on the other side of the mirror and knew her face for one of those rare faces that possess an absolute symmetry, each feature the exact equivalent of the other, so one of her profiles could serve as the template for both. Her skull was like a proposition in geometry. Irreducible as stone, finite as a syllogism, she was always indistinguishable from herself whichever way she went.

But the imperturbably knitting androgyne had turned its face contrariwise. One half of its face was always masculine and the other, no matter what, was feminine; yet these had been changed about, so that all the balances of the planes of the face and the lines of the brow were the opposite of what they had been before, although one half of the face was still feminine and the other masculine. Nevertheless, the quality of the difference made it seem that this altered yet similar face was the combination of the reflection of the female side of the face and the masculine side of the face that *did not appear* in the face I had seen beyond the mirror; the effect was as of the reflection of a reflection, like an example of perpetual regression, the perfect, self-sufficient nirvana of the hermaphrodite. She was Tiresias, capable of prophetic projection, whichever side of the mirror she chose to offer herself to my sight upon; and she went on knitting and knitting and knitting, with an infernal suburban complacency.

When I turned from the mirror, Anna was holding out her right or left hand towards me but, although I felt sure I was walking towards her and lifted up my legs and set them down again with the utmost determination, Anna receded further and further away from me. Niece and aunt emitted a titter and I guessed that, in order to come to Anna, I must go away from her. Therefore I stepped sturdily backwards and, in less than a second, her hard, thin, sunburned hand grasped mine.

The touch of her hand filled me with a wild loneliness.

With her other hand, she opened the door. I was terribly afraid of that door, for the room that contained the mirror was all that I knew, and therefore my only safety, in this unknown world that Anna, who now smiled inscrutably at me, negotiated as skillfully as if she herself, the solstice in person, went on curious hinges between this place and that place unlike her aunt, who, since she was crippled, could not move unless her condition of permanent stasis meant she was moving too fast for me to see, with a speed the inertia of the eye registered as immobility.

But, when the door creaked open on everyday, iron hinges that had never been oiled in this world or any other world, I saw only the staircase up which Anna had led me, down which she would now lead me, and the muffler that still curled down to the hall. The air was dank, just as it had been. Only, all the alignments of the stairwell had been subtly altered and the light was composed of a reversed spectrum.

The webs of the spiders presented structures of white fire so minutely altered from those I had passed on my way upstairs that only memory made me apprehend how their geometrical engineering had all been executed backwards. So we passed under the spectral arch they had prepared for us and out into the open air that did not refresh my bewildered brain, for it was as solid as water, dense and compact, of an impermeable substance that transmitted neither sound nor odor. To move through this liquid silence demanded the utmost exertion of physical energy and intellectual concentration, for gravity, beyond the mirror, was not a property of the ground but of the atmosphere. Then Anna, who understood the physical laws of this world, exerted a negative pressure upon me by some willed absence of impulse and to my amazement I now moved as if propelled sharply from behind along the path to the gate, past flowers that distilled inexpressible colors from the black sky above us, colors whose names only exist in an inverted language you could never understand if I were to speak it. But the colors were virtually independent of the forms of the plants. Haloes of incandescence, they had arbitrarily settled about spread umbrellas of petals as thin yet as hard as the shoulder blade of a rabbit, for the fresh of the flowers was calcified and lifeless; no plant was sentient in this coral garden. All had suffered a dead sea change.

And the black sky possessed no dimension of distance, nor gave none; it did not arch above us but looked as if it were pasted behind the flat outlines of the half-ruinous house that now lay behind us, a shipwreck bearing a marvelous freight, the female man or virile woman clicking away at her needles in a visible silence. A visible silence, yes; for the dense fluidity of the atmosphere did not transmit sound to me as sound, but, instead, as irregular kinetic abstractions etched upon its interior, so that, once in the new wood, a sinister, mineral, realm of undiminishable darkness, to listen to the blackbird was to watch a moving point inside a block of deliquescent glass. I saw these sounds because my eyes took in a different light than the light that shone on my breast when my heart beat on the other side of it, although the wood through whose now lateral gravity Anna negotiated me was the same wood in which I had been walking when I first heard her sing. And I cannot tell you, since there is no language in this world to do so, how strange the antithetical wood and sweet June day were, for both had become the systematic negation of its others.

Anna, in some reversed fashion, must still have been menacing me with her gun, since it was her impulse that moved me; on we went, just as we had come—but Anna, now, went before me, with the muzzle of her gun pressed in the belly of nothingness, and the dog, her familiar, this time in the van. And this dog was white as snow and its balls were gone; on this side of the mirror, all dogs were bitches and vice versa.

I saw wild garlic and ground elder and the buttercups and daisies in the fossilized undergrowth now rendered in vivacious yet unnamable colors, as immobile arabesques without depth. But the sweetness of the wild roses rang in my ears like a peal of windbells for the vibrations of the perfumes echoed on my eardrums like the pulse of my own blood since, though they had become a kind of sound, they could not carry in the same way that sound did. I could not, for the life of me, make up my mind which world was which for I understood this world was coexistent in time and space with the other wood—was, as it were, the polarization of that other wood, although it was in no way similar to the reflection the other wood, or this wood, might have made in a mirror.

The more my eyes grew accustomed to the dark, the less in common did the petrified flora seem to have with anything I knew. I perceived all had been starkly invaded with, yes, shells, enormous shells, giant and uninhabited shells, so we might have been walking in the ruins of a marine city; the cool, pale coloring of those huge shells now glowed with a ghostly otherness and they were piled and heaped upon one another to parody the landscape of the woodland, unless the trees parodied them; all were whorled the wrong way round, all had that deathly weight, the supernatural resonance of the shell which seduced me and Anna told me in a soundless language I understood immediately that the transfigured wood, fertile now, only of metamorphoses, was—for how could it be anything else—the Sea of Fertility. The odor of her violence deafened me.

Then, once again, she began to sing; I saw the mute, dark fire burning like Valhalla in *Götterdämmerung*. She sang a funeral pyre, the swan's song, death itself, and, with a brusque motion of her gun, she forced me forward on my knees while the dog stood over me as she tore open my clothes. The serenade smoldered all around us and I was so much at the mercy of the weight of the air, which pressed down on me like a coffin lid, and of the viscosity of the atmosphere, that I could do nothing to defend myself, even if I had known how, and soon she had me, poor, forked thing, stretched out upon a bank of shells with my trousers around my knees. She smiled but I could not tell what the smile meant; on this side of the mirror, a smile was no clue whatsoever to intention or to feeling and I did not think she meant to do me a good deed as she unbuckled her uncouth leather belt and stepped out of her jeans.

Parting the air with the knives of her arms, she precipitated herself upon me like a quoit on a peg. I screamed; the notes of my scream rose up on the air like Ping-Pong balls on a jet of water at a fun-fair. She raped me; perhaps her gun, in this system, gave her the power to do so.

I shouted and swore but the shell grotto in which she ravished me did not reverberate and I only emitted gobs of light. Her rape, her violation of me, caused me atrocious physical and mental pain. My being leaked away from me under the visitation of her aggressive flesh. My self grew less in agony under the piston thrust of her slender loins, as if she were a hammer and were forging me into some other substance than flesh and spirit. I knew the dreadful pleasure of abandonment; she had lit my funeral pyre and now would kill me. I felt such outrage I beat in the air behind my head with my helpless fists as she pumped away indefatigably at my sex, and to my surprise, I saw her face cloud and bruises appear on it, although my hands were nowhere near her. She was a brave girl; she only fucked the harder, for she was intransigent and now resembled the Seljuk Turks sacking Constantinople. I knew there was no hope for me if I did not act immediately.

Her gun lay propped against the shells beside us. I reached the other way and seized it. I shot at the black sky while she straddled me. The bullet pierced a neat, round, empty hole in the flat vault of the heavens but no light, no sound, leaked through; I had made a hole without quality but Anna let out a ripping shriek that sent a jagged scar across the surface of the wood. She tumbled backwards and twitched a little. The dog growled at me, a terrible sight, and leaped at my throat but I quickly shot her, also, in this negative way and, now free, there remained only the problem of the return to the mirror, the return to the right-hand side of the world. But I kept tight hold of the gun, by grasping it loosely, because of the guardian of the mirror.

To return to the house, I struck out from the shell grotto where Anna lay, in the opposite direction from the one we had come from. I must have fallen into a mirror elision of reflected time, or else I stumbled upon a physical law I could not have guessed at, for the wood dissolved, as if the blood that leaked from Anna's groin was a solvent for its petrified substance, and now I found myself back at the crumbling gate before her juices were dry on my cock. I paused to do up my fly before I made my way to the door; I used my arms like scissors to snip through the thickness of the atmosphere, for it grew, moment by moment, less liquid and more impalpable. I did not ring the bell, so great was my outrage, so vivid my sense of having been the plaything of these mythic and monstrous beings.

The knitting curled down the stairs, just as I expected, and, in another moment, I saw, on a staccato stave, the sound of the needles.

She, he, it, Tiresias, though she knitted on remorselessly, was keening over a whole dropped row of stitches, trying to repair the damage as best she could. Her keening filled the room with a Walpurgisnacht of crazy shapes and, when she saw I was alone, she flung back her head and howled. In that decompression chamber between here and there, I heard a voice as clear as crystal describe a wordless song of accusation.

"Oh, my Anna, what have you done with my Anna—?"

"I shot her," I cried. "With her own weapon."

"A rape! She's raped!" screamed the androgyne as I dragged the gilt chair to the mirror and clambered upon it. In the silvered depths before me, I saw the new face of a murderer I had put on behind the mirror.

The androgyne, still knitting, kicked with her bare heels upon the floor to drive her bathchair over the wreathing muffler towards me, in order to attack me. The bathchair cannoned into the chair on which I stood and she rose up in it as far as she could and began to beat me with her tender fists. But, because she did not stop knitting, she offered no resistance when I brought my ham-hand crashing down on her working face. I broke her nose; bright blood sprang out. I turned to the mirror as she screamed and dropped her knitting.

She dropped her knitting as I crashed through the glass
through the glass, glass splintered round me driving
unmercifully into my face
through the glass, glass splintered
through the glass—
half through.

Then the glass gathered itself together like a skillful whore and expelled me. The glass rejected me; it sealed itself again into nothing but mysterious, reflective opacity. It became a mirror and it was impregnable.

Balked, I stumbled back. In Tiresias's bed-sitting room, there was the most profound silence, and nothing moved; the flow of time might have stopped. Tiresias held her empty hands to her face that was now irretrievably changed; each one snapped clean in two, her knitting needles lay on the floor. Then she sobbed and flung out her arms in a wild, helpless gesture. Blood and tears splashed down on her robe, but in a baleful, hopeless way she began to laugh, although time must have started again and now moved with such destructive speed that, before my eyes, that ageless being withered—a quick frost touched her. Wrinkles sprang out on her pale forehead while her hair fell from her head in great armfuls and her negligé turned brown and crumbled away, to reveal all the flesh that sagged from the bone as I watched it. She was the ruins of time. She grasped her throat and choked. Perhaps she was dying. The muffler was blowing away like dead leaves in a wind that sprang up from nowhere and raced through the room, although the windows stayed shut tight. But Tiresias spoke to me; she spoke to me once again.

"The umbilical cord is cut," she said. "The thread is broken. Did you not realize who I was? That I was the synthesis in person? For I could go any way the world goes and so I was knitting the thesis and the antithesis together, this world and that world. Over the leaves and under the leaves. Cohesion gone. Ah!"

Down she tumbled, the bald old crone, upon a pile of wisps of unraveled grey wool as the ormolu furniture split apart and the paper unfurled from the wall. But I was arrogant; I was undefeated. Had I not killed her? Proud as a man, I once again advanced to meet my image in the mirror. Full of self-confidence, I held out my hands to embrace my self, my anti-self, my self not-self, my assassin, my death, the world's death.

Cathedral

by Raymond Carver

Introduced by Tobias Wolff

A HOT NIGHT, SUMMER OF 1982. I WAS LYING ON THE COUCH WITH A story of Ray's that had recently come out in the *Atlantic*. I'd had it around for several days but hadn't yet read it because I tend to avoid stories by my contemporaries when I'm hard at work on something of my own, as I was then. Tolstoy, that's the ticket. Hemingway. Flaubert. Someone monumental, someone impossible to imitate or envy. No complications. When you get to the end, you think, Man, that Tolstoy sure could write!—and go on about your business.

But a new story of Ray's always exerted a tidal pull on me. I was bound to succumb; it was just a matter of time, and the time had arrived. The story was "Cathedral." I began it with the excitement you feel when granting yourself a deferred pleasure, but before long I began to feel this pleasure give way to discomfort and even resistance, for reasons I will describe later. I was fighting the story. But after a few pages it disarmed me and I surrendered to it, and as I read on I felt myself drawn up by it. I felt as if I were levitating there above the couch. I was weightless, filled with a sense of profound, inexplicable joy. Blessed, and conscious of it, I understood that I was in the presence of a masterpiece.

No doubt Ray knew what he had wrought. He never bragged, but humble as he was in his dealings with other people, he did not pretend humility about his work. He had a pretty good idea what he was doing, and what he'd done. Still, a story like this demands a response. You might know you've written something extraordinary, but you can't help wondering if other people know it too. That's the point, after all, unless you're keeping a diary. Anyway, it gave me great satisfaction to track him down—he was on the road somewhere—and tell him how his story had affected me. And I feel the same kind of pleasure now, introducing "Cathedral" in this volume. It is good to be able to say, This is good.

But I did not jump to that conclusion. At first, as I've mentioned, I found myself resisting the story. It's hard to say now exactly what my problem was then, but it had to do with the tone. It seemed, in its terse, brittle factuality, to verge on self-parody: "His wife had died. So he was visiting the dead wife's relatives in Connecticut. He called my wife from his in-laws'. Arrangements were made." That affectless voice has its source, naturally, in the character of the narrator, a hard, grudging man whose idea of a joke is to ask his blind guest, Robert, which side of the train he sat on. He seems incapable of generosity, understanding, love, or pity. He doesn't even have a name. There seems to be nothing to him. Ray had an amused contempt for the term "minimalism" as a way of describing his work, but after the first few pages of "Cathedral" I started to wonder if he hadn't written a truly minimal story.

And then everything changes. There is no one moment you can point to and say, There's the hinge. It comes on you by almost imperceptible degrees, a gathering apprehension of the fear that drives the narrator's harshness and cruel humor. He's a frightened man, trapped in terrible, self-enforced solitude and unable to imagine a way out of it. Robert's blindness and the recent death of his wife form a mirror image of the narrator's fear of dependency and loss. No wonder, as he says, "A blind man in my house was not something I looked forward to."

He reveals his humanity almost in spite of himself. It may seem a stunted, ineducable sort of humanity, but wonder enough that it's there at all. And then something else happens. The narrator begins to enjoy Robert's company. He even allows himself to say so. And in the course of a night spent "watching" a special on cathedrals—that's right, he's got Robert planted in front of the tube—the two men come together to build a cathedral of their own, a space of perfect fellowship and freedom, wherein each is granted a miracle of sight by taking on the vision of the other. The effect is complex and mysterious, laying bare our hunger for human connection and the unexpected possibilities inherent in that connection. It is a triumphant ending, yet achieved without any falsification of voice or character. The apparently minimal terms of the story have become the foundations of a soaring act of artistry and hope.

Cathedral

Raymond Carver

This blind man, an old friend of my wife's, he was on his way to spend the night. His wife had died. So he was visiting the dead wife's relatives in Connecticut. He called my wife from his in-laws'. Arrangements were made. He would come by train, a five-hour trip, and my wife would meet him at the station. She hadn't seen him since she worked for him one summer in Seattle ten years ago. But she and the blind man had kept in touch. They made tapes and mailed them back and forth. I wasn't enthusiastic about his visit. He was no one I knew. And his being blind bothered me. My idea of blindness came from the movies. In the movies, the blind moved slowly and never laughed. Sometimes they were led by seeing-eye dogs. A blind man in my house was not something I looked forward to.

That summer in Seattle she had needed a job. She didn't have any money. The man she was going to marry at the end of the summer was in officers' training school. He didn't have any money, either. But she was in love with the guy, and he was in love with her, etc. She'd seen something in the paper: HELP WANTED—*Reading to Blind Man,* and a telephone number. She phoned and went over, was hired on the spot. She'd worked with this blind man all summer. She read stuff to him, case studies, reports, that sort of thing. She helped him organize his little office in the county social-service department. They'd become good friends, my wife and the blind man. How do I know these things? She told me. And she told me something else. On her last day in the office, the blind man asked if he could touch her face. She agreed to this. She told me he touched his fingers to every part of her face, her nose—even her neck! She never forgot it. She even tried to write a poem about it. She was always trying to write a poem. She wrote a poem or two every year, usually after something really important had happened to her.

When we first started going out together, she showed me the poem. In the poem, she recalled his fingers and the way they had moved around over her face. In the poem, she talked about what she had felt at the time, about what went through her mind when the blind man touched her nose and lips. I can remember I didn't think much of the poem. Of course, I didn't tell her that. Maybe I just don't understand poetry. I admit it's not the first thing I reach for when I pick up something to read.

Anyway, this man who'd first enjoyed her favors, the officer-to-be, he'd been her childhood sweetheart. So okay. I'm saying that at the end of the summer she let the blind man run his hands over her face, said good-bye to him, married her childhood etc., who was now a commissioned officer, and she moved away from Seattle. But they'd kept in touch, she and the blind man. She made the first contact after a year or so. She called him up one night from an Air Force base in Alabama. She wanted to talk. They talked. He asked her to send him a tape and tell him about her life. She did this. She sent the tape. On the tape, she told the blind man about her husband and about their life together in the military. She told the blind man she loved her husband but she didn't like it where they lived and she didn't like it that he was a part of the military-industrial thing. She told the blind man she'd written a poem and he was in it. She told him that she was writing a poem about what it was like to be an Air Force officer's wife. The poem wasn't finished yet. She was still writing it. The blind man made a tape. He sent her the tape. She made a tape. This went on for years. My wife's officer was posted to one base and then another. She sent tapes from Moody AFB, McGuire, McConnell, and finally Travis, near Sacramento, where one night she got to feeling lonely and cut off from people she kept losing in that moving-around life. She got to feeling she couldn't go it another step. She went in and swallowed all the pills and capsules in the medicine chest and washed them down with a bottle of gin. Then she got into a hot bath and passed out.

But instead of dying, she got sick. She threw up. Her officer—why should he have a name? he was the childhood sweetheart, and what more does he want?—came home from somewhere, found her, and called the ambulance. In time, she put it all on a tape and sent the tape to the blind man. Over the years, she put all kinds of stuff on tapes and sent the tapes off lickety-split. Next to writing a poem every year, I think it was her chief means of recreation. On one tape, she told the blind man she'd decided to live away from her officer for a time. On another tape, she told him about her divorce. She and I began going out, and of course she told her blind man about it. She told him everything, or so it seemed to me. Once she asked me if I'd like to hear the latest tape from the blind man. This was a year ago. I was on the tape, she said. So I said okay, I'd listen to it. I got us drinks and we settled down in the living room. We made ready to listen. First she inserted the tape into the player and adjusted a couple of dials. Then she pushed a lever. The tape squeaked and someone began to talk in this loud voice. She lowered the volume. After a few minutes of harmless chitchat, I heard my own name in the mouth of this stranger, this blind man I didn't even know! And then this: "From all you've said about him, I can only conclude—" But we were interrupted, a knock at the door, something, and we didn't ever get back to the tape. Maybe it was just as well. I'd heard all I wanted to.

Now this same blind man was coming to sleep in my house.

"Maybe I could take him bowling," I said to my wife. She was at the draining board doing scalloped potatoes. She put down the knife she was using and turned around.

"If you love me," she said, "you can do this for me. If you don't love me, okay. But if you had a friend, any friend, and the friend came to visit, I'd make him feel comfortable." She wiped her hands with the dish towel.

"I don't have any blind friends," I said.

"You don't have *any* friends," she said. "Period. Besides," she said, "goddamn it, his wife's just died! Don't you understand that? The man's lost his wife!"

I didn't answer. She'd told me a little about the blind man's wife. Her name was Beulah. Beulah! That's a name for a colored woman.

"Was his wife a Negro?" I asked.

"Are you crazy?" my wife said. "Have you just flipped or something?" She picked up a potato. I saw it hit the floor, then roll under the stove. "What's wrong with you?" she said. "Are you drunk?"

"I'm just asking," I said.

Right then my wife filled me in with more detail than I cared to know. I made a drink and sat at the kitchen table to listen. Pieces of the story began to fall into place.

Beulah had gone to work for the blind man the summer after my wife had stopped working for him. Pretty soon Beulah and the blind man had themselves a church wedding. It was a little wedding—who'd want to go to such a wedding in the first place?—just the two of them, plus the minister and the minister's wife. But it was a church wedding just the same. It was what Beulah had wanted, he'd said. But even then Beulah must have been carrying the cancer in her glands. After they had been inseparable for eight years—my wife's word, *inseparable*—Beulah's health went into a rapid decline. She died in a Seattle hospital room, the blind man sitting beside the bed and holding on to her hand. They'd married, lived and worked together, slept together—had sex, sure—and then the blind man had to bury her. All this without his having ever seen what the goddamned woman looked like. It was beyond my understanding. Hearing this, I felt sorry for the blind man for a little bit. And then I found myself thinking what a pitiful life this woman must have led. Imagine a woman who could never see herself as she was seen in the eyes of her loved one. A woman who could go on day after day and never receive the smallest compliment from her beloved. A woman whose husband could never read the expression on her face, be it misery or something better. Someone who could wear makeup or not—what difference to him? She could, if she wanted, wear green eye-shadow around one eye, a straight pin in her nostril, yellow slacks, and purple shoes, no matter. And then to slip off into death, the blind man's hand on her hand, his blind eyes streaming tears—I'm imagining now—her last thought maybe this: that he never even knew what she looked like, and she on an express to the grave. Robert was left with a small insurance policy and half of a twenty-peso Mexican coin. The other half of the coin went into the box with her. Pathetic.

So when the time rolled around, my wife went to the depot to pick him up. With nothing to do but wait—sure, I blamed him for that—I was having a drink and watching the TV when I heard the car pull into the drive. I got up from the sofa with my drink and went to the window to have a look.

I saw my wife laughing as she parked the car. I saw her get out of the car and shut the door. She was still wearing a smile. Just amazing. She went around to the other side of the car to where the blind man was already starting to get out. This blind man, feature this, he was wearing a full beard! A beard on a blind man! Too much, I say. The blind man reached into the backseat and dragged out a suitcase. My wife took his arm, shut the car door, and, talking all the way, moved him down the drive and then up the steps to the front porch. I turned off the TV. I finished my drink, rinsed the glass, dried my hands. Then I went to the door.

My wife said, "I want you to meet Robert. Robert, this is my husband. I've told you all about him." She was beaming. She had this blind man by his coat sleeve.

The blind man let go of his suitcase and up came his hand.

I took it. He squeezed hard, held my hand, and then he let it go.

"I feel like we've already met," he boomed.

"Likewise," I said. I didn't know what else to say. Then I said, "Welcome. I've heard a lot about you." We began to move then, a little group, from the porch into the living room, my wife guiding him by the arm. The blind man was carrying his suitcase in his other hand. My wife said things like, "To your left here, Robert. That's right. Now watch it, there's a chair. That's it. Sit down right here. This is the sofa. We just bought this sofa two weeks ago."

I started to say something about the old sofa. I'd liked that old sofa. But I didn't say anything. Then I wanted to say something else, small-talk, about the scenic ride along the Hudson. How going *to* New York, you should sit on the right-hand side of the train, and coming *from* New York, the left-hand side.

"Did you have a good train ride?" I said. "Which side of the train did you sit on, by the way?"

"What a question, which side!" my wife said. "What's it matter which side?" she said.

"I just asked," I said.

"Right side," the blind man said. "I hadn't been on a train in nearly forty years. Not since I was a kid. With my folks. That's been a long time. I'd nearly forgotten the sensation. I have winter in my beard now," he said. "So I've been told, anyway. Do I look distinguished, my dear?" the blind man said to my wife.

"You look distinguished, Robert," she said. "Robert," she said. "Robert, it's just so good to see you."

My wife finally took her eyes off the blind man and looked at me. I had the feeling she didn't like what she saw. I shrugged.

I've never met, or personally known, anyone who was blind. This blind man was late forties, a heavy-set, balding man with stooped shoulders, as if he carried a great weight there. He wore brown slacks, brown shoes, a light-brown shirt, a tie, a sports coat. Spiffy. He also had this full beard. But he didn't use a cane and he didn't wear dark glasses. I'd always thought dark glasses were a must for the blind. Fact was, I wished he had a pair. At first glance, his eyes looked like anyone else's eyes. But if you looked close, there was something different about them. Too much white in the iris, for one thing, and the pupils seemed to move around in the sockets without his knowing it or being able to stop it. Creepy. As I stared at his face, I saw the left pupil turn in toward his nose while the other made an effort to keep in one place. But it was only an effort, for that eye was on the roam without his knowing it or wanting it to be.

I said, "Let me get you a drink. What's your pleasure? We have a little of everything. It's one of our pastimes."

"Bub, I'm a Scotch man myself," he said fast enough in this big voice.

"Right," I said. Bub! "Sure you are. I knew it."

He let his fingers touch his suitcase, which was sitting alongside the sofa. He was taking his bearings. I didn't blame him for that.

"I'll move that up to your room," my wife said.

"No, that's fine," the blind man said loudly. "It can go up when I go up."

"A little water with the Scotch?" I said.

"Very little," he said.

"I knew it," I said.

He said, "Just a tad. The Irish actor, Barry Fitzgerald? I'm like that fellow. When I drink water, Fitzgerald said, I drink water. When I drink whiskey, I drink whiskey." My wife laughed. The blind man brought his hand up under his beard. He lifted his beard slowly and let it drop.

I did the drinks, three big glasses of Scotch with a splash of water in each. Then we made ourselves comfortable and talked about Robert's travels. First the long flight from the West Coast to Connecticut, we covered that. Then from Connecticut up here by train. We had another drink concerning that leg of the trip.

I remembered having read somewhere that the blind didn't smoke because, as speculation had it, they couldn't see the smoke they exhaled. I thought I knew that much and that much only about blind people. But this blind man smoked his cigarette down to the nubbin and then lit another one. This blind man filled his ashtray and my wife emptied it.

When we sat down at the table for dinner, we had another drink. My wife heaped Robert's plate with cube steak, scalloped potatoes, green beans. I buttered him up two slices of bread. I said, "Here's bread and butter for you." I swallowed some of my drink. "Now let us pray," I said, and the blind man lowered his head. My wife looked at me, her mouth agape. "Pray the phone won't ring and the food doesn't get cold," I said.

We dug in. We ate everything there was to eat on the table. We ate like there was no tomorrow. We didn't talk. We ate. We scarfed. We grazed that table. We were into serious eating. The blind man had right away located his foods, he knew just where everything was on his plate. I watched with admiration as he used his knife and fork on the meat. He'd cut two pieces of meat, fork the meat into his mouth, and then go all out for the scalloped potatoes, the beans next, and then he'd tear off a hunk of buttered bread and eat that. He'd follow this up with a big drink of milk. It didn't seem to bother him to use his fingers once in a while, either.

We finished everything, including half a strawberry pie. For a few moments, we sat as if stunned. Sweat beaded on our faces. Finally, we got up from the table and left the dirty plates. We didn't look back. We took ourselves into the living room and sank into our places again. Robert and my wife sat on the sofa. I took the big chair. We had us two or three more drinks while they talked about the major things that had come to pass for them in the past ten years. For the most part, I just listened. Now and then I joined in. I didn't want him to think I'd left the room, and I didn't want her to think I was feeling left out. They talked of things that had happened to them—to them!—these past ten years. I waited in vain to hear my name on my wife's sweet lips: "And then my dear husband came into my life"—something like that. But I heard nothing of the sort. More talk of Robert. Robert had done a little of everything, it seemed, a regular blind jack-of-all-trades. But most recently he and his wife had had an Amway distributorship, from which, I gathered, they'd earned their living, such as it was. The blind man was also a ham radio operator. He talked in his loud voice about conversations he'd had with fellow operators in Guam, in the Philippines, in Alaska, and even in Tahiti. He said he'd have a lot of friends there if he ever wanted to go visit those places. From time to time, he'd turn his blind face toward me, put his hand under his beard, ask me something. How long had I been in my present position? (Three years.) Did I like my work? (I didn't.) Was I going to stay with it? (What were the options?) Finally, when I thought he was beginning to run down, I got up and turned on the TV.

My wife looked at me with irritation. She was heading toward a boil. Then she looked at the blind man and said, "Robert, do you have a TV?"

The blind man said, "My dear, I have two TVs. I have a color set and a black-and-white thing, an old relic. It's funny, but if I turn the TV on, and I'm always turning it on, I turn on the color set. It's funny, don't you think?"

I didn't know what to say to that. I had absolutely nothing to say to that. No opinion. So I watched the news program and tried to listen to what the announcer was saying.

"This is a color TV," the blind man said. "Don't ask me how, but I can tell."

"We traded up a while ago," I said.

The blind man had another taste of his drink. He lifted his beard, sniffed it, and let it fall. He leaned forward on the sofa. He positioned his ashtray on the coffee table, then put the lighter to his cigarette. He leaned back on the sofa and crossed his legs at the ankles.

My wife covered her mouth, and then she yawned. She stretched. She said, "I think I'll go upstairs and put on my robe. I think I'll change into something else. Robert, you make yourself comfortable," she said.

"I'm comfortable," the blind man said.

"I want you to feel comfortable in this house," she said.

"I am comfortable," the blind man said.

After she'd left the room, he and I listened to the weather report and then to the sports roundup. By that time, she'd been gone so long I didn't know if she was going to come back. I thought she might have gone to bed. I wished she'd come back downstairs. I didn't want to be left alone with a blind man. I asked him if he wanted another drink, and he said sure. Then I asked if he wanted to smoke some dope with me. I said I'd just rolled a number. I hadn't, but I planned to do so in about two shakes.

"I'll try some with you," he said.

"Damn right," I said. "That's the stuff."

I got our drinks and sat down on the sofa with him. Then I rolled us two fat numbers. I lit one and passed it. I brought it to his fingers. He took it and inhaled.

"Hold it as long as you can," I said. I could tell he didn't know the first thing.

My wife came back downstairs wearing her pink robe and her pink slippers.

"What do I smell?" she said.

"We thought we'd have us some cannabis," I said.

My wife gave me a savage look. Then she looked at the blind man and said, "Robert, I didn't know you smoked."

He said, "I do now, my dear. There's a first time for everything. But I don't feel anything yet."

"This stuff is pretty mellow," I said. "This stuff is mild. It's dope you can reason with," I said. "It doesn't mess you up."

"Not much it doesn't, bub," he said, and laughed.

My wife sat on the sofa between the blind man and me. I passed her the number. She took it and toked and then passed it back to me. "Which way is this going?" she said. Then she said, "I shouldn't be smoking this. I can hardly keep my eyes open as it is. That dinner did me in. I shouldn't have eaten so much."

"It was the strawberry pie," the blind man said. "That's what did it," he said, and he laughed his big laugh. Then he shook his head.

"There's more strawberry pie," I said.

"Do you want some more, Robert?" my wife said.

"Maybe in a little while," he said.

We gave our attention to the TV. My wife yawned again. She said, "Your bed is made up when you feel like going to bed, Robert. I know you must have had a long day. When you're ready to go to bed, say so." She pulled his arm. "Robert?"

He came to and said, "I've had a real nice time. This beats tapes, doesn't it?"

I said, "Coming at you," and I put the number between his fingers. He inhaled, held the smoke, and then let it go. It was like he'd been doing it since he was nine years old.

"Thanks, bub," he said. "But I think this is all for me. I think I'm beginning to feel it," he said. He held the burning roach out for my wife.

"Same here," she said. "Ditto. Me, too." She took the roach and passed it to me. "I may just sit here for a while between you two guys with my eyes closed. But don't let me bother you, okay? Either one of you. If it bothers you, say so. Otherwise, I may just sit here with my eyes closed until you're ready to go to bed," she said. "Your bed's made up, Robert, when you're ready. It's right next to our room at the top of the stairs. We'll show you up when you're ready. You wake me up now, you guys, if I fall asleep." She said that and then she closed her eyes and went to sleep.

The news program ended. I got up and changed the channel. I sat back down on the sofa. I wished my wife hadn't pooped out. Her head lay across the back of the sofa, her mouth open. She'd turned so that her robe had slipped away from her legs, exposing a juicy thigh. I reached to draw her robe back over her, and it was then that I glanced at the blind man. What the hell! I flipped the robe open again.

"You say when you want some strawberry pie," I said.

"I will," he said.

I said, "Are you tired? Do you want me to take you up to your bed? Are you ready to hit the hay?"

"Not yet," he said. "No, I'll stay up with you, bub. If that's all right. I'll stay up until you're ready to turn in. We haven't had a chance to talk. Know what I mean? I feel like me and her monopolized the evening." He lifted his beard and he let it fall. He picked up his cigarettes and his lighter.

"That's all right," I said. Then I said, "I'm glad for the company."

And I guess I was. Every night I smoked dope and stayed up as long as I could before I fell asleep. My wife and I hardly ever went to bed at the same time. When I did go to sleep, I had these dreams. Sometimes I'd wake up from one of them, my heart going crazy.

Something about the church and the Middle Ages was on the TV. Not your run-of-the-mill TV fare. I wanted to watch something else. I turned to the other channels. But there was nothing on them, either. So I turned back to the first channel and apologized.

"Bub, it's all right," the blind man said. "It's fine with me. Whatever you want to watch is okay. I'm always learning something. Learning never ends. It won't hurt me to learn something tonight. I got ears," he said.

* * *

We didn't say anything for a time. He was leaning forward with his head turned at me, his right ear aimed in the direction of the set. Very disconcerting. Now and then his eyelids drooped and then they snapped open again. Now and then he put his fingers into his beard and tugged, like he was thinking about something he was hearing on the television.

On the screen, a group of men wearing cowls was being set upon and tormented by men dressed in skeleton costumes and men dressed as devils. The men dressed as devils wore devil masks, horns, and long tails. This pageant was part of a procession. The Englishman who was narrating the thing said it took place in Spain once a year. I tried to explain to the blind man what was happening.

"Skeletons," he said. "I know about skeletons," he said, and he nodded.

The TV showed this one cathedral. Then there was a long, slow look at another one. Finally, the picture switched to the famous one in Paris, with its flying buttresses and its spires reaching up to the clouds. The camera pulled away to show the whole of the cathedral rising above the skyline.

There were times when the Englishman who was telling the thing would shut up, would simply let the camera move around over the cathedrals. Or else the camera would tour the countryside, men in fields walking behind oxen. I waited as long as I could. Then I felt I had to say something. I said, "They're showing the outside of this cathedral now. Gargoyles. Little statues carved to look like monsters. Now I guess they're in Italy. Yeah, they're in Italy. There's paintings on the walls of this one church."

"Are those fresco paintings, bub?" he asked, and he sipped from his drink.

I reached for my glass. But it was empty. I tried to remember what I could remember. "You're asking me are those frescoes?" I said. "That's a good question. I don't know."

The camera moved to a cathedral outside Lisbon. The differences in the Portuguese cathedral compared with the French and Italian were not that great. But they were there. Mostly the interior stuff. Then something occurred to me, and I said, "Something has occurred to me. Do you have any idea what a cathedral is? What they look like, that is? Do you follow me? If somebody says cathedral to you, do you have any notion what they're talking about? Do you know the difference between that and a Baptist church, say?"

He let the smoke dribble from his mouth. "I know they took hundreds of workers fifty or a hundred years to build," he said. "I just heard the man say that, of course. I know generations of the same families worked on a cathedral. I heard him say that, too. The men who began their life's work on them, they never lived to see the completion of their work. In that wise, bub, they're no different from the rest of us, right?" He laughed. Then his eyelids drooped again. His head nodded. He seemed to be snoozing. Maybe he was imagining himself in Portugal. The TV was showing another cathedral now. This one was in Germany. The Englishman's voice droned on.

"Cathedrals," the blind man said. He sat up and rolled his head back and forth. "If you want the truth, bub, that's about all I know. What I just said. What I heard him say. But maybe you could describe one to me? I wish you'd do it. I'd like that. If you want to know, I really don't have a good idea."

I stared hard at the shot of the cathedral on the TV. How could I even begin to describe it? But say my life depended on it. Say my life was being threatened by an insane guy who said I had to do it or else.

I stared some more at the cathedral before the picture flipped off into the countryside. There was no use. I turned to the blind man and said, "To begin with, they're very tall." I was looking around the room for clues. "They reach way up. Up and up. Toward the sky. They're so big, some of them, they have to have these supports. To help hold them up, so to speak. These supports are called buttresses. They remind me of viaducts, for some reason. But maybe you don't know viaducts, either? Sometimes the cathedrals have devils and such carved into the front. Sometimes lords and ladies. Don't ask me why this is," I said.

He was nodding. The whole upper part of his body seemed to be moving back and forth.

"I'm not doing so good, am I?" I said.

He stopped nodding and leaned forward on the edge of the sofa. As he listened to me, he was running his fingers through his beard. I wasn't getting through to him, I could see that. But he waited for me to go on just the same. He nodded, like he was trying to encourage me. I tried to think what else to say. "They're really big," I said. "They're massive. They're built of stone. Marble, too, sometimes. In those olden days, when they built cathedrals, men wanted to be close to God. In those olden days, God was an important part of everyone's life. You could tell this from their cathedral-building. I'm sorry," I said, "but it looks like that's the best I can do for you. I'm just no good at it."

"That's all right, bub," the blind man said. "Hey, listen. I hope you don't mind my asking you. Can I ask you something? Let me ask you a simple question, yes or no. I'm just curious and there's no offense. You're my host. But let me ask if you are in any way religious? You don't mind my asking?"

I shook my head. He couldn't see that, though. A wink is the same as a nod to a blind man. "I guess I don't believe in it. In anything. Sometimes it's hard. You know what I'm saying?"

"Sure, I do," he said.

"Right," I said.

The Englishman was still holding forth. My wife sighed in her sleep. She drew a long breath and went on with her sleeping.

"You'll have to forgive me," I said. "But I can't tell you what a cathedral looks like. It just isn't in me to do it. I can't do any more than I've done."

The blind man sat very still, his head down, as he listened to me.

I said, "The truth is, cathedrals don't mean anything special to me. Nothing. Cathedrals. They're something to look at on late-night TV. That's all they are."

It was then that the blind man cleared his throat. He brought something up. He took a handkerchief from his back pocket. Then he said, "I get it, bub. It's okay. It happens. Don't worry about it," he said. "Hey, listen to me. Will you do me a favor? I got an idea. Why don't you find us some heavy paper? And a pen. We'll do something. We'll draw one together. Get us a pen and some heavy paper. Go on, bub, get the stuff," he said.

So I went upstairs. My legs felt like they didn't have any strength in them. They felt like they did after I'd done some running. In my wife's room, I looked around. I found some ballpoints in a little basket on her table. And then I tried to think where to look for the kind of paper he was talking about.

Downstairs, in the kitchen, I found a shopping bag with onion skins in the bottom of the bag. I emptied the bag and shook it. I brought it into the living room and sat down with it near his legs. I moved some things, smoothed the wrinkles from the bag, spread it out on the coffee table.

The blind man got down from the sofa and sat next to me on the carpet.

He ran his fingers over the paper. He went up and down the sides of the paper. The edges, even the edges. He fingered the corners.

"All right," he said. "All right, let's do her."

He found my hand, the hand with the pen. He closed his hand over my hand. "Go ahead, bub, draw," he said. "Draw. You'll see. I'll follow along with you. It'll be okay. Just begin now like I'm telling you. You'll see. Draw," the blind man said.

So I began. First I drew a box that looked like a house. It could have been the house I lived in. Then I put a roof on it. At either end of the roof, I drew spires. Crazy.

"Swell," he said. "Terrific. You're doing fine," he said. "Never thought anything like this could happen in your lifetime, did you, bub? Well, it's a strange life, we all know that. Go on now. Keep it up."

I put in windows with arches. I drew flying buttresses. I hung great doors. I couldn't stop. The TV station went off the air. I put down the pen and closed and opened my fingers. The blind man felt around over the paper. He moved the tips of his fingers over the paper, all over what I had drawn, and he nodded.

"Doing fine," the blind man said.

I took up the pen again, and he found my hand. I kept at it. I'm no artist. But I kept drawing just the same.

My wife opened up her eyes and gazed at us. She sat up on the sofa, her robe hanging open. She said, "What are you doing? Tell me, I want to know."

I didn't answer her.

The blind man said, "We're drawing a cathedral. Me and him are working on it. Press hard," he said to me. "That's right. That's good," he said.

"Sure. You got it, bub. I can tell. You didn't think you could. But you can, can't you? You're cooking with gas now. You know what I'm saying? We're going to really have us something here in a minute. How's the old arm?" he said. "Put some people in there now. What's a cathedral without people?"

My wife said, "What's going on? Robert, what are you doing? What's going on?"

"It's all right," he said to her. "Close your eyes now," the blind man said to me.

I did it. I closed them just like he said.

"Are they closed?" he said. "Don't fudge."

"They're closed," I said.

"Keep them that way," he said. He said, "Don't stop now. Draw."

So we kept on with it. His fingers rode my fingers as my hand went over the paper. It was like nothing else in my life up to now.

Then he said, "I think that's it. I think you got it," he said. "Take a look. What do you think?"

But I had my eyes closed. I thought I'd keep them that way for a little longer. I thought it was something I ought to do.

"Well?" he said. "Are you looking?"

My eyes were still closed. I was in my house. I knew that. But I didn't feel like I was inside anything.

"It's really something," I said.

Goodbye, My Brother

by John Cheever

Introduced by Allan Gurganus

WE WATCH A MASTER POTTER WORK THE WHEEL. HE STRADDLES A spinning disk topped by a lump of muck, and in hands this able, this scarily practiced, this rigged with sheer killing power, the vessel's walls lift like some fine mouth singing its only vowel straight up.

The consolations of mastery are evident in John Cheever's own favorite John Cheever story, "Goodbye, My Brother." To read this admission of fratricidal impulses, this hymn of family continuity, is to participate in the very act of its shaping. "What is a masterpiece?" Gertrude Stein liked to ask. By asking, she showed the immodesty of daily inquiring, "Mirror, mirror on the wall . . ." But surely one way to recognize roaming Masterworks involves: human breath.

What gauge is simpler yet more profound? If you find your gray matter clicking like some car hood at the last pit stop of the Indy 500, that's a start; if your heart becomes aware of its surrounding bell tower, that's an early warning sign; should the sound of the fire alarm clanging in the next room dwindle to gnat-sized distraction, that might give a hint; but if you hold your breath till a ravishing relentless emotional sentence's period says, "You may breathe . . . *now*"—then you might be reading "Goodbye, My Brother" for the first time or, more especially, the sixtieth.

The pleasures of Cheever begin in something as mysterious as tone. This is a pitch that can accommodate the most casual turn of conversation ("I don't think about the family much"). But it's a voice that can suddenly push the all-too-human offhandedness of address toward surprising universal topics like honor, shelter, love, compromise, lust. Though most stories might be said to concern family reunions gone ruinously wrong, the very familiarity of the present tale's material—a single unregenerate brother's return and exit—serves only to highlight the mastery itself.

Artists are notoriously poor judges of their own work. But in this instance, John Cheever knew precisely what he had (and had not) done. He ignored chronology and placed "Goodbye, my Brother" first in *The Stories of John Cheever*. There it belongs.

Cheever ends his brief introduction to the collected stories:

> It was under the canopy of a Fifty-ninth Street apartment house that I wrote, aloud, the closing of "Goodbye, My Brother." "Oh, what can you do with a man like that?" I asked, and closed by saying, "I watched the naked women walk out of the sea." "You're talking to yourself, Mr. Cheever," the doorman said politely . . . correct, friendly, and content with his ten-dollar tip at Christmas.

The more you love a story, the stronger is your impulse to illuminate its virtues by simply quoting from the thing. That urge will be beautifully sated by "Goodbye, My Brother" appearing, whole, just ahead. I would urge you, fellow reader, to drink it all before you return to sip this particular appreciation. I loathe those chatterers who give away the ends of movies. Though the Cheever story concludes in a way that seems inevitable, I don't want its final beautiful chord change anticipated or diminished by my meddling love for it. So absorb the story first.

According to Scott Donaldson's biography, in Cheever's original draft, there was no "bad" brother. No "Tifty," named with a family's fond cruelty for the sound of his childhood bedroom slippers. In the beginning, the schoolteacher narrator himself shouldered both roles; he enacted all those mixed emotions about his own pretentious, endearing, fallen family. The struggle remained inward. By subdividing the fight, by embodying the naysayer in the peevish, heightened character of Lawrence—a nondrinking, ungambler en route from sad Cleveland to sadder Albany—Cheever elevates what might've been a soured inward story to one as simple and resounding as myth.

Of course, the tale is also what teachers of advanced-placement ninth grade lit might call "a contemporary reworking of the Cain and Abel legend." So much of Cheever's work can be traced to the Old Testament or the *Bulfinch's Mythology,* required reading at Quincy Academy, his only school (the world excepted).

Here the author of many longer works embodies (and all but retires) most of his own recurrent themes. Cheever, born under the sign of Gemini, the twin brothers, played out the urge toward fratricide again and again. Never did he render it more successfully. By making the history of the Pommeroys a long one, by leaning hard on the image of the new "old" home place created from borrowed shingles, the writer plainly posits this family's long struggle as paralleling our myth-gorged American Experiment itself.

> The branch of the Pommeroys to which we belong was founded by a minister who was eulogized by Cotton Mather for his untiring abjuration of the Devil. The Pommeroys were ministers until the middle of the nineteenth century, and the harshness of their thought—man is full of misery, and all earthly beauty is lustful and corrupt—has been preserved in books and sermons. The temper of our family changed somewhat and became more lighthearted, but when I was of school age, I can remember a cousinage of old men and women who seem to hark back to the dark days of the ministry and to be animated by perpetual guilt and the deification of the scourge.

How beautiful a paragraph! It is theologically sound. Note that new old Gothick word "cousinage," the uninsisted-upon internal ryhme of "to hark back to the dark days of the ministry." And, of course, the suggestion that cocktail banter, the love of the natural world, the sophisticated treatment of sexuality as a comic subject might constitute recent familial achievements, not mere slippage into the sea. The story hints that these are as much a part of the Pommeroys' recombinant mythology at the end of the twentieth century as was the abjured "Devil" striding the end of the eighteenth.

Along with one of the editors of this volume, I was John Cheever's student at the Iowa Writers Workshop in the early seventies. It was during this dark period of his later life that we came to know what a disciplined, funny, and joyful person he could be. We reveled in his company and in the example of his faultless prose. At the time, of course, he seemed somewhat antiquated; I mean his curious method of beginning stories at their starts (see Genesis, line one) and closing them as they concluded. We were then gaga over the backflip antics of Donald Barthleme. Still, we knew—by the very meter of our breath—that Cheever had shaped some of the best sentences ever written by a Flaubert-inspired American. (Flaubert, as teacher and model, is pitiless, and therefore supremely useful.) But it was a pitching back and forth, between clay as mud and clay as porcelain, that so marked everybody's dealings with John Cheever. Despite evidence otherwise, he once confessed to writing this story in a single sitting: confessed and boasted. But the boast was couched in the humility of a potter confronting the daily merciless judgment of centrifugal force. Cheever said he liked best to work in the back guest bedroom of his beautiful homeplace in Ossining, New York. I later saw this room, the sort of at-the-ugly-end-of-the-hall warren where the sewing machine is stowed, where dotty visiting great-aunts are sent with genial grace, knowing that such sparseness will discourage long stays. There, at a card table, he pounded out his stories and novels. All on a little black machine that possessed no electrical plug.

How beautiful to recall—as if trying to remember the snuffboxes of the devilish eighteenth century—a writing device that depended only on the strength of downrushing human fingers. I mean a gizmo constructed to answer Newtonian physics; it had no moving part that was not rubber or metal and therefore replaceable in two minutes. The shifting roller was called the "carriage"—another shade of things antique. The carriage reaching the end of a line was signaled by something as literally primitive as the ringing of a bell. Today's computer salespersons might refer to unecessary options as "bells and whistles." But, I tell you, the bell was necessary then. This present story could not, I think, have been composed without the faintly churchlike gratitude of a silver bell, half nautical, achievable, and sonorous. Perhaps the bell's metronomic contribution made pre-computer prose more pulsating, the typical sentences shorter, purer—unlike the snaking silent toxic run-ons of today? That bell and simple wizardry colluded in the composition of this story, a lash of consciousness perfectly outcurling, snapping exact at its end. It must be regarded both as music and as gift. John Cheever certainly saw it that way.

* * *

The story remains so fresh. Only one word dates it. A certain breakfast roll is herein called a "crescent" and not, as every American can now boldly say, a "croissant."

"Goodbye, My Brother" makes promises so often forgotten these days—an assurance that the ocean is the source of life, that beautiful women are—in Cheever's un-P.C. daringly prelapsarian relation to womankind—easier to be around than the other sort; that all family relations, though strained and harrowing and violent as human birth, must eventually empty into acceptance, self-knowledge, and a kind of resignation that can pass, in dealing with our brothers and sisters, for love: that often *is* love.

The architecture of Cheever's narrative possesses all the frontal force of eighteenth-century New England ecclesiastical design. The white symmetry (unmarked by the blue chalk of its makings) aims upward, a frame structure that—in its very starchiness—recalls the Puritan self-purging. It mortally reflects a region's will to ethical beauty, life at its more orderly, its most civic and transcendental, yet contained.

Cheever's best short fiction is even better than most people think. There is a distance between his greatest stories and the mere surface joys of the others. But in a tale like this one, a complex morality keeps burning through the surface heraldry. There is a relentless vision at work. The theology is notable for rerouting Cotton Mather's aseptic values: Lawrence stands accused of *not* drinking, *not* gambling, *not* flirting, and therefore *not* enjoying; his damnation is no less fixed than an earlier generation's certainty. "The harsh surface beauty of life," as the story terms it, seems what we have these days. To our narrator—the harried schoolmaster with just two weeks a year to experience pure fun, pure masquerade, pure simplifying natural pleasure—such a return to courtesy (and class entitlement) replaces an early ethical "absolute good." The unabashed lyrical passages are reserved here for a single person's experiencing of the elements. Such a Winslow Homer watercolor of a sentence our narrator commits:

> Most of the sailing that I do these days is in Manhasset, and I am used to setting a homeward course by the gasoline barge and the tin roofs of the boat shed, and it was a pleasure that afternoon, as we returned, to keep the bow on a white church spire in the village and to find even the inshore water green and clear.

The sentence is constructed as a set of waves, resisted. Cheever's every word is operative; there's no filler, no cornstarch, no MSG to interfere with the taste of sea spray and eternity. The mundane landmarks, the gasoline barge and the roofs, manage—instead of impeding the sense of speed and joy—to heighten the feel of our being fully at home on the water itself, the very briny depths where patriarch Pommeroy met his traditional doom.

But Cheever's tale of a misspent family reunion allows the natural world's pleasure to serve as more than mere comfort margin and counterpoint to human discord. The water and the land, the scent of beach grapes, the perfect vistas observed from a house sinking into the sea—these, as human relations strain and fray, become, like the gaming social rituals of the cliffside house itself, sacramental.

> We drank our gin; the abuse seemed to reach a crescendo, and then, one by one, we went swimming in the solid green water. But when we came out no one mentioned Lawrence unkindly; the line of abusive conversation had been cut, as if swimming had the cleansing force claimed for baptism.

Cheever is preparing us for the glorious final chord change of the story. It is that most generous sort of account, and hardest to achieve: a sad, sad story about the possibility of beauty in this life, a hymn to pleasure and order that, on ending, leaves one soaked in a strange soaring sense of creature well-being.

The writer has been setting up that exquisite last line when his sister, Diana, and his wife, Helen—till now, never named in a shared sentence—are finally joined, to emerge, glistening, redeemed, redeeming. Cheever finally lets us reflect on these two names from Myth and from that Myth called History. It is typical of Cheever that the names should be so characteristic of WASPs of this and earlier generations. But the surprise of alchemically allowing these women to emerge nude from the unimprovable sea is just part of the writer's revised theology of pleasure.

At the top of his form, Cheever can function both as a social historian and as a magic realist, both as a creator of supreme entertainments and as a moralist who'll be remembered like the best Pommeroy preachers "in sermons and books." In the final exit from the sea, what lifts is not simply that last lush symphonic swell after the brutalities family life exacts from the best of us. No, we are returned to mere Eden, before the falling of a house into the sea might be of concern, before there was a need for houses, before God sent rain to Eden—because rain might inconvenience the couple placed there for pleasure-seeking only. We are returned to the childhood happiness of pure noun. A tree is to climb. Anything red needs eating. The human form is incorruptible.

"The great value of art," Delmore Schwartz wrote, "is in the exercise of an observing faculty able to confer on commonplace experience a universal value and thus restore significance to the life of the individual."

And so, godless yet a believer, I choose to end my admiration of this perfect vessel of a story with two awed simple syllables—ones that constitute every reader's psalm of praise to a work that seems so true. I mean our sweetest, most succinct form of literary criticism, of loving praise: "Amen."

Goodbye, My Brother

John Cheever

We are a family that has always been very close in spirit. Our father was drowned in a sailing accident when we were young, and our mother has always stressed the fact that our familial relationships have a kind of permanence that we will never meet with again. I don't think about the family much, but when I remember its members and the coast where they lived and the sea salt that I think is in our blood, I am happy to recall that I am a Pommeroy—that I have the nose, the coloring, and the promise of longevity—and that while we are not a distinguished family, we enjoy the illusion, when we are together, that the Pommeroys are unique. I don't say any of this because I'm interested in family history or because this sense of uniqueness is deep or important to me but in order to advance the point that we are loyal to one another in spite of our differences, and that any rupture in this loyalty is a source of confusion and pain.

We are four children: there is my sister Diana and the three men—Chaddy, Lawrence, and myself. Like most families in which the children are out of their twenties, we have been separated by business, marriage, and war. Helen and I live on Long Island now, with our four children. I teach in a secondary school, and I am past the age where I expect to be made headmaster—or principal, as we say—but I respect the work. Chaddy, who has done better than the rest of us, lives in Manhattan, with Odette and their children. Mother lives in Philadelphia, and Diana, since her divorce, has been living in France, but she comes back to the States in the summer to spend a month at Laud's Head. Laud's Head is a summer place on the shore of one of the Massachusetts islands. We used to have a cottage there, and in the twenties our father built the big house. It stands on a cliff above the sea and, excepting St. Tropez and some of the Apennine villages, it is my favorite place in the world. We each have an equity in the place and we contribute some money to help keep it going.

Our youngest brother, Lawrence, who is a lawyer, got a job with a Cleveland firm after the war, and none of us saw him for four years. When he decided to leave Cleveland and go to work for a firm in Albany, he wrote Mother that he would, between jobs, spend ten days at Laud's Head, with his wife and their two children. This was when I had planned to take my vacation—I had been teaching summer school—and Helen and Chaddy and Odette and Diana were all going to be there, so the family would be together. Lawrence is the member of the family with whom the rest of us have least in common. We have never seen a great deal of him, and I suppose that's why we still call him Tifty—a nickname he was given when he was a child, because when he came down the hall toward the dining room for breakfast, his slippers made a noise that sounded like "Tifty, tifty, tifty." That's what Father called him, and so did everyone else. When he grew older, Diana sometimes used to call him Little Jesus, and Mother often called him the Croaker. We had disliked Lawrence, but we looked forward to his return with a mixture of apprehension and loyalty, and with some of the joy and delight of reclaiming a brother.

Lawrence crossed over from the mainland on the four-o'clock boat one afternoon late in the summer, and Chaddy and I went down to meet him. The arrivals and departures of the summer ferry have all the outward signs that suggest a voyage—whistles, bells, hand trucks, reunions, and the smell of brine—but it is a voyage of no import, and when I watched the boat come into the blue harbor that afternoon and thought that it was completing a voyage of no import, I realized that I had hit on exactly the kind of observation that Lawrence would have made. We looked for his face behind the windshields as the cars drove off the boat, and we had no trouble in recognizing him. And we ran over and shook his hand and clumsily kissed his wife and the children. "Tifty!" Chaddy shouted. "Tifty!" It is difficult to judge changes in the appearance of a brother, but both Chaddy and I agreed, as we drove back to Laud's Head, that Lawrence still looked very young. He got to the house first, and we took the suitcases out of his car. When I came in, he was standing in the living room, talking with Mother and Diana. They were in their best clothes and all their jewelry, and they were welcoming him extravagantly, but even then, when everyone was endeavoring to seem most affectionate and at a time when these endeavors come easiest, I was aware of a faint tension in the room. Thinking about this as I carried Lawrence's heavy suitcases up the stairs, I realized that our dislikes are as deeply ingrained as our better passions, and I remembered that once, twenty-five years ago, when I had hit Lawrence on the head with a rock, he had picked himself up and gone directly to our father to complain.

I carried the suitcases up to the third floor, where Ruth, Lawrence's wife, had begun to settle her family. She is a thin girl, and she seemed very tired from the journey, but when I asked her if she didn't want me to bring a drink upstairs to her, she said she didn't think she did.

When I got downstairs, Lawrence wasn't around, but the others were all ready for cocktails, and we decided to go ahead. Lawrence is the only member of the family who has never enjoyed drinking. We took our cocktails onto the terrace, so that we could see the bluffs and the sea and the islands in the east, and the return of Lawrence and his wife, their presence in the house, seemed to refresh our responses to the familiar view; it was as if the pleasure they would take in the sweep and the color of that coast, after such a long absence, had been imparted to us. While we were there, Lawrence came up the path from the beach.

"Isn't the beach fabulous, Tifty?" Mother asked. "Isn't it fabulous to be back? Will you have a Martini?"

"I don't care," Lawrence said. "Whiskey, gin—I don't care what I drink. Give me a little rum."

"We don't have any *rum,*" Mother said. It was the first note of asperity. She had taught us never to be indecisive, never to reply as Lawrence had. Beyond this, she is deeply concerned with the propriety of her house, and anything irregular by her standards, like drinking straight rum or bringing a beer can to the dinner table, excites in her a conflict that she cannot, even with her capacious sense of humor, surmount. She sensed the asperity and worked to repair it. "Would you like some Irish, Tifty dear?" she said. "Isn't Irish what you've always liked? There's some Irish on the sideboard. Why don't you get yourself some Irish?" Lawrence said that he didn't care. He poured himself a Martini, and then Ruth came down and we went in to dinner.

In spite of the fact that we had, through waiting for Lawrence, drunk too much before dinner, we were all anxious to put our best foot forward and to enjoy a peaceful time. Mother is a small woman whose face is still a striking reminder of how pretty she must have been, and whose conversation is unusually light, but she talked that evening about a soil-reclamation project that is going on up-island. Diana is as pretty as Mother must have been; she is an animated and lovely woman who likes to talk about the dissolute friends that she has made in France, but she talked that night about the school in Switzerland where she had left her two children. I could see that the dinner had been planned to please Lawrence. It was not too rich, and there was nothing to make him worry about extravagance.

After supper, when we went back onto the terrace, the clouds held that kind of light that looks like blood, and I was glad that Lawrence had such a lurid sunset for his homecoming. When we had been out there a few minutes, a man named Edward Chester came to get Diana. She had met him in France, or on the boat home, and he was staying for ten days at the inn in the village. He was introduced to Lawrence and Ruth, and then he and Diana left.

"Is that the one she's sleeping with now?" Lawrence asked.

"What a horrid thing to say!" Helen said.

"You ought to apologize for that, Tifty," Chaddy said.

"I don't know," Mother said tiredly. "I don't know, Tifty. Diana is in a position to do whatever she wants, and I don't ask sordid questions. She's my only daughter. I don't see her often."

"Is she going back to France?"

"She's going back the week after next."

Lawrence and Ruth were sitting at the edge of the terrace, not in the chairs, not in the circle of chairs. With his mouth set, my brother looked to me then like a Puritan cleric. Sometimes, when I try to understand his frame of mind, I think of the beginnings of our family in this country, and his disapproval of Diana and her lover reminded me of this. The branch of the Pommeroys to which we belong was founded by a minister who was eulogized by Cotton Mather for his untiring abjuration of the Devil. The Pommeroys were ministers until the middle of the nineteenth century, and the harshness of their thought—man is full of misery, and all earthly beauty is lustful and corrupt—has been preserved in books and sermons. The temper of our family changed somewhat and became more lighthearted, but when I was of school age, I can remember a cousinage of old men and women who seemed to hark back to the dark days of the ministry and to be animated by perpetual guilt and the deification of the scourge. If you are raised in this atmosphere—and in a sense we were—I think it is a trial of the spirit to reject its habits of guilt, self-denial, taciturnity, and penitence, and it seemed to me to have been a trial of the spirit in which Lawrence had succumbed.

"Is that Cassiopeia?" Odette asked.

"No, dear," Chaddy said. "That isn't Cassiopeia."

"Who was Cassiopeia?" Odette said.

"She was the wife of Cepheus and the mother of Andromeda," I said.

"The cook is a Giants fan," Chaddy said. "She'll give you even money that they win the pennant."

It had grown so dark that we could see the passage of light through the sky from the lighthouse at Cape Heron. In the dark below the cliff, the continual detonations of the surf sounded. And then, as she often does when it is getting dark and she has drunk too much before dinner, Mother began to talk about the improvements and additions that would someday be made on the house, the wings and bathrooms and gardens.

"This house will be in the sea in five years," Lawrence said.

"Tifty the Croaker," Chaddy said.

"Don't call me Tifty," Lawrence said.

"Little Jesus," Chaddy said.

"The sea wall is badly cracked," Lawrence said. "I looked at it this afternoon. You had it repaired four years ago, and it cost eight thousand dollars. You can't do that every four years."

"Please, Tifty," Mother said.

"Facts are facts," Lawrence said, "and it's a damned-fool idea to build a house at the edge of the cliff on a sinking coastline. In my lifetime, half the garden has washed away and there's four feet of water where we used to have a bathhouse."

"Let's have a very *general* conversation," Mother said bitterly. "Let's talk about politics or the boat-club dance."

"As a matter of fact," Lawrence said, "the house is probably in some danger now. If you had an unusually high sea, a hurricane sea, the wall would crumble and the house would go. We could all be drowned."

"I can't *bear* it," Mother said. She went into the pantry and came back with a full glass of gin.

I have grown too old now to think that I can judge the sentiments of others, but I was conscious of the tension between Lawrence and Mother, and I knew some of the history of it. Lawrence couldn't have been more than sixteen years old when he decided that Mother was frivolous, mischievous, destructive, and overly strong. When he had determined this, he decided to separate himself from her. He was at boarding school then, and I remember that he did not come home for Christmas. He spent Christmas with a friend. He came home very seldom after he had made his unfavorable judgment on Mother, and when he did come home, he always tried, in his conversation, to remind her of his estrangement. When he married Ruth, he did not tell Mother. He did not tell her when his children were born. But in spite of these principled and lengthy exertions he seemed, unlike the rest of us, never to have enjoyed any separation, and when they are together, you feel at once a tension, an unclearness.

And it was unfortunate, in a way, that Mother should have picked that night to get drunk. It's her privilege, and she doesn't get drunk often, and fortunately she wasn't bellicose, but we were all conscious of what was happening. As she quietly drank her gin, she seemed sadly to be parting from us; she seemed to be in the throes of travel. Then her mood changed from travel to injury, and the few remarks she made were petulant and irrelevant. When her glass was nearly empty, she stared angrily at the dark air in front of her nose, moving her head a little, like a fighter. I knew that there was not room in her mind then for all the injuries that were crowding into it. Her children were stupid, her husband was drowned, her servants were thieves, and the chair she sat in was uncomfortable. Suddenly she put down her empty glass and interrupted Chaddy, who was talking about baseball. "I know one *thing*," she said hoarsely. "I know that if there is an afterlife, I'm going to have a very different kind of family. I'm going to have nothing but fabulously rich, witty, and enchanting children." She got up and, starting for the door, nearly fell. Chaddy caught her and helped her up the stairs. I could hear their tender good-nights, and then Chaddy came back. I thought that Lawrence by now would be tired from his journey and his return, but he remained on the terrace, as if he were waiting to see the final malfeasance, and the rest of us left him there and went swimming in the dark.

When I woke the next morning, or half woke, I could hear the sound of someone rolling the tennis court. It is a fainter and deeper sound than the iron buoy bells off the point—an unrhythmic iron chiming—that belongs in my mind to the beginnings of a summer day, a good portent. When I went downstairs, Lawrence's two kids were in the living room, dressed in ornate cowboy suits. They are frightened and skinny children. They told me their father was rolling the tennis court but that they did not want to go out because they had seen a snake under the doorstep. I explained to them that their cousins—all the other children—ate breakfast in the kitchen and that they'd better run along in there. At this announcement, the boy began to cry. Then his sister joined him. They cried as if to go in the kitchen and eat would destroy their most precious rights. I told them to sit down with me. Lawrence came in, and I asked him if he wanted to play some tennis. He said no, thanks, although he thought he might play some singles with Chaddy. He was in the right here, because both he and Chaddy play better tennis than I, and he did play some singles with Chaddy after breakfast, but later on, when the others came down to play family doubles, Laurence disappeared. This made me cross—unreasonably so, I suppose—but we play darned interesting family doubles and he could have played in a set for the sake of courtesy.

Late in the morning, when I came up from the court alone, I saw Tifty on the terrace, prying up a shingle from the wall with his jackknife. "What's the matter, Lawrence?" I said. "Termites?" There are termites in the wood and they've given us a lot of trouble.

He pointed out to me, at the base of each row of shingles, a faint blue line of carpenter's chalk. "This house is about twenty-two years old," he said. "These shingles are about two hundred years old. Dad must have bought shingles from all the farms around here when he built the place, to make it look venerable. You can still see the carpenter's chalk put down where these antiques were nailed into place."

It was true about the shingles, although I had forgotten it. When the house was built, our father, or his architect, had ordered it covered with lichened and weather-beaten shingles. I didn't follow Lawrence's reasons for thinking that this was scandalous.

"And look at these doors," Lawrence said. "Look at these doors and window frames." I followed him over to a big Dutch door that opens onto the terrace and looked at it. It was a relatively new door, but someone had worked hard to conceal its newness. The surface had been deeply scored with some metal implement, and white paint had been rubbed into the incisions to imitate brine, lichen, and weather rot. "Imagine spending thousands of dollars to make a sound house look like a wreck," Lawrence said. "Imagine the frame of mind this implies. Imagine wanting to live so much in the past that you'll pay men carpenters' wages to disfigure your front door." Then I remembered Lawrence's sensitivity to time and his sentiments and opinions about our feelings for the past. I had heard him say, years ago, that we and our friends and our part of the nation, finding ourselves unable to cope with the problems of the present, had, like a wretched adult, turned back to what we supposed was a happier and a simpler time, and that our taste for reconstruction and candlelight was a measure of this irremediable failure. The faint blue line of chalk had reminded him of these ideas, the scarified door had reinforced them, and now clue after clue presented itself to him—the stern light at the door, the bulk of the chimney, the width of the floorboards and the pieces set into them to resemble pegs. While Lawrence was lecturing me on these frailties, the others came up from the court. As soon as Mother saw Lawrence, she responded, and I saw that there was little hope of any rapport between the matriarch and the changeling. She took Chaddy's arm. "Let's go swimming and have Martinis on the beach," she said. "Let's have a *fabulous* morning."

The sea that morning was a solid color, like verd stone. Everyone went to the beach but Tifty and Ruth. "I don't mind *him,*" Mother said. She was excited, and she tipped her glass and spilled some gin into the sand. "I don't mind *him.* It doesn't matter to me how *rude* and *horrid* and *gloomy* he is, but what I can't bear are the faces of his wretched little children, those fabulously unhappy little children." With the height of the cliff between us, everyone talked wrathfully about Lawrence; about how he had grown worse instead of better, how unlike the rest of us he was, how he endeavored to spoil every pleasure. We drank our gin; the abuse seemed to reach a crescendo, and then, one by one, we went swimming in the solid green water. But when we came out no one mentioned Lawrence unkindly; the line of abusive conversation had been cut, as if swimming had the cleansing force claimed for baptism. We dried our hands and lighted cigarettes, and if Lawrence was mentioned, it was only to suggest, kindly, something that might please him. Wouldn't he like to sail to Barin's cove, or go fishing?

And now I remember that while Lawrence was visiting us, we went swimming oftener than we usually do, and I think there was a reason for this. When the irritability that accumulated as a result of his company began to lessen our patience, not only with Lawrence but with one another, we would all go swimming and shed our animus in the cold water. I can see the family now, smarting from Lawrence's rebukes as they sat on the sand, and I can see them wading and diving and surface-diving and hear in their voices the restoration of patience and the rediscovery of inexhaustible good will. If Lawrence noticed this change—this illusion of purification—I suppose that he would have found in the vocabulary of psychiatry, or the mythology of the Atlantic, some circumspect name for it, but I don't think he noticed the change. He neglected to name the curative powers of the open sea, but it was one of the few chances for diminution that he missed.

The cook we had that year was a Polish woman named Anna Ostrovick, a summer cook. She was first-rate—a big, fat, hearty, industrious woman who took her work seriously. She liked to cook and to have the food she cooked appreciated and eaten, and whenever we saw her, she always urged us to eat. She cooked hot bread—crescents and brioches—for breakfast two or three times a week, and she would bring these into the dining room herself and say, "Eat, eat, eat!" When the maid took the serving dishes back into the pantry, we could sometimes hear Anna, who was standing there, say, "Good! They eat." She fed the garbage man, the milkman, and the gardener. "Eat!" she told them. "Eat, eat!" On Thursday afternoons, she went to the movies with the maid, but she didn't enjoy the movies, because the actors were all so thin. She would sit in the dark theatre for an hour and a half watching the screen anxiously for the appearance of someone who had enjoyed his food. Bette Davis merely left with Anna the impression of a woman who has not eaten well. "They are all so skinny," she would say when she left the movies. In the evenings, after she had gorged all of us, and washed the pots and pans, she would collect the table scraps and go out to feed the creation. We had a few chickens that year, and although they would have roosted by then, she would dump food into their troughs and urge the sleeping fowl to eat. She fed the songbirds in the orchard and the chipmunks in the yard. Her appearance at the edge of the garden and her urgent voice—we could hear her calling "Eat, eat, eat"—had become, like the sunset gun at the boat club and the passage of light from Cape Heron, attached to that hour. "Eat, eat, eat," we could hear Anna say. "Eat, eat . . ." Then it would be dark.

When Lawrence had been there three days, Anna called me into the kitchen. "You tell your mother," she said, "that *he* doesn't come into my kitchen. If *he* comes into my kitchen all the time, I go. *He* is always coming into my kitchen to tell me what a sad woman I am. He is always telling me that I work too hard and that I don't get paid enough and that I should belong to a union with vacations. Ha! He is so skinny but he is always coming into my kitchen when I am busy to pity me, but I am as good as him, I am as good as *anybody,* and I do not have to have people like that getting into my way all the time and feeling sorry for me. I am a famous and a wonderful cook and I have jobs everywhere and the only reason I come here to work this summer is because I was never before on an island, but I can have other jobs tomorrow, and if he is always coming into my kitchen to pity me, you tell your mother I am going. I am as good as *anybody* and I do not have to have that skinny all the time telling how poor I am."

I was pleased to find that the cook was on our side, but I felt that the situation was delicate. If Mother asked Lawrence to stay out of the kitchen, he would make a grievance out of the request. He could make a grievance out of anything, and it sometimes seemed that as he sat darkly at the dinner table, every word of disparagement, wherever it was aimed, came home to him. I didn't mention the cook's complaint to anyone, but somehow there wasn't any more trouble from that quarter.

The next cause for contention that I had from Lawrence came over our backgammon games.

When we are at Laud's Head, we play a lot of backgammon. At eight o'clock, after we have drunk our coffee, we usually get out the board. In a way, it is one of our pleasantest hours. The lamps in the room are still unlighted, Anna can be seen in the dark garden, and in the sky above her head there are continents of shadow and fire. Mother turns on the light and rattles the dice as a signal. We usually play three games apiece, each with the others. We play for money, and you can win or lose a hundred dollars on a game, but the stakes are usually much lower. I think that Lawrence used to play—I can't remember—but he doesn't play any more. He doesn't gamble. This is not because he is poor or because he has any principles about gambling but because he thinks the game is foolish and a waste of time. He was ready enough, however, to waste his time watching the rest of us play. Night after night, when the game began, he pulled a chair up beside the board, and watched the checkers and the dice. His expression was scornful, and yet he watched carefully. I wondered why he watched us night after night, and, through watching his face, I think that I may have found out.

Lawrence doesn't gamble, so he can't understand the excitement of winning and losing money. He has forgotten how to play the game, I think, so that its complex odds can't interest him. His observations were bound to include the facts that backgammon is an idle game and a game of chance, and that the board, marked with points, was a symbol of our worthlessness. And since he doesn't understand gambling or the odds of the game, I thought that what interested him must be the members of his family. One night when I was playing with Odette—I had won thirty-seven dollars from Mother and Chaddy—I think I saw what was going on in his mind.

Odette has black hair and black eyes. She is careful never to expose her white skin to the sun for long, so the striking contrast of blackness and pallor is not changed in the summer. She needs and deserves admiration—it is the element that contents her—and she will flirt, unseriously, with any man. Her shoulders were bare that night, her dress was cut to show the division of her breasts and to show her breasts when she leaned over the board to play. She kept losing and flirting and making her losses seem like a part of the flirtation. Chaddy was in the other room. She lost three games, and when the third game ended, she fell back on the sofa and, looking at me squarely, said something about going out on the dunes to settle the score. Lawrence heard her. I looked at Lawrence. He seemed shocked and gratified at the same time, as if he had suspected all along that we were not playing for anything so insubstantial as money. I may be wrong, of course, but I think that Lawrence felt that in watching our backgammon he was observing the progress of a mordant tragedy in which the money we won and lost served as a symbol for more vital forfeits. It is like Lawrence to try to read significance and finality into every gesture that we make, and it is certain of Lawrence that when he finds the inner logic to our conduct, it will be sordid.

Chaddy came in to play with me. Chaddy and I have never liked to lose to each other. When we were younger, we used to be forbidden to play games together, because they always ended in a fight. We think we know each other's mettle intimately. I think he is prudent; he thinks I am foolish. There is always bad blood when we play anything—tennis or backgammon or softball or bridge—and it does seem at times as if we were playing for the possession of each other's liberties. When I lose to Chaddy, I can't sleep. All this is only half the truth of our competitive relationship, but it was the half-truth that would be discernible to Lawrence, and his presence at the table made me so self-conscious that I lost two games. I tried not to seem angry when I got up from the board. Lawrence was watching me. I went out onto the terrace to suffer there in the dark the anger I always feel when I lose to Chaddy.

When I came back into the room, Chaddy and Mother were playing. Lawrence was still watching. By his lights, Odette had lost her virtue to me, I had lost my self-esteem to Chaddy, and now I wondered what he saw in the present match. He watched raptly, as if the opaque checkers and the marked board served for an exchange of critical power. How dramatic the board, in its ring of light, and the quiet players and the crash of the sea outside must have seemed to him! Here was spiritual cannibalism made visible; here, under his nose, were the symbols of the rapacious use human beings make of one another.

Mother plays a shrewd, an ardent, and an interfering game. She always has her hands in her opponent's board. When she plays with Chaddy, who is her favorite, she plays intently. Lawrence would have noticed this. Mother is a sentimental woman. Her heart is good and easily moved by tears and frailty, a characteristic that, like her handsome nose, has not been changed at all by age. Grief in another provokes her deeply, and she seems at times to be trying to divine in Chaddy some grief, some loss, that she can succor and redress, and so re-establish the relationship that she enjoyed with him when he was sickly and young. She loves defending the weak and the child-like, and now that we are old, she misses it. The world of debts and business, men and war, hunting and fishing has on her an exacerbating effect. (When Father drowned, she threw away his fly rods and his guns.) She has lectured us all endlessly on self-reliance, but when we come back to her for comfort and for help—particularly Chaddy—she seems to feel most like herself. I suppose Lawrence thought that the old woman and her son were playing for each other's soul.

She lost. "Oh *dear,*" she said. She looked stricken and bereaved, as she always does when she loses. "Get me my glasses, get me my checkbook, get me something to drink." Lawrence got up at last and stretched his legs. He looked at us all bleakly. The wind and the sea had risen, and I thought that if he heard the waves, he must hear them only as a dark answer to all his dark questions; that he would think that the tide had expunged the embers of our picnic fires. The company of a lie is unbearable, and he seemed like the embodiment of a lie. I couldn't explain to him the simple and intense pleasures of playing for money, and it seemed to me hideously wrong that he should have sat at the edge of the board and concluded that we were playing for one another's soul. He walked restlessly around the room two or three times and then, as usual, gave us a parting shot. "I should think you'd go crazy," he said, "cooped up with one another like this, night after night. Come on, Ruth. I'm going to bed."

* * *

That night, I dreamed about Lawrence. I saw his plain face magnified into ugliness, and when I woke in the morning, I felt sick, as if I had suffered a great spiritual loss while I slept, like the loss of courage and heart. It was foolish to let myself be troubled by my brother. I needed a vacation. I needed to relax. At school, we live in one of the dormitories, we eat at the house table, and we never get away. I not only teach English winter and summer but I work in the principal's office and fire the pistol at track meets. I needed to get away from this and from every other form of anxiety, and I decided to avoid my brother. Early that day, I took Helen and the children sailing, and we stayed out until suppertime. The next day, we went on a picnic. Then I had to go to New York for a day, and when I got back, there was the costume dance at the boat club. Lawrence wasn't going to this, and it's a party where I always have a wonderful time.

The invitations that year said to come as you wish you were. After several conversations, Helen and I had decided what to wear. The thing she most wanted to be again, she said, was a bride, and so she decided to wear her wedding dress. I thought this was a good choice—sincere, lighthearted, and inexpensive. Her choice influenced mine, and I decided to wear an old football uniform. Mother decided to go as Jenny Lind, because there was an old Jenny Lind costume in the attic. The others decided to rent costumes, and when I went to New York, I got the clothes. Lawrence and Ruth didn't enter into any of this.

Helen was on the dance committee, and she spent most of Friday decorating the club. Diana and Chaddy and I went sailing. Most of the sailing that I do these days is in Manhasset, and I am used to setting a homeward course by the gasoline barge and the tin roofs of the boat shed, and it was a pleasure that afternoon, as we returned, to keep the bow on a white church spire in the village and to find even the inshore water green and clear. At the end of our sail, we stopped at the club to get Helen. The committee had been trying to give a submarine appearance to the ballroom, and the fact that they had nearly succeeded in accomplishing this illusion made Helen very happy. We drove back to Laud's Head. It had been a brilliant afternoon, but on the way home we could smell the east wind—the dark wind, as Lawrence would have said—coming in from the sea.

My wife, Helen, is thirty-eight, and her hair would be gray, I guess, if it were not dyed, but it is dyed an unobtrusive yellow—a faded color—and I think it becomes her. I mixed cocktails that night while she was dressing, and when I took a glass upstairs to her, I saw her for the first time since our marriage in her wedding dress. There would be no point in saying that she looked to me more beautiful than she did on our wedding day, but because I have grown older and have, I think, a greater depth of feeling, and because I could see in her face that night both youth and age, both her devotion to the young woman that she had been and the positions that she had yielded graciously to time, I think I have never been so deeply moved. I had already put on the football uniform, and the weight of it, the heaviness of the pants and the shoulder guards, had worked a change in me, as if in putting on these old clothes I had put off the reasonable anxieties and troubles of my life. It felt as if we had both returned to the years before our marriage, the years before the war.

The Collards had a big dinner party before the dance, and our family—excepting Lawrence and Ruth—went to this. We drove over to the club, through the fog, at about half past nine. The orchestra was playing a waltz. While I was checking my raincoat, someone hit me on the back. It was Chucky Ewing, and the funny thing was that Chucky had on a football uniform. This seemed comical as hell to both of us. We were laughing when we went down the hall to the dance floor. I stopped at the door to look at the party, and it was beautiful. The committee had hung fish nets around the sides and over the high ceiling. The nets on the ceiling were filled with colored balloons. The light was soft and uneven, and the people—our friends and neighbors—dancing in the soft light to "Three O'Clock in the Morning" made a pretty picture. Then I noticed the number of women dressed in white, and I realized that they, like Helen, were wearing wedding dresses. Patsy Hewitt and Mrs. Gear and the Lackland girl waltzed by, dressed as brides. Then Pep Talcott came over to where Chucky and I were standing. He was dressed to be Henry VIII, but he told us that the Auerbach twins and Henry Barrett and Dwight MacGregor were all wearing football uniforms, and that by the last count there were ten brides on the floor.

This coincidence, this funny coincidence, kept everybody laughing, and made this one of the most lighthearted parties we've ever had at the club. At first I thought that the women had planned with one another to wear wedding dresses, but the ones that I danced with said it was a coincidence and I'm sure that Helen had made her decision alone. Everything went smoothly for me until a little before midnight. I saw Ruth standing at the edge of the floor. She was wearing a long red dress. It was all wrong. It wasn't the spirit of the party at all. I danced with her, but no one cut in, and I was darned if I'd spend the rest of the night dancing with her and I asked her where Lawrence was. She said he was out on the dock, and I took her over to the bar and left her and went out to get Lawrence.

The east fog was thick and wet, and he was alone on the dock. He was not in costume. He had not even bothered to get himself up as a fisherman or a sailor. He looked particularly saturnine. The fog blew around us like a cold smoke. I wished that it had been a clear night, because the easterly fog seemed to play into my misanthropic brother's hands. And I knew that the buoys—the groaners and bells that we could hear then—would sound to him like half-human, half-drowned cries, although every sailor knows that buoys are necessary and reliable fixtures, and I knew that the foghorn at the lighthouse would mean wanderings and losses to him and that he could misconstrue the vivacity of the dance music. "Come on in, Tifty," I said, "and dance with your wife or get her some partners."

"Why should I?" he said. "Why should I?" And he walked to the window and looked in at the party. "Look at it," he said. "Look at that. . . ."

Chucky Ewing had got hold of a balloon and was trying to organize a scrimmage line in the middle of the floor. The others were dancing a samba. And I knew that Lawrence was looking bleakly at the party as he had looked at the weather-beaten shingles on our house, as if he saw here an abuse and a distortion of time; as if in wanting to be brides and football players we exposed the fact that, the lights of youth having been put out in us, we had been unable to find other lights to go by and, destitute of faith and principle, had become foolish and sad. And that he was thinking this about so many kind and happy and generous people made me angry, made me feel for him such an unnatural abhorrence that I was ashamed, for he is my brother and a Pommeroy. I put my arm around his shoulders and tried to force him to come in, but he wouldn't.

I got back in time for the Grand March, and after the prizes had been given out for the best costumes, they let the balloons down. The room was hot, and someone opened the big doors onto the dock, and the easterly wind circled the room and went out, carrying across the dock and out onto the water most of the balloons. Chucky Ewing went running out after the balloons, and when he saw them pass the dock and settle on the water, he took off his football uniform and dove in. Then Eric Auerbach dove in and Lew Phillips dove in and I dove in, and you know how it is at a party after midnight when people start jumping into the water. We recovered most of the balloons and dried off and went on dancing, and we didn't get home until morning.

The next day was the day of the flower show. Mother and Helen and Odette all had entries. We had a pickup lunch, and Chaddy drove the women and children over to the show. I took a nap, and in the middle of the afternoon I got some trunks and a towel and, on leaving the house, passed Ruth in the laundry. She was washing clothes. I don't know why she should seem to have so much more work to do than anyone else, but she is always washing or ironing or mending clothes. She may have been taught, when she was young, to spend her time like this, or she may be at the mercy of an expiatory passion. She seems to scrub and iron with a penitential fervor, although I can't imagine what it is that she thinks she's done wrong. Her children were with her in the laundry. I offered to take them to the beach, but they didn't want to go.

It was late in August, and the wild grapes that grow profusely all over the island made the land wind smell of wine. There is a little grove of holly at the end of the path, and then you climb the dunes, where nothing grows but that coarse grass. I could hear the sea, and I remember thinking how Chaddy and I used to talk mystically about the sea. When we were young, we had decided that we could never live in the West because we would miss the sea. "It is very nice here," we used to say politely when we visited people in the mountains, "but we miss the Atlantic." We used to look down our noses at people from Iowa and Colorado who had been denied this revelation, and we scorned the Pacific. Now I could hear the waves, whose heaviness sounded like a reverberation, like a tumult, and it pleased me as it had pleased me when I was young, and it seemed to have a purgative force, as if it had cleared my memory of, among other things, the penitential image of Ruth in the laundry.

But Lawrence was on the beach. There he sat. I went in without speaking. The water was cold, and when I came out, I put on a shirt. I told him that I was going to walk up to Tanners Point, and he said that he would come with me. I tried to walk beside him. His legs are no longer than mine, but he always likes to stay a little ahead of his companion. Walking along behind him, looking at his bent head and his shoulders, I wondered what he could make of that landscape.

There were the dunes and cliffs, and then, where they declined, there were some fields that had begun to turn from green to brown and yellow. The fields were used for pasturing sheep, and I guess Lawrence would have noticed that the soil was eroded and that the sheep would accelerate this decay. Beyond the fields there are a few coastal farms, with square and pleasant buildings, but Lawrence could have pointed out the hard lot of an island farmer. The sea, at our other side, was the open sea. We always tell guests that there, to the east, lies the coast of Portugal, and for Lawrence it would be an easy step from the coast of Portugal to the tyranny in Spain. The waves broke with a noise like a "hurrah, hurrah, hurrah," but to Lawrence they would say *"Vale, vale."* I suppose it would have occurred to his baleful and incisive mind that the coast was terminal moraine, the edge of the prehistoric world, and it must have occurred to him that we walked along the edge of the known world in spirit as much as in fact. If he should otherwise have overlooked this, there were some Navy planes bombing an uninhabited island to remind him.

That beach is a vast and preternaturally clean and simple landscape. It is like a piece of the moon. The surf had pounded the floor solid, so it was easy walking, and everything left on the sand had been twice changed by the waves. There was the spine of a shell, a broomstick, part of a bottle and part of a brick, both of them milled and broken until they were nearly unrecognizable, and I suppose Lawrence's sad frame of mind—for he kept his head down—went from one broken thing to another. The company of his pessimism began to infuriate me, and I caught up with him and put a hand on his shoulder. "It's only a summer day, Tifty," I said. "It's only a summer day. What's the matter? Don't you like it here?"

"I don't like it here," he said blandly, without raising his eyes. "I'm going to sell my equity in the house to Chaddy. I didn't expect to have a good time. The only reason I came back was to say goodbye."

I let him get ahead again and I walked behind him, looking at his shoulders and thinking of all the goodbyes he had made. When Father drowned, he went to church and said goodbye to Father. It was only three years later that he concluded that Mother was frivolous and said goodbye to her. In his freshman year at college, he had been very good friends with his roommate, but the man drank too much, and at the beginning of the spring term Lawrence changed roommates and said goodbye to his friend. When he had been in college for two years, he concluded that the atmosphere was too sequestered and he said goodbye to Yale. He enrolled at Columbia and got his law degree there, but he found his first employer dishonest, and at the end of six months he said goodbye to a good job. He married Ruth in City Hall and said goodbye to the Protestant Episcopal Church; they went to live on a back street in Tuckahoe and said goodbye to the middle class. In 1938, he went to Washington to work as a government lawyer, saying goodbye to private enterprise, but after eight months in Washington he concluded that the Roosevelt administration was sentimental and he said goodbye to it. They left Washington for a suburb of Chicago, where he said goodbye to his neighbors, one by one, on counts of drunkenness, boorishness, and stupidity. He said goodbye to Chicago and went to Kansas; he said goodbye to Kansas and went to Cleveland. Now he had said goodbye to Cleveland and come East again, stopping at Laud's Head long enough to say goodbye to the sea.

It was elegiac and it was bigoted and narrow, it mistook circumspection for character, and I wanted to help him. "Come out of it," I said. "Come out of it, Tifty."

"Come out of what?"

"Come out of this gloominess. Come out of it. It's only a summer day. You're spoiling your own good time and you're spoiling everyone else's. We need a vacation, Tifty. I need one. I need to rest. We all do. And you've made everything tense and unpleasant. I only have two weeks in the year. Two weeks. I need to have a good time and so do all the others. We need to rest. You think that your pessimism is an advantage, but it's nothing but an unwillingness to grasp realities."

"What are the realities?" he said. "Diana is a foolish and a promiscuous woman. So is Odette. Mother is an alcoholic. If she doesn't discipline herself, she'll be in a hospital in a year or two. Chaddy is dishonest. He always has been. The house is going to fall into the sea." He looked at me and added, as an afterthought, "You're a fool."

"You're a gloomy son of a bitch," I said. "You're a gloomy son of a bitch."

"Get your fat face out of mine," he said. He walked along.

Then I picked up a root and, coming at his back—although I have never hit a man from the back before—I swung the root, heavy with seawater, behind me, and the momentum sped my arm and I gave him, my brother, a blow on the head that forced him to his knees on the sand, and I saw the blood come out and begin to darken his hair. Then I wished that he was dead, dead and about to be buried, not buried but about to be buried, because I did not want to be denied ceremony and decorum in putting him away, in putting him out of my consciousness, and I saw the rest of us—Chaddy and Mother and Diana and Helen—in mourning in the house on Belvedere Street that was torn down twenty years ago, greeting our guests and our relatives at the door and answering their mannerly condolences with mannerly grief. Nothing decorous was lacking so that even if he had been murdered on a beach, one would feel before the tiresome ceremony ended that he had come into the winter of his life and that it was a law of nature, and a beautiful one, that Tifty should be buried in the cold, cold ground.

He was still on his knees. I looked up and down. No one had seen us. The naked beach, like a piece of the moon, reached to invisibility. The spill of a wave, in a glancing run, shot up to where he knelt. I would still have liked to end him, but now I had begun to act like two men, the murderer and the Samaritan. With a swift roar, like hollowness made sound, a white wave reached him and encircled him, boiling over his shoulders, and I held him against the undertow. Then I led him to a higher place. The blood had spread all through his hair, so that it looked black. I took off my shirt and tore it to bind up his head. He was conscious, and I didn't think he was badly hurt. He didn't speak. Neither did I. Then I left him there.

I walked a little way down the beach and turned to watch him, and I was thinking of my own skin then. He had got to his feet and he seemed steady. The daylight was still clear, but on the sea wind fumes of brine were blowing in like a light fog, and when I had walked a little way from him, I could hardly see his dark figure in this obscurity. All down the beach I could see the heavy salt air blowing in. Then I turned my back on him, and as I got near to the house, I went swimming again, as I seem to have done after every encounter with Lawrence that summer.

When I got back to the house, I lay down on the terrace. The others came back. I could hear Mother defaming the flower arrangements that had won prizes. None of ours had won anything. Then the house quieted, as it always does at that hour. The children went into the kitchen to get supper and the others went upstairs to bathe. Then I heard Chaddy making cocktails, and the conversation about the flower-show judges was resumed. Then Mother cried, "Tifty! Tifty! Oh, Tifty!"

He stood in the door, looking half dead. He had taken off the bloody bandage and he held it in his hand. "My brother did this," he said. "My brother did it. He hit me with a stone—something—on the beach." His voice broke with self-pity. I thought he was going to cry. No one else spoke. "Where's Ruth?" he cried. "Where's Ruth? Where in hell is Ruth? I want her to start packing. I don't have any more time to waste here. I have important things to do. I have *important* things to do." And he went up the stairs.

They left for the mainland the next morning, taking the six-o'clock boat. Mother got up to say goodbye, but she was the only one, and it is a harsh and an easy scene to imagine—the matriarch and the changeling, looking at each other with a dismay that would seem like the powers of love reversed. I heard the children's voices and the car go down the drive, and I got up and went to the window, and what a morning that was! Jesus, what a morning! The wind was northerly. The air was clear. In the early heat, the roses in the garden smelled like strawberry jam. While I was dressing, I heard the boat whistle, first the warning signal and then the double blast, and I could see the good people on the top deck drinking coffee out of fragile paper cups, and Lawrence at the bow, saying to the sea, "*Thalassa, thalassa,*" while his timid and unhappy children watched the creation from the encirclement of their mother's arms. The buoys would toll mournfully for Lawrence, and while the grace of the light would make it an exertion not to throw out your arms and swear exultantly, Lawrence's eyes would trace the black sea as it fell astern: he would think of the bottom, dark and strange, where full fathom five our father lies.

Oh, what can you do with a man like that? What can you do? How can you dissuade his eye in a crowd from seeking out the cheek with acne, the infirm hand; how can you teach him to respond to the inestimable greatness of the race, the harsh surface beauty of life; how can you put his finger for him on the obdurate truths before which fear and horror are powerless? The sea that morning was iridescent and dark. My wife and my sister were swimming—Diana and Helen—and I saw their uncovered heads, black and gold in the dark water. I saw them come out and I saw that they were naked, unshy, beautiful, and full of grace, and I watched the naked women walk out of the sea.

Gooseberries

by Anton Chekhov

Introduced by Eudora Welty

THE REVOLUTION BROUGHT ABOUT BY THE GENTLE CHEKHOV TO the short story was in every sense not destructive but constructive. By removing the formal plot he did not leave the story structureless; he endowed it with another kind of structure—one which embodied the principle of growth. And it was one that had no cause to repeat itself; in each and every story, short or long, it was a structure open to human meaning and answerable to that meaning. It took form from within.

It does so in a way that is endlessly provocative in the story "Gooseberries."

Let us recall what happens when two friends turn aside from a walk in the country to seek shelter from the rain. They chance to be near the house of a friend. They arrive at a working farm, a place of mud and mire; their host is grimy, his house appears dark and forbidding. But everything changes. In their honor the host takes a bath; a whole year's grime is shed like a snakeskin. The guests are invited to bathe too, and Ivan plunges into the river. Swimming and diving and shouting and floating on his back in the river in the rain, among the water lilies, he feels an elation such as he'd felt in youth. A great release is taking place in him. And something with the quality of enchantment begins to surround the party. All now clean, dressed in dry clothing, they move upstairs into the elegant part of the farmhouse; in warm, peaceful, quiet rooms they are attended by a young woman of startling beauty.

Here Ivan tells them a story, and all this seems to have been a preparation for it. It is the story of his brother Nickolay, who had worked all his life for a house and a farm just such as this one. As Ivan talks, the farm, the day, the house with its encrustations of time, the seductive room with its beautiful attendant, its romantic portraits of ladies and generals around the walls, and the rain falling outside, all stand about the story he tells like screens of varying substance of reality and dream.

Nickolay's story is really a terrible story of *getting,* of stinginess and callousness and obsessive greed, costing the woman he married her very life. Above all, he must raise his own gooseberries! When Ivan visited him, after his dream of possessing all this had come true, and was given the first of the gooseberries to taste, and found them hard and sour, Ivan's own life underwent a change.

"The real tragedies of life are enacted somewhere behind the scenes," he tells his friends now. "Someone ought to stand with a hammer at the door of every happy contented man, continually banging on it to remind him that there are unhappy people around and that however happy *he* may be at the time, sooner or later life will show him its claws and disaster will overtake him in the form of illness, poverty, bereavement and there will be no one to hear and see him. But there isn't anyone holding a hammer . . ."

Quite naturally, his listeners find Ivan's story unsatisfactory. The host, a man of only forty, is even inattentive. Here in his own beautifully prepared room, he thinks "the story had no direct bearing on his life."

The extraordinary structure of "Gooseberries" is purely subjective. The swing, the breathtaking arc, from the exhilaration of Ivan's swimming in the river to the profound despair into which the telling of his brother's story finally brings him might be a plunge from youth to age, from the rejuvenated swimmer to the old man whose head is ablaze with ideas, who can only cry, "If I were young!" When we recall that, swimming, he kept diving down and touching bottom, we could as easily say he moves from the profundities of joy to the heights of despair. It doesn't matter which we say; in the river, Ivan has experienced happiness of such purity that it is forgetful of self. He can only shout, "Good God! Good God!" In the end, reaching that same pitch of self-forgetfulness in despair, he changes the cry to "Doing good!"

We are left, the story's swing being brought to rest, the memory of the gooseberries, the smell of Ivan's pipe in the bedroom, and the rain that has never stopped.

Gooseberries

Anton Chekhov

Translated by Constance Garnett

The whole sky had been overcast with rain-clouds from early morning; it was a still day, not hot, but heavy, as it is in grey dull weather when the clouds have been hanging over the country for a long while, when one expects rain and it does not come. Ivan Ivanovitch, the veterinary surgeon, and Burkin, the high-school teacher, were already tired from walking, and the fields seemed to them endless. Far ahead of them they could just see the windmills of the village of Mironositskoe; on the right stretched a row of hillocks which disappeared in the distance behind the village, and they both knew that this was the bank of the river, that there were meadows, green willows, homesteads there, and that if one stood on one of the hillocks one could see from it the same vast plain, telegraph-wires, and a train which in the distance looked like a crawling caterpillar, and that in clear weather one could even see the town. Now, in still weather, when all nature seemed mild and dreamy, Ivan Ivanovitch and Burkin were filled with love of that countryside, and both thought how great, how beautiful a land it was.

"Last time we were in Prokofy's barn," said Burkin, "you were about to tell me a story."

"Yes; I meant to tell you about my brother."

Ivan Ivanovitch heaved a deep sigh and lighted a pipe to begin to tell his story, but just at that moment the rain began. And five minutes later heavy rain came down, covering the sky, and it was hard to tell when it would be over. Ivan Ivanovitch and Burkin stopped in hesitation; the dogs, already drenched, stood with their tails between their legs gazing at them feelingly.

"We must take shelter somewhere," said Burkin. "Let us go to Alehin's; it's close by."

"Come along."

They turned aside and walked through mown fields, sometimes going straight forward, sometimes turning to the right, till they came out on the road. Soon they saw poplars, a garden, then the red roofs of barns; there was a gleam of the river, and the view opened on to a broad expanse of water with a windmill and a white bath-house: this was Sofino, where Alehin lived.

The watermill was at work, drowning the sound of the rain; the dam was shaking. Here wet horses with drooping heads were standing near their carts, and men were walking about covered with sacks. It was damp, muddy, and desolate; the water looked cold and malignant. Ivan Ivanovitch and Burkin were already conscious of a feeling of wetness, messiness, and discomfort all over; their feet were heavy with mud, and when, crossing the dam, they went up to the barns, they were silent, as though they were angry with one another.

In one of the barns there was the sound of a winnowing machine, the door was open, and clouds of dust were coming from it. In the doorway was standing Alehin himself, a man of forty, tall and stout, with long hair, more like a professor or an artist than a landowner. He had on a white shirt that badly needed washing, a rope for a belt, drawers instead of trousers, and his boots, too, were plastered up with mud and straw. His eyes and nose were black with dust. He recognized Ivan Ivanovitch and Burkin, and was apparently much delighted to see them.

"Go into the house, gentlemen," he said, smiling; "I'll come directly, this minute."

It was a big two-storeyed house. Alehin lived in the lower storey, with arched ceilings and little windows, where the bailiffs had once lived; here everything was plain, and there was a smell of rye bread, cheap vodka, and harness. He went upstairs into the best rooms only on rare occasions, when visitors came. Ivan Ivanovitch and Burkin were met in the house by a maid-servant, a young woman so beautiful that they both stood still and looked at one another.

"You can't imagine how delighted I am to see you, my friends," said Alehin, going into the hall with them. "It is a surprise! Pelagea," he said, addressing the girl, "give our visitors something to change into. And, by the way, I will change too. Only I must first go and wash, for I almost think I have not washed since spring. Wouldn't you like to come into the bath-house? and meanwhile they will get things ready here."

Beautiful Pelagea, looking so refined and soft, brought them towels and soap, and Alehin went to the bath-house with his guests.

"It's a long time since I had a wash," he said, undressing. "I have got a nice bath-house, as you see—my father built it—but I somehow never have time to wash."

He sat down on the steps and soaped his long hair and his neck, and the water round him turned brown.

"Yes, I must say," said Ivan Ivanovitch meaningly, looking at his head.

"It's a long time since I washed . . ." said Alehin with embarrassment, giving himself a second soaping, and the water near him turned dark blue, like ink.

Ivan Ivanovitch went outside, plunged into the water with a loud splash, and swam in the rain, flinging his arms out wide. He stirred the water into waves which set the white lilies bobbing up and down; he swam to the very middle of the millpond and dived, and came up a minute later in another place, and swam on, and kept on diving, trying to touch the bottom.

"Oh, my goodness!" he repeated continually, enjoying himself thoroughly. "Oh, my goodness!" He swam to the mill, talked to the peasants there, then returned and lay on his back in the middle of the pond, turning his face to the rain. Burkin and Alehin were dressed and ready to go, but he still went on swimming and diving. "Oh, my goodness! . . ." he said. "Oh, Lord, have mercy on me! . . ."

"That's enough!" Burkin shouted to him.

They went back to the house. And only when the lamp was lighted in the big drawing-room upstairs, and Burkin and Ivan Ivanovitch, attired in silk dressing-gowns and warm slippers, were sitting in arm-chairs; and Alehin, washed and combed, in a new coat, was walking about the drawing-room, evidently enjoying the feeling of warmth, cleanliness, dry clothes, and light shoes; and when lovely Pelagea, stepping noiselessly on the carpet and smiling softly, handed tea and jam on a tray—only then Ivan Ivanovitch began on his story, and it seemed as though not only Burkin and Alehin were listening, but also the ladies, young and old, and the officers who looked down upon them sternly and calmly from their gold frames.

"There are two of us brothers," he began—"I, Ivan Ivanovitch, and my brother, Nikolay Ivanovitch, two years younger. I went in for a learned profession and became a veterinary surgeon, while Nikolay sat in a government office from the time he was nineteen. Our father, Tchimsha-Himalaisky, was a kantonist, but he rose to be an officer and left us a little estate and the rank of nobility. After his death the little estate went in debts and legal expenses; but, anyway, we had spent our childhood running wild in the country. Like peasant children, we passed our days and nights in the fields and the woods, looked after horses, stripped the bark off the trees, fished, and so on. . . . And, you know, whoever has once in his life caught perch or has seen the migrating of the thrushes in autumn, watched how they float in flocks over the village on bright, cool days, he will never be a real townsman, and will have a yearning for freedom to the day of his death. My brother was miserable in the government office. Years passed by, and he went on sitting in the same place, went on writing the same papers and thinking of one and the same thing—how to get into the country. And this yearning by degrees passed into a definite desire, into a dream of buying himself a little farm somewhere on the banks of a river or a lake.

"He was a gentle, good-natured fellow, and I was fond of him, but I never sympathized with this desire to shut himself up for the rest of his life in a little farm of his own. It's the correct thing to say that a man needs no more than six feet of earth. But six feet is what a corpse needs, not a man. And they say, too, now, that if our intellectual classes are attracted to the land and yearn for a farm, it's a good thing. But these farms are just the same as six feet of earth. To retreat from town, from the struggle, from the bustle of life, to retreat and bury oneself in one's farm—it's not life, it's egoism, laziness, it's monasticism of a sort, but monasticism without good works. A man does not need six feet of earth or a farm, but the whole globe, all nature, where he can have room to display all the qualities and peculiarities of his free spirit.

"My brother Nikolay, sitting in his government office, dreamed of how he would eat his own cabbages, which would fill the whole yard with such a savoury smell, take his meals on the green grass, sleep in the sun, sit for whole hours on the seat by the gate gazing at the fields and the forest. Gardening books and the agricultural hints in calendars were his delight, his favourite spiritual sustenance; he enjoyed reading newspapers, too, but the only things he read in them were the advertisements of so many acres of arable land and a grass meadow with farm-houses and buildings, a river, a garden, a mill and millponds, for sale. And his imagination pictured the garden-paths, flowers and fruit, starling cotes, the carp in the pond, and all that sort of thing, you know. These imaginary pictures were of different kinds according to the advertisements which he came across, but for some reason in every one of them he had always to have gooseberries. He could not imagine a homestead, he could not picture an idyllic nook, without gooseberries.

"'Country life has its conveniences,' he would sometimes say. 'You sit on the verandah and you drink tea, while your ducks swim on the pond, there is a delicious smell everywhere, and . . . and the gooseberries are growing.'

"He used to draw a map of his property, and in every map there were the same things—(a) house for the family, (b) servants' quarters, (c) kitchen-garden, (d) gooseberry-bushes. He lived parsimoniously, was frugal in food and drink, his clothes were beyond description; he looked like a beggar, but kept on saving and putting money in the bank. He grew fearfully avaricious. I did not like to look at him, and I used to give him something and send him presents for Christmas and Easter, but he used to save that too. Once a man is absorbed by an idea there is no doing anything with him.

"Years passed: he was transferred to another province. He was over forty, and he was still reading the advertisements in the papers and saving up. Then I heard he was married. Still with the same object of buying a farm and having gooseberries, he married an elderly and ugly widow without a trace of feeling for her, simply because she had filthy lucre. He went on living frugally after marrying her, and kept her short of food, while he put her money in the bank in his name.

"Her first husband had been a postmaster, and with him she was accustomed to pies and home-made wines, while with her second husband she did not get enough black bread; she began to pine away with this sort of life, and three years later she gave up her soul to God. And I need hardly say that my brother never for one moment imagined that he was responsible for her death. Money, like vodka, makes a man queer. In our town there was a merchant who, before he died, ordered a plateful of honey and ate up all his money and lottery tickets with the honey, so that no one might get the benefit of it. While I was inspecting cattle at a railway-station, a cattle-dealer fell under an engine and had his leg cut off. We carried him into the waiting-room, the blood was flowing—it was a horrible thing—and he kept asking them to look for his leg and was very much worried about it; there were twenty roubles in the boot on the leg that had been cut off, and he was afraid they would be lost."

"That's a story from a different opera," said Burkin.

"After his wife's death," Ivan Ivanovitch went on, after thinking for half a minute, "my brother began looking out for an estate for himself. Of course, you may look about for five years and yet end by making a mistake, and buying something quite different from what you have dreamed of. My brother Nikolay bought through an agent a mortgaged estate of three hundred and thirty acres, with a house for the family, with servants' quarters, with a park, but with no orchard, no gooseberry-bushes, and no duck-pond; there was a river, but the water in it was the colour of coffee, because on one side of the estate there was a brickyard and on the other a factory for burning bones. But Nikolay Ivanovitch did not grieve much; he ordered twenty gooseberry-bushes, planted them, and began living as a country gentleman.

"Last year I went to pay him a visit. I thought I would go and see what it was like. In his letters my brother called his estate 'Tchumbaroklov Waste, alias Himalaiskoe.' I reached 'alias Himalaiskoe' in the afternoon. It was hot. Everywhere there were ditches, fences, hedges, fir-trees planted in rows, and there was no knowing how to get to the yard, where to put one's horse. I went up to the house, and was met by a fat red dog that looked like a pig. It wanted to bark, but it was too lazy. The cook, a fat, barefooted woman, came out of the kitchen, and she, too, looked like a pig, and said that her master was resting after dinner. I went in to see my brother. He was sitting up in bed with a quilt over his legs; he had grown older, fatter, wrinkled; his cheeks, his nose, and his mouth all stuck out—he looked as though he might begin grunting into the quilt at any moment.

"We embraced each other, and shed tears of joy and of sadness at the thought that we had once been young and now were both grey-headed and near the grave. He dressed, and led me out to show me the estate.

"'Well, how are you getting on here?' I asked.

"'Oh, all right, thank God; I am getting on very well.'

"He was no more a poor timid clerk, but a real landowner, a gentleman. He was already accustomed to it, had grown used to it, and liked it. He ate a great deal, went to the bath-house, was growing stout, was already at law with the village commune and both factories, and was very much offended when the peasants did not call him 'Your Honour.' And he concerned himself with the salvation of his soul in a substantial, gentlemanly manner, and performed deeds of charity, not simply, but with an air of consequence. And what deeds of charity! He treated the peasants for every sort of disease with soda and castor oil, and on his name-day had a thanksgiving service in the middle of the village, and then treated the peasants to a gallon of vodka—he thought that was the thing to do. Oh, those horrible gallons of vodka! One day the fat landowner hauls the peasants up before the district captain for trespass, and next day, in honour of a holiday, treats them to a gallon of vodka, and they drink and shout 'Hurrah!' and when they are drunk bow down to his feet. A change of life for the better, and being well-fed and idle develop in a Russian the most insolent self-conceit. Nikolay Ivanovitch, who at one time in the government office was afraid to have any views of his own, now could say nothing that was not gospel truth, and uttered such truths in the tone of a prime minister. 'Education is essential, but for the peasants it is premature.' 'Corporal punishment is harmful as a rule, but in some cases it is necessary and there is nothing to take its place.'

"'I know the peasants and understand how to treat them,' he would say. 'The peasants like me. I need only to hold up my little finger and the peasants will do anything I like.'

"And all this, observe, was uttered with a wise, benevolent smile. He repeated twenty times over 'We noblemen,' 'I as a noble'; obviously he did not remember that our grandfather was a peasant, and our father a soldier. Even our surname Tchimsha-Himalaisky, in reality so incongruous, seemed to him now melodious, distinguished, and very agreeable.

"But the point just now is not he, but myself. I want to tell you about the change that took place in me during the brief hours I spent at his country place. In the evening, when we were drinking tea, the cook put on the table a plateful of gooseberries. They were not bought, but his own gooseberries, gathered for the first time since the bushes were planted. Nikolay Ivanovitch laughed and looked for a minute in silence at the gooseberries, with tears in his eyes; he could not speak for excitement. Then he put one gooseberry in his mouth, looked at me with the triumph of a child who has at last received his favourite toy, and said:

"'How delicious!'

"And he ate them greedily, continually repeating, 'Ah, how delicious! Do taste them!'

"They were sour and unripe, but, as Pushkin says:

"'Dearer to us the falsehood that exalts
Than hosts of baser truths.'

"I saw a happy man whose cherished dream was so obviously fulfilled, who had attained his object in life, who had gained what he wanted, who was satisfied with his fate and himself. There is always, for some reason, an element of sadness mingled with my thoughts of human happiness, and, on this occasion, at the sight of a happy man I was overcome by an oppressive feeling that was close upon despair. It was particularly oppressive at night. A bed was made up for me in the room next to my brother's bedroom, and I could hear that he was awake, and that he kept getting up and going to the plate of gooseberries and taking one. I reflected how many satisfied, happy people there really are! What a suffocating force it is! You look at life: the insolence and idleness of the strong, the ignorance and brutishness of the weak, incredible poverty all about us, overcrowding, degeneration, drunkenness, hypocrisy, lying. . . . Yet all is calm and stillness in the houses and in the streets; of the fifty thousand living in a town, there is not one who would cry out, who would give vent to his indignation aloud. We see the people going to market for provisions, eating by day, sleeping by night, talking their silly nonsense, getting married, growing old, serenely escorting their dead to the cemetery; but we do not see and we do not hear those who suffer, and what is terrible in life goes on somewhere behind the scenes. . . . Everything is quiet and peaceful, and nothing protests but mute statistics: so many people gone out of their minds, so many gallons of vodka drunk, so many children dead from malnutrition. . . . And this order of things is evidently necessary; evidently the happy man only feels at ease because the unhappy bear their burdens in silence, and without that silence happiness would be impossible. It's a case of general hypnotism. There ought to be behind the door of every happy, contented man someone standing with a hammer continually reminding him with a tap that there are unhappy people; that however happy he may be, life will show him her laws sooner or later, trouble will come for him—disease, poverty, losses, and no one will see or hear, just as now he neither sees nor hears others. But there is no man with a hammer; the happy man lives at his ease, and trivial daily cares faintly agitate him like the wind in the aspen-tree—and all goes well.

"That night I realized that I, too, was happy and contented," Ivan Ivanovitch went on, getting up. "I, too, at dinner and at the hunt liked to lay down the law on life and religion, and the way to manage the peasantry. I, too, used to say that science was light, that culture was essential, but for the simple people reading and writing was enough for the time. Freedom is a blessing, I used to say; we can no more do without it than without air, but we must wait a little. Yes, I used to talk like that, and now I ask, 'For what reason are we to wait?'" asked Ivan Ivanovitch, looking angrily at Burkin. "Why wait, I ask you? What grounds have we for waiting? I shall be told, it can't be done all at once; every idea takes shape in life gradually, in its due time. But who is it says that? Where is the proof that it's right? You will fall back upon the natural order of things, the uniformity of phenomena; but is there order and uniformity in the fact that I, a living, thinking man, stand over a chasm and wait for it to close of itself, or to fill up with mud at the very time when perhaps I might leap over it or build a bridge across it? And again, wait for the sake of what? Wait till there's no strength to live? And meanwhile one must live, and one wants to live!

"I went away from my brother's early in the morning, and ever since then it has been unbearable for me to be in town. I am oppressed by its peace and quiet; I am afraid to look at the windows, for there is no spectacle more painful to me now than the sight of a happy family sitting round the table drinking tea. I am old and am not fit for the struggle; I am not even capable of hatred; I can only grieve inwardly, feel irritated and vexed; but at night my head is hot from the rush of ideas, and I cannot sleep. . . . Ah, if I were young!"

Ivan Ivanovitch walked backwards and forwards in excitement, and repeated: "If I were young!"

He suddenly went up to Alehin and began pressing first one of his hands and then the other.

"Pavel Konstantinovitch," he said in an imploring voice, "don't be calm and contented, don't let yourself be put to sleep! While you are young, strong, confident, be not weary in well-doing! There is no happiness, and there ought not to be; but if there is a meaning and an object in life, that meaning and object is not our happiness, but something greater and more rational. Do good!"

And all this Ivan Ivanovitch said with a pitiful, imploring smile, as though he were asking him a personal favour.

Then all three sat in arm-chairs at different ends of the drawing-room and were silent. Ivan Ivanovitch's story had not satisfied either Burkin or Alehin. When the generals and ladies gazed down from their gilt frames, looking in the dusk as though they were alive, it was dreary to listen to the story of the poor clerk who ate gooseberries. They felt inclined, for some reason, to talk about elegant people, about women. And their sitting in the drawing-room where everything—the chandeliers in their covers, the arm-chairs, and the carpet under their feet—reminded them that those very people who were now looking down from their frames had once moved about, sat, drunk tea in this room, and the fact that lovely Pelagea was moving noiselessly about was better than any story.

Alehin was fearfully sleepy; he had got up early, before three o'clock in the morning, to look after his work, and now his eyes were closing; but he was afraid his visitors might tell some interesting story after he had gone, and he lingered on. He did not go into the question whether what Ivan Ivanovitch had just said was right and true. His visitors did not talk of groats, nor of hay, nor of tar, but of something that had no direct bearing on his life, and he was glad and wanted them to go on.

"It's bed-time, though," said Burkin, getting up. "Allow me to wish you good-night."

Alehin said good-night and went downstairs to his own domain, while the visitors remained upstairs. They were both taken for the night to a big room where there stood two old wooden beds decorated with carvings, and in the corner was an ivory crucifix. The big cool beds, which had been made by the lovely Pelagea, smelt agreeably of clean linen.

Ivan Ivanovitch undressed in silence and got into bed.

"Lord forgive us sinners!" he said, and put his head under the quilt.

His pipe lying on the table smelt strongly of stale tobacco, and Burkin could not sleep for a long while, and kept wondering where the oppressive smell came from.

The rain was pattering on the window-panes all night.

A Christmas Carol

by Charles Dickens

Introduced by John Irving

IN JANUARY OF 1990, I WAS LIVING WITH THE GREAT ROYAL CIRCUS IN Junagadh, Gujarat, in the northwest of India. The TV and VCR were almost as common in the troupe tents of the performers and their families as they are where I more frequently live—in Vermont and in Toronto. That January, the popular Hindu epic the *Mahabharata* was continuing its Sunday morning journey of ninety-three televised episodes, each an hour long; at that pace, the story wouldn't end (at the gates of heaven) until the coming summer. A record number of robberies had occurred during the broadcasts because the thieves knew that a great majority of Indians would be glued to their television sets. That Sunday, in the troupe tent of the Great Royal's ringmaster and lion tamer, Mr. Pratap Singh, the TV was faithfully encircled; the only members of the circus not watching the *Mahabharata* were a half-dozen elephants and two dozen lions and tigers, in addition to a dozen horses and as many chimpanzees, and uncounted cockatoos and parrots—and dozens of dogs. But of the 150 *human* members of the Great Royal Circus, including almost a dozen dwarfs, everyone was enjoying the epic.

The rest of the week, the videocassette players in the troupe tents treated the acrobats and wild-animal trainers to various wonders and excesses of the Hindi cinema. Nowadays, the Great Royal rarely travels outside the states of Maharashtra and Gujarat; the movies that are hits in Bombay are similarly successful with the circus performers. But that Sunday, after the conclusion of the weekly episode of the *Mahabharata,* I wandered away from the television set and into the family kitchen of the ringmaster's troupe tent. Sumi, the lion tamer's wife, made me a cup of tea. From the VCR, I heard a surprisingly familiar burst of dialogue—in English. I couldn't see the TV screen, but I knew that the speaker was none other than that most literary of ghosts, Jacob Marley—the dead business partner of the infamous Ebenezer Scrooge. It was that part when Marley's Ghost is rejecting Scrooge's compliment: "But you were always a good man of business, Jacob." Marley's Ghost cries out, "Business! Mankind was my business. The common welfare was my business; charity, mercy, forbearance, and benevolence, were, all, my business. The dealings of my trade were but a drop of water in the comprehensive ocean of my business!" It's a stirring speech, followed by the rattling of the ghost's chains.

I repaired to the television set in the Singh family's troupe tent to watch the video of *A Christmas Carol;* it was the Alastair Sim version. There—in Junagadh, at an Indian circus—the child acrobats were seated on the rugs that covered the tent's dirt floor; they were illiterate Hindu children but they were riveted to the story, which was as fascinating to them as it remains to our children. If the principal point of *A Christmas Carol* is that Scrooge reforms—that he learns "how to keep Christmas well"—these child acrobats had never kept Christmas at all; moreover, they would never keep it. Also, they spoke and understood little English, yet they knew and loved the tale.

One of them—a twelve-year-old contortionist, a girl named Laxmi who was also skilled as a tightrope walker—saw me looking at the TV. Since I was the foreigner among them, I suppose Laxmi thought I needed to be told something about *A Christmas Carol;* she mistook my astonishment at what I was seeing and where I was seeing it, and assumed I was ignorant of the characters and the narrative.

"Scrooge," she said, identifying old Ebenezer for me. "A ghost," Laxmi said, indicating the shade of the late Jacob Marley. "More coming," she added.

"A Christmas Carol," I replied; this didn't impress Laxmi; I don't know if she knew the title.

It was then that the ringmaster and lion tamer, who was also the chief trainer of the child performers, spoke to me. Pratap Singh was not a man who kept Christmas either. "The children's favorite ghost story," Pratap explained. I remember thinking that Charles Dickens would have been pleased.

A Christmas Carol was originally subtitled "Ghost Story of Christmas"; the accent on the ghostly (*not* the Christmas-y) elements of the tale was further emphasized in Dickens's Preface to the 1843 edition. "I have endeavoured in this Ghostly little book, to raise the Ghost of an Idea, which shall not put my readers out of humour with themselves, with each other, with the season, or with me."

If that doesn't alert his readers sufficiently, Dickens titles the first stave of his carol "Marley's Ghost," *and* the author states no less than four times in the first four paragraphs that Marley is dead. "Marley was dead: to begin with"—the first sentence of the first paragraph. "Old Marley was as dead as a door-nail"—the last sentence of the first paragraph. "You will therefore permit me to repeat, emphatically, that Marley was as dead as a door-nail"—the last sentence of the second paragraph. And, finally: "There is no doubt that Marley was dead. This must be distinctly understood, or nothing wonderful can come of the story I am going to relate"—the second and third sentences of the fourth paragraph. I think we get the idea. An editor of today's less-is-more school of fiction would doubtless have found this repetitious, but Dickens never suffered a minimalist's sensibilities; in Dickens's prose, the refrain is as common as the semicolon.

From the beginning, Scrooge's cantankerous character is unsparing with his cynicism; his miserliness—more so, his utter shunning of humanity—makes him seem a fair match for any ghost. "The cold within him froze his old features," as Dickens describes him. "He carried his own low temperature always about with him; he iced his office in the dog-days; and didn't thaw it one degree at Christmas." Beggars don't dare to approach him. "Even the blindmen's dogs" give Scrooge a wide berth. "It was the very thing he liked. To edge his way along the crowded paths of life, warning all human sympathy to keep its distance"—Ebenezer Scrooge is the original Bah-Humbug man. "If I could work my will," Scrooge declares, "every idiot who goes about with 'Merry Christmas,' on his lips, should be boiled with his own pudding, and buried with a stake of holly through his heart."

Scrooge is such a pillar of skepticism, he at first resists believing in Marley's Ghost. "You may be an undigested bit of beef, a blot of mustard, a crumb of cheese, a fragment of an underdone potato. There's more of gravy than of grave about you, whatever you are!" Yet Scrooge is converted; beyond the seasonal lessons of Christian charity, *A Christmas Carol* teaches us that a man—even a man as hard as Ebenezer Scrooge—can change. What is heartening about the change in Scrooge is that he learns to love his fellowman; in the politically correct language of our insipid times, Scrooge learns to be *more caring*. But, typical of Dickens, Scrooge has undergone a deeper transformation; that he is persuaded to believe in ghosts, for example, means that Scrooge has been miraculously returned to his childhood—and to a child's powers of imagination and make-believe.

Dickens's celebration of ghosts, and of Christmas, is but a small part of the author's abiding faith in the innocence and magic of children; Dickens believed that his own imagination—in fact, his overall well-being—depended on the contact he kept with his childhood. Furthermore, his popularity with his fellow Victorians, which is reflected by the ongoing interest of young readers today, is rooted in Dickens's remarkable ability for rendering *realistically* what many adults condescendingly call "fantasy."

Additionally, it was Dickens's "fullness of heart" that caused Thackeray to praise *A Christmas Carol* to the skies. "Who can listen to objections regarding such a book as this?" Thackeray wrote. "It seems to be a national benefit, and to every man or woman who reads it a personal kindness." Even the dour Thomas Carlyle was so moved by *A Christmas Carol* that he was (in the words of his wife) "seized with a perfect *convulsion* of hospitality"; apparently, this was quite contrary to the Scots philosopher's nature. George Hogarth, Dickens's future father-in-law, had reviewed the young author (when Charles was only twenty-four): "A close observer of character and manners, with a strong sense of the ridiculous and a graphic faculty of placing in the most whimsical and amusing lights the follies and absurdities of human nature. He has the power, too, of producing tears as well as laughter. His pictures of the vices and wretchedness which abound in this vast city are sufficient to strike the heart of the most careless and insensitive reader." Or, as Chesterton once wrote of Dickens, "The man led a mob." Part of the reason is that relationship which Dickens forces his readers to maintain with children.

* * *

As for the ghosts—"You will be haunted by Three Spirits," Marley's Ghost warns Scrooge—they have become emblematic of *our* Christmases, too. The first of these phantoms is the easiest to bear. "It was a strange figure—like a child: yet not so like a child as like an old man, viewed through some supernatural medium, which gave him the appearance of having receded from the view, and being diminished to a child's proportions."

Shortly thereafter, the spirit introduces himself: "I am the Ghost of Christmas Past."

"Long past?" Scrooge asks.

"No. Your past," the ghost answers—a chilling reply.

It is from the Ghost of Christmas Present that Scrooge is confronted by his own words; his own insensitivity is thrown back at him and leaves him "overcome with penitence and grief." This happens because Scrooge asks the spirit if Tiny Tim will live. "I see a vacant seat in the poor chimney-corner," replies the ghost, in a ghostly fashion, "and a crutch without an owner, carefully preserved." When Scrooge protests, the spirit quotes Scrooge verbatim: "If he be like to die, he had better do it, and decrease the surplus population."

As for the last visitor, that silent but most terrifying phantom, the Ghost of Christmas Yet to Come appears before Scrooge "draped and hooded, coming, like a mist along the ground, towards him." This ghost is taking no prisoners; this spirit shows Scrooge his own corpse. "He lay in the dark empty house, with not a man, a woman, or a child, to say that he was kind to me in this or that, and for the memory of one kind word I will be kind to him. A cat was tearing at the door, and there was a sound of gnawing rats beneath the hearth-stone. What *they* wanted in the room of death, and why they were so restless and disturbed, Scrooge did not dare to think."

This is a Christmas story, yes; yet it is first and foremost a cautionary tale. *We* are that corpse whose face is covered with a veil; we dare not take the veil away, for fear we shall see ourselves lying there. ("Oh cold, cold, rigid, dreadful Death, set up thine altar here, and dress it with such terrors as thou hast at thy command: for this is thy dominion!") This is a Christmas story, yes; as such, it has a happy ending. But, as Marley's Ghost tells Scrooge, the tale is truly a warning. We had best improve our capacity for human sympathy—or else! We must love one another or die unloved.

Most of us have seen so many renditions of *A Christmas Carol* that we imagine we know the story, but how long has it been since we've actually *read* it? Each Christmas, we are assaulted with a new carol; indeed, we're fortunate if all we see is the delightful Alastair Sim. One year, we suffer through some treacle in a western setting; Scrooge is a grizzled cattle baron, tediously unkind to his cows. Another year, poor Tiny Tim hobbles about in the Bronx or in Brooklyn; old Ebenezer is an unrepentant slum landlord. In a few years, I'll be old enough to play the role of Scrooge in one of those countless amateur theatrical events which commemorate (and ruin) *A Christ-*

mas Carol every season. We should spare ourselves these sentimentalized enactments and reread the original—or read it for the first time, as the case may be.

It may surprise us to learn that there is not one scene of Scrooge "interacting" with Tiny Tim, although that is a cherished moment in many made-for-television versions; it is also surprising that, in the epilogue, Dickens anticipates his own detractors. Of Scrooge, the author writes: "Some people laughed to see the alteration in him, but he let them laugh, and little heeded them; for he was wise enough to know that nothing ever happened on this globe, for good, at which some people did not have their fill of laughter in the outset; and knowing that such as these would be blind anyway, he thought it quite as well that they should wrinkle up their eyes in grins, as have the malady in less attractive forms. His own heart laughed: and that was quite enough for him.

"He had no further intercourse with Spirits," the author adds in the final paragraph.

To his readers, Charles Dickens called himself "Their faithful Friend and Servant." In his Preface to the 1843 edition of *A Christmas Carol,* Dickens bestowed a generous benediction; he confessed his hopes for his "Ghostly little book" *and* for his readers—"May it haunt their houses pleasantly." In truth, even in the troupe tent of an Indian circus—not to mention here and now, 150 years after the carol was written—Dickens's "Ghost Story of Christmas" continues to haunt us pleasantly. "And so, as Tiny Tim observed, God bless Us, Every One!"

A Christmas Carol

Charles Dickens

Stave One

MARLEY'S GHOST

Marley was dead: to begin with. There is no doubt whatever about that. The register of his burial was signed by the clergyman, the clerk, the undertaker, and the chief mourner. Scrooge signed it: and Scrooge's name was good upon 'Change, for anything he chose to put his hand to. Old Marley was as dead as a door-nail.

Mind! I don't mean to say that I know, of my own knowledge, what there is particularly dead about a door-nail. I might have been inclined, myself, to regard a coffin-nail as the deadest piece of ironmongery in the trade. But the wisdom of our ancestors is in the simile; and my unhallowed hands shall not disturb it, or the Country's done for. You will therefore permit me to repeat, emphatically, that Marley was as dead as a door-nail.

Scrooge knew he was dead? Of course he did. How could it be otherwise? Scrooge and he were partners for I don't know how many years. Scrooge was his sole executor, his sole administrator, his sole assign, his sole residuary legatee, his sole friend and sole mourner. And even Scrooge was not so dreadfully cut up by the sad event, but that he was an excellent man of business on the very day of the funeral, and solemnised it with an undoubted bargain.

The mention of Marley's funeral brings me back to the point I started from. There is no doubt that Marley was dead. This must be distinctly understood, or nothing wonderful can come of the story I am going to relate. If we were not perfectly convinced that Hamlet's Father died before the play began, there would be nothing more remarkable in his taking a stroll at night, in an easterly wind, upon his own ramparts, than there would be in any other middle-aged gentleman rashly turning out after dark in a breezy spot—say Saint Paul's Churchyard for instance—literally to astonish his son's weak mind.

Scrooge never painted out Old Marley's name. There it stood, years afterwards, above the warehouse door: Scrooge and Marley. The firm was known as Scrooge and Marley. Sometimes people new to the business called

Scrooge Scrooge, and sometimes Marley, but he answered to both names: it was all the same to him.

Oh! But he was a tight-fisted hand at the grindstone, Scrooge! a squeezing, wrenching, grasping, scraping, clutching, covetous, old sinner! Hard and sharp as flint, from which no steel had ever struck out generous fire; secret, and self-contained, and solitary as an oyster. The cold within him froze his old features, nipped his pointed nose, shrivelled his cheek, stiffened his gait; made his eyes red, his thin lips blue; and spoke out shrewdly in his grating voice. A frosty rime was on his head, and on his eyebrows, and his wiry chin. He carried his own low temperature always about with him; he iced his office in the dog-days; and didn't thaw it one degree at Christmas.

External heat and cold had little influence on Scrooge. No warmth could warm, nor wintry weather chill him. No wind that blew was bitterer than he, no falling snow was more intent upon its purpose, no pelting rain less open to entreaty. Foul weather didn't know where to have him. The heaviest rain, and snow, and hail, and sleet, could boast of the advantage over him in only one respect. They often "came down" handsomely, and Scrooge never did.

Nobody ever stopped him in the street to say, with gladsome looks, "My dear Scrooge, how are you? When will you come to see me?" No beggars implored him to bestow a trifle, no children asked him what it was o'clock, no man or woman ever once in all his life inquired the way to such and such a place, of Scrooge. Even the blind men's dogs appeared to know him; and when they saw him coming on, would tug their owners into doorways and up courts; and then would wag their tails as though they said, "No eye at all is better than an evil eye, dark master!"

But what did Scrooge care? It was the very thing he liked. To edge his way along the crowded paths of life, warning all human sympathy to keep its distance, was what the knowing ones call "nuts" to Scrooge.

Once upon a time—of all the good days in the year, on Christmas Eve—old Scrooge sat busy in his counting-house. It was cold, bleak, biting weather: foggy withal: and he could hear the people in the court outside go wheezing up and down, beating their hands upon their breasts, and stamping their feet upon the pavement-stones to warm them. The City clocks had only just gone three, but it was quite dark already: it had not been light all day: and candles were flaring in the windows of the neighbouring offices, like ruddy smears upon the palpable brown air. The fog came pouring in at every chink and keyhole, and was so dense without, that although the court was of the narrowest, the houses opposite were mere phantoms. To see the dingy cloud come drooping down, obscuring everything, one might have thought that Nature lived hard by, and was brewing on a large scale.

The door of Scrooge's counting-house was open that he might keep his eye upon his clerk, who in a dismal little cell beyond, a sort of tank, was copying letters. Scrooge had a very small fire, but the clerk's fire was so very much smaller that it looked like one coal. But he couldn't replenish it, for Scrooge kept the coal-box in his own room; and so surely as the clerk came in with the shovel, the master predicted that it would be necessary for them to part. Wherefore the clerk put on his white comforter, and tried to warm himself at the candle; in which effort, not being a man of a strong imagination, he failed.

"A Merry Christmas, uncle! God save you!" cried a cheerful voice. It was the voice of Scrooge's nephew, who came upon him so quickly that this was the first intimation he had of his approach.

"Bah!" said Scrooge. "Humbug!"

He had so heated himself with rapid walking in the fog and frost, this nephew of Scrooge's, that he was all in a glow; his face was ruddy and handsome; his eyes sparkled, and his breath smoked again.

"Christmas a humbug, uncle!" said Scrooge's nephew. "You don't mean that, I am sure."

"I do," said Scrooge. "Merry Christmas! What right have you to be merry? What reason have you to be merry? You're poor enough."

"Come, then," returned the nephew, gayly. "What right have you to be dismal? What reason have you to be morose? You're rich enough."

Scrooge having no better answer ready on the spur of the moment, said, "Bah!" again; and followed it up with "Humbug."

"Don't be cross, uncle," said the nephew.

"What else can I be," returned the uncle, "when I live in such a world of fools as this? Merry Christmas! Out upon merry Christmas! What's Christmas time to you but a time for paying bills without money; a time for finding yourself a year older, but not an hour richer; a time for balancing your books and having every item in 'em through a round dozen of months presented dead against you? If I could work my will," said Scrooge, indignantly, "every idiot who goes about with 'Merry Christmas,' on his lips, should be boiled with his own pudding, and buried with a stake of holly through his heart. He should!"

"Uncle!" pleaded the nephew.

"Nephew!" returned the uncle, sternly, "keep Christmas in your own way, and let me keep it in mine."

"Keep it!" repeated Scrooge's nephew. "But you don't keep it."

"Let me leave it alone, then," said Scrooge. "Much good may it do you! Much good it has ever done you!"

"There are many things from which I might have derived good, by which I have not profited, I dare say," returned the nephew: "Christmas among the rest. But I am sure I have always thought of Christmas time, when it has come round—apart from the veneration due to its sacred name and origin, if anything belonging to it can be apart from that—as a good time: a kind, forgiving, charitable, pleasant time: the only time I know of, in the long calendar of the year, when men and women seem by one consent to open their shut-up hearts freely, and to think of people below them as if they really were fellow-passengers to the grave, and not another race of creatures bound on other journeys. And therefore, uncle, though it has never put a scrap of gold or silver in my pocket, I believe that it *has* done me good, and *will* do me good; and I say, God bless it!"

The clerk in the Tank involuntarily applauded: becoming immediately sensible of the impropriety, he poked the fire, and extinguished the last frail spark forever.

"Let me hear another sound from *you,*" said Scrooge, "and you'll keep your Christmas by losing your situation." "You're quite a powerful speaker, Sir," he added, turning to his nephew. "I wonder you don't go into Parliament."

"Don't be angry, uncle. Come! Dine with us to-morrow."

Scrooge said that he would see him—yes, indeed he did. He went the whole length of the expression and said that he would see him in that extremity first.

"But why?" cried Scrooge's nephew. "Why?"

"Why did you get married?" said Scrooge.

"Because I fell in love."

"Because you fell in love!" growled Scrooge, as if that were the only thing in the world more ridiculous than a merry Christmas. "Good afternoon!"

"Nay, uncle, but you never came to see me before that happened. Why give it as a reason for not coming now?"

"Good afternoon," said Scrooge.

"I want nothing from you; I ask nothing of you; why cannot we be friends?"

"Good afternoon," said Scrooge.

"I am sorry, with all my heart, to find you so resolute. We have never had any quarrel, to which I have been a party. But I have made the trial in homage to Christmas, and I'll keep my Christmas humour to the last. So A Merry Christmas, uncle!"

"Good afternoon!" said Scrooge.

"And A Happy New Year!"

"Good afternoon!" said Scrooge.

His nephew left the room without an angry word, notwithstanding. He stopped at the outer door to bestow the greetings of the season on the clerk, who, cold as he was, was warmer than Scrooge; for he returned them cordially.

"There's another fellow," muttered Scrooge; who overheard him: "my clerk, with fifteen shillings a week, and a wife and family, talking about a merry Christmas. I'll retire to Bedlam."

This lunatic, in letting Scrooge's nephew out, had let two other people in. They were portly gentlemen, pleasant to behold, and now stood, with their hats off, in Scrooge's office. They had books and papers in their hands, and bowed to him.

"Scrooge and Marley's, I believe," said one of the gentlemen, referring to his list. "Have I the pleasure of addressing Mr. Scrooge, or Mr. Marley?"

"Mr. Marley has been dead these seven years," Scrooge replied. "He died seven years ago, this very night."

"We have no doubt his liberality is well represented by his surviving partner," said the gentleman, presenting his credentials.

It certainly was; for they had been two kindred spirits. At the ominous word "liberality," Scrooge frowned, and shook his head, and handed the credentials back.

"At this festive season of the year, Mr. Scrooge," said the gentleman, taking up a pen, "it is more than usually desirable that we should make some slight provision for the poor and destitute, who suffer greatly at the present time. Many thousands are in want of common necessaries; hundreds of thousands are in want of common comforts, Sir."

"Are there no prisons?" asked Scrooge.

"Plenty of prisons," said the gentleman, laying down the pen again.

"And the Union workhouses?" demanded Scrooge. "Are they still in operation?"

"They are. Still," returned the gentleman, "I wish I could say they were not."

"The Treadmill and the Poor Law are in full vigour, then?" said Scrooge.

"Both very busy, Sir."

"Oh! I was afraid, from what you said at first, that something had occurred to stop them in their useful course," said Scrooge. "I'm very glad to hear it."

"Under the impression that they scarcely furnish Christian cheer of mind or body to the multitude," returned the gentleman, "a few of us are endeavouring to raise a fund to buy the Poor some meat and drink, and means of warmth. We choose this time, because it is a time of all others, when Want is keenly felt, and Abundance rejoices. What shall I put you down for?"

"Nothing!" Scrooge replied.

"You wish to be anonymous?"

"I wish to be left alone," said Scrooge. "Since you ask me what I wish, gentlemen, that is my answer. I don't make merry myself at Christmas and I can't afford to make idle people merry. I help to support the establishments I have mentioned: they cost enough: and those who are badly off must go there."

"Many can't go there; and many would rather die."

"If they would rather die," said Scrooge, "they had better do it, and decrease the surplus population. Besides—excuse me—I don't know that."

"But you might know it," observed the gentleman.

"It's not my business," Scrooge returned. "It's enough for a man to understand his own business, and not to interfere with other people's. Mine occupies me constantly. Good afternoon, gentlemen!"

Seeing clearly that it would be useless to pursue their point, the gentlemen withdrew. Scrooge resumed his labours with an improved opinion of himself, and in a more facetious temper than was usual with him.

Meanwhile the fog and darkness thickened so, that people ran about with flaring links, proffering their services to go before horses in carriages, and conduct them on their way. The ancient tower of a church, whose gruff old bell was always peeping slyly down at Scrooge out of a gothic window in the wall, became invisible, and struck the hours and quarters in the clouds, with tremulous vibrations afterwards as if its teeth were chattering in its frozen head up there. The cold became intense. In the main street at the corner of the court, some labourers were repairing the gas-pipes, and had lighted a great fire in a brazier, round which a party of ragged men and boys were gathered: warming their hands and winking their eyes before the blaze in rapture. The water-plug being left in solitude, its overflowings sullenly congealed, and turned to misanthropic ice. The brightness of the shops where holly sprigs and berries crackled in the lamp heat of the windows, made pale faces ruddy as they passed. Poulterers' and grocers' trades became a splendid joke: a glorious pageant, with which it was next to impossible to believe that such dull principles as bargain and sale had anything to do. The Lord Mayor, in the stronghold of the mighty Mansion House, gave orders to his fifty cooks and butlers to keep Christmas as a Lord Mayor's household should; and even the little tailor, whom he had fined five shillings on the previous Monday for being drunk and bloodthirsty in the streets, stirred up to-morrow's pudding in his garret, while his lean wife and the baby sallied out to buy the beef.

Foggier yet, and colder! Piercing, searching, biting, cold. If the good Saint Dunstan had but nipped the Evil Spirit's nose with a touch of such weather as that, instead of using his familiar weapons, then indeed he would have roared to lusty purpose. The owner of one scant young nose, gnawed and mumbled by the hungry cold as bones are gnawed by dogs, stooped down at Scrooge's keyhole to regale him with a Christmas carol: but at the first sound of

"God bless you, merry gentleman!
May nothing you dismay!"

Scrooge seized the ruler with such energy of action, that the singer fled in terror, leaving the keyhole to the fog and even more congenial frost.

At length the hour of shutting up the counting-house arrived. With an ill-will Scrooge dismounted from his stool, and tacitly admitted the fact to the expectant clerk in the Tank, who instantly snuffed his candle out, and put on his hat.

"You'll want all day to-morrow, I suppose?" said Scrooge.

"If quite convenient, Sir."

"It's not convenient," said Scrooge, "and it's not fair. If I was to stop half-a-crown for it, you'd think yourself ill-used, I'll be bound?"

The clerk smiled faintly.

"And yet," said Scrooge, "you don't think *me* ill-used, when I pay a day's wages for no work."

The clerk observed that it was only once a year.

"A poor excuse for picking a man's pocket every twenty-fifth of December!" said Scrooge, buttoning his great-coat to the chin. "But I suppose you must have the whole day. Be here all the earlier next morning!"

The clerk promised that he would; and Scrooge walked out with a growl. The office was closed in a twinkling, and the clerk, with the long ends of his white comforter dangling below his waist (for he boasted no great-coat), went down a slide on Cornhill, at the end of a lane of boys, twenty times, in honour of its being Christmas Eve, and then ran home to Camden Town as hard as he could pelt, to play at blindman's-buff.

Scrooge took his melancholy dinner in his usual melancholy tavern; and having read all the newspapers, and beguiled the rest of the evening with his banker's-book, went home to bed. He lived in chambers which had once belonged to his deceased partner. They were a gloomy suite of rooms, in a lowering pile of building up a yard, where it had so little business to be, that one could scarcely help fancying it must have run there when it was a young house, playing at hide-and-seek with other houses, and have forgotten the way out again. It was old enough now, and dreary enough, for nobody lived in it but Scrooge, the other rooms being all let out as offices. The yard was so dark that even Scrooge, who knew its every stone, was fain to grope with his hands. The fog and frost so hung about the black old gateway of the house, that it seemed as if the Genius of the Weather sat in mournful meditation on the threshold.

Now, it is a fact, that there was nothing at all particular about the knocker on the door, except that it was very large. It is also a fact, that Scrooge had seen it, night and morning, during his whole residence in that place; also that Scrooge had as little of what is called fancy about him as any man in the City of London, even including—which is a bold word—the corporation, aldermen, and livery. Let it also be borne in mind that Scrooge had not bestowed one thought on Marley, since his last mention of his seven-years-dead partner that afternoon. And then let any man explain to me, if he can, how it happened that Scrooge, having his key in the lock of the door, saw in the knocker, without its undergoing any intermediate process of change: not a knocker, but Marley's face.

Marley's face. It was not in impenetrable shadow as the other objects in the yard were, but had a dismal light about it, like a bad lobster in a dark cellar. It was not angry or ferocious, but looked at Scrooge as Marley used to look: with ghostly spectacles turned up on its ghostly forehead. The hair was curiously stirred, as if by breath or hot air; and, though the eyes were wide open, they were perfectly motionless. That, and its livid colour, made it horrible; but its horror seemed to be in spite of the face and beyond its control, rather than a part of its own expression.

As Scrooge looked fixedly at this phenomenon, it was a knocker again.

To say that he was not startled, or that his blood was not conscious of a terrible sensation to which it had been a stranger from infancy, would be untrue. But he put his hand upon the key he had relinquished, turned it sturdily, walked in, and lighted his candle.

He *did* pause, with a moment's irresolution, before he shut the door; and he *did* look cautiously behind it first, as if he half-expected to be terrified with the sight of Marley's pigtail sticking out into the hall. But there was nothing on the back of the door, except the screws and nuts that held the knocker on; so he said "Pooh, pooh!" and closed it with a bang.

The sound resounded through the house like thunder. Every room above, and every cask in the wine-merchant's cellars below, appeared to have a separate peal of echoes of its own. Scrooge was not a man to be frightened by echoes. He fastened the door, and walked across the hall, and up the stairs: slowly too: trimming his candle as he went.

You may talk vaguely about driving a coach-and-six up a good old flight of stairs, or through a bad young Act of Parliament; but I mean to say you might have got a hearse up that staircase, and taken it broadwise, with the splinter-bar towards the wall, and the door towards the balustrades: and done it easy. There was plenty of width for that, and room to spare; which is perhaps the reason why Scrooge thought he saw a locomotive hearse going on before him in the gloom. Half-a-dozen gas-lamps out of the street wouldn't have lighted the entry too well, so you may suppose that it was pretty dark with Scrooge's dip.

Up Scrooge went, not caring a button for that: darkness is cheap, and Scrooge liked it. But before he shut his heavy door, he walked through his rooms to see that all was right. He had just enough recollection of the face to desire to do that.

Sitting-room, bedroom, lumber-room. All as they should be. Nobody under the table, nobody under the sofa; a small fire in the grate; spoon and basin ready; and the little saucepan of gruel (Scrooge had a cold in his head) upon the hob. Nobody under the bed; nobody in the closet; nobody in his dressing-gown, which was hanging up in a suspicious attitude against the wall. Lumber-room as usual. Old fire-guard, old shoes, two fish-baskets, washing-stand on three legs, and a poker.

Quite satisfied, he closed his door, and locked himself in; double-locked himself in, which was not his custom. Thus secured against surprise, he took off his cravat; put on his dressing-gown and slippers, and his nightcap; and sat down before the fire to take his gruel.

It was a very low fire indeed; nothing on such a bitter night. He was obliged to sit close to it, and brood over it, before he could extract the least sensation of warmth from such a handful of fuel. The fireplace was an old one, built by some Dutch merchant long ago, and paved all round with quaint Dutch tiles, designed to illustrate the Scriptures. There were Cains and Abels, Pharaohs' daughters, Queens of Sheba, Angelic messengers descending through the air on clouds like feather-beds, Abrahams, Belshazzars, Apostles putting off to sea in butter-boats, hundreds of figures, to attract his thoughts; and yet that face of Marley, seven years dead, came like the ancient Prophet's rod, and swallowed up the whole. If each smooth tile had been a blank at first, with power to shape some picture on its surface from the disjointed fragments of his thoughts, there would have been a copy of old Marley's head on every one.

"Humbug!" said Scrooge; and walked across the room.

After several turns, he sat down again. As he threw his head back in the chair, his glance happened to rest upon a bell, a disused bell, that hung in the room, and communicated for some purpose now forgotten with a chamber in the highest story of the building. It was with great astonishment, and with a strange, inexplicable dread, that as he looked, he saw this bell begin to swing. It swung so softly in the outset that it scarcely made a sound; but soon it rang out loudly, and so did every bell in the house.

This might have lasted half a minute, or a minute, but it seemed an hour. The bells ceased as they had begun, together. They were succeeded by a clanking noise, deep down below; as if some person were dragging a heavy chain over the casks in the wine-merchant's cellar. Scrooge then remembered to have heard that ghosts in haunted houses were described as dragging chains.

The cellar-door flew open with a booming sound, and then he heard the noise much louder, on the floors below; then coming up the stairs; then coming straight towards his door.

"It's humbug still!" said Scrooge. "I won't believe it."

His colour changed though, when, without a pause, it came on through the heavy door, and passed into the room before his eyes. Upon its coming in, the dying flame leaped up, as though it cried "I know him! Marley's Ghost!" and fell again.

The same face: the very same. Marley in his pigtail, usual waistcoat, tights and boots; the tassels on the latter bristling, like his pigtail, and his coat-skirts, and the hair upon his head. The chain he drew was clasped about his middle. It was long, and wound about him like a tail; and it was made (for Scrooge observed it closely) of cash-boxes, keys, padlocks, ledgers, deeds, and heavy purses wrought in steel. His body was transparent; so that Scrooge, observing him, and looking through his waistcoat, could see the two buttons on his coat behind.

Scrooge had often heard it said that Marley had no bowels, but he had never believed it until now.

No, nor did he believe it even now. Though he looked the phantom through and through, and saw it standing before him; though he felt the chilling influence of its death-cold eyes; and marked the very texture of the folded kerchief bound about its head and chin, which wrapper he had not observed before: he was still incredulous, and fought against his senses.

"How now!" said Scrooge, caustic and cold as ever. "What do you want with me?"

"Much!"—Marley's voice, no doubt about it.

"Who are you?"

"Ask me who I *was*."

"Who *were* you then?" said Scrooge, raising his voice. "You're particular—for a shade." He was going to say "*to* a shade," but substituted this, as more appropriate.

"In life I was your partner, Jacob Marley."

"Can you—can you sit down?" asked Scrooge, looking doubtfully at him.

"I can."

"Do it then."

Scrooge asked the question, because he didn't know whether a ghost so transparent might find himself in a condition to take a chair; and felt that in the event of its being impossible, it might involve the necessity of an embarrassing explanation. But the Ghost sat down on the opposite side of the fireplace, as if he were quite used to it.

"You don't believe in me," observed the Ghost.

"I don't," said Scrooge.

"What evidence would you have of my reality beyond that of your senses?"

"I don't know," said Scrooge.

"Why do you doubt your senses?"

"Because," said Scrooge, "a little thing affects them. A slight disorder of the stomach makes them cheats. You may be an undigested bit of beef, a blot of mustard, a crumb of cheese, a fragment of an underdone potato. There's more of gravy than of grave about you, whatever you are!"

Scrooge was not much in the habit of cracking jokes, nor did he feel, in his heart, by any means waggish then. The truth is, that he tried to be smart, as a means of distracting his own attention, and keeping down his terror; for the spectre's voice disturbed the very marrow in his bones.

To sit, staring at those fixed, glazed eyes, in silence for a moment, would play, Scrooge felt, the very deuce with him. There was something very awful, too, in the spectre's being provided with an infernal atmosphere of its own. Scrooge could not feel it himself, but this was clearly the case; for though the Ghost sat perfectly motionless, its hair, and skirts, and tassels, were still agitated as by the hot vapour from an oven.

"You see this toothpick?" said Scrooge, returning quickly to the charge, for the reason just assigned; and wishing, though it were only for a second, to divert the vision's stony gaze from himself.

"I do," replied the Ghost.

"You are not looking at it," said Scrooge.

"But I see it," said the Ghost, "notwithstanding."

"Well!" returned Scrooge. "I have but to swallow this, and be for the rest of my days persecuted by a legion of goblins, all of my own creation. Humbug, I tell you—humbug!"

At this the spirit raised a frightful cry, and shook its chain with such a dismal and appalling noise, that Scrooge held on tight to his chair to save himself from falling in a swoon. But how much greater was his horror, when the phantom taking off the bandage round its head, as if it were too warm to wear indoors, its lower jaw dropped down upon its breast!

Scrooge fell upon his knees, and clasped his hands before his face.

"Mercy!" he said. "Dreadful apparition, why do you trouble me?"

"Man of the worldly mind!" replied the Ghost, "do you believe in me or not?"

"I do," said Scrooge. "I must. But why do spirits walk the earth, and why do they come to me?"

"It is required of every man," the Ghost returned, "that the spirit within him should walk abroad among his fellow-men, and travel far and wide; and if that spirit goes not forth in life, it is condemned to do so after death. It is doomed to wander through the world—oh, woe is me!—and witness what it cannot share, but might have shared on earth, and turned to happiness!"

Again the spectre raised a cry, and shook its chain, and wrung its shadowy hands.

"You are fettered," said Scrooge, trembling. "Tell me why?"

"I wear the chain I forged in life," replied the Ghost. "I made it link by link, and yard by yard; I girded it on of my own free will, and of my own free will I wore it. Is its pattern strange to *you?*"

Scrooge trembled more and more.

"Or would you know," pursued the Ghost, "the weight and length of the strong coil you bear yourself? It was full as heavy and as long as this, seven Christmas Eves ago. You have laboured on it, since. It is a ponderous chain!"

Scrooge glanced about him on the floor, in the expectation of finding himself surrounded by some fifty or sixty fathoms of iron cable: but he could see nothing.

"Jacob," he said imploringly. "Old Jacob Marley, tell me more. Speak comfort to me, Jacob."

"I have none to give," the Ghost replied. "It comes from other regions, Ebenezer Scrooge, and is conveyed by other ministers, to other kinds of men. Nor can I tell you what I would. A very little more, is all permitted to me. I cannot rest, I cannot stay, I cannot linger anywhere. My spirit never walked beyond our counting-house—mark me—in life my spirit never roved beyond the narrow limits of our money-changing hole; and weary journeys lie before me!"

It was a habit with Scrooge, whenever he became thoughtful, to put his hands in his breeches pockets. Pondering on what the Ghost had said, he did so now, but without lifting up his eyes, or getting off his knees.

"You must have been very slow about it, Jacob," Scrooge observed, in a business-like manner, though with humility and deference.

"Slow!" the Ghost repeated.

"Seven years dead," mused Scrooge. "And travelling all the time!"

"The whole time," said the Ghost. "No rest, no peace. Incessant torture of remorse."

"You travel fast?" said Scrooge.

"On the wings of the wind," replied the Ghost.

"You might have got over a great quantity of ground in seven years," said Scrooge.

The Ghost, on hearing this, set up another cry, and clanked its chain so hideously in the dead silence of the night, that the Ward would have been justified in indicting it for a nuisance.

"Oh! captive, bound, and double-ironed," cried the phantom, "not to know, that ages of incessant labour, by immortal creatures, for this earth must pass into eternity before the good of which it is susceptible is all developed. Not to know that any Christian spirit working kindly in its little sphere, whatever it may be, will find its mortal life too short for its vast means of usefulness. Not to know that no space of regret can make amends for one life's opportunity misused! Yet such was I! Oh! such was I!"

"But you were always a good man of business, Jacob," faltered Scrooge, who now began to apply this to himself.

"Business!" cried the Ghost, wringing its hands again. "Mankind was my business. The common welfare was my business; charity, mercy, forbearance, and benevolence, were, all, my business. The dealings of my trade were but a drop of water in the comprehensive ocean of my business!"

It held up its chain at arm's length, as if that were the cause of all its unavailing grief, and flung it heavily upon the ground again.

"At this time of the rolling year," the spectre said, "I suffer most. Why did I walk through crowds of fellow-beings with my eyes turned down, and never raise them to that blessed Star which led the Wise Men to a poor abode! Were there no poor homes to which its light would have conducted *me!*"

Scrooge was very much dismayed to hear the spectre going on at this rate, and began to quake exceedingly.

"Hear me!" cried the Ghost. "My time is nearly gone."

"I will," said Scrooge. "But don't be hard upon me! Don't be flowery, Jacob! Pray!"

"How it is that I appear before you in a shape that you can see, I may not tell. I have sat invisible beside you many and many a day."

It was not an agreeable idea. Scrooge shivered, and wiped the perspiration from his brow.

"That is no light part of my penance," pursued the Ghost. "I am here to-night to warn you, that you have yet a chance and hope of escaping my fate. A chance and hope of my procuring, Ebenezer."

"You were always a good friend to me," said Scrooge. "Thank'ee!"

"You will be haunted," resumed the Ghost, "by Three Spirits."

Scrooge's countenance fell almost as low as the Ghost's had done.

"Is that the chance and hope you mentioned, Jacob?" he demanded, in a faltering voice.

"It is."

"I—I think I'd rather not," said Scrooge.

"Without their visits," said the Ghost, "you cannot hope to shun the path I tread. Expect the first to-morrow, when the bell tolls one."

"Couldn't I take 'em all at once, and have it over, Jacob?" hinted Scrooge.

"Expect the second on the next night at the same hour. The third upon the next night when the last stroke of twelve has ceased to vibrate. Look to see me no more; and look that, for your own sake, you remember what has passed between us!"

When it had said these words, the spectre took its wrapper from the table, and bound it round its head, as before. Scrooge knew this, by the smart sound its teeth made, when the jaws were brought together by the bandage. He ventured to raise his eyes again, and found his supernatural visitor confronting him in an erect attitude, with its chain wound over and about its arm.

The apparition walked backward from him; and at every step it took, the window raised itself a little, so that when the spectre reached it, it was wide open. It beckoned Scrooge to approach, which he did. When they were within two paces of each other, Marley's Ghost held up its hand, warning him to come no nearer. Scrooge stopped.

Not so much in obedience, as in surprise and fear: for on the raising of the hand, he became sensible of confused noises in the air; incoherent sounds of lamentation and regret; wailings inexpressibly sorrowful and self-accusatory. The spectre, after listening for a moment, joined in the mournful dirge; and floated out upon the bleak, dark night.

Scrooge followed to the window: desperate in his curiosity. He looked out.

The air was filled with phantoms, wandering hither and thither in restless haste, and moaning as they went. Every one of them wore chains like Marley's Ghost; some few (they might be guilty governments) were linked together; none were free. Many had been personally known to Scrooge in their lives. He had been quite familiar with one old ghost, in a white waistcoat, with a monstrous iron safe attached to its ankle, who cried piteously at being unable to assist a wretched woman with an infant, whom it saw below, upon a door-step. The misery with them all was, clearly, that they sought to interfere, for good, in human matters, and had lost the power forever.

Whether these creatures faded into mist, or mist enshrouded them, he could not tell. But they and their spirit voices faded together; and the night became as it had been when he walked home.

Scrooge closed the window, and examined the door by which the Ghost had entered. It was double-locked, as he had locked it with his own hands, and the bolts were undisturbed. He tried to say "Humbug!" but stopped at the first syllable. And being, from the emotion he had undergone, or the fatigues of the day, or his glimpse of the Invisible World, or the dull conversation of the Ghost, or the lateness of the hour, much in need of repose, went straight to bed, without undressing, and fell asleep upon the instant.

Stave Two

THE FIRST OF THE THREE SPIRITS

When Scrooge awoke, it was so dark, that looking out of bed, he could scarcely distinguish the transparent window from the opaque walls of his chamber. He was endeavouring to pierce the darkness with his ferret eyes, when the chimes of a neighbouring church struck the four quarters. So he listened for the hour.

To his great astonishment the heavy bell went on from six to seven, and from seven to eight, and regularly up to twelve; then stopped. Twelve! It was past two when he went to bed. The clock was wrong. An icicle must have got into the works. Twelve!

He touched the spring of his repeater, to correct this most preposterous clock. Its rapid little pulse beat twelve; and stopped.

"Why, it isn't possible," said Scrooge, "that I can have slept through a whole day and far into another night. It isn't possible that anything has happened to the sun, and this is twelve at noon!"

The idea being an alarming one, he scrambled out of bed, and groped his way to the window. He was obliged to rub the frost off with the sleeve of his dressing-gown before he could see anything; and could see very little then. All he could make out was, that it was still very foggy and extremely cold, and that there was no noise of people running to and fro, and making a great stir, as there unquestionably would have been if night had beaten off bright day, and taken possession of the world. This was a great relief, because "three days after sight of this First of Exchange pay to Mr. Ebenezer Scrooge or his order," and so forth, would have become a mere United States' security if there were no days to count by.

Scrooge went to bed again, and thought, and thought, and thought it over and over and over, and could make nothing of it. The more he thought, the more perplexed he was; and the more he endeavoured not to think, the more he thought. Marley's Ghost bothered him exceedingly. Every time he resolved within himself, after mature inquiry, that it was all a dream, his mind flew back again, like a strong spring released, to its first position, and presented the same problem to be worked all through, "Was it a dream or not?"

Scrooge lay in this state until the chimes had gone three quarters more, when he remembered, on a sudden, that the Ghost had warned him of a visitation when the bell tolled one. He resolved to lie awake until the hour was passed; and, considering that he could no more go to sleep than go to Heaven, this was perhaps the wisest resolution in his power.

The quarter was so long, that he was more than once convinced he must have sunk into a doze unconsciously, and missed the clock. At length it broke upon his listening ear.

"Ding, dong!"

"A quarter past," said Scrooge, counting.

"Ding, dong!"

"Half-past!" said Scrooge.

"Ding, dong!"

"A quarter to it," said Scrooge.

"Ding, dong!"

"The hour itself," said Scrooge, triumphantly, "and nothing else!"

He spoke before the hour bell sounded, which it now did with a deep, dull, hollow, melancholy ONE. Light flashed up in the room upon the instant, and the curtains of his bed were drawn.

The curtains of his bed were drawn aside, I tell you, by a hand. Not the curtains at his feet, nor the curtains at his back, but those to which his face was addressed. The curtains of his bed were drawn aside; and Scrooge, starting up into a half-recumbent attitude, found himself face to face with the unearthly visitor who drew them: as close to it as I am now to you, and I am standing in the spirit at your elbow.

It was a strange figure—like a child: yet not so like a child as like an old man, viewed through some supernatural medium, which gave him the appearance of having receded from the view, and being diminished to a child's proportions. Its hair, which hung about its neck and down its back, was white as if with age; and yet the face had not a wrinkle in it, and the tenderest bloom was on the skin. The arms were very long and muscular; the hands the same, as if its hold were of uncommon strength. Its legs and feet, most delicately formed, were, like those upper members, bare. It wore a tunic of the purest white; and round its waist was bound a lustrous belt, the sheen of which was beautiful. It held a branch of fresh green holly in its hand; and, in singular contradiction of that wintry emblem, had its dress trimmed with summer flowers. But the strangest thing about it was, that from the crown of its head there sprang a bright clear jet of light, by which all this was visible; and which was doubtless the occasion of its using, in its duller moments, a great extinguisher for a cap, which it now held under its arm.

Even this, though, when Scrooge looked at it with increasing steadiness, was *not* its strangest quality. For as its belt sparkled and glittered now in one part and now in another, and what was light one instant, at another time was dark, so the figure itself fluctuated in its distinctness: being now a thing with one arm, now with one leg, now with twenty legs, now a pair of legs without a head, now a head without a body: of which dissolving parts, no outline would be visible in the dense gloom wherein they melted away. And in the very wonder of this, it would be itself again; distinct and clear as ever.

"Are you the Spirit, Sir, whose coming was foretold to me?" asked Scrooge.

"I am!"

The voice was soft and gentle. Singularly low, as if instead of being so close beside him, it were at a distance.

"Who, and what are you?" Scrooge demanded.

"I am the Ghost of Christmas Past."

"Long past?" inquired Scrooge: observant of its dwarfish stature.

"No. Your past."

Perhaps, Scrooge could not have told anybody why, if anybody could have asked him; but he had a special desire to see the Spirit in his cap; and begged him to be covered.

"What!" exclaimed the Ghost, "would you so soon put out, with worldly hands, the light I give? Is it not enough that you are one of those whose passions made this cap, and force me through whole trains of years to wear it low upon my brow!"

Scrooge reverently disclaimed all intention to offend, or any knowledge of having wilfully "bonneted" the Spirit at any period of his life. He then made bold to inquire what business brought him there.

"Your welfare!" said the Ghost.

Scrooge expressed himself much obliged, but could not help thinking that a night of unbroken rest would have been more conducive to that end. The Spirit must have heard him thinking, for it said immediately:—

"Your reclamation, then. Take heed!"

It put out its strong hand as it spoke, and clasped him gently by the arm.

"Rise! and walk with me!"

It would have been in vain for Scrooge to plead that the weather and the hour were not adapted to pedestrian purposes; that bed was warm, and the thermometer a long way below freezing; that he was clad but lightly in his slippers, dressing-gown, and nightcap; and that he had a cold upon him at that time. The grasp, though gentle as a woman's hand, was not to be resisted. He rose: but finding that the Spirit made towards the window, clasped its robe in supplication.

"I am a mortal," Scrooge remonstrated, "and liable to fall."

"Bear but a touch of my hand *there,*" said the Spirit, laying it upon his heart, "and you shall be upheld in more than this!"

As the words were spoken, they passed through the wall, and stood upon an open country road, with fields on either hand. The city had entirely vanished. Not a vestige of it was to be seen. The darkness and the mist had vanished with it, for it was a clear, cold, winter day, with snow upon the ground.

"Good Heaven!" said Scrooge, clasping his hands together, as he looked about him. "I was bred in this place. I was a boy here!"

The Spirit gazed upon him mildly. Its gentle touch, though it had been light and instantaneous, appeared still present to the old man's sense of feeling. He was conscious of a thousand odours floating in the air, each one connected with a thousand thoughts, and hopes, and joys, and cares long, long forgotten!

"Your lip is trembling," said the Ghost. "And what is that upon your cheek?"

Scrooge muttered, with an unusual catching in his voice, that it was a pimple; and begged the Ghost to lead him where he would.

"You recollect the way?" inquired the Spirit.

"Remember it!" cried Scrooge with fervour—"I could walk it blindfold."

"Strange to have forgotten it for so many years!" observed the Ghost. "Let us go on."

They walked along the road, Scrooge recognizing every gate, and post, and tree; until a little market-town appeared in the distance, with its bridge, its church, and winding river. Some shaggy ponies now were seen trotting towards them with boys upon their backs, who called to other boys in country gigs and carts, driven by farmers. All these boys were in great spirits, and shouted to each other, until the broad fields were so full of merry music, that the crisp air laughed to hear it.

"These are but shadows of the things that have been," said the Ghost. "They have no consciousness of us."

The jocund travellers came on; and as they came, Scrooge knew and named them every one. Why was he rejoiced beyond all bounds to see them! Why did his cold eye glisten, and his heart leap up as they went past! Why was he filled with gladness when he heard them give each other Merry Christmas, as they parted at cross-roads and by-ways, for their several homes! What was merry Christmas to Scrooge? Out upon merry Christmas. What good had it ever done to him?

"The school is not quite deserted," said the Ghost. "A solitary child, neglected by his friends, is left there still."

Scrooge said he knew it. And he sobbed.

They left the high-road, by a well-remembered lane, and soon approached a mansion of dull red brick, with a little weathercock-surmounted cupola, on the roof, and a bell hanging in it. It was a large house, but one of broken fortunes; for the spacious offices were little used, their walls were damp and mossy, their windows broken, and their gates decayed. Fowls clucked and strutted in the stables; and the coach-houses and sheds were overrun with grass. Nor was it more retentive of its ancient state, within; for entering the dreary hall, and glancing through the open doors of many rooms, they found them poorly furnished, cold, and vast. There was an earthy savour in the air, a chilly bareness in the place, which associated itself somehow with too much getting up by candle-light, and not too much to eat.

They went, the Ghost and Scrooge, across the hall, to a door at the back of the house. It opened before them, and disclosed a long, bare, melancholy room, made barer still by lines of plain deal forms and desks. At one of these a lonely boy was reading near a feeble fire; and Scrooge sat down upon a form, and wept to see his poor forgotten self as he had used to be.

Not a latent echo in the house, not a squeak and scuffle from the mice behind the panelling, not a drip from the half-thawed water-spout in the dull yard behind, not a sigh among the leafless boughs of one despondent poplar, not the idle swinging of an empty store-house door, no, not a clicking in the fire, but fell upon the heart of Scrooge with softening influence, and gave a freer passage to his tears.

The Spirit touched him on the arm, and pointed to his younger self, intent upon his reading. Suddenly a man, in foreign garments: wonderfully real and distinct to look at: stood outside the window, with an axe stuck in his belt, and leading an ass laden with wood by the bridle.

"Why, it's Ali Baba!" Scrooge exclaimed in ecstasy. "It's dear old honest Ali Baba! Yes, yes, I know! One Christmas time, when yonder solitary child was left here all alone, he *did* come, for the first time, just like that. Poor boy! And Valentine," said Scrooge, "and his wild brother, Orson; there they go! And what's his name, who was put down in his drawers, asleep, at the Gate of Damascus; don't you see him! And the Sultan's Groom turned upside down by the Genii; there he is upon his head! Serve him right. I'm glad of it. What business had *he* to be married to the Princess!"

To hear Scrooge expending all the earnestness of his nature on such subjects, in a most extraordinary voice between laughing and crying; and to see his heightened and excited face; would have been a surprise to his business friends in the City, indeed.

"There's the Parrot!" cried Scrooge. "Green body and yellow tail, with a thing like a lettuce growing out of the top of his head; there he is! Poor Robin Crusoe, he called him, when he came home again after sailing round the island. 'Poor Robin Crusoe, where have you been, Robin Crusoe?' The man thought he was dreaming, but he wasn't. It was the Parrot, you know. There goes Friday, running for his life to the little creek! Halloa! Hoop! Halloo!"

Then, with a rapidity of transition very foreign to his usual character, he said, in pity for his former self, "Poor boy!" and cried again.

"I wish," Scrooge muttered, putting his hand in his pocket, and looking about him, after drying his eyes with his cuff: "but it's too late now."

"What is the matter?" asked the Spirit.

"Nothing," said Scrooge. "Nothing. There was a boy singing a Christmas Carol at my door last night. I should like to have given him something: that's all."

The Ghost smiled thoughtfully, and waved its hand: saying as it did so, "Let us see another Christmas!"

Scrooge's former self grew larger at the words, and the room became a little darker and more dirty. The panels shrank, the windows cracked; fragments of plaster fell out of the ceiling, and the naked laths were shown instead; but how all this was brought about, Scrooge knew no more than you do. He only knew that it was quite correct; that everything had happened so; that there he was, alone again, when all the other boys had gone home for the jolly holidays.

He was not reading now, but walking up and down despairingly. Scrooge looked at the Ghost, and with a mournful shaking of his head, glanced anxiously towards the door.

It opened; and a little girl, much younger than the boy, came darting in, and putting her arms about his neck, and often kissing him, addressed him as her "Dear, dear brother."

"I have come to bring you home, dear brother!" said the child, clapping her tiny hands, and bending down to laugh. "To bring you home, home, home!"

"Home, little Fan?" returned the boy.

"Yes!" said the child, brimful of glee. "Home, for good and all. Home, for ever and ever. Father is so much kinder than he used to be, that home's like Heaven! He spoke so gently to me one dear night when I was going to bed, that I was not afraid to ask him once more if you might come home; and he said Yes, you should; and sent me in a coach to bring you. And you're to be a man!" said the child, opening her eyes, "and are never to come back here; but first, we're to be together all the Christmas long, and have the merriest time in all the world."

"You are quite a woman, little Fan!" exclaimed the boy.

She clapped her hands and laughed, and tried to touch his head; but being too little, laughed again, and stood on tiptoe to embrace him. Then she began to drag him, in her childish eagerness, towards the door; and he, nothing loath to go, accompanied her.

A terrible voice in the hall cried, "Bring down Master Scrooge's box, there!" and in the hall appeared the schoolmaster himself, who glared on Master Scrooge with a ferocious condescension, and threw him into a dreadful state of mind by shaking hands with him. He then conveyed him and his sister into the veriest old well of a shivering best-parlour that ever was seen, where the maps upon the wall, and the celestial and terrestrial globes in the windows, were waxy with cold. Here he produced a decanter of curiously light wine, and a block of curiously heavy cake, and administered instalments of those dainties to the young people: at the same time, sending out a meagre servant to offer a glass of "something" to the postboy, who answered that he thanked the gentleman, but if it was the same tap as he had tasted before, he had rather not. Master Scrooge's trunk being by this time tied on to the top of the chaise, the children bade the schoolmaster good-by right willingly; and getting into it, drove gayly down the garden-sweep: the quick wheels dashing the hoar-frost and snow from off the dark leaves of the evergreens like spray.

"Always a delicate creature, whom a breath might have withered," said the Ghost. "But she had a large heart!"

"So she had," cried Scrooge. "You're right. I'll not gainsay it, Spirit. God forbid!"

"She died a woman," said the Ghost, "and had, as I think, children."

"One child," Scrooge returned.

"True," said the Ghost. "Your nephew!"

Scrooge seemed uneasy in his mind; and answered briefly, "Yes."

Although they had but that moment left the school behind them, they were now in the busy thoroughfares of a city, where shadowy passengers passed and repassed; where shadowy carts and coaches battled for the way, and all the strife and tumult of a real city were. It was made plain enough, by the dressing of the shops, that here too it was Christmas time again; but it was evening, and the streets were lighted up.

The Ghost stopped at a certain warehouse door, and asked Scrooge if he knew it.

"Know it!" said Scrooge. "Was I apprenticed here?"

They went in. At sight of an old gentleman in a Welsh wig, sitting behind such a high desk, that if he had been two inches taller he must have knocked his head against the ceiling, Scrooge cried in great excitement:—

"Why, it's old Fezziwig! Bless his heart; it's Fezziwig alive again!"

Old Fezziwig laid down his pen, and looked up at the clock, which pointed to the hour of seven. He rubbed his hands; adjusted his capacious waistcoat; laughed all over himself, from his shoes to his organ of benevolence; and called out in a comfortable, oily, rich, fat, jovial voice:—

"Yo ho, there! Ebenezer! Dick!"

Scrooge's former self, now grown a young man, came briskly in, accompanied by his fellow-'prentice.

"Dick Wilkins, to be sure!" said Scrooge to the Ghost. "Bless me, yes. There he is. He was very much attached to me, was Dick. Poor Dick! Dear, dear!"

"Yo ho, my boys!" said Fezziwig. "No more work to-night. Christmas Eve, Dick. Christmas, Ebenezer! Let's have the shutters up," cried old Fezziwig, with a sharp clap of his hands, "before a man can say Jack Robinson!"

You wouldn't believe how those two fellows went at it! They charged into the street with the shutters—one, two, three—had 'em up in their places—four, five, six—barred 'em and pinned 'em—seven, eight, nine—and came back before you could have got to twelve, panting like race-horses.

"Hilli-ho!" cried old Fezziwig, skipping down from the high desk, with wonderful agility. "Clear away, my lads, and let's have lots of room here! Hilli-ho, Dick! Chirrup, Ebenezer!"

Clear away! There was nothing they wouldn't have cleared away, or couldn't have cleared away, with old Fezziwig looking on. It was done in a minute. Every movable was packed off, as if it were dismissed from public life for evermore; the floor was swept and watered, the lamps were trimmed, fuel was heaped upon the fire; and the warehouse was as snug, and warm, and dry, and bright a ball-room, as you would desire to see upon a winter's night.

In came a fiddler with a music-book, and went up to the lofty desk, and made an orchestra of it, and tuned like fifty stomach-aches. In came Mrs. Fezziwig, one vast substantial smile. In came the three Miss Fezziwigs, beaming and lovable. In came the six young followers whose hearts they broke. In came all the young men and women employed in the business. In came the housemaid, with her cousin, the baker. In came the cook, with her brother's particular friend, the milkman. In came the boy from over the way, who was suspected of not having board enough from his master; trying to hide himself behind the girl from next door but one, who was proved to have had her ears pulled by her mistress. In they all came, one after another; some shyly, some boldly, some gracefully, some awkwardly, some pushing, some pulling; in they all came, anyhow and everyhow. Away they all went, twenty couples at once, hands half round and back again the other way; down the middle and up again; round and round in various stages of affectionate grouping; old top couple always turning up in the wrong place; new top couple starting off again, as soon as they got there; all top couples at last, and not a bottom one to help them. When this result was brought about, old Fezziwig, clapping his hands to stop the dance, cried out, "Well done!" and the fiddler plunged his hot face into a pot of porter, especially provided for that purpose. But scorning rest upon his reappearance, he instantly began again, though there were no dancers yet, as if the other fiddler had been carried home, exhausted, on a shutter; and he were a bran-new man resolved to beat him out of sight, or perish.

There were more dances, and there were forfeits, and more dances, and there was cake, and there was negus, and there was a great piece of Cold Roast, and there was a great piece of Cold Boiled, and there were mince-pies, and plenty of beer. But the great effect of the evening came after the Roast and Boiled, when the fiddler (an artful dog, mind! The sort of man who knew his business better than you or I could have told it him!) struck up "Sir Roger de Coverley." Then old Fezziwig stood out to dance with Mrs. Fezziwig. Top couple, too; with a good stiff piece of work cut out for them; three or four and twenty pair of partners; people who were not to be trifled with; people who *would* dance, and had no notion of walking.

But if they had been twice as many: ah, four times: old Fezziwig would have been a match for them, and so would Mrs. Fezziwig. As to *her,* she was worthy to be his partner in every sense of the term. If that's not high praise, tell me higher, and I'll use it. A positive light appeared to issue from Fezziwig's calves. They shone in every part of the dance like moons. You couldn't have predicted, at any given time, what would become of 'em next. And when old Fezziwig and Mrs. Fezziwig had gone all through the dance; advance and retire, hold hands with your partner; bow and courtesy; corkscrew; thread-the-needle, and back again to your place; Fezziwig "cut"—cut so deftly, that he appeared to wink with his legs, and came upon his feet again without a stagger.

When the clock struck eleven, this domestic ball broke up. Mr. and Mrs. Fezziwig took their stations, one on either side the door, and shaking hands with every person individually as he or she went out, wished him or her a Merry Christmas. When everybody had retired but the two 'prentices, they did the same to them; and thus the cheerful voices died away, and the lads were left to their beds; which were under a counter in the back-shop.

During the whole of this time, Scrooge had acted like a man out of his wits. His heart and soul were in the scene, and with his former self. He corroborated everything, remembered everything, enjoyed everything, and underwent the strangest agitation. It was not until now, when the bright faces of his former self and Dick were turned from them, that he remembered the Ghost, and became conscious that it was looking full upon him, while the light upon its head burnt very clear.

"A small matter," said the Ghost, "to make these silly folks so full of gratitude."

"Small!" echoed Scrooge.

The Spirit signed to him to listen to the two apprentices, who were pouring out their hearts in praise of Fezziwig: and when he had done so, said,

"Why! Is it not? He has spent but a few pounds of your mortal money: three or four, perhaps. Is that so much that he deserves this praise?"

"It isn't that," said Scrooge, heated by the remark, and speaking unconsciously like his former, not his latter, self. "It isn't that, Spirit. He has the power to render us happy or unhappy; to make our service light or burdensome; a pleasure or a toil. Say that his power lies in words and looks; in things so slight and insignificant that it is impossible to add and count 'em up: what then? The happiness he gives, is quite as great as if it cost a fortune."

He felt the Spirit's glance, and stopped.

"What is the matter?" asked the Ghost.

"Nothing particular," said Scrooge.

"Something, I think?" the Ghost insisted.

"No," said Scrooge, "No. I should like to be able to say a word or two to my clerk just now! That's all."

His former self turned down the lamps as he gave utterance to the wish; and Scrooge and the Ghost again stood side by side in the open air.

"My time grows short," observed the Spirit. "Quick!"

This was not addressed to Scrooge, or to any one whom he could see, but it produced an immediate effect. For again Scrooge saw himself. He was older now; a man in the prime of life. His face had not the harsh and rigid lines of later years; but it had begun to wear the signs of care and avarice. There was an eager, greedy, restless motion in the eye, which showed the passion that had taken root, and where the shadow of the growing tree would fall.

He was not alone, but sat by the side of a fair young girl in a mourning-dress: in whose eyes there were tears, which sparkled in the light that shone out of the Ghost of Christmas Past.

"It matters little," she said, softly. "To you, very little. Another idol has displaced me; and if it can cheer and comfort you in time to come, as I would have tried to do, I have no just cause to grieve."

"What idol has displaced you?" he rejoined.

"A golden one."

"This is the even-handed dealing of the world!" he said. "There is nothing on which it is so hard as poverty; and there is nothing it professes to condemn with such severity as the pursuit of wealth!"

"You fear the world too much," she answered, gently. "All your other hopes have merged into the hope of being beyond the chance of its sordid reproach. I have seen your nobler aspirations fall off one by one, until the master passion, Gain, engrosses you. Have I not?"

"What then?" he retorted. "Even if I have grown so much wiser, what then? I am not changed towards you."

She shook her head.

"Am I?"

"Our contract is an old one. It was made when we were both poor and content to be so, until, in good season, we could improve our worldly fortune by our patient industry. You *are* changed. When it was made, you were another man."

"I was a boy," he said impatiently.

"Your own feeling tells you that you were not what you are," she returned. "I am. That which promised happiness when we were one in heart, is fraught with misery now that we are two. How often and how keenly I have thought of this, I will not say. It is enough that I *have* thought of it, and can release you."

"Have I ever sought release?"

"In words? No. Never."

"In what, then?"

"In a changed nature; in an altered spirit; in another atmosphere of life; another Hope as its great end. In everything that made my love of any worth or value in your sight. If this had never been between us," said the girl, looking mildly, but with steadiness, upon him; "tell me, would you seek me out and try to win me now? Ah, no!"

He seemed to yield to the justice of this supposition, in spite of himself. But he said with a struggle, "You think not."

"I would gladly think otherwise if I could," she answered, "Heaven knows! When *I* have learned a Truth like this, I know how strong and irresistible it must be. But if you were free to-day, to-morrow, yesterday, can even I believe that you would choose a dowerless girl—you who, in your very confidence with her, weigh everything by Gain: or, choosing her, if for a moment you were false enough to your one guiding principle to do so, do I not know that your repentance and regret would surely follow? I do; and I release you. With a full heart, for the love of him you once were."

He was about to speak; but with her head turned from him, she resumed.

"You may—the memory of what is past half makes me hope you will—have pain in this. A very, very brief time, and you will dismiss the recollection of it, gladly, as an unprofitable dream, from which it happened well that you awoke. May you be happy in the life you have chosen!"

She left him, and they parted.

"Spirit!" said Scrooge, "show me no more! Conduct me home. Why do you delight to torture me?"

"One shadow more!" exclaimed the Ghost.

"No more!" cried Scrooge. "No more. I don't wish to see it. Show me no more!"

But the relentless Ghost pinioned him in both his arms, and forced him to observe what happened next.

They were in another scene and place: a room, not very large or handsome, but full of comfort. Near to the winter fire sat a beautiful young girl, so like the last that Scrooge believed it was the same, until he saw *her,* now a comely matron, sitting opposite her daughter. The noise in this room was perfectly tumultuous, for there were more children there, than Scrooge in his agitated state of mind could count; and, unlike the celebrated herd in the poem, they were not forty children conducting themselves like one, but every child was conducting itself like forty. The consequences were uproarious beyond belief; but no one seemed to care; on the contrary, the mother and daughter laughed heartily, and enjoyed it very much; and the latter, soon beginning to mingle in the sports, got pillaged by the young brigands most ruthlessly. What would I not have given to be one of them! Though I never could have been so rude, no, no! I wouldn't for the wealth of all the world have crushed that braided hair, and torn it down; and for the precious little shoe, I wouldn't have plucked it off, God bless my soul! to save my life. As to measuring her waist in sport, as they did, bold young brood, I couldn't have done it; I should have expected my arm to have grown round it for a punishment, and never come straight again. And yet I should have dearly liked, I own, to have touched her lips; to have questioned her, that she might have opened them; to have looked upon the lashes of her downcast eyes, and never raised a blush; to have let loose waves of hair, an inch of which would be a keepsake beyond price: in short, I should have liked, I do confess, to have had the lightest license of a child, and yet been man enough to know its value.

But now a knocking at the door was heard, and such a rush immediately ensued that she with laughing face and plundered dress was borne towards it the centre of a flushed and boisterous group just in time to greet the father, who came home attended by a man laden with Christmas toys and presents. Then the shouting and the struggling, and the onslaught that was made on the defenseless porter! The scaling him with chairs for ladders to dive into his pockets, despoil him of brown-paper parcels, hold on tight by his cravat, hug him round the neck, pommel his back, and kick his legs in irrepressible affection! The shouts of wonder and delight with which the development of every package was received! The terrible announcement that the baby had been taken in the act of putting a doll's frying-pan into his mouth, and was more than suspected of having swallowed a fictitious turkey, glued on a wooden platter! The immense relief of finding this a false alarm! The joy, and gratitude, and ecstasy! They are all indescribable alike. It is enough that by degrees the children and their emotions got out of the parlour and by one stair at a time, up to the top of the house; where they went to bed, and so subsided.

And now Scrooge looked on more attentively than ever, when the master of the house, having his daughter leaning fondly on him, sat down with her and her mother at his own fireside; and when he thought that such another creature, quite as graceful and as full of promise, might have called him father, and been a spring-time in the haggard winter of his life, his sight grew very dim indeed.

"Belle," said the husband, turning to his wife with a smile, "I saw an old friend of yours this afternoon."

"Who was it?"

"Guess!"

"How can I? Tut, don't I know?" she added in the same breath, laughing as he laughed. "Mr. Scrooge."

"Mr. Scrooge it was. I passed his office window; and as it was not shut up, and he had a candle inside, I could scarcely help seeing him. His partner lies upon the point of death, I hear; and there he sat alone. Quite alone in the world, I do believe."

"Spirit!" said Scrooge in a broken voice, "remove me from this place."

"I told you these were shadows of the things that have been," said the Ghost. "That they are what they are, do not blame me!"

"Remove me!" Scrooge exclaimed. "I cannot bear it!"

He turned upon the Ghost, and seeing that it looked upon him with a face, in which in some strange way there were fragments of all the faces it had shown him, wrestled with it.

"Leave me! Take me back. Haunt me no longer!"

In the struggle, if that can be called a struggle in which the Ghost with no visible resistance on its own part was undisturbed by any effort of its adversary, Scrooge observed that its light was burning high and bright; and dimly connecting that with its influence over him, he seized the extinguisher-cap, and by a sudden action pressed it down upon his head.

The Spirit dropped beneath it, so that the extinguisher covered its whole form; but though Scrooge pressed it down with all his force, he could not hide the light which streamed from under it, in an unbroken flood upon the ground.

He was conscious of being exhausted, and overcome by an irresistible drowsiness; and, further, of being in his own bedroom. He gave the cap a parting squeeze, in which his hand relaxed; and had barely time to reel to bed, before he sank into a heavy slumber.

Stave Three

THE SECOND OF THE THREE SPIRITS

Awaking in the middle of a prodigiously tough snore, and sitting up in bed to get his thoughts together, Scrooge had no occasion to be told that the bell was again upon the stroke of One. He felt that he was restored to consciousness in the right nick of time, for the especial purpose of holding a conference with the second messenger despatched to him through Jacob Marley's intervention. But, finding that he turned uncomfortably cold when he began to wonder which of his curtains this new spectre would draw back, he put them every one aside with his own hands, and lying down again, established a sharp lookout all round the bed. For he wished to challenge the Spirit on the moment of its appearance, and did not wish to be taken by surprise and made nervous.

Gentlemen of the free-and-easy sort, who plume themselves on being acquainted with a move or two, and begin usually equal to the time-of-day, express the wide range of their capacity for adventure by observing that they are good for anything from pitch-and-toss to manslaughter; between which opposite extremes, no doubt, there lies a tolerably wide and comprehensive range of subjects. Without venturing for Scrooge quite as hardily as this, I don't mind calling on you to believe that he was ready for a good broad field of strange appearances, and that nothing between a baby and rhinoceros would have astonished him very much.

Now, being prepared for almost anything, he was not by any means prepared for nothing; and, consequently, when the Bell struck One, and no shape appeared, he was taken with a violent fit of trembling. Five minutes, ten minutes, a quarter of an hour went by, yet nothing came. All this time, he lay upon his bed, the very core and centre of a blaze of ruddy light, which streamed upon it when the clock proclaimed the hour; and which, being only light, was more alarming than a dozen ghosts, as he was powerless to make out what it meant, or would be at; and was sometimes apprehensive that he might be at that very moment an interesting case of spontaneous combustion, without having the consolation of knowing it. At last, however, he began to think—as you or I would have thought at first; for it is always the person not in the predicament who knows what ought to have been done in it, and would unquestionably have done it too—at last, I say, he began to think that the source and secret of this ghostly light might be in the adjoining room, from whence, on further tracing it, it seemed to shine. This idea taking full possession of his mind, he got up softly and shuffled in his slippers to the door.

The moment Scrooge's hand was on the lock, a strange voice called him by his name, and bade him enter. He obeyed.

It was his own room. There was no doubt about that. But it had undergone a surprising transformation. The walls and ceiling were so hung with living green, that it looked a perfect grove, from every part of which, bright gleaming berries glistened. The crisp leaves of holly, mistletoe, and ivy reflected back the light, as if so many little mirrors had been scattered there; and such a mighty blaze went roaring up the chimney, as that dull petrifaction of a hearth had never known in Scrooge's time, or Marley's, or for many and many a winter season gone. Heaped up on the floor, to form a kind of throne, were turkeys, geese, game, poultry, brawn, great joints of meat, sucking-pigs, long wreaths of sausages, mince-pies, plum-puddings, barrels of oysters, red-hot chestnuts, cherry-cheeked apples, juicy oranges, luscious pears, immense twelfth-cakes, and seething bowls of punch, that made the chamber dim with their delicious steam. In easy state upon this couch, there sat a jolly Giant, glorious to see; who bore a glowing torch, in shape not unlike Plenty's horn, and held it up, high up, to shed its light on Scrooge, as he came peeping round the door.

"Come in!" exclaimed the Ghost. "Come in! and know me better, man!"

Scrooge entered timidly, and hung his head before this Spirit. He was not the dogged Scrooge he had been; and though the Spirit's eyes were clear and kind, he did not like to meet them.

"I am the Ghost of Christmas Present," said the Spirit. "Look upon me!"

Scrooge reverently did so. It was clothed in one simple deep green robe, or mantle, bordered with white fur. This garment hung so loosely on the figure, that its capacious breast was bare, as if disdaining to be warded or concealed by any artifice. Its feet, observable beneath the ample folds of the garment, were also bare; and on its head it wore no other covering than a holly wreath set here and there with shining icicles. Its dark brown curls were long and free; free as its genial face, its sparkling eye, its open hand, its cheery voice, its unconstrained demeanour, and its joyful air. Girded round its middle was an antique scabbard; but no sword was in it, and the ancient sheath was eaten up with rust.

"You have never seen the like of me before!" exclaimed the Spirit.

"Never," Scrooge made answer to it.

"Have never walked forth with the younger members of my family; meaning (for I am very young) my elder brothers born in these later years?" pursued the Phantom.

"I don't think I have," said Scrooge. "I am afraid I have not. Have you had many brothers, Spirit?"

"More than eighteen hundred," said the Ghost.

"A tremendous family to provide for!" muttered Scrooge.

The Ghost of Christmas Present rose.

"Spirit," said Scrooge, submissively, "conduct me where you will. I went forth last night on compulsion, and I learnt a lesson which is working now. To-night, if you have aught to teach me, let me profit by it."

"Touch my robe!"

Scrooge did as he was told, and held it fast,

Holly, mistletoe, red berries, ivy, turkeys, geese, game, poultry, brawn, meat, pigs, sausages, oysters, pies, puddings, fruit, and punch, all vanished instantly. So did the room, the fire, the ruddy glow, the hour of night, and they stood in the city streets on Christmas morning, where (for the weather was severe) the people made a rough, but brisk and not unpleasant kind of music, in scraping the snow from the pavement in front of their dwellings, and from the tops of their houses: whence it was mad delight to the boys to see it come plumping down into the road below, and splitting into artificial little snow-storms.

The house fronts looked black enough, and the windows blacker, contrasting with the smooth white sheet of snow upon the roofs, and with the dirtier snow upon the ground; which last deposit had been ploughed up in deep furrows by the heavy wheels of carts and wagons; furrows that crossed and recrossed each other hundreds of times where the great streets branched off, and made intricate channels, hard to trace, in the thick yellow mud and icy water. The sky was gloomy, and the shortest streets were choked up with a dingy mist, half thawed, half frozen, whose heavier particles descended in a shower of sooty atoms, as if all the chimneys in Great Britain had, by one consent, caught fire, and were blazing away to their dear hearts' content. There was nothing very cheerful in the climate or the town, and yet was there an air of cheerfulness abroad that the clearest summer air and brightest summer sun might have endeavoured to diffuse in vain.

For, the people who were shovelling away on the housetops were jovial and full of glee; calling out to one another from the parapets, and now and then exchanging a facetious snow-ball—better-natured missile far than many a wordy jest—laughing heartily if it went right and not less heartily if it went wrong. The poulterers' shops were still half open, and the fruiterers' were radiant in their glory. There were great, round, pot-bellied baskets of chestnuts, shaped like the waistcoats of jolly old gentlemen, lolling at the doors, and tumbling out into the street in their apoplectic opulence. There were ruddy, brown-faced, broad-girthed Spanish Onions, shining in the fatness of their growth like Spanish Friars; and winking from their shelves in wanton slyness at the girls as they went by, and glanced demurely at the hung-up mistletoe. There were pears and apples, clustered high in blooming pyramids; there were bunches of grapes, made, in the shopkeepers' benevolence, to dangle from conspicuous hooks, that people's mouths might water gratis as they passed; there were piles of filberts, mossy and brown, recalling, in their fragrance, ancient walks among the woods, and pleasant shufflings ankle deep through withered leaves; there were Norfolk Biffins, squab, and swarthy, setting off the yellow of the oranges and lemons, and, in the great compactness of their juicy persons, urgently entreating and beseeching to be carried home in paper bags and eaten after dinner. The very gold and silver fish, set forth among these choice fruits in a bowl, though members of a dull and stagnant-blooded race, appeared to know that there was something going on; and, to a fish, went gasping round and round their little world in slow and passionless excitement.

The Grocers'! oh the Grocers'! nearly closed, with perhaps two shutters down, or one; but through those gaps such glimpses! It was not alone that the scales descending on the counter made a merry sound, or that the twine and roller parted company so briskly, or that the canisters were rattled up and down like juggling tricks, or even that the blended scents of tea and coffee were so grateful to the nose, or even that the raisins were so plentiful and rare, the almonds so extremely white, the sticks of cinnamon so long and straight, the other spices so delicious, the candied fruits so caked and spotted with molten sugar as to make the coldest lookers-on feel faint and subsequently bilious. Nor was it that the figs were moist and pulpy, or that the French plums blushed in modest tartness from their highly decorated boxes, or that everything was good to eat and in its Christmas dress: but the customers were all so hurried and so eager in the hopeful promise of the day, that they tumbled up against each other at the door, clashing their wicker baskets wildly, and left their purchases upon the counter, and came running back to fetch them, and committed hundreds of the like mistakes in the best humour possible; while the Grocer and his people were so frank and fresh that the polished hearts with which they fastened their aprons behind might have been their own, worn outside for general inspection, and for Christmas daws to peck at if they chose.

But soon the steeples called good people all, to church and chapel, and away they came, flocking through the streets in their best clothes, and with their gayest faces. And at the same time there emerged from scores of by-streets, lanes, and nameless turnings, innumerable people, carrying their dinners to the bakers' shops. The sight of these poor revellers appeared to interest the Spirit very much, for he stood with Scrooge beside him in a baker's doorway, and taking off the covers as their bearers passed, sprinkled incense on their dinners from his torch. And it was a very uncommon kind of torch, for once or twice when there were angry words between some dinner carriers who had jostled with each other, he shed a few drops of water on them from it, and their good humour was restored directly. For they said, it was a shame to quarrel upon Christmas Day. And so it was! God love it, so it was!

In time the bells ceased, and the bakers were shut up; and yet there was a genial shadowing forth of all these dinners and the progress of their cooking, in the thawed blotch of wet above each baker's oven; where the pavement smoked as if its stones were cooking too.

"Is there a peculiar flavour in what you sprinkle from your torch?" asked Scrooge.

"There is. My own."

"Would it apply to any kind of dinner on this day?" asked Scrooge.

"To any kindly given. To a poor one most."

"Why to a poor one most?" asked Scrooge.

"Because it needs it most."

"Spirit," said Scrooge, after a moment's thought, "I wonder you, of all the beings in the many worlds about us, should desire to cramp these people's opportunities of innocent enjoyment."

"I!" cried the Spirit.

"You would deprive them of their means of dining every seventh day, often the only day on which they can be said to dine at all," said Scrooge. "Wouldn't you?"

"I!" cried the Spirit.

"You seek to close these places on the Seventh Day?" said Scrooge. "And it comes to the same thing."

"*I* seek!" exclaimed the Spirit.

"Forgive me if I am wrong. It has been done in your name, or at least in that of your family," said Scrooge.

"There are some upon this earth of yours," returned the Spirit, "who lay claim to know us, and who do their deeds of passion, pride, ill-will, hatred, envy, bigotry, and selfishness in our name, who are as strange to us and all our kith and kin, as if they had never lived. Remember that, and charge their doings on themselves, not us."

Scrooge promised that he would; and they went on, invisible, as they had been before, into the suburbs of the town. It was a remarkable quality of the Ghost (which Scrooge had observed at the baker's), that notwithstanding his gigantic size, he could accommodate himself to any place with ease; and that he stood beneath a low roof quite as gracefully and like a supernatural creature, as it was possible he could have done in any lofty hall.

And perhaps it was the pleasure the good Spirit had in showing off this power of his, or else it was his own kind, generous, hearty nature, and his sympathy with all poor men, that led him straight to Scrooge's clerk's; for there he went, and took Scrooge with him, holding to his robe; and on the threshold of the door the Spirit smiled, and stopped to bless Bob Cratchit's dwelling with the sprinklings of his torch. Think of that! Bob had but fifteen "Bob" a-week himself; he pocketed on Saturdays but fifteen copies of his Christian name; and yet the Ghost of Christmas Present blessed his four-roomed house!

Then up rose Mrs. Cratchit, Cratchit's wife, dressed out but poorly in a twice-turned gown, but brave in ribbons, which are cheap and make a goodly show for sixpence; and she laid the cloth, assisted by Belinda Cratchit, second of her daughters, also brave in ribbons; while Master Peter Cratchit plunged a fork into the saucepan of potatoes, and getting the corners of his monstrous shirt collar (Bob's private property, conferred upon his son and heir in honour of the day) into his mouth, rejoiced to find himself so gallantly attired, and yearned to show his linen in the fashionable Parks. And now two smaller Cratchits, boy and girl, came tearing in, screaming that outside the baker's they had smelt the goose, and known it for their own; and basking in luxurious thoughts of sage-and-onion, these young Cratchits danced about the table, and exalted Master Peter Cratchit to the skies, while he (not proud, although his collars nearly choked him) blew the fire, until the slow potatoes bubbling up, knocked loudly at the saucepan-lid to be let out and peeled.

"What has ever got your precious father then?" said Mrs. Cratchit. "And your brother, Tiny Tim! And Martha warn't as late last Christmas Day by half-an-hour!"

"Here's Martha, mother!" said a girl, appearing as she spoke.

"Here's Martha, mother!" cried the two young Cratchits. "Hurrah! There's *such* a goose, Martha!"

"Why, bless your heart alive, my dear, how late you are!" said Mrs. Cratchit, kissing her a dozen times, and taking off her shawl and bonnet for her with officious zeal.

"We'd a deal of work to finish up last night," replied the girl, "and had to clear away this morning, mother!"

"Well! Never mind so long as you are come," said Mrs. Cratchit. "Sit ye down before the fire, my dear, and have a warm, Lord bless ye!"

"No, no! There's father coming," cried the two young Cratchits, who were everywhere at once. "Hide, Martha, hide!"

So Martha hid herself, and in came little Bob, the father, with at least three feet of comforter exclusive of the fringe, hanging down before him; and his threadbare clothes darned up and brushed, to look seasonable; and Tiny Tim upon his shoulder. Alas for Tiny Tim, he bore a little crutch, and had his limbs supported by an iron frame!

"Why, where's our Martha?" cried Bob Cratchit, looking round.

"Not coming," said Mrs. Cratchit.

"Not coming!" said Bob, with a sudden declension in his high spirits; for he had been Tim's blood horse all the way from church, and had come home rampant. "Not coming upon Christmas Day!"

Martha didn't like to see him disappointed, if it were only in joke; so she came out prematurely from behind the closet door, and ran into his arms, while the two young Cratchits hustled Tiny Tim, and bore him off into the wash-house, that he might hear the pudding singing in the copper.

"And how did little Tim behave?" asked Mrs. Cratchit, when she had rallied Bob on his credulity, and Bob had hugged his daughter to his heart's content.

"As good as gold," said Bob, "and better. Somehow he gets thoughtful, sitting by himself so much, and thinks the strangest things you ever heard. He told me, coming home, that he hoped the people saw him in the church, because he was a cripple, and it might be pleasant to them to remember upon Christmas Day, who made lame beggars walk and blind men see."

Bob's voice was tremulous when he told them this, and trembled more when he said that Tiny Tim was growing strong and hearty.

His active little crutch was heard upon the floor, and back came Tiny Tim before another word was spoken, escorted by his brother and sister to his stool before the fire; and while Bob, turning up his cuffs—as if, poor fellow, they were capable of being made more shabby—compounded some hot mixture in a jug with gin and lemons, and stirred it round and round and put it on the hob to simmer; Master Peter and the two ubiquitous young Cratchits went to fetch the goose, with which they soon returned in high procession.

Such a bustle ensued that you might have thought a goose the rarest of all birds; a feathered phenomenon, to which a black swan was a matter of course—and in truth it was something very like it in that house. Mrs. Cratchit made the gravy (ready beforehand in a little saucepan) hissing hot; Master Peter mashed the potatoes with incredible vigour; Miss Belinda sweetened up the apple-sauce; Martha dusted the hot plates; Bob took Tiny Tim beside him in a tiny corner at the table; the two young Cratchits set chairs for everybody, not forgetting themselves, and mounting guard upon their posts, crammed spoons into their mouths, lest they should shriek for goose before their turn came to be helped. At last the dishes were set on, and grace was said. It was succeeded by a breathless pause, as Mrs. Cratchit, looking slowly all along the carving-knife, prepared to plunge it in the breast; but when she did, and when the long expected gush of stuffing issued forth, one murmur of delight arose all around the board, and even Tiny Tim, excited by the two young Cratchits, beat on the table with the handle of his knife, and feebly cried Hurrah!

There never was such a goose. Bob said he didn't believe there ever was such a goose cooked. Its tenderness and flavour, size and cheapness, were the themes of universal admiration. Eked out by the apple-sauce and mashed potatoes, it was a sufficient dinner for the whole family; indeed, as Mrs. Cratchit said with great delight (surveying one small atom of a bone upon the dish), they hadn't ate it all at last! Yet every one had had enough, and the youngest Cratchits, in particular, were steeped in sage and onion to the eyebrows! But now, the plates being changed by Miss Belinda, Mrs. Cratchit left the room alone—too nervous to bear witnesses—to take the pudding up and bring it in.

Suppose it should not be done enough! Suppose it should break in turning out! Suppose somebody should have got over the wall of the back-yard, and stolen it, while they were merry with the goose—a supposition at which the two young Cratchits became livid! All sorts of horrors were supposed.

Hallo! A great deal of steam! The pudding was out of the copper. A smell like a washing-day! That was the cloth. A smell like an eating-house and a pastrycook's next door to each other, with a laundress's next door to that! That was the pudding! In half a minute Mrs. Cratchit entered—flushed, but smiling proudly—with the pudding, like a speckled cannon-ball, so hard and firm, blazing in half of half-a-quartern of ignited brandy, and bedight with Christmas holly stuck into the top.

Oh, a wonderful pudding! Bob Cratchit said, and calmly too, that he regarded it as the greatest success achieved by Mrs. Cratchit since their marriage. Mrs. Cratchit said that now the weight was off her mind, she would confess she had had her doubts about the quantity of flour. Everybody had something to say about it, but nobody said or thought it was at all a small pudding for a large family. It would have been flat heresy to do so. Any Cratchit would have blushed to hint at such a thing.

At last the dinner was all done, the cloth was cleared, the hearth swept, and the fire made up. The compound in the jug being tasted, and considered perfect, apples and oranges were put upon the table, and a shovel-full of chestnuts on the fire. Then all the Cratchit family drew around the hearth, in what Bob Cratchit called a circle, meaning half a one; and at Bob Cratchit's elbow stood the family display of glass. Two tumblers, and a custard-cup without a handle.

These held the hot stuff from the jug, however, as well as golden goblets would have done; and Bob served it out with beaming looks, while the chestnuts on the fire sputtered and cracked noisily. Then Bob proposed:—

"A Merry Christmas to us all, my dears. God bless us!"

Which all the family re-echoed.

"God bless us every one!" said Tiny Tim, the last of all.

He sat very close to his father's side upon his little stool. Bob held his withered little hand in his, as if he loved the child, and wished to keep him by his side, and dreaded that he might be taken from him.

"Spirit," said Scrooge, with an interest he had never felt before, "tell me if Tiny Tim will live."

"I see a vacant seat," replied the Ghost, "in the poor chimney-corner, and a crutch without an owner, carefully preserved. If these shadows remain unaltered by the Future, the child will die."

"No, no," said Scrooge. "Oh, no, kind Spirit! Say he will be spared."

"If these shadows remain unaltered by the Future, none other of my race," returned the Ghost, "will find him here. What then? If he be like to die, he had better do it, and decrease the surplus population."

Scrooge hung his head to hear his own words quoted by the Spirit, and was overcome with penitence and grief.

"Man," said the Ghost, "if man you be in heart, not adamant, forbear that wicked cant until you have discovered What the surplus is, and Where it is. Will you decide what men shall live, what men shall die? It may be, that in the sight of Heaven, you are more worthless and less fit to live than millions like this poor man's child. Oh, God! to hear the Insect on the leaf pronouncing on the too much life among his hungry brothers in the dust!"

Scrooge bent before the Ghost's rebuke, and trembling cast his eyes upon the ground. But he raised them speedily, on hearing his own name.

"Mr. Scrooge!" said Bob; "I'll give you Mr. Scrooge, the Founder of the Feast!"

"The Founder of the Feast indeed!" cried Mrs. Cratchit, reddening. "I wish I had him here. I'd give him a piece of my mind to feast upon, and I hope he'd have a good appetite for it."

"My dear," said Bob, "the children! Christmas Day."

"It should be Christmas Day, I am sure," said she, "on which one drinks the health of such an odious, stingy, hard, unfeeling man as Mr. Scrooge. You know he is, Robert! Nobody knows it better than you do, poor fellow!"

"My dear," was Bob's mild answer, "Christmas Day."

"I'll drink his health for your sake and the Day's," said Mrs. Cratchit, "not for his. Long life to him! A Merry Christmas and a Happy New Year! He'll be very merry and happy, I have no doubt!"

The children drank the toast after her. It was the first of their proceedings which had no heartiness in it. Tiny Tim drank it last of all, but he didn't care twopence for it. Scrooge was the Ogre of the family. The mention of his name cast a dark shadow on the party, which was not dispelled for full five minutes.

After it had passed away, they were ten times merrier than before, from the mere relief of Scrooge the Baleful being done with. Bob Cratchit told them how he had a situation in his eye for Master Peter, which would bring in, if obtained, full five-and-sixpence weekly. The two young Cratchits laughed tremendously at the idea of Peter's being a man of business; and Peter himself looked thoughtfully at the fire from between his collars, as if he were deliberating what particular investments he should favour when he came into the receipt of that bewildering income. Martha, who was a poor apprentice at a milliner's, then told them what kind of work she had to do, and how many hours she worked at a stretch, and how she meant to lie abed to-morrow morning for a good long rest; to-morrow being a holiday she passed at home. Also how she had seen a countess and a lord some days before, and how the lord "was much about as tall as Peter;" at which Peter pulled up his collars so high that you couldn't have seen his head if you had been there. All this time the chestnuts and the jug went round and round; and by-and-by they had a song about a lost child travelling in the snow, from Tiny Tim, who had a plaintive little voice, and sang it very well indeed.

There was nothing of high mark in this. They were not a handsome family; they were not well dressed; their shoes were far from being waterproof; their clothes were scanty; and Peter might have known, and very likely did, the inside of a pawnbroker's. But, they were happy, grateful, pleased with one another, and contented with the time; and when they faded, and looked happier yet in the bright sprinklings of the Spirit's torch at parting, Scrooge had his eye upon them, and especially on Tiny Tim, until the last.

By this time it was getting dark, and snowing pretty heavily; and as

Scrooge and the Spirit went along the streets, the brightness of the roaring fires in kitchens, parlours, and all sorts of rooms, was wonderful. Here, the flickering of the blaze showed preparations for a cozy dinner, with hot plates baking through and through before the fire, and deep red curtains, ready to be drawn to shut out cold and darkness. There, all the children of the house were running out into the snow to meet their married sisters, brothers, cousins, uncles, aunts, and be the first to greet them. Here, again, were shadows on the window-blind of guests assembling; and there a group of handsome girls, all hooded and fur-booted, and all chattering at once, tripped lightly off to some near neighbour's house; where woe upon the single man who saw them enter—artful witches! well they knew it—in a glow!

But if you had judged from the numbers of people on their way to friendly gatherings, you might have thought that no one was at home to give them welcome when they got there, instead of every house expecting company, and piling up its fires half-chimney high. Blessings on it, how the Ghost exulted! How it bared its breadth of breast, and opened its capacious palm, and floated on outpouring, with a generous hand, its bright and harmless mirth, on everything within its reach! The very lamplighter, who ran on before dotting the dusky street with specks of light, and who was dressed to spend the evening somewhere, laughed out loudly as the Spirit passed: though little kenned the lamplighter that he had any company but Christmas!

And now, without a word of warning from the Ghost, they stood upon a bleak and desert moor, where monstrous masses of rude stone were cast about, as though it were the burial-place of giants; and water spread itself wheresoever it listed, or would have done so, but for the frost that held it prisoner; and nothing grew but moss and furze, and coarse, rank grass. Down in the west the setting sun had left a streak of fiery red, which glared upon the desolation for an instant, like a sullen eye, and frowning lower, lower, lower yet, was lost in the thick gloom of darkest night.

"What place is this?" asked Scrooge.

"A place where Miners live who labour in the bowels of the earth," returned the Spirit. "But they know me. See!"

A light shone from the window of a hut, and swiftly they advanced towards it. Passing through the wall of mud and stone, they found a cheerful company assembled round a glowing fire. An old, old man and woman, with their children and their children's children, and another generation beyond that, all decked out gayly in their holiday attire. The old man in a voice that seldom rose above the howling of the wind upon the barren waste, was singing them a Christmas song; it had been a very old song when he was a boy; and from time to time they all joined in the chorus. So surely as they raised their voices, the old man got quite blithe and loud; and so surely as they stopped, his vigour sank again.

The Spirit did not tarry here, but bade Scrooge hold his robe, and passing on above the moor, sped whither? Not to sea? To sea. To Scrooge's horror, looking back, he saw the last of the land, a frightful range of rocks, behind them; and his ears were deafened by the thundering of water, as it rolled, and roared, and raged among the dreadful caverns it had worn and fiercely tried to undermine the earth.

Built upon a dismal reef of sunken rocks, some league or so from shore, on which the waters chafed and dashed, the wild year through, there stood a solitary lighthouse. Great heaps of seaweed clung to its base, and storm-birds—born of the wind one might suppose as seaweed of the water—rose and fell about it, like the waves they skimmed.

But even here, two men who watched the light had made a fire, that through the loophole in the thick stone wall shed out a ray of brightness on the awful sea. Joining their horny hands over the rough table at which they sat, they wished each other Merry Christmas in their can of grog; and one of them: the elder, too, with his face all damaged and scarred with hard weather, as the figure head of an old ship might be: struck up a sturdy song that was like a Gale in itself.

Again the Ghost sped on, above the black and heaving sea—on, on—until, being far away, as he told Scrooge, from any shore, they lighted on a ship. They stood beside the helmsman at the wheel, the look-out in the bow, the officers who had the watch; dark, ghostly figures in their several stations; but every man among them hummed a Christmas tune, or had a Christmas thought, or spoke below his breath to his companion of some by-gone Christmas Day, with homeward hopes belonging to it. And every man on board, waking or sleeping, good or bad, had had a kinder word for another on that day than on any day in the year; and had shared to some extent in its festivities; and had remembered those he cared for at a distance, and had known that they delighted to remember him.

It was a great surprise to Scrooge, while listening to the moaning of the wind, and thinking what a solemn thing it was to move on through the lonely darkness over an unknown abyss, whose depths were secrets as profound as Death: it was a great surprise to Scrooge, while thus engaged, to hear a hearty laugh. It was a much greater surprise to Scrooge to recognize it as his own nephew's and to find himself in a bright, dry, gleaming room, with the Spirit standing smiling by his side, and looking at that same nephew with approving affability.

"Ha, ha!" laughed Scrooge's nephew. "Ha, ha, ha!"

If you should happen, by any unlikely chance, to know a man more blest in a laugh than Scrooge's nephew, all I can say is, I should like to know him too. Introduce him to me, and I'll cultivate his acquaintance.

It is a fair, even-handed, noble adjustment of things, that while there is infection in disease and sorrow, there is nothing in the world so irresistibly contagious as laughter and good-humour. When Scrooge's nephew laughed in this way: holding his sides, rolling his head, and twisting his face into the most extravagant contortions: Scrooge's niece, by marriage, laughed as heartily as he. And their assembled friends being not a bit behindhand, roared out lustily.

"Ha, ha! Ha, ha, ha, ha!"

"He said that Christmas was a humbug, as I live!" cried Scrooge's nephew. "He believed it too!"

"More shame for him, Fred!" said Scrooge's niece, indignantly. Bless those women; they never do anything by halves. They are always in earnest.

She was very pretty: exceedingly pretty. With a dimpled, surprised-looking, capital face; a ripe little mouth, that seemed made to be kissed—as no doubt it was; all kinds of good little dots about her chin, that melted into one another when she laughed; and the sunniest pair of eyes you ever saw in any little creature's head. Altogether she was what you would have called provoking, you know; but satisfactory, too. Oh, perfectly satisfactory!

"He's a comical old fellow," said Scrooge's nephew, "that's the truth; and not so pleasant as he might be. However, his offences carry their own punishment, and I have nothing to say against him."

"I'm sure he is very rich, Fred," hinted Scrooge's niece. "At least you always tell *me* so."

"What of that, my dear!" said Scrooge's nephew. "His wealth is of no use to him. He don't do any good with it. He don't make himself comfortable with it. He hasn't the satisfaction of thinking—ha, ha, ha!—that he is ever going to benefit Us with it."

"I have no patience with him," observed Scrooge's niece. Scrooge's niece's sisters, and all the other ladies, expressed the same opinion.

"Oh, I have!" said Scrooge's nephew. "I am sorry for him; I couldn't be angry with him if I tried. Who suffers by his ill whims? Himself, always. Here, he takes it into his head to dislike us, and he won't come and dine with us. What's the consequence? He don't lose much of a dinner."

"Indeed, I think he loses a very good dinner," interrupted Scrooge's niece. Everybody else said the same, and they must be allowed to have been competent judges, because they had just had dinner; and, with the dessert upon the table, were clustered round the fire, by lamplight.

"Well! I'm very glad to hear it," said Scrooge's nephew, "because I haven't any great faith in these young housekeepers. What do *you* say, Topper?"

Topper had clearly got his eye upon one of Scrooge's niece's sisters, for he answered that a bachelor was a wretched outcast, who had no right to express an opinion on the subject. Whereat Scrooge's niece's sister—the plump one with the lace tucker: not the one with the roses—blushed.

"Do go on, Fred," said Scrooge's niece, clapping her hands. "He never finishes what he begins to say! He is such a ridiculous fellow!"

Scrooge's nephew revelled in another laugh, and as it was impossible to keep the infection off; though the plump sister tried hard to do it with aromatic vinegar; his example was unanimously followed.

"I was only going to say," said Scrooge's nephew, "that the consequence of his taking a dislike to us, and not making merry with us, is, as I think, that he loses some pleasant moments, which could do him no harm. I am sure he loses pleasanter companions than he can find in his own thoughts, either in his mouldy old office, or his dusty chambers. I mean to give him the same chance every year, whether he likes it or not, for I pity him. He may rail at Christmas till he dies, but he can't help thinking better of it—I defy him—if he finds me going there, in good temper, year after year, and saying 'Uncle Scrooge, how are you?' If it only puts him in the vein to leave his poor clerk fifty pounds, *that's* something; and I think I shook him yesterday."

It was their turn to laugh now at the notion of his shaking Scrooge. But being thoroughly good-natured, and not much caring what they laughed at, so that they laughed at any rate, he encouraged them in their merriment, and passed the bottle joyously.

After tea, they had some music. For they were a musical family, and knew what they were about, when they sang a Glee or Catch, I can assure you: especially Topper, who could growl away in the bass like a good one, and never swell the large veins in his forehead, or get red in the face over it. Scrooge's niece played well upon the harp; and played among other tunes a simple little air (a mere nothing: you might learn to whistle it in two minutes), which had been familiar to the child who fetched Scrooge from the boarding-school, as he had been reminded by the Ghost of Christmas Past. When this strain of music sounded, all the things that Ghost had shown him, came upon his mind; he softened more and more; and thought that if he could have listened to it often, years ago, he might have cultivated the kindnesses of life for his own happiness with his own hands, without resorting to the sexton's spade that buried Jacob Marley.

But they didn't devote the whole evening to music. After a while they played at forfeits; for it is good to be children sometimes, and never better than at Christmas, when its mighty Founder was a child himself. Stop! There was first a game at blind-man's buff. Of course there was. And I no more believe Topper was really blind than I believe he had eyes in his boots. My opinion is, that it was a done thing between him and Scrooge's nephew: and that the Ghost of Christmas Present knew it. The way he went after that plump sister in the lace tucker, was an outrage on the credulity of human nature. Knocking down the fire-irons, tumbling over the chairs, bumping up against the piano, smothering himself among the curtains, wherever she went, there went he. He always knew where the plump sister was. He wouldn't catch anybody else. If you had fallen up against him, as some of them did, and stood there; he would have made a feint of endeavouring to seize you, which would have been an affront to your understanding; and would instantly have sidled off in the direction of the plump sister. She often cried out that it wasn't fair; and it really was not. But when at last, he caught her; when, in spite of all her silken rustlings, and her rapid flutterings past him, he got her into a corner whence there was no escape; then his conduct was the most execrable. For his pretending not to know her; his pretending that it was necessary to touch her head-dress, and further to assure himself of her identity by pressing a certain ring upon her finger, and a certain chain about her neck; was vile, monstrous! No doubt she told him her opinion of it, when, another blind man being in office, they were so very confidential together, behind the curtains.

Scrooge's niece was not one of the blind-man's buff party, but was made comfortable with a large chair and a footstool, in a snug corner, where the Ghost and Scrooge were close behind her. But she joined in the forfeits, and loved her love to admiration with all the letters of the alphabet. Likewise at the game of How, When, and Where, she was very great, and to the secret joy of Scrooge's nephew, beat her sisters hollow: though they were sharp girls too, as Topper could have told you. There might have been twenty people there, young and old, but they all played, and so did Scrooge; for, wholly forgetting in the interest he had in what was going on, that his voice made no sound in their ears, he sometimes came out with his guess quite loud, and very often guessed quite right, too; for the sharpest needle, best Whitechapel, warranted not to cut in the eye was not sharper than Scrooge; blunt as he took it in his head to be.

The Ghost was greatly pleased to find him in this mood and looked upon him with such favour that he begged like a boy to be allowed to stay until the guest departed. But this the Spirit said could not be done.

"Here is a new game," said Scrooge. "One half-hour, Spirit, only one!"

It is a Game called Yes and No, where Scrooge's nephew had to think of something, and the rest must find out what; he only answering to their questions yes or no, as the case was. The brisk fire of questioning to which he was exposed, elicited from him that he was thinking of an animal, a live animal, rather a disagreeable animal, a savage animal, an animal that growled and grunted sometimes, and talked sometimes, and lived in London, and walked about the streets, and wasn't made a show of, and wasn't led by anybody, and didn't live in a menagerie, and was never killed in a market, and was not a horse, or an ass, or a cow, or a bull, or a tiger, or a dog, or a pig, or a cat, or a bear. At every fresh question that was put to him, this nephew burst into a fresh roar of laughter; and was so inexpressibly tickled, that he was obliged to get up off the sofa and stamp. At last the plump sister, falling into a similar state, cried out:—

"I have found it out! I know what it is, Fred! I know what it is!"

"What is it?" cried Fred.

"It's your Uncle Scro-o-o-o-oge!"

Which it certainly was. Admiration was the universal sentiment, though some objected that the reply to "Is it a bear?" ought to have been "Yes;" inasmuch as an answer in the negative was sufficient to have diverted their thoughts from Mr. Scrooge, supposing they had ever had any tendency that way.

"He has given us plenty of merriment, I am sure," said Fred, "and it would be ungrateful not to drink his health. Here is a glass of mulled wine ready to our hand at the moment; and I say, 'Uncle Scrooge!'"

"Well! Uncle Scrooge!" they cried.

"A Merry Christmas and a Happy New Year to the old man, whatever he is!" said Scrooge's nephew. "He wouldn't take it from me, but may he have it, nevertheless. Uncle Scrooge!"

Uncle Scrooge had imperceptibly become so gay and light of heart, that he would have pledged the unconscious company in return, and thanked them in an inaudible speech, if the Ghost had given him time. But the whole scene passed off in the breath of the last word spoken by his nephew; and he and the Spirit were again upon their travels.

Much they saw, and far they went, and many homes they visited, but always with a happy end. The Spirit stood beside sick beds, and they were cheerful; on foreign lands, and they were close at home; by struggling men, and they were patient in their greater hope; by poverty, and it was rich. In almshouse, hospital, and jail, in misery's every refuge, where vain man in his little brief authority had not made fast the door, and barred the Spirit out, he left his blessing, and taught Scrooge his precepts.

It was a long night, if it were only a night; but Scrooge had his doubts of this, because the Christmas Holidays appeared to be condensed into the space of time they passed together. It was, strange, too, that while Scrooge remained unaltered in his outward form, the Ghost grew older, clearly older. Scrooge had observed this change, but never spoke of it, until they left a children's Twelfth Night party, when, looking at the Spirit as they stood together in an open place, he noticed that its hair was gray.

"Are spirits' lives so short?" asked Scrooge.

"My life upon this globe, is very brief," replied the Ghost. "It ends to-night."

"To-night!" cried Scrooge.

"To-night at midnight. Hark! The time is drawing near."

The chimes were ringing the three quarters past eleven at that moment.

"Forgive me if I am not justified in what I ask," said Scrooge, looking intently at the Spirit's robe, "but I see something strange, and not belonging to yourself, protruding from your skirts. Is it a foot or a claw?"

"It might be a claw, for the flesh there is upon it," was the Spirit's sorrowful reply. "Look here."

From the foldings of its robe, it brought two children; wretched, abject, frightful, hideous, miserable. They knelt down at its feet, and clung upon the outside of its garment.

"Oh, Man! look here. Look, look, down here!" exclaimed the Ghost.

They were a boy and girl. Yellow, meagre, ragged, scowling, wolfish; but prostrate, too, in their humility. Where graceful youth should have filled their features out, and touched them with its freshest tints, a stale and shrivelled hand, like that of age, had pinched, and twisted them and pulled them into shreds. Where angels might have sat enthroned, devils lurked, and glared out menacing. No change, no degradation, no perversion of humanity, in any grade, through all the mysteries of wonderful creation, has monsters half so horrible and dread.

Scrooge started back, appalled. Having them shown to him in this way, he tried to say they were fine children, but the words choked themselves, rather than be parties to a lie of such enormous magnitude.

"Spirit! are they yours?" Scrooge could say no more.

"They are Man's," said the Spirit, looking down upon them. "And they cling to me, appealing from their fathers. This boy is Ignorance. This girl is Want. Beware them both, and all of their degree, but most of all beware this boy, for on his brow I see that written which is Doom, unless the writing be erased. Deny it!" cried the Spirit, stretching out its hand toward the city. "Slander those who tell it ye! Admit it for your factious purposes, and make it worse! And bide the end!"

"Have they no refuge or resource?" cried Scrooge.

"Are there no prisons?" said the Spirit, turning on him for the last time with his own words. "Are there no workhouses?"

The bell struck twelve.

Scrooge looked about him for the Ghost, and saw it not. As the last stroke ceased to vibrate, he remembered the prediction of old Jacob Marley, and lifting up his eyes, beheld a solemn Phantom, draped and hooded, coming, like a mist along the ground, towards him.

Stave Four

The Last of the Spirits

The Phantom slowly, gravely, silently approached. When it came near him, Scrooge bent down upon his knee; for in the very air through which this Spirit moved it seemed to scatter gloom and mystery.

It was shrouded in a deep black garment, which concealed its head, its face, its form, and left nothing of it visible save one outstretched hand. But for this it would have been difficult to detach its figure from the night, and separate it from the darkness by which it was surrounded.

He felt that it was tall and stately when it came beside him, and that its mysterious presence filled him with a solemn dread. He knew no more, for the Spirit neither spoke nor moved.

"I am in the presence of the Ghost of Christmas Yet To Come?" said Scrooge.

The Spirit answered not, but pointed downward with its hand.

"You are about to show me shadows of the things that have not happened, but will happen in the time before us," Scrooge pursued. "Is that so, Spirit?"

The upper portion of the garment was contracted for an instant in its folds, as if the Spirit had inclined its head. That was the only answer he received.

Although well used to ghostly company by this time, Scrooge feared the silent shape so much that his legs trembled beneath him, and he found that he could hardly stand when he prepared to follow it. The Spirit paused a moment, as observing his condition, and giving him time to recover.

But Scrooge was all the worse for this. It thrilled him with a vague uncertain horror, to know that behind the dusky shroud there were ghostly eyes intently fixed upon him, while he, though he stretched his own to the utmost could see nothing but a spectral hand and one great heap of black.

"Ghost of the Future!" he exclaimed, "I fear you more than any Spectre I have seen. But, as I know your purpose is to do me good, and as I hope to live to be another man from what I was, I am prepared to bear you company, and do it with a thankful heart. Will you not speak to me?"

It gave him no reply. The hand was pointed straight before them.

"Lead on!" said Scrooge. "Lead on! The night is waning fast, and it is precious time to me, I know. Lead on, Spirit!"

The Phantom moved away as it had come towards him. Scrooge followed in the shadow of its dress, which bore him up, he thought, and carried him along.

They scarcely seemed to enter the city; for the city rather seemed to spring up about them, and encompass them of its own act. But there they were, in the heart of it; on 'Change, amongst the merchants; who hurried up and down, and chinked the money in their pockets, and conversed in groups, and looked at their watches, and trifled thoughtfully with their great gold seals; and so forth, as Scrooge had seen them often.

The Spirit stopped beside one little knot of business men. Observing that the hand was pointed to them, Scrooge advanced to listen to their talk.

"No," said a great fat man with a monstrous chin, "I don't know much about it, either way. I only know he's dead."

"When did he die?" inquired another.

"Last night, I believe."

"Why, what was the matter with him?" asked a third, taking a vast quantity of snuff out of a very large snuff-box. "I thought he'd never die."

"God knows," said the first, with a yawn.

"What has he done with his money?" asked a red-faced gentleman with a pendulous excrescence on the end of his nose, that shook like the gills of a turkey-cock.

"I haven't heard," said the man with the large chin, yawning again. "Left it to his Company, perhaps. He hasn't left it to *me*. That's all I know."

This pleasantry was received with a general laugh.

"It's likely to be a very cheap funeral," said the same speaker; "for upon my life I don't know of anybody to go to it. Suppose we make up a party and volunteer?"

"I don't mind going if a lunch is provided," observed the gentleman with the excrescence on his nose. "But I must be fed, if I make one."

Another laugh.

"Well, I am the most disinterested among you, after all," said the first speaker, "for I never wear black gloves, and I never eat lunch. But I'll offer to go, if anybody else will. When I come to think of it, I'm not at all sure that I wasn't his most particular friend; for we used to stop and speak whenever we met. Bye, bye!"

Speakers and listeners strolled away, and mixed with other groups. Scrooge knew the men, and looked toward the Spirit for an explanation.

The Phantom glided on into a street. Its finger pointed to two persons meeting. Scrooge listened again, thinking that the explanation might lie here.

He knew these men, also, perfectly. They were men of business: very wealthy, and of great importance. He had made a point always of standing well in their esteem: in a business point of view, that is; strictly in a business point of view.

"How are you?" said one.

"How are you?" returned the other.

"Well!" said the first. "Old Scratch has got his own at last, hey?"

"So I am told," returned the second. "Cold, isn't it?"

"Seasonable for Christmas time. You're not a skater, I suppose?"

"No. No. Something else to think of. Good morning!"

Not another word. That was their greeting, their conversation, and their parting.

Scrooge was at first inclined to be surprised that the Spirit should attach importance to conversations apparently so trivial; but feeling assured that they must have some hidden purpose, he set himself to consider what it was likely to be. They could scarcely be supposed to have any bearing, on the death of Jacob, his old partner, for that was Past, and this Ghost's province was the Future. Nor could he think of any one immediately connected with himself, to whom he could apply them. But nothing doubting that to whomsoever they applied they had some latent moral for his own improvement, he resolved to treasure up every word he heard, and everything he saw; and especially to observe the shadow of himself when it appeared. For he had an expectation that the conduct of his future self would give him the clew he missed, and would render the solution of these riddles easy.

He looked about in that very place for his own image; but another man stood in his accustomed corner, and though the clock pointed to his usual time of day for being there, he saw no likeness of himself among the multitudes that poured in through the Porch. It gave him little surprise, however; for he had been revolving in his mind a change of life, and thought and hoped he saw his newborn resolutions carried out in this.

Quiet and dark, beside him stood the Phantom, with its outstretched hand. When he aroused himself from his thoughtful quest, he fancied from the turn of the hand, and its situation in reference to himself, that the Unseen Eyes were looking at him keenly. It made him shudder, and feel very cold.

They left the busy scene, and went into an obscure part of the town, where Scrooge had never penetrated before, although he recognized its situation, and its bad repute. The ways were foul and narrow; the shops and houses wretched; the people half-naked, drunken, slipshod, ugly. Alleys and archways, like so many cesspools, disgorged their offences of smell, and dirt, and life, upon the straggling streets; and the whole quarter reeked with crime, with filth, and misery.

Far in this den of infamous resort, there was a low-browed, beetling shop, below a pent-house roof, where iron, old rags, bottles, bones, and greasy offal, were bought. Upon the floor within, were piled up heaps of rusty keys, nails, chains, hinges, files, scales, weights, and refuse iron of all kinds. Secrets that few would like to scrutinize were bred and hidden in mountains of unseemly rags, masses of corrupt fat, and sepulchres of bones. Sitting in among the wares he dealt in, by a charcoal-stove, made of old bricks, was a gray-haired rascal, nearly seventy years of age; who had screened himself from the cold air without, by a frowzy curtaining of miscellaneous tatters, hung upon a line; and smoked his pipe in all the luxury of calm retirement.

Scrooge and the Phantom came into the presence of this man, just as a woman with a heavy bundle slunk into the shop. But she had scarcely entered, when another woman, similarly laden, came in too; and she was closely followed by a man in faded black, who was no less startled by the sight of them, than they had been upon the recognition of each other. After a short period of blank astonishment, in which the old man with the pipe had joined them, they all three burst into a laugh.

"Let the charwoman alone to be the first!" cried she who had entered first. "Let the laundress alone to be the second; and let the undertaker's man alone to be the third. Look here, old Joe, here's a chance! If we haven't all three met here without meaning it!"

"You couldn't have met in a better place," said old Joe, removing his pipe from his mouth. "Come into the parlour. You were made free of it long ago, you know; and the other two an't strangers. Stop till I shut the door of the shop. Ah! How it skreeks! There an't such a rusty bit of metal in the place as its own hinges, I believe; and I'm sure there's no such old bones here, as mine. Ha, ha! We're all suitable to our calling, we're well matched. Come into the parlour. Come into the parlour."

The parlour was the space behind the screen of rags. The old man raked the fire together with an old stair-rod and having trimmed his smoky lamp (for it was night) with the stem of his pipe, put it in his mouth again.

While he did this, the woman who had already spoken threw her bundle on the floor, and sat down in a flaunting manner on a stool; crossing her elbows on her knees, and looking with a bold defiance at the other two.

"What odds then! What odds, Mrs. Dilber?" said the woman. "Every person has a right to take care of themselves. *He* always did!"

"That's true, indeed!" said the laundress. "No man more so."

"Why, then, don't stand staring as if you was afraid, woman; who's the wiser? We're not going to pick holes in each other's coats, I suppose?"

"No, indeed!" said Mrs. Dilber and the man together. "We should hope not."

"Very well, then!" cried the woman. "That's enough. Who's the worse for the loss of a few things like these? Not a dead man, I suppose."

"No, indeed," said Mrs. Dilber, laughing.

"If he wanted to keep 'em after he was dead, a wicked old screw," pursued the woman, "why wasn't he natural in his lifetime? If he had been, he'd have had somebody to look after him when he was struck with Death, instead of lying gasping out his last there, alone by himself."

"It's the truest word that ever was spoke," said Mrs. Dilber. "It's a judgment on him."

"I wish it was a little heavier one," replied the woman; "and it should have been, you may depend upon it, if I could have laid my hands on anything else. Open that bundle, old Joe, and let me know the value of it. Speak out plain. I'm not afraid to be the first, nor afraid for them to see it. We knew pretty well that we were helping ourselves, before we met here, I believe. It's no sin. Open the bundle, Joe."

But the gallantry of her friends would not allow of this; and the man in faded black, mounting the breach first, produced *his* plunder. It was not extensive. A seal or two, a pencil-case, a pair of sleeve-buttons, and a brooch of no great value, were all. They were severally examined and appraised by old Joe, who chalked the sums he was disposed to give for each, upon the wall, and added them up into a total when he found there was nothing more to come.

"That's your account," said Joe, "and I wouldn't give another sixpence, if I was to be boiled for not doing it. Who's next?"

Mrs. Dilber was next. Sheets and towels, a little wearing apparel, two old-fashioned silver teaspoons, a pair of sugar-tongs, and a few boots. Her account was stated on the wall in the same manner.

"I always give too much to ladies. It's a weakness of mine, and that's the way I ruin myself," said old Joe. "That's your account. If you asked me for another penny, and made it an open question, I'd repent of being so liberal and knock off half-a-crown."

"And now undo *my* bundle, Joe," said the first woman.

Joe went down on his knees for the greater convenience of opening it, and having unfastened a great many knots, dragged out a large and heavy roll of some dark stuff.

"What do you call this?" said Joe. "Bed-curtains!"

"Ah!" returned the woman, laughing and leaning forward on her crossed arms. "Bed-curtains!"

"You don't mean to say you took 'em down, rings and all, with him lying there?" said Joe.

"Yes I do," replied the woman. "Why not?"

"You were born to make your fortune," said Joe, "and you'll certainly do it."

"I certainly shan't hold my hand, when I can get anything in it by reaching it out, for the sake of such a man as He was, I promise you, Joe," returned the woman coolly. "Don't drop that oil upon the blankets, now."

"His blankets?" asked Joe.

"Whose else's do you think?" replied the woman. "He isn't likely to take cold without 'em, I dare say."

"I hope he didn't die of anything catching? Eh?" said old Joe, stopping in his work, and looking up.

"Don't you be afraid of that," returned the woman. "I an't so fond of his company that I'd loiter about him for such things, if he did. Ah! you may look through that shirt till your eyes ache; but you won't find a hole in it, nor a threadbare place. It's the best he had, and a fine one too. They'd have wasted it, if it hadn't been for me."

"What do you call wasting of it?" asked old Joe.

"Putting it on him to be buried in, to be sure," replied the woman with a laugh. "Somebody was fool enough to do it, but I took it off again. If calico ain't good enough for such a purpose, it isn't good enough for anything. It's quite as becoming to the body. He can't look uglier than he did in that one."

Scrooge listened to this dialogue in horror. As they sat grouped about their spoil, in the scanty light afforded by the old man's lamp, he viewed them with a detestation and disgust, which could hardly have been greater, though they had been obscene demons, marketing the corpse itself.

"Ha, ha!" laughed the same woman, when old Joe, producing a flannel bag with money in it, told out their several gains upon the ground. "This is the end of it, you see! He frightened every one away from him when he was alive, to profit us when he was dead! Ha, ha, ha!"

"Spirit!" said Scrooge, shuddering from head to foot. "I see, I see. The case of this unhappy man might be my own. My life tends that way, now. Merciful Heaven, what is this!"

He recoiled in terror, for the scene had changed, and now he almost touched a bed: a bare, uncurtained bed: on which, beneath a ragged sheet, there lay a something covered up, which, though it was dumb, announced itself in awful language.

The room was very dark, too dark to be observed with any accuracy, though Scrooge glanced round it in obedience to a secret impulse, anxious to know what kind of room it was. A pale light, rising in the outer air, fell straight upon the bed; and on it, plundered and bereft, unwatched, unwept, uncared for, was the body of this man.

Scrooge glanced towards the Phantom. Its steady hand was pointed to the head. The cover was so carelessly adjusted that the slightest raising of it, the motion of a finger upon Scrooge's part, would have disclosed the face. He thought of it, felt how easy it would be to do, and longed to do it; but had no more power to withdraw the veil than to dismiss the spectre at his side.

Oh cold, cold, rigid, dreadful Death, set up thine altar here, and dress it with such terrors as thou hast at thy command: for this is thy dominion! But of the loved, revered, and honoured head, thou canst not turn one hair to thy dread purposes, or make one feature odious. It is not that the hand is heavy and will fall down when released; it it not that the heart and pulse are still; but that the hand WAS open, generous, and true; the heart brave, warm, and tender; and the pulse a man's. Strike, Shadow, strike! And see his good deeds springing from the wound, to sow the world with life immortal!

No voice pronounced these words in Scrooge's ears, and yet he heard them when he looked upon the bed. He thought, if this man could be raised up now, what would be his foremost thoughts? Avarice, hard dealing, griping cares? They have brought him to a rich end, truly!

He lay in the dark empty house, with not a man, a woman, or a child, to say that he was kind to me in this or that, and for the memory of one kind word I will be kind to him. A cat was tearing at the door, and there was a sound of gnawing rats beneath the hearth-stone. What *they* wanted in the room of death, and why they were so restless and disturbed, Scrooge did not dare to think.

"Spirit!" he said, "this is a fearful place. In leaving it, I shall not leave its lesson, trust me. Let us go!"

Still the Ghost pointed with an unmoved finger to the head.

"I understand you," Scrooge returned, "and I would do it, if I could. But I have not the power, Spirit. I have not the power."

Again it seemed to look upon him.

"If there is any person in the town, who feels emotion caused by this man's death," said Scrooge quite agonized, "show that person to me, Spirit, I beseech you!"

The Phantom spread its dark robe before him for a moment, like a wing; and withdrawing it, revealed a room by daylight, where a mother and her children were.

She was expecting some one, and with anxious eagerness; for she walked up and down the room; started at every sound; looked out from the window; glanced at the clock; tried, but in vain, to work with her needle; and could hardly bear the voices of the children in their play.

At length the long-expected knock was heard. She hurried to the door, and met her husband; a man whose face was careworn and depressed, though he was young. There was a remarkable expression in it now; a kind of serious delight of which he felt ashamed, and which he struggled to repress.

He sat down to the dinner that had been hoarding for him by the fire; and when she asked him faintly what news (which was not until after a long silence), he appeared embarrassed how to answer.

"Is it good," she said, "or bad?"—to help him.

"Bad," he answered.

"We are quite ruined?"

"No. There is hope yet, Caroline."

"If *he* relents," she said, amazed, "there is! Nothing is past hope, if such a miracle has happened."

"He is past relenting," said her husband. "He is dead."

She was a mild and patient creature if her face spoke truth; but she was thankful in her soul to hear it, and she said so, with clasped hands. She prayed forgiveness the next moment, and was sorry; but the first was the emotion of the heart.

"What the half-drunken woman whom I told you of last night, said to me, when I tried to see him and obtain a week's delay; and what I thought was a mere excuse to avoid me; turns out to have been quite true. He was not only very ill, but dying, then."

"To whom will our debt be transferred?"

"I don't know. But before that time we shall be ready with the money; and even though we were not, it would be bad fortune indeed to find so merciless a creditor in his successor. We may sleep to-night with light hearts, Caroline!"

Yes. Soften it as they would, their hearts were lighter. The children's faces, hushed, and clustered round to hear what they so little understood, were brighter; and it was a happier house for this man's death! The only emotion that the Ghost could show him, caused by the event, was one of pleasure.

"Let me see some tenderness connected with a death," said Scrooge; "or that dark chamber, Spirit, which we left just now, will be forever present to me."

The Ghost conducted him through several streets familiar to his feet; and as they went along, Scrooge looked here and there to find himself, but nowhere was he to be seen. They entered poor Bob Cratchit's house; the dwelling he had visited before; and found the mother and the children seated round the fire.

Quiet. Very quiet. The noisy little Cratchits were as still as statues in one corner, and sat looking up at Peter, who had a book before him. The mother and her daughters were engaged in sewing. But surely they were very quiet!

"'And he took a child, and set him in the midst of them.'"

Where had Scrooge heard those words? He had not dreamed them. The boy must have read them out, as he and the Spirit crossed the threshold. Why did he not go on?

The mother laid her work upon the table, and put her hand up to her face.

"The colour hurts my eyes," she said.

The colour? Ah, poor Tiny Tim!

"They're better now again," said Cratchit's wife. "It makes them weak by candlelight; and I wouldn't show weak eyes to your father when he comes home, for the world. It must be near his time."

"Past it rather," Peter answered, shutting up his book. "But I think he's walked a little slower than he used, these few last evenings, mother."

They were very quiet again. At last she said, and in a steady cheerful voice, that only faltered once:—

"I have known him walk with—I have known him walk with Tiny Tim upon his shoulder, very fast indeed."

"And so have I," cried Peter. "Often."

"And so have I," exclaimed another. So had all.

"But he was so very light to carry," she resumed, intent upon her work, "and his father loved him so, that it was no trouble—no trouble. And there is your father at the door!"

She hurried out to meet him; and little Bob in his comforter—he had need of it, poor fellow—came in. His tea was ready for him on the hob, and they all tried who should help him to it most. Then the two young Cratchits got upon his knees and laid, each child a little cheek, against his face, as if they said, "Don't mind it, father. Don't be grieved!"

Bob was very cheerful with them, and spoke pleasantly to all the family. He looked at the work upon the table, and praised the industry and speed of Mrs. Cratchit and the girls. They would be done long before Sunday he said.

"Sunday! You went to-day, then, Robert?" said his wife.

"Yes, my dear," returned Bob. "I wish you could have gone. It would have done you good to see how green a place it is. But you'll see it often. I promised him that I would walk there on a Sunday. My little, little child!" cried Bob. "My little child!"

He broke down all at once. He couldn't help it. If he could have helped it, he and his child would have been farther apart perhaps than they were.

He left the room, and went up stairs into the room above, which was lighted cheerfully, and hung with Christmas. There was a chair set close beside the child, and there were signs of some one having been there lately. Poor Bob sat down in it, and when he had thought a little and composed himself, he kissed the little face. He was reconciled to what had happened, and went down again quite happy.

They drew about the fire, and talked; the girls and mother working still. Bob told them of the extraordinary kindness of Mr. Scrooge's nephew, whom he had scarcely seen but once, and who, meeting him in the street that day, and seeing that he looked a little—"just a little down you know," said Bob, inquired what had happened to distress him. "On which," said Bob, "for he is the pleasantest-spoken gentleman you ever heard, I told him. 'I am heartily sorry for it, Mr. Cratchit,' he said, 'and heartily sorry for your good wife.' By the bye, how he ever knew *that,* I don't know."

"Knew what, my dear?"

"Why, that you were a good wife," replied Bob.

"Everybody knows that!" said Peter.

"Very well observed, my boy!" cried Bob. "I hope they do. 'Heartily sorry,' he said, 'for your good wife. If I can be of service to you in any way,' he said, giving me his card, 'that's where I live. Pray come to me.' Now, it wasn't," cried Bob, "for the sake of anything he might be able to do for us, so much as for his kind way, that this was quite delightful. It really seemed as if he had known our Tiny Tim, and felt with us."

"I'm sure he's a good soul!" said Mrs. Cratchit.

"You would be surer of it, my dear," returned Bob, "if you saw and spoke to him. I shouldn't be at all surprised, mark what I say, if he got Peter a better situation."

"Only hear that, Peter," said Mrs. Cratchit.

"And then," cried one of the girls, "Peter will be keeping company with some one, and setting up for himself."

"Get along with you!" retorted Peter, grinning.

"It's just as likely as not," said Bob, "one of these days; though there's plenty of time for that, my dear. But however and whenever we part from one another, I am sure we shall none of us forget poor Tiny Tim—shall we—or this first parting that there was among us?"

"Never, father!" cried they all.

"And I know," said Bob, "I know, my dears, that when we recollect how patient and how mild he was; although he was a little, little child; we shall not quarrel easily among ourselves, and forget poor Tiny Tim in doing it."

"No, never, father!" they all cried again.

"I am very happy," said little Bob, "I am very happy!"

Mrs. Cratchit kissed him, his daughters kissed him, the two young Cratchits kissed him, and Peter and himself shook hands. Spirit of Tiny Tim, thy childish essence was from God!

"Spectre," said Scrooge, "something informs me that our parting moment is at hand. I know it, but I know not how. Tell me what man that was whom we saw lying dead?"

The Ghost of Christmas Yet To Come conveyed him, as before—though at a different time, he thought: indeed, there seemed no order in these latter visions, save that they were in the Future—into the resorts of business men, but showed him not himself. Indeed, the Spirit did not stay for anything, but went straight on, as to the end just now desired, until besought by Scrooge to tarry for a moment.

"This court," said Scrooge, "through which we hurry now, is where my place of occupation is, and has been for a length of time. I see the house. Let me behold what I shall be, in days to come!"

The Spirit stopped; the hand was pointed elsewhere.

"The house is yonder," Scrooge exclaimed. "Why do you point away?"

The inexorable finger underwent no change.

Scrooge hastened to the window of his office, and looked in. It was an office still, but not his. The furniture was not the same, and the figure in the chair was not himself. The Phantom pointed as before.

He joined it once again, and wondering why and whither he had gone, accompanied it until they reached an iron gate. He paused to look round before entering.

A churchyard. Here, then, the wretched man whose name he had now to learn, lay underneath the ground. It was a worthy place. Walled in by houses; overrun by grass and weeds, the growth of vegetation's death, not life; choked up with too much burying; fat with repleted appetite. A worthy place!

The Spirit stood among the graves, and pointed down to One. He advanced towards it trembling. The Phantom was exactly as it had been, but he dreaded that he saw new meaning in its solemn shape.

"Before I draw nearer to that stone to which you point," said Scrooge, "answer me one question. Are these the shadows of the things that Will be, or are they shadows of things that May be, only?"

Still the Ghost pointed downward to the grave by which it stood.

"Men's courses will foreshadow certain ends, to which, if persevered in, they must lead," said Scrooge. "But if the courses be departed from, the ends will change. Say it is thus with what you show me!"

The Spirit was immovable as ever.

Scrooge crept towards it, trembling as he went; and following the finger, read upon the stone of the neglected grave his own name, EBENEZER SCROOGE.

"Am *I* that man who lay upon the bed?" he cried, upon his knees.

The finger pointed from the grave to him, and back again.

"No, Spirit! Oh, no, no!"

The finger still was there.

"Spirit!" he cried, tight clutching at its robe, "hear me! I am not the man I was. I will not be the man I must have been but for this intercourse. Why show me this, if I am past all hope!"

For the first time the hand appeared to shake.

"Good Spirit," he pursued, as down upon the ground he fell before it: "Your nature intercedes for me, and pities me. Assure me that I yet may change these shadows you have shown me, by an altered life!"

The kind hand trembled.

"I will honour Christmas in my heart, and try to keep it all the year. I will live in the Past, the Present, and the Future. The Spirits of all Three shall strive within me. I will not shut out the lessons that they teach. Oh, tell me I may sponge away the writing on this stone!"

In his agony, he caught the spectral hand. It sought to free itself, but he was strong in his entreaty, and detained it. The Spirit, stronger yet, repulsed him.

Holding up his hands in one last prayer to have his fate reversed, he saw an alteration in the Phantom's hood and dress. It shrank, collapsed, and dwindled down to a bedpost.

Stave Five

THE END OF IT

Yes! and the bedpost was his own. The bed was his own, the room was his own. Best and happiest of all, the Time before his was his own, to make amends in!

"I will live in the Past, the Present, and the Future!" Scrooge repeated, as he scrambled out of bed. "The Spirits of all Three shall strive within me. Oh Jacob Marley! Heaven, and the Christmas Time be praised for this! I say it on my knees, old Jacob, on my knees!"

He was so fluttered and so glowing with his good intentions, that his broken voice would scarcely answer to his call. He had been sobbing violently in his conflict with the Spirit, and his face was wet with tears.

"They are not torn down," cried Scrooge, folding one of his bed-curtains in his arms, "they are not torn down, rings and all. They are here: I am here: the shadows of the things that would have been, may be dispelled. They will be. I know they will!"

His hands were busy with his garments all this time: turning them inside out, putting them on upside down, tearing them, mislaying them, making them parties to every kind of extravagance.

"I don't know what to do!" cried Scrooge, laughing and crying in the same breath; and making a perfect Laocoön of himself with his stockings. "I am as light as a feather, I am as happy as an angel, I am as merry as a schoolboy. I am as giddy as a drunken man. A Merry Christmas to everybody! A Happy New Year to all the world. Hallo here! Whoop! Hallo!"

He had frisked into the sitting room, and was now standing there: perfectly winded.

"There's the saucepan that the gruel was in!" cried Scrooge, starting off again and frisking round the fireplace. "There's the door, by which the Ghost of Jacob Marley entered! There's the corner where the Ghost of Christmas Present sat! There's the window where I saw the wandering Spirits! It's all right, it's all true, it all happened. Ha, ha, ha!"

Really, for a man who had been out of practice for so many years, it was a splendid laugh, a most illustrious laugh. The father of a long, long line of brilliant laughs!

"I don't know what day of the month it is!" said Scrooge. "I don't know how long I've been among the Spirits. I don't know anything. I'm quite a baby. Never mind. I don't care. I'd rather be a baby. Hallo! Whoop! Hallo here!"

He was checked in his transports by the churches ringing out the lustiest peals he had ever heard. Clash, clang, hammer, ding, dong, bell. Bell, dong, ding, hammer, clang, clash! Oh, glorious, glorious!

Running to the window, he opened it, and put out his head. No fog, no mist; clear, bright, jovial, stirring, cold; cold, piping for the blood to dance to; golden sunlight; heavenly sky; sweet fresh air; merry bells. Oh, glorious. Glorious!

"What's to-day?" cried Scrooge, calling downward to a boy in Sunday clothes, who perhaps had loitered in to look about him.

"EH?" returned the boy, with all his might of wonder.

"What's to-day, my fine fellow?" said Scrooge.

"To-day!" replied the boy. "Why, CHRISTMAS DAY."

"It's Christmas Day!" said Scrooge to himself. "I haven't missed it. The Spirits have done it all in one night. They can do anything they like. Of course they can. Of course they can. Hallo, my fine fellow?"

"Hallo!" returned the boy.

"Do you know the Poulterer's, in the next street but one, at the corner?" Scrooge inquired.

"I should hope I did," replied the lad.

"An intelligent boy!" said Scrooge. "A remarkable boy! Do you know whether they've sold the prize Turkey that was hanging up there? Not the little prize Turkey: the big one?"

"What, the one as big as me?" returned the boy.

"What a delightful boy!" said Scrooge. "It's a pleasure to talk to him. Yes, my buck!"

"It's hanging there now," replied the boy.

"Is it?" said Scrooge. "Go and buy it."

"Walk-ER!" exclaimed the boy.

"No, no," said Scrooge, "I am in earnest. Go and buy it, and tell 'em to bring it here, that I may give them the direction where to take it. Come back with the man, and I'll give you a shilling. Come back with him in less than five minutes, and I'll give you half-a-crown!"

The boy was off like a shot. He must have had a steady hand at a trigger who could have got a shot off half so fast.

"I'll send it to Bob Cratchit's!" whispered Scrooge, rubbing his hands, and splitting with a laugh. "He shan't know who sends it. It's twice the size of Tiny Tim. Joe Miller never made such a joke as sending it to Bob's will be!"

The hand in which he wrote the address was not a steady one, but write it he did, somehow, and went down stairs to open the street door, ready for the coming of the poulterer's man. As he stood there, waiting his arrival, the knocker caught his eye.

"I shall love it, as long as I live!" cried Scrooge, patting it with his hand. "I scarcely ever looked at it before. What an honest expression it has in its face! It's a wonderful knocker!—Here's the Turkey. Hallo! Whoop! How are you! Merry Christmas!"

It *was* a Turkey! He could never have stood upon his legs, that bird. He would have snapped 'em short off in a minute, like sticks of sealing-wax.

"Why, it's impossible to carry that to Camden Town," said Scrooge. "You must have a cab."

The chuckle with which he said this, and the chuckle with which he paid for the turkey, and the chuckle with which he paid for the cab, and the chuckle with which he recompensed the boy, were only to be exceeded by the chuckle with which he sat down breathless in his chair again, and chuckled till he cried.

Shaving was not an easy task, for his hand continued to shake very much; and shaving requires attention, even when you don't dance while you are at it. But if he had cut the end of his nose off, he would have put a piece of sticking-plaster over it, and been quite satisfied.

He dressed himself "all in his best," and at last got out into the streets. The people were by this time pouring forth, as he had seen them with the Ghost of Christmas Present; and walking with his hands behind him, Scrooge regarded every one with a delighted smile. He looked so irresistibly pleasant, in a word, that three or four good-humoured fellows said, "Good morning, Sir! A Merry Christmas to you!" And Scrooge said often afterwards, that of all the blithe sounds he had ever heard, those were the blithest in his ears.

He had not gone far, when coming on towards him he beheld the portly gentleman, who had walked into his counting-house the day before and said, "Scrooge and Marley's, I believe?" It sent a pang across his heart to think how this old gentleman would look upon him when they met; but he knew what path lay straight before him, and he took it.

"My dear Sir," said Scrooge, quickening his pace, and taking the old gentleman by both his hands. "How do you do? I hope you succeeded yesterday. It was very kind of you. A Merry Christmas to you, Sir!"

"Mr. Scrooge?"

"Yes," said Scrooge. "That is my name, and I fear it may not be pleasant to you. Allow me to ask your pardon. And will you have the goodness"—here Scrooge whispered in his ear.

"Lord bless me!" cried the gentleman, as if his breath were gone. "My dear Mr. Scrooge, are you serious?"

"If you please," said Mr. Scrooge. "Not a farthing less. A great many back-payments are included in it, I assure you. Will you do me that favour?"

"My dear Sir," said the other, shaking hands with him. "I don't know what to say to such munifi—"

"Don't say anything, please," retorted Scrooge. "Come and see me. Will you come and see me?"

"I will!" cried the old gentleman. And it was clear he meant to do it.

"Thank'ee," said Scrooge. "I am much obliged to you. I thank you fifty times. Bless you!"

He went to church, and walked about the streets, and watched the people hurrying to and fro, and patted children on the head, and questioned beggars, and looked down into the kitchens of houses, and up to the windows; and found that everything could yield him pleasure. He had never dreamed that any walk—that anything—could give him so much happiness. In the afternoon, he turned his steps towards his nephew's house.

He passed the door a dozen times, before he had the courage to go up and knock. But he made a dash, and did it:—

"Is your master at home, my dear?" said Scrooge to the girl. Nice girl! Very.

"Yes, Sir."

"Where is he, my love?" said Scrooge.

"He's in the dining-room, Sir, along with mistress. I'll show you up stairs, if you please."

"Thank'ee. He knows me," said Scrooge, with his hand already on the dining-room lock. "I'll go in here, my dear."

He turned it gently, and sidled his face in round the door. They were looking at the table (which was spread out in great array); for these young housekeepers are always nervous on such points, and like to see that everything is right.

"Fred!" said Scrooge.

Dear heart alive, how his niece by marriage started! Scrooge had forgotten, for the moment, about her sitting in the corner with the footstool, or he wouldn't have done it, on any account.

"Why, bless my soul!" cried Fred, "who's that?"

"It's I. Your uncle Scrooge. I have come to dinner. Will you let me in, Fred?"

Let him in! It is a mercy he didn't shake his arm off. He was at home in five minutes. Nothing could be heartier. His niece looked just the same. So did Topper when *he* came. So did the plump sister, when *she* came. So did every one when *they* came. Wonderful party, wonderful games, wonderful unanimity, won-der-ful happiness!

But he was early at the office next morning. Oh, he was early there. If he could only be there first, and catch Bob Cratchit coming late! That was the thing he had set his heart upon.

And he did it; yes he did! The clock struck nine. No Bob. A quarter past. No Bob. He was full eighteen minutes and a half behind his time. Scrooge sat with his door wide open, that he might see him come into the Tank.

His hat was off, before he opened the door; his comforter too. He was on his stool in a jiffy; driving away with his pen, as if he were trying to overtake nine o'clock.

"Hallo!" growled Scrooge, in his accustomed voice as near as he could feign it. "What do you mean by coming here at this time of day?"

"I am very sorry, Sir," said Bob. "I *am* behind my time."

"You are?" repeated Scrooge. "Yes. I think you are. Step this way, Sir, if you please."

"It's only once a year, Sir," pleaded Bob, appearing from the Tank. "It shall not be repeated. I was making rather merry yesterday, Sir."

"Now, I'll tell you what, my friend," said Scrooge, "I am not going to stand this sort of thing any longer. And therefore," he continued, leaping from his stool, and giving Bob such a dig in the waistcoat that he staggered back into the Tank again: "and therefore I am about to raise your salary!"

Bob trembled, and got a little nearer to the ruler. He had a momentary idea of knocking Scrooge down with it; holding him; and calling to the people in the court for help and a strait waistcoat.

"A Merry Christmas, Bob!" said Scrooge, with an earnestness that could not be mistaken, as he clapped him on the back. "A merrier Christmas, Bob, my good fellow, than I have given you for many a year! I'll raise your salary, and endeavour to assist your struggling family, and we will discuss your affairs this very afternoon, over a Christmas bowl of smoking bishop, Bob! Make up the fires, and buy another coal-scuttle before you dot another i, Bob Cratchit!"

Scrooge was better than his word. He did it all, and infinitely more; and to Tiny Tim, who did NOT die, he was a second father. He became as good a friend, as good a master, and as good a man, as the good old city knew, or any other good old city, town, or borough, in the good old world. Some people laughed to see the alteration in him, but he let them laugh, and little heeded them; for he was wise enough to know that nothing ever happened on this globe, for good, at which some people did not have their fill of laughter in the outset; and knowing that such as these would be blind anyway, he thought it quite as well that they should wrinkle up their eyes in grins, as have the malady in less attractive forms. His own heart laughed: and that was quite enough for him.

He had no further intercourse with Spirits, but lived upon the Total Abstinence Principle, ever afterwards; and it was always said of him, that he knew how to keep Christmas well, if any man alive possessed the knowledge. May that be truly said of us, and all of us! And so, as Tiny Tim observed, God Bless Us, Every One!

Pie Dance

by Molly Giles

Introduced by Amy Tan

SOME TIME AGO, I WENT TO MY FIRST WRITERS' WORKSHOP, THE Squaw Valley Community of Writers. In part I wanted to see if I had what it takes to write fiction. I chose Squaw Valley because one of the staff was a writer and teacher named Molly Giles. I had read a story of hers called "Self-Defense" in *Editor's Choice* and was hoping I might be able to wangle some advice from her.

At Squaw, Molly read aloud a story called "Pie Dance." I sat in the darkened theater along with everyone else and I was immediately caught by the first line of the story: "I don't know what to do about my husband's new wife."

This same wry and observant voice then proceeds to lay out the situation in matter-of-fact fashion, as if she were setting a table with everyday plates and stainless. But what a feast of images and emotions Molly Giles is capable of conjuring up! In a single paragraph, there's dramatic tension between two characters, a sense of place, humor, creaks and clicks, harsh light, *and* a mutt who goes on point.

What follows seems to be a conversation about nothing in particular, polite offers from the ex-wife, polite refusals from the new wife. The chitchat goes down easily enough, but the uneasiness and fear of the new wife is palpable and the narrator knows it. This is a narrator who has the power and precision of a brain surgeon; if she wants, she can go beneath the surface and expose a nerve. Instead, she stands on her porch and merely observes her successor with analytic patience: every small gesture, every awkward pause, her "layered look," her heavy bottom. Curiously, she has enough sympathy for the new wife to want to tell her "who among us is perfect, Pauline."

The story takes place almost entirely outside on the porch and in bright sunlight that hurts the eyes. And in the end, we see what lies within the dark house, within the heart of the narrator.

It's a wonderful story, and to my mind perfectly crafted. When Molly Giles finished reading "Pie Dance," I knew without a doubt that I didn't have all it takes to be a fiction writer. But hearing that story, I also knew—as deeply as you can know something about yourself—that it would be worth a lifetime to try.

Pie Dance

Molly Giles

I don't know what to do about my husband's new wife. She won't come in. She sits on the front porch and smokes. She won't knock or ring the bell, and the only way I know she's there at all is because the dog points in the living room. The minute I see Stray standing with one paw up and his tail straight out I say, "Shhh. It's Pauline." I stroke his coarse fur and lean on the broom and we wait. We hear the creak of a board, the click of a purse, a cigarette being lit, a sad, tiny cough. At last I give up and open the door. "Pauline?" The afternoon light hurts my eyes. "Would you like to come in?"

"No," says Pauline.

Sometimes she sits on the stoop, picking at the paint, and sometimes she sits on the edge of an empty planter box. Today she's perched on the railing. She frowns when she sees me and lifts her small chin. She wears the same black velvet jacket she always wears, the same formal silk blouse, the same huge dark glasses. "Just passing by," she explains.

I nod. Pauline lives thirty miles to the east, in the city, with Konrad. "Passing by" would take her one toll bridge, one freeway, and two back-country roads from their flat. But lies are the least of our problems, Pauline's and mine, so I nod again, bunch my bathrobe a little tighter around my waist, try to cover one bare foot with the other, and repeat my invitation. She shakes her head so vigorously the railing lurches. "Konrad," she says in her high young voice, "expects me. You know how he is."

I do, or I did—I'm not sure I know now—but I nod, and she flushes, staring so hard at something right behind me that I turn too and tell Stray, who is still posing in the doorway, to cancel the act and come say hello. Stray drops his front paw and pads forward, nose to the ground. Pauline blows cigarette smoke into the wisteria vine and draws her feet close to the railing. "What kind is it?" she asks, looking down.

I tell her we don't know, we think he's part Irish setter and part golden retriever; what happened was someone drove him out here to the country and abandoned him and he howled outside our house until one of the children let him come in. Pauline nods as if this were very interesting and says, "Oh really?" but I stop abruptly; I know I am boring. I am growing dull as Mrs. Dixon, Konrad's mother, who goes on and on about her poodle and who, for a time, actually sent us birthday cards and Christmas presents signed with a poodle paw print. I clasp the broom with both hands and gaze fondly at Stray. I am too young to love a dog; at the same time I am beginning to realize there isn't that much to love in this world. So when Pauline says, "Can it do tricks?" I try to keep the rush of passion from my eyes; I try to keep my voice down.

"He can dance," I admit.

"How great," she says, swaying on the railing. "Truly great."

"Yes," I agree. I do not elaborate. I do not tell Pauline that at night, when the children are asleep, I often dance with him. Nor do I confess that the two of us, Stray and I, have outgrown the waltz and are deep into reggae. Stray is a gay and affable partner, willing to learn, delighted to lead. I could boast about him forever, but Pauline, I see, already looks tired. "And you?" I ask. "How have you been?"

For answer she coughs, flexing her small hand so the big gold wedding ring flashes a lot in the sun; she smiles for the first time and makes a great show of pounding her heart as she coughs. She doesn't look well. She's lost weight since the marriage and seems far too pale. "Water?" I ask. "Or how about tea? We have peppermint, jasmine, mocha, and lemon."

"Oh no!" she cries, choking.

"We've honey. We've cream."

"Oh no! But thank you! So much!"

After a bit she stops coughing and resumes smoking and I realize we both are staring at Stray again. "People," Pauline says with a sigh, "are so cruel. Don't you think?"

I do; I think yes. I tell her Stray was half-starved and mangy when we found him; he had been beaten and kicked, but we gave him raw eggs and corn oil for his coat and had his ear sewn up and took him to the vet's for all the right shots and look at him now. We continue to look at him now. Stray, glad to be noticed, and flattered, immediately trots to the driveway and pees on the wheel of Pauline's new Mustang. "Of course," I complain, "he's worse than a child."

Pauline bows her head and picks one of Stray's hairs off her black velvet jacket. "I guess," she says. She smiles. She really has a very nice smile. It was the first thing I noticed when Konrad introduced us; it's a wide smile, glamorous and trembly, like a movie star's. I once dreamt I had to kiss her and it wasn't bad, I didn't mind. In the dream Konrad held us by the hair with our faces shoved together. It was claustrophobic but not at all disgusting. I remember thinking, when I awoke: Poor Konrad, he doesn't even know how to punish people, and it's a shame, because he wants to so much. Later I noticed that Pauline's lips, when she's not smiling, are exactly like Konrad's, full and loose and purplish, sad. I wonder if when they kiss they feel they're making a mirror; I would. Whether the rest of Pauline mirrors Konrad is anyone's guess. I have never seen her eyes, of course, because of the dark glasses. Her hair is blond and so fine that the tips of her ears poke through. She is scarcely taller than one of the children, and it is difficult to think of her as Konrad's "executive assistant"; she seems a child, dressed up. She favors what the magazines call the "layered look"—I suspect because she is ashamed of her bottom. She has thin shoulders but a heavy bottom. Well, I want to tell her, who is not ashamed of their bottom. If not their bottom their thighs or their breasts or their wobbly female bellies; who among us is perfect, Pauline.

Instead of saying a word of this, of course, I sigh and say, "Some days it seems all I do is sweep up after that dog." Stray, good boy, rolls in dry leaves and vomits some grass. As if more were needed, as if Stray and I together are conducting an illustrated lecture, I swish the broom several times on the painted porch floor. The straw scrapes my toes. What Pauline doesn't know—because I haven't told her and because she won't come inside—is that I keep the broom by the front door for show. I keep it to show the Moonies, Mormons, and Jehovah's Witnesses who stop by the house that I've no time to be saved, can't be converted. I use it to lean on when I'm listening, lean on when I'm not; I use it to convince prowlers of my prowess and neighbors of my virtue; I use it for everything, in fact, but cleaning the house. I feel no need to clean house, and certainly not with a broom. The rooms at my back are stacked to the rafters with dead flowers and song sheets, stuffed bears and bird nests, junk mail and seashells, but to Pauline, perhaps, my house is vast, scoured, and full of light—to Pauline, perhaps, my house is in order. But who knows, with Pauline. She gives me her beautiful smile, then drops her eyes to my bathrobe hem and gives me her faint, formal frown. She pinches the dog hair between her fingers and tries to wipe it behind a leaf on the yellowing vine.

"I don't know how you manage" is what she says. She shakes her head. "Between the dog," she says, grinding her cigarette out on the railing, "and the children . . . " She sits huddled in the wan freckled sunlight with the dead cigarette curled in the palm of her hand, and after a minute, during which neither of us can think of one more thing to say, she lights up another. "It was the children," she says at last, "I really wanted to see."

"They'll be sorry they missed you," I tell her politely.

"Yes," Pauline says. "I'd hoped . . . "

"Had you but phoned," I add, just as politely, dropping my eyes and sweeping my toes. The children are not far away. They said they were going to the end of the lane to pick blackberries for pie, but what they are actually doing is showing their bare bottoms to passing cars and screaming "Hooey hooey." I know this because little Dixie Steadman, who used to baby-sit before she got her Master's Degree in Female Processes, saw them and called me. "Why are you letting your daughters celebrate their femininity in this burlesque?" Dixie asked. Her voice was calm and reasonable and I wanted to answer, but before I could there was a brisk papery rustle and she began to read rape statistics to me, and I had to hold the phone at arm's length and finally I put it to Stray's ear and even he yawned, showing all his large yellow teeth, and then I put the receiver down, very gently, and we tiptoed away. What I'm wondering now is what "hooey" means. I'd ask Pauline, who would be only too glad to look it up for me (her curiosity and industry made her, Konrad said, an invaluable assistant, right from the start), but I'm afraid she'd mention it to Konrad and then he would start threatening to take the children away; he does that; he can't help it; it's like a nervous tic. He loves to go to court. Of course he's a lawyer, he has to. Even so, I think he overdoes it. I never understood the rush to divorce me and marry Pauline; we were fine as we were, but he says my problem is that I have no morals and perhaps he's right, perhaps I don't. Both my divorce and Pauline's wedding were executed in court, and I think both by Judge Benson. The marriage couldn't have been statelier than the dissolution, and if I were Pauline, only twenty-four and getting married for the very first time, I would have been bitter. I would have insisted on white lace or beige anyway and candles and lots of fresh flowers, but Pauline is not one to complain. Perhaps she feels lucky to be married at all; perhaps she feels lucky to be married to Konrad. Her shoulders always droop a little when she's with him, I've noticed, and she listens to him with her chin tucked in and her wrists poised, as if she were waiting to take dictation. Maybe she adores him. But if she does she must learn not to take him too seriously or treat him as if he matters; he hates that; he can't deal with that at all. I should tell her this, but there are some things she'll have to find out for herself. All I tell her is that the girls are gone, up the lane, picking berries.

"How wonderful," she says, exhaling. "Berries."

"Blackberries," I tell her. "They grow wild here. They grow all over."

"In the city," she says, making an effort, "a dinky little carton costs eighty-nine cents." She smiles. "Say you needed three cartons to make one pie," she asks me, "how much would that cost?"

I blink, one hand on my bathrobe collar.

"Two-sixty-seven." Her smile deepens, dimples. "Two-sixty-seven plus tax when you can buy a whole frozen pie for one-fifty-six, giving you a savings of one-eleven at least. They don't call them convenience foods," Pauline says, "for nothing."

"Are you sure," I ask, after a minute, "you don't want some tea?"

"Oh no!"

"Some coffee?"

"Oh no!"

"A fast glass of wine?"

She chuckles, cheerful, but will not answer. I scan the sky. It's close, but cloudless. If there were to be a thunderstorm—and we often have thunderstorms this time of year—Pauline would have to come in. Or would she? I see her, erect and dripping, defiant.

"Mrs. Dixon," I offer, "had a wonderful recipe for blackber . . . "

"Mrs. Dixon?"

For a second I almost see Pauline's eyes. They are small and tired and very angry. Then she tips her head to the sun and the glasses cloud over again.

"Konrad's mother."

"Yes," she says. She lights another cigarette, shakes the match out slowly. "I know."

"A wonderful recipe for blackberry cake. She used to say that Konrad never liked pie."

"I know."

"Just cake."

"I know."

"What I found out, Pauline, is that he likes both."

"We never eat dessert," Pauline says, her lips small and sad again. "It isn't good for us and we just don't have it."

Stray begins to bark and wheel around the garden and a second later the children appear, Letty first, her blond hair tangled and brambly like mine, then Alicia, brown-eyed like Konrad, and then Sophie, who looks like no one unless—yes—with her small proud head, a bit like Pauline. The children are giggling and they deliberately smash into each other as they zigzag down the driveway. "Oops," they cry, with elaborate formality, "do forgive me. My mistake." As they come closer we see that all three are scratched and bloody with berry juice. One holds a Mason jar half full and one has a leaky colander and one boasts a ruined pocket. Pauline closes her eyes tight behind her dark glasses and holds out her arms. The girls, giggling, jostle toward her. They're wild for Pauline. She tells them stories about kidnappers and lets them use her calculator. With each kiss the wooden railing rocks and lurches; if these visits keep up I will have to rebuild the porch, renew the insurance. I carry the berries into the kitchen, rinse them off, and set them to drain. When I come back outside Pauline stands alone on the porch. Stains bloom on her blouse and along her out-thrust chin.

"Come in," I urge, "and wash yourself off."

She shakes her head very fast and smiles at the floor. "No," she says. "You see, I have to go."

The children are turning handsprings on the lawn, calling "Watch me! me! me!" as Stray dashes between them, licking their faces. I walk down the driveway to see Pauline off. As I lift my hand to wave she turns and stares past me, toward the house; I turn too, see nothing, no one, only an old wooden homestead, covered with yellowing vines, a curtain aflutter in an upstairs window, a red door ajar on a dark brown room.

"Thank you," she cries. Then she throws her last cigarette onto the gravel and grinds it out and gets into her car and backs out the driveway and down to the street and away.

Once she turns the corner I drop my hand and bite the knuckles, hard. Then I look back at the house. Konrad steps out, a towel gripped to his waist. He is scowling; angry, I know, because he's spent the last half hour hiding in the shower with the cat litter box and the tortoise. He shouts for his shoes. I find them toed out in flight, one in the bedroom, one down the hall. As he hurries to tie them I tell him a strange thing has happened: it seems I've grown morals.

"What?" Konrad snaps. He combs his hair with his fingers when he can't find my brush.

"Us," I say. "You. Me. Pauline. It's a lot of hooey," I tell Konrad. "It is."

Konrad turns his face this way, that way, scrubs a space clear in the mirror. "Do you know what you're saying?" he says to the mirror.

I think. I think, Yes. I know what I'm saying. I'm saying good-bye. I'm saying, Go home.

And when he has gone and the girls are asleep and the house is night-still, I remember the pie. I roll out the rich dough, flute it, and fill it with berries and sugar, lemons and spice. We'll have it for breakfast, the children and I; we'll share it with Stray. "Would you like that?" I ask him. Stray thumps his tail, but he's not looking at me; his head is cocked, he's listening to something else. I listen too. A faint beat comes from the radio on the kitchen counter. Even before I turn it up I can tell it's a reggae beat, strong and sassy. I'm not sure I can catch it. Not sure I should try. Still, when Stray bows, I curtsy. And when the song starts, we dance.

Greatness Strikes Where It Pleases

by Lars Gustafsson

Introduced by Charles Baxter

HE HAD BEEN INVITED TO INTRODUCE A STORY AND WAS PULLING down books from the shelves to reread a few of the old obscure favorites. They had to be obscure, he thought, or there was no point in introducing one of them. The books were scattered on the floor, and he had to be careful to avoid tripping over them or kicking one of them into the corner. Some of the stories, once reread, no longer seemed quite so appropriate for the occasion, however. Conrad Aiken's "The Woman-Hater" still had its shockingly beautiful paragraph two pages from the end, when the college kid is kissed by a woman he doesn't know and wakes up like Sleeping Beauty, but the rest of the story seemed too drab, too perfunctorily written. Aiken's "Silent Snow, Secret Snow," about a boy's descent into schizophrenia, was still perfect in its evocation of a child's mental vertigo but was, it seemed, constantly anthologized. Evan Connell's "Arcturus" was too long for inclusion in an anthology, as was Isak Dinesen's "Sorrow-acre." Kipling's "'They'" could effectively give anyone the shivers. All the same, it seemed, upon reexamination, too tricky by half and culturally unpleasant in the way Kipling could sometimes be. Anyone introducing such a story might feel an urge to apologize for it—a bad way to start. Katherine Anne Porter's "Noon Wine" was bulletproof but, like "Arcturus," too long and hardly obscure. He didn't know enough about some writers and their traditions, Yasunari Kawabata's or Bessie Head's, for example, to introduce one of their stories. And he didn't feel like introducing writers who needed no introduction, at least from him: Chekhov or Alice Munro or Italo Calvino. Dozens of others.

Sighing happily, he took down Lars Gustafsson's *Stories of Happy People* and reread "Greatness Strikes Where It Pleases." Probably it was the story he had wanted to introduce all along.

This story, translated by Yvonne L. Sandstroem and John Weinstock, is part of a book first published in Sweden in 1981 whose concern is that most complex and elusive fictional subject, happiness. Happiness is fundamentally antidramatic. For the most part, it resists conflict altogether, having passed beyond it or finessed it. In this sense it is distinct from the emotions of triumph or contentment. There are probably no stories in Paradise, and there are very few stories *about* Paradise. In America we secretly tend to think of happiness as rather dull and banal, middle class, unworthy of our attention, possessed by the likes of Ozzie and Harriet. Gustafsson's protagonists in this book, by contrast, approach happiness warily and treat it as the utterly mysterious condition that it is.

In one story we follow Nietzsche, floating in and out of excruciating migraines in his pension room on the shore of Lago Maggiore, discovering that he himself is part of a great truth, a wildly humorous and very clever joke in which he is the perfect thing that makes the world not-perfect. In another, we follow two obsessed lovers; in a third, an old Swedish industrial engineer who discovers in the quotations from Chairman Mao a catalyst for remembering a truth buried in his memory and almost obliterated by historical trauma. Whatever happiness Gustafsson's protagonists find, it always has the virtue of a pleasing complexity, like a very oddly shaped crystal.

The subject of, and virtually only character in, "Greatness Strikes Where It Pleases" is what we would call a retarded person, a sort of boy who grows to be a sort of man. The story has no interest in the pathos of this situation, none whatever. It is hardly interested in this character as a *person* at all: his actions and decisions are virtually irrelevant to the story's progress, which is genuine but minimal. All the same, the story is something of a miracle: it induces in the reader a bit of a trance, and in this trance it convincingly portrays its subject as mysteriously exceptional, godlike.

"Greatness Strikes Where It Pleases" is one of the few stories I know of where time virtually stands still throughout the entire story. Or rather it is experienced in nearly frozen narrative events of almost pure feeling. The story has eliminated transitions: one moment the boy is with his parents; at the next moment he is in a home; then he is a man. Man and boy are virtually the same. Nothing leads to anything else. Nothing has to. Instead, one scene *yields* to another, as dough in the oven yields to the heat to become bread, or as the front of a crowd changes direction because of some pressure from the rear. Everything within the story—grass, mushrooms, wood saws—is defamiliarized, an object for endless contemplation.

The protagonist (he has no name) has almost no words, does not own the words that are used against him, but recognizes that the strong, unlike him, *do* own the words and use them to punish others, including himself, and to order the business of the world. Gustafsson's story is involved in a very tricky maneuver here, because all this must come to us through words and a literary language that the boy and subsequently the man do not possess. The words of the story must induce a feeling for his perceptions even though the perceptions do not come to him in exactly this form.

"He had no words for the world, and birds' suddenly flying up was one of the thousand ways in which the world would turn *unreliable*." That's the horror. But the story is dominated by pleasures, slow-seeming ones: "*The trees are so happy, he thought, when the wind comes. That gives them something to do.*"

We all have intuitions that we don't exactly have the words for, especially when we're children. These intuitions probably have the form of shaped sensory perceptions or emotions that have what amounts to a distinct outline. Henry James, in his preface to *What Maisie Knew,* argues that fiction, or at least *his* kind of fiction, shouldn't be stuck with only the language that the characters themselves possess. By a certain sleight-of-hand, the writer gives to the character the language that the character deserves, a language that honors the character's intuitions. Our feelings can be sophisticated even when our language is not.

The narrator of "Greatness Strikes Where It Pleases," as I've said, never takes pity on the subject of the story. What he does is much odder. He gives him instead the benefit of his intelligent and informed fascination and curiosity. He engages in a thought experiment in which the young man is granted *nobility,* free from condescension. This character gradually becomes an ambassador from and then a monarch of a country that the rest of us know almost nothing about but can still perceive. It is the country of contemplation-without-thought.

> In a world that had no center, he reigned like a quiet monarch, too self-evident ever to feel that his own order was being threatened, too rich to demand anything from the poor, an envoy in chaos serving an order so noble that it was also able to accept the necessity of disorder.

That's beautiful. And in its simple complexity—there *is* such a condition—it gives an inkling of the almost stationary beauty of the story's conclusion, where Gustafsson's protagonist begins to take on the mind of a mushroom, which is also the mind of God.

Sitting in his chair, so fat he spills out over the edges, this nameless character ends in an exalted, ethereal state, both weighed down and lifted up, that cannot truly be shared by anyone capable of reading this story. The boy who has been excluded from everything wordly, worldly, and human has now attained a state that you, the reader, can only read about but never have in quite the way he has it.

The final six paragraphs of this story are remarkable and hair-raising. The story has stopped progressing, in its unusual manner. Instead, and at some distance from you, it turns, very very slowly, like a wheel in the sky. The chords are slow and sustained, and they are in no hurry to get anywhere because they have already arrived at their destination. It is like the music of Thomas Tallis or what we know of the conversation of angels. Light floods through everything, and we enter something like the mind of the infinite, which is still the mind of a retarded boy, shockingly apart from the rest of us, hugely beautiful, and great.

Greatness Strikes Where It Pleases

Lars Gustafsson

Translated by Yvonne L. Sandstroem and John Weinstock

He came from one of the small farms up by the woods; strange things come from there now and then.

Tumbledown barns in the meadows, sometimes with the ridge of the roof broken right in the middle, small cow barns made from cinderblock, unusable after the milk trucks got too wide for the small roads.

And the road into the woods: like a green tunnel. When he was a boy, he played between the barn and the house and was always forbidden to go behind the barn into the woods.

The woods were marshy, with all kinds of mushrooms and toadstools, a place rich in different species the way it sometimes happens where the shadows linger a long time and different kinds of rock mingle.

It was quite a small place; his brother and sister were both older, by two and three years.

His first school was the woodshed; his brother and sister were often there, whittling boats and cars out of wood. They were practising their way into tools. He himself had a horror of them, perhaps due to some unsuccessful early attempts, a horror of the sharp edges of the chisels that could cut into your nail like a knife into butter, the axes and the big timber cleavers with their worn handles, and, worst of all, the saws hanging in a long row on their nails, from the big two-handed lumberman's saws with their bows and clasps to the crosscut saws, the joiner's saws with their buckle pegs that clattered so merrily when you released the tension, the one-man crosscut saws that, oddly enough, were called "tails" although they had nothing to do with tails—grownups had such funny names for their things: that was their peculiarity, and they had a *right* to all those names which he didn't have. He always laughed awkwardly and crept into a corner when his brother and sister tried to teach him those names.

Those things belonged to them: dovetail saws, punches. The old wooden mallet used for pounding in fence posts, made from curly birch, battered by tens of thousands of strikes of wood against wood, impossible to lift.

And above them all, hanging majestically: the ice saw, absolutely forbidden to touch, a cruel giant with dragon's teeth, a magnification of the other saws, crueller than they, but also silent, waiting, never used.

He would dream of the teeth of all the saws.

Sometimes they hit him, but not very badly. Anyway, they hit him when he came from the woodshed with wounds and gashes from the tools in the woodshed. They were afraid that he'd really hurt himself. They wanted to keep him away from the tools.

His brother and sister, who knew how, were allowed to handle them. It gave him the feeling that the words, too, belonged to them.

Sometimes they might send him to fetch tools that did not exist, "bench marks," things like that.

It gave him a feeling that it would always be vague and uncertain which things existed in the world and which did not. Evidently using words was harder than you might imagine.

They always laughed loudly, doubled up with laughter when he returned empty-handed, or when they had fooled him into going to the far end of the barn searching for impossible objects.

In actual fact, the strong decided what words should be used for.

Mushrooms were better. They didn't care about having names. They had smells instead, strong, earthy smells, smells of decaying leaves, of heated iron, of oxidizing copper, some of them like rotting animals and some with mysterious smells that didn't exist anywhere else.

And their shapes: most of them round, but all of them round in different ways. Some had a depression in the middle, as if the whole thing had been rotated around the midpoint at enormous speed, just once, then solidifying; some had indentations, wavy shapes; some had tall, narrow stems; some had a collar; some, delicate gills under the cap, so fragile that they crumbled at the slightest touch. And there were some with organworks of fine pipes.

Sometimes they were covered with slime that made you pull your hand back quickly. Sometimes they were dry, brown, friendly to your fingers, as if they'd pulled the sunshine into themselves and still preserved this sunshine like a secret force under the skin.

And then those strange things that came up late in the fall, smelling like mushrooms but still not looking like mushrooms but like something else: a red finger groping its way between two rocks, a strangely solid pat of butter forgotten on a cranberry leaf, something indescribably gray fermenting, growing, turning in the fissures of a rotting tree trunk.

He felt a kinship, a friendship between himself and these cool objects without names that changed day by day and which always disappeared again like formless clumps of decomposing life in the moss.

He minded the ban on going to the mushrooms more than the ban on going to the tools.

* * *

The fall when he turned seven and was going to start school turned into a disaster.

It was a small school, down by the lake, a one-room school with a single teacher, a small, broad man with gold-rimmed glasses and strong, blunt hands.

Decades later, he could still remember the teacher's broad, strong fingernails with a kind of approval. They looked like those objects that really exist.

He was going to learn to read, and the teacher was both kind and helpful. He sat for a long time on a chair beside him, smelling of strange smells, tobacco and Palmolive soap.

The letters were easy to tell apart, but he never got any words out of them. They didn't want to speak.

That wasn't anything to wonder at. He didn't have any words to counter them with, nothing to meet them with. Nothing at all. He tried copying them, and they turned into mushrooms.

It seemed natural that he should walk around by himself during recess, digging with a stick in the gravel, while his brother and sister played with their friends.

There was nothing that wasn't completely self-evident, and he simply couldn't understand what he was doing in school. It was noisy. It bothered him to hear too many children laughing and shouting to each other at the same time.

He was homesick, and when it got to be afternoon, a wind came through the big ash trees outside the schoolhouse.

The trees are so happy, he thought, when the wind comes. That gives them something to do.

Actually he only went to school for a week.

What he could remember of it afterward was that it was where he first smelled a smell that would later become very familiar to him: the smell of scouring powder and disinfectant, the smell of hospitals, the smell in the waiting room at the county doctor's, strong in some places and weaker in others, but always the same, varying in one way or the other: *the smell of those who wanted something from him.*

The lunch music and the voices on the radio. The voices on the radio became important to him later on; they affirmed his continued existence, they hovered around him, especially at dinner time, cheery, sometimes persuasive, voices that filled the air, music that filled the air and didn't want anything from him.

That was later. After they'd come to get him.

They came and got him one afternoon that fall. His parents evidently were expecting it, his mother in her good dress and with a cardboard suitcase tied with a piece of string (he would encounter it again and again for a couple of decades; at last it became identified with his mother); wartime taxi with a producer-gas unit rumbling dully in the rear, roads and carsick vomiting on the way to the city.

Then the House, large, white, behind trees and a fence. And the smell of those who wanted something from him.

All new smells. The aides, in their dresses with high collars and maternal aprons—they were often older women, round and sturdy—had a different smell. The food smelled different, was different, starchy, gravyish, floating, wetter than at home in the woods. It was eaten in a common dining room during terrible rattling and spilling. Some of his new schoolmates had a hard time managing their spoons. Some of them let the food run out of the corners of their mouths.

He was afraid of them.

They didn't do anything to him. Most of them moved slowly; some were so deep in their own worlds that nothing could have disturbed them.

They were all so far beyond language, the language of the others, the foreign languages, that there was nothing for them to quarrel about.

They shared the same living space, and there was enough food for everybody.

The food was important: it was like a maternal outflowing, a welcoming smell, a connection to the other world which was not a prohibition.

That took time to discover.

The first fall he was too paralysed to feel such things. He still missed his own world, the woodshed, his mushrooms, the smell of milk strained in the barn while it was still warm; the funny, wet snouts of the pigs, the laces high up on his father's boots, always muddy, swinging rhythmically around the bootlegs when he went out in the morning.

He missed a world.

He found a spider under his bed that he used to play with silently in the evening, until he happened to pick it apart, leg by leg.

He was too interested in seeing how it was made.

The boy in the bed next to him was shapelessly fat, wet his bed regularly, and cried in his sleep. When he had the chance, he made little paper balls and ate them. He could tear them out of a magazine someone had forgotten in the dayroom, or tear strips from a bag left behind on a table in the large, dark hall. He tore at the wallpaper by the door until someone told him he wasn't allowed to do that.

Sometimes he'd feed the boy paper. It was fun to see how fast it disappeared.

The boy in the bed on the other side of him wasn't much fun. He was silent.

But the wallpaper, especially in the morning, with its faded blue and pink lines, the wallpaper was almost the first thing that comforted him. The lines crossed and veered apart again; they made shapes. You could make trees, big, intricate trees with limbs that branched off and then branched off again, all the way up to the ceiling.

You could let one tree copy another, so that there were two mirror trees opposite one another on each wall, one in the shade and the other in the sun.

He could lie like that for such a long time, building trees, that they thought he was sick in the morning.

He was just making a tree that was reflecting itself inside itself when the aide came and made him get up. She looked curiously at his sheets.

He belonged to those who washed themselves. He had a habit of sucking the celluloid handle of his toothbrush for a long time.

The knots in his shoelaces were the worst. The knot was a small, evil animal that the lace passed through. The lace and the knot weren't the same thing, for you could make the same knot with different kinds of lace.

His knots were always terribly complicated.

Spring came, and suddenly, in the space of one day, they were all sent home. It was April 1940, and the House was going to be used for something else.

His mother came. She praised him and said he'd grown.

She had coffee with the aides, and it sounded as if they were talking in pretend voices.

At home, the snow was melting. His brother and sister had grown a lot more than he had, and the old horse had died and was buried by the pasture.

He'd never liked it. It had large, yellow, menacing teeth, and it had a way of tossing its head around in the half-light of the barn that scared him.

It was gone, and that was as it should be.

After he'd been home a week, he almost drowned in a brook when he went too far out on the crumbling edge of the ice close to a waterfall. He got a good hiding.

It was his brother who pulled him out. One of his red boots stuck in the mud. His brother poked around for it with a fence pole for quite some time, while the boy stood there shivering. He cried, for he knew that the worst was yet to come.

The water still stung in his nose; water you inhale deeply has a strange way of stinging.

The first coltsfoot was growing beside his own foot, which was heavy with mud. His nose was running, he shook with cold, his thin overalls smelled damp and putrid from the brook water. He stood quite still, freezing, and someone somewhere owed him infinite love.

Not a trace of mushrooms in April.

* * *

The spring of 1945, just when World War II was ending, he learned to masturbate.

He thought he had made a fantastic discovery: he could surprise himself.

He rubbed the thing which grew more and more like a mushroom, preferably against the right side of his bed, and pondered his wallpaper trees, went deeper and deeper into them, and had done it many times with increasing desire, with excitement, a feeling that the world was becoming *denser* that way, the first time he discovered that there was an ending. The first time it scared him: his body knew something he didn't know it knew. It could do something he'd never believed it could do.

How many such secrets did it hold? How many new, secret pockets could it open?

And was he the only one in the world who could do it? In a way, it was the happiest spring of his life.

They made it clear to him that he was doing something forbidden, especially the older aides, who had a way of being *disgusted* by it. But they weren't too severe. It was to be expected.

Now he had himself for a playmate, for a mirror. He was no longer alone. He started to grow and got quite tall. Mirror and reflection grew together and couldn't be separated. And still they had their secret conversations. The trees in the wallpaper acquired depth.

At this time, between 1945 and 1950 approximately, he was very close to something that might have been an awakening.

He was moved to another room—without wallpaper—and stood in the door of the wood shop, following with an interested gaze those who could carve.

A new teacher came, a lean, rather tall young man with gentle brown eyes who allowed him to straighten up, to sort pieces of wood in the lumber room from the very beginning; who didn't let on when the older students laughed at him.

He was not allowed close to the saws and the chisels, but he was allowed to use the sandpaper and to help hold the glue clamps when they were put around pieces of wood on which the glue was still bubbling from the heat in the pot.

The new teacher—he never knew his name—was almost as silent as he was himself. He moved with calm, determined steps between the tool cabinets and the benches, kept the paint cans and the lumber in order. He always looked him in the eye when he gave him something to do, a board to carry, a floor to sweep. He looked him in the eye and let it be known that he actually existed. When he handed him a pail of wood shavings to empty, it became a living sign saying that he existed.

The students in this workshop were of different kinds and different ages. Some things happened that frightened him a bit and that amused him almost as much. Clumsy as calves, older and younger boys moved around each other, joked, butted each other. Jokes and taunts occurred, glue pots in the hair and boards nailed to the floor when you went to pick them up.

It disturbed him and frightened him when it was directed against him. The laughter was something they tried to force on him.

The board in the floor was a surprise directed at someone they wanted him to be. Something to laugh at. But that wasn't where he was.

The new teacher knew how to quiet such things down; with a calm hand, without harsh words, he separated the combatants when the boys got into a fight, dragging each other around a bench, keeping a strong hold on each other's hair. Patiently, he showed that you can't plane a board from both directions without ripping up the fibers. He never allowed dirt to accumulate under his short, broad nails.

He was, in a way, the center of the world.

In a world that had no center, he reigned like a quiet monarch, too self-evident ever to feel that his own order was being threatened, too rich to demand anything from the poor, an envoy in chaos serving an order so noble that it was also able to accept the necessity of disorder.

There were those who urinated in the pails of wood shavings because they didn't have time to get to the toilets inside the main entrance.

They had to clean it up themselves, but no harsh words were spoken.

It was somewhat different with the women aides. They were so divided between disgust and maternity, or locked into a maternity which was disgust at the same time, that they always created anxiety.

They smelled different. Their large, white forearms, often a bit reddened, fascinated him, and he often tried to touch them, but they nudged him gently aside. He was "in the way," as they called it.

He suspected great secrets in them, sniffed out that he was only seeing a narrow strip of their lives, but he wasn't able to formulate it.

They changed often, so that there was no possibility of keeping a face in your memory: as the years passed, their faces merged into a single face, and it was gentle and mute.

He himself slipped away, too. The wood shop teacher moved after a couple of years; the shop was closed, since the students who had worked there moved to another kind of institution. Quite a few disappeared, and only the hopeless ones remained.

The traffic along the road increased during those years. In the spring of 1952, a trailer truck loaded with grain lost control swerving to avoid a youth on a Husqvarna 125 cc; the trailer went through the loose sand on the shoulder of the road, and the whole thing turned over in their hedge.

The driver climbed out, a bit shaken up, and saw two hydrocephalic boys tumbling like little seals in the yellow grain that filled the ditch.

He thought he'd landed in another world.

The salvage went quickly, but they scooped up wheat for weeks down in the ditch, played with it, filled their pockets with it. The aides found wheat under the beds, in the pillow cases, everywhere.

It was a mysterious gift, and it came from outside.

It was the last big event for a long time. His senses were asleep: there was nothing that made enough of a claim on them. He lived for mealtimes, and when he was around thirty, he became grotesquely fat. His blue carpenter's pants with suspender buckles had to be let out.

Traffic along the road increased. He was always led across the road when he was going to help in the apple orchard on the other side. He wasn't much use. For the most part he walked around raking, and often he would rake under a single tree until the ground was all torn up and some laughing foreman came and moved him.

He had a profound horror of the motorized cultivator that arrived in 1956: one of the regular gardeners had got his foot caught that spring, and it looked awful: toes hanging loose, blood flowing, but that wasn't what frightened him. It was the helpless cry when everyone came running. After that, he refused to stay in the orchard when the cultivator got going and rushed back to the Home, across the road. They let him be.

He didn't want to hear that cry again.

He had another peculiarity which amused the men in the market garden: he was afraid of birds.

Not birds flying, not flights of wild geese and cranes and swifts tumbling high in the air in the summer evenings.

It was birds that flew up suddenly out of bushes that frightened him, sparrows fluttering up from a new-plowed field would make him beside himself with terror. Even after he had turned thirty, he would still, in spite of all prohibitions, run into the kitchen, babbling incomprehensibly.

Good-natured aides would try to comfort him with a piece of coffeecake: he could sit for a long time, trembling and stiff, until his terror slowly wore off.

He had no words for the world, and birds' suddenly flying up was one of the thousand ways in which the world would turn *unreliable*.

The bird wasn't something that fluttered through the world, the bird was a corner of the cloth of the world which had worked loose and started to flutter.

Of course there was terror in it, but also liberation: the dream he was dreaming would have an ending.

At the end of the '50s, his parents died. Nobody tried to explain it to him, and he didn't know in what order they died or when, but when he hadn't seen them for a few years—his mother would visit him regularly twice a year and always brought him candy and apples, an anxious lot of apples, as if the lack of apples were his problem—he started to miss them, in some vague fashion, about the way you might all of a sudden long for mustard or honey or a certain kind of floury gravy with just a taste of burned pork.

He remembered the buildings better than he did his parents—the horse, the woodshed—the only thing left of his parents was the sound when they shut the door to the porch and stamped the snow off their boots in the winter.

But this sound was an important sound. It meant that the lamps would be lit, that the atmosphere in the room would change.

At the end of September every year, the willow herb, the evening primrose, has no more flowers left, but its seed pods ride on the wind, and if they get into a yard, they respond to even the slightest changes in temperature by rising and falling rhythmically. And at last they settle down, in small, quick drafts, which the wind can easily carry off again.

That was the way September was that year, in 1977.

He was sitting in the dayroom in the new Home, sixty miles from the old one, which had been torn down in 1963.

He had his favorite spot by the window. Here was an asphalt yard, without trees, without flowers, only a wilted flowerbed edging the drive and the three parking places.

Here the seeds of the willow herb came drifting in. It was the kind of September day when the air is *quite still and waiting*.

He was shapeless in his lounger; he swelled over its edges. For ten years he had been quite empty.

The drifting seed pods, unbelievably light, moved on winds so slight that no one could discern them.

Slowly the shadow of the curtain moved across the polished floor of the dayroom.

The hourglass-shaped ribbon of light moved across the surface of the planet, dawn line and dusk line rushing forward like great wings across distant plains and mountains. Slowly or swiftly, depending on how you chose to measure it, the earth moved in its orbit and would never return to the same point where it had once been. Slowly or swiftly, the solar system moved in its orbit, and with silent, dizzying speed; like a disk of light, the galaxy moved in its mysterious rotation around itself.

In the wombs of the mothers, unborn embryos were growing, membranes and tissues folded and pleated themselves cleverly around each other, exploring without sorrow, without hesitation, the possibilities of topological space.

Of this he knew nothing: heavy and huge like a boulder in the woods, he sat in his chair, moving it with effort a few inches every hour so that it always remained in the patch of sun.

He was as slow as the galaxy and as mysterious.

In the shadows of the leaves which moved more and more insistently against the wall, he saw the old mushrooms growing once more, from the first soft mound shooting up through the moss to the last black-brown pyramid of shapeless, pungent tissue in December.

For years, he allowed them to grow freely as he sat there; he made them more and more remarkable, more and more fantastic; each and every one the only one of its kind, saw them live and die; knew since long ago that all time and everything that grew were as mysterious and great as he was himself.

The Interview

by Ruth Prawer Jhabvala

Introduced by Jane Smiley

I READ "THE INTERVIEW" IN THE WINTER OF 1978, WHEN I WAS LIVING in one room at the University of Iceland and shirking my research duties by borrowing lots of books from the library at the U.S. Information Agency. At the end of January, it was light for about two and a half hours every day, and since I didn't like to rise before dawn, that meant I ate breakfast at about one-thirty in the afternoon and finally fell into bed again around four or five in the morning. I was depressed. I hid out in my room and read S. J. Perelman, Christina Stead, Tolstoy, Halldór Laxness, and the anthology of *New Yorker* stories from the fifties where "The Interview" was printed. During the daily ration of sunlight, I sat at my portable typewriter and wrote fiction. After a while it dawned on me that on the days I wrote I felt that life was worth living, and on the days I didn't write I felt that it was not worth living. I foresaw that when I got back to the States, life would not present itself to me in such stark terms, but I learned my lesson anyway and returned from Iceland in May a far more committed writer than I had felt myself to be in September. When I recall that period now, I don't remember *being* depressed, only that I *was* depressed. What I remember are all the worlds I visited, self-contained and exquisite and lit by the experience and imagination of writers like Ruth Prawer Jhabvala.

Jhabvala lived for a long time in India. "The Interview" was written in the fifties when she was young, but it struck me in Iceland and it strikes me now as a very wise story. The narrator, a young husband of the educated caste, speaks of his day (and his life) with disarming honesty. He is observant, intelligent, possessed of a degree of self-knowledge. In Iceland, I was transported to Bombay by the picture he draws of the life that swirls around him in his house and out on the street. But what I found both splendid and exciting about the story was how much about the young man Jhabvala made me understand—not only who he felt himself to be but how he came to be the way he was, and how who he was fit into his world. And yet she does not write about him as if he were a specimen. I think two moments in the story are as poignant as any I have ever read: the moment in the office when he sees another applicant tear his dhoti on a nail, and his own final moment of regret. I hesitate to say more about the story because I find one of its best pleasures to be its complex unfolding. I would like to have written something as observant and as wise as "The Interview."

The Interview

Ruth Prawer Jhabvala

I am always very careful of my appearance, so you could not say that I spent much more time than usual over myself that morning. It is true, I trimmed and oiled my moustache, but then I often do that; I always like it to look very neat, like Raj Kapoor's, the film star's. But I knew my sister-in-law and my wife were watching me. My sister-in-law was smiling, and she had one hand on her hip; my wife only looked anxious. I knew she was anxious. All night she had been whispering to me. She had whispered, "Get this job and take me away to live somewhere alone, only you and I and our children." I had answered, "Yes," because I wanted to go to sleep. I don't know where and why she has taken this notion that we should go and live alone.

When I had finished combing my hair, I sat on the floor and my sister-in-law brought me my food on a tray. It may sound strange that my sister-in-law should serve me, and not my wife, but it is so in our house. It used to be my mother who brought me my food, even after I was married; she would never allow my wife to do this for me, though my wife wanted to very much. Then, when my mother got so old, my sister-in-law began to serve me. I know that my wife feels deeply hurt by this, but she doesn't dare to say anything. My mother doesn't notice many things anymore, otherwise she certainly would not allow my sister-in-law to bring me my food; she has always been very jealous of this privilege herself, though she never cared who served my brother. Now she has become so old that she can hardly see anything, and most of the time she sits in the corner by the family trunks and folds and strokes her pieces of cloth. For years now she has been collecting pieces of cloth. Some of them are very old and dirty, but she doesn't care, she loves them all equally. Nobody is allowed to touch them. Once there was a great quarrel, because my wife had taken one of them to make a dress for our child. My mother shouted at her—it was terrible to hear her: but then, she has never liked my wife—and my wife was very much afraid and cried and tried to excuse herself. I hit her across the face, not very hard and not because I wanted to, but only to satisfy my mother. The old woman kept quiet then and went back to folding and stroking her pieces of cloth.

All the time I was eating, I could feel my sister-in-law looking at me and smiling. It made me uncomfortable. I thought she might be smiling because she knew I wouldn't get the job for which I had to go and be interviewed. I also knew I wouldn't get it, but I didn't like her to smile like that. It was as if she were saying, "You see, you will always have to be dependent on us." It is clearly my brother's duty to keep me and my family until I can get work and contribute my own earnings to the family household. There is no need for her to smile about it. But it is true that I am more dependent on her now than on anyone else. Since my mother has got so old, my sister-in-law has become more and more the most important person in the house, so that she even keeps the keys and the household stores. At first I didn't like this. As long as my mother managed the household, I was sure of getting many extra tidbits. But now I find that my sister-in-law is also very kind to me—much more kind than she is to her husband. It is not for him that she saves the tidbits, nor for her children, but for me; and when she gives them to me, she never says anything and I never say anything, but she smiles and then I feel confused and rather embarrassed. My wife has noticed what she does for me.

I have found that women are usually kind to me. I think they realize that I am a rather sensitive person and that therefore I must be treated very gently. My mother has always treated me very gently. I am her youngest child, and I am fifteen years younger than my brother who is next to me (she did have several children in between us, but they all died). Right from the time when I was a tiny baby, she understood that I needed greater care and tenderness than other children. She always made me sleep close beside her in the night, and in the day I usually sat with her and my grandmother and my widowed aunt, who were also very fond of me. When I got bigger, my father sometimes wanted to take me to help in his stall (he had a little grocer's stall, where he sold lentils and rice and cheap cigarettes and colored drinks in bottles) but my mother and grandmother and aunt never liked to let me go. Once he did take me with him, and he made me pour some lentils out of paper bags into a tin. I rather liked pouring the lentils—they made such a nice noise as they landed in the tin—but suddenly my mother came and was very angry with my father for making me do this work. She took me home at once, and when she told my grandmother and aunt what had happened, they stroked me and kissed me and then they gave me a hot fritter to eat. The fact is, right from childhood I have been a person who needs a lot of peace and rest, and my food too has to be rather more delicate than that of other people. I have often tried to explain this to my wife, but as she is not very intelligent, she doesn't seem to understand.

Now my wife was watching me while I ate. She was squatting on the floor, washing our youngest baby; the baby's head was in her lap, and all one could see of it was the back of its legs and its naked bottom. My wife did not watch me as openly as my sister-in-law did; only from time to time she raised her eyes to me, I could feel it, and they were very worried and troubled. She too was thinking about the job for which I was going to be interviewed, but she was anxious that I should get it. "We will go and live somewhere alone," she had said. Why did she say it? When she knows that it is not possible and never will be.

And even if it were possible, I would not like it. I can't live away from my mother; and I don't think I would like to live away from my sister-in-law. I often look at her and it makes me happy. Even though she is not young anymore, she is still beautiful. She is tall, with big hips and big breasts and eyes that flash; she often gets angry, and when she is angry, she is the most beautiful of all. Then her eyes are like fire and she shows all her teeth, which are very strong and white, and her head is proud with the black hair flying loose. My wife is not beautiful at all. I was very disappointed in her when they first married me to her. Now I have got used to her and I even like her, because she is so good and quiet and never troubles me at all. I don't think anybody else in our house likes her. My sister-in-law always calls her "that beauty," but she does not mean it; and she makes her do all the most difficult household tasks, and often she shouts at her and even beats her. This is not right; my wife has never done anything to her—on the contrary, she always treats her with respect. But I cannot interfere in their quarrels.

Then I was ready to go, though I didn't want to go. I knew only too well what would happen at the interview. My mother blessed me, and my sister-in-law looked at me over her shoulder and her great eyes flashed with laughter. I didn't look at my wife, who still sat squatting on the floor, but I knew she was pleading with me to get the job like she had pleaded in the night. As I walked down the stairs, the daughter of the carpenter, who lives in one of the rooms on the lower floor, came out of her door and she walked up the stairs as I walked down, and she passed very close beside me, with her eyes lowered but her arm just touching my sleeve. She always waits for me to come out and then she passes me on the stairs. We have never spoken together. She is a very young girl, her breasts are only just forming; her blouse has short sleeves and her arms are beautiful, long and slender. I think soon she is to be married, I have heard my sister-in-law say so. My sister-in-law laughed when she told me, she said, "It is high time" and then she said something coarse. Perhaps she has noticed that the girl waits for me to pass on the stairs.

No, I did not want to go to the interview. I had been to so many during the last few months, and always the same things happened. I know I have to work, in order to earn money and give it to my mother or my sister-in-law for the household, but there is no pleasure for me in the work. Last time I had work, it was in an insurance office and all day they made me sit at a desk and write figures. What pleasure could there be for me in that? I am a very thoughtful person, and I like always to sit and think my own thoughts; but while I thought my own thoughts in the office, I sometimes made mistakes over the figures and then my superiors were very angry with me. I was always afraid of their anger, and I begged their forgiveness and admitted that I was much at fault. When they forgave me, I was no longer afraid and I continued doing my work and thinking my thoughts. But the last time they would not forgive me again, though I begged and begged and cried what a faulty, bad man I was and what good men they were, and how they were my mother and my father and how I looked only to them for my life and the lives of my children. But when they still said I must go, I saw that the work there was really finished and I stopped crying. I went into the washroom and combed my hair and folded my soap in my towel, and then I took my money from the accountant without a word and I left the office with my eyes lowered. But I was no longer afraid, because what is finished is finished, and my brother still had work and probably one day I would get another job.

Ever since then my brother has been trying to get me into government service. He himself is a clerk in government service and enjoys many advantages: every five years he gets an increase of ten rupees in his salary and he has ten days sick leave in the year and when he retires he will get a pension. It would be good for me also to have such a job; but it is difficult to get, because first there is an interview at which important people sit at a desk and ask many questions. I am afraid of them, and I cannot understand properly what they are saying, so I answer what I think they want me to answer. But it seems that my answers are not after all the right ones, because up till now they have not given me a job.

On my way to this interview, I thought how much nicer it would be to go to the cinema instead. If I had had ten annas, perhaps I would have gone; it was just time for the morning show. The young clerks and the students would be collecting in a queue outside the cinema now. They would be standing and not talking much, holding their ten annas and waiting for the box office to open. I enjoy these morning shows, perhaps because the people who come to them are all young men like myself, all silent and rather sad. I am often sad; it would even be right to say that I am sad most of the time. But when the film begins, I am happy. I love to see the beautiful women, dressed in golden clothes with heavy earrings and necklaces and bracelets covering their arms, and their handsome lovers who are all the things I would like to be. And when they sing their love songs, so full of deep feelings, the tears sometimes come into my eyes; but not because I am sad, no, on the contrary, because I am so happy. After the film is over, I never go home straightaway, but I walk around the streets and think about how wonderful life could be.

When I arrived at the place where the interview was, I had to walk down many corridors and ask directions from many peons before I could find the right room. The peons were all rude to me, because they knew what I had come for. They lounged on benches outside the offices, and when I asked them, they looked me up and down before answering, and sometimes they made jokes about me with one another. I was very polite to them, for even though they were only peons, they had uniforms and jobs and belonged here, and they knew the right way whereas I did not. At last I came to the room where I had to wait. Many others were already sitting there, on chairs that were drawn up all around the room against the wall. No one was talking. I also sat on a chair, and after a while an official came in with a list and he asked if anyone else had come. I got up and he asked my name, and then he looked down the list and made a tick with a pencil. He said to me very sternly, "Why are you late?" I begged pardon and told him the bus in which I had come had had an accident. He said, "When you are called for interview, you have to be here exactly on time, otherwise your name is crossed off the list." I begged pardon again and asked him very humbly please not to cross me off this time. I knew that all the others were listening, though none of them looked at us. He was very stern with me and even scornful, but in the end he said, "Wait here, and when your name is called, you must go in at once."

I did not count the number of people waiting in the room, but there were many. Perhaps there was one job free, perhaps two or three. I knew that all the others were very worried and anxious to get the job, so I became worried and anxious too. The walls of the room were painted green halfway up and white above that and were quite bare. There was a fan turning from the ceiling, but it was not turning fast enough to give much breeze. Behind the big door the interview was going on; one by one we would all be called in behind this closed door.

I began to worry desperately. It always happens like this. When I come to an interview, I don't want the job at all, but when I see all the others waiting and worrying, I want it terribly. Yet at the same time I know that I don't want it. It would only be the same thing over again: writing figures and making mistakes and then being afraid when they found out. And there would be a superior officer to whom I would have to be very deferential, and every time I saw him or heard his voice I would begin to be afraid that he had found out something against me. For weeks and months I would sit and write figures, getting wearier of it and wearier, so that more and more I would be thinking my own thoughts. Then the mistakes would come, and my superior officer would be angry and I afraid.

My brother never makes mistakes. For years he has been sitting in the same office, writing figures and being deferential to his superior officer; he concentrates very hard on his work, and so he doesn't make mistakes. But all the same he is afraid; that is why he concentrates so hard—because he is afraid that he will make a mistake and they will be angry with him and take away his job. He is afraid of this all the time. And he is right: what would become of us all if he also lost his job? It is not the same with me. I think I am afraid to lose my job only because that is a thing of which one is expected to be afraid. When I have actually lost it, I am really relieved. But I am very different from my brother; even in appearance I am very different. It is true, he is fifteen years older than I am, but even when he was my age, he never looked like I do. My appearance has always attracted others, and up to the time I was married, my mother used to stroke my hair and my face and say many tender things to me. Once, when I was walking on my way to school through the bazaar, a man called to me, very softly, and when I came he gave me a ripe mango, and then he took me into a dark passage that led to a disused mosque, and he touched me under my clothes and he said, "You are so nice, so nice." He was very kind to me. I love wearing fine clothes, very thin white muslin kurtas that have been freshly washed and starched and are embroidered at the shoulders. Sometimes I also use scent, a fine khas smell; my hair oil also smells of khas. Some years ago, when the carpenter's daughter was still a small child and did not yet wait for me on the stairs, there was a girl living in the tailor's shop opposite our house and she used to follow me when I went out. But it is my brother who is married to a beautiful wife, and my wife is not beautiful at all. He is not happy with his wife; when she talks to him, she talks in a hard scornful way; and it is not for him that she saves the best food, but for me, even though I have not brought money home for many months.

The big closed door opened and the man who had been in there for interview came out. We all looked at him, but he walked out in a great hurry, with a preoccupied expression on his face; probably he was going over in his mind all that had been said at the interview. I could feel the anxiety in the other men getting stronger, so mine got stronger too. The official with the list came and we all looked at him. He read out another name and the man whose name was called jumped up from his chair; he did not notice that his dhoti had got caught on a nail in the chair and he wondered why he could not go farther. When he realized what had happened, he tried to disentangle himself, but his fingers shook so much that he could not get the dhoti off the nail. The official watched him and said, "Hurry, now, do you think the gentlemen will wait for you for as long as you please?" Then the man also dropped the umbrella he was carrying and now he was trying both to disentangle the dhoti and to pick up the umbrella. When he could not get the dhoti loose, he became so desperate that he tore at the cloth and ripped it free. It was a pity to see the dhoti torn because it was a new one, which he was probably wearing for the first time and had put on specially for the interview. He clasped his umbrella to his chest and walked in a great hurry to the interviewing room, with his dhoti hanging about his legs and his face swollen with embarrassment and confusion.

We all sat and waited. The fan, which seemed to be a very old one, made a creaking noise. One man kept cracking his finger joints—*tik,* we heard, *tik* (it made my own finger joints long to be cracked too). All the rest of us kept very still. From time to time the official with the list came in, he walked around the room very slowly, tapping his list, and then we all looked down at our feet and the man who had been cracking his finger joints stopped doing it. A faint and muffled sound of voices came from behind the closed door. Sometimes a voice was raised, but even then I could not make out what was being said, though I strained very hard.

The last time I had an interview, it was very unpleasant for me. One of the people who was interviewing took a dislike to me and shouted at me very loudly. He was a large fat man and he wore an English suit; his teeth were quite yellow, and when he became angry and shouted, he showed them all, and even though I was very upset, I couldn't help looking at them and wondering how they had become so yellow. I don't know why he was angry. He shouted: "Good God, man, can't you understand what's said to you?" It was true, I could not understand, but I had been trying so hard to answer well. What more did he expect of me? Probably there was something in my appearance that he did not like. It happens that way sometimes—they take a dislike to you, and then of course there is nothing you can do.

When I thought of the man with the yellow teeth, I became more anxious than ever. I need great calm in my life. Whenever anything worries me too much, I have to cast the thought of it off immediately, otherwise there is a danger that I may become very ill. All my limbs were itching so that it was difficult for me to sit still, and I could feel blood rushing into my brain. It was this room that was doing me so much harm: all the other men waiting, anxious and silent, and the noise from the fan and the official with the list walking around, tapping his list or striking it against his thigh, and the big closed door behind which the interview was going on. I felt great need to get up and go away. I didn't *want* the job. I wasn't even thinking about it anymore—I was thinking only about how to avoid having to sit here and wait.

Now the door opened again and the man with the torn new dhoti came out. He was biting his lip and scratching the back of his neck, and he too walked straight out without looking at us at all. The big door was left slightly open for a moment, and I could see a man's arm in a white shirt-sleeve and part of the back of his head. His shirt was very white and of good material, and his ears stood away from his head so that one could see how his spectacles fitted into the backs of his ears. I realized at once that this man would be my enemy and that he would make things very difficult for me and perhaps even shout at me. Then I knew it was no use for me to stay there. The official with the list came back and great panic seized me that he would read out my name. I got up quickly, murmuring, "Please excuse me—bathroom," and went out. The official with the list called after me, "Hey mister, where are you going?" so I lowered my head and walked faster. I would have started to run, but that might have caused suspicion, so I just walked as fast as I could, down the long corridors and right out of the building. There at last I was able to stop and take a deep breath, and I felt much better.

I stood still for only a little while, then I moved on, though not in any particular direction. There were many clerks and peons moving around in the street, hurrying from one office building to another and carrying files and papers. Everyone seemed to have something to do. I was glad when I had moved out of this block and on to the open space where people like myself, who had nothing to do, sat under the trees or in any other patch of shade they could find. But I couldn't sit there; it was too close to the office blocks, and any moment someone might come and say to me, "Why did you go away?" So I walked farther. I was feeling quite light-hearted; it was such a relief for me not to have to be interviewed.

I came to a row of eating stalls, and I sat down on a wooden bench outside one of them, which was called the Paris Hotel, and asked for tea. I felt badly in need of tea, and since I intended to walk part of the way home, I was in a position to pay for it. There were two Sikhs sitting at the end of my bench who were eating with great appetite, dipping their hands very rapidly into brass bowls. In between eating they exchanged remarks with the proprietor of the Paris Hotel, who sat high up inside his stall, stirring in a big brass pot in which he was cooking the day's food. He was chewing a betel leaf, and from time to time he spat out the red betel juice far over the cooking pot and onto the ground between the wooden benches and tables.

I sat quietly at my end of the bench and drank my tea. The food smelled very good, and it made me realize that I was hungry. I decided that if I walked all the way home, I could afford a little cake (I am very fond of sweet things). The cake was not new, but it had a beautiful piece of bright-green peel inside it. On reaching home I would lie down at once to sleep and not wake up again till tomorrow morning. That way no one would be able to ask me any questions. I would not look at my wife at all, so I would be able to avoid her eyes. I would not look at my sister-in-law either; but she would be smiling, that I knew already—leaning against the wall with her hand on her hip, looking at me and smiling. She would know that I had run away, but she would not say anything.

Let her know! What does it matter? It is true I have no job and no immediate prospect of getting one. It is true that I am dependent on my brother. Everybody knows that. There is no shame in it: there are many people without jobs. And she has been so kind to me up till now, there is no reason why she should not continue to be kind to me. Though I know she is not by nature a kind woman; she speaks mostly with a very harsh tongue and her actions also are harsh. Only to me she has been kind.

The Sikhs at the end of the bench had finished eating. They licked their fingers and belched deeply, the way one does after a good meal. They started to laugh and joke with the proprietor. I sat quiet and alone at my end of the bench. Of course they did not laugh and joke with me. They knew that I was superior to them, for whereas they work with their hands, I am a lettered man who does not have to sweat for a living but sits on a chair in an office and writes figures and can speak in English. My brother is very proud of his superiority, and he has great contempt for carpenters and mechanics and such people who work with their hands. I am also proud of being a lettered man, but when I listened to the Sikhs laughing and joking, the thought came to me that perhaps their life was happier than mine. It was a thought that had come to me before. There is the carpenter who lives downstairs in our house, the one whose daughter waits for me on the stairs, and though he is poor, there is always great eating in his house and many people come and I hear them laughing and singing and even dancing. The carpenter is a big strong man and he always looks happy, never anxious and sick with worry the way my brother does. He doesn't wear shoes and clean white clothes like my brother and I do, nor does he speak any English, but all the same he is happy. Even though his work is inferior, I don't think he gets as weary of it as I do of mine, and he has no superior officer to make him afraid.

Then I thought again about my sister-in-law and I thought that if I were kind to her, she would continue to be kind to me. I became quite excited when I thought of being kind to her. I would know then how her big breasts felt under the blouse, how warm they were and how soft. And I would know about the inside of her mouth with the big strong teeth. Her tongue and palate are very pink, like the pink satin blouse she wears on festive occasions, and I had often wondered whether they felt as soft as the blouse too. Her eyes would be shut and perhaps there would be tears on the lashes; and she would be making warm animal sounds and her big body too would be warm like an animal's. I became very excited when I thought of it; but when the excitement had passed, I was sad. Because then I thought of my wife, who is thin and not beautiful and there is no excitement in her body. But she does whatever I want and always tries to please me. I remembered her whispering to me in the night, "Take me away, let us go and live somewhere alone, only you and I and our children." That can never be, and so always she will have to be unhappy.

I was very sad when I thought of her being unhappy; because it is not only she who is unhappy but I also and many others. Everywhere there is unhappiness. I thought of the man whose new dhoti had been torn and who would now have to go home and sew it carefully so that the tear would not be seen. I thought of all the other men sitting and waiting to be interviewed, all but one or two of whom would not get the job for which they had come to be interviewed, and so again they would have to go to another interview and another and another, to sit and wait and be anxious. And my brother who has a job, but is frightened that he will lose it; and my mother so old that she can only sit on the floor and stroke her pieces of cloth; and my sister-in-law who does not care for her husband; and the carpenter's daughter who is to be married and perhaps she also will not be happy. Yet life could be so different. When I go to the cinema and hear the beautiful songs they sing, I know how different it could be; and also sometimes when I sit alone and think my thoughts, then I have a feeling that everything could be so beautiful. But now my tea was finished and also my cake, and I wished I had not bought them, because it was a long way to walk home and I was tired.

The Dead

by James Joyce

Introduced by Mary Gordon

It begins with a slap in the face. "Lily, the caretaker's daughter, was literally run off her feet."

Well, and did you fall for that one? Literally? Don't you know the difference between literally and figuratively? You're no better than Lily herself, are you? Or perhaps you're not Lily, but the garrulous speaker of the second paragraph, the platitude-spouting fool. "It was always a great affair, the Misses Morkan's annual dance. . . . Never once had it fallen flat. For years and years it had gone off in splendid style as long as anyone could remember. . . . Though their life was modest they believed in eating well; the best of everything: diamond-bone sirloins, three-shilling tea and the best bottled stout."

"The Dead" is built around a party, and for most of its duration we, like partygoers, swim in a clamor of voices, not only Gabriel's and the omniscient narrator's. Even Gabriel has many voices. There is the self-conscious Gabriel, the prissy Gabriel, the pompous Gabriel, the affectionate Gabriel, the lustful Gabriel. But many others speak: Miss Ivors, the political nettler; Mr. Browne with his forced jokes; Freddy Malins, who's just a little bit "screwed"; his mother, who tells us everything is "beautiful," including the fish her son-in-law caught in Scotland and had boiled for their dinner by the innkeeper. There is the novelettish voice of such sentences as "Aunt Kate was making frank use of her handkerchief," and the society-page gabble of "the acclamation which followed was taken up beyond the door of the supper-room by many of the other guests and renewed time after time." There is Aunt Julia's voice singing "Arrayed for the Bridal" and Bartell D'Arcy's singing "The Lass of Aughrim." There is the voice of Patrick Morkan, Gabriel's grandfather, imitated by Gabriel: the very model of a stuffy twit when his horse makes a fool of him by walking round and round the statue of the King; "Go on, sir! What do you mean, sir? . . . Most extraordinary conduct! Can't understand the horse!"

To add to the tumult, Joyce offers us a series of lists, giving us information we have no need of: things that are only there for the pleasure of their naming. Guests are introduced briefly, for the sound of their names: Mr. Bergin, Mr. Kerrigan, Miss Power, Miss Furlong, Miss Daly. There are the secondhand booksellers on the Dublin quays: Hickey's on Bachelor's Walk, Webb's and Massey's on Aston's Quay, O'Clohissey's in the by-street. And, most important, the meal spread out before us, like Homer's catalogue of ships. Followed by dessert, the sweetmeats joined together by their jumpy integument of "and's."

This is the hubbub of realism, the buzz and Babel of the nineteenth century. Words, words, words, talk talk talk, and in so many voices, such an abundance that of course there must be misunderstandings and mistakes. "The Dead" is chock full of mistakes, beginning with Gabriel's ill-considered joshing of Lily about her beau, to which she replies, "The men that is now is only all palaver and what they can get out of you." Twice, Aunt Julia misunderstands: she doesn't know what galoshes are and doesn't get Gabriel's reference to the Three Graces. Browne repeatedly calls Freddy Malins Teddy and embarrasses the young ladies by telling the kind of joke they don't like. Errors of tone abound. Gabriel takes the wrong tone in responding to Miss Ivors's political challenge, and he mistakes the pressure of her hand for a conciliatory gesture, when it is really a prelude to her standing on tiptoe to whisper into his ear: "West Briton." Aunt Kate offers an ill-considered criticism of the pope's decision to banish women from choirs in favor of young boys, and she is chastised for doing this in the presence of Mr. Browne, who is of "the other persuasion." A conversation about monks sleeping in their coffin is dropped because it is too "lugubrious." And Freddy is ready to pick a fight in defense of a black opera singer whom no one, in fact, has criticized. "And why couldn't he have a voice too? Is it because he's only a black?"

The mistakes and misunderstandings seem to be smoothed over by Gabriel's speech in praise of his aunts and cousin, whom he compliments for their hospitality, their harmoniousness. There is the bustle of leave-taking, when Freddy Malins and Mr. Browne can't make the cabdriver understand them, and everyone shouts directions from the door, only adding to the confusion. Finally, the cab takes off, and upstairs there is the sound of music.

In the quiet surrounded by music, Gabriel sees his wife standing on the stairs. "There was grace and mystery in her attitude as if she were a symbol of something. He asked himself what is a woman standing on the stairs in the shadow, listening to distant music, a symbol of."

We usually think of mistakes as affairs of language, a by-blow of the very separateness that causes us to wish to communicate with one another. But what Gabriel perceives and tries to create in silence—a woman who is a symbol—constitutes the central mistake both of his life and of the story. He assumes that the light in her eyes and the color on her cheeks have to do with him, as he will later assume that she has understood his desire for her and shared it. In his silent creation of Gretta—a creation brought about without a word from her—Gabriel has misconstrued the woman he has lived beside. Just as the narrator refers to Gretta only as Mrs. Conroy or Gabriel's wife, Gabriel assumes that Gretta's whole identity is connected to him. It is only after she speaks what is in her heart, after she tells her story, that the vision which both takes in and transcends separateness can occur.

She tells him of a boy she knew as a young girl in the West Country, a boy who died for love of her. Afterward, she sleeps. And in this silence, the silence which comes after true speech, Gabriel is transformed from petty if dutiful pedant to a man of vision.

The process happens in stages. He is dully angry, and this anger rekindles his lust. He is jealous. He is ironic. He feels humiliated, seeing himself as far less than the boy who died for her. When he speaks, his voice is "humble and indifferent," the humility and indifference Joyce thought to be the necessary conditions of the true artist. Then he is terrified at the "impalpable and vindictive being . . . coming against him, gathering forces against him in its vague world." He notes that Gretta's not as young as she used to be and feels disgust for the reality of her body, represented by her petticoat string and the limp upper of her boot.

He thinks of his Aunt Julia's impending death, and this thought, born of benevolence, leads him to understand that to be alive is to be in the process of becoming a shade. Tears fill his eyes, and his blurred physical vision allows him to imagine the dead boy—a shade, to be sure, but standing near, under a dripping tree. Gabriel loses him*self,* that distinct and separate self by which he has been able to be named. He is among the dead.

"His own identity was fading out into a grey impalpable world: the solid world in itself which these had one time reared and lived in was dissolving and dwindling." What a strange word, the word "reared." What does it imply? That the dead have nurtured the world we think of as the real one as parents "rear" a child, feeding it, sheltering it, educating it, until it is ready to leave them?

Gabriel's vision takes him to the graveyard where the boy is buried. The snow is falling. In the extraordinary last paragraph of "The Dead," the word "falling" is repeated seven times: seven, the theologically magic number, the number of the seven deadly sins, the seven moral virtues, the seven corporal and spiritual works of mercy.

The vagueness of the flickering shades subsides. Gabriel sees the snow on "the crooked crosses and headstones, on the spears of the little gate, on the barren thorns," those singular sharp things asserting, inexorably, their individuality, their separateness from their fellows. But the snow that is falling generally falls on them all alike and muffles their sharpness, their distinctness. "His soul swooned slowly as he heard the snow falling faintly through the universe and faintly falling, like the descent of their last end, upon all the living and the dead."

Consider the daring of Joyce's final repetitions and reversals: "falling faintly, faintly falling"—a triumph of pure sound, of language as music. No one has ever equaled it; it makes those who have come after him pause for a minute, in awed gratitude, in discouragement. How can any of us come up to it? Only, perhaps, humbly, indifferently, in its honor and its name, to try.

And he did it all when he was twenty-five. The bastard.

The Dead

James Joyce

Lily, the caretaker's daughter, was literally run off her feet. Hardly had she brought one gentleman into the little pantry behind the office on the ground floor and helped him off with his overcoat than the wheezy hall-door bell clanged again and she had to scamper along the bare hallway to let in another guest. It was well for her she had not to attend to the ladies also. But Miss Kate and Miss Julia had thought of that and had converted the bathroom upstairs into a ladies' dressing-room. Miss Kate and Miss Julia were there, gossiping and laughing and fussing, walking after each other to the head of the stairs, peering down over the banisters and calling down to Lily to ask her who had come.

It was always a great affair, the Misses Morkan's annual dance. Everybody who knew them came to it, members of the family, old friends of the family, the members of Julia's choir, any of Kate's pupils that were grown up enough and even some of Mary Jane's pupils too. Never once had it fallen flat. For years and years it had gone off in splendid style as long as anyone could remember; ever since Kate and Julia, after the death of their brother Pat, had left the house in Stoney Batter and taken Mary Jane, their only niece, to live with them in the dark gaunt house on Usher's Island, the upper part of which they had rented from Mr Fulham, the corn-factor on the ground floor. That was a good thirty years ago if it was a day. Mary Jane, who was then a little girl in short clothes, was now the main prop of the household for she had the organ in Haddington Road. She had been through the Academy and gave a pupils' concert every year in the upper room of the Antient Concert Rooms. Many of her pupils belonged to better-class families on the Kingstown and Dalkey line. Old as they were, her aunts also did their share. Julia, though she was quite grey, was still the leading soprano in Adam and Eve's, and Kate, being too feeble to go about much, gave music lessons to beginners on the old square piano in the back room. Lily, the caretaker's daughter, did housemaid's work for them. Though their life was modest they believed in eating well; the best of everything: diamond-bone sirloins, three-shilling tea and the best bottled stout. But Lily seldom made a mistake in the orders so that she got on well with her three mistresses. They were fussy, that was all. But the only thing they would not stand was back answers.

Of course they had good reason to be fussy on such a night. And then it was long after ten o'clock and yet there was no sign of Gabriel and his wife.

Besides they were dreadfully afraid that Freddy Malins might turn up screwed. They would not wish for worlds that any of Mary Jane's pupils should see him under the influence; and when he was like that it was sometimes very hard to manage him. Freddy Malins always came late but they wondered what could be keeping Gabriel: and that was what brought them every two minutes to the banisters to ask Lily had Gabriel or Freddy come.

—O, Mr Conroy, said Lily to Gabriel when she opened the door for him, Miss Kate and Miss Julia thought you were never coming. Good-night, Mrs Conroy.

—I'll engage they did, said Gabriel, but they forget that my wife here takes three mortal hours to dress herself.

He stood on the mat, scraping the snow from his goloshes, while Lily led his wife to the foot of the stairs and called out:

—Miss Kate, here's Mrs Conroy.

Kate and Julia came toddling down the dark stairs at once. Both of them kissed Gabriel's wife, said she must be perished alive and asked was Gabriel with her.

—Here I am as right as the mail, Aunt Kate! Go on up. I'll follow, called out Gabriel from the dark.

He continued scraping his feet vigorously while the three women went upstairs, laughing, to the ladies' dressing-room. A light fringe of snow lay like a cape on the shoulders of his overcoat and like toecaps on the toes of his goloshes; and, as the buttons of his overcoat slipped with a squeaking noise through the snow-stiffened frieze, a cold fragrant air from out-of-doors escaped from crevices and folds.

—Is it snowing again, Mr Conroy? asked Lily.

She had preceded him into the pantry to help him off with his overcoat. Gabriel smiled at the three syllables she had given his surname and glanced at her. She was a slim, growing girl, pale in complexion and with hay-coloured hair. The gas in the pantry made her look still paler. Gabriel had known her when she was a child and used to sit on the lowest step nursing a rag doll.

—Yes, Lily, he answered, and I think we're in for a night of it.

He looked up at the pantry ceiling, which was shaking with the stamping and shuffling of feet on the floor above, listened for a moment to the piano and then glanced at the girl, who was folding his overcoat carefully at the end of a shelf.

—Tell me, Lily, he said in a friendly tone, do you still go to school?

—O no, sir, she answered. I'm done schooling this year and more.

—O, then, said Gabriel gaily, I suppose we'll be going to your wedding one of these fine days with your young man, eh?

The girl glanced back at him over her shoulder and said with great bitterness:

—The men that is now is only all palaver and what they can get out of you.

Gabriel coloured as if he felt he had made a mistake and, without looking at her, kicked off his goloshes and flicked actively with his muffler at his patent-leather shoes.

He was a stout tallish young man. The high colour of his cheeks pushed upwards even to his forehead where it scattered itself in a few formless patches of pale red; and on his hairless face there scintillated restlessly the polished lenses and the bright gilt rims of the glasses which screened his delicate and restless eyes. His glossy black hair was parted in the middle and brushed in a long curve behind his ears where it curled slightly beneath the groove left by his hat.

When he had flicked lustre into his shoes he stood up and pulled his waistcoat down more tightly on his plump body. Then he took a coin rapidly from his pocket.

—O Lily, he said, thrusting it into her hands, it's Christmas-time, isn't it? Just . . . here's a little. . . .

He walked rapidly towards the door.

—O no, sir! cried the girl, following him. Really, sir, I wouldn't take it.

—Christmas-time! Christmas-time! said Gabriel, almost trotting to the stairs and waving his hand to her in deprecation.

The girl, seeing that he had gained the stairs, called out after him:

—Well, thank you, sir.

He waited outside the drawing-room door until the waltz should finish, listening to the skirts that swept against it and to the shuffling of feet. He was still discomposed by the girl's bitter and sudden retort. It had cast a gloom over him which he tried to dispel by arranging his cuffs and the bows of his tie. Then he took from his waistcoat pocket a little paper and glanced at the headings he had made for his speech. He was undecided about the lines from Robert Browning for he feared they would be above the heads of his hearers. Some quotation that they could recognise from Shakespeare or from the Melodies would be better. The indelicate clacking of the men's heels and the shuffling of their soles reminded him that their grade of culture differed from his. He would only make himself ridiculous by quoting poetry to them which they could not understand. They would think that he was airing his superior education. He would fail with them just as he had failed with the girl in the pantry. He had taken up a wrong tone. His whole speech was a mistake from first to last, an utter failure.

Just then his aunts and his wife came out of the ladies' dressing-room. His aunts were two small plainly dressed old women. Aunt Julia was an inch or so the taller. Her hair, drawn low over the tops of her ears, was grey; and grey also, with darker shadows, was her large flaccid face. Though she was stout in build and stood erect her slow eyes and parted lips gave her the appearance of a woman who did not know where she was or where she was going. Aunt Kate was more vivacious. Her face, healthier than her sister's, was all puckers and creases, like a shrivelled red apple, and her hair, braided in the same old-fashioned way, had not lost its ripe nut colour.

They both kissed Gabriel frankly. He was their favourite nephew, the son of their dead elder sister, Ellen, who had married T. J. Conroy of the Port and Docks.

—Gretta tells me you're not going to take a cab back to Monkstown to-night, Gabriel, said Aunt Kate.

—No, said Gabriel, turning to his wife, we had quite enough of that last year, hadn't we. Don't you remember, Aunt Kate, what a cold Gretta got out of it? Cab windows rattling all the way, and the east wind blowing in after we passed Merrion. Very jolly it was. Gretta caught a dreadful cold.

Aunt Kate frowned severely and nodded her head at every word.

—Quite right, Gabriel, quite right, she said. You can't be too careful.

—But as for Gretta there, said Gabriel, she'd walk home in the snow if she were let.

Mrs Conroy laughed.

—Don't mind him, Aunt Kate, she said. He's really an awful bother, what with green shades for Tom's eyes at night and making him do the dumb-bells, and forcing Eva to eat the stirabout. The poor child! And she simply hates the sight of it! . . . O, but you'll never guess what he makes me wear now!

She broke out into a peal of laughter and glanced at her husband, whose admiring and happy eyes had been wandering from her dress to her face and hair. The two aunts laughed heartily too, for Gabriel's solicitude was a standing joke with them.

—Goloshes! said Mrs Conroy. That's the latest. Whenever it's wet underfoot I must put on my goloshes. To-night even he wanted me to put them on, but I wouldn't. The next thing he'll buy me will be a diving suit.

Gabriel laughed nervously and patted his tie reassuringly while Aunt Kate nearly doubled herself, so heartily did she enjoy the joke. The smile soon faded from Aunt Julia's face and her mirthless eyes were directed towards her nephew's face. After a pause she asked:

—And what are goloshes, Gabriel?

—Goloshes, Julia! exclaimed her sister. Goodness me, don't you know what goloshes are? You wear them over your . . . over your boots, Gretta, isn't it?

—Yes, said Mrs Conroy. Guttapercha things. We both have a pair now. Gabriel says everyone wears them on the continent.

—O, on the continent, murmured Aunt Julia, nodding her head slowly.

Gabriel knitted his brows and said, as if he were slightly angered:

—It's nothing very wonderful but Gretta thinks it very funny because she says the word reminds her of Christy Minstrels.

—But tell me, Gabriel, said Aunt Kate, with brisk tact. Of course, you've seen about the room. Gretta was saying . . .

—O, the room is all right, replied Gabriel. I've taken one in the Gresham.

—To be sure, said Aunt Kate, by far the best thing to do. And the children, Gretta, you're not anxious about them?

—O, for one night, said Mrs Conroy. Besides, Bessie will look after them.

—To be sure, said Aunt Kate again. What a comfort it is to have a girl like that, one you can depend on! There's that Lily, I'm sure I don't know what has come over her lately. She's not the girl she was at all.

Gabriel was about to ask his aunt some questions on this point but she broke off suddenly to gaze after her sister who had wandered down the stairs and was craning her neck over the banisters.

—Now, I ask you, she said, almost testily, where is Julia going? Julia! Julia! Where are you going?

Julia, who had gone halfway down one flight, came back and announced blandly:

—Here's Freddy.

At the same moment a clapping of hands and a final flourish of the pianist told that the waltz had ended. The drawing-room door was opened from within and some couples came out. Aunt Kate drew Gabriel aside hurriedly and whispered into his ear:

—Slip down, Gabriel, like a good fellow and see if he's all right, and don't let him up if he's screwed. I'm sure he's screwed. I'm sure he is.

Gabriel went to the stairs and listened over the banisters. He could hear two persons talking in the pantry. Then he recognised Freddy Malins' laugh. He went down the stairs noisily.

—It's such a relief, said Aunt Kate to Mrs Conroy, that Gabriel is here. I always feel easier in my mind when he's here. . . . Julia, there's Miss Daly and Miss Power will take some refreshment. Thanks for your beautiful waltz, Miss Daly. It made lovely time.

A tall wizen-faced man, with a stiff grizzled moustache and swarthy skin, who was passing out with his partner said:

—And may we have some refreshment, too, Miss Morkan?

—Julia, said Aunt Kate summarily, and here's Mr Browne and Miss Furlong. Take them in, Julia, with Miss Daly and Miss Power.

—I'm the man for the ladies, said Mr Browne, pursing his lips until his moustache bristled and smiling in all his wrinkles. You know, Miss Morkan, the reason they are so fond of me is—

He did not finish his sentence, but, seeing that Aunt Kate was out of earshot, at once led the three young ladies into the back room. The middle of the room was occupied by two square tables placed end to end, and on these Aunt Julia and the caretaker were straightening and smoothing a large cloth. On the sideboard were arrayed dishes and plates, and glasses and bundles of knives and forks and spoons. The top of the closed square piano served also as a sideboard for viands and sweets. At a smaller sideboard in one corner two young men were standing, drinking hop-bitters.

Mr Browne led his charges thither and invited them all, in jest, to some ladies' punch, hot, strong and sweet. As they said they never took anything strong he opened three bottles of lemonade for them. Then he asked one of the young men to move aside, and, taking hold of the decanter, filled out for himself a goodly measure of whisky. The young men eyed him respectfully while he took a trial sip.

—God help me, he said, smiling, it's the doctor's orders.

His wizened face broke into a broader smile, and the three young ladies laughed in musical echo to his pleasantry, swaying their bodies to and fro, with nervous jerks of their shoulders. The boldest said:

—O, now, Mr Browne, I'm sure the doctor never ordered anything of the kind.

Mr Browne took another sip of his whisky and said, with sidling mimicry:

—Well, you see, I'm like the famous Mrs Cassidy, who is reported to have said: *Now, Mary Grimes, if I don't take it, make me take it, for I feel I want it.*

His hot face had leaned forward a little too confidentially and he had assumed a very low Dublin accent so that the young ladies, with one instinct, received his speech in silence. Miss Furlong, who was one of Mary Jane's pupils, asked Miss Daly what was the name of the pretty waltz she had played; and Mr Browne, seeing that he was ignored, turned promptly to the two young men who were more appreciative.

A red-faced young woman, dressed in pansy, came into the room, excitedly clapping her hands and crying:

—Quadrilles! Quadrilles!

Close on her heels came Aunt Kate, crying:

—Two gentlemen and three ladies, Mary Jane!

—O, here's Mr Bergin and Mr Kerrigan, said Mary Jane.

Mr Kerrigan, will you take Miss Power? Miss Furlong, may I get you a partner, Mr Bergin. O, that'll just do now.

—Three ladies, Mary Jane, said Aunt Kate.

The two young gentlemen asked the ladies if they might have the pleasure, and Mary Jane turned to Miss Daly.

—O, Miss Daly, you're really awfully good, after playing for the last two dances, but really we're so short of ladies to-night.

—I don't mind in the least, Miss Morkan.

—But I've a nice partner for you, Mr Bartell D'Arcy, the tenor. I'll get him to sing later on. All Dublin is raving about him.

—Lovely voice, lovely voice! said Aunt Kate.

As the piano had twice begun the prelude to the first figure Mary Jane led her recruits quickly from the room. They had hardly gone when Aunt Julia wandered slowly into the room, looking behind her at something.

—What is the matter, Julia? asked Aunt Kate anxiously. Who is it?

Julia, who was carrying in a column of table-napkins, turned to her sister and said, simply, as if the question had surprised her:

—It's only Freddy, Kate, and Gabriel with him.

In fact right behind her Gabriel could be seen piloting Freddy Malins across the landing. The latter, a young man of about forty, was of Gabriel's size and build, with very round shoulders. His face was fleshy and pallid, touched with colour only at the thick hanging lobes of his ears and at the wide wings of his nose. He had coarse features, a blunt nose, a convex and receding brow, tumid and protruded lips. His heavy-lidded eyes and the disorder of his scanty hair made him look sleepy. He was laughing heartily in a high key at a story which he had been telling Gabriel on the stairs and at the same time rubbing the knuckles of his left fist backwards and forwards into his left eye.

—Good-evening, Freddy, said Aunt Julia.

Freddy Malins bade the Misses Morkan good-evening in what seemed an offhand fashion by reason of the habitual catch in his voice and then, seeing that Mr Browne was grinning at him from the sideboard, crossed the room on rather shaky legs and began to repeat in an undertone the story he had just told to Gabriel.

—He's not so bad, is he? said Aunt Kate to Gabriel.

Gabriel's brows were dark but he raised them quickly and answered:

—O no, hardly noticeable.

—Now, isn't he a terrible fellow! she said. And his poor mother made him take the pledge on New Year's Eve. But come on, Gabriel, into the drawing-room.

Before leaving the room with Gabriel she signalled to Mr Browne by frowning and shaking her forefinger in warning to and fro. Mr Browne nodded in answer and, when she had gone, said to Freddy Malins:

—Now, then, Teddy, I'm going to fill you out a good glass of lemonade just to buck you up.

Freddy Malins, who was nearing the climax of his story, waved the offer aside impatiently but Mr Browne, having first called Freddy Malins' attention to a disarray in his dress, filled out and handed him a full glass of lemonade. Freddy Malins' left hand accepted the glass mechanically, his right hand being engaged in the mechanical readjustment of his dress. Mr Browne, whose face was once more wrinkling with mirth, poured out for himself a glass of whisky while Freddy Malins exploded, before he had well reached the climax of his story, in a kink of high-pitched bronchitic laughter and, setting down his untasted and overflowing glass, began to rub the knuckles of his left fist backwards and forwards into his left eye, repeating words of his last phrase as well as his fit of laughter would allow him.

Gabriel could not listen while Mary Jane was playing her Academy piece, full of runs and difficult passages, to the hushed drawing-room. He liked music but the piece she was playing had no melody for him and he doubted whether it had any melody for the other listeners, though they had begged Mary Jane to play something. Four young men, who had come from the refreshment-room to stand in the doorway at the sound of the piano, had gone away quietly in couples after a few minutes. The only persons who seemed to follow the music were Mary Jane herself, her hands racing along the key-board or lifted from it at the pauses like those of a priestess in momentary imprecation, and Aunt Kate standing at her elbow to turn the page.

Gabriel's eyes, irritated by the floor, which glittered with beeswax under the heavy chandelier, wandered to the wall above the piano. A picture of the balcony scene in *Romeo and Juliet* hung there and beside it was a picture of the two murdered princes in the Tower which Aunt Julia had worked in red, blue and brown wools when she was a girl. Probably in the school they had gone to as girls that kind of work had been taught, for one year his mother had worked for him as a birthday present a waistcoat of purple tabinet, with little foxes' heads upon it, lined with brown satin and having round mulberry buttons. It was strange that his mother had had no musical talent though Aunt Kate used to call her the brains carrier of the Morkan family. Both she and Julia had always seemed a little proud of their serious and matronly sister. Her photograph stood before the pierglass. She held an open book on her knees and was pointing out something in it to Constantine who, dressed in a man-o'-war suit, lay at her feet. It was she who had chosen the names for her sons for she was very sensible of the dignity of family life. Thanks to her, Constantine was now senior curate in Balbriggan and, thanks to her, Gabriel himself had taken his degree in the Royal University. A shadow passed over his face as he remembered her sullen opposition to his marriage. Some slighting phrases she had used still rankled in his memory; she had once spoken of Gretta as being country cute and that was not true of Gretta at all. It was Gretta who had nursed her during all her last long illness in their house at Monkstown.

He knew that Mary Jane must be near the end of her piece for she was playing again the opening melody with runs of scales after every bar and while he waited for the end the resentment died down in his heart. The piece ended with a trill of octaves in the treble and a final deep octave in the bass. Great applause greeted Mary Jane as, blushing and rolling up her music nervously, she escaped from the room. The most vigorous clapping came from the four young men in the doorway who had gone away to the refreshment-room at the beginning of the piece but had come back when the piano had stopped.

Lancers were arranged. Gabriel found himself partnered with Miss Ivors. She was a frank-mannered talkative young lady, with a freckled face and prominent brown eyes. She did not wear a low-cut bodice and the large brooch which was fixed in the front of her collar bore on it an Irish device.

When they had taken their places she said abruptly:

—I have a crow to pluck with you.

—With me? said Gabriel.

She nodded her head gravely.

—What is it? asked Gabriel, smiling at her solemn manner.

—Who is G. C.? answered Miss Ivors, turning her eyes upon him.

Gabriel coloured and was about to knit his brows, as if he did not understand, when she said bluntly:

—O, innocent Amy! I have found out that you write for *The Daily Express*. Now, aren't you ashamed of yourself?

—Why should I be ashamed of myself? asked Gabriel, blinking his eyes and trying to smile.

—Well, I'm ashamed of you, said Miss Ivors frankly. To say you'd write for a rag like that. I didn't think you were a West Briton.

A look of perplexity appeared on Gabriel's face. It was true that he wrote a literary column every Wednesday in *The Daily Express,* for which he was paid fifteen shillings. But that did not make him a West Briton surely. The books he received for review were almost more welcome than the paltry cheque. He loved to feel the covers and turn over the pages of newly printed books. Nearly every day when his teaching in the college was ended he used to wander down the quays to the second-hand booksellers, to Hickey's on Bachelor's Walk, to Webb's or Massey's on Aston's Quay, or to O'Clohissey's in the by-street. He did not know how to meet her charge. He wanted to say that literature was above politics. But they were friends of many years' standing and their careers had been parallel, first at the University and then as teachers: he could not risk a grandiose phrase with her. He continued blinking his eyes and trying to smile and murmured lamely that he saw nothing political in writing reviews of books.

When their turn to cross had come he was still perplexed and inattentive. Miss Ivors promptly took his hand in a warm grasp and said in a soft friendly tone:

—Of course, I was only joking. Come, we cross now.

When they were together again she spoke of the University question and Gabriel felt more at ease. A friend of hers had shown her his review of Browning's poems. That was how she had found out the secret: but she liked the review immensely. Then she said suddenly:

—O, Mr Conroy, will you come for an excursion to the Aran Isles this summer? We're going to stay there a whole month. It will be splendid out in the Atlantic. You ought to come. Mr Clancy is coming, and Mr Kilkelly and Kathleen Kearney. It would be splendid for Gretta too if she'd come. She's from Connacht, isn't she?

—Her people are, said Gabriel shortly.

—But you will come, won't you? said Miss Ivors, laying her warm hand eagerly on his arm.

—The fact is, said Gabriel, I have already arranged to go—

—Go where? asked Miss Ivors.

—Well, you know, every year I go for a cycling tour with some fellows and so—

—But where? asked Miss Ivors.

—Well, we usually go to France or Belgium or perhaps Germany, said Gabriel awkwardly.

—And why do you go to France and Belgium, said Miss Ivors, instead of visiting your own land?

—Well, said Gabriel, it's partly to keep in touch with the languages and partly for a change.

—And haven't you your own language to keep in touch with—Irish? asked Miss Ivors.

—Well, said Gabriel, if it comes to that, you know, Irish is not my language.

Their neighbours had turned to listen to the cross-examination. Gabriel glanced right and left nervously and tried to keep his good humour under the ordeal which was making a blush invade his forehead.

—And haven't you your own land to visit, continued Miss Ivors, that you know nothing of, your own people, and your own country?

—O, to tell you the truth, retorted Gabriel suddenly, I'm sick of my own country, sick of it!

—Why? asked Miss Ivors.

Gabriel did not answer for his retort had heated him.

—Why? repeated Miss Ivors.

They had to go visiting together and, as he had not answered her, Miss Ivors said warmly:

—Of course, you've no answer.

Gabriel tried to cover his agitation by taking part in the dance with great energy. He avoided her eyes for he had seen a sour expression on her face. But when they met in the long chain he was surprised to feel his hand firmly pressed. She looked at him from under her brows for a moment quizzically until he smiled. Then, just as the chain was about to start again, she stood on tiptoe and whispered into his ear:

—West Briton!

When the lancers were over Gabriel went away to a remote corner of the room where Freddy Malins' mother was sitting. She was a stout feeble old woman with white hair. Her voice had a catch in it like her son's and she stuttered slightly. She had been told that Freddy had come and that he was nearly all right. Gabriel asked her whether she had had a good crossing. She lived with her married daughter in Glasgow and came to Dublin on a visit once a year. She answered placidly that she had had a beautiful crossing and that the captain had been most attentive to her. She spoke also of the beautiful house her daughter kept in Glasgow, and of all the nice friends they had there. While her tongue rambled on Gabriel tried to banish from his mind all memory of the unpleasant incident with Miss Ivors. Of course the girl or woman, or whatever she was, was an enthusiast but there was a time for all things. Perhaps he ought not to have answered her like that. But she had no right to call him a West Briton before people, even in joke. She had tried to make him ridiculous before people, heckling him and staring at him with her rabbit's eyes.

He saw his wife making her way towards him through the waltzing couples. When she reached him she said into his ear:

—Gabriel, Aunt Kate wants to know won't you carve the goose as usual. Miss Daly will carve the ham and I'll do the pudding.

—All right, said Gabriel.

—She's sending in the younger ones first as soon as this waltz is over so that we'll have the table to ourselves.

—Were you dancing? asked Gabriel.

—Of course I was. Didn't you see me? What words had you with Molly Ivors?

—No words. Why? Did she say so?

—Something like that. I'm trying to get that Mr D'Arcy to sing. He's full of conceit, I think.

—There were no words, said Gabriel moodily, only she wanted me to go for a trip to the west of Ireland and I said I wouldn't.

His wife clasped her hands excitedly and gave a little jump.

—O, do go, Gabriel, she cried. I'd love to see Galway again.

—You can go if you like, said Gabriel coldly.

She looked at him for a moment, then turned to Mrs Malins and said:

—There's a nice husband for you, Mrs Malins.

While she was threading her way back across the room Mrs Malins, without adverting to the interruption, went on to tell Gabriel what beautiful places there were in Scotland and beautiful scenery. Her son-in-law brought them every year to the lakes and they used to go fishing. Her son-in-law was a splendid fisher. One day he caught a fish, a beautiful big big fish, and the man in the hotel boiled it for their dinner.

Gabriel hardly heard what she said. Now that supper was coming near he began to think again about his speech and about the quotation. When he saw Freddy Malins coming across the room to visit his mother Gabriel left the chair free for him and retired into the embrasure of the window. The room had already cleared and from the back room came the clatter of plates and knives. Those who still remained in the drawing-room seemed tired of dancing and were conversing quietly in little groups. Gabriel's warm trembling fingers tapped the cold pane of the window. How cool it must be outside! How pleasant it would be to walk out alone, first along by the river and then through the park! The snow would be lying on the branches of the trees and forming a bright cap on the top of the Wellington Monument. How much more pleasant it would be there than at the supper-table!

He ran over the headings of his speech: Irish hospitality, sad memories, the Three Graces, Paris, the quotation from Browning. He repeated to himself a phrase he had written in his review: *One feels that one is listening to a thought-tormented music*. Miss Ivors had praised the review. Was she sincere? Had she really any life of her own behind all her propagandism? There had never been any ill-feeling between them until that night. It unnerved him to think that she would be at the supper-table, looking up at him while he spoke with her critical quizzing eyes. Perhaps she would not be sorry to see him fail in his speech. An idea came into his mind and gave him courage. He would say, alluding to Aunt Kate and Aunt Julia: *Ladies and Gentlemen, the generation which is now on the wane among us may have had its faults but for my part I think it had certain qualities of hospitality, of humour, of humanity, which the new and very serious and hypereducated generation that is growing up around us seems to me to lack.* Very good: that was one for Miss Ivors. What did he care that his aunts were only two ignorant old women?

A murmur in the room attracted his attention. Mr Browne was advancing from the door, gallantly escorting Aunt Julia, who leaned upon his arm, smiling and hanging her head. An irregular musketry of applause escorted her also as far as the piano and then, as Mary Jane seated herself on the stool, and Aunt Julia, no longer smiling, half turned so as to pitch her voice fairly into the room, gradually ceased. Gabriel recognised the prelude. It was that of an old song of Aunt Julia's—*Arrayed for the Bridal.* Her voice, strong and clear in tone, attacked with great spirit the runs which embellish the air and though she sang very rapidly she did not miss even the smallest of the grace notes. To follow the voice, without looking at the singer's face, was to feel and share the excitement of swift and secure flight. Gabriel applauded loudly with all the others at the close of the song and loud applause was borne in from the invisible supper-table. It sounded so genuine that a little colour struggled into Aunt Julia's face as she bent to replace in the music-stand the old leather-bound song-book that had her initials on the cover. Freddy Malins, who had listened with his head perched sideways to hear her better, was still applauding when everyone else had ceased and talking animatedly to his mother who nodded her head gravely and slowly in acquiescence. At last, when he could clap no more, he stood up suddenly and hurried across the room to Aunt Julia whose hand he seized and held in both his hands, shaking it when words failed him or the catch in his voice proved too much for him.

—I was just telling my mother, he said, I never heard you sing so well, never. No, I never heard your voice so good as it is to-night. Now! Would you believe that now? That's the truth. Upon my word and honour that's the truth. I never heard your voice sound so fresh and so . . . so clear and fresh, never.

Aunt Julia smiled broadly and murmured something about compliments as she released her hand from his grasp. Mr Browne extended his open hand towards her and said to those who were near him in the manner of a showman introducing a prodigy to an audience:

—Miss Julia Morkan, my latest discovery!

He was laughing very heartily at this himself when Freddy Malins turned to him and said:

—Well, Browne, if you're serious you might make a worse discovery. All I can say is I never heard her sing half so well as long as I am coming here. And that's the honest truth.

—Neither did I, said Mr Browne. I think her voice has greatly improved.

Aunt Julia shrugged her shoulders and said with meek pride:

—Thirty years ago I hadn't a bad voice as voices go.

—I often told Julia, said Aunt Kate emphatically, that she was simply thrown away in that choir. But she never would be said by me.

She turned as if to appeal to the good sense of the others against a refractory child while Aunt Julia gazed in front of her, a vague smile of reminiscence playing on her face.

—No, continued Aunt Kate, she wouldn't be said or led by anyone, slaving there in that choir night and day, night and day. Six o'clock on Christmas morning! And all for what?

—Well, isn't it for the honour of God, Aunt Kate? asked Mary Jane, twisting round on the piano-stool and smiling.

Aunt Kate turned fiercely on her niece and said:

—I know all about the honour of God, Mary Jane, but I think it's not at all honourable for the pope to turn out the women out of the choirs that have slaved there all their lives and put little whipper-snappers of boys over their heads. I suppose it is for the good of the Church if the pope does it. But it's not just, Mary Jane, and it's not right.

She had worked herself into a passion and would have continued in defence of her sister for it was a sore subject with her but Mary Jane, seeing that all the dancers had come back, intervened pacifically:

—Now, Aunt Kate, you're giving scandal to Mr Browne who is of the other persuasion.

Aunt Kate turned to Mr Browne, who was grinning at this allusion to his religion, and said hastily:

—O, I don't question the pope's being right. I'm only a stupid old woman and I wouldn't presume to do such a thing. But there's such a thing as common everyday politeness and gratitude. And if I were in Julia's place I'd tell that Father Healy straight up to his face . . .

—And besides, Aunt Kate, said Mary Jane, we really are all hungry and when we are hungry we are all very quarrelsome.

—And when we are thirsty we are also quarrelsome, added Mr Browne.

—So that we had better go to supper, said Mary Jane, and finish the discussion afterwards.

On the landing outside the drawing-room Gabriel found his wife and Mary Jane trying to persuade Miss Ivors to stay for supper. But Miss Ivors, who had put on her hat and was buttoning her cloak, would not stay. She did not feel in the least hungry and she had already overstayed her time.

—But only for ten minutes, Molly, said Mrs Conroy. That won't delay you.

—To take a pick itself, said Mary Jane, after all your dancing.

—I really couldn't, said Miss Ivors.

—I am afraid you didn't enjoy yourself at all, said Mary Jane hopelessly.

—Ever so much, I assure you, said Miss Ivors, but you really must let me run off now.

—But how can you get home? asked Mrs Conroy.

—O, it's only two steps up the quay.

Gabriel hesitated a moment and said:

—If you will allow me, Miss Ivors, I'll see you home if you really are obliged to go.

But Miss Ivors broke away from them.

—I won't hear of it, she cried. For goodness sake go in to your suppers and don't mind me. I'm quite well able to take care of myself.

—Well, you're the comical girl, Molly, said Mrs Conroy frankly.

—*Beannacht libh,* cried Miss Ivors, with a laugh, as she ran down the staircase.

Mary Jane gazed after her, a moody puzzled expression on her face, while Mrs Conroy leaned over the banisters to listen for the hall-door. Gabriel asked himself was he the cause of her abrupt departure. But she did not seem to be in ill humour: she had gone away laughing. He stared blankly down the staircase.

At that moment Aunt Kate came toddling out of the supper-room, almost wringing her hands in despair.

—Where is Gabriel? she cried. Where on earth is Gabriel? There's everyone waiting in there, stage to let, and nobody to carve the goose!

—Here I am, Aunt Kate! cried Gabriel, with sudden animation, ready to carve a flock of geese, if necessary.

A fat brown goose lay at one end of the table and at the other end, on a bed of creased paper strewn with sprigs of parsley, lay a great ham, stripped of its outer skin and peppered over with crust crumbs, a neat paper frill round its shin and beside this was a round of spiced beef. Between these rival ends ran parallel lines of side-dishes: two little minsters of jelly, red and yellow; a shallow dish full of blocks of blancmange and red jam, a large green leaf-shaped dish with a stalk-shaped handle, on which lay bunches of purple raisins and peeled almonds, a companion dish on which lay a solid rectangle of Smyrna figs, a dish of custard topped with grated nutmeg, a small bowl full of chocolates and sweets wrapped in gold and silver papers and a glass vase in which stood some tall celery stalks. In the centre of the table there stood, as sentries to a fruit-stand which upheld a pyramid of oranges and American apples, two squat old-fashioned decanters of cut glass, one containing port and the other dark sherry. On the closed square piano a pudding in a huge yellow dish lay in waiting and behind it were three squads of bottles of stout and ale and minerals, drawn up according to the colours of their uniforms, the first two black, with brown and red labels, the third and smallest squad white, with transverse green sashes.

Gabriel took his seat boldly at the head of the table and, having looked to the edge of the carver, plunged his fork firmly into the goose. He felt quite at ease now for he was an expert carver and liked nothing better than to find himself at the head of a well-laden table.

—Miss Furlong, what shall I send you? he asked. A wing or a slice of the breast?

—Just a small slice of the breast.

—Miss Higgins, what for you?

—O, anything at all, Mr Conroy.

While Gabriel and Miss Daly exchanged plates of goose and plates of ham and spiced beef Lily went from guest to guest with a dish of hot floury potatoes wrapped in a white napkin. This was Mary Jane's idea and she had also suggested apple sauce for the goose but Aunt Kate had said that plain roast goose without apple sauce had always been good enough for her and she hoped she might never eat worse. Mary Jane waited on her pupils and saw that they got the best slices and Aunt Kate and Aunt Julia opened and carried across from the piano bottles of stout and ale for the gentlemen and bottles of minerals for the ladies. There was a great deal of confusion and laughter and noise, the noise of orders and counter-orders, of knives and forks, of corks and glass-stoppers. Gabriel began to carve second helpings as soon as he had finished the first round without serving himself. Everyone protested loudly so that he compromised by taking a long draught of stout for he had found the carving hot work. Mary Jane settled down quietly to her supper but Aunt Kate and Aunt Julia were still toddling round the table, walking on each other's heels, getting in each other's way and giving each other unheeded orders. Mr Browne begged of them to sit down and eat their suppers and so did Gabriel but they said there was time enough so that, at last, Freddy Malins stood up and, capturing Aunt Kate, plumped her down on her chair amid general laughter.

When everyone had been well served Gabriel said, smiling:

—Now, if anyone wants a little more of what vulgar people call stuffing let him or her speak.

A chorus of voices invited him to begin his own supper and Lily came forward with three potatoes which she had reserved for him.

—Very well, said Gabriel amiably, as he took another preparatory draught, kindly forget my existence, ladies and gentlemen, for a few minutes.

He set to his supper and took no part in the conversation with which the table covered Lily's removal of the plates. The subject of talk was the opera company which was then at the Theatre Royal. Mr Bartell D'Arcy, the tenor, a dark-complexioned young man with a smart moustache, praised very highly the leading contralto of the company but Miss Furlong thought she had a rather vulgar style of production. Freddy Malins said there was a negro chieftain singing in the second part of the Gaiety pantomime who had one of the finest tenor voices he had ever heard.

—Have you heard him? he asked Mr Bartell D'Arcy across the table.

—No, answered Mr Bartell D'Arcy carelessly.

—Because, Freddy Malins explained, now I'd be curious to hear your opinion of him. I think he has a grand voice.

—It takes Teddy to find out the really good things, said Mr Browne familiarly to the table.

—And why couldn't he have a voice too? asked Freddy Malins sharply. Is it because he's only a black?

Nobody answered this question and Mary Jane led the table back to the legitimate opera. One of her pupils had given her a pass for *Mignon*. Of course it was very fine, she said, but it made her think of poor Georgina Burns. Mr Browne could go back farther still, to the old Italian companies that used to come to Dublin—Tietjens, Ilma de Murzka, Campanini, the great Trebelli, Giuglini, Ravelli, Aramburo. Those were the days, he said, when there was something like singing to be heard in Dublin. He told too of how the top gallery of the old Royal used to be packed night after night, of how one night an Italian tenor had sung five encores to *Let Me Like a Soldier Fall,* introducing a high C every time, and of how the gallery boys would sometimes in their enthusiasm unyoke the horses from the carriage of some great *prima donna* and pull her themselves through the streets to her hotel. Why did they never play the grand old operas now, he asked, *Dinorah, Lucrezia Borgia?* Because they could not get the voices to sing them: that was why.

—O, well, said Mr Bartell D'Arcy, I presume there are as good singers to-day as there were then.

—Where are they? asked Mr Browne defiantly.

—In London, Paris, Milan, said Mr Bartell D'Arcy warmly. I suppose Caruso, for example, is quite as good, if not better than any of the men you have mentioned.

—Maybe so, said Mr Browne. But I may tell you I doubt it strongly.

—O, I'd give anything to hear Caruso sing, said Mary Jane.

—For me, said Aunt Kate, who had been picking a bone, there was only one tenor. To please me, I mean. But I suppose none of you ever heard of him.

—Who was he, Miss Morkan? asked Mr Bartell D'Arcy politely.

—His name, said Aunt Kate, was Parkinson. I heard him when he was in his prime and I think he had then the purest tenor voice that was ever put into a man's throat.

—Strange, said Mr Bartell D'Arcy. I never even heard of him.

—Yes, yes, Miss Morkan is right, said Mr Browne. I remember hearing of old Parkinson but he's too far back for me.

—A beautiful pure sweet mellow English tenor, said Aunt Kate with enthusiasm.

Gabriel having finished, the huge pudding was transferred to the table.

The clatter of forks and spoons began again. Gabriel's wife served out spoonfuls of the pudding and passed the plates down the table. Midway down they were held up by Mary Jane, who replenished them with raspberry or orange jelly or with blancmange and jam. The pudding was of Aunt Julia's making and she received praises for it from all quarters. She herself said that it was not quite brown enough.

—Well, I hope, Miss Morkan, said Mr Browne, that I'm brown enough for you because, you know, I'm all brown.

All the gentlemen, except Gabriel, ate some of the pudding out of compliment to Aunt Julia. As Gabriel never ate sweets the celery had been left for him. Freddy Malins also took a stalk of celery and ate it with his pudding. He had been told that celery was a capital thing for the blood and he was just then under doctor's care. Mrs Malins, who had been silent all through the supper, said that her son was going down to Mount Melleray in a week or so. The table then spoke of Mount Melleray, how bracing the air was down there, how hospitable the monks were and how they never asked for a penny-piece from their guests.

—And do you mean to say, asked Mr Browne incredulously, that a chap can go down there and put up there as if it were a hotel and live on the fat of the land and then come away without paying a farthing?

—O, most people give some donation to the monastery when they leave, said Mary Jane.

—I wish we had an institution like that in our Church, said Mr Browne candidly.

He was astonished to hear that the monks never spoke, got up at two in the morning and slept in their coffins. He asked what they did it for.

—That's the rule of the order, said Aunt Kate firmly.

—Yes, but why? asked Mr Browne.

Aunt Kate repeated that it was the rule, that was all. Mr Browne still seemed not to understand. Freddy Malins explained to him, as best he could, that the monks were trying to make up for the sins committed by all the sinners in the outside world. The explanation was not very clear for Mr Browne grinned and said:

—I like that idea very much but wouldn't a comfortable spring bed do them as well as a coffin?

—The coffin, said Mary Jane, is to remind them of their last end.

As the subject had grown lugubrious it was buried in a silence of the table during which Mrs Malins could be heard saying to her neighbour in an indistinct undertone:

—They are very good men, the monks, very pious men.

The raisins and almonds and figs and apples and oranges and chocolates and sweets were now passed about the table and Aunt Julia invited all the guests to have either port or sherry. At first Mr Bartell D'Arcy refused to take either but one of his neighbours nudged him and whispered something to him upon which he allowed his glass to be filled. Gradually as the last glasses were being filled the conversation ceased. A pause followed, broken only by the noise of the wine and by unsettlings of chairs. The Misses Morkan, all three, looked down at the tablecloth. Someone coughed once or twice and then a few gentlemen patted the table gently as a signal for silence. The silence came and Gabriel pushed back his chair and stood up.

The patting at once grew louder in encouragement and then ceased altogether. Gabriel leaned his ten trembling fingers on the tablecloth and smiled nervously at the company. Meeting a row of upturned faces he raised his eyes to the chandelier. The piano was playing a waltz tune and he could hear the skirts sweeping against the drawing-room door. People, perhaps, were standing in the snow on the quay outside, gazing up at the lighted windows and listening to the waltz music. The air was pure there. In the distance lay the park where the trees were weighted with snow. The Wellington Monument wore a gleaming cap of snow that flashed westward over the white field of Fifteen Acres.

He began:

—Ladies and Gentlemen.

—It has fallen to my lot this evening, as in years past, to perform a very pleasing task but a task for which I am afraid my poor powers as a speaker are all too inadequate.

—No, no! said Mr Browne.

—But, however that may be, I can only ask you to-night to take the will for the deed and to lend me your attention for a few moments while I endeavour to express to you in words what my feelings are on this occasion.

—Ladies and Gentlemen. It is not the first time that we have gathered together under this hospitable roof, around this hospitable board. It is not the first time that we have been the recipients—or perhaps, I had better say, the victims—of the hospitality of certain good ladies.

He made a circle in the air with his arms and paused. Everyone laughed or smiled at Aunt Kate and Aunt Julia and Mary Jane who all turned crimson with pleasure. Gabriel went on more boldly:

—I feel more strongly with every recurring year that our country has no tradition which does it so much honour and which it should guard so jealously as that of its hospitality. It is a tradition that is unique as far as my experience goes (and I have visited not a few places abroad) among the modern nations. Some would say, perhaps, that with us it is rather a failing than anything to be boasted of. But granted even that, it is, to my mind, a princely failing, and one that I trust will long be cultivated among us. Of one thing, at least, I am sure. As long as this one roof shelters the good ladies aforesaid—and I wish from my heart it may do so for many and many a long year to come—the tradition of genuine warm-hearted courteous Irish hospitality, which our forefathers have handed down to us and which we in turn must hand down to our descendants, is still alive among us.

A hearty murmur of assent ran round the table. It shot through Gabriel's mind that Miss Ivors was not there and that she had gone away discourteously: and he said with confidence in himself:

—Ladies and Gentlemen.

—A new generation is growing up in our midst, a generation actuated by new ideas and new principles. It is serious and enthusiastic for these new ideas and its enthusiasm, even when it is misdirected, is, I believe, in the main sincere. But we are living in a sceptical and, if I may use the phrase, a thought-tormented age: and sometimes I fear that this new generation, educated or hypereducated as it is, will lack those qualities of humanity, of hospitality, of kindly humour which belonged to an older day. Listening to-night to the names of all those great singers of the past it seemed to me, I must confess, that we were living in a less spacious age. Those days might, without exaggeration, be called spacious days: and if they are gone beyond recall let us hope, at least, that in gatherings such as this we shall still speak of them with pride and affection, still cherish in our hearts the memory of those dead and gone great ones whose fame the world will not willingly let die.

—Hear, hear! said Mr Browne loudly.

—But yet, continued Gabriel, his voice falling into a softer inflection, there are always in gatherings such as this sadder thoughts that will recur to our minds: thoughts of the past, of youth, of changes, of absent faces that we miss here to-night. Our path through life is strewn with many such sad memories: and were we to brood upon them always we could not find the heart to go on bravely with our work among the living. We have all of us living duties and living affections which claim, and rightly claim, our strenuous endeavours.

—Therefore, I will not linger on the past. I will not let any gloomy moralising intrude upon us here to-night. Here we are gathered together for a brief moment from the bustle and rush of our everyday routine. We are met here as friends, in the spirit of good-fellowship, as colleagues, also to a certain extent, in the true spirit of *camaraderie,* and as the guests of—what shall I call them?—the Three Graces of the Dublin musical world.

The table burst into applause and laughter at this sally. Aunt Julia vainly asked each of her neighbours in turn to tell her what Gabriel had said.

—He says we are the Three Graces, Aunt Julia, said Mary Jane.

Aunt Julia did not understand but she looked up, smiling, at Gabriel, who continued in the same vein:

—Ladies and Gentlemen.

—I will not attempt to play to-night the part that Paris played on another occasion. I will not attempt to choose between them. The task would be an invidious one and one beyond my poor powers. For when I view them in turn, whether it be our chief hostess herself, whose good heart, whose too good heart, has become a byword with all who know her, or her sister, who seems to be gifted with perennial youth and whose singing must have been a surprise and a revelation to us all to-night, or, last but not least, when I consider our youngest hostess, talented, cheerful, hard-working and the best of nieces, I confess, Ladies and Gentlemen, that I do not know to which of them I should award the prize.

Gabriel glanced down at his aunts and, seeing the large smile on Aunt Julia's face and the tears which had risen to Aunt Kate's eyes, hastened to his close. He raised his glass of port gallantly, while every member of the company fingered a glass expectantly, and said loudly:

—Let us toast them all three together. Let us drink to their health, wealth, long life, happiness and prosperity and may they long continue to hold the proud and self-won position which they hold in their profession and the position of honour and affection which they hold in our hearts.

All the guests stood up, glass in hand, and, turning towards the three seated ladies, sang in unison, with Mr Browne as leader:

For they are jolly gay fellows,
For they are jolly gay fellows,
For they are jolly gay fellows,
Which nobody can deny.

Aunt Kate was making frank use of her handkerchief and even Aunt Julia seemed moved. Freddy Malins beat time with his pudding-fork and the singers turned towards one another, as if in melodious conference, while they sang, with emphasis:

Unless he tells a lie,
Unless he tells a lie.

Then, turning once more towards their hostesses, they sang:

For they are jolly gay fellows,
For they are jolly gay fellows,
For they are jolly gay fellows,
Which nobody can deny.

The acclamation which followed was taken up beyond the door of the supper-room by many of the other guests and renewed time after time, Freddy Malins acting as officer with his fork on high.

The piercing morning air came into the hall where they were standing so that Aunt Kate said:

—Close the door, somebody. Mrs Malins will get her death of cold.

—Browne is out there, Aunt Kate, said Mary Jane.

—Browne is everywhere, said Aunt Kate, lowering her voice.

Mary Jane laughed at her tone.

—Really, she said archly, he is very attentive.

—He has been laid on here like the gas, said Aunt Kate in the same tone, all during the Christmas.

She laughed herself this time good-humouredly and then added quickly:

—But tell him to come in, Mary Jane, and close the door. I hope to goodness he didn't hear me.

At that moment the hall-door was opened and Mr Browne came in from the doorstep, laughing as if his heart would break. He was dressed in a long green overcoat with mock astrakhan cuffs and collar and wore on his head an oval fur cap. He pointed down the snow-covered quay from where the sound of shrill prolonged whistling was borne in.

—Teddy will have all the cabs in Dublin out, he said.

Gabriel advanced from the little pantry behind the office, struggling into his overcoat and, looking round the hall, said:

—Gretta not down yet?

—She's getting on her things, Gabriel, said Aunt Kate.

—Who's playing up there? asked Gabriel.

—Nobody. They're all gone.

—O no, Aunt Kate, said Mary Jane. Bartell D'Arcy and Miss O'Callaghan aren't gone yet.

—Someone is strumming at the piano, anyhow, said Gabriel.

Mary Jane glanced at Gabriel and Mr Browne and said with a shiver:

—It makes me feel cold to look at you two gentlemen muffled up like that. I wouldn't like to face your journey home at this hour.

—I'd like nothing better this minute, said Mr Browne stoutly, than a rattling fine walk in the country or a fast drive with a good spanking goer between the shafts.

—We used to have a very good horse and trap at home, said Aunt Julia sadly.

—The never-to-be-forgotten Johnny, said Mary Jane, laughing.

Aunt Kate and Gabriel laughed too.

—Why, what was wonderful about Johnny? asked Mr Browne.

—The late lamented Patrick Morkan, our grandfather, that is, explained Gabriel, commonly known in his later years as the old gentleman, was a glue-boiler.

—O, now, Gabriel, said Aunt Kate, laughing, he had a starch mill.

—Well, glue or starch, said Gabriel, the old gentleman had a horse by the name of Johnny. And Johnny used to work in the old gentleman's mill, walking round and round in order to drive the mill. That was all very well; but now comes the tragic part about Johnny. One fine day the old gentleman thought he'd like to drive out with the quality to a military review in the park.

—The Lord have mercy on his soul, said Aunt Kate compassionately.

—Amen, said Gabriel. So the old gentleman, as I said, harnessed Johnny and put on his very best tall hat and his very best stock collar and drove out in grand style from his ancestral mansion somewhere near Back Lane, I think.

Everyone laughed, even Mrs Malins, at Gabriel's manner and Aunt Kate said:

—O now, Gabriel, he didn't live in Back Lane, really. Only the mill was there.

—Out from the mansion of his forefathers, continued Gabriel, he drove with Johnny. And everything went on beautifully until Johnny came in sight of King Billy's statue: and whether he fell in love with the horse King Billy sits on or whether he thought he was back again in the mill, anyhow he began to walk round the statue.

Gabriel paced in a circle round the hall in his goloshes amid the laughter of the others.

—Round and round he went, said Gabriel, and the old gentleman, who was a very pompous old gentleman, was highly indignant. *Go on, sir! What do you mean, sir? Johnny! Johnny! Most extraordinary conduct! Can't understand the horse!*

The peals of laughter which followed Gabriel's imitation of the incident were interrupted by a resounding knock at the hall-door. Mary Jane ran to open it and let in Freddy Malins. Freddy Malins, with his hat well back on his head and his shoulders humped with cold, was puffing and steaming after his exertions.

—I could only get one cab, he said.

—O, we'll find another along the quay, said Gabriel.

—Yes, said Aunt Kate. Better not keep Mrs Malins standing in the draught.

Mrs Malins was helped down the front steps by her son and Mr Browne and, after many manœuvres, hoisted into the cab. Freddy Malins clambered in after her and spent a long time settling her on the seat, Mr Browne helping him with advice. At last she was settled comfortably and Freddy Malins invited Mr Browne into the cab. There was a good deal of confused talk, and then Mr Browne got into the cab. The cabman settled his rug over his knees, and bent down for the address. The confusion grew greater and the cabman was directed differently by Freddy Malins and Mr Browne, each of whom had his head out through a window of the cab. The difficulty was to know where to drop Mr Browne along the route and Aunt Kate, Aunt Julia and Mary Jane helped the discussion from the doorstep with cross-directions and contradictions and abundance of laughter. As for Freddy Malins he was speechless with laughter. He popped his head in and out of the window every moment, to the great danger of his hat, and told his mother how the discussion was progressing till at last Mr Browne shouted to the bewildered cabman above the din of everybody's laughter:

—Do you know Trinity College?

—Yes, sir, said the cabman.

—Well, drive bang up against Trinity College gates, said Mr Browne, and then we'll tell you where to go. You understand now?

—Yes, sir, said the cabman.

—Make like a bird for Trinity College.

—Right, sir, cried the cabman.

The horse was whipped up and the cab rattled off along the quay amid a chorus of laughter and adieus.

Gabriel had not gone to the door with the others. He was in a dark part of the hall gazing up the staircase. A woman was standing near the top of the first flight, in the shadow also. He could not see her face but he could see the terracotta and salmonpink panels of her skirt which the shadow made appear black and white. It was his wife. She was leaning on the banisters, listening to something. Gabriel was surprised at her stillness and strained his ear to listen also. But he could hear little save the noise of laughter and dispute on the front steps, a few chords struck on the piano and a few notes of a man's voice singing.

He stood still in the gloom of the hall, trying to catch the air that the voice was singing and gazing up at his wife. There was grace and mystery in her attitude as if she were a symbol of something. He asked himself what is a woman standing on the stairs in the shadow, listening to distant music, a symbol of. If he were a painter he would paint her in that attitude. Her blue felt hat would show off the bronze of her hair against the darkness and the dark panels of her skirt would show off the light ones. *Distant Music* he would call the picture if he were a painter.

The hall-door was closed; and Aunt Kate, Aunt Julia and Mary Jane came down the hall, still laughing.

—Well, isn't Freddy terrible? said Mary Jane. He's really terrible.

Gabriel said nothing but pointed up the stairs towards where his wife was standing. Now that the hall-door was closed the voice and the piano could be heard more clearly. Gabriel held up his hand for them to be silent. The song seemed to be in the old Irish tonality and the singer seemed uncertain both of his words and of his voice. The voice, made plaintive by distance and by the singer's hoarseness, faintly illuminated the cadence of the air with words expressing grief:

O, the rain falls on my heavy locks
And the dew wets my skin,
My babe lies cold . . .

—O, exclaimed Mary Jane. It's Bartell D'Arcy singing and he wouldn't sing all the night. O, I'll get him to sing a song before he goes.

—O do, Mary Jane, said Aunt Kate.

Mary Jane brushed past the others and ran to the staircase but before she reached it the singing stopped and the piano was closed abruptly.

—O, what a pity! she cried. Is he coming down, Gretta?

Gabriel heard his wife answer yes and saw her come down towards them. A few steps behind her were Mr Bartell D'Arcy and Miss O'Callaghan.

—O, Mr D'Arcy, cried Mary Jane, it's downright mean of you to break off like that when we were all in raptures listening to you.

—I have been at him all the evening, said Miss O'Callaghan, and Mrs Conroy too and he told us he had a dreadful cold and couldn't sing.

—O, Mr D'Arcy, said Aunt Kate, now that was a great fib to tell.

—Can't you see that I'm as hoarse as a crow? said Mr D'Arcy roughly.

He went into the pantry hastily and put on his overcoat. The others, taken aback by his rude speech, could find nothing to say. Aunt Kate wrinkled her brows and made signs to the others to drop the subject. Mr D'Arcy stood swathing his neck carefully and frowning.

—It's the weather, said Aunt Julia, after a pause.

—Yes, everybody has colds, said Aunt Kate readily, everybody.

—They say, said Mary Jane, we haven't had snow like it for thirty years; and I read this morning in the newspapers that the snow is general all over Ireland.

—I love the look of snow, said Aunt Julia sadly.

—So do I, said Miss O'Callaghan. I think Christmas is never really Christmas unless we have the snow on the ground.

—But poor Mr D'Arcy doesn't like the snow, said Aunt Kate, smiling.

Mr D'Arcy came from the pantry, fully swathed and buttoned, and in a repentant tone told them the history of his cold. Everyone gave him advice and said it was a great pity and urged him to be very careful of his throat in the night air. Gabriel watched his wife who did not join in the conversation. She was standing right under the dusty fanlight and the flame of the gas lit up the rich bronze of her hair which he had seen her drying at the fire a few days before. She was in the same attitude and seemed unaware of the talk about her. At last she turned towards them and Gabriel saw that there was colour on her cheeks and that her eyes were shining. A sudden tide of joy went leaping out of his heart.

—Mr D'Arcy, she said, what is the name of that song you were singing?

—It's called *The Lass of Aughrim,* said Mr D'Arcy, but I couldn't remember it properly. Why? Do you know it?

—*The Lass of Aughrim,* she repeated. I couldn't think of the name.

—It's a very nice air, said Mary Jane. I'm sorry you were not in voice to-night.

—Now, Mary Jane, said Aunt Kate, don't annoy Mr D'Arcy. I won't have him annoyed.

Seeing that all were ready to start she shepherded them to the door where good-night was said:

—Well, good-night, Aunt Kate, and thanks for the pleasant evening.

—Good-night, Gabriel. Good-night, Gretta!

—Good-night, Aunt Kate, and thanks ever so much. Good-night, Aunt Julia.

—O, good-night, Gretta, I didn't see you.

—Good-night, Mr D'Arcy. Good-night, Miss O'Callaghan.

—Good-night, Miss Morkan.

—Good-night, again.

—Good-night, all. Safe home.

—Good-night. Good-night.

The morning was still dark. A dull yellow light brooded over the houses and the river; and the sky seemed to be descending. It was slushy underfoot; and only streaks and patches of snow lay on the roofs, on the parapets of the quay and on the area railings. The lamps were still burning redly in the murky air and, across the river, the palace of the Four Courts stood out menacingly against the heavy sky.

She was walking on before him with Mr Bartell D'Arcy, her shoes in a brown parcel tucked under one arm and her hands holding her skirt up from the slush. She had no longer any grace of attitude but Gabriel's eyes were still bright with happiness. The blood went bounding along his veins; and the thoughts went rioting through his brain, proud, joyful, tender, valorous.

She was walking on before him so lightly and so erect that he longed to run after her noiselessly, catch her by the shoulders and say something foolish and affectionate into her ear. She seemed to him so frail that he longed to defend her against something and then to be alone with her. Moments of their secret life together burst like stars upon his memory. A heliotrope envelope was lying beside his breakfast-cup and he was caressing it with his hand. Birds were twittering in the ivy and the sunny web of the curtain was shimmering along the floor: he could not eat for happiness. They were standing on the crowded platform and he was placing a ticket inside the warm palm of her glove. He was standing with her in the cold, looking in through a grated window at a man making bottles in a roaring furnace. It was very cold. Her face, fragrant in the cold air, was quite close to his; and suddenly she called out to the man at the furnace:

—Is the fire hot, sir?

But the man could not hear her with the noise of the furnace. It was just as well. He might have answered rudely.

A wave of yet more tender joy escaped from his heart and went coursing in warm flood along his arteries. Like the tender fires of stars moments of their life together, that no one knew of or would ever know of, broke upon and illumined his memory. He longed to recall to her those moments, to make her forget the years of their dull existence together and remember only their moments of ecstasy. For the years, he felt, had not quenched his soul or hers. Their children, his writing, her household cares had not quenched all their souls' tender fire. In one letter that he had written to her then he had said: *Why is it that words like these seem to me so dull and cold? Is it because there is no word tender enough to be your name?*

Like distant music these words that he had written years before were borne towards him from the past. He longed to be alone with her. When the others had gone away, when he and she were in their room in the hotel, then they would be alone together. He would call her softly:

—Gretta!

Perhaps she would not hear at once: she would be undressing. Then something in his voice would strike her. She would turn and look at him. . . .

At the corner of Winetavern Street they met a cab. He was glad of its rattling noise as it saved him from conversation. She was looking out of the window and seemed tired. The others spoke only a few words, pointing out some building or street. The horse galloped along wearily under the murky morning sky, dragging his old rattling box after his heels, and Gabriel was again in a cab with her, galloping to catch the boat, galloping to their honeymoon.

As the cab drove across O'Connell Bridge Miss O'Callaghan said:

—They say you never cross O'Connell Bridge without seeing a white horse.

—I see a white man this time, said Gabriel.

—Where? asked Mr Bartell D'Arcy.

Gabriel pointed to the statue, on which lay patches of snow. Then he nodded familiarly to it and waved his hand.

—Good-night, Dan, he said gaily.

When the cab drew up before the hotel Gabriel jumped out and, in spite of Mr Bartell D'Arcy's protest, paid the driver. He gave the man a shilling over his fare. The man saluted and said:

—A prosperous New Year to you, sir.

—The same to you, said Gabriel cordially.

She leaned for a moment on his arm in getting out of the cab and while standing at the curbstone, bidding the others good-night. She leaned lightly on his arm, as lightly as when she had danced with him a few hours before. He had felt proud and happy then, happy that she was his, proud of her grace and wifely carriage. But now, after the kindling again of so many memories, the first touch of her body, musical and strange and perfumed, sent through him a keen pang of lust. Under cover of her silence he pressed her arm closely to his side; and, as they stood at the hotel door, he felt that they had escaped from their lives and duties, escaped from home and friends and run away together with wild and radiant hearts to a new adventure.

An old man was dozing in a great hooded chair in the hall. He lit a candle in the office and went before them to the stairs. They followed him in silence, their feet falling in soft thuds on the thickly carpeted stairs. She mounted the stairs behind the porter, her head bowed in the ascent, her frail shoulders curved as with a burden, her skirt girt tightly about her. He could have flung his arms about her hips and held her still for his arms were trembling with desire to seize her and only the stress of his nails against the palms of his hands held the wild impulse of his body in check. The porter halted on the stairs to settle his guttering candle. They halted too on the steps below him. In the silence Gabriel could hear the falling of the molten wax into the tray and the thumping of his own heart against his ribs.

The porter led them along a corridor and opened a door. Then he set his unstable candle down on a toilet-table and asked at what hour they were to be called in the morning.

—Eight, said Gabriel.

The porter pointed to the tap of the electric-light and began a muttered apology but Gabriel cut him short.

—We don't want any light. We have light enough from the street. And I say, he added, pointing to the candle, you might remove that handsome article, like a good man.

The porter took up his candle again, but slowly for he was surprised by such a novel idea. Then he mumbled good-night and went out. Gabriel shot the lock to.

A ghostly light from the street lamp lay in a long shaft from one window to the door. Gabriel threw his overcoat and hat on a couch and crossed the room towards the window. He looked down into the street in order that his emotion might calm a little. Then he turned and leaned against a chest of drawers with his back to the light. She had taken off her hat and cloak and was standing before a large swinging mirror, unhooking her waist. Gabriel paused for a few moments, watching her, and then said:

—Gretta!

She turned away from the mirror slowly and walked along the shaft of light towards him. Her face looked so serious and weary that the words would not pass Gabriel's lips. No, it was not the moment yet.

—You looked tired, he said.

—I am a little, she answered.

—You don't feel ill or weak?

—No, tired: that's all.

She went on to the window and stood there, looking out. Gabriel waited again and then, fearing that diffidence was about to conquer him, he said abruptly:

—By the way, Gretta!

—What is it?

—You know that poor fellow Malins? he said quickly.

—Yes. What about him?

—Well, poor fellow, he's a decent sort of chap after all, continued Gabriel in a false voice. He gave me back that sovereign I lent him and I didn't expect it really. It's a pity he wouldn't keep away from that Browne, because he's not a bad fellow at heart.

He was trembling now with annoyance. Why did she seem so abstracted? He did not know how he could begin. Was she annoyed, too, about something? If she would only turn to him or come to him of her own accord! To take her as she was would be brutal. No, he must see some ardour in her eyes first. He longed to be master of her strange mood.

—When did you lend him the pound? she asked, after a pause.

Gabriel strove to restrain himself from breaking out into brutal language about the sottish Malins and his pound. He longed to cry to her from his soul, to crush her body against his, to overmaster her. But he said:

—O, at Christmas, when he opened that little Christmas-card shop in Henry Street.

He was in such a fever of rage and desire that he did not hear her come from the window. She stood before him for an instant, looking at him strangely. Then, suddenly raising herself on tiptoe and resting her hands lightly on his shoulders, she kissed him.

—You are a very generous person, Gabriel, she said.

Gabriel, trembling with delight at her sudden kiss and at the quaintness of her phrase, put his hands on her hair and began smoothing it back, scarcely touching it with his fingers. The washing had made it fine and brilliant. His heart was brimming over with happiness. Just when he was wishing for it she had come to him of her own accord. Perhaps her thoughts had been running with his. Perhaps she had felt the impetuous desire that was in him and then the yielding mood had come upon her. Now that she had fallen to him so easily he wondered why he had been so diffident.

He stood, holding her head between his hands. Then, slipping one arm swiftly about her body and drawing her towards him, he said softly:

—Gretta dear, what are you thinking about?

She did not answer nor yield wholly to his arm. He said again, softly:

—Tell me what it is, Gretta. I think I know what is the matter. Do I know?

She did not answer at once. Then she said in an outburst of tears:

—O, I am thinking about that song, *The Lass of Aughrim*.

She broke loose from him and ran to the bed and, throwing her arms across the bed-rail, hid her face. Gabriel stood stock-still for a moment in astonishment and then followed her. As he passed in the way of the cheval-glass he caught sight of himself in full length, his broad, well-filled shirt-front, the face whose expression always puzzled him when he saw it in a mirror and his glimmering gilt-rimmed eyeglasses. He halted a few paces from her and said:

—What about the song? Why does that make you cry?

She raised her head from her arms and dried her eyes with the back of her hand like a child. A kinder note than he had intended went into his voice.

—Why, Gretta? he asked.

—I am thinking about a person long ago who used to sing that song.

—And who was the person long ago? asked Gabriel, smiling.

—It was a person I used to know in Galway when I was living with my grandmother, she said.

The smile passed away from Gabriel's face. A dull anger began to gather again at the back of his mind and the dull fires of his lust began to glow angrily in his veins.

—Someone you were in love with? he asked ironically.

—It was a young boy I used to know, she answered, named Michael Furey. He used to sing that song, *The Lass of Aughrim*. He was very delicate.

Gabriel was silent. He did not wish her to think that he was interested in this delicate boy.

—I can see him so plainly, she said after a moment. Such eyes as he had: big dark eyes! And such an expression in them—an expression!

—O then, you were in love with him? said Gabriel.

—I used to go out walking with him, she said, when I was in Galway.

A thought flew across Gabriel's mind.

—Perhaps that was why you wanted to go to Galway with that Ivors girl? he said coldly.

She looked at him and asked in surprise:

—What for?

Her eyes made Gabriel feel awkward. He shrugged his shoulders and said:

—How do I know? To see him perhaps.

She looked away from him along the shaft of light towards the window in silence.

—He is dead, she said at length. He died when he was only seventeen. Isn't it a terrible thing to die so young as that?

—What was he? asked Gabriel, still ironically.

—He was in the gasworks, she said.

Gabriel felt humiliated by the failure of his irony and by the evocation of this figure from the dead, a boy in the gasworks. While he had been full of memories of their secret life together, full of tenderness and joy and desire, she had been comparing him in her mind with another. A shameful consciousness of his own person assailed him. He saw himself as a ludicrous figure, acting as a pennyboy for his aunts, a nervous well-meaning sentimentalist, orating to vulgarians and idealising his own clownish lusts, the pitiable fatuous fellow he had caught a glimpse of in the mirror. Instinctively he turned his back more to the light lest she might see the shame that burned upon his forehead.

He tried to keep up his tone of cold interrogation but his voice when he spoke was humble and indifferent.

—I suppose you were in love with this Michael Furey, Gretta, he said.

—I was great with him at that time, she said.

Her voice was veiled and sad. Gabriel, feeling now how vain it would be to try to lead her whither he had purposed, caressed one of her hands and said, also sadly:

—And what did he die of so young, Gretta? Consumption, was it?

—I think he died for me, she answered.

A vague terror seized Gabriel at this answer as if, at that hour when he had hoped to triumph, some impalpable and vindictive being was coming against him, gathering forces against him in its vague world. But he shook himself free of it with an effort of reason and continued to caress her hand. He did not question her again for he felt that she would tell him of herself. Her hand was warm and moist: it did not respond to his touch but he continued to caress it just as he had caressed her first letter to him that spring morning.

—It was in the winter, she said, about the beginning of the winter when I was going to leave my grandmother's and come up here to the convent. And he was ill at the time in his lodgings in Galway and wouldn't be let out and his people in Oughterard were written to. He was in decline, they said, or something like that. I never knew rightly.

She paused for a moment and sighed.

—Poor fellow, she said. He was very fond of me and he was such a gentle boy. We used to go out together, walking, you know, Gabriel, like the way they do in the country. He was going to study singing only for his health. He had a very good voice, poor Michael Furey.

—Well; and then? asked Gabriel.

—And then when it came to the time for me to leave Galway and come up to the convent he was much worse and I wouldn't be let see him so I wrote a letter saying I was going up to Dublin and would be back in the summer and hoping he would be better then.

She paused for a moment to get her voice under control and then went on:

—Then the night before I left I was in my grandmother's house in Nuns' Island, packing up, and I heard gravel thrown up against the window. The window was so wet I couldn't see so I ran downstairs as I was and slipped out the back into the garden and there was the poor fellow at the end of the garden, shivering.

—And did you not tell him to go back? asked Gabriel.

—I implored of him to go home at once and told him he would get his death in the rain. But he said he did not want to live. I can see his eyes as well as well! He was standing at the end of the wall where there was a tree.

—And did he go home? asked Gabriel.

—Yes, he went home. And when I was only a week in the convent he died and he was buried in Oughterard where his people came from. O, the day I heard that, that he was dead!

She stopped, choking with sobs, and, overcome by emotion, flung herself face downward on the bed, sobbing in the quilt. Gabriel held her hand for a moment longer, irresolutely, and then, shy of intruding on her grief, let it fall gently and walked quietly to the window.

She was fast asleep.

Gabriel, leaning on his elbow, looked for a few moments unresentfully on her tangled hair and half-open mouth, listening to her deep-drawn breath. So she had had that romance in her life: a man had died for her sake. It hardly pained him now to think how poor a part he, her husband, had played in her life. He watched her while she slept as though he and she had never lived together as man and wife. His curious eyes rested long upon her face and on her hair: and, as he thought of what she must have been then, in that time of her first girlish beauty, a strange friendly pity for her entered his soul. He did not like to say even to himself that her face was no longer beautiful but he knew that it was no longer the face for which Michael Furey had braved death.

Perhaps she had not told him all the story. His eyes moved to the chair over which she had thrown some of her clothes. A petticoat string dangled to the floor. One boot stood upright, its limp upper fallen down: the fellow of it lay upon its side. He wondered at his riot of emotions of an hour before. From what had it proceeded? From his aunt's supper, from his own foolish speech, from the wine and dancing, the merrymaking when saying good-night in the hall, the pleasure of the walk along the river in the snow. Poor Aunt Julia! She, too, would soon be a shade with the shade of Patrick Morkan and his horse. He had caught that haggard look upon her face for a moment when she was singing *Arrayed for the Bridal*. Soon, perhaps, he would be sitting in that same drawing-room, dressed in black, his silk hat on his knees. The blinds would be drawn down and Aunt Kate would be sitting beside him, crying and blowing her nose and telling him how Julia had died. He would cast about in his mind for some words that might console her, and would find only lame and useless ones. Yes, yes: that would happen very soon.

The air of the room chilled his shoulders. He stretched himself cautiously along under the sheets and lay down beside his wife. One by one they were all becoming shades. Better pass boldly into that other world, in the full glory of some passion, than fade and wither dismally with age. He thought of how she who lay beside him had locked in her heart for so many years that image of her lover's eyes when he had told her that he did not wish to live.

Generous tears filled Gabriel's eyes. He had never felt like that himself towards any woman but he knew that such a feeling must be love. The tears gathered more thickly in his eyes and in the partial darkness he imagined he saw the form of a young man standing under a dripping tree. Other forms were near. His soul had approached that region where dwell the vast hosts of the dead. He was conscious of, but could not apprehend, their wayward and flickering existence. His own identity was fading out into a grey impalpable world: the solid world itself which these dead had one time reared and lived in was dissolving and dwindling.

A few light taps upon the pane made him turn to the window. It had begun to snow again. He watched sleepily the flakes, silver and dark, falling obliquely against the lamplight. The time had come for him to set out on his journey westward. Yes, the newspapers were right: snow was general all over Ireland. It was falling on every part of the dark central plain, on the treeless hills, falling softly upon the Bog of Allen and, farther westward, softly falling into the dark mutinous Shannon waves. It was falling, too, upon every part of the lonely churchyard on the hill where Michael Furey lay buried. It lay thickly drifted on the crooked crosses and headstones, on the spears of the little gate, on the barren thorns. His soul swooned slowly as he heard the snow falling faintly through the universe and faintly falling, like the descent of their last end, upon all the living and the dead.

In the Penal Colony

by Franz Kafka

Introduced by Joyce Carol Oates

THIS GREAT, VEXING, HEARTRENDING PARABLE OF A STORY: ONCE READ, never forgotten. Especially if read in late adolescence, when you are a university undergraduate of the 1950s for whom the world of outsized, unnameable, oceanic passions is a world illuminated sheerly by books. A world of books. *An ax,* as Franz Kafka said, *to break the frozen sea within.*

In a diary entry for 25 September 1917, Franz Kafka noted that happiness for him consisted in raising the world "into the pure, the true, and the immutable."

When you are eighteen years old, you know this is true. It must be true! Yet how is such a transformation of the self, very like a levitation of the soul, to be accomplished?

Then again, Kafka has made it obvious: the cruel wisdom of "In the Penal Colony" *is* happiness.

Guilt is never to be doubted.

Kafka's mysticism consists in taking the side of the other: the worst news you can imagine, as it slips into your life, and *is,* from that hour onward, *you.*

There is a wisdom of adults you understand, as you hover on the very threshold of adulthood, that must be true precisely because it is so pitiless, cruel, and funny. Because it seems to illuminate a condition of the world and of humankind's place in it that "your" religion—in my case, a mildly emotional, thoroughly unexamined, and utterly unintellectual Roman Catholicism—has not suggested.

It's a remarkable piece of apparatus.

"In the Penal Colony"—the parable as autobiography, as prophecy, as memory. "In the Penal Colony"—written in 1914, decades before Auschwitz, Dachau, Belsen, Treblinka (in which, indeed, relatives of Franz Kafka, including his sisters, would die). "In the Penal Colony"—called by its melancholy, self-mocking author nothing more than "personal proofs of my weakness . . . evidence of solitude."

This most matter-of-fact and logical of nightmares. Each moment yielding readily to the next, and to the next—fluid, inevitable. We are the unnamed explorer-witness to the catastrophe, yet at the same time we are the unnamed officer whose passion "In the Penal Colony" records. His pointless martyrdom! (Is all "martyrdom" pointless?) We witness, in the collapse of the *remarkable piece of apparatus,* the end of a human epoch.

What had once been *sacred,* Kafka predicts, will now be *secular.*

What had once been *God-directed* will now be *human-directed;* which is to say, *humane.*

No more torture. No more idiotic superstition. But—no more transcendence?

> But how quiet [the condemned man] grows at just about the sixth hour! Enlightenment comes to the most dull-witted. It begins around the eyes. From there it radiates. A moment that might tempt one to get under the Harrow oneself. Nothing more happens than that the man begins to understand the inscription, he purses his mouth as if he were listening. You have seen how difficult it is to decipher the script with one's eyes; but our man deciphers it with his wounds. To be sure, that is a hard task; he needs six hours to accomplish it. . . . Then the judgment has been fulfilled, and we, the soldier and I, bury him.

Except, unfortunately, at this point in the history of the Penal Colony, the old machine of salvation is breaking down. We learn that the old Commandant is dead, his very grave neglected, defiled—in a teahouse! The new Commandant is hostile to the machine and its sacred scripture. With what elegant deadpan silent-film looniness the *remarkable piece of apparatus* self-destructs, there before the explorer's amazed eyes. And the officer's fate, his promised salvation? We, the explorer, look anxiously into the face of a corpse.

> It was as it had been in life; no sign was visible of the promised redemption; what the others had found in the machine the officer had not found; the lips were pressed firmly together, the eyes were open, with the same expression as in life, the look was calm and convinced, through the forehead went the point of the great iron spike.

Can one outgrow Kafka, our great poet of solitude, of tragedy comprehended as farce? I think so, yes. In the impatient, zestful still-youthful adulthood of one's life. When at last one *takes control* of one's life. Or believes one can, or has. Franz Kafka's melancholy passivity, his celebration of the absurd, his parables of *bad luck* may baffle the ear, like words in a foreign tongue. Or they may strike the ear as too shrill. Or like faint, failing screams. Echoes of outgrown nightmares.

You outgrow Kafka. But then one day, abruptly, you return to Kafka. As the brash arc of youthful adulthood begins to wan. It's like discovering yourself in a corridor you would have sworn you'd never been in before—yet you know it. This staircase, this door to be opened, this room. *It's all there. Always has been there. Unchanged. Waiting for you.*

In the Penal Colony

Franz Kafka

Translated by Willa and Edwin Muir

It's a remarkable piece of apparatus," said the officer to the explorer and surveyed with a certain air of admiration the apparatus which was after all quite familiar to him. The explorer seemed to have accepted merely out of politeness the Commandant's invitation to witness the execution of a soldier condemned to death for disobedience and insulting behavior to a superior. Nor did the colony itself betray much interest in this execution. At least, in the small sandy valley, a deep hollow surrounded on all sides by naked crags, there was no one present save the officer, the explorer, the condemned man, who was a stupid-looking, wide-mouthed creature with bewildered hair and face, and the soldier who held the heavy chain controlling the small chains locked on the prisoner's ankles, wrists, and neck, chains that were themselves attached to each other by communicating links. In any case, the condemned man looked so like a submissive dog that one might have thought he could be left to run free on the surrounding hills and would only need to be whistled for when the execution was due to begin.

The explorer did not much care about the apparatus and walked up and down behind the prisoner with almost visible indifference while the officer made the last adjustments, now creeping beneath the structure, which was bedded deep in the earth, now climbing a ladder to inspect its upper parts. These were tasks that might well have been left to a mechanic, but the officer performed them with great zeal, whether because he was a devoted admirer of the apparatus or because of other reasons the work could be entrusted to no one else. "Ready now!" he called at last and climbed down from the ladder. He looked uncommonly limp, breathed with his mouth wide open, and had tucked two fine ladies' handkerchiefs under the collar of his uniform. "These uniforms are too heavy for the tropics, surely," said the explorer, instead of making some inquiry about the apparatus, as the officer had expected. "Of course," said the officer, washing his oily and greasy hands in a bucket of water that stood ready, "but they mean home to us; we don't want to forget about home. Now just have a look at this machine," he added at once, simultaneously drying his hands on a towel and indicating the apparatus. "Up till now a few things still had to be set by hand, but from this moment it works all by itself." The explorer nodded and followed him. The officer, anxious to secure himself against all contingencies, said: "Things sometimes go wrong, of course; I hope that nothing goes wrong today, but we have to allow for the possibility. The machinery should go on working continuously for twelve hours. But if anything does go wrong it will only be some small matter that can be set right at once.

"Won't you take a seat?" he asked finally, drawing a cane chair out from among a heap of them and offering it to the explorer, who could not refuse it. He was now sitting at the edge of a pit, into which he glanced for a fleeting moment. It was not very deep. On one side of the pit the excavated soil had been piled up in a rampart, on the other side of it stood the apparatus. "I don't know," said the officer, "if the Commandant has already explained this apparatus to you." The explorer waved one hand vaguely; the officer asked for nothing better, since now he could explain the apparatus himself. "This apparatus," he said, taking hold of a crank handle and leaning against it, "was invented by our former Commandant. I assisted at the very earliest experiments and had a share in all the work until its completion. But the credit of inventing it belongs to him alone. Have you ever heard of our former Commandant? No? Well, it isn't saying too much if I tell you that the organization of the whole penal colony is his work. We who were his friends knew even before he died that the organization of the colony was so perfect that his successor, even with a thousand new schemes in his head, would find it impossible to alter anything, at least for many years to come. And our prophecy has come true; the new Commandant has had to acknowledge its truth. A pity you never met the old Commandant!—But," the officer interrupted himself, "I am rambling on, and here stands his apparatus before us. It consists, as you see, of three parts. In the course of time each of these parts has acquired a kind of popular nickname. The lower one is called the 'Bed,' the upper one the 'Designer,' and this one here in the middle that moves up and down is called the 'Harrow.'" "The Harrow?" asked the explorer. He had not been listening very attentively, the glare of the sun in the shadeless valley was altogether too strong, it was difficult to collect one's thoughts. All the more did he admire the officer, who in spite of his tight-fitting full-dress uniform coat, amply befrogged and weighed down by epaulettes, was pursuing his subject with such enthusiasm and, besides talking, was still tightening a screw here and there with a spanner. As for the soldier, he seemed to be in much the same condition as the explorer. He had wound the prisoner's chain around both his wrists, propped himself on his rifle, let his head hang, and was paying no attention to anything. That did not surprise the explorer, for the officer was speaking French, and certainly neither the soldier nor the prisoner understood a word of French. It was all the more remarkable, therefore, that the prisoner was nonetheless making an effort to follow the officer's explanations. With a kind of drowsy persistence he directed his gaze wherever the officer pointed a finger, and at the interruption of the explorer's question he, too, as well as the officer, looked around.

"Yes, the Harrow," said the officer, "a good name for it. The needles are set in like the teeth of a harrow and the whole thing works something like a harrow, although its action is limited to one place and contrived with much more artistic skill. Anyhow, you'll soon understand it. On the Bed here the condemned man is laid—I'm going to describe the apparatus first before I set it in motion. Then you'll be able to follow the proceedings better. Besides, one of the cogwheels in the Designer is badly worn; it creaks a lot when it's working; you can hardly hear yourself speak; spare parts, unfortunately, are difficult to get here.—Well, here is the Bed, as I told you. It is completely covered with a layer of cotton wool; you'll find out why later. On this cotton wool the condemned man is laid, face down, quite naked, of course; here are straps for the hands, here for the feet, and here for the neck, to bind him fast. Here at the head of the Bed, where the man, as I said, first lays down his face, is this little gag of felt, which can be easily regulated to go straight into his mouth. It is meant to keep him from screaming and biting his tongue. Of course the man is forced to take the felt into his mouth, for otherwise his neck would be broken by the strap." "Is that cotton wool?" asked the explorer, bending forward. "Yes, certainly," said the officer, with a smile, "feel it for yourself." He took the explorer's hand and guided it over the Bed. "It's specially prepared cotton wool, that's why it looks so different; I'll tell you presently what it's for." The explorer already felt a dawning interest in the apparatus; he sheltered his eyes from the sun with one hand and gazed up at the structure. It was a huge affair. The Bed and the Designer were of the same size and looked like two dark wooden chests. The Designer hung about two meters above the Bed; each of them was bound at the corners with four rods of brass that almost flashed out rays in the sunlight. Between the chests shuttled the Harrow on a ribbon of steel.

The officer had scarcely noticed the explorer's previous indifference, but he was now well aware of his dawning interest; so he stopped explaining in order to leave a space of time for quiet observation. The condemned man imitated the explorer; since he could not use a hand to shelter his eyes he gazed upwards without shade.

"Well, the man lies down," said the explorer, leaning back in his chair and crossing his legs.

"Yes," said the officer, pushing his cap back a little and passing one hand over his heated face, "now listen! Both the Bed and the Designer have an electric battery each; the Bed needs one for itself, the Designer for the Harrow. As soon as the man is strapped down, the Bed is set in motion. It quivers in minute, very rapid vibrations, both from side to side and up and down. You will have seen similar apparatus in hospitals; but in our Bed the movements are all precisely calculated; you see, they have to correspond very exactly to the movements of the Harrow. And the Harrow is the instrument for the actual execution of the sentence."

"And how does the sentence run?" asked the explorer.

"You don't know that either?" said the officer in amazement, and bit his lips. "Forgive me if my explanations seem rather incoherent. I do beg your pardon. You see, the Commandant always used to do the explaining; but the new Commandant shirks this duty; yet that such an important visitor"—the explorer tried to deprecate the honor with both hands; the officer, however, insisted—"that such an important visitor should not even be told about the kind of sentence we pass is a new development, which—" He was just on the point of using strong language but checked himself and said only: "I was not informed, it is not my fault. In any case, I am certainly the best person to explain our procedure, since I have here"—he patted his breast pocket—"the relevant drawings made by our former Commandant."

"The Commandant's own drawings?" asked the explorer. "Did he combine everything in himself, then? Was he soldier, judge, mechanic, chemist, and draughtsman?"

"Indeed he was," said the officer, nodding assent, with a remote, glassy look. Then he inspected his hands critically; they did not seem clean enough to him for touching the drawings; so he went over to the bucket and washed them again. Then he drew out a small leather wallet and said: "Our sentence does not sound severe. Whatever commandment the prisoner has disobeyed is written upon his body by the Harrow. This prisoner, for instance"—the officer indicated the man—"will have written on his body: HONOR THY SUPERIORS!"

The explorer glanced at the man; he stood, as the officer pointed him out, with bent head, apparently listening with all his ears in an effort to catch what was being said. Yet the movement of his blubber lips, closely pressed together, showed clearly that he could not understand a word. Many questions were troubling the explorer, but at the sight of the prisoner he asked only: "Does he know his sentence?" "No," said the officer, eager to go on with his exposition, but the explorer interrupted him: "He doesn't know the sentence that has been passed on him?" "No," said the officer again, pausing a moment as if to let the explorer elaborate his question, and then said: "There would be no point in telling him. He'll learn it on his body." The explorer intended to make no answer, but he felt the prisoner's gaze turned on him; it seemed to ask if he approved such goings-on. So he bent forward again, having already leaned back in his chair, and put another question: "But surely he knows that he has been sentenced?" "Nor that either," said the officer, smiling at the explorer as if expecting him to make further surprising remarks. "No," said the explorer, wiping his forehead, "then he can't know either whether his defense was effective?" "He has had no chance of putting up a defense," said the officer, turning his eyes away as if speaking to himself and so sparing the explorer the shame of hearing self-evident matters explained. "But he must have had some chance of defending himself," said the explorer, and rose from his seat.

The officer realized that he was in danger of having his exposition of the apparatus held up for a long time; so he went up to the explorer, took him by the arm, waved a hand toward the condemned man, who was standing very straight now that he had so obviously become the center of attention—the soldier had also given the chain a jerk—and said: "This is how the matter stands. I have been appointed judge in this penal colony. Despite my youth. For I was the former Commandant's assistant in all penal matters and know more about the apparatus than anyone. My guiding principle is this: Guilt is never to be doubted. Other courts cannot follow that principle, for they consist of several opinions and have higher courts to scrutinize them. That is not the case here, or at least, it was not the case in the former Commandant's time. The new man has certainly shown some inclination to interfere with my judgments, but so far I have succeeded in fending him off and will go on succeeding. You wanted to have the case explained; it is quite simple, like all of them. A captain reported to me this morning that this man, who had been assigned to him as a servant and sleeps before his door, had been asleep on duty. It is his duty, you see, to get up every time the hour strikes and salute the captain's door. Not an exacting duty, and very necessary, since he has to be a sentry as well as a servant, and must be alert in both functions. Last night the captain wanted to see if the man was doing his duty. He opened the door as the clock struck two and there was his man curled up asleep. He took his riding whip and lashed him across the face. Instead of getting up and begging pardon, the man caught hold of his master's legs, shook him, and cried: 'Throw that whip away or I'll eat you alive.'—That's the evidence. The captain came to me an hour ago; I wrote down his statement and appended the sentence to it. Then I had the man put in chains. That was all quite simple. If I had first called the man before me and interrogated him, things would have got into a confused tangle. He would have told lies, and had I exposed these lies he would have backed them up with more lies, and so on and so forth. As it is, I've got him and I won't let him go.—Is that quite clear now? But we're wasting time, the execution should be beginning and I haven't finished explaining the apparatus yet." He pressed the explorer back into his chair, went up again to the apparatus, and began: "As you see, the shape of the Harrow corresponds to the human form; here is the harrow for the torso, here are the harrows for the legs. For the head there is only this one small spike. Is that quite clear?" He bent amiably forward toward the explorer, eager to provide the most comprehensive explanations.

The explorer considered the Harrow with a frown. The explanation of the judicial procedure had not satisfied him. He had to remind himself that this was in any case a penal colony where extraordinary measures were needed and that military discipline must be enforced to the last. He also felt that some hope might be set on the new Commandant, who was apparently of a mind to bring in, although gradually, a new kind of procedure which the officer's narrow mind was incapable of understanding. This train of thought prompted his next question: "Will the Commandant attend the execution?" "It is not certain," said the officer, wincing at the direct question, and his friendly expression darkened. "That is just why we have to lose no time. Much as I dislike it, I shall have to cut my explanations short. But of course tomorrow, when the apparatus has been cleaned—its one drawback is that it gets so messy—I can recapitulate all the details. For the present, then, only the essentials.—When the man lies down on the Bed and it begins to vibrate, the Harrow is lowered onto his body. It regulates itself automatically so that the needles barely touch his skin; once contact is made the steel ribbon stiffens immediately into a rigid band. And then the performance begins. An ignorant onlooker would see no difference between one punishment and another. The Harrow appears to do its work with uniform regularity. As it quivers, its points pierce the skin of the body which is itself quivering from the vibration of the Bed. So that the actual progress of the sentence can be watched, the Harrow is made of glass. Getting the needles fixed in the glass was a technical problem, but after many experiments we overcame the difficulty. No trouble was too great for us to take, you see. And now anyone can look through the glass and watch the inscription taking form on the body. Wouldn't you care to come a little nearer and have a look at the needles?"

The explorer got up slowly, walked across, and bent over the Harrow. "You see," said the officer, "there are two kinds of needles arranged in multiple patterns. Each long needle has a short one beside it. The long needle does the writing, and the short needle sprays a jet of water to wash away the blood and keep the inscription clear. Blood and water together are then conducted here through small runnels into this main runnel and down a waste pipe into the pit." With his finger the officer traced the exact course taken by the blood and water. To make the picture as vivid as possible he held both hands below the outlet of the waste pipe as if to catch the outflow, and when he did this the explorer drew back his head and feeling behind him with one hand sought to return to his chair. To his horror he found that the condemned man too had obeyed the officer's invitation to examine the Harrow at close quarters and had followed him. He had pulled forward the sleepy soldier with the chain and was bending over the glass. One could see that his uncertain eyes were trying to perceive what the two gentlemen had been looking at, but since he had not understood the explanation he could not make head or tail of it. He was peering this way and that way. He kept running his eyes along the glass. The explorer wanted to drive him away, since what he was doing was probably culpable. But the officer firmly restrained the explorer with one hand and with the other took a clod of earth from the rampart and threw it at the soldier. He opened his eyes with a jerk, saw what the condemned man had dared to do, let his rifle fall, dug his heels into the ground, dragged his prisoner back so that he stumbled and fell immediately, and then stood looking down at him, watching him struggling and rattling in his chains. "Set him on his feet!" yelled the officer, for he noticed that the explorer's attention was being too much distracted by the prisoner. In fact he was even leaning right across the Harrow, without taking any notice of it, intent only on finding out what was happening to the prisoner. "Be careful with him!" cried the officer again. He ran around the apparatus, himself caught the condemned man under the shoulders, and with the soldier's help got him up on his feet, which kept slithering from under him.

"Now I know all about it," said the explorer as the officer came back to him. "All except the most important thing," he answered, seizing the explorer's arm and pointing upwards: "In the Designer are all the cogwheels that control the movements of the Harrow, and this machinery is regulated according to the inscription demanded by the sentence. I am still using the guiding plans drawn by the former Commandant. Here they are"—he extracted some sheets from the leather wallet—"but I'm sorry I can't let you handle them, they are my most precious possessions. Just take a seat and I'll hold them in front of you like this, then you'll be able to see everything quite well." He spread out the first sheet of paper. The explorer would have liked to say something appreciative, but all he could see was a labyrinth of lines crossing and recrossing each other, which covered the paper so thickly that it was difficult to discern the blank spaces between them. "Read it," said the officer. "I can't," said the explorer. "Yet it's clear enough," said the officer. "It's very ingenious," said the explorer evasively, "but I can't make it out." "Yes," said the officer with a laugh, putting the paper away again, "it's no calligraphy for school children. It needs to be studied closely. I'm quite sure that in the end you would understand it too. Of course the script can't be a simple one; it's not supposed to kill a man straight off, but only after an interval of, on an average, twelve hours; the turning point is reckoned to come at the sixth hour. So there have to be lots and lots of flourishes around the actual script; the script itself runs around the body only in a narrow girdle; the rest of the body is reserved for the embellishments. Can you appreciate now the work accomplished by the Harrow and the whole apparatus?—Just watch it!" He ran up the ladder, turned a wheel, called down: "Look out, keep to one side!" and everything started working. If the wheel had not creaked, it would have been marvelous. The officer, as if surprised by the noise of the wheel, shook his fist at it, then spread out his arms in excuse to the explorer, and climbed down rapidly to peer at the working of the machine from below. Something perceptible to no one save himself was still not in order; he clambered up again, did something with both hands in the interior of the Designer, then slid down one of the rods, instead of using the ladder, so as to get down quicker, and with the full force of his lungs, to make himself heard at all in the noise, yelled in the explorer's ear: "Can you follow it? The Harrow is beginning to write; when it finishes the first draft of the inscription on the man's back, the layer of cotton wool begins to roll and slowly turns the body over, to give the Harrow fresh space for writing. Meanwhile the raw part that has been written on lies on the cotton wool, which is specially prepared to staunch the bleeding and so makes all ready for a new deepening of the script. Then these teeth at the edge of the Harrow, as the body turns further around, tear the cotton wool away from the wounds, throw it into the pit, and there is more work for the Harrow. So it keeps on writing deeper and deeper for the whole twelve hours. The first six hours the condemned man stays alive almost as before, he suffers only pain. After two hours the felt gag is taken away, for he has no longer strength to scream. Here, into this electrically heated basin at the head of the Bed, some warm rice pap is poured, from which the man, if he feels like it, can take as much as his tongue can lap. Not one of them ever misses the chance. I can remember none, and my experience is extensive. Only about the sixth hour does the man lose all desire to eat. I usually kneel down here at that moment and observe what happens. The man rarely swallows his last mouthful, he only rolls it around his mouth and spits it out into the pit. I have to duck just then or he would spit it in my face. But how quiet he grows at just about the sixth hour! Enlightenment comes to the most dull-witted. It begins around the eyes. From there it radiates. A moment that might tempt one to get under the Harrow oneself. Nothing more happens than that the man begins to understand the inscription, he purses his mouth as if he were listening. You have seen how difficult it is to decipher the script with one's eyes; but our man deciphers it with his wounds. To be sure, that is a hard task; he needs six hours to accomplish it. By that time the Harrow has pierced him quite through and casts him into the pit, where he pitches down upon the blood and water and the cotton wool. Then the judgment has been fulfilled, and we, the soldier and I, bury him."

The explorer had inclined his ear to the officer and with his hands in his jacket pockets watched the machine at work. The condemned man watched it too, but uncomprehendingly. He bent forward a little and was intent on the moving needles when the soldier, at a sign from the officer, slashed through his shirt and trousers from behind with a knife, so that they fell off; he tried to catch at his falling clothes to cover his nakedness, but the soldier lifted him into the air and shook the last remnants from him. The officer stopped the machine, and in the sudden silence the condemned man was laid under the Harrow. The chains were loosened and the straps fastened on instead; in the first moment that seemed almost a relief to the prisoner. And now the Harrow was adjusted a little lower, since he was a thin man. When the needle points touched him a shudder ran over his skin; while the soldier was busy strapping his right hand, he flung out his left hand blindly; but it happened to be in the direction toward where the explorer was standing. The officer kept watching the explorer sideways, as if seeking to read from his face the impression made on him by the execution, which had been at least cursorily explained to him.

The wrist strap broke; probably the soldier had drawn it too tight. The officer had to intervene, the soldier held up the broken piece of strap to show him. So the officer went over to him and said, his face still turned toward the explorer: "This is a very complex machine, it can't be helped that things are breaking or giving way here and there; but one must not thereby allow oneself to be diverted in one's general judgment. In any case, this strap is easily made good; I shall simply use a chain; the delicacy of the vibrations for the right arm will of course be a little impaired." And while he fastened the chains, he added: "The resources for maintaining the machine are now very much reduced. Under the former Commandant I had free access to a sum of money set aside entirely for this purpose. There was a store, too, in which spare parts were kept for repairs of all kinds. I confess I have been almost prodigal with them, I mean in the past, not now as the new Commandant pretends, always looking for an excuse to attack our old way of doing things. Now he has taken charge of the machine money himself, and if I send for a new strap they ask for the broken old strap as evidence, and the new strap takes ten days to appear and then is of shoddy material and not much good. But how I am supposed to work the machine without a strap, that's something nobody bothers about."

The explorer thought to himself: It's always a ticklish matter to intervene decisively in other people's affairs. He was neither a member of the penal colony nor a citizen of the state to which it belonged. Were he to denounce this execution or actually try to stop it, they could say to him: You are a foreigner, mind your own business. He could make no answer to that, unless he were to add that he was amazed at himself in this connection, for he traveled only as an observer, with no intention at all of altering other people's methods of administering justice. Yet here he found himself strongly tempted. The injustice of the procedure and the inhumanity of the execution were undeniable. No one could suppose that he had any selfish interest in the matter, for the condemned man was a complete stranger, not a fellow countryman or even at all sympathetic to him. The explorer himself had recommendations from high quarters, had been received here with great courtesy, and the very fact that he had been invited to attend the execution seemed to suggest that his views would be welcome. And this was all the more likely since the Commandant, as he had heard only too plainly, was no upholder of the procedure and maintained an attitude almost of hostility to the officer.

At that moment the explorer heard the officer cry out in rage. He had just, with considerable difficulty, forced the felt gag into the condemned man's mouth when the man in an irresistible access of nausea shut his eyes and vomited. Hastily the officer snatched him away from the gag and tried to hold his head over the pit; but it was too late, the vomit was running all over the machine. "It's all the fault of that Commandant!" cried the officer, senselessly shaking the brass rods in front, "the machine is befouled like a pigsty." With trembling hands he indicated to the explorer what had happened. "Have I not tried for hours at a time to get the Commandant to understand that the prisoner must fast for a whole day before the execution. But our new, mild doctrine thinks otherwise. The Commandant's ladies stuff the man with sugar candy before he's led off. He has lived on stinking fish his whole life long and now he has to eat sugar candy! But it could still be possible, I should have nothing to say against it, but why won't they get me a new felt gag, which I have been begging for the last three months. How should a man not feel sick when he takes a felt gag into his mouth which more than a hundred men have already slobbered and gnawed in their dying moments?"

The condemned man had laid his head down and looked peaceful, the soldier was busy trying to clean the machine with the prisoner's shirt. The officer advanced toward the explorer who in some vague presentiment fell back a pace, but the officer seized him by the hand, and drew him to one side. "I should like to exchange a few words with you in confidence," he said, "may I?" "Of course," said the explorer, and listened with downcast eyes.

"This procedure and method of execution, which you are now having the opportunity to admire, has at the moment no longer any open adherents in our colony. I am its sole advocate, and at the same time the sole advocate of the old Commandant's tradition. I can no longer reckon on any further extension of the method, it takes all my energy to maintain it as it is. During the old Commandant's lifetime the colony was full of his adherents; his strength of conviction I still have in some measure, but not an atom of his power; consequently the adherents have skulked out of sight, there are still many of them but none of them will admit it. If you were to go into the tea-house today, on execution day, and listen to what is being said, you would perhaps hear only ambiguous remarks. These would all be made by adherents, but under the present Commandant and his present doctrines they are of no use to me. And now I ask you: because of this Commandant and the women who influence him, is such a piece of work, the work of a lifetime"—he pointed to the machine—"to perish? Ought one to let that happen? Even if one has only come as a stranger to our island for a few days? But there's no time to lose, an attack of some kind is impending on my function as judge; conferences are already being held in the Commandant's office from which I am excluded; even your coming here today seems to me a significant move; they are cowards and use you as a screen, you, a stranger.—How different an execution was in the old days! A whole day before the ceremony the valley was packed with people; they all came only to look on; early in the morning the Commandant appeared with his ladies; fanfares roused the whole camp; I reported that everything was in readiness; the assembled company—no high official dared to absent himself—arranged itself around the machine; this pile of cane chairs is a miserable survival from that epoch. The machine was freshly cleaned and glittering, I got new spare parts for almost every execution. Before hundreds of spectators—all of them standing on tiptoe as far as the heights there—the condemned man was laid under the Harrow by the Commandant himself. What is left today for a common soldier to do was then my task, the task of the presiding judge, and was an honor for me. And then the execution began! No discordant noise spoiled the working of the machine. Many did not care to watch it but lay with closed eyes in the sand; they all knew: Now Justice is being done. In the silence one heard nothing but the condemned man's sighs, half-muffled by the felt gag. Nowadays the machine can no longer wring from anyone a sigh louder than the felt gag can stifle; but in those days the writing needles let drop an acid fluid, which we're no longer permitted to use. Well, and then came the sixth hour! It was impossible to grant all the requests to be allowed to watch it from nearby. The Commandant in his wisdom ordained that the children should have the preference; I, of course, because of my office had the privilege of always being at hand; often enough I would be squatting there with a small child in either arm. How we all absorbed the look of transfiguration on the face of the sufferer, how we bathed our cheeks in the radiance of that justice, achieved at last and fading so quickly! What times these were, my comrade!" The officer had obviously forgotten whom he was addressing; he had embraced the explorer and laid his head on his shoulder. The explorer was deeply embarrassed, impatiently he stared over the officer's head. The soldier had finished his cleaning job and was now pouring rice pap from a pot into the basin. As soon as the condemned man, who seemed to have recovered entirely, noticed this action he began to reach for the rice with his tongue. The soldier kept pushing him away, since the rice pap was certainly meant for a later hour, yet it was just as unfitting that the soldier himself should thrust his dirty hands into the basin and eat out of it before the other's avid face.

The officer quickly pulled himself together. "I didn't want to upset you," he said, "I know it is impossible to make those days credible now. Anyhow, the machine is still working and it is still effective in itself. It is effective in itself even though it stands alone in this valley. And the corpse still falls at the last into the pit with an incomprehensibly gentle wafting motion, even though there are no hundreds of people swarming around like flies as formerly. In those days we had to put a strong fence around the pit, it has long since been torn down."

The explorer wanted to withdraw his face from the officer and looked around him at random. The officer thought he was surveying the valley's desolation; so he seized him by the hands, turned him around to meet his eyes, and asked: "Do you realize the shame of it?"

But the explorer said nothing. The officer left him alone for a little; with legs apart, hands on hips, he stood very still, gazing at the ground. Then he smiled encouragingly at the explorer and said: "I was quite near you yesterday when the Commandant gave you the invitation. I heard him giving it. I know the Commandant. I divined at once what he was after. Although he is powerful enough to take measures against me, he doesn't dare to do it yet, but he certainly means to use your verdict against me, the verdict of an illustrious foreigner. He has calculated it carefully: this is your second day on the island, you did not know the old Commandant and his ways, you are conditioned by European ways of thought, perhaps you object on principle to capital punishment in general and to such mechanical instruments of death in particular, besides you will see that the execution has no support from the public, a shabby ceremony—carried out with a machine already somewhat old and worn—now, taking all that into consideration, would it not be likely (so thinks the Commandant) that you might disapprove of my methods? And if you disapprove, you wouldn't conceal the fact (I'm still speaking from the Commandant's point of view), for you are a man to feel confidence in your own well-tried conclusions. True, you have seen and learned to appreciate the peculiarities of many peoples, and so you would not be likely to take a strong line against our proceedings, as you might do in your own country. But the Commandant has no need of that. A casual, even an unguarded remark will be enough. It doesn't even need to represent what you really think, so long as it can be used speciously to serve his purpose. He will try to prompt you with sly questions, of that I am certain. And his ladies will sit around you and prick up their ears; you might be saying something like this: 'In our country we have a different criminal procedure,' or 'In our country the prisoner is interrogated before he is sentenced,' or 'We haven't used torture since the Middle Ages.' All these statements are as true as they seem natural to you, harmless remarks that pass no judgment on my methods. But how would the Commandant react to them? I can see him, our good Commandant, pushing his chair away immediately and rushing onto the balcony, I can see his ladies streaming out after him, I can hear his voice—the ladies call it a voice of thunder—well, and this is what he says: 'A famous Western investigator, sent out to study criminal procedure in all the countries of the world, has just said that our old tradition of administering justice is inhumane. Such a verdict from such a personality makes it impossible for me to countenance these methods any longer. Therefore from this very day I ordain . . . ' and so on. You may want to interpose that you never said any such thing, that you never called my methods inhumane, on the contrary your profound experience leads you to believe they are most humane and most in consonance with human dignity, and you admire the machine greatly—but it will be too late; you won't even get onto the balcony, crowded as it will be with ladies; you may try to draw attention to yourself; you may want to scream out; but a lady's hand will close your lips—and I and the work of the old Commandant will be done for."

The explorer had to suppress a smile; so easy, then, was the task he had felt to be so difficult. He said evasively: "You overestimate my influence; the Commandant has read my letters of recommendation, he knows that I am no expert in criminal procedure. If I were to give an opinion, it would be as a private individual, an opinion no more influential than that of any ordinary person, and in any case much less influential than that of the Commandant, who, I am given to understand, has very extensive powers in this penal colony. If his attitude to your procedure is as definitely hostile as you believe, then I fear the end of your tradition is at hand, even without any humble assistance from me."

Had it dawned on the officer at last? No, he still did not understand. He shook his head emphatically, glanced briefly around at the condemned man and the soldier, who both flinched away from the rice, came close up to the explorer, and without looking at his face but fixing his eye on some spot on his coat said in a lower voice than before: "You don't know the Commandant; you feel yourself—forgive the expression—a kind of outsider so far as all of us are concerned; yet, believe me, your influence cannot be rated too highly. I was simply delighted when I heard that you were to attend the execution all by yourself. The Commandant arranged it to aim a blow at me, but I shall turn it to my advantage. Without being distracted by lying whispers and contemptuous glances—which could not have been avoided had a crowd of people attended the execution—you have heard my explanations, seen the machine, and are now in course of watching the execution. You have doubtless already formed your own judgment; if you still have some small uncertainties the sight of the execution will resolve them. And now I make this request to you: help me against the Commandant!"

The explorer would not let him go on. "How could I do that," he cried, "it's quite impossible. I can neither help nor hinder you."

"Yes, you can," the officer said. The explorer saw with a certain apprehension that the officer had clenched his fists. "Yes, you can," repeated the officer, still more insistently. "I have a plan that is bound to succeed. You believe your influence is insufficient. I know that it is sufficient. But even granted that you are right, is it not necessary, for the sake of preserving this tradition, to try even what might prove insufficient? Listen to my plan, then. The first thing necessary for you to carry it out is to be as reticent as possible today regarding your verdict on these proceedings. Unless you are asked a direct question you must say nothing at all; but what you do say must be brief and general; let it be remarked that you would prefer not to discuss the matter, that you are out of patience with it, that if you are to let yourself go you would use strong language. I don't ask you to tell any lies; by no means; you should only give curt answers, such as: 'Yes, I saw the execution,' or 'Yes, I had it explained to me.' Just that, nothing more. There are grounds enough for any impatience you betray, although not such as will occur to the Commandant. Of course, he will mistake your meaning and interpret it to please himself. That's what my plan depends on. Tomorrow in the Commandant's office there is to be a large conference of all the high administrative officials, the Commandant presiding. Of course the Commandant is the kind of man to have turned these conferences into public spectacles. He has had a gallery built that is always packed with spectators. I am compelled to take part in the conferences, but they make me sick with disgust. Now, whatever happens, you will certainly be invited to this conference; if you behave today as I suggest, the invitation will become an urgent request. But if for some mysterious reason you're not invited, you'll have to ask for an invitation; there's no doubt of your getting it then. So tomorrow you're sitting in the Commandant's box with the ladies. He keeps looking up to make sure you're there. After various trivial and ridiculous matters, brought in merely to impress the audience—mostly harbor works, nothing but harbor works!—our judicial procedure comes up for discussion too. If the Commandant doesn't introduce it, or not soon enough, I'll see that it's mentioned. I'll stand up and report that today's execution has taken place. Quite briefly, only a statement. Such a statement is not usual, but I shall make it. The Commandant thanks me, as always, with an amiable smile, and then he can't restrain himself, he seizes the excellent opportunity. 'It has just been reported,' he will say, or words to that effect, 'that an execution has taken place. I should like merely to add that this execution was witnessed by the famous explorer who has, as you all know, honored our colony so greatly by his visit to us. His presence at today's session of our conference also contributes to the importance of this occasion. Should we not now ask the famous explorer to give us his verdict on our traditional mode of execution and the procedure that leads up to it?' Of course there is loud applause, general agreement, I am more insistent than anyone. The Commandant bows to you and says: 'Then in the name of the assembled company, I put the question to you.' And now you advance to the front of the box. Lay your hands where everyone can see them, or the ladies will catch them and press your fingers.—And then at last you can speak out. I don't know how I'm going to endure the tension of waiting for that moment. Don't put any restraint on yourself when you make your speech, publish the truth aloud, lean over the front of the box, shout, yes indeed, shout your verdict, your unshakable conviction, at the Commandant. Yet perhaps you wouldn't care to do that, it's not in keeping with your character, in your country perhaps people do these things differently, well, that's all right too, that will be quite as effective, don't even stand up, just say a few words, even in a whisper, so that only the officials beneath you will hear them, that will be quite enough, you don't even need to mention the lack of public support for the execution, the creaking wheel, the broken strap, the filthy gag of felt, no, I'll take all that upon me, and, believe me, if my indictment doesn't drive him out of the conference hall, it will force him to his knees to make the acknowledgment: Old Commandant, I humble myself before you.—That is my plan; will you help me to carry it out? But of course you are willing, what is more, you must." And the officer seized the explorer by both arms and gazed, breathing heavily, into his face. He had shouted the last sentence so loudly that even the soldier and the condemned man were startled into attending; they had not understood a word but they stopped eating and looked over at the explorer, chewing their previous mouthfuls.

From the very beginning the explorer had no doubt about what answer he must give; in his lifetime he had experienced too much to have any uncertainty here; he was fundamentally honorable and unafraid. And yet now, facing the soldier and the condemned man, he did hesitate, for as long as it took to draw one breath. At last, however, he said, as he had to: "No." The officer blinked several times but did not turn his eyes away. "Would you like me to explain?" asked the explorer. The officer nodded wordlessly. "I do not approve of your procedure," said the explorer then, "even before you took me into your confidence—of course I shall never in any circumstances betray your confidence—I was already wondering whether it would be my duty to intervene and whether my intervention would have the slightest chance of success. I realized to whom I ought to turn: to the Commandant, of course. You have made that fact even clearer, but without having strengthened my resolution, on the contrary, your sincere conviction has touched me, even though it cannot influence my judgment."

The officer remained mute, turned to the machine, caught hold of a brass rod, and then, leaning back a little, gazed at the Designer as if to assure himself that all was in order. The soldier and the condemned man seemed to have come to some understanding; the condemned man was making signs to the soldier, difficult though his movements were because of the tight straps; the soldier was bending down to him; the condemned man whispered something and the soldier nodded.

The explorer followed the officer and said: "You don't know yet what I mean to do. I shall tell the Commandant what I think of the procedure, certainly, but not at a public conference, only in private; nor shall I stay here long enough to attend any conference; I am going away early tomorrow morning, or at least embarking on my ship."

It did not look as if the officer had been listening. "So you did not find the procedure convincing," he said to himself and smiled, as an old man smiles at childish nonsense and yet pursues his own meditations behind the smile.

"Then the time has come," he said at last, and suddenly looked at the explorer with bright eyes that held some challenge, some appeal for cooperation. "The time for what?" asked the explorer uneasily, but got no answer.

"You are free," said the officer to the condemned man in the native tongue. The man did not believe it at first. "Yes, you are set free," said the officer. For the first time the condemned man's face woke to real animation. Was it true? Was it only a caprice of the officer's, that might change again? Had the foreign explorer begged him off? What was it? One could read these questions on his face. But not for long. Whatever it might be, he wanted to be really free if he might, and he began to struggle so far as the Harrow permitted him.

"You'll burst my straps," cried the officer, "lie still! We'll soon loosen them." And signing the soldier to help him, he set about doing so. The condemned man laughed wordlessly to himself, now he turned his face left toward the officer, now right toward the soldier, nor did he forget the explorer.

"Draw him out," ordered the officer. Because of the Harrow this had to be done with some care. The condemned man had already torn himself a little in the back through his impatience.

From now on, however, the officer paid hardly any attention to him. He went up to the explorer, pulled out the small leather wallet again, turned over the papers in it, found the one he wanted, and showed it to the explorer. "Read it," he said. "I can't," said the explorer, "I told you before that I can't make out these scripts." "Try taking a close look at it," said the officer and came quite near to the explorer so that they might read it together. But when even that proved useless, he outlined the script with his little finger, holding it high above the paper as if the surface dared not be sullied by touch, in order to help the explorer to follow the script in that way. The explorer did make an effort, meaning to please the officer in this respect at least, but he was quite unable to follow. Now the officer began to spell it, letter by letter, and then read out the words. "'BE JUST!' is what is written there," he said, "surely you can read it now." The explorer bent so close to the paper that the officer feared he might touch it and drew it farther away; the explorer made no remark, yet it was clear that he still could not decipher it. "'BE JUST!' is what is written there," said the officer once more. "Maybe," said the explorer, "I am prepared to believe you." "Well, then," said the officer, at least partly satisfied, and climbed up the ladder with the paper; very carefully he laid it inside the Designer and seemed to be changing the disposition of all the cogwheels; it was a troublesome piece of work and must have involved wheels that were extremely small, for sometimes the officer's head vanished altogether from sight inside the Designer, so precisely did he have to regulate the machinery.

The explorer, down below, watched the labor uninterruptedly, his neck grew stiff and his eyes smarted from the glare of sunshine over the sky. The soldier and the condemned man were now busy together. The man's shirt and trousers, which were already lying in the pit, were fished out by the point of the soldier's bayonet. The shirt was abominably dirty and its owner washed it in the bucket of water. When he put on the shirt and trousers both he and the soldier could not help guffawing, for the garments were of course slit up behind. Perhaps the condemned man felt it incumbent on him to amuse the soldier, he turned around and around in his slashed garments before the soldier, who squatted on the ground beating his knees with mirth. All the same, they presently controlled their mirth out of respect for the gentlemen.

When the officer had at length finished his task aloft, he surveyed the machinery in all its details once more, with a smile, but this time shut the lid of the Designer, which had stayed open till now, climbed down, looked into the pit and then at the condemned man, noting with satisfaction that the clothing had been taken out, then went over to wash his hands in the water bucket, perceived too late that it was disgustingly dirty, was unhappy because he could not wash his hands, in the end thrust them into the sand—this alternative did not please him, but he had to put up with it—then stood upright and began to unbutton his uniform jacket. As he did this, the two ladies' handkerchiefs he had tucked under his collar fell into his hands. "Here are your handkerchiefs," he said, and threw them to the condemned man. And to the explorer he said in explanation: "A gift from the ladies."

In spite of the obvious haste with which he was discarding first his uniform jacket and then all his clothing, he handled each garment with loving care, he even ran his fingers caressingly over the silver lace on the jacket and shook a tassel into place. This loving care was certainly out of keeping with the fact that as soon as he had a garment off he flung it at once with a kind of unwilling jerk into the pit. The last thing left to him was his short sword with the sword belt. He drew it out of the scabbard, broke it, then gathered all together, the bits of the sword, the scabbard, and the belt, and flung them so violently down that they clattered into the pit.

Now he stood naked there. The explorer bit his lips and said nothing. He knew very well what was going to happen, but he had no right to obstruct the officer in anything. If the judicial procedure which the officer cherished were really so near its end—possibly as a result of his own intervention, as to which he felt himself pledged—then the officer was doing the right thing; in his place the explorer would not have acted otherwise.

The soldier and the condemned man did not understand at first what was happening, at first they were not even looking on. The condemned man was gleeful at having got the handkerchiefs back, but he was not allowed to enjoy them for long, since the soldier snatched them with a sudden, unexpected grab. Now the condemned man in turn was trying to twitch them from under the belt where the soldier had tucked them, but the soldier was on his guard. So they were wrestling, half in jest. Only when the officer stood quite naked was their attention caught. The condemned man especially seemed struck with the notion that some great change was impending. What had happened to him was now going to happen to the officer. Perhaps even to the very end. Apparently the foreign explorer had given the order for it. So this was revenge. Although he himself had not suffered to the end, he was to be revenged to the end. A broad, silent grin now appeared on his face and stayed there all the rest of the time.

The officer, however, had turned to the machine. It had been clear enough previously that he understood the machine well, but now it was almost staggering to see how he managed it and how it obeyed him. His hand had only to approach the Harrow for it to rise and sink several times till it was adjusted to the right position for receiving him; he touched only the edge of the Bed and already it was vibrating; the felt gag came to meet his mouth, one could see that the officer was really reluctant to take it but he shrank from it only a moment, soon he submitted and received it. Everything was ready, only the straps hung down at the sides, yet they were obviously unnecessary, the officer did not need to be fastened down. Then the condemned man noticed the loose straps, in his opinion the execution was incomplete unless the straps were buckled, he gestured eagerly to the soldier and they ran together to strap the officer down. The latter had already stretched out one foot to push the lever that started the Designer; he saw the two men coming up; so he drew his foot back and let himself be buckled in. But now he could not reach the lever; neither the soldier nor the condemned man would be able to find it, and the explorer was determined not to lift a finger. It was not necessary; as soon as the straps were fastened the machine began to work; the Bed vibrated, the needles flickered above the skin, the Harrow rose and fell. The explorer had been staring at it quite a while before he remembered that a wheel in the Designer should have been creaking; but everything was quiet, not even the slightest hum could be heard.

Because it was working so silently the machine simply escaped one's attention. The explorer observed the soldier and the condemned man. The latter was the more animated of the two, everything in the machine interested him, now he was bending down and now stretching up on tiptoe, his forefinger was extended all the time pointing out details to the soldier. This annoyed the explorer. He was resolved to stay till the end, but he could not bear the sight of these two. "Go back home," he said. The soldier would have been willing enough, but the condemned man took the order as a punishment. With clasped hands he implored to be allowed to stay, and when the explorer shook his head and would not relent, he even went down on his knees. The explorer saw that it was no use merely giving orders, he was on the point of going over and driving them away. At that moment he heard a noise above him in the Designer. He looked up. Was that cogwheel going to make trouble after all? But it was something quite different. Slowly the lid of the Designer rose up and then clicked wide open. The teeth of a cogwheel showed themselves and rose higher, soon the whole wheel was visible, it was as if some enormous force were squeezing the Designer so that there was no longer room for the wheel, the wheel moved up till it came to the very edge of the Designer, fell down, rolled along the sand a little on its rim, and then lay flat. But a second wheel was already rising after it, followed by many others, large and small and indistinguishably minute, the same thing happened to all of them, at every moment one imagined the Designer must now really be empty, but another complex of numerous wheels was already rising into sight, falling down, trundling along the sand, and lying flat. This phenomenon made the condemned man completely forget the explorer's command, the cogwheels fascinated him, he was always trying to catch one and at the same time urging the soldier to help, but always drew back his hand in alarm, for another wheel always came hopping along which, at least on its first advance, scared him off.

The explorer, on the other hand, felt greatly troubled; the machine was obviously going to pieces; its silent working was a delusion; he had a feeling that he must now stand by the officer, since the officer was no longer able to look after himself. But while the tumbling cogwheels absorbed his whole attention he had forgotten to keep an eye on the rest of the machine; now that the last cogwheel had left the Designer, however, he bent over the Harrow and had a new and still more unpleasant surprise. The Harrow was not writing, it was only jabbing, and the Bed was not turning the body over but only bringing it up quivering against the needles. The explorer wanted to do something, if possible, to bring the whole machine to a standstill, for this was no exquisite torture such as the officer desired, this was plain murder.

He stretched out his hands. But at that moment the Harrow rose with the body spitted on it and moved to the side, as it usually did only when the twelfth hour had come. Blood was flowing in a hundred streams, not mingled with water, the water jets too had failed to function. And now the last action failed to fulfill itself, the body did not drop off the long needles, streaming with blood it went on hanging over the pit without falling into it. The Harrow tried to move back to its old position, but as if it had itself noticed that it had not yet got rid of its burden it stuck after all where it was, over the pit. "Come and help!" cried the explorer to the other two, and himself seized the officer's feet. He wanted to push against the feet while the others seized the head from the opposite side and so the officer might be slowly eased off the needles. But the other two could not make up their minds to come; the condemned man actually turned away; the explorer had to go over to them and force them into position at the officer's head. And here, almost against his will, he had to look at the face of the corpse. It was as it had been in life; no sign was visible of the promised redemption; what the others had found in the machine the officer had not found; the lips were firmly pressed together, the eyes were open, with the same expression as in life, the look was calm and convinced, through the forehead went the point of the great iron spike.

As the explorer, with the soldier and the condemned man behind him, reached the first houses of the colony, the soldier pointed to one of them and said: "There is the teahouse."

In the ground floor of the house was a deep, low, cavernous space, its walls and ceiling blackened with smoke. It was open to the road all along its length. Although this teahouse was very little different from the other houses of the colony, which were all very dilapidated, even up to the Commandant's palatial headquarters, it made on the explorer the impression of a historic tradition of some kind, and he felt the power of past days. He went near to it, followed by his companions, right up between the empty tables that stood in the street before it, and breathed the cool, heavy air that came from the interior. "The old man's buried here," said the soldier, "the priest wouldn't let him lie in the churchyard. Nobody knew where to bury him for a while, but in the end they buried him here. The officer never told you about that, for sure, because of course that's what he was most ashamed of. He even tried several times to dig the old man up by night, but he was always chased away." "Where is the grave?" asked the explorer, who found it impossible to believe the soldier. At once both of them, the soldier and the condemned man, ran before him pointing with outstretched hands in the direction where the grave should be. They led the explorer right up to the back wall, where guests were sitting at a few tables. They were apparently dock laborers, strong men with short, glistening, full black beards. None had a jacket, their shirts were torn, they were poor, humble creatures. As the explorer drew near, some of them got up, pressed close to the wall, and stared at him. "It's a foreigner," ran the whisper around him, "he wants to see the grave." They pushed one of the tables aside, and under it there was really a gravestone. It was a simple stone, low enough to be covered by a table. There was an inscription on it in very small letters, the explorer had to kneel down to read it. This was what it said: "Here rests the old Commandant. His adherents, who now must be nameless, have dug this grave and set up this stone. There is a prophecy that after a certain number of years the Commandant will rise again and lead his adherents from this house to recover the colony. Have faith and wait!" When the explorer had read this and risen to his feet he saw all the bystanders around him smiling, as if they too had read the inscription, had found it ridiculous, and were expecting him to agree with them. The explorer ignored this, distributed a few coins among them, waiting till the table was pushed over the grave again, quitted the teahouse, and made for the harbor.

The soldier and the condemned man had found some acquaintances in the teahouse, who detained them. But they must have soon shaken them off, for the explorer was only halfway down the long flight of steps leading to the boats when they came rushing after him. Probably they wanted to force him at the last minute to take them with him. While he was bargaining below with a ferryman to row him to the steamer, the two of them came headlong down the steps, in silence, for they did not dare to shout. But by the time they reached the foot of the steps the explorer was already in the boat, and the ferryman was just casting off from the shore. They could have jumped into the boat, but the explorer lifted a heavy knotted rope from the floor boards, threatened them with it, and so kept them from attempting the leap.

Girl

by Jamaica Kincaid

Introduced by Stephanie Vaughn

JAMAICA KINCAID'S "GIRL" ALWAYS ASTONISHES ME. IT PASSES OVER the conventions of preamble and lights upon the page in full motion: "Wash the white clothes on Monday and put them on the stone heap; wash the color clothes on Tuesday. . . ." Maybe it is the seduction of the implied "you" which pulls me in; maybe it is the irresistible voice of the command, or the precision and certitude of the short declarative statement: This is the way to live in my feminine domain, it says; read on. The story spills out in a single breath, a gusty exhalation of urgency and passion, which is also a single sentence. The sentence plunges down the page like a waterfall, like liquid lava, in a violent splendor barely contained by the white margins. Its exhilarating motion gives me the sense of a writer carried over the precipice by the energy of her own vision, by the imperatives and declarations of the story, by the turbulence of anger and love crashing to the bottom of something. Here is a writer who is not working from outlines and complacencies. Here is a writer who can take whatever might seem ordinary and commonplace in their namings—pumpkin fritters, table settings, salt fish, the gum-sizing in new cotton—and elevate them to beauty with her extraordinary voice, its humor, and its scorn, and its pulsing, incantatory, even biblical rhythms. The story seems to have a linear motion, this downward sweep of nouns and injunctions, from the menstrual cloths at the beginning to the abortion medicine toward the end, from the "girl" of the title to the "woman" of the last line. But no, the story transfigures itself into circularities—the return to "slut" and to "slut" and to "slut." It is a dilating story, a widening story, opening into the dark intimate spaces of peril. The girl may be cheated by a cloth merchant, repudiated by a butcher, she may conceive a child she does not want, she may throw a stone at a blackbird which is not a blackbird, she may endlessly, in the timeless present tense of the mother's voice fail to be the right kind of girl. And where is the "girl" of the title, the prospective "woman" of the last line? She is trapped between two sets of semicolons. She is feathered into abjection and weightlessness by the italic typeface. She is imprisoned in her own mother's voice, a tower of language. But isn't the girl also the magician in this story, the enchantress who has escaped into womanhood and come back to ventriloquize her mother? Surely the girl is the writer—not Jamaica Kincaid in the literal autobiographical sense but the invented writer who pulls a whole childhood of memory into a single perfectly managed sentence and makes me laugh at the mother every time she breaks down and says "slut"? Whenever I read this story (and I have read it perhaps a hundred times), I return at once to the first sentence and begin to read it aloud, so that I can experience the story on my tongue and in the resonant cavities of my body. I find that it is best to stand up when you read this story aloud, and to take a breath from the deepest region of your belly. When your lungs are full, when your shoulders are back, you begin to speak the story, and then you find that you are singing.

Girl

Jamaica Kincaid

Wash the white clothes on Monday and put them on the stone heap; wash the color clothes on Tuesday and put them on the clothesline to dry; don't walk barehead in the hot sun; cook pumpkin fritters in very hot sweet oil; soak your little cloths right after you take them off; when buying cotton to make yourself a nice blouse, be sure that it doesn't have gum on it, because that way it won't hold up well after a wash; soak salt fish overnight before you cook it; is it true that you sing benna in Sunday school?; always eat your food in such a way that it won't turn someone else's stomach; on Sundays try to walk like a lady and not like the slut you are so bent on becoming; don't sing benna in Sunday school; you mustn't speak to wharf-rat boys, not even to give directions; don't eat fruits on the street—flies will follow you; *but I don't sing benna on Sundays at all and never in Sunday school;* this is how to sew on a button; this is how to make a buttonhole for the button you have just sewed on; this is how to hem a dress when you see the hem coming down and so to prevent yourself from looking like the slut I know you are so bent on becoming; this is how you iron your father's khaki shirt so that it doesn't have a crease; this is how you iron your father's khaki pants so that they don't have a crease; this is how you grow okra—far from the house, because okra tree harbors red ants; when you are growing dasheen, make sure it gets plenty of water or else it makes your throat itch when you are eating it; this is how you sweep a corner; this is how you sweep a whole house; this is how you sweep a yard; this how you smile to someone you don't like too much; this is how you smile to someone you don't like at all; this is how you smile to someone you like completely; this is how you set a table for tea; this is how you set a table for dinner; this is how you set a table for dinner with an important guest; this is how you set a table for lunch; this is how you set a table for breakfast; this is how to behave in the presence of men who don't know you very well, and this way they won't recognize immediately the slut I have warned you against becoming; be sure to wash every day, even if it is with your own spit; don't squat down to play marbles—you are not a boy, you know; don't pick people's flowers—you might catch something; don't throw stones at blackbirds, because it might not be a blackbird at all; this is how to make a bread pudding; this is how to make doukona; this is how to make pepper pot; this is how to make a good medicine for a cold; this is how to make a good medicine to throw away a child before it even becomes a child; this is how to catch a fish; this is how to throw back a fish you don't like, and that way something bad won't fall on you; this is how to bully a man; this is how a man bullies you; this is how to love a man, and if this doesn't work there are other ways, and if they don't work don't feel too bad about giving up; this is how to spit up in the air if you feel like it, and this is how to move quick so that it doesn't fall on you; this is how to make ends meet; always squeeze bread to make sure it's fresh, *but what if the baker won't let me feel the bread?;* you mean to say that after all you are really going to be the kind of woman who the baker won't let near the bread?

The Smallest Woman in the World

by Clarice Lispector

Introduced by Julia Alvarez

STORIES THAT HOLD ME SPELLBOUND REMIND ME OF THE TALE THE Ancient Mariner has to tell. He finds just the person whom he knows has to hear his story, and then he holds his listener with the glittering eye of his narrative. The listener might resist at first, but when the tale is told, he feels the deep *ah yes* of having heard just the thing he needed to hear.

There are stories I admire, ones I adore, ones I wish I had written. But the story that holds me spellbound is the one I feel was written because someone like me had to read it.

I first read Clarice Lispector's story "The Smallest Woman in the World" about sixteen–seventeen years ago, before the great push in anthologies, colleges, curriculum to include "minority voices." I had been trained back in those days when you read only *the* great books—Milton, Shakespeare, Chaucer—and you went to anthropology, or in my case home to the Island, to learn about *the other*. Literature, for me, was definitely the colony of the powerful, and I was fully identified with them. When I read *The Tempest,* I too held Caliban at arm's length, never giving a thought to what his rights were to the island Prospero had conquered. When I heard the lover's plaint in the Sonnets about his dark lady's looks, I understood how a fair one would have made him feel better. In other words, I looked at *the other* with a cold, dominant Yeatsian eye, though my own personal experience, of course, negated my literary one. All the women authors I did finally read, and all the "minority" women authors that saved my work and psyche from total divorce from my own roots and culture and being, I read long after graduate school, on my own.

When I picked up the Lispector story, I was just beginning this process of reading on my own. The Ancient Mariner story is obviously compelling because the listener is ripe for the telling. Encountering that first paragraph I was all set, with my training, for Joseph Conrad and the trek into deepest Africa to encounter horror, the horror. "Imagine my surprise" when I came upon the seventeen and three-quarter inch, full-grown, black, silent, and very pregnant smallest woman in the world! I burst out laughing.

It was a heady, gleeful, refreshing laughter—aimed at myself mostly. How could I have missed her in all my reading? The answer came almost at once: of course, she is *so* small—and silent and black and pregnant—that I and, it seemed, most of western tradition had overlooked her.

It is hard to know who she really is. We are first introduced to her through the point of view of the explorer. Instantly upon meeting her, he names her, giving her a ridiculous, prettifying name, reminiscent of her obvious opposite, Saint Teresa, the Little Flower. But the explorer himself is being transformed by the encounter: as he studies her before naming her, he feels "a delicacy of feeling" of which his wife would never have thought him capable. To this sweet, deeply moving biblical moment of Adam naming in the garden, the newly baptized Little Flower responds by scratching her crotch. The explorer looks away, embarrassed, I suppose.

The story, too, looks away for a long while; instead of staying in Africa, we head back for "civilization." (Part of the transforming effect of this story is that the reader starts saying all these words with a sense of irony.) Now we hear reaction after reaction to Little Flower—all having more to do with the readers of the Sunday Papers than they do with the oblivious little woman still, we assume, in deepest Africa, scratching where it itches.

I do wonder why almost all of the responders are women—except for one little boy and an absent, uneasy father, coughing behind his paper. Is it because, as the wife of the uneasy father accuses, "You're the insensitive one"? We women are the responders. It's the next best thing if we can't go on the adventures. After all, the world might not be our apple, but it can be our Rorschach, goddammit! Then, too, Little Flower is pregnant, a condition that binds her to other females. But this sense of resemblance makes the women uneasy. One woman at her mirror rolling her hair draws away from this black, crude face, placing a distance of "insuperable millenniums" between the creature and herself. "It isn't human," another mother reminds her daughter. I can understand their reluctance—they are fully identified with their dominant status as the refined and beautiful wives and daughters of the powerful.

By moving away from Little Flower into the drawing room, the story charts a common impulse: always we want to come back to what we know. To bring back the strange into the cozy safety of our living room and *respond*. To theorize and coopt it with our love and misinformed understanding, p.c.-ing her to death. And at the same time to distance ourselves from it—to respond to it but not identify with it.

The story has wandered far from the original creature herself—just as I had in my own training when I first came upon the story. As I said, it is difficult to encounter the unadulterated rare thing herself and not interpose our selves, our faces, our prejudices upon it. But finally the narrator returns us to the source. Now, we will get "the secret of her own secret": what we've wanted to know all along, Who is Little Flower? What does she mean? In other words, the story raises in the reader the same curiosity about Little Flower as symbol that the explorer and his civilized ladies felt toward the little figure herself.

But wait, Little Flower is laughing! At us? No, not really. For if she were laughing at us, we would be speaking the same language. Unlike the sad women we met in the drawing rooms who have learned—or are beginning to intuit—the wisdom that "sorrow is endless," Little Flower posits joy with her laughter. She is still close to her irreducible being, and she is joyous because she has not been eaten, and she is in love with the explorer because she likes his boots and his shiny ring. She responds to these feelings in a frankly sexual way. Little Flower is free of the cruel refinements of these feelings that must be making the other women in their little golden cages so unhappy.

Or so we understand from our author, who must be intuiting what Little Flower is feeling, for the smallest woman doesn't speak. She does finally say one word, one quoted word in the whole story, "Yes." All we hear of her is her wonderful laughter, which serves, at least for me, the same function as the Ancient Mariner's glittering eye. That laughter holds me and echoes in my head long after the story is over. And then, I realize—and I remember the shock of that first reading—that the laughter was coming from deep inside me.

Yes!

What I suddenly understood that first time I read the story—and my laughter each time I reread the story confirms it—was that I was Little Flower. *Yes.* I am really—in the hiddenmost parts of the deepest Africa in me—the smallest woman in the world. I've learned English perfectly without an accent. Due to vitamins and good nutrition, I have grown to a sizable small size and weight. I know how to throw this small weight and American voice around. I have the degrees, the training on how to respond to literature, I have a car, a house, a closet full of pretty clothes, because it is good to own, good to own.

But it's not just me who is Little Flower. Everyone who reads the story knows he or she is Little Flower, and he or she is also the overlay of responses and note-taking that keeps the little being invisible and minuscule inside us: our little pregnancy, the first atom of our being, the creature who has not been eaten. But cruel refinements interfere. And we forget the visceral first and truest response of our being to the world

Sometimes I know I forget who I am under the overlay of Sunday papers, of work, of clothes, of the feminine, of the American girl, of netted hats, of words, words, words.

But this little story always reminds me and that is why it holds me, spellbound.

The Smallest Woman in the World

Clarice Lispector

Translated by Elizabeth Bishop

In the depths of Equatorial Africa the French explorer, Marcel Pretre, hunter and man of the world, came across a tribe of surprisingly small pygmies. Therefore he was even more surprised when he was informed that a still smaller people existed, beyond forests and distances. So he plunged farther on.

In the Eastern Congo, near Lake Kivu, he really did discover the smallest pygmies in the world. And—like a box within a box within a box—obedient, perhaps, to the necessity nature sometimes feels of outdoing herself—among the smallest pygmies in the world there was the smallest of the smallest pygmies in the world.

Among mosquitoes and lukewarm trees, among leaves of the most rich and lazy green, Marcel Pretre found himself facing a woman seventeen and three-quarter inches high, full-grown, black, silent—"Black as a monkey," he informed the press—who lived in a treetop with her little spouse. In the tepid miasma of the jungle, that swells the fruits so early and gives them an almost intolerable sweetness, she was pregnant.

So there she stood, the smallest woman in the world. For an instant, in the buzzing heat, it seemed as if the Frenchman had unexpectedly reached his final destination. Probably only because he was not insane, his soul neither wavered nor broke its bounds. Feeling an immediate necessity for order and for giving names to what exists, he called her Little Flower. And in order to be able to classify her among the recognizable realities, he immediately began to collect facts about her.

Her race will soon be exterminated. Few examples are left of this species, which, if it were not for the sly dangers of Africa, might have multiplied. Besides disease, the deadly effluvium of the water, insufficient food, and ranging beasts, the great threat to the Likoualas are the savage Bahundes, a threat that surrounds them in the silent air, like the dawn of battle. The Bahundes hunt them with nets, like monkeys. And eat them. Like that: they catch them in nets and *eat* them. The tiny race, retreating, always retreating, has finished hiding away in the heart of Africa, where the lucky explorer discovered it. For strategic defense, they live in the highest trees. The women descend to grind and cook corn and to gather greens; the men, to hunt. When a child is born, it is left free almost immediately. It is true that, what with the beasts, the child frequently cannot enjoy this freedom for very long. But then it is true that it cannot be lamented that for such a short life there had been any long, hard work. And even the language that the child learns is short and simple, merely the essentials. The Likoualas use few names; they name things by gestures and animal noises. As for things of the spirit, they have a drum. While they dance to the sound of the drum, a little male stands guard against the Bahundes, who come from no one knows where.

That was the way, then, that the explorer discovered, standing at his very feet, the smallest existing human thing. His heart beat, because no emerald in the world is so rare. The teachings of the wise men of India are not so rare. The richest man in the world has never set eyes on such strange grace. Right there was a woman that the greed of the most exquisite dream could never have imagined. It was then that the explorer said timidly, and with a delicacy of feeling of which his wife would never have thought him capable: "You are Little Flower."

At that moment, Little Flower scratched herself where no one scratches. The explorer—as if he were receiving the highest prize for chastity to which an idealistic man dares aspire—the explorer, experienced as he was, looked the other way.

A photograph of Little Flower was published in the colored supplement of the Sunday Papers, life-size. She was wrapped in a cloth, her belly already very big. The flat nose, the black face, the splay feet. She looked like a dog.

On that Sunday, in an apartment, a woman seeing the picture of Little Flower in the paper didn't want to look a second time because "It gives me the creeps."

In another apartment, a lady felt such perverse tenderness for the smallest of the African women that—an ounce of prevention being worth a pound of cure—Little Flower could never be left alone to the tenderness of that lady. Who knows to what murkiness of love tenderness can lead? The woman was upset all day, almost as if she were missing something. Besides, it was spring and there was a dangerous leniency in the air.

In another house, a little girl of five, seeing the picture and hearing the comments, was extremely surprised. In a houseful of adults, this little girl had been the smallest human being up until now. And, if this was the source of all caresses, it was also the source of the first fear of the tyranny of love. The existence of Little Flower made the little girl feel—with a deep uneasiness that only years and years later, and for very different reasons, would turn into thought—made her feel, in her first wisdom, that "sorrow is endless."

In another house, in the consecration of spring, a girl about to be married felt an ecstasy of pity: "Mama, look at her little picture, poor little thing! Just look how sad she is!"

"But," said the mother, hard and defeated and proud, "it's the sadness of an animal. It isn't human sadness."

"Oh, Mama!" said the girl, discouraged.

In another house, a clever little boy had a clever idea: "Mummy, if I could put this little woman from Africa in little Paul's bed when he's asleep? When he woke up wouldn't he be frightened? Wouldn't he howl? When he saw her sitting on his bed? And then we'd play with her! She would be our toy!"

His mother was setting her hair in front of the bathroom mirror at the moment, and she remembered what a cook had told her about life in an orphanage. The orphans had no dolls, and, with terrible maternity already throbbing in their hearts, the little girls had hidden the death of one of the children from the nun. They kept the body in a cupboard and when the nun went out they played with the dead child, giving her baths and things to eat, punishing her only to be able to kiss and console her. In the bathroom, the mother remembered this, and let fall her thoughtful hands, full of curlers. She considered the cruel necessity of loving. And she considered the malignity of our desire for happiness. She considered how ferociously we need to play. How many times we will kill for love. Then she looked at her clever child as if she were looking at a dangerous stranger. And she had a horror of her own soul that, more than her body, had engendered that being, adept at life and happiness. She looked at him attentively and with uncomfortable pride, that child who had already lost two front teeth, evolution evolving itself, teeth falling out to give place to those that could bite better. "I'm going to buy him a new suit," she decided, looking at him, absorbed. Obstinately, she adorned her gap-toothed son with fine clothes; obstinately, she wanted him very clean, as if his cleanliness could emphasize a soothing superficiality, obstinately perfecting the polite side of beauty. Obstinately drawing away from, and drawing him away from, something that ought to be "black as a monkey." Then, looking in the bathroom mirror, the mother gave a deliberately refined and social smile, placing a distance of insuperable millenniums between the abstract lines of her features and the crude face of Little Flower. But, with years of practice, she knew that this was going to be a Sunday on which she would have to hide from herself anxiety, dreams, and lost millenniums.

In another house, they gave themselves up to the enthralling task of measuring the seventeen and three-quarter inches of Little Flower against the wall. And, really, it was a delightful surprise: she was even smaller than the sharpest imagination could have pictured. In the heart of each member of the family was born, nostalgic, the desire to have that tiny and indomitable thing for itself, that thing spared having been eaten, that permanent source of charity. The avid family soul wanted to devote itself. To tell the truth, who hasn't wanted to own a human being just for himself? Which, it is true, wouldn't always be convenient; there are times when one doesn't want to have feelings.

"I bet if she lived here it would end in a fight," said the father, sitting in the armchair and definitely turning the page of the newspaper. "In this house everything ends in a fight."

"Oh, you, José—always a pessimist," said the mother.

"But, Mama, have you thought of the size her baby's going to be?" said the oldest little girl, aged thirteen, eagerly.

The father stirred uneasily behind his paper.

"It should be the smallest black baby in the world," the mother answered, melting with pleasure. "Imagine her serving our table, with her big little belly!"

"That's enough!" growled father.

"But you have to admit," said the mother, unexpectedly offended, "that it is something very rare. You're the insensitive one."

And the rare thing itself?

In the meanwhile, in Africa, the rare thing herself, in her heart—and who knows if the heart wasn't black, too, since once nature has erred she can no longer be trusted—the rare thing herself had something even rarer in her heart, like the secret of her own secret: a minimal child. Methodically, the explorer studied that little belly of the smallest mature human being. It was at this moment that the explorer, for the first time since he had known her, instead of feeling curiosity, or exhalation, or victory, or the scientific spirit, felt sick.

The smallest woman in the world was laughing.

She was laughing, warm, warm—Little Flower was enjoying life. The rare thing herself was experiencing the ineffable sensation of not having been eaten yet. Not having been eaten yet was something that at any other time would have given her the agile impulse to jump from branch to branch. But, in this moment of tranquility, amid the thick leaves of the Eastern Congo, she was not putting this impulse into action—it was entirely concentrated in the smallness of the rare thing itself. So she was laughing. It was a laugh such as only one who does not speak laughs. It was a laugh that the explorer, constrained, couldn't classify. And she kept on enjoying her own soft laugh, she who wasn't being devoured. Not to be devoured is the most perfect feeling. Not to be devoured is the secret goal of a whole life. While she was not being eaten, her bestial laughter was as delicate as joy is delicate. The explorer was baffled.

In the second place, if the rare thing herself was laughing, it was because, within her smallness, a great darkness had begun to move.

The rare thing herself felt in her breast a warmth that might be called love. She loved that sallow explorer. If she could have talked and had told him that she loved him, he would have been puffed up with vanity. Vanity that would have collapsed when she added that she also loved the explorer's ring very much, and the explorer's boots. And when that collapse had taken place, Little Flower would not have understood why. Because her love for the explorer—one might even say "profound love," since, having no other resources, she was reduced to profundity—her profound love for the explorer would not have been at all diminished by the fact that she also loved his boots. There is an old misunderstanding about the word love, and, if many children are born from this misunderstanding, many others have lost the unique chance of being born, only because of the susceptibility that demands that it be me! me! that is loved, and not my money. But in the humidity of the forest these cruel refinements do not exist, and love is not to be eaten, love is to find a boot pretty, love is to like the strange color of a man who isn't black, is to laugh for love of a shiny ring. Little Flower blinked with love, and laughed warmly, small, gravid, warm.

The explorer tried to smile back, without knowing exactly to what abyss his smile responded, and then he was embarrassed as only a very big man can be embarrassed. He pretended to adjust his explorer's hat better; he colored, prudishly. He turned a lovely color, a greenish-pink, like a lime at sunrise. He was undoubtedly sour.

Perhaps adjusting the symbolic helmet helped the explorer to get control of himself, severely recapture the discipline of his work, and go on with his note-taking. He had learned how to understand some of the tribe's few articulate words, and to interpret their signs. By now, he could ask questions.

Little Flower answered "Yes." That it was very nice to have a tree of her own to live in. Because—she didn't say this but her eyes became so dark that they said it—because it is good to own, good to own, good to own. The explorer winked several times.

Marcel Pretre had some difficult moments with himself. But at least he kept busy taking notes. Those who didn't take notes had to manage as best they could:

"Well," suddenly declared one old lady, folding up the newspaper decisively, "well, as I always say: God knows what He's doing."

The Daughters of the Late Colonel

by Katherine Mansfield

Introduced by Deborah Eisenberg

ALL OF US WHOM THE EDITORS CALLED MUST HAVE BEEN THROWN into consternation. How to designate as one's favorite a single story when one has scores of favorite stories? The editors were prepared for the problem; they had devised three criteria: What about a story that received insufficient attention, they said. Or a story that had influenced our own writing. Or a story that pointed us toward trying to write in the first place.

But every good piece of writing receives insufficient attention. Do people grab each other by the lapel in elevators or on the subway and shout, waving works by Jane Bowles, Isaac Babel, Junichiro Tanizaki, Mavis Gallant, Heinrich von Kleist? And as far as influence goes, no matter how devotional my reading, no matter how susceptible I'd like to be, I can't figure out for the life of me how to *get* influenced!

But as to the third criterion, yes, certainly there were things I read as a child that left me absolutely agog—and in a way that now seems to me premonitory. Stories that caused me to understand literature as a thing that is effected, a conjuring from the inexpressible that brings into our perceptible world the evidence of something essential; I remember the sensation vividly—of receiving a communiqué, of something *arriving*. I didn't actually dare to begin writing myself until I was in my thirties, and even in my childhood I don't believe I ever thought, Oh, I could do that, I want to do that. But I did think something along the lines of, That is a thing that can be done; the thing that was done here is impossible and yet it has been done. And the more I try to remember those moments, the more it seems to me that my selection for this volume was made by the time I was seven or eight years old.

There had always been on my parents' bookshelf a book that was, due to its physical characteristics, irresistible to me. It was hugely tall (ten inches, I discover) like a storybook, but an inch thick, with a mysterious fawn-colored binding. On the spine was a picture of a pretty dog, and on the front cover a strange atmospheric line drawing. Inside there were similar drawings. The pages were thick, porous, and rough-edged, and the print, floating in calm space, was large, emphatic, and delicious.

This was Alfred A. Knopf's 1930 edition of twelve Katherine Mansfield stories, selected by J. Middleton Murry with illustrations by Zhenya Gay. I don't remember a particular moment at which I began to read, rather than simply to look at it, and, in fact, at first I understood so little of it there could have been no great difference between reading and looking. Still, it exerted some powerful allure for me, because I returned to it again and again—at what sort of intervals I do not remember—until I was able actually to comprehend some of the stories, which revealed their shapes and natures to me with maddening and provocative slowness, pretty much at the pace my own nature and the shape of my life were being revealed to me.

What was it that kept me reading that book, aside from the pleasure of holding and seeing it? Something powerful enough that the candied splendor of Mansfield's prose, her crystalline imagery, and her potently eliptical style of observation ran through my life like an electric current—something powerful enough that my early enthusiasm easily withstood the spasms of unpopularity her writing underwent during my adolescence, as well as my ready disdain, throughout the same years, for just about everything.

Perhaps children are especially responsive to loveliness of prose and imagery; lovely prose and imagery are intrinsically pleasurable, so one can enjoy their values long before one can make one's way through their complex adult adjuncts. Perhaps all children are designed to love all Mansfield. But the two stories in that volume that particularly fascinated me when I was a child, "Prelude" and "Daughters of the Late Colonel," are—I've been startled to notice as I look them over now—*about* children. And their success depends largely on Mansfield's breathtaking plunge into the unformulated, plastic, and intense life of children—a confined species, whose explorations of the world proceed by means of the mental and the sensual, rather than by means of what we casually call information.

One might say that Mansfield's best stories convey themselves through accretions of exquisitely precise instants. But these two—tense, almost explosive as they are—are perhaps especially unfettered by exposition and narrative convention, by any superimposition of form or artificial drama. Here, Mansfield restricts us to the rich prison of domestic strangeness and to the haunted terrain children are forced to wander, which is animated by presences everywhere—in furniture, in plants, in puddings, in the sun and the moon.

The children in "Daughters of the Late Colonel" are both, one learns late in the story though without much surprise, around forty. But from the first word of the title these two are characterized as children, and the likelihood that the condition will be permanent is clear from the first sentence, which tells us that the one event that can occur to define the course of their lives has occurred already.

Adults are clearly not the best judges of what is truly childlike, but neither, apparently, are children, and what drew me to the story was not, in any case, the extent to which the characters and their perceptions are plausibly childlike, but the extent to which they are like life. Although almost every line of the story—up until the shattering final section—is hilarious, this fact was lost on me for years. Mansfield's fluent tracing of cognitive events, the innocence of the sisters, the unruly hallucinatory specificity of their experience, their speculative musings on their protean and intractable household, their flustered improvisatory responses to the pressures bearing down on them from all sides, their terror of their death-resistant father, their embattled dignity, the way they must keep their wits about them at all times in the company of dangerous and uncomprehending aliens (adults) like Nurse Andrews and Kate and Mr. Farolles, the swift elisions of internal and external occurrence, the menace of the father's mobile spirit, which at any moment might flare up out of the chair or the wardrobe or his grave or a corset box—well, it all seemed entirely real to me. And although these are the very things that make the story so funny, even now when I read it, I find the "girls'" view of the world—their fears—so strikingly clear and accurate as to be inarguable.

But the most fascinating thing for me was—and is, still—that there were words, lined up to say one thing and another, but one's response was not exactly to the words, and what they appeared to be saying, but to something enormous and living beyond that, which the words exactly entailed. And as I remember it, there was one day when I first "comprehended" the ending of the story. It's hard to say if this is in fact an actual single memory or the conflation of several experiences, because I always sat in the same chair when I read the story, in *my* family's living room, from which I dreamed of escape, and the story always rewarded me with the same odd and ephemeral sensations I courted from it. But in this memory there was a moment when the grief of the ending—the story's arc off the page and into everywhere—was clear to me. And I remember actually staring at the print to see how those feathery sentences could contain anything so cold or hard or painful, something that wasn't the same as them but could be made by them and by nothing else.

The Daughters of the Late Colonel

Katherine Mansfield

I

The week after was one of the busiest weeks of their lives. Even when they went to bed it was only their bodies that lay down and rested; their minds went on, thinking things out, talking things over, wondering, deciding, trying to remember where. . . .

Constantia lay like a statue, her hands by her sides, her feet just overlapping each other, the sheet up to her chin. She stared at the ceiling.

"Do you think father would mind if we gave his top-hat to the porter?"

"The porter?" snapped Josephine. "Why ever the porter? What a very extraordinary idea!"

"Because," said Constantia slowly, "he must often have to go to funerals. And I noticed at—at the cemetery that he only had a bowler." She paused. "I thought then how very much he'd appreciate a top-hat. We ought to give him a present, too. He was always very nice to father."

"But," cried Josephine, flouncing on her pillow and staring across the dark at Constantia, "father's head!" And suddenly, for one awful moment, she nearly giggled. Not, of course, that she felt in the least like giggling. It must have been habit. Years ago, when they had stayed awake at night talking, their beds had simply heaved. And now the porter's head, disappearing, popped out, like a candle, under father's hat. . . . The giggle mounted, mounted; she clenched her hands; she fought it down; she frowned fiercely at the dark and said "Remember" terribly sternly.

"We can decide to-morrow," she sighed.

Constantia had noticed nothing; she sighed.

"Do you think we ought to have our dressing-gowns dyed as well?"

"Black?" almost shrieked Josephine.

"Well, what else?" said Constantia. "I was thinking—it doesn't seem quite sincere, in a way, to wear black out of doors and when we're fully dressed, and then when we're at home—"

"But nobody sees us," said Josephine. She gave the bedclothes such a twitch that both her feet became uncovered, and she had to creep up the pillows to get them well under again.

"Kate does," said Constantia. "And the postman very well might."

Josephine thought of her dark-red slippers, which matched her dressing-gown, and of Constantia's favourite indefinite green ones which went with hers. Black! Two black dressing-gowns and two pairs of black woolly slippers, creeping off to the bathroom like black cats.

"I don't think it's absolutely necessary," said she.

Silence. Then Constantia said, "We shall have to post the papers with the notice in them tomorrow to catch the Ceylon mail. . . . How many letters have we had up till now?"

"Twenty-three."

Josephine had replied to them all, and twenty-three times when she came to "We miss our dear father so much" she had broken down and had to use her handkerchief, and on some of them even to soak up a very light-blue tear with an edge of blotting-paper. Strange! She couldn't have put it on—but twenty-three times. Even now, though, when she said over to herself sadly "We miss our dear father *so* much" she could have cried if she'd wanted to.

"Have you got enough stamps?" came from Constantia.

"Oh, how can I tell?" said Josephine crossly. "What's the good of asking me that now?"

"I was just wondering," said Constantia mildly.

Silence again. There came a little rustle, a scurry, a hop.

"A mouse," said Constantia.

"It can't be a mouse because there aren't any crumbs," said Josephine.

"But it doesn't know there aren't," said Constantia.

A spasm of pity squeezed her heart. Poor little thing! She wished she'd left a tiny piece of biscuit on the dressing-table. It was awful to think of it not finding anything. What would it do?

"I can't think how they manage to live at all," she said slowly.

"Who?" demanded Josephine.

And Constantia said more loudly than she meant to, "Mice."

Josephine was furious. "Oh, what nonsense, Con!" she said. "What have mice got to do with it? You're asleep."

"I don't think I am," said Constantia. She shut her eyes to make sure. She was.

Josephine arched her spine, pulled up her knees, folded her arms so that her fists came under her ears, and pressed her cheek hard against the pillow.

II

Another thing which complicated matters was they had Nurse Andrews staying on with them that week. It was their own fault; they had asked her. It was Josephine's idea. On the morning—well, on the last morning, when the doctor had gone, Josephine had said to Constantia, "Don't you think it would be rather nice if we asked Nurse Andrews to stay on for a week as our guest?"

"Very nice," said Constantia.

"I thought," went on Josephine quickly, "I should just say this afternoon, after I've paid her, 'My sister and I would be very pleased, after all you've done for us, Nurse Andrews, if you would stay on for a week as our guest.' I'd have to put that in about being our guest in case—"

"Oh, but she could hardly expect to be paid!" cried Constantia.

"One never knows," said Josephine sagely.

Nurse Andrews had, of course, jumped at the idea. But it was a bother. It meant they had to have regular sit-down meals at the proper times, whereas if they'd been alone they could just have asked Kate if she wouldn't have minded bringing them a tray wherever they were. And meal-times now that the strain was over were rather a trial.

Nurse Andrews was simply fearful about butter. Really they couldn't help feeling that about butter, at least, she took advantage of their kindness. And she had that maddening habit of asking for just an inch more bread to finish what she had on her plate, and then, at the last mouthful, absent-mindedly—of course it wasn't absent-mindedly—taking another helping. Josephine got very red when this happened, and she fastened her small, bead-like eyes on the tablecloth as if she saw a minute strange insect creeping through the web of it. But Constantia's long, pale face lengthened and set, and she gazed away—away—far over the desert, to where that line of camels unwound like a thread of wool. . . .

"When I was with Lady Tukes," said Nurse Andrews, "she had such a dainty little contrayvance for the buttah. It was a silvah Cupid balanced on the—on the bordah of a glass dish, holding a tayny fork. And when you wanted some buttah you simply pressed his foot and he bent down and speared you a piece. It was quite a gayme."

Josephine could hardly bear that. But "I think those things are very extravagant" was all she said.

"But whey?" asked Nurse Andrews, beaming through her eyeglasses. "No one, surely, would take more buttah than one wanted—would one?"

"Ring, Con," cried Josephine. She couldn't trust herself to reply.

And proud young Kate, the enchanted princess, came in to see what the old tabbies wanted now. She snatched away their plates of mock something or other and slapped down a white, terrified blancmange.

"Jam, please, Kate," said Josephine kindly.

Kate knelt and burst open the sideboard, lifted the lid of the jam-pot, saw it was empty, put it on the table, and stalked off.

"I'm afraid," said Nurse Andrews a moment later, "there isn't any."

"Oh, what a bother!" said Josephine. She bit her lip. "What had we better do?"

Constantia looked dubious. "We can't disturb Kate again," she said softly.

Nurse Andrews waited, smiling at them both. Her eyes wandered, spying at everything behind her eyeglasses. Constantia in despair went back to her camels. Josephine frowned heavily—concentrated. If it hadn't been for this idiotic woman she and Con would, of course, have eaten their blanc-mange without. Suddenly the idea came.

"I know," she said. "Marmalade. There's some marmalade in the side-board. Get it, Con."

"I hope," laughed Nurse Andrews, and her laugh was like a spoon tinkling against a medicine-glass—"I hope it's not very bittah marmalayde."

III

But, after all, it was not long now, and then she'd be gone for good. And there was no getting over the fact that she had been very kind to father. She had nursed him day and night at the end. Indeed, both Constantia and Josephine felt privately she had rather overdone the not leaving him at the very last. For when they had gone in to say good-bye Nurse Andrews had sat beside his bed the whole time, holding his wrist and pretending to look at her watch. It couldn't have been necessary. It was so tactless, too. Supposing father had wanted to say something—something private to them. Not that he had. Oh, far from it! He lay there, purple, a dark, angry purple in the face, and never even looked at them when they came in. Then, as they were standing there, wondering what to do, he had suddenly opened one eye. Oh, what a difference it would have made, what a difference to their memory of him, how much easier to tell people about it, if he had only opened both! But no—one eye only. It glared at them a moment and then . . . went out.

IV

It had made it very awkward for them when Mr. Farolles, of St. John's, called the same afternoon.

"The end was quite peaceful, I trust?" were the first words he said as he glided towards them through the dark drawing-room.

"Quite," said Josephine faintly. They both hung their heads. Both of them felt certain that eye wasn't at all a peaceful eye.

"Won't you sit down?" said Josephine.

"Thank you, Miss Pinner," said Mr. Farolles gratefully. He folded his coat-tails and began to lower himself into father's arm-chair, but just as he touched it he almost sprang up and slid into the next chair instead.

He coughed. Josephine clasped her hands; Constantia looked vague.

"I want you to feel, Miss Pinner," said Mr. Farolles, "and you, Miss Constantia, that I'm trying to be helpful. I want to be helpful to you both, if you will let me. These are the times," said Mr. Farolles, very simply and earnestly, "when God means us to be helpful to one another."

"Thank you very much, Mr. Farolles," said Josephine and Constantia.

"Not at all," said Mr. Farolles gently. He drew his kid gloves through his fingers and leaned forward. "And if either of you would like a little Communion, either or both of you, here *and* now, you have only to tell me. A little Communion is often very help—a great comfort," he added tenderly.

But the idea of a little Communion terrified them. What! In the drawing-room by themselves—with no—no altar or anything! The piano would be much too high, thought Constantia, and Mr. Farolles could not possibly lean over it with the chalice. And Kate would be sure to come bursting in and interrupt them, thought Josephine. And supposing the bell rang in the middle? It might be somebody important—about their mourning. Would they get up reverently and go out, or would they have to wait . . . in torture?

"Perhaps you will send round a note by your good Kate if you would care for it later," said Mr. Farolles.

"Oh yes, thank you very much!" they both said.

Mr. Farolles got up and took his black straw hat from the round table.

"And about the funeral," he said softly. "I may arrange that—as your dear father's old friend and yours, Miss Pinner—and Miss Constantia?"

Josephine and Constantia got up too.

"I should like it to be quite simple," said Josephine firmly, "and not too expensive. At the same time, I should like—"

"A good one that will last," thought dreamy Constantia, as if Josephine were buying a nightgown. But of course Josephine didn't say that. "One suitable to our father's position." She was very nervous.

"I'll run round to our good friend Mr. Knight," said Mr. Farolles soothingly. "I will ask him to come and see you. I am sure you will find him very helpful indeed."

V

Well, at any rate, all that part of it was over, though neither of them could possibly believe that father was never coming back. Josephine had had a moment of absolute terror at the cemetery, while the coffin was lowered, to think that she and Constantia had done this thing without asking his permission. What would father say when he found out? For he was bound to find out sooner or later. He always did. "Buried. You two girls had me *buried!*" She heard his stick thumping. Oh, what would they say? What possible excuse could they make? It sounded such an appallingly heartless thing to do. Such a wicked advantage to take of a person because he happened to be helpless at the moment. The other people seemed to treat it all as a matter of course. They were strangers; they couldn't be expected to understand that father was the very last person for such a thing to happen to. No, the entire blame for it all would fall on her and Constantia. And the expense, she thought, stepping into the tight-buttoned cab. When she had to show him the bills. What would he say then?

She heard him absolutely roaring, "And do you expect me to pay for this gimcrack excursion of yours?"

"Oh," groaned poor Josephine aloud, "we shouldn't have done it, Con!"

And Constantia, pale as a lemon in all that blackness, said in a frightened whisper, "Done what, Jug?"

"Let them bu-bury father like that," said Josephine, breaking down and crying into her new, queer-smelling mourning handkerchief.

"But what else could we have done?" asked Constantia wonderingly. "We couldn't have kept him, Jug—we couldn't have kept him unburied. At any rate, not in a flat that size."

Josephine blew her nose; the cab was dreadfully stuffy.

"I don't know," she said forlornly. "It is all so dreadful. I feel we ought to have tried to, just for a time at least. To make perfectly sure. One thing's certain"—and her tears sprang out again—"father will never forgive us for this—never!"

VI

Father would never forgive them. That was what they felt more than ever when, two mornings later, they went into his room to go through his things. They had discussed it quite calmly. It was even down on Josephine's list of things to be done. *Go through father's things and settle about them.* But that was a very different matter from saying after breakfast:

"Well, are you ready, Con?"

"Yes, Jug—when you are."

"Then I think we'd better get it over."

It was dark in the hall. It had been a rule for years never to disturb father in the morning, whatever happened. And now they were going to open the door without knocking even. . . . Constantia's eyes were enormous at the idea; Josephine felt weak in the knees.

"You—you go first," she gasped, pushing Constantia.

But Constantia said, as she always had said on those occasions, "No, Jug, that's not fair. You're eldest."

Josephine was just going to say—what at other times she wouldn't have owned to for the world—what she kept for her very last weapon, "But you're tallest," when they noticed that the kitchen door was open, and there stood Kate. . . .

"Very stiff," said Josephine, grasping the door handle and doing her best to turn it. As if anything ever deceived Kate!

It couldn't be helped. That girl was . . . Then the door was shut behind them, but—but they weren't in father's room at all. They might have suddenly walked through the wall by mistake into a different flat altogether. Was the door just behind them? They were too frightened to look. Josephine knew that if it was it was holding itself tight shut; Constantia felt that, like the doors in dreams, it hadn't any handle at all. It was the coldness which made it so awful. Or the whiteness—which? Everything was covered. The blinds were down, a cloth hung over the mirror, a sheet hid the bed; a huge fan of white paper filled the fireplace. Constantia timidly put out her hand; she almost expected a snowflake to fall. Josephine felt a queer tingling in her nose, as if her nose was freezing. Then a cab klop-klopped over the cobbles below, and the quiet seemed to shake into little pieces.

"I had better pull up a blind," said Josephine bravely.

"Yes, it might be a good idea," whispered Constantia.

They only gave the blind a touch, but it flew up and the cord flew after, rolling round the blind-stick, and the little tassel tapped as if trying to get free. That was too much for Constantia.

"Don't you think—don't you think we might put it off for another day?" she whispered.

"Why?" snapped Josephine, feeling, as usual, much better now that she knew for certain that Constantia was terrified. "It's got to be done. But I do wish you wouldn't whisper, Con."

"I didn't know I was whispering," whispered Constantia.

"And why do you keep on staring at the bed?" said Josephine, raising her voice almost defiantly. "There's nothing *on* the bed."

"Oh, Jug, don't say so!" said poor Connie. "At any rate, not so loudly."

Josephine felt herself that she had gone too far. She took a wide swerve over to the chest of drawers, put out her hand, but quickly drew it back again.

"Connie!" she gasped, and she wheeled round and leaned with her back against the chest of drawers.

"Oh, Jug—what?"

Josephine could only glare. She had the most extraordinary feeling that she had just escaped something simply awful. But how could she explain to Constantia that father was in the chest of drawers? He was in the top drawer with his handkerchiefs and neckties, or in the next with his shirts and pyjamas, or in the lowest of all with his suits. He was watching there, hidden away—just behind the door-handle—ready to spring.

She pulled a funny old-fashioned face at Constantia, just as she used to in the old days when she was going to cry.

"I can't open," she nearly wailed.

"No, don't, Jug," whispered Constantia earnestly. "It's much better not to. Don't let's open anything. At any rate, not for a long time."

"But—but it seems so weak," said Josephine, breaking down.

"But why not be weak for once, Jug?" argued Constantia, whispering quite fiercely. "If it is weak." And her pale stare flew from the locked writing-table—so safe—to the huge glittering wardrobe, and she began to breathe in a queer, panting way. "Why shouldn't we be weak for once in our lives, Jug? It's quite excusable. Let's be weak—be weak, Jug. It's much nicer to be weak than to be strong."

And then she did one of those amazingly bold things that she'd done about twice before in their lives; she marched over to the wardrobe, turned the key, and took it out of the lock. Took it out of the lock and held it up to Josephine, showing Josephine by her extraordinary smile that she knew what she'd done, she'd risked deliberately father being in there among his overcoats.

If the huge wardrobe had lurched forward, had crashed down on Constantia, Josephine wouldn't have been surprised. On the contrary, she would have thought it the only suitable thing to happen. But nothing happened.

Only the room seemed quieter than ever, and bigger flakes of cold air fell on Josephine's shoulders and knees. She began to shiver.

"Come, Jug," said Constantia, still with that awful callous smile, and Josephine followed just as she had that last time, when Constantia had pushed Benny into the round pond.

VII

But the strain told on them when they were back in the dining-room. They sat down, very shaky, and looked at each other.

"I don't feel I can settle to anything," said Josephine, "until I've had something. Do you think we could ask Kate for two cups of hot water?"

"I really don't see why we shouldn't," said Constantia carefully. She was quite normal again. "I won't ring. I'll go to the kitchen door and ask her."

"Yes, do," said Josephine, sinking down into a chair. "Tell her, just two cups, Con, nothing else—on a tray."

"She needn't even put the jug on, need she?" said Constantia, as though Kate might very well complain if the jug had been there.

"Oh no, certainly not! The jug's not at all necessary. She can pour it direct out of the kettle," cried Josephine, feeling that would be a labour-saving indeed.

Their cold lips quivered at the greenish brims. Josephine curved her small red hands round the cup; Constantia sat up and blew on the wavy stream, making it flutter from one side to the other.

"Speaking of Benny," said Josephine.

And though Benny hadn't been mentioned Constantia immediately looked as though he had.

"He'll expect us to send him something of father's, of course. But it's so difficult to know what to send to Ceylon."

"You mean things get unstuck so on the voyage," murmured Constantia.

"No, lost," said Josephine sharply. "You know there's no post. Only runners."

Both paused to watch a black man in white linen drawers running through the pale fields for dear life, with a large brown-paper parcel in his hands. Josephine's black man was tiny; he scurried along glistening like an ant. But there was something blind and tireless about Constantia's tall, thin fellow, which made him, she decided, a very unpleasant person indeed. . . . On the veranda, dressed all in white and wearing a cork helmet, stood Benny. His right hand shook up and down, as father's did when he was impatient. And behind him, not in the least interested, sat Hilda, the unknown sister-in-law. She swung in a cane rocker and flicked over the leaves of the *Tatler.*

"I think his watch would be the most suitable present," said Josephine.

Constantia looked up; she seemed surprised.

"Oh, would you trust a gold watch to a native?"

"But of course I'd disguise it," said Josephine. "No one would know it was a watch." She liked the idea of having to make a parcel such a curious shape that no one could possibly guess what it was. She even thought for a moment of hiding the watch in a narrow cardboard corset-box that she'd kept by her for a long time, waiting for it to come in for something. It was such beautiful firm cardboard. But, no, it wouldn't be appropriate for this occasion. It had lettering on it: *Medium Women's 28. Extra Firm Busks.* It would be almost too much of a surprise for Benny to open that and find father's watch inside.

"And of course it isn't as though it would be going—ticking, I mean," said Constantia, who was still thinking of the native love of jewellery. "At least," she added, "it would be very strange if after all that time it was."

VIII

Josephine made no reply. She had flown off on one of her tangents. She had suddenly thought of Cyril. Wasn't it more usual for the only grandson to have the watch? And then dear Cyril was so appreciative, and a gold watch meant so much to a young man. Benny, in all probability, had quite got out of the habit of watches; men so seldom wore waistcoats in those hot climates. Whereas Cyril in London wore them from year's end to year's end. And it would be so nice for her and Constantia, when he came to tea, to know it was there. "I see you've got on grandfather's watch, Cyril." It would be somehow so satisfactory.

Dear boy! What a blow his sweet, sympathetic little note had been! Of course they quite understood; but it was most unfortunate.

"It would have been such a point, having him," said Josephine.

"And he would have enjoyed it so," said Constantia, not thinking what she was saying.

However, as soon as he got back he was coming to tea with his aunties. Cyril to tea was one of their rare treats.

"Now, Cyril, you mustn't be frightened of our cakes. Your Auntie Con and I bought them at Buszard's this morning. We know what a man's appetite is. So don't be ashamed of making a good tea."

Josephine cut recklessly into the rich dark cake that stood for her winter gloves or the soling and heeling of Constantia's only respectable shoes. But Cyril was most unmanlike in appetite.

"I say, Aunt Josephine, I simply can't. I've only just had lunch, you know."

"Oh, Cyril, that can't be true! It's after four," cried Josephine. Constantia sat with her knife poised over the chocolate-roll.

"It is, all the same," said Cyril. "I had to meet a man at Victoria, and he kept me hanging about till . . . there was only time to get lunch and to come on here. And he gave me—phew"—Cyril put his hand to his forehead—"a terrific blow-out," he said.

It was disappointing—to-day of all days. But still he couldn't be expected to know.

"But you'll have a meringue, won't you, Cyril?" said Aunt Josephine. "These meringues were bought specially for you. Your dear father was so fond of them. We were sure you are, too."

"I *am,* Aunt Josephine," cried Cyril ardently. "Do you mind if I take half to begin with?"

"Not at all, dear boy; but we mustn't let you off with that."

"Is your dear father still so fond of meringues?" asked Auntie Con gently. She winced faintly as she broke through the shell of hers.

"Well, I don't quite know, Auntie Con," said Cyril breezily.

At that they both looked up.

"Don't know?" almost snapped Josephine. "Don't know a thing like that about your own father, Cyril?"

"Surely," said Aunty Con softly.

Cyril tried to laugh it off. "Oh, well," he said, "it's such a long time since—" He faltered. He stopped. Their faces were too much for him.

"Even *so,*" said Josephine.

And Auntie Con looked.

Cyril put down his teacup. "Wait a bit," he cried. "Wait a bit, Aunt Josephine. What am I thinking of?"

He looked up. They were beginning to brighten. Cyril slapped his knee.

"Of course," he said, "it was meringues. How could I have forgotten? Yes, Aunt Josephine, you're perfectly right. Father's most frightfully keen on meringues."

They didn't only beam. Aunt Josephine went scarlet with pleasure; Auntie Con gave a deep, deep sigh.

"And now, Cyril, you must come and see father," said Josephine. "He knows you were coming today."

"Right," said Cyril, very firmly and heartily. He got up from his chair; suddenly he glanced at the clock.

"I say, Auntie Con, isn't your clock a bit slow? I've got to meet a man at—at Paddington just after five. I'm afraid I shan't be able to stay very long with grandfather."

"Oh, he won't expect you to stay *very* long!" said Aunt Josephine.

Constantia was still gazing at the clock. She couldn't make up her mind if it was fast or slow. It was one or the other, she felt almost certain of that. At any rate, it had been.

Cyril still lingered. "Aren't you coming along, Auntie Con?"

"Of course," said Josephine, "we shall all go. Come on, Con."

IX

They knocked at the door, and Cyril followed his aunts into grandfather's hot, sweetish room.

"Come on," said Grandfather Pinner. "Don't hang about. What is it? What've you been up to?"

He was sitting in front of a roaring fire, clasping his stick. He had a thick rug over his knees. On his lap there lay a beautiful pale yellow silk handkerchief.

"It's Cyril, father," said Josephine shyly. And she took Cyril's hand and led him forward.

"Good afternoon, grandfather," said Cyril, trying to take his hand out of Aunt Josephine's. Grandfather Pinner shot his eyes at Cyril in the way he was famous for. Where was Auntie Con? She stood on the other side of Aunt Josephine; her long arms hung down in front of her; her hands were clasped. She never took her eyes off grandfather.

"Well," said Grandfather Pinner, beginning to thump, "what have you got to tell me?"

What had he, what had he got to tell him? Cyril felt himself smiling like a perfect imbecile. The room was stifling, too.

But Aunt Josephine came to his rescue. She cried brightly, "Cyril says his father is still very fond of meringues, father dear."

"Eh?" said Grandfather Pinner, curving his hand like a purple meringue-shell over one ear.

Josephine repeated, "Cyril says his father is still very fond of meringues."

"Can't hear," said old Colonel Pinner. And he waved Josephine away with his stick, then pointed with his stick to Cyril. "Tell me what she's trying to say," he said.

(My God!) "Must I?" said Cyril, blushing and staring at Aunt Josephine.

"Do, dear," she smiled. "It will please him so much."

"Come on, out with it!" cried Colonel Pinner testily, beginning to thump again.

And Cyril leaned forward and yelled, "Father's still very fond of meringues."

At that Grandfather Pinner jumped as though he had been shot.

"Don't shout!" he cried. "What's the matter with the boy? *Meringues!* What about 'em?"

"Oh, Aunt Josephine, must we go on?" groaned Cyril desperately.

"It's quite all right, dear boy," said Aunt Josephine, as though he and she were at the dentist's together. "He'll understand in a minute." And she whispered to Cyril, "He's getting a bit deaf, you know." Then she leaned forward and really bawled at Grandfather Pinner, "Cyril only wanted to tell you, father dear, that *his* father is still very fond of meringues."

Colonel Pinner heard that time, heard and brooded, looking Cyril up and down.

"What an esstrordinary thing!" said old Grandfather Pinner. "What an esstrordinary thing to come all this way here to tell me!"

And Cyril felt it *was*.

"Yes, I shall send Cyril the watch," said Josephine.

"That would be very nice," said Constantia. "I seem to remember last time he came there was some little trouble about the time."

X

They were interrupted by Kate bursting through the door in her usual fashion, as though she had discovered some secret panel in the wall.

"Fried or boiled?" asked the bold voice.

Fried or boiled? Josephine and Constantia were quite bewildered for the moment. They could hardly take it in.

"Fried or boiled what, Kate?" asked Josephine, trying to begin to concentrate.

Kate gave a loud sniff. "Fish."

"Well, why didn't you say so immediately?" Josephine reproached her gently. "How could you expect us to understand, Kate? There are a great many things in this world, you know, which are fried or boiled." And after such a display of courage she said quite brightly to Constantia, "Which do you prefer, Con?"

"I think it might be nice to have it fried," said Constantia. "On the other hand, of course boiled fish is very nice. I think I prefer both equally well. . . . Unless you . . . In that case—"

"I shall fry it," said Kate, and she bounced back, leaving their door open and slamming the door of her kitchen.

Josephine gazed at Constantia; she raised her pale eyebrows until they rippled away into her pale hair. She got up. She said in a very lofty, imposing way, "Do you mind following me into the drawing-room, Constantia? I've something of great importance to discuss with you."

For it was always to the drawing-room they retired when they wanted to talk over Kate.

Josephine closed the door meaningly. "Sit down, Constantia," she said, still very grand. She might have been receiving Constantia for the first time. And Con looked round vaguely for a chair, as though she felt indeed quite a stranger.

"Now the question is," said Josephine, bending forward, "whether we shall keep her or not."

"That is the question," agreed Constantia.

"And this time," said Josephine firmly, "we must come to a definite decision."

Constantia looked for a moment as though she might begin going over all the other times, but she pulled herself together and said, "Yes, Jug."

"You see, Con," explained Josephine, "everything is so changed now." Constantia looked up quickly. "I mean," went on Josephine, "we're not dependent on Kate as we were." And she blushed faintly. "There's not father to cook for."

"That is perfectly true," agreed Constantia. "Father certainly doesn't want any cooking now, whatever else—"

Josephine broke in sharply, "You're not sleepy, are you, Con?"

"Sleepy, Jug?" Constantia was wide-eyed.

"Well, concentrate more," said Josephine sharply, and she returned to the subject. "What it comes to is, if we did"—and this she barely breathed, glancing at the door—"give Kate notice"—she raised her voice again—"we could manage our own food."

"Why not?" cried Constantia. She couldn't help smiling. The idea was so exciting. She clasped her hands. "What should we live on, Jug?"

"Oh, eggs in various forms!" said Jug, lofty again. "And, besides, there are all the cooked foods."

"But I've always heard," said Constantia, "they are considered so very expensive."

"Not if one buys them in moderation," said Josephine. But she tore herself away from this fascinating bypath and dragged Constantia after her.

"What we've got to decide now, however, is whether we really do trust Kate or not."

Constantia leaned back. Her flat little laugh flew from her lips.

"Isn't it curious, Jug," said she, "that just on this one subject I've never been able to quite make up my mind?"

XI

She never had. The whole difficulty was to prove anything. How did one prove things, how could one? Suppose Kate had stood in front of her and deliberately made a face. Mightn't she very well have been in pain? Wasn't it impossible, at any rate, to ask Kate if she was making a face at her? If Kate answered "No"—and of course she would say "No"—what a position! How undignified! Then again Constantia suspected, she was almost certain that Kate went to her chest of drawers when she and Josephine were out, not to take things but to spy. Many times she had come back to find her amethyst cross in the most unlikely places, under her lace ties or on top of her evening Bertha. More than once she had laid a trap for Kate. She had arranged things in a special order and then called Josephine to witness.

"You see, Jug?"

"Quite, Con."

"Now we shall be able to tell."

But, oh dear, when she did go to look, she was as far off from a proof as ever! If anything was displaced, it might so very well have happened as she closed the drawer; a jolt might have done it so easily.

"You come, Jug, and decide. I really can't. It's too difficult."

But after a pause and a long glare Josephine would sigh. "Now you've put the doubt into my mind, Con, I'm sure I can't tell myself."

"Well, we can't postpone it again," said Josephine. "If we postpone it this time—"

XII

But at that moment in the street below a barrel-organ struck up. Josephine and Constantia sprang to their feet together.

"Run, Con," said Josephine. "Run quickly. There's sixpence on the—"

Then they remembered. It didn't matter. They would never have to stop the organ-grinder again. Never again would she and Constantia be told to make that monkey take his noise somewhere else. Never would sound that loud, strange bellow when father thought they were not hurrying enough. The organ-grinder might play there all day and the stick would not thump.

It never will thump again,
It never will thump again,

played the barrel-organ.

What was Constantia thinking? She had such a strange smile; she looked different. She couldn't be going to cry.

"Jug, Jug," said Constantia softly, pressing her hands together. "Do you know what day it is? It's Saturday. It's a week to-day, a whole week."

A week since father died,
A week since father died,

cried the barrel-organ. And Josephine, too, forgot to be practical and sensible; she smiled faintly, strangely. On the Indian carpet there fell a square of sunlight, pale red; it came and went and came—and stayed, deepened—until it shone almost golden.

"The sun's out," said Josephine, as though it really mattered.

A perfect fountain of bubbling notes shook from the barrel-organ, round, bright notes, carelessly scattered.

Constantia lifted her big, cold hands as if to catch them, and then her hands fell again. She walked over to the mantelpiece to her favourite Buddha. And the stone and gilt image, whose smile always gave her such a queer feeling, almost a pain and yet a pleasant pain, seemed to-day to be more than smiling. He knew something; he had a secret. "I know something that you don't know," said her Buddha. Oh, what was it, what could it be? And yet she had always felt there was . . . something.

The sunlight pressed through the windows, thieved its way in, flashed its light over the furniture and the photographs. Josephine watched it. When it came to mother's photograph, the enlargement over the piano, it lingered as though puzzled to find so little remained of mother, except the earrings shaped like tiny pagodas and a black feather boa. Why did the photographs of dead people always fade so? wondered Josephine. As soon as a person was dead their photograph died too. But, of course, this one of mother was very old. It was thirty-five years old. Josephine remembered standing on a chair and pointing out that feather boa to Constantia and telling her that it was a snake that had killed their mother in Ceylon. . . . Would everything have been different if mother hadn't died? She didn't see why. Aunt Florence had lived with them until they had left school, and they had moved three times and had their yearly holiday and . . . and there'd been changes of servants, of course.

Some little sparrows, young sparrows they sounded, chirped on the window-ledge. *Yeep—eyeep—yeep.* But Josephine felt they were not sparrows, not on the window-ledge. It was inside her, that queer little crying noise. *Yeep—eyeep—yeep.* Ah, what was it crying, so weak and forlorn?

If mother had lived, might they have married? But there had been nobody for them to marry. There had been father's Anglo-Indian friends before he quarrelled with them. But after that she and Constantia never met a single man except clergymen. How did one meet men? Or even if they'd met them, how could they have got to know men well enough to be more than strangers? One read of people having adventures, being followed, and so on. But nobody had ever followed Constantia and her. Oh yes, there had been one year at Eastbourne a mysterious man at their boarding-house who had put a note on the jug of hot water outside their bedroom door! But by the time Connie had found it the steam had made the writing too faint to read; they couldn't even make out to which of them it was addressed. And he had left next day. And that was all. The rest had been looking after father, and at the same time keeping out of father's way. But now? But now? The thieving sun touched Josephine gently. She lifted her face. She was drawn over to the window by gentle beams. . . .

Until the barrel-organ stopped playing Constantia stayed before the Buddha, wondering, but not as usual, not vaguely. This time her wonder was like longing. She remembered the times she had come in here, crept out of bed in her nightgown when the moon was full, and lain on the floor with her arms outstretched, as though she was crucified. Why? The big, pale moon had made her do it. The horrible dancing figures on the carved screen had leered at her and she hadn't minded. She remembered too how, whenever they were at the seaside, she had gone off by herself and got as close to the sea as she could, and sung something, something she had made up, while she gazed all over the restless water. There had been this other life, running out, bringing things home in bags, getting things on approval, discussing them with Jug, and taking them back to get more things on approval, and arranging father's trays and trying not to annoy father. But it all seemed to have happened in a kind of tunnel. It wasn't real. It was only when she came out of the tunnel into the moonlight or by the sea or into a thunderstorm that she really felt herself. What did it mean? What was it she was always wanting? What did it all lead to? Now? Now?

She turned away from the Buddha with one of her vague gestures. She went over to where Josephine was standing. She wanted to say something to Josephine, something frightfully important, about—about the future and what . . .

"Don't you think perhaps—" she began.

But Josephine interrupted her. "I was wondering if now—" she murmured. They stopped; they waited for each other.

"Go on, Con," said Josephine.

"No, no, Jug; after you," said Constantia.

"No, say what you were going to say. You began," said Josephine.

"I . . . I'd rather hear what your were going to say first," said Constantia.

"Don't be absurd, Con."

"Really, Jug."

"Connie!"

"Oh, *Jug!*"

A pause. Then Constantia said faintly, "I can't say what I was going to say, Jug, because I've forgotten what it was . . . that I was going to say."

Josephine was silent for a moment. She stared at a big cloud where the sun had been. Then she replied shortly, "I've forgotten too."

Labor Day Dinner

by Alice Munro

Introduced by David Leavitt

FEW STORIES MEAN AS MUCH TO ME AS ALICE MUNRO'S "LABOR DAY Dinner." I remember feeling astonished the first time I read it and, on subsequent readings, my astonishment giving way to a kind of respectful awe. Munro's sensitivity to the nuances of family life humbles me, as does the elegant simplicity of her prose; the seeming effortlessness with which she alternates points of view; the delicacy of her humor; above all, the craftsmanly skill with which she resolves a panoply of elements into a denouement that makes the reader (like the heroine) quite literally catch his breath. "Lightness of touch"; this is the phrase that always comes to mind when I try to characterize "Labor Day Dinner"; and as any writer knows, it takes a lot of hammering to make a story seem light. Another phrase that comes to mind is from E. M. Forster's *Howards End*. Indeed, Forster might have been thinking of Munro when he wrote of Mrs. Wilcox: "One knew that she worshipped the past, and that the instinctive wisdom the past can alone bestow had descended upon her: that wisdom to which we give the clumsy name of aristocracy." She is indeed an aristocrat among writers.

But I think that finally the reason "Labor Day Dinner" will always be among my favorite stories is that reading it made me want to write. It suggested to me vast possibilities, novelistic possibilities, of which I had not previously imagined the short story capable, and at which I wanted to try my hand. Well, at present I am still doing my apprenticeship; when I read her stories, and then my own, I wince at the clattering sound my sets make as they're moved around backstage, I shake my head at the infelicity of the costume changes. In Munro's stories, by contrast, there is only silence on the other side of silence.

She is Forster's heir; and no story proves that ancestry more perfectly than "Labor Day Dinner."

Labor Day Dinner

Alice Munro

Just before six o'clock in the evening, George and Roberta and Angela and Eva get out of George's pickup truck—he traded his car for a pickup when he moved to the country—and walk across Valerie's front yard, under the shade of two aloof and splendid elm trees that have been expensively preserved. Valerie says those trees cost her a trip to Europe. The grass underneath them has been kept green all summer, and is bordered by fiery dahlias. The house is of pale-red brick, and around the doors and windows there is a decorative outline of lighter-colored bricks, originally white. This style is often found in Grey County; perhaps it was a specialty of one of the early builders.

George is carrying the folding lawn chairs Valerie asked them to bring. Roberta is carrying a dessert, a raspberry bombe made from raspberries picked on their own farm—George's farm—earlier in the summer. She has packed it in ice cubes and wrapped it in dish towels, but she is eager to get it into the freezer. Angela and Eva carry bottles of wine. Angela and Eva are Roberta's daughters. It has been arranged between Roberta and her husband that they spend the summers with her and George and the school year in Halifax with him. Roberta's husband is in the Navy. Angela is seventeen, Eva is twelve.

These four people are costumed in a way that would suggest they were going to different dinner parties. George, who is a stocky, dark, barrel-chested man, with a daunting, professional look of self-assurance and impatience (he used to be a teacher), wears a clean T-shirt and nondescript pants. Roberta is wearing faded tan cotton pants and a loose raw-silk top of mud-brick color—a color that suits her dark hair and pale skin well enough when she is at her best, but she is not at her best today. When she made herself up in the bathroom, she thought her skin looked like a piece of waxed paper that had been crumpled into a tight ball and then smoothed out. She was momentarily pleased with her thinness and had planned to wear a slinky silver halter top she owns—a glamorous joke—but at the last minute she changed her mind. She is wearing dark glasses, and the reason is that she has taken to weeping in spurts, never at the really bad times but in between; the spurts are as unbidden as sneezes.

As for Angela and Eva, they are dramatically arrayed in outfits contrived from a box of old curtains found in the upstairs of George's house. Angela wears emerald-green damask with long, sun-faded stripes, draped so as to leave one golden shoulder bare. She has cut vine leaves out of the same damask, pasted them on cardboard, and arranged them in her hair. Angela is tall and fair-haired, and embarrassed by her recently acquired beauty. She will go to great trouble to flaunt it, as she does now, and then will redden and frown and look stubbornly affronted when somebody tells her she looks like a goddess. Eva is wearing several fragile, yellowed lace curtains draped and bunched up, and held together with pins, ribbons, and nosegays of wild phlox already drooping and scattering. One of the curtains is pinned across her forehead and flows behind her, like a nineteen-twenties bridal veil. She has put her shorts on underneath, in case anybody should glimpse underpants through the veiling. Eva is puritanical, outrageous—an acrobat, a parodist, an optimist, a disturber. Her face, under the pinned veil, is lewdly painted with green eyeshadow and dark lipstick and rouge and mascara. The violent colors emphasize her childish look of recklessness and valor.

Angela and Eva have ridden here in the back of the truck, stretched out on the lawn chairs. It is only three miles from George's place to Valerie's, but Roberta did not think riding like that was safe—she wanted them to get down and sit on the truck bed. To her surprise, George spoke up on their behalf, saying it would be ignominious for them to have to huddle down on the floor in their finery. He said he would drive slowly and avoid bumps; so he did. Roberta was a little nervous, but she was relieved to see him sympathetic and indulgent about the very things—self-dramatization, self-display—that she had expected would annoy him. She herself has given up wearing long skirts and caftans because of what he has said about disliking the sight of women trailing around in such garments, which announce to him, he says, not only a woman's intention of doing no serious work but her persistent wish to be admired and courted. This is a wish George has no patience with and has spent some energy, throughout his adult life, in thwarting.

Roberta thought that after speaking in such a friendly way to the girls, and helping them into the truck, he might speak to her when he got into the cab, might even take her hand, brushing away her undisclosed crimes, but it did not happen. Shut up together, driving over the hot gravel roads at an almost funereal pace, they are pinned down by a murderous silence. On the edge of it, Roberta feels herself curling up like a jaundiced leaf. She knows this to be a hysterical image. Also hysterical is the notion of screaming and opening the door and throwing herself on the gravel. She ought to make an effort not to be hysterical, not to exaggerate. But surely it is hatred—what else can it be?—that George is steadily manufacturing and wordlessly pouring out at her, and surely it is a deadly gas. She tries to break the silence herself, making little clucks of worry as she tightens the towels over the bombe and then sighing—a noisy imitation sigh meant to sound tired, pleased, and comfortable. They are driving between high stands of corn, and she thinks how ugly the corn looks—a monotonous, coarse-leaved crop, a foolish army. How long has this been going on? Since yesterday morning: she felt it in him before they got out of bed. They went out and got drunk last night to try to better things, but the relief didn't last.

Before they left for Valerie's Roberta was in the bedroom, fastening her halter top, and George came in and said, "Is that what you're wearing?"

"I thought I would, yes. Doesn't it look all right?"

"Your armpits are flabby."

"Are they? I'll put on something with sleeves."

In the truck, now that she knows he isn't going to make up, she lets herself hear him say that. A harsh satisfaction in his voice. The satisfaction of airing disgust. He is disgusted by her aging body. That could have been foreseen. She starts humming something, feeling the lightness, the freedom, the great tactical advantage of being the one to whom the wrong has been done, the bleak challenge offered, the unforgivable thing said.

But suppose he doesn't think it's unforgivable, suppose in his eyes she's the one who's unforgivable? She's always the one; disasters overtake her daily. It used to be that as soon as she noticed some deterioration she would seek strenuously to remedy it. Now the remedies bring more problems. She applies cream frantically to her wrinkles, and her face breaks out in spots, like a teen-ager's. Dieting until her waist was thin enough to please produced a haggard look about her cheeks and throat. Flabby armpits—how can you exercise the armpits? What is to be done? Now the payment is due, and what for? For vanity. Hardly even for that. Just for having those pleasing surfaces once, and letting them speak for you; just for allowing an arrangement of hair and shoulders and breasts to have its effect. You don't stop in time, don't know what to do instead; you lay yourself open to humiliation. So thinks Roberta, with self-pity—what she knows to be self-pity—rising and sloshing around in her like bitter bile.

She must get away, live alone, wear sleeves.

Valerie calls to them from a darkened window under the vines, "Go on in, go in. I'm just putting on my panty hose."

"Don't put on your panty hose!" cry George and Roberta together. You would think from the sound of their voices that all the way over here they had been engaged in tender and lively conversation.

"Don't put on your *panty* hose," wail Angela and Eva.

"Oh, all right, if there's all that much prejudice against panty hose," says Valerie behind her window. "I won't even put on a dress. I'll come as I am."

"Not that!" cries George, and staggers, holding the lawn chairs up in front of his face.

But Valerie, appearing in the doorway, is dressed beautifully, in a loose gown of green and gold and blue. She doesn't have to worry about George's opinion of long dresses. She is absolved of blame anyway, because you could never say that Valerie is looking to be courted or admired. She is a tall, flat-chested woman, whose long, plain face seems to be crackling with welcome, eager understanding, with humor and intelligence and appreciation. Her hair is thick, gray-black, and curly. This summer she recklessly cut it off, so that all that is left is a curly crewcut, revealing her long, corded neck and the creases at the edge of her cheeks, and her large, flat ears.

"I think it makes me look like a goat," she has said. "I like goats. I love their eyes. Wouldn't it be wonderful to have those horizontal pupils. Bizarre!"

Her children tell her she is bizarre enough already.

Here come Valerie's children now, as George and Roberta and Angela and Eva crowd into the hall, Roberta saying that she is dripping ice and must get this pretentious concoction into the freezer. First Ruth, who is twenty-five and nearly six feet tall and looks a lot like her mother. She has given up wanting to be an actress and is learning to teach disturbed children. Her arms are full of goldenrod and Queen Anne's lace and dahlias—weeds and flowers all mixed up together—and she throws them on the hall floor with a theatrical gesture and embraces the bombe.

"Dessert," she says lovingly. "Oh, bliss! Angela, you look incredibly lovely! Eva, too. I know who Eva is. She's the Bride of Lammermoor!"

Angela will allow, even delight in, such open praise from Ruth, because Ruth is the person she admires most in the world—possibly the only person she admires.

"The Bride of who?" Eva is asking happily. "The Bride of *who?*"

David, Valerie's twenty-one-year-old son, a history student, is standing in the living-room doorway, smiling tolerantly and affectionately at the excitement. David is tall and lean, dark-haired and dark-skinned, like his mother and sister, but he is deliberate, low-voiced, never rash. In this household of many delicate checks and balances it is noticeable that the lively, outspoken women defer to David in some ceremonial way, seeming to ask for the gesture of his protection, though protection itself is something they are not likely to need.

When the greetings die down David says, "This is Kimberly," and introduces them each in turn to the young woman standing under his arm. She is very clean and trim, in a white skirt and a short-sleeved pink shirt. She wears glasses and no makeup; her hair is short and straight and tidy, and a pleasant light-brown color. She shakes hands with each of them and looks each of them in the eye, through her glasses, and though her manner is entirely polite, even subdued, there is a slight feeling of an official person greeting the members of an unruly, outlandish delegation.

Valerie has known both George and Roberta for years. She knew them long before they knew each other. She and George were on the staff of the same Toronto high school. George was head of the art department; Valerie was school counsellor. She knew George's wife, a jittery, well-dressed women, who was killed in a plane crash in Florida. George and his wife were separated by that time.

And, of course, Valerie knew Roberta because Roberta's husband, Andrew, is her cousin. They never cared much for each other—Valerie and

Roberta's husband—and each of them has described the other to Roberta as a stick. Andrew used to say that Valerie was a queer-looking stick and utterly sexless, and when Roberta told Valerie that she was leaving him Valerie said, "Oh, good. He is such a stick." Roberta was pleased to find such sympathy and pleased that she wouldn't have to dredge up acceptable reasons; apparently Valerie thought his being a stick was reason enough. At the same time Roberta had a wish to defend her husband and to inquire how on earth Valerie could presume to know whether he was a stick or wasn't. She can't get over wishing to defend him; she feels he had such bad luck marrying her.

When Roberta moved out and left Halifax, she came and stayed with Valerie in Toronto. There she met George, and he took her off to see his farm. Now Valerie says they are her creation, the result of her totally inadvertent matchmaking.

"It was the first time I ever saw love bloom at close quarters," she says. "It was like watching an amaryllis. Astounding."

But Roberta has the idea that, much as she likes them both and wishes them well, love is really something Valerie could do without being reminded of. In Valerie's company you do wonder sometimes what all the fuss is about. Valerie wonders. Her life and her presence, more than any opinion she expresses, remind you that love is not kind or honest and does not contribute to happiness in any reliable way.

When she talked to Roberta about George (this was before she knew Roberta was in love with him), Valerie said, "He's a mysterious man, really. I think he's very idealistic, though he'd hate to hear me say that. This farm he's bought. This self-sufficient, remote, productive life in the country." She went on to talk about how he had grown up in Timmins, the son of a Hungarian shoemaker, youngest of six children and the first to finish high school, let alone go to university. "He's the sort of person who would know what to do in a street fight but doesn't know how to swim. He brought his old crabby, bent-over father down to Toronto and took care of him till he died. I think he drops women rather hard."

Roberta listened to all this with great interest and a basic disregard, because what other people knew about George already seemed inessential to her. She was full of alarm and delight. Being in love was nothing she had counted on. The most she'd hoped for was a life like Valerie's. She had illustrated a couple of children's books and thought she could get more commissions; she could rent a room out in the Beaches, in East Toronto, paint the walls white, sit on cushions instead of chairs, and learn to be self-disciplined and self-indulgent, as she thought solitary people must be.

Valerie and Roberta walk through the house, carrying a bottle of cold wine and two of Valerie's grandmother's water goblets. Roberta thinks Valerie's house is exactly what people have in mind when they say longingly "a house in the country" or, more particularly, "an old brick farmhouse." The warm, pale-red brick with the light brick trim, the vines and elms, the sanded floors and hooked rugs and white walls, the chipped wash-jug set on a massive chest of drawers in front of a dim mirror. Of course, Valerie has had fifteen years to bring this about. She and her husband bought the house as a summer place, and then when he died she sold their city house and moved to an apartment and put her money and her energy into this. George bought his house and land two years ago, having been introduced to this part of the country by Valerie, and fourteen months ago he left his teaching job and moved up here for good. On the heels of that move came his first meeting with Roberta. Last December she came to live with him. She thought that it would take them about a year to get the place fixed up, and then George could get back to doing his sculpting. A sculptor is what he really wants to be. That is why he wanted to give up teaching and live cheaply in the country—raise a lot of vegetables, keep chickens. He hasn't started on the chickens yet.

Roberta meant to keep busy illustrating books. Why hasn't she done this? No time, nowhere to work: no room, no light, no table. No clear moments of authority, now that life has got this new kind of grip on her.

What they have done so far—what George has done, mostly, while Roberta sweeps and cooks—is put a new roof on the house, put in aluminum-frame windows, pour bag after bag of dusty pebble-like insulation into the space behind the walls, fit batts of yellow, woolly-looking fibre glass against the attic roof, clean all the stovepipes and replace some of them and re-brick part of the chimney, replace the rotting eaves. After all these essential and laborious repairs the house is still unattractive on the outside, with its dark-red imitation-brick covering and its sagging porch heaped with drying new lumber and salvaged old lumber and extra batts of fibre glass and other useful debris. And it is dark and sour-smelling within. Roberta would like to rip up the linoleum and tear down the dismal wallpaper, but everything must be done in order, and George has figured out the order; it is no use ripping up and tearing down until the wiring and insulating have been finished and the shell of the house reconstructed. Lately he has been saying that before he starts on the inside of the house or puts the siding on the outside he must do a major job on the barn; if he doesn't get the beam structure propped and strengthened the whole building may come down in next winter's storms.

As well as this there is the garden: the apple and cherry trees, which have been pruned; the raspberry canes, which have been cleaned out; the lawn, which has been reseeded, reclaimed from patches of long wild grass and patches of bare ground and rubble under the shade of some ragged pines. At first Roberta kept an idea of the whole place in her mind—all the things that had been done, that were being done, and that were yet to do. Now she doesn't think of the work that way—she has no general picture of it—but stays in the kitchen and does jobs as they arise. Dealing with the produce of the garden—making chili sauce, preparing tomatoes and peppers and beans and corn for the freezer, making tomato juice, making cherry jam—has taken up a lot of her time. Sometimes she looks into the freezer and wonders who will eat all this—George and who else? She can feel her own claims shrinking.

The table is laid on the long screened verandah at the back of the house. Valerie and Roberta go out a door at the end of the verandah, down some shallow steps, and into a little brick-walled, brick-paved area that Valerie has had made this summer but does not like to call a patio. She says you can't have a patio on a farmhouse. She hasn't decided yet what she does like to call it. She hasn't decided, either, whether to get heavy wooden lawn chairs, which she likes the look of, or comfortable lightweight metal-and-plastic chairs, like those which George and Roberta brought.

They pour the wine and lift their glasses, the capacious old water goblets they love to drink wine from. They can hear Ruth and Eva and Angela laughing in Ruth's bedroom. Ruth has said they must help her get into costume, too—she is going to think of something that will outdo them all. And they can hear the swish of George's scythe, which he has brought to cut the long grass and burdocks around Valerie's little stone dairy house.

"The dairy house would make a lovely studio," Valerie says. "I should rent it to an artist. George? You? I'd rent it for the scything and a raspberry bombe. George is going to make a studio in the barn, though, isn't he?"

"Eventually," says Roberta. At present all George's work is in the front of the house, in the old parlor. Some half-finished and nearly finished pieces are there, covered up with dusty sheets, and also some blocks of wood (George works only in wood)—a big chunk of seasoned oak and pieces of kiln-dried butternut and cherry. His ripsaw, his chisels and gouges, his linseed oil and turpentine and beeswax and resins are all there, the lids dusty and screwed tight. Eva and Angela used to go around and, standing on tiptoe in the rubble and weeds, peer in the front window at the shrouded shapes.

"Ugh, they look spooky," Eva said to George. "What are they underneath?"

"Wooden doughnuts," George said. "Pop sculpt."

"Really?"

"A potato and a two-headed baby."

Next time they went to look they found a sheet tacked up over the window. This was a grayish-colored sheet, torn at the top. To anybody driving by it made the house look even more bleak and neglected.

"Do you know I had cigarettes all the time?" Valerie says. "I have half a carton. I hid them in the cupboard in my room."

She has sent David and Kimberly into town, telling them she's out of cigarettes. Valerie can't stop smoking, though she takes vitamin pills and is careful not to eat anything with red food coloring in it. "I couldn't think of anything else to say I was out of, and I had to have them clear off for a while. Now I don't dare smoke one or they'll smell it when they get back and know I was a liar. And I want one."

"Drink instead," says Roberta. When she got here she thought she couldn't talk to anybody—she was going to say her head ached and ask if she could lie down. But Valerie steadies her, as always. Valerie makes what isn't bearable interesting.

"So how are you?" Valerie says.

"Ohhh," says Roberta.

"Life would be grand if it weren't for the people," says Valerie moodily. "That sounds like a quotation, but I think I just made it up. The problem is that Kimberly is a Christian. Well, that's fine. We could use a Christian or two. For that matter, I am not an un-Christian. But she is very noticeably a Christian, don't you think? I'm amazed how mean she makes me feel."

George is enjoying the scything. For one thing, he likes working without spectators. Whenever he works at home these days, he is aware of a crowd of female spectators. Even if they're nowhere in sight, he feels as if they're watching—taking their ease, regarding his labors with mystification and amusement. He admits, if he thinks about it, that Roberta does do some work, though she has done nothing to earn money as far as he knows; she hasn't been in touch with her publishers, and she hasn't worked on ideas of her own. She permits her daughters to do nothing all day long, all summer long. Yesterday morning he got up feeling tired and disheartened—he had gone to sleep thinking of the work he had to do on the barn, and this preoccupation had seeped into his dreams, which were full of collapses, miscalculations, structural treacheries—and he went out to the deck off the kitchen, thinking to eat his eggs there and brood about the day's jobs. This deck is the only thing he has built as yet, the only change he has made in the house. He built it last spring in response to Roberta's complaints about the darkness of the house and the bad ventilation. He told her that the people who built these houses did so much work in the sun that they never thought of sitting in it.

He came out on the deck, then, carrying his plate and mug, and all three of them were already there. Angela was dressed in a sapphire-blue leotard; she was doing ballet exercises by the deck railing. Eva was sitting with her back against the wall of the house, spooning up bran flakes out of a soup bowl; she did this with such enthusiasm that many were spilled on the deck floor. Roberta, in a deck chair, had the everlasting mug of coffee clasped in both hands. She had one knee up and her back hunched, and with her dark glasses on she looked tense and mournful. He knows she weeps behind those glasses. It seems to him that she has let the children draw the sap right out of her body. She spends her time placating them, picking up after them; she has to beg them to make their beds and clean up their rooms; he has heard her pleading with them to collect their dirty dishes, so that she can wash them. Or that is what it sounds like to him. Is this the middle-class fashion of bringing up children? Here she was admiring Angela, meekly admiring her own daughter—the naked, lifted, golden leg, the disdainful profile. If either of his sisters had ventured on such a display, his mother would have belted them.

Angela lowered her leg and said, "Greetings, Master!"

"I don't see you bumping your head on the ground," said George. He usually joked with the girls no matter what he felt like. Rough joking was his habit, and it had been hugely successful in the classroom, where he had maintained a somewhat overdrawn, occasionally brutal, consistently entertaining character. He had done this with most of the other teachers as well, expressing his contempt for them so colorfully that they could not believe he meant it.

Eva loved to act out any suggestion of this sort. She stretched herself full length on the deck and knocked her head hard on the boards.

"You'll get a concussion," Roberta said.

"No, I won't. I'll just give myself a lobotomy."

"George, do you realize that in four brief days we will be gone?" said Angela. "Isn't your heart broken?"

"In twain."

"But will you let Mom take care of Diana when we're gone?" said Eva, sitting upright and feeling her head for bruises. Diana was a stray cat she was feeding in the barn.

"What do you mean, *let?*" said Roberta, and George at the same time said, "Certainly not. I'll tie her to the bedpost if she ever tries to go near the barn."

This cat is a sore point. If Angela sees the farm as a stage for herself, or sometimes as Nature—a begetter of thoughts and poems, to which she yields herself, wandering and dreaming—Eva sees it as a place to look for animals, with some of her attention left over for insects, minnows, rocks, and slugs. Both of them see it, certainly, as vacationland, spread out before them for whatever use or pleasure they can get out of it; neither sees the jobs waiting to be done under their noses. Eva has spent the summer stalking groundhogs and rabbits, trapping frogs and letting them go, catching minnows in a jar, trying to figure out how various animals could be housed in the barn. George holds her responsible—out of the very strength of her desire—for luring the deer out of the bush, so that he had to stop everything else that he was doing and build an eight-foot-high wire fence around the garden. The only animal she has managed to install in the barn is Diana, rail-thin, ugly, and half wild, whose dangling teats show that she is maintaining a family of kittens elsewhere. Much of Eva's time has been spent trying to discover the whereabouts of these kittens.

George sees the cat as a freeloader, a potential great nuisance, an invader of his property. By feeding it and encouraging it, Eva has embarked on a course of minor but significant treachery, which Roberta has implicitly supported. He knows his feelings on this matter are exaggerated, even comical; that does not help him. One of the things he has never wanted to be, and has avoided being, is a comic dad, a fulminator, a bungler. But it is Roberta's behavior that bothers him, more than Eva's. Here Roberta shows most plainly the mistake she has made in bringing up her children. In his mind he can hear Roberta talking to somebody at a party. "Eva has adopted a horrible cat, a really nasty-looking vagabond—that's her summer achievement. And Angela spends the whole day doing jetés and sulking at us." He has not actually heard Roberta say this—they have not been to any parties—but he can well imagine it. She would summon her children up for the entertainment of others; she would make them into characters, from whom nothing serious was to be expected. This seems to George not only frivolous but heartless. Roberta, who is so indulgent with her children, who worries constantly that they may find her insufficiently loving, interested, understanding, is nevertheless depriving them. She is not taking them seriously; she is not bringing them up. And what is George to do in the face of this? They are not his children. One of the reasons he has not had children is that he doubts if he could give his attention unreservedly, and for as long as would be needed, to this very question of bringing them up. As a teacher, he knows how to make a lot of noise and keep several steps ahead of them, but it is exhausting to have to do that on the home front. And it was boys, chiefly, whom he learned to outmaneuver; boys were the threat in a class. The girls he never bothered much about, beyond some careful sparring with the sexy ones. That is not in order here.

Aside from all this, he often can't help liking Angela and Eva. They seem to him confused and appealing. They think him highly amusing, which irks him sometimes and pleases him at other times. His way with people is to be very reserved or very entertaining, and he believes that his preference is to be reserved. Therefore, he likes the entertainment to be appreciated.

But when he finished his breakfast and got two six-quart baskets and went down to the garden to pick the tomatoes, nobody stirred to help him. Roberta continued her moody thinking and her coffee drinking. Angela had finished her exercises and was writing in the notebook she uses for a journal. Eva had taken off for the barn.

Angela sits down at the piano in Valerie's living room. There is no piano in George's house, and she misses one. Doesn't her mother miss one? Her mother has become a person who doesn't ask for anything.

"I have seen her change," Angela has written in her journal, "from a person I deeply respected into a person on the verge of being a nervous wreck.

If this is love I want no part of it. He wants to enslave her and us all and she walks a tightrope trying to keep him from getting mad. She doesn't enjoy anything and if you gave her the choice she would like best to lie down in a dark room with a cloth over her eyes and not see anybody or do anything. This is an intelligent woman who used to believe in freedom."

She starts to play the "Turkish March," which brings to her mind the picture of a house her parents sold when she was five. There was a little shelf up near the ceiling in the dining room, where her mother had set the dessert plates for decoration. A tree, or bush, in the yard had lettuce-colored leaves as big as plates.

She has written in her journal: "I know nostalgia is a futile emotion. Sometimes I feel like tearing out some things I have written where perhaps I have been too harsh in judging certain people or situations but I have decided to leave everything because I want to have a record of what I really felt at the time. I want to have a truthful record of my whole life. How to keep oneself from lying I see as the main problem everywhere."

During the summer Angela has spent a lot of time reading. She has read *Anna Karenina, The Second Sex, Emily of New Moon, The Norton Anthology of Poetry, The Autobiography of W. B. Yeats, The Happy Hooker, The Act of Creation, Seven Gothic Tales*. Some of these, to be accurate, she has not read all the way through. Her mother used to read all the time, too. Angela would come home from school at noon, and again in the afternoon, and find her mother reading. Her mother read about the conquest of Mexico, she read *The Tale of Genji*. Angela marvels at how safe her mother seemed then.

Angela has one picture in her mind of Eva before Eva was born. The three of them—Angela, her mother, and her father—are on a beach. Her father is scooping out a large hole in the sand. Her father is a gifted builder of sand castles with road and irrigation systems, so Angela watches with interest any projects he undertakes. But the hole has nothing to do with a sand castle. When it is finished her mother rolls over, giggling, and fits her stomach into it. In her stomach is Eva, and the hollow is like a spoon for an egg. The beach is wide, mile after mile of white sand sloping delicately into the blue-green water. No rocky lakefront or stingy bit of cove. A radiant, generous place. Where could it have been?

She proceeds from the "Turkish March" to a try at "Eine Kleine Nachtmusik." Roberta, listening to the piano at the same time she's listening to Valerie talking humorously and despairingly about her fear of Kimberly, her dislike of intruders, her indefensible reluctance to relinquish her children, thinks, No, it wasn't a mistake. What does she mean by that? She means it wasn't a mistake to leave her husband. Whatever happens, it wasn't a mistake. It was necessary. Otherwise she wouldn't have known.

"This is a bad time for you," Valerie says judiciously. "There is just a spectacular lot of strain."

"That's what I say to myself," says Roberta. "But sometimes I think that's not it. It's not the house, it's not the children. It's just something black that rises."

"Oh, there's always something black," says Valerie, grumbling.

"I think about Andrew—what was I doing to him? Setting things up to find the failure in him, railing at him, then getting cold feet and making up. Gradually the need to get rid of him would build again, but I was always sure it was his fault—if he'd just do this or that I could love him. So horrible for him that he turned into—remember what you said he was? A stick."

"He was a stick," says Valerie. "He always was. You're not responsible for everything."

"I think about it, because I wonder if that's what George is doing to me. He wants to be rid of me, then he doesn't, then he does, then he can't admit that, even to himself; he has to set up failures. I feel I know what Andrew went through. Not that I'd go back. Never. But I see it."

"I doubt if things happen so symmetrically."

"I don't think so, either, really. I don't think you get your punishment in such a simple way. Isn't it funny how you're attracted—I am—to the idea of a pattern like that? I mean, the idea is attractive, of there being that balance. But not the experience. I'd like to avoid them."

"You forget how happy you are when you're happy."

"And vice versa. It's like childbirth."

George has finished scything and is cleaning the blade. He can hear the piano through the open windows of Valerie's house, and erratic streams of sweet, cold air are coming up from the river. He feels much better now, either because of the simple exercise or from the relief of feeling unobserved; perhaps it's just good to get away from the mountainous demands of his own place. He wonders if it's Roberta playing. The music fits in nicely with what he's doing: first the cheerful, workaday "Turkish March," to go along with the scything; now, as he stands cleaning the blade and smelling the cut grass, the subtle congratulations—even if a bit uncertainly delivered—of "Eine Kleine Nachtmusik." As always, when his mood truly lifts, when the dawn breaks, he wants to go and find Roberta and envelop her, assure her—assure himself—that no real damage has been done. He hoped to be able to do that last night when they went drinking, but he couldn't; something still held him back.

He recalls Roberta's first visit to his house. That was in late August or early September, about a year ago now. They staged an indecorous sort of picnic, cooking feasts and playing records, hauling a mattress out into the yard. Clear nights, with Roberta pointing out to him the unlikely ways the stars tie up into their constellations, and every day pure gold. Roberta saying he must get it all straight now: she is forty-three years old, which is six years too old for him; she has left her husband because everything between them seemed artificial; but she hates saying that, because it may be just cant, she isn't sure what she means, and above all, she doesn't know what she's capable of. She seemed to him courageous, truthful, without vanity. How out of this could come such touchiness, tearfulness, weariness, such a threat of collapse he cannot imagine.

But the first impression is worth respecting, he thinks.

Eva and Ruth are decorating the dinner table on the verandah. Ruth is wearing a white shirt belonging to her brother, his striped pajama bottoms, and a monumental black turban. She looks like a proud but good-natured Sikh.

"I think the table ought to be strewn," says Ruth. "Subtlety is out, Eva."

At intervals they set orange and gold dahlias and beautifully striped pepper squash, zucchini, yellow gourds, Indian corn.

Under cover of the music Eva says, "Angela has more problems living here than I do. She thinks that whenever they fight it's about her."

"Do they fight?" says Ruth softly. Then she says, "It's none of my business." She was in love with George when she was thirteen or fourteen. It was when her mother first became friends with him. She used to hate his wife, and was glad when they separated. She remembers that the wife was the daughter of a gynecologist, and that this was cited by her mother as a reason George and his wife could never get on. It was probably the father's prosperity her mother was talking about, or the way the daughter had been brought up. But to Ruth the word "gynecologist" seemed sharp and appalling, and she saw the gynecologist's daughter dressed in an outfit of cold, jagged metal.

"They have silent fights. We can tell. Angela is so self-interested she thinks everything revolves around her. That's what happens when you become an adolescent. I don't want it to happen to me."

There is a pause in Angela's playing, and Eva says sharply, "Oh, I don't want to leave! I hate leaving."

"Do you?"

"I hate to leave Diana. I don't know what will happen to her. I don't know if I'll ever see her again. I don't think I'll ever see the deer again. I hate having to leave things."

Now that the piano is silent, Eva can be heard outside, where Valerie and Roberta are sitting. Roberta hears what Eva says, and waits, expecting to hear her say something about next summer. She braces herself to hear it.

Instead, Eva says, "You know, I understand George. I don't mind about him the way Angela does. I know how to be jokey. I understand him."

Roberta and Valerie look at each other, and Roberta smiles, shakes her head, and shivers. She has been afraid, sometimes, that George would hurt her children, not physically but by some turnabout, some revelation of dislike, that they could never forget. It seems to her that she has instructed them, by example, that he is to be accommodated, his silences respected, his joking responded to. What if he should turn, within this safety, and deal them a memorable blow? If it happened, it would be she who would have betrayed them into it. And she can feel a danger. For instance, when George was pruning the apple trees she heard Angela say, "My father's got an apple tree and a cherry tree now."

(That was information. Would he take it as competition?)

"I suppose he has some minions come and prune them for him?" George said.

"He has hundreds," said Angela cheerfully. "Dwarfs. He makes them all wear little Navy uniforms."

Angela was on thin ice at that moment. But Roberta thinks now that the real danger is not to Angela, who would find a way to welcome insult, would be ready to reap some advantage. (Roberta has read parts of the journal.) It is Eva, with her claims of understanding, her hopes of all-round conciliation, who could be smashed and stranded.

Over cold apple-and-watercress soup Eva has switched back to her *enfant terrible* style to tell the table, "They went out and got drunk last night. They were polluted."

David says he hasn't heard that expression in a long time.

Valerie says, "How awful for you little ones."

"We considered phoning the Children's Aid," says Angela, looking very unchildlike in the candlelight—looking like a queen, in fact—and aware that David is watching her, though with David it's hard to say whether he's watching with approval or with reservations. It seems as if it might be approval. Kimberly has taken over his reservations.

"Did you have a dissolute time?" said Valerie. "Roberta, you never told me. Where did you go?"

"It was highly respectable," says Roberta. "We went to the Queen's Hotel in Logan. To the Lounge—that's what they call it. The posh place to drink."

"George wouldn't take you out to any old beer parlor," says Ruth. "George is a closet conservative."

"It's true," says Valerie. "George believes you should take ladies only to nice places."

"And children should be seen and not heard," says Angela.

"Not seen, either," says George.

"Which is confusing to everyone, because he comes on like a raving radical," says Ruth.

"This is a treat," says George, "getting a free analysis. Actually, it was quite dissolute, and Roberta probably doesn't remember, on account of being so polluted, as Eva says. She bewitched a fellow who did toothpick tricks."

Roberta says it was a game where you made a word out of toothpicks, then took a toothpick away or rearranged what was there and made another word, and so on.

"I hope not dirty words?" says Eva.

"I never talked like that when I was her age," Angela says. "I was your pre-permissive child."

"And after we got tired of the game, or after he did, because I was tired of it quite soon, he showed me pictures of his wife and himself on their Mediterranean cruise. He was with another lady last night, because his wife is dead now, and if he forgot where the pictures were taken this lady reminded him. She said she didn't think he'd ever get over it."

"The cruise or his wife?" says Ruth, while George is saying that he had a conversation with a couple of Dutch farmers who wanted to take him for a ride in their plane.

"I don't think I went," George adds.

"I dissuaded you," says Roberta, not looking at him.

" 'Dissuaded' sounds so lovely," says Ruth. "It's so smooth. I must be thinking of suède."

Eva asks what it means.

"Persuaded not to," says Roberta. "I persuaded George not to go for a plane ride at one o'clock in the morning with the rich Dutch farmers. Instead, we all had an adventure getting the man from the Mediterranean cruise into his car so his girlfriend could drive him home."

Ruth and Kimberly get up to remove the soup bowls, and David goes to put on a record of Dvořák's "New World" Symphony. This is his mother's request. David says it's syrupy.

They are quiet, waiting for the music to start. Eva says, "How did you guys fall in love anyway? Was it a physical attraction?"

Ruth knocks her gently on the head with a soup bowl. "You ought to have your jaws wired shut," she says. "Don't forget I'm learning how to cope with disturbed children."

"Didn't it bother you, Mom being so much older?"

"You see what I mean about her?" Angela says.

"What do you know about love?" says George grandly. "Love suffereth long, and is kind. Similar to myself in that respect. Love is not puffed up . . . "

"I think that is a particular kind of love," says Kimberly, setting down the vegetables. "If you're quoting."

Under cover of a conversation about translation and the meanings of words (a subject of which George knows little but about which he is soon making sweeping, provocative statements, true to his classroom technique), Roberta says to Valerie, "The man's girlfriend said that the wonderful thing was that his wife had done the whole Mediterranean cruise with a front-end loader."

"A what?"

"Front-end loader. I looked blank, too, so she said, 'You know, his wife had one of those operations and she had to wear one of those bag things.' "

"Oh, God help us."

"She had big fat arms and a sprayed blond hairdo. The wife did, in the pictures. The girlfriend was something the same, but trimmer. The wife had such a lewd, happy look. A good-times look."

"And a front-end loader."

So you see against what odds, and with what unpromising-looking persons, love takes root and flourishes, and I myself have no front-end loader, merely some wrinkles and slackness and sallowness and subtle withering. This is what Roberta is saying to herself. It's not my fault, she says to herself, as she has said so often before. Usually when she says it it's a whine, a plea, a whimper. Now it says itself matter-of-factly in her head; the tone in which it is stated is bored and tired. It seems as if this could be the truth.

By dessert the conversation has shifted to architecture. The only light on the verandah is from the candles on the table. Ruth has taken the big candles away and set in front of each place a single small candle in a black metal holder with a handle, like the candle in the nursery rhyme. Valerie and Roberta say it together: " 'Here comes a candle to light you to bed. Here comes a chopper to chop off your head!' "

Neither of them taught that rhyme to her children, and their children have never heard it before.

"I've heard it," says Kimberly.

"The pointed arch, for instance—that was just a fad," George is saying. "It was an architectural fashion, very like fashions today."

"Well, it wasn't only that," says David, temporizing. "It was more than a fashion. The people who built the cathedrals were not entirely like us."

"They were very unlike us," Kimberly says.

"I'm sure I was always taught, if I was taught at all in those far-off days," says Valerie, "that the pointed arch was a development of the Romanesque arch. It suddenly occurred to them to carry it further. And it looked more religious."

"Bull," says George happily. "Beggin' your pardon. I know that's what they used to say, but in fact the pointed arch is the most primitive. It's the easiest arch; it's not a development from the round arch at all—how could it be? They had pointed arches in Egypt. The round arch, the keystone arch, is the most sophisticated arch you can build. The whole thing has been reported ass backwards to favor Christianity."

"Well, it may be sophisticated, but I think it's depressing," says Ruth. "I think they're very depressing, those round arches. They're monotonous; they just go along blah-blah-blah—they don't exactly make your spirits soar."

"It must have expressed something the people deeply wanted," Kimberly says. "You can hardly call that a fad. They built those cathedrals, the people did; the plan wasn't dictated by some architect."

"A misconception. They did have architects. In some cases we even know who they were."

"Nevertheless, I think Kimberly's right," says Valerie. "In those cathedrals you feel so much of the aspirations of those people; you feel the Christian emotion in the architecture—"

"Never mind what you feel. The fact is, the Crusaders brought the pointed arch back from the Arab world. Just as they brought back a taste for spicy food. It wasn't dreamed up by the collective unconscious to honor Jesus any more than I was. It was the latest style. The earliest examples you can see are in Italy, and then it worked north."

Kimberly is very pink in the face but is benignly, tightly smiling. Valerie, just because she so much dislikes Kimberly, is feeling a need to say anything at all to come to her rescue. Valerie never minds if she sounds silly; she will throw herself headlong into any conversation to turn it off its contentious course, to make people laugh and calm down. Ruth also has a knack for lightening things, though in her case it seems to be done not so deliberately but serenely and almost inadvertently, as a result of her faithful following of her own line of thought. What about David? At this moment David is caught up by Angela and not paying as much attention as he might be. Angela is trying out her powers; she will try them out even on a cousin she has known since she was a child. Kimberly is endangered on two sides, Roberta thinks. But she will manage. She is strong enough to hold on to David through any number of Angelas, and strong enough to hold her smile in the face of George's attack on her faith. Does her smile foresee how he will burn? Not likely. She foresees, instead, how all of them will stumble and wander around and tie themselves in knots; what does it matter who wins the argument? For Kimberly all the arguments have already been won.

Thinking this, pinning them all down this way, Roberta feels competent, relieved. Indifference has rescued her. The main thing is to be indifferent to George—that's the great boon. But her indifference flows past him; it's generous, it touches everybody. She is drunk enough to feel like reporting some findings. "Sexual abdication is not enough," she might say to Valerie. She is sober enough to keep quiet.

Valerie has got George talking about Italy. Ruth and David and Kimberly and Angela have started talking about something else. Roberta hears Angela's voice speaking with impatience and authority, and with an eagerness, a shyness, only she can detect.

"Acid rain . . . " Angela is saying.

Eva flicks her fingers against Roberta's arm. "What are you thinking?" she says.

"I don't know."

"You can't not know. What are you thinking?"

"About life."

"What about life?"

"About people."

"What about people?"

"About the dessert."

Eva flicks harder, giggling. "What about the dessert?"

"I thought it was O.K."

Sometime later Valerie has occasion to say that she was not born in the nineteenth century, in spite of what David may think. David says that everybody born in this country before the Second World War was to all intents and purposes brought up in the nineteenth century, and that their thinking is archaic.

"We are more than products of our upbringing," Valerie says. "As you yourself must hope, David." She says that she has been listening to all this talk about overpopulation, ecological disaster, nuclear disaster, this and that disaster, destroying the ozone layer—it's been going on and on, on and on for years, talk of disaster—but here they sit, all healthy, relatively sane, with a lovely dinner and lovely wine inside them, in the beautiful, undestroyed countryside.

"The Incas eating off gold plates while Pizarro was landing on the coast," says David.

"Don't talk as if there's no solution," says Kimberly.

"I think maybe we're destroyed already," Ruth says dreamily. "I think maybe we're anachronisms. No, that's not what I mean. I mean relics. In some way we are already. Relics."

Eva raises her head from her folded arms on the table. Her curtain veil is pulled down over one eye; her makeup has leaked beyond its boundaries, so that her whole face is a patchy flower. She says in a loud, stern voice, "I am not a relic," and they all laugh.

"Certainly not!" says Valerie, and then begins the yawning, the pushing back of chairs, the rather sheepish and formal smiles, the blowing out of candles: time to go home.

"Smell the river now!" Valerie tells them. Her voice sounds forlorn and tender, in the dark.

"A gibbous moon."

It was Roberta who told George what a gibbous moon was, and so his saying this is always an offering. It is an offering now, as they drive between the black cornfields.

"So there is."

Roberta doesn't reject the offering with silence, but she doesn't welcome it, either. She is polite. She yawns, and there is a private sound to her yawn. This isn't tactics, though she knows indifference is attractive. The real thing is. He can spot an imitation; he can always withstand tactics. She has to go all the way, to where she doesn't care. Then he feels how light and distant she is and his love revives. She has power. But the minute she begins to value it it will begin to leave her. So she is thinking, as she yawns and wavers on the edge of caring and not caring. She'd stay on this edge if she could.

The half-ton truck bearing George and Roberta, with Eva and Angela in the back, is driving down the third concession road of Weymouth Township, known locally as the Telephone Road. It is a gravel road, fairly wide and well travelled. They turned on to it from the River Road, a much narrower road, which runs past Valerie's place. From the corner of the River Road to

George's gate is a distance of about two and a quarter miles. Two side roads cut this stretch of the Telephone Road at right angles. Both these roads have stop signs; the Telephone Road is a through road. The first crossroad they have already passed. Along the second crossroad, from the west, a dark-green 1969 Dodge is travelling at between eighty and ninety miles an hour. Two young men are returning from a party to their home in Logan. One has passed out. The other is driving. He hasn't remembered to put the lights on. He sees the road by the light of the moon.

There isn't time to say a word. Roberta doesn't scream. George doesn't touch the brake. The big car flashes before them, a huge, dark flash, without lights, seemingly without sound. It comes out of the dark corn and fills the air right in front of them the way a big flat fish will glide into view suddenly in an aquarium tank. It seems to be no more than a yard in front of their headlights. Then it's gone—it has disappeared into the corn on the other side of the road. They drive on. They drive on down the Telephone Road and turn into the lane and come to a stop and are sitting in the truck in the yard in front of the dark shape of the half-improved house. What they feel is not terror or thanksgiving—not yet. What they feel is strangeness. They feel as strange, as flattened out and borne aloft, as unconnected with previous and future events as the ghost car was, the black fish. The shaggy branches of the pine trees are moving overhead, and under those branches the moonlight comes clear on the hesitant grass of their new lawn.

"Are you guys dead?" Eva says, rousing them. "Aren't we home?"

Spring in Fialta

by Vladimir Nabokov

Introduced by Jim Shepard

THE FIRST TIME I ENCOUNTERED "SPRING IN FIALTA" I NOT ONLY READ it in one sitting, I inhabited it long after I put the book down. For the greater part of the following afternoon, I wandered around the house not quite hearing things. I later learned the story had been a favorite of Nabokov's, and I can well imagine the number of ways it pleased him: from the delight it takes in demolishing any expected lyricism in its opening gesture (After the title we read, "Spring in Fialta is cloudy and dull"), to its quiet series of multiplying alter egos, down to the plus-foured Englishman whose lustful eye shifts from Nina to a "compact furry moth, which he deftly slipped into a pillbox," to the elegance and the wit with which huge expositional apparatuses are dealt away with ("quite a long time ago, around 1917 I should say, judging by certain left-wing theater rumblings backstage"). The story clearly owes to Anton Chekhov's "The Kiss" and "The Lady with the Little Dog" some of its thematic heart: that pervasive and disorienting sense that the false part of one's life is happening openly while the real and interesting part remains hidden. But only some of its thematic heart, and the rest has a lot to do with the story's greatness.

Victor, an émigré, recounts a chance meeting in the seaside resort of Fialta ("a blend of the Adriatic's Fiume and the Black Sea's Yalta," biographer Brian Boyd informs us) with Nina, a woman who inexplicably kissed him on a snowy path on a Russian winter night fifteen years earlier, before they had exchanged a word. Victor, who for most of the story has hovered nearby an "island of happiness" represented by home and family, is nonetheless a man given to slight boredom, gloomy thoughts, and stirring recollections, in the manner of one of those Chekhovian intellectuals who combines human decency with an inability in his private life to do anything useful, a man who seems to be in a kind of continuous stumble. Over the course of the story he relives his entire tenuous relationship with her. The ways in which their connection—a history consisting almost entirely of gaps—takes on a compelling force precisely parallels the ways in which a short story's few perfectly chosen trifles cohere to create the illusion of a dense, substantial, and extensive world.

Victor tells us that he can never "find the precise term" for the kind of relationship he shares with Nina; the story can be seen as the attempt to enlarge our vocabulary by that one word. Nina fits her "generous, dutiful lips" to his in their first meeting, and the nature of that generosity and dutifulness—that "sunburst of kindness" of which she seemed always capable—is what Victor never fully comprehends; he allows her to remain a figure of fantasy, imagined in his own image. How familiar to him, he says, were her "hesitations, second thoughts, third thoughts mirroring first ones, ephemeral worries"; how familiar, indeed. His quintessential image of her is one that encapsulates not only the transience of his own émigré existence but the nature of his emotional life: "She had always either just arrived or was about to leave." Everything in the story seems to take place in "that life-quickening atmosphere of a big railway station where everything is something trembling on the brink of something else, thus to be clutched and cherished," all of it, in the manner of train traveler Nina, "slipping away with beautiful smoothness."

He goes about the business of life, ignoring his idealized love for his Nina, who remains an unstable mix of the woman he occasionally observes so acutely and the solipsized creation of his own melancholy. He announces: "were I a writer, I should allow only my heart to have imagination, and for the rest rely upon memory, that long-drawn sunset shadow of one's personal truth." That's precisely what he does, while we watch. His story is about the relationship of memory to imagination, especially in the face of loss. We watch him cobble together only what he can remember and may have occasionally imagined: trifles.

But what trifles! That little pantless infant boy, "trying to carry three oranges at once, but continually dropping the variable third, until he fell himself"; Nina's "yellow scarf already on the move like those dogs that recognize you before their owners do"; his gazing into her train compartment as though "spying upon an utterly unsuspecting life moving in that aquarium dimness"; his registering, upon telling her that he'd hoped she'd come to his room the night they shared a château, both her dismay at having disappointed him and her rapid estimating glance at the receding back of her husband.

These are trifles designed to disclose the wistful helplessness of human beings: the not-so-very young man who made such a discreet mess of his life, the young woman who will never be happy.

As the story progresses, the intimations of Nina's mortality become more gently insistent, and with them the story's sadness begins to bloom and grow, a sadness that suffuses everything in the manner of Fialta's saturated sunshine. And yet the painful absurdity of the situation never recedes. (Nabokov remarked that Chekhov wrote "sad books for humorous people; that is, only a reader with a sense of humor can really appreciate their sadness.") Nearly all of Victor's memories point the inexorable way to loss: consider the moment he views her surrounded by acquaintances "who stood in a circle gaping at her as idlers gape at a street row, a lost child, or the victim of an accident," all three examples heartbreakingly indicating to her final fate. And all such memories lead to the story's climactic scene, the moment when they find themselves alone "on a rough kind of terrace" with a view that brings together all the bright bits of memory strewn throughout the story: dove-colored Mount St. George, the train that brought Victor to Fialta, the cypress that first leads the way up that slope, and, of course, Nina's kiss. "With an unbearable force" our hero relives "all that had ever been between us beginning with a similar kiss" and is finally forced to say, "Look here—what if I love you?" And Nina glances at him, puzzled and then embarrassed. And he, to his everlasting regret, recants: never mind, he was only joking.

She is gone forever, and he never really knew her. A standard romantic lament. His earlier apprehensions are correct: "something lovely, delicate, and unrepeatable was being wasted: something which I abused by snapping off poor bright bits in gross haste while neglecting the modest but true core which perhaps it kept offering me in a pitiful whisper." There may have been, to quote *Lolita*'s Humbert Humbert, "a garden, and a twilight, and a palace gate" behind that face he so closely observed, but he never troubled himself, never disturbed the smooth flow of his life, to find out. And if he had? "But then what should I have done with you, Nina, how should I have disposed of the store of sadness that had gradually accumulated as a result of our seemingly carefree, but really hopeless meetings?"

But then something mysterious—and utterly Nabokovian—happens. The moment of greatest sadness becomes the moment when we suddenly understand something we had been seeing without understanding: a radiance that had been present throughout the story, in Fialta, in Nina, and in what both engender in Victor. There *is,* it turns out, "something in the very somnolence of [Fialta's] humid Lent that especially anoints one's soul," and that something is what Victor—and we—are left with. "*This time,*" Victor tells us, "*we had met in warm and misty Fialta, and I could not have celebrated the occasion with greater art.*" Exactly. Victor's twin poles of "truth" and "imagination" are blended here not by presence, but by absence—an irony hiding within the supposed stripping away of irony—and here again Victor's lyricism, like his whole relation to Nina, is dependent on these aspects of removal, absence, untouchability. Imagination is what he always had, not memory; imagination is what is being celebrated, and indicted. What has happened does not conform, strictly, to common sense. But as Nabokov has told us, common sense at its worst is a sense made common. What has happened leaves us with a story which, as he once said of Chekhov's work, "will live as long as there are birchwoods and sunsets and the urge to write."

Spring in Fialta

Vladimir Nabokov

Spring in Fialta is cloudy and dull. Everything is damp: the piebald trunks of the plane trees, the juniper shrubs, the railings, the gravel. Far away, in a watery vista between the jagged edges of pale bluish houses, which have tottered up from their knees to climb the slope (a cypress indicating the way), the blurred Mount St. George is more than ever remote from its likeness on the picture post cards which since 1910, say (those straw hats, those youthful cabmen), have been courting the tourist from the sorry-go-round of their prop, among amethyst-toothed lumps of rock and the mantelpiece dreams of sea shells. The air is windless and warm, with a faint tang of burning. The sea, its salt drowned in a solution of rain, is less glaucous than gray with waves too sluggish to break into foam.

It was on such a day in the early thirties that I found myself, all my senses wide open, on one of Fialta's steep little streets, taking in everything at once, that marine rococo on the stand, and the coral crucifixes in a shop-window, and the dejected poster of a visiting circus, one corner of its drenched paper detached from the wall, and a yellow bit of unripe orange peel on the old, slate-blue sidewalk, which retained here and there a fading memory of ancient mosaic design. I am fond of Fialta; I am fond of it because I feel in the hollow of those violaceous syllables the sweet dark dampness of the most rumpled of small flowers, and because the altolike name of a lovely Crimean town is echoed by its viola; and also because there is something in the very somnolence of its humid Lent that especially anoints one's soul. So I was happy to be there again, to trudge uphill in inverse direction to the rivulet of the gutter, hatless, my head wet, my skin already suffused with warmth although I wore only a light mackintosh over my shirt.

I had come on the Capparabella express, which, with that reckless gusto peculiar to trains in mountainous country, had done its thundering best to collect throughout the night as many tunnels as possible. A day or two, just as long as a breathing spell in the midst of a business trip would allow me, was all I expected to stay. I had left my wife and children at home, and that was an island of happiness always present in the clear north of my being, always floating beside me, and even through me, I dare say, but yet keeping on the outside of me most of the time.

A pantless infant of the male sex, with a taut mud-gray little belly, jerkily stepped down from a doorstep and waddled off, bowlegged, trying to carry three oranges at once, but continuously dropping the variable third, until he fell himself, and then a girl of twelve or so, with a string of heavy beads around her dusky neck and wearing a skirt as long as that of a gypsy, promptly took away the whole lot with her more nimble and more numerous hands. Nearby, on the wet terrace of a café, a waiter was wiping the slabs of tables; a melancholy brigand hawking local lollipops, elaborate-looking things with a lunar gloss, had placed a hopelessly full basket on the cracked balustrade, over which the two were conversing. Either the drizzle had stopped or Fialta had got so used to it that she herself did not know whether she was breathing moist air or warm rain. Thumb-filling his pipe from a rubber pouch as he walked, a plus-foured Englishman of the solid exportable sort came from under an arch and entered a pharmacy, where large pale sponges in a blue vase were dying a thirsty death behind their glass. What luscious elation I felt rippling through my veins, how gratefully my whole being responded to the flutters and effluvia of that gray day saturated with a vernal essence which itself it seemed slow in perceiving! My nerves were unusually receptive after a sleepless night; I assimilated everything: the whistling of a thrush in the almond trees beyond the chapel, the peace of the crumbling houses, the pulse of the distant sea, panting in the mist, all this together with the jealous green of bottle glass bristling along the top of a wall and the fast colors of a circus advertisement featuring a feathered Indian on a rearing horse in the act of lassoing a boldly endemic zebra, while some thoroughly fooled elephants sat brooding upon their star-spangled thrones.

Presently the same Englishman overtook me. As I absorbed him along with the rest, I happened to notice the sudden side-roll of his big blue eye straining at its crimson canthus, and the way he rapidly moistened his lips—because of the dryness of those sponges, I thought; but then I followed the direction of his glance, and saw Nina.

Every time I had met her during the fifteen years of our—well, I fail to find the precise term for our kind of relationship—she had not seemed to recognize me at once; and this time too she remained quite still for a moment, on the opposite sidewalk, half turning toward me in sympathetic incertitude mixed with curiosity, only her yellow scarf already on the move like those dogs that recognize you before their owners do—and then she uttered a cry, her hands up, all her ten fingers dancing, and in the middle of the street, with merely the frank impulsiveness of an old friendship (just as she would rapidly make the sign of the cross over me every time we parted), she kissed me thrice with more mouth than meaning, and then walked beside me, hanging on to me, adjusting her stride to mine, hampered by her narrow brown skirt perfunctorily slit down the side.

"Oh yes, Ferdie is here too," she replied and immediately in her turn inquired nicely after Elena.

"Must be loafing somewhere around with Segur," she went on in reference to her husband. "And I have some shopping to do; we leave after lunch. Wait a moment, where are you leading me, Victor dear?"

Back into the past, back into the past, as I did every time I met her, repeating the whole accumulation of the plot from the very beginning up to the last increment—thus in Russian fairy tales the already told is bunched up again at every new turn of the story. This time we had met in warm and misty Fialta, and I could not have celebrated the occasion with greater art, could not have adorned with brighter vignettes the list of fate's former services, even if I had known that this was to be the last one; the last one, I maintain, for I cannot imagine any heavenly firm of brokers that might consent to arrange me a meeting with her beyond the grave.

My introductory scene with Nina had been laid in Russia quite a long time ago, around 1917 I should say, judging by certain left-wing theater rumblings backstage. It was at some birthday party at my aunt's on her country estate, near Luga, in the deepest folds of winter (how well I remember the first sign of nearing the place: a red barn in a white wilderness). I had just graduated from the Imperial Lyceum; Nina was already engaged: although she was of my age and of that of the century, she looked twenty at least, and this in spite or perhaps because of her neat slender build, whereas at thirty-two that very slightness of hers made her look younger. Her fiancé was a guardsman on leave from the front, a handsome heavy fellow, incredibly well-bred and stolid, who weighed every word on the scales of the most exact common sense and spoke in a velvety baritone, which grew even smoother when he addressed her; his decency and devotion probably got on her nerves, and he is now a successful if somewhat lonesome engineer in a most distant tropical country.

Windows light up and stretch their luminous lengths upon the dark billowy snow, making room for the reflection of the fan-shaped light above the front door between them. Each of the two side-pillars is fluffily fringed with white, which rather spoils the lines of what might have been a perfect ex libris for the book of our two lives. I cannot recall why we had all wandered out of the sonorous hall into the still darkness, peopled only with firs, snow-swollen to twice their size; did the watchmen invite us to look at a sullen red glow in the sky, portent of nearing arson? Possibly. Did we go to admire an equestrian statue of ice sculptured near the pond by the Swiss tutor of my cousins? Quite as likely. My memory revives only on the way back to the brightly symmetrical mansion toward which we tramped in single file along a narrow furrow between snowbanks, with that crunch-crunch-crunch which is the only comment that a taciturn winter night makes upon humans. I walked last; three singing steps ahead of me walked a small bent shape; the firs gravely showed their burdened paws. I slipped and dropped the dead flashlight someone had forced upon me; it was devilishly hard to retrieve; and instantly attracted by my curses, with an eager, low laugh in anticipation of fun, Nina dimly veered toward me. I call her Nina, but I could hardly have known her name yet, hardly could we have had time, she and I, for any preliminary; "Who's that?" she asked with interest—and I was already kissing her neck, smooth and quite fiery hot from the long fox fur of her coat collar, which kept getting into my way until she clasped my shoulder, and with the candor so peculiar to her gently fitted her generous, dutiful lips to mine.

But suddenly parting us by its explosion of gaiety, the theme of a snowball fight started in the dark, and someone, fleeing, falling, crunching, laughing and panting, climbed a drift, tried to run, and uttered a horrible groan: deep snow had performed the amputation of an arctic. And soon after, we all dispersed to our respective homes, without my having talked with Nina, nor made any plans about the future, about those fifteen itinerant years that had already set out toward the dim horizon, loaded with the parts of our unassembled meetings; and as I watched her in the maze of gestures and shadows of gestures of which the rest of that evening consisted (probably parlor games—with Nina persistently in the other camp), I was astonished, I remember, not so much by her inattention to me after that warmth in the snow as by the innocent naturalness of that inattention, for I did not yet know that had I said a word it would have changed at once into a wonderful sunburst of kindness, a cheerful, compassionate attitude with all possible co-operation, as if woman's love were spring water containing salubrious salts which at the least notice she ever so willingly gave anyone to drink.

"Let me see, where did we last meet," I began (addressing the Fialta version of Nina) in order to bring to her small face with prominent cheekbones and dark-red lips a certain expression I knew; and sure enough, the shake of her head and the puckered brow seemed less to imply forgetfulness than to deplore the flatness of an old joke; or to be more exact, it was as if all those cities where fate had fixed our various rendezvous without ever attending them personally, all those platforms and stairs and three-walled rooms and dark back alleys, were trite settings remaining after some other lives all brought to a close long before and were so little related to the acting out of our own aimless destiny that it was almost bad taste to mention them.

I accompanied her into a shop under the arcades; there, in the twilight beyond a beaded curtain, she fingered some red leather purses stuffed with tissue paper, peering at the price tags, as if wishing to learn their museum names. She wanted, she said, exactly that shape but in fawn, and when after ten minutes of frantic rustling the old Dalmatian found such a freak by a miracle that has puzzled me ever since, Nina, who was about to pick some money out of my hand, changed her mind and went through the streaming beads without having bought anything.

Outside it was just as milky dull as before; the same smell of burning, stirring my Tartar memories, drifted from the bare windows of the pale houses; a small swarm of gnats was busy darning the air above a mimosa, which bloomed listlessly, her sleeves trailing to the very ground; two workmen in broad-brimmed hats were lunching on cheese and garlic, their backs against a circus billboard, which depicted a red hussar and an orange tiger of sorts; curious—in his effort to make the beast as ferocious as possible, the artist had gone so far that he had come back from the other side, for the tiger's face looked positively human.

"*Au fond,* I wanted a comb," said Nina with belated regret.

How familiar to me were her hesitations, second thoughts, third thoughts mirroring first ones, ephemeral worries between trains. She had always either just arrived or was about to leave, and of this I find it hard to think without feeling humiliated by the variety of intricate routes one feverishly follows in order to keep that final appointment which the most confirmed dawdler knows to be unavoidable. Had I to submit before judges of our earthly existence a specimen of her average pose, I would have perhaps placed her leaning upon a counter at Cook's, left calf crossing right shin, left toe tapping floor, sharp elbows and coin-spilling bag on the counter, while the employee, pencil in hand, pondered with her over the plan of an eternal sleeping car.

After the exodus from Russia, I saw her—and that was the second time—in Berlin at the house of some friends. I was about to get married; she had just broken with her fiancé. As I entered that room I caught sight of her at once and, having glanced at the other guests, I instinctively determined which of the men knew more about her than I. She was sitting in the corner of a couch, her feet pulled up, her small comfortable body folded in the form of a Z; an ash tray stood aslant on the couch near one of her heels; and, having squinted at me and listened to my name, she removed her stalk-like cigarette holder from her lips and proceeded to utter slowly and joyfully, "Well, of all people—" and at once it became clear to everyone, beginning with her, that we had long been on intimate terms: unquestionably, she had forgotten all about the actual kiss, but somehow because of that trivial occurrence she found herself recollecting a vague stretch of warm, pleasant friendship, which in reality had never existed between us. Thus the whole cast of our relationship was fraudulently based upon an imaginary amity—which had nothing to do with her random good will. Our meeting proved quite insignificant in regard to the words we said, but already no barriers divided us; and when that night I happened to be seated beside her at supper, I shamelessly tested the extent of her secret patience.

Then she vanished again; and a year later my wife and I were seeing my brother off to Posen, and when the train had gone, and we were moving toward the exit along the other side of the platform, suddenly near a car of the Paris express I saw Nina, her face buried in the bouquet she held, in the midst of a group of people whom she had befriended without my knowledge and who stood in a circle gaping at her as idlers gape at a street row, a lost child, or the victim of an accident. Brightly she signaled to me with her flowers; I introduced her to Elena, and in that life-quickening atmosphere of a big railway station where everything is something trembling on the brink of something else, thus to be clutched and cherished, the exchange of a few words was enough to enable two totally dissimilar women to start calling each other by their pet names the very next time they met. That day, in the blue shade of the Paris car, Ferdinand was first mentioned: I learned with a ridiculous pang that she was about to marry him. Doors were beginning to slam; she quickly but piously kissed her friends, climbed into the vestibule, disappeared; and then I saw her through the glass settling herself in her compartment, having suddenly forgotten about us or passed into another world, and we all, our hands in our pockets, seemed to be spying upon an utterly unsuspecting life moving in that aquarium dimness, until she grew aware of us and drummed on the windowpane, then raised her eyes, fumbling at the frame as if hanging a picture, but nothing happened; some fellow passenger helped her, and she leaned out, audible and real, beaming with pleasure; one of us, keeping up with the stealthily gliding car, handed her a magazine and a Tauchnitz (she read English only when traveling); all was slipping away with beautiful smoothness, and I held a platform ticket crumpled beyond recognition, while a song of the last century (connected, it has been rumored, with some Parisian drama of love) kept ringing and ringing in my head, having emerged, God knows why, from the music box of memory, a sobbing ballad which often used to be sung by an old maiden aunt of mine, with a face as yellow as Russian church wax, but whom nature had given such a powerful, ecstatically full voice that it seemed to swallow her up in the glory of a fiery cloud as soon as she would begin:

> On dit que tu te maries,
> tu sais que j'en vais mourir,

and that melody, the pain, the offense, the link between hymen and death evoked by the rhythm, and the voice itself of the dead singer, which accompanied the recollection as the sole owner of the song, gave me no rest for several hours after Nina's departure and even later arose at increasing intervals like the last flat little waves sent to the beach by a passing ship, lapping ever more infrequently and dreamily, or like the bronze agony of a vibrating belfry after the bell ringer has already reseated himself in the cheerful circle of his family. And another year or two later, I was in Paris on business; and one morning on the landing of a hotel, where I had been looking up a film-actor fellow, there she was again, clad in a gray tailored suit, waiting for the elevator to take her down, a key dangling from her fingers. "Ferdinand has gone fencing," she said conversationally; her eyes rested on the lower part of my face as if she were lip reading, and after a moment of reflection (her amatory comprehension was matchless), she turned and rapidly swaying on slender ankles led me along the sea-blue carpeted passage. A chair at the door of her room supported a tray with the remains of breakfast—a honey-stained knife, crumbs on the gray porcelain; but the room had already been done, and because of our sudden draft a wave of muslin embroidered with white dahlias got sucked in, with a shudder and knock, between the responsive halves of the French window, and only when the door had been locked did they let go that curtain with something like a blissful sigh; and a little later I stepped out on the diminutive cast-iron balcony beyond to inhale a combined smell of dry maple leaves and gasoline—the dregs of the hazy blue morning street; and as I did not yet realize the presence of that growing morbid pathos which was to embitter so my subsequent meetings with Nina, I was probably quite as collected and carefree as she was, when from the hotel I accompanied her to some office or other to trace a suitcase she had lost, and thence to the café where her husband was holding session with his court of the moment.

I will not mention the name (and what bits of it I happen to give here appear in decorous disguise) of that man, that Franco-Hungarian writer. . . . I would rather not dwell upon him at all, but I cannot help it—he is surging up from under my pen. Today one does not hear much about him; and this is good, for it proves that I was right in resisting his evil spell, right in experiencing a creepy chill down my spine whenever this or that new book of his touched my hand. The fame of his likes circulates briskly but soon grows heavy and stale; and as for history it will limit his life story to the dash between two dates. Lean and arrogant, with some poisonous pun ever ready to fork out and quiver at you, and with a strange look of expectancy in his dull brown veiled eyes, this false wag had, I daresay, an irresistible effect on small rodents. Having mastered the art of verbal invention to perfection, he particularly prided himself on being a weaver of words, a title he valued higher than that of writer; personally, I never could understand what was the good of thinking up books, of penning things that had not really happened in some way or other; and I remember once saying to him as I braved the mockery of his encouraging nods that, were I a writer, I should allow only my heart to have imagination, and for the rest rely upon memory, that long-drawn sunset shadow of one's personal truth.

I had known his books before I knew him; a faint disgust was already replacing the aesthetic pleasure which I had suffered his first novel to give me. At the beginning of his career, it had been possible perhaps to distinguish some human landscape, some old garden, some dream-familiar disposition of trees through the stained glass of his prodigious prose . . . but with every new book the tints grew still more dense, the gules and purpure still more ominous; and today one can no longer see anything at all through that blazoned, ghastly rich glass, and it seems that were one to break it, nothing but a perfectly black void would face one's shivering soul. But how dangerous he was in his prime, what venom he squirted, with what whips he lashed when provoked! The tornado of his passing satire left a barren waste where felled oaks lay in a row, and the dust still twisted, and the unfortunate author of some adverse review, howling with pain, spun like a top in the dust.

At the time we met, his "*Passage à niveau*" was being acclaimed in

Paris; he was, as they say, "surrounded," and Nina (whose adaptability was an amazing substitute for the culture she lacked) had already assumed if not the part of a muse at least that of a soul mate and subtle adviser, following Ferdinand's creative convolutions and loyally sharing his artistic tastes; for although it is wildly improbable that she had ever waded through a single volume of his, she had a magic knack of gleaning all the best passages from the shop talk of literary friends.

An orchestra of women was playing when we entered the café; first I noted the ostrich thigh of a harp reflected in one of the mirror-faced pillars, and then I saw the composite table (small ones drawn together to form a long one) at which, with his back to the plush wall, Ferdinand was presiding; and for a moment his whole attitude, the position of his parted hands, and the faces of his table companions all turned toward him reminded me in a grotesque, nightmarish way of something I did not quite grasp, but when I did so in retrospect, the suggested comparison struck me as hardly less sacrilegious than the nature of his art itself. He wore a white turtle-neck sweater under a tweed coat; his glossy hair was combed back from the temples, and above it cigarette smoke hung like a halo; his bony, Pharaohlike face was motionless: the eyes alone roved this way and that, full of dim satisfaction. Having forsaken the two or three obvious haunts where naïve amateurs of Montparnassian life would have expected to find him, he had started patronizing this perfectly bourgeois establishment because of his peculiar sense of humor, which made him derive ghoulish fun from the pitiful *specialité de la maison*—this orchestra composed of half a dozen weary-looking, self-conscious ladies interlacing mild harmonies on a crammed platform and not knowing, as he put it, what to do with their motherly bosoms, quite superfluous in the world of music. After each number he would be convulsed by a fit of epileptic applause, which the ladies had stopped acknowledging and which was already arousing, I thought, certain doubts in the minds of the proprietor of the café and its fundamental customers, but which seemed highly diverting to Ferdinand's friends. Among these I recall: an artist with an impeccably bald though slightly chipped head, which under various pretexts he constantly painted into his eye-and-guitar canvases; a poet, whose special gag was the ability to represent, if you asked him, Adam's Fall by means of five matches; a humble business man who financed surrealist ventures (and paid for the *apértifs*) if permitted to print in a corner eulogistic allusions to the actress he kept; a pianist, presentable insofar as the face was concerned, but with a dreadful expression of the fingers; a jaunty but linguistically impotent Soviet writer fresh from Moscow, with an old pipe and a new wrist watch, who was completely and ridiculously unaware of the sort of company he was in; there were several other gentlemen present who have become confused in my memory, and doubtless two or three of the lot had been intimate with Nina. She was the only woman at the table; there she stooped, eagerly sucking at a straw, the level of her lemonade sinking with a kind of childish celerity, and only when the last drop had gurgled and squeaked, and she had pushed away the straw with her tongue, only then did I finally catch her eye, which I had been obstinately seeking, still not being able to cope with the fact that she had had time to forget what had occurred earlier in the morning—to forget it so thoroughly that upon meeting my glance, she replied with a blank questioning smile, and only after peering more closely did she remember suddenly what kind of answering smile I was expecting. Meanwhile, Ferdinand (the ladies having temporarily left the platform after pushing away their instruments like so many pieces of furniture) was juicily drawing his cronies' attention to the figure of an elderly luncher in a far corner of the café, who had, as some Frenchmen for some reason or other have, a little red ribbon or something on his coat lapel and whose gray beard combined with his mustaches to form a cosy yellowish nest for his sloppily munching mouth. Somehow the trappings of old age always amused Ferdie.

I did not stay long in Paris, but that week proved sufficient to engender between him and me that fake chumminess the imposing of which he had such a talent for. Subsequently I even turned out to be of some use to him: my firm acquired the film rights of one of his more intelligible stories, and then he had a good time pestering me with telegrams. As the years passed, we found ourselves every now and then beaming at each other in some place, but I never felt at ease in his presence, and that day in Fialta, too, I experienced a familiar depression upon learning that he was on the prowl nearby; one thing, however, considerably cheered me up: the flop of his recent play.

And here he was coming toward us, garbed in an absolutely waterproof coat with belt and pocket flaps, a camera across his shoulder, double rubber soles to his shoes, sucking with an imperturbability that was meant to be funny a long stick of moonstone candy, that specialty of Fialta's. Beside him, walked the dapper, doll-like, rosy Segur, a lover of art and a perfect fool; I never could discover for what purpose Ferdinand needed him; and I still hear Nina exclaiming with a moaning tenderness that did not commit her to anything: "Oh, he is such a darling, Segur!" They approached; Ferdinand and I greeted each other lustily, trying to crowd into hand shake and back slap as much fervor as possible, knowing by experience that actually that was all but pretending it was only a preface; and it always happened like that: after every separation we met to the accompaniment of strings being excitedly tuned, in a bustle of geniality, in the hubbub of sentiments taking their seats; but the ushers would close the doors, and after that no one was admitted.

Segur complained to me about the weather, and at first I did not understand what he was talking about; even if the moist, gray, greenhouse essence of Fialta might be called "weather," it was just as much outside of anything that could serve us as a topic of conversation as was, for instance, Nina's slender elbow, which I was holding between finger and thumb, or a bit of tin foil someone had dropped, shining in the middle of the cobbled street in the distance.

We four moved on, vague purchases still looming ahead. "God, what an Indian!" Ferdinand suddenly exclaimed with fierce relish, violently nudging me and pointing at a poster. Further on, near a fountain, he gave his stick of candy to a native child, a swarthy girl with beads round her pretty neck; we stopped to wait for him: he crouched saying something to her, addressing her sooty-black lowered eyelashes, and then he caught up with us, grinning and making one of those remarks with which he loved to spice his speech. Then his attention was drawn by an unfortunate object exhibited in a souvenir shop: a dreadful marble imitation of Mount St. George showing a black tunnel at its base, which turned out to be the mouth of an inkwell, and with a compartment for pens in the semblance of railroad tracks. Open-mouthed, quivering, all agog with sardonic triumph, he turned that dusty, cumbersome, and perfectly irresponsible thing in his hands, paid without bargaining, and with his mouth still open came out carrying the monster. Like some autocrat who surrounds himself with hunchbacks and dwarfs, he would become attached to this or that hideous object; this infatuation might last from five minutes to several days or even longer if the thing happened to be animate.

Nina wistfully alluded to lunch, and seizing the opportunity when Ferdinand and Segur stopped at a post office, I hastened to lead her away. I still wonder what exactly she meant to me, that small dark woman of the narrow shoulders and "lyrical limbs" (to quote the expression of a mincing émigré poet, one of the few men who had sighed platonically after her), and still less do I understand what was the purpose of fate in bringing us constantly together. I did not see her for quite a long while after my sojourn in Paris, and then one day when I came home from my office I found her having tea with my wife and examining on her silk-hosed hand, with her wedding ring gleaming through, the texture of some stockings bought cheap in Tauentzienstrasse. Once I was shown her photograph in a fashion magazine full of autumn leaves and gloves and wind-swept golf links. On a certain Christmas she sent me a picture post card with snow and stars. On a Riviera beach she almost escaped my notice behind her dark glasses and terra-cotta tan. Another day, having dropped in on an ill-timed errand at the house of some strangers where a party was in progress, I saw her scarf and fur coat among alien scarecrows on a coat rack. In a bookshop she nodded to me from a page of one of her husband's stories, a page referring to an episodic servant girl, but smuggling in Nina in spite of the author's intention: "Her face," he wrote, "was rather nature's snapshot than a meticulous portrait, so that when . . . tried to imagine it, all he could visualize were fleeting glimpses of disconnected features: the downy outline of her pommettes in the sun, the amber-tinted brown darkness of quick eyes, lips shaped into a friendly smile which was always ready to change into an ardent kiss."

Again and again she hurriedly appeared in the margins of my life, without influencing in the least its basic text. One summer morning (Friday—because housemaids were thumping out carpets in the sun-dusted yard), my family was away in the country and I was lolling and smoking in bed when I heard the bell ring with tremendous violence—and there she was in the hall having burst in to leave (incidentally) a hairpin and (mainly) a trunk illuminated with hotel labels, which a fortnight later was retrieved for her by a nice Austrian boy, who (according to intangible but sure symptoms) belonged to the same very cosmopolitan association of which I was a member. Occasionally, in the middle of a conversation her name would be mentioned, and she would run down the steps of a chance sentence, without turning her head. While traveling in the Pyrenees, I spent a week at the château belonging to people with whom she and Ferdinand happened to be staying, and I shall never forget my first night there: how I waited, how certain I was that without my having to tell her she would steal to my room, how she did not come, and the din thousands of crickets made in the delirious depth of the rocky garden dripping with moonlight, the mad bubbling brooks, and my struggle between blissful southern fatigue after a long day of hunting on the screes and the wild thirst for her stealthy coming, low laugh, pink ankles above the swan's down trimming of high-heeled slippers; but the night raved on, and she did not come, and when next day, in the course of a general ramble in the mountains, I told her of my waiting, she clasped her hands in dismay—and at once with a rapid glance estimated whether the backs of the gesticulating Ferd and his friend had sufficiently receded. I remember talking to her on the telephone across half of Europe (on her husband's business) and not recognizing at first her eager barking voice; and I remember once dreaming of her: I dreamt that my eldest girl had run in to tell me the doorman was sorely in trouble—and when I had gone down to him, I saw lying on a trunk, a roll of burlap under her head, pale-lipped and wrapped in a woolen kerchief, Nina fast asleep, as miserable refugees sleep in Godforsaken railway stations. And regardless of what happened to me or to her, in between, we never discussed anything, as we never thought of each other during the intervals in our destiny, so that when we met the pace of life altered at once, all its atoms were recombined, and we lived in another, lighter time-medium, which was measured not by the lengthy separations but by those few meetings of which a short, supposedly frivolous life was thus artificially formed. And with each new meeting I grew more and more apprehensive; no—I did not experience any inner emotional collapse, the shadow of tragedy did not haunt our revels, my married life remained unimpaired, while on the other hand her eclectic husband ignored her casual affairs although deriving some profit from them in the way of pleasant and useful connections. I grew apprehensive because something lovely, delicate, and unrepeatable was being wasted: something which I abused by snapping off poor bright bits in gross haste while neglecting the modest but true core which perhaps it kept offering me in a pitiful whisper. I was apprehensive because, in the long run, I was somehow accepting Nina's life, the lies, the futility, the gibberish of that life. Even in the absence of any sentimental discord, I felt myself bound to seek for a rational, if not moral, interpretation of my existence, and this meant choosing between the world in which I sat for my portrait, with my wife, my young daughters, the Doberman pinscher (idyllic garlands, a signet ring, a slender cane), between that happy, wise, and good world . . . and what? Was there any practical chance of life together with Nina, life I could barely imagine, for it would be penetrated, I knew, with a passionate, intolerable bitterness and every moment of it would be aware of a past, teeming with protean partners. No, the thing was absurd. And moreover was she not chained to her husband by something stronger than love—the stanch friendship between two convicts? Absurd! But then what should I have done with you, Nina, how should I have disposed of the store of sadness that had gradually accumulated as a result of our seemingly carefree, but really hopeless meetings?

Fialta consists of the old town and of the new one; here and there, past and present are interlaced, struggling either to disentangle themselves or to thrust each other out; each one has its own methods: the newcomer fights honestly—importing palm trees, setting up smart tourist agencies, painting with creamy lines the red smoothness of tennis courts; whereas the sneaky old-timer creeps out from behind a corner in the shape of some little street on crutches or the steps of stairs leading nowhere. On our way to the hotel, we passed a half-built white villa, full of litter within, on a wall of which again the same elephants, their monstrous baby knees wide apart, sat on huge, gaudy drums; in ethereal bundles the equestrienne (already with a penciled mustache) was resting on a broad-backed steed; and a tomato-nosed clown was walking a tightrope, balancing an umbrella ornamented with those recurrent stars—a vague symbolic recollection of the heavenly fatherland of circus performers. Here, in the Riviera part of Fialta, the wet gravel crunched in a more luxurious manner, and the lazy sighing of the sea was more audible. In the back yard of the hotel, a kitchen boy armed with a knife was pursuing a hen which was clucking madly as it raced for its life. A bootblack offered me his ancient throne with a toothless smile. Under the plane trees stood a motorcycle of German make, a mud-bespattered limousine, and a yellow long-bodied Icarus that looked like a giant scarab: ("That's ours—Segur's, I mean," said Nina, adding, "Why don't you come with us, Victor?" although she knew very well that I could not come); in the lacquer of its elytra a gouache of sky and branches was engulfed; in the metal of one of the bomb-shaped lamps we ourselves were momentarily reflected, lean filmland pedestrians passing along the convex surface; and then, after a few steps, I glanced back and foresaw, in an almost optical sense, as it were, what really happened an hour or so later: the three of them wearing motoring helmets, getting in, smiling and waving to me, transparent to me like ghosts, with the color of the world shining through them, and then they were moving, receding, diminishing (Nina's last ten-fingered farewell); but actually the automobile was still standing quite motionless, smooth and whole like an egg, and Nina under my outstretched arm was entering a laurel-flanked doorway, and as we sat down we could see through the window Ferdinand and Segur, who had come by another way, slowly approaching.

There was no one on the veranda where we lunched except the Englishman I had recently observed; in front of him, a long glass containing a bright crimson drink threw an oval reflection on the tablecloth. In his eyes, I noticed the same bloodshot desire, but now it was in no sense related to Nina; that avid look was not directed at her at all, but was fixed on the upper right-hand corner of the broad window near which he was sitting.

Having pulled the gloves off her small thin hands, Nina, for the last time in her life, was eating the shellfish of which she was so fond. Ferdinand also busied himself with food, and I took advantage of his hunger to begin a conversation which gave me the semblance of power over him: to be specific, I mentioned his recent failure. After a brief period of fashionable religious conversion, during which grace descended upon him and he undertook some rather ambiguous pilgrimages, which ended in a decidedly scandalous adventure, he had turned his dull eyes toward barbarous Moscow. Now, frankly speaking, I have always been irritated by the complacent conviction that a ripple of stream consciousness, a few healthy obscenities, and a dash of communism in any old slop pail will alchemically and automatically produce ultramodern literature; and I will contend until I am shot that art as soon as it is brought into contact with politics inevitably sinks to the level of any ideological trash. In Ferdinand's case, it is true, all this was rather irrelevant: the muscles of his muse were exceptionally strong, to say nothing of the fact that he didn't care a damn for the plight of the underdog; but because of certain obscurely mischievous undercurrents of that sort, his art had become still more repulsive. Except for a few snobs none had understood the play; I had not seen it myself, but could well imagine that elaborate Kremlinesque night along the impossible spirals of which he spun various wheels of dismembered symbols; and now, not without pleasure, I asked him whether he had read a recent bit of criticism about himself.

"Criticism!" he exclaimed. "Fine criticism! Every slick jackanapes sees fit to read me a lecture. Ignorance of my work is their bliss. My books are touched gingerly, as one touches something that may go bang. Criticism! They are examined from every point of view except the essential one. It is as if a naturalist, in describing the equine genus, started to jaw about saddles or Mme. de V. (he named a well-known literary hostess, who indeed strongly resembled a grinning horse). I would like some of that pigeon's blood, too," he continued in the same loud, ripping voice, addressing the waiter, who understood his desire only after he had looked in the direction of the long-nailed finger which unceremoniously pointed at the Englishman's glass. For some reason or other, Segur mentioned Ruby Rose, the lady who painted flowers on her breast, and the conversation took on a less insulting character. Meanwhile the big Englishman suddenly made up his mind, got up on a chair, stepped from there on to the window sill, and stretched up till he reached that coveted corner of the frame where rested a compact furry moth, which he deftly slipped into a pillbox.

". . . rather like Wouwerman's white horse," said Ferdinand, in regard to something he was discussing with Segur.

"*Tu es très hippique ce matin,*" remarked the latter.

Soon they both left to telephone. Ferdinand was particularly fond of long-distance calls, and particularly good at endowing them, no matter what the distance, with a friendly warmth when it was necessary, as for instance now, to make sure of free lodgings.

From afar came the sounds of music—a trumpet, a zither. Nina and I set out to wander again. The circus on its way to Fialta had apparently sent out runners: an advertising pageant was tramping by; but we did not catch its head, as it had turned uphill into a side alley: the gilded back of some carriage was receding, a man in a burnoose led a camel, a file of four mediocre Indians carried placards on poles, and behind them, by special permission, a tourist's small son in a sailor suit sat reverently on a tiny pony.

We wandered by a café where the tables were now almost dry but still empty; the waiter was examining (I hope he adopted it later) a horrible foundling, the absurd inkstand affair, stowed by Ferdinand on the banisters in passing. At the next corner we were attracted by an old stone stairway, and we climbed up, and I kept looking at the sharp angle of Nina's step as she ascended, raising her skirt, its narrowness requiring the same gesture as formerly length had done; she diffused a familiar warmth, and going up beside her, I recalled the last time we had come together. It had been in a Paris house, with many people around, and my dear friend Jules Darboux, wishing to do me a refined aesthetic favor, had touched my sleeve and said, "I want you to meet—" and led me to Nina, who sat in the corner of a couch, her body folded Z-wise, with an ash tray at her heel, and she took a long turquoise cigarette holder from her lips and joyfully, slowly exclaimed, "Well, of all people—" and then all evening my heart felt like breaking, as I passed from group to group with a sticky glass in my fist, now and then looking at her from a distance (she did not look . . .), and listened to scraps of conversation, and overheard one man saying to another, "Funny, how they all smell alike, burnt leaf through whatever perfume they use, those angular dark-haired girls," and as it often happens, a trivial remark related to some unknown topic coiled and clung to one's own intimate recollection, a parasite of its sadness.

At the top of the steps, we found ourselves on a rough kind of terrace. From here one could see the delicate outline of the dove-colored Mount St. George with a cluster of bone-white flecks (some hamlet) on one of its slopes; the smoke of an indiscernible train undulated along its rounded base—and suddenly disappeared; still lower, above the jumble of roofs, one could perceive a solitary cypress, resembling the moist-twirled black tip of a water-color brush; to the right, one caught a glimpse of the sea, which was gray, with silver wrinkles. At our feet lay a rusty old key, and on the wall of the half-ruined house adjoining the terrace, the ends of some wire still remained hanging. . . . I reflected that formerly there had been life here, a family had enjoyed the coolness at nightfall, clumsy children had colored pictures by the light of a lamp. . . . We lingered there as if listening to something; Nina, who stood on higher ground, put a hand on my shoulder and smiled, and carefully, so as not to crumple her smile, kissed me. With an unbearable force, I relived (or so it now seems to me) all that had ever been between us beginning with a similar kiss; and I said (substituting for our cheap, formal "thou" that strangely full and expressive "you" to which the circumnavigator, enriched all around, returns), "Look here—what if I love you?" Nina glanced at me, I repeated those words, I wanted to add . . . but something like a bat passed swiftly across her face, a quick, queer, almost ugly expression, and she, who would utter coarse words with perfect simplicity, became embarrassed; I also felt awkward. . . . "Never mind, I was only joking," I hastened to say, lightly encircling her waist. From somewhere a firm bouquet of small dark, unselfishly smelling violets appeared in her hands, and before she returned to her husband and car, we stood for a little while longer by the stone parapet, and our romance was even more hopeless than it had ever been. But the stone was as warm as flesh, and suddenly I understood something I had been seeing without understanding—why a piece of tin foil had sparkled so on the pavement, why the gleam of a glass had trembled on a tablecloth, why the sea was ashimmer: somehow, by imperceptible degrees, the white sky above Fialta had got saturated with sunshine, and now it was sun-pervaded throughout, and this brimming white radiance grew broader and broader, all dissolved in it, all vanished, all passed, and I stood on the station platform of Mlech with a freshly bought newspaper, which told me that the yellow car I had seen under the plane trees had suffered a crash beyond Fialta, having run at full speed into the truck of a traveling circus entering the town, a crash from which Ferdinand and his friend, those invulnerable rogues, those salamanders of fate, those basilisks of good fortune, had escaped with local and temporary injury to their scales, while Nina, in spite of her long-standing, faithful imitation of them, had turned out after all to be mortal.

The Things They Carried

by Tim O'Brien

Introduced by Bobbie Ann Mason

OF ALL THE STORIES I'VE READ IN THE LAST DECADE, TIM O'BRIEN'S "The Things They Carried" hit me hardest. It knocked me down, just as if a hundred-pound rucksack had been thrown right at me. The weight of the things the American soldiers carried on their interminable journey through the jungle in Vietnam sets the tone for this story. But the power of it is not just the poundage they were humping on their backs. The story's list of "things they carried" extends to the burden of memory and desire and confusion and grief. It's the weight of America's involvement in the war. You can hardly bear to contemplate all that this story evokes with its matter-of-fact yet electrifying details.

The way this story works makes me think of the Vietnam Veterans Memorial in Washington. The memorial is just a list of names, in a simple, dark—yet soaring—design. Its power is in the simplicity of presentation and in what lies behind each of those names.

In the story, there is a central incident, the company's first casualty on its march through the jungle. But the immediate drama is the effort—by the main character, by the narrator, by the writer himself—to contain the emotion, to carry it. When faced with a subject almost too great to manage or confront, the mind wants to organize, to categorize, to simplify. Restraint and matter-of-factness are appropriate deflective techniques for dealing with pain, and they work on several levels in the story. Sometimes it is more affecting to see someone dealing with pain than it is to know about the pain itself. That's what's happening here.

By using the simplicity of a list and trying to categorize the simple items the soldiers carried, O'Brien reveals the real terror of the war itself. And the categories go from the tangible—foot powder, photographs, chewing gum—to the intangible. They carried disease; memory. When it rained, they carried the sky. The weight of what they carried moves expansively, opens out, grows from the stuff in the rucksack to the whole weight of the American war chest, with its litter of ammo and packaging through the landscape of Vietnam. And then it moves back, away from the huge outer world, back into the interior of the self. The story details the way they carried themselves (dignity, laughter, words) as well as what they carried inside (fear, "emotional baggage").

And within the solemn effort to list and categorize, a story unfolds. PFC Ted Lavender, a grunt who carries tranquilizers, is on his way back from relieving himself in the jungle when he is shot by a sniper. The irony and horror of it are unbearable. Almost instantaneously, it seems, the central character, Lieutenant Cross, changes from a romantic youth to a man of action and duty. With his new, hard clarity, he is carried forward by his determination not to be caught unprepared again. And the way he prepares to lead his group is to list his resolves. He has to assert power over the event by detaching himself. It is a life-and-death matter.

So this effort to detach and control becomes both the drama and the technique of the story. For it is our impulse to deal with unspeakable horror and sadness by fashioning some kind of order, a story, to clarify and contain our emotions. As the writer, Tim O'Brien stands back far enough not to be seen but not so far that he isn't in charge.

"They carried all they could bear, and then some, including a silent awe for the terrible power of the things they carried."

The Things They Carried

Tim O'Brien

First Lieutenant Jimmy Cross carried letters from a girl named Martha, a junior at Mount Sebastian College in New Jersey. They were not love letters, but Lieutenant Cross was hoping, so he kept them folded in plastic at the bottom of his rucksack. In the late afternoon, after a day's march, he would dig his foxhole, wash his hands under a canteen, unwrap the letters, hold them with the tips of his fingers, and spend the last hour of light pretending. He would imagine romantic camping trips into the White Mountains in New Hampshire. He would sometimes taste the envelope flaps, knowing her tongue had been there. More than anything, he wanted Martha to love him as he loved her, but the letters were mostly chatty, elusive on the matter of love. She was a virgin, he was almost sure. She was an English major at Mount Sebastian, and she wrote beautifully about her professors and roommates and midterm exams, about her respect for Chaucer and her great affection for Virginia Woolf. She often quoted lines of poetry; she never mentioned the war, except to say, Jimmy, take care of yourself. The letters weighed 10 ounces. They were signed Love, Martha, but Lieutenant Cross understood that Love was only a way of signing and did not mean what he sometimes pretended it meant. At dusk, he would carefully return the letters to his rucksack. Slowly, a bit distracted, he would get up and move among his men, checking the perimeter; then at full dark he would return to his hole and watch the night and wonder if Martha was a virgin.

The things they carried were largely determined by necessity. Among the necessities or near-necessities were P-38 can openers, pocket knives, heat tabs, wristwatches, dog tags, mosquito repellent, chewing gum, candy, cigarettes, salt tablets, packets of Kool-Aid, lighters, matches, sewing kits, Military Payment Certificates, C rations, and two or three canteens of water. Together, these items weighed between 15 and 20 pounds, depending upon a man's habits or rate of metabolism. Henry Dobbins, who was a big man, carried extra rations; he was especially fond of canned peaches in heavy syrup over pound cake. Dave Jensen, who practiced field hygiene, carried a toothbrush, dental floss, and several hotel-sized bars of soap he'd stolen on R&R in Sydney, Australia. Ted Lavender, who was scared, carried tranquilizers until he was shot in the head outside the village of Than Khe in mid-April. By necessity, and because it was SOP, they all carried steel helmets that weighed 5 pounds including the liner and camouflage cover. They carried the standard fatigue jackets and trousers. Very few carried underwear. On their feet they carried jungle boots—2.1 pounds—and Dave Jensen carried three pairs of socks and a can of Dr. Scholl's foot powder as a precaution against trench foot. Until he was shot, Ted Lavender carried six or seven ounces of premium dope, which for him was a necessity. Mitchell Sanders, the RTO, carried condoms. Norman Bowker carried a diary. Rat Kiley carried comic books. Kiowa, a devout Baptist, carried an illustrated New Testament that had been presented to him by his father, who taught Sunday school in Oklahoma City, Oklahoma. As a hedge against bad times, however, Kiowa also carried his grandmother's distrust of the white man, his grandfather's old hunting hatchet. Necessity dictated. Because the land was mined and booby-trapped, it was SOP for each man to carry a steel-centered, nylon-covered flak jacket, which weighed 6.7 pounds, but which on hot days seemed much heavier. Because you could die so quickly, each man carried at least one large compress bandage, usually in the helmet band for easy access. Because the nights were cold, and because the monsoons were wet, each carried a green plastic poncho that could be used as a raincoat or groundsheet or makeshift tent. With its quilted liner, the poncho weighed almost two pounds, but it was worth every ounce. In April, for instance, when Ted Lavender was shot, they used his poncho to wrap him up, then to carry him across the paddy, then to lift him into the chopper that took him away.

They were called legs or grunts.

To carry something was to hump it, as when Lieutenant Jimmy Cross humped his love for Martha up the hills and through the swamps. In its intransitive form, to hump meant to walk, or to march, but it implied burdens far beyond the intransitive.

Almost everyone humped photographs. In his wallet, Lieutenant Cross carried two photographs of Martha. The first was a Kodacolor snapshot signed Love, though he knew better. She stood against a brick wall. Her eyes were gray and neutral, her lips slightly open as she stared straight-on at the camera. At night, sometimes, Lieutenant Cross wondered who had taken the picture, because he knew she had boyfriends, because he loved her so much, and because he could see the shadow of the picture-taker spreading out against the brick wall. The second photograph had been clipped from the 1968 Mount Sebastian yearbook. It was an action shot—women's volleyball—and Martha was bent horizontal to the floor, reaching, the palms of her hands in sharp focus, the tongue taut, the expression frank and competitive. There was no visible sweat. She wore white gym shorts. Her legs, he thought, were almost certainly the legs of a virgin, dry and without hair, the left knee cocked and carrying her entire weight, which was just over one hundred pounds. Lieutenant Cross remembered touching that left knee. A dark theater, he remembered, and the movie was *Bonnie and Clyde,* and Martha wore a tweed skirt, and during the final scene, when he touched her knee, she turned and looked at him in a sad, sober way that made him pull his hand back, but he would always remember the feel of the tweed skirt and the knee beneath it and the sound of the gunfire that killed Bonnie and Clyde, how embarrassing it was, how slow and oppressive. He remembered kissing her good night at the dorm door. Right then, he thought, he should've done something brave. He should've carried her up the stairs to her room and tied her to the bed and touched that left knee all night long. He should've risked it. Whenever he looked at the photographs, he thought of new things he should've done.

What they carried was partly a function of rank, partly of field specialty.

As a first lieutenant and platoon leader, Jimmy Cross carried a compass, maps, code books, binoculars, and a .45-caliber pistol that weighed 2.9 pounds fully loaded. He carried a strobe light and the responsibility for the lives of his men.

As an RTO, Mitchell Sanders carried the PRC-25 radio, a killer, 26 pounds with its battery.

As a medic, Rat Kiley carried a canvas satchel filled with morphine and plasma and malaria tablets and surgical tape and comic books and all the things a medic must carry, including M&M's for especially bad wounds, for a total weight of nearly 20 pounds.

As a big man, therefore a machine gunner, Henry Dobbins carried the M-60, which weighed 23 pounds unloaded, but which was almost always loaded. In addition, Dobbins carried between 10 and 15 pounds of ammunition draped in belts across his chest and shoulders.

As PFCs or Spec 4s, most of them were common grunts and carried the standard M-16 gas-operated assault rifle. The weapon weighed 7.5 pounds unloaded, 8.2 pounds with its full 20-round magazine. Depending on numerous factors, such as topography and psychology, the riflemen carried anywhere from 12 to 20 magazines, usually in cloth bandoliers, adding on another 8.4 pounds at minimum, 14 pounds at maximum. When it was available, they also carried M-16 maintenance gear—rods and steel brushes and swabs and tubes of LSA oil—all of which weighed about a pound. Among the grunts, some carried the M-79 grenade launcher, 5.9 pounds unloaded, a reasonably light weapon except for the ammunition, which was heavy. A single round weighed 10 ounces. The typical load was 25 rounds. But Ted Lavender, who was scared, carried 34 rounds when he was shot and killed outside Than Khe, and he went down under an exceptional burden, more than 20 pounds of ammunition, plus the flak jacket and helmet and rations and water and toilet paper and tranquilizers and all the rest, plus the unweighed fear. He was dead weight. There was no twitching or flopping. Kiowa, who saw it happen, said it was like watching a rock fall, or a big sandbag or something—just boom, then down—not like the movies where the dead guy rolls around and does fancy spins and goes ass over teakettle—not like that, Kiowa said, the poor bastard just flat-fuck fell. Boom.

Down. Nothing else. It was a bright morning in mid-April. Lieutenant Cross felt the pain. He blamed himself. They stripped off Lavender's canteens and ammo, all the heavy things, and Rat Kiley said the obvious, the guy's dead, and Mitchell Sanders used his radio to report one U.S. KIA and to request a chopper. Then they wrapped Lavender in his poncho. They carried him out to a dry paddy, established security, and sat smoking the dead man's dope until the chopper came. Lieutenant Cross kept to himself. He pictured Martha's smooth young face, thinking he loved her more than anything, more than his men, and now Ted Lavender was dead because he loved her so much and could not stop thinking about her. When the dustoff arrived, they carried Lavender aboard. Afterward they burned Than Khe. They marched until dusk, then dug their holes, and that night Kiowa kept explaining how you had to be there, how fast it was, how the poor guy just dropped like so much concrete. Boom-down, he said. Like cement.

In addition to the three standard weapons—the M-60, M-16, and M-79—they carried whatever presented itself, or whatever seemed appropriate as a means of killing or staying alive. They carried catch-as-catch-can. At various times, in various situations, they carried M-14s and CAR-15s and Swedish Ks and grease guns and captured AK-47s and Chi-Coms and RPGs and Simonov carbines and black market Uzis and .38-caliber Smith & Wesson handguns and 66 mm LAWs and shotguns and silencers and blackjacks and bayonets and C-4 plastic explosives. Lee Strunk carried a slingshot; a weapon of last resort, he called it. Mitchell Sanders carried brass knuckles. Kiowa carried his grandfather's feathered hatchet. Every third or fourth man carried a Claymore antipersonnel mine—3.5 pounds with its firing device. They all carried fragmentation grenades—14 ounces each. They all carried at least one M-18 colored smoke grenade—24 ounces. Some carried CS or tear gas grenades. Some carried white phosphorus grenades. They carried all they could bear, and then some, including a silent awe for the terrible power of the things they carried.

In the first week of April, before Lavender died, Lieutenant Jimmy Cross received a good-luck charm from Martha. It was a simple pebble, an ounce at most. Smooth to the touch, it was a milky white color with flecks of orange and violet, oval-shaped, like a miniature egg. In the accompanying letter, Martha wrote that she had found the pebble on the Jersey shoreline, precisely where the land touched water at high tide, where things came together but also separated. It was this separate-but-together quality, she wrote, that had inspired her to pick up the pebble and to carry it in her breast pocket for several days, where it seemed weightless, and then to send it through the mail, by air, as a token of her truest feelings for him. Lieutenant Cross found this romantic. But he wondered what her truest feelings were, exactly, and what she meant by separate-but-together. He wondered how the tides and waves had come into play on that afternoon along the

Jersey shoreline when Martha saw the pebble and bent down to rescue it from geology. He imagined bare feet. Martha was a poet, with the poet's sensibilities, and her feet would be brown and bare, the toenails unpainted, the eyes chilly and somber like the ocean in March, and though it was painful, he wondered who had been with her that afternoon. He imagined a pair of shadows moving along the strip of sand where things came together but also separated. It was phantom jealousy, he knew, but he couldn't help himself. He loved her so much. On the march, through the hot days of early April, he carried the pebble in his mouth, turning it with his tongue, tasting sea salt and moisture. His mind wandered. He had difficulty keeping his attention on the war. On occasion he would yell at his men to spread out the column, to keep their eyes open, but then he would slip away into daydreams, just pretending, walking barefoot along the Jersey shore, with Martha, carrying nothing. He would feel himself rising. Sun and waves and gentle winds, all love and lightness.

What they carried varied by mission.

When a mission took them to the mountains, they carried mosquito netting, machetes, canvas tarps, and extra bug juice.

If a mission seemed especially hazardous, or if it involved a place they knew to be bad, they carried everything they could. In certain heavily mined AOs, where the land was dense with Toe Poppers and Bouncing Betties, they took turns humping a 28-pound mine detector. With its headphones and big sensing plate, the equipment was a stress on the lower back and shoulders, awkward to handle, often useless because of the shrapnel in the earth, but they carried it anyway, partly for safety, partly for the illusion of safety.

On ambush, or other night missions, they carried peculiar little odds and ends. Kiowa always took along his New Testament and a pair of moccasins for silence. Dave Jensen carried night-sight vitamins high in carotene. Lee Strunk carried his slingshot; ammo, he claimed, would never be a problem. Rat Kiley carried brandy and M&M's candy. Until he was shot, Ted Lavender carried the starlight scope, which weighed 6.3 pounds with its aluminum carrying case. Henry Dobbins carried his girlfriend's pantyhose wrapped around his neck as a comforter. They all carried ghosts. When dark came, they would move out single file across the meadows and paddies to their ambush coordinates, where they would quietly set up the Claymores and lie down and spend the night waiting.

Other missions were more complicated and required special equipment. In mid-April, it was their mission to search out and destroy the elaborate tunnel complexes in the Than Khe area south of Chu Lai. To blow the tunnels, they carried one-pound blocks of pentrite high explosives, four blocks to a man, 68 pounds in all. They carried wiring, detonators, and battery-powered clackers. Dave Jensen carried earplugs. Most often, before blowing the tunnels, they were ordered by higher command to search them, which was considered bad news, but by and large they just shrugged and carried out orders. Because he was a big man, Henry Dobbins was excused from tunnel duty. The others would draw numbers. Before Lavender died there were 17 men in the platoon, and whoever drew the number 17 would strip off his gear and crawl in headfirst with a flashlight and Lieutenant Cross's .45-caliber pistol. The rest of them would fan out as security. They would sit down or kneel, not facing the hole, listening to the ground beneath them, imagining cobwebs and ghosts, whatever was down there—the tunnel walls squeezing in—how the flashlight seemed impossibly heavy in the hand and how it was tunnel vision in the very strictest sense, compression in all ways, even time, and how you had to wiggle in—ass and elbows—a swallowed-up feeling—and how you found yourself worrying about odd things: Will your flashlight go dead? Do rats carry rabies? If you screamed, how far would the sound carry? Would your buddies hear it? Would they have the courage to drag you out? In some respects, though not many, the waiting was worse than the tunnel itself. Imagination was a killer.

On April 16, when Lee Strunk drew the number 17, he laughed and muttered something and went down quickly. The morning was hot and very still. Not good, Kiowa said. He looked at the tunnel opening, then out across a dry paddy toward the village of Than Khe. Nothing moved. No clouds or birds or people. As they waited, the men smoked and drank Kool-Aid, not talking much, feeling sympathy for Lee Strunk but also feeling the luck of the draw. You win some, you lose some, said Mitchell Sanders, and sometimes you settle for a rain check. It was a tired line and no one laughed.

Henry Dobbins ate a tropical chocolate bar. Ted Lavender popped a tranquilizer and went off to pee.

After five minutes, Lieutenant Jimmy Cross moved to the tunnel, leaned down, and examined the darkness. Trouble, he thought—a cave-in maybe. And then suddenly, without willing it, he was thinking about Martha. The stresses and fractures, the quick collapse, the two of them buried alive under all that weight. Dense, crushing love. Kneeling, watching the hole, he tried to concentrate on Lee Strunk and the war, all the dangers, but his love was too much for him, he felt paralyzed, he wanted to sleep inside her lungs and breathe her blood and be smothered. He wanted her to be a virgin and not a virgin, all at once. He wanted to know her. Intimate secrets: Why poetry? Why so sad? Why that grayness in her eyes? Why so alone? Not lonely, just alone—riding her bike across campus or sitting off by herself in the cafeteria—even dancing, she danced alone—and it was the aloneness that filled him with love. He remembered telling her that one evening. How she nodded and looked away. And how, later, when he kissed her, she received the kiss without returning it, her eyes wide open, not afraid, not a virgin's eyes, just flat and uninvolved.

Lieutenant Cross gazed at the tunnel. But he was not there. He was buried with Martha under the white sand at the Jersey shore. They were pressed together, and the pebble in his mouth was her tongue. He was smiling. Vaguely, he was aware of how quiet the day was, the sullen paddies, yet he could not bring himself to worry about matters of security. He was beyond that. He was just a kid at war, in love. He was twenty-four years old. He couldn't help it.

A few moments later Lee Strunk crawled out of the tunnel. He came up grinning, filthy but alive. Lieutenant Cross nodded and closed his eyes while the others clapped Strunk on the back and made jokes about rising from the dead.

Worms, Rat Kiley said. Right out of the grave. Fuckin' zombie.

The men laughed. They all felt great relief.

Spook city, said Mitchell Sanders.

Lee Strunk made a funny ghost sound, a kind of moaning, yet very happy, and right then, when Strunk made that high happy moaning sound, when he went *Ahhooooo,* right then Ted Lavender was shot in the head on his way back from peeing. He lay with his mouth open. The teeth were broken. There was a swollen black bruise under his left eye. The cheekbone was gone. Oh shit, Rat Kiley said, the guy's dead. The guy's dead, he kept saying, which seemed profound—the guy's dead. I mean really.

The things they carried were determined to some extent by superstition. Lieutenant Cross carried his good-luck pebble. Dave Jensen carried a rabbit's foot. Norman Bowker, otherwise a very gentle person, carried a thumb that had been presented to him as a gift by Mitchell Sanders. The thumb was dark brown, rubbery to the touch, and weighed four ounces at most. It had been cut from a VC corpse, a boy of fifteen or sixteen. They'd found him at the bottom of an irrigation ditch, badly burned, flies in his mouth and eyes. The boy wore black shorts and sandals. At the time of his death he had been carrying a pouch of rice, a rifle, and three magazines of ammunition.

You want my opinion, Mitchell Sanders said, there's a definite moral here.

He put his hand on the dead boy's wrist. He was quiet for a time, as if counting a pulse, then he patted the stomach, almost affectionately, and used Kiowa's hunting hatchet to remove the thumb.

Henry Dobbins asked what the moral was.

Moral?

You know. *Moral.*

Sanders wrapped the thumb in toilet paper and handed it across to Norman Bowker. There was no blood. Smiling, he kicked the boy's head, watched the flies scatter, and said, It's like with that old TV show—Paladin. Have gun, will travel.

Henry Dobbins thought about it.

Yeah, well, he finally said. I don't see no moral.

There it *is,* man.

Fuck off.

* * *

They carried USO stationery and pencils and pens. They carried Sterno, safety pins, trip flares, signal flares, spools of wire, razor blades, chewing tobacco, liberated joss sticks and statuettes of the smiling Buddha, candles, grease pencils, *The Stars and Stripes,* fingernail clippers, Psy Ops leaflets, bush hats, bolos, and much more. Twice a week, when the resupply choppers came in, they carried hot chow in green mermite cans and large canvas bags filled with iced beer and soda pop. They carried plastic water containers, each with a two-gallon capacity. Mitchell Sanders carried a set of starched tiger fatigues for special occasions. Henry Dobbins carried Black Flag insecticide. Dave Jensen carried empty sandbags that could be filled at night for added protection. Lee Strunk carried tanning lotion. Some things they carried in common. Taking turns, they carried the big PRC-77 scrambler radio, which weighed 30 pounds with its battery. They shared the weight of memory. They took up what others could no longer bear. Often, they carried each other, the wounded or weak. They carried infections. They carried chess sets, basketballs, Vietnamese-English dictionaries, insignia of rank, Bronze Stars and Purple Hearts, plastic cards imprinted with the Code of Conduct. They carried diseases, among them malaria and dysentery. They carried lice and ringworm and leeches and paddy algae and various rots and molds. They carried the land itself—Vietnam, the place, the soil—a powdery orange-red dust that covered their boots and fatigues and faces. They carried the sky. The whole atmosphere, they carried it, the humidity, the monsoons, the stink of fungus and decay, all of it, they carried gravity. They moved like mules. By daylight they took sniper fire, at night they were mortared, but it was not battle, it was just the endless march, village to village, without purpose, nothing won or lost. They marched for the sake of the march. They plodded along slowly, dumbly, leaning forward against the heat, unthinking, all blood and bone, simple grunts, soldiering with their legs, toiling up the hills and down into the paddies and across the rivers and up again and down, just humping, one step and then the next and then another, but no volition, no will, because it was automatic, it was anatomy, and the war was entirely a matter of posture and carriage, the hump was everything, a kind of inertia, a kind of emptiness, a dullness of desire and intellect and conscience and hope and human sensibility. Their principles were in their feet. Their calculations were biological. They had no sense of strategy or mission. They searched the villages without knowing what to look for, not caring, kicking over jars of rice, frisking children and old men, blowing tunnels, sometimes setting fires and sometimes not, then forming up and moving on to the next village, then other villages, where it would always be the same. They carried their own lives. The pressures were enormous. In the heat of early afternoon, they would remove their helmets and flak jackets, walking bare, which was dangerous but which helped ease the strain. They would often discard things along the route of march. Purely for comfort, they would throw away rations, blow their Claymores and grenades, no matter, because by nightfall the resupply choppers would arrive with more of the same, then a day or two later still more, fresh watermelons and crates of ammunition and sunglasses and woolen sweaters—the resources were stunning—sparklers for the Fourth of July, colored eggs for Easter—it was the great American war chest—the fruits of science, the smokestacks, the canneries, the arsenals at Hartford, the Minnesota forests, the machine shops, the vast fields of corn and wheat—they carried like freight trains; they carried it on their backs and shoulders—and for all the ambiguities of Vietnam, all the mysteries and unknowns, there was at least the single abiding certainty that they would never be at a loss for things to carry.

After the chopper took Lavender away, Lieutenant Jimmy Cross led his men into the village of Than Khe. They burned everything. They shot chickens and dogs, they trashed the village well, they called in artillery and watched the wreckage, then they marched for several hours through the hot afternoon, and then at dusk, while Kiowa explained how Lavender died, Lieutenant Cross found himself trembling.

He tried not to cry. With his entrenching tool, which weighed five pounds, he began digging a hole in the earth.

He felt shame. He hated himself. He had loved Martha more than his men, and as a consequence Lavender was now dead, and this was something he would have to carry like a stone in his stomach for the rest of the war.

All he could do was dig. He used his entrenching tool like an ax, slashing, feeling both love and hate, and then later, when it was full dark, he sat at the bottom of his foxhole and wept. It went on for a long while. In part, he was grieving for Ted Lavender, but mostly it was for Martha, and for himself, because she belonged to another world, which was not quite real, and because she was a junior at Mount Sebastian College in New Jersey, a poet and a virgin and uninvolved, and because he realized she did not love him and never would.

Like cement, Kiowa whispered in the dark. I swear to God—boom, down. Not a word.

I've heard this, said Norman Bowker.

A pisser, you know? Still zipping himself up. Zapped while zipping.

All right, fine. That's enough.

Yeah, but you had to see it, the guy just—

I *heard,* man. Cement. So why not shut the fuck *up?*

Kiowa shook his head sadly and glanced over at the hole where Lieutenant Jimmy Cross sat watching the night. The air was thick and wet. A warm dense fog had settled over the paddies and there was the stillness that precedes rain.

After a time Kiowa sighed.

One thing for sure, he said. The lieutenant's in some deep hurt. I mean that crying jag—the way he was carrying on—it wasn't fake or anything, it was real heavy-duty hurt. The man cares.

Sure, Norman Bowker said.

Say what you want, the man does care.

We all got problems.

Not Lavender.

No, I guess not, Bowker said. Do me a favor, though.

Shut up?

That's a smart Indian. Shut up.

Shrugging, Kiowa pulled off his boots. He wanted to say more, just to lighten up his sleep, but instead he opened his New Testament and arranged it beneath his head as a pillow. The fog made things seem hollow and unattached. He tried not to think about Ted Lavender, but then he was thinking how fast it was, no drama, down and dead, and how it was hard to feel anything except surprise. It seemed unchristian. He wished he could find some great sadness, or even anger, but the emotion wasn't there and he couldn't make it happen. Mostly he felt pleased to be alive. He liked the smell of the New Testament under his cheek, the leather and ink and paper and glue, whatever the chemicals were. He liked hearing the sounds of night. Even his fatigue, it felt fine, the stiff muscles and the prickly awareness of his own body, a floating feeling. He enjoyed not being dead. Lying there, Kiowa admired Lieutenant Jimmy Cross's capacity for grief. He wanted to share the man's pain, he wanted to care as Jimmy Cross cared. And yet when he closed his eyes, all he could think was Boom-down, and all he could feel was the pleasure of having his boots off and the fog curling in around him and the damp soil and the Bible smells and the plush comfort of night.

After a moment Norman Bowker sat up in the dark.

What the hell, he said. You want to talk, *talk*. Tell it to me.

Forget it.

No, man, go on. One thing I hate, it's a silent Indian.

For the most part they carried themselves with poise, a kind of dignity. Now and then, however, there were times of panic, when they squealed or wanted to squeal but couldn't, when they twitched and made moaning sounds and covered their heads and said Dear Jesus and flopped around on the earth and fired their weapons blindly and cringed and sobbed and begged for the noise to stop and went wild and made stupid promises to themselves and to God and to their mothers and fathers, hoping not to die. In different ways, it happened to all of them. Afterward, when the firing ended, they would blink and peek up. They would touch their bodies, feeling shame, then quickly hiding it. They would force themselves to stand. As if in slow motion, frame by frame, the world would take on the old logic—absolute silence, then the wind, then sunlight, then voices. It was the burden of being alive. Awkwardly, the men would reassemble themselves, first in private, then in groups, becoming soldiers again. They would repair the leaks in their eyes. They would check for casualties, call in dustoffs, light cigarettes, try to smile, clear their throats and spit and begin cleaning their weapons. After a time someone would shake his head and say, No lie, I almost shit my pants, and someone else would laugh, which meant it was bad, yes, but the guy had obviously not shit his pants, it wasn't that bad, and in any case nobody would ever do such a thing and then go ahead and talk about it. They would squint into the dense, oppressive sunlight. For a few moments, perhaps, they would fall silent, lighting a joint and tracking its passage from man to man, inhaling, holding in the humiliation. Scary stuff, one of them might say. But then someone else would grin or flick his eyebrows and say, Roger-dodger, almost cut me a new asshole, *almost.*

There were numerous such poses. Some carried themselves with a sort of wistful resignation, others with pride or stiff soldierly discipline or good humor or macho zeal. They were afraid of dying but they were even more afraid to show it.

They found jokes to tell.

They used a hard vocabulary to contain the terrible softness. *Greased* they'd say. *Offed, lit up, zapped while zipping.* It wasn't cruelty, just stage presence. They were actors. When someone died, it wasn't quite dying, because in a curious way it seemed scripted, and because they had their lines mostly memorized, irony mixed with tragedy, and because they called it by other names, as if to encyst and destroy the reality of death itself. They kicked corpses. They cut off thumbs. They talked grunt lingo. They told stories about Ted Lavender's supply of tranquilizers, how the poor guy didn't feel a thing, how incredibly tranquil he was.

There's a moral here, said Mitchell Sanders.

They were waiting for Lavender's chopper, smoking the dead man's dope.

The moral's pretty obvious, Sanders said, and winked. Stay away from drugs. No joke, they'll ruin your day every time.

Cute, said Henry Dobbins.

Mind blower, get it? Talk about wiggy. Nothing left, just blood and brains.

They made themselves laugh.

There it is, they'd say. Over and over—there it is, my friend, there it is—as if the repetition itself were an act of poise, a balance between crazy and almost crazy, knowing without going, there it is, which meant be cool, let it ride, because Oh yeah, man, you can't change what can't be changed, there it is, there it absolutely and positively and fucking well *is.*

They were tough.

They carried all the emotional baggage of men who might die. Grief, terror, love, longing—these were intangibles, but the intangibles had their own mass and specific gravity, they had tangible weight. They carried shameful memories. They carried the common secret of cowardice barely restrained, the instinct to run or freeze or hide, and in many respects this was the heaviest burden of all, for it could never be put down, it required perfect balance and perfect posture. They carried their reputations. They carried the soldier's greatest fear, which was the fear of blushing. Men killed, and died, because they were embarrassed not to. It was what had brought them to the war in the first place, nothing positive, no dreams of glory or honor, just to avoid the blush of dishonor. They died so as not to die of embarrassment. They crawled into tunnels and walked point and advanced under fire. Each morning, despite the unknowns, they made their legs move. They endured. They kept humping. They did not submit to the obvious alternative, which was simply to close the eyes and fall. So easy, really. Go limp and tumble to the ground and let the muscles unwind and not speak and not budge until your buddies picked you up and lifted you into the chopper that would roar and dip its nose and carry you off to the world. A mere matter of falling, yet no one ever fell. It was not courage, exactly; the object was not valor. Rather, they were too frightened to be cowards.

By and large they carried these things inside, maintaining the masks of composure. They sneered at sick call. They spoke bitterly about guys who had found release by shooting off their own toes or fingers. Pussies, they'd say. Candy-asses. It was fierce, mocking talk, with only a trace of envy or awe, but even so the image played itself out behind their eyes.

They imagined the muzzle against flesh. So easy: squeeze the trigger and blow away a toe. They imagined it. They imagined the quick, sweet pain, then the evacuation to Japan, then a hospital with warm beds and cute geisha nurses.

And they dreamed of freedom birds.

At night, on guard, staring into the dark, they were carried away by jumbo jets. They felt the rush of takeoff. *Gone!* they yelled. And then velocity—wings and engines—a smiling stewardess—but it was more than a plane, it was a real bird, a big sleek silver bird with feathers and talons and high screeching. They were flying. The weights fell off; there was nothing to bear. They laughed and held on tight, feeling the cold slap of wind and altitude, soaring, thinking *It's over, I'm gone!*—they were naked, they were light and free—it was all lightness, bright and fast and buoyant, light as light, a helium buzz in the brain, a giddy bubbling in the lungs as they were taken up over the clouds and the war, beyond duty, beyond gravity and mortification and global entanglements—*Sin loi!* they yelled. *I'm sorry, mother-fuckers, but I'm out of it, I'm goofed, I'm on a space cruise, I'm gone!*—and it was a restful, unencumbered sensation, just riding the light waves, sailing that big silver freedom bird over the mountains and oceans, over America, over the farms and great sleeping cities and cemeteries and highways and the golden arches of McDonald's, it was flight, a kind of fleeing, a kind of falling, falling higher and higher, spinning off the edge of the earth and beyond the sun and through the vast, silent vacuum where there were no burdens and where everything weighed exactly nothing—*Gone!* they screamed. *I'm sorry but I'm gone!*—and so at night, not quite dreaming, they gave themselves over to lightness, they were carried, they were purely borne.

On the morning after Ted Lavender died, First Lieutenant Jimmy Cross crouched at the bottom of his foxhole and burned Martha's letters. Then he burned the two photographs. There was a steady rain falling, which made it difficult, but he used heat tabs and Sterno to build a small fire, screening it with his body, holding the photographs over the tight blue flame with the tips of his fingers.

He realized it was only a gesture. Stupid, he thought. Sentimental, too, but mostly just stupid.

Lavender was dead. You couldn't burn the blame.

Besides, the letters were in his head. And even now, without photographs, Lieutenant Cross could see Martha playing volleyball in her white gym shorts and yellow T-shirt. He could see her moving in the rain.

When the fire died out, Lieutenant Cross pulled his poncho over his shoulders and ate breakfast from a can.

There was no great mystery, he decided.

In those burned letters Martha had never mentioned the war, except to say, Jimmy, take care of yourself. She wasn't involved. She signed the letters Love, but it wasn't love, and all the fine lines and technicalities did not matter. Virginity was no longer an issue. He hated her. Yes, he did. He hated her. Love, too, but it was a hard, hating kind of love.

The morning came up wet and blurry. Everything seemed part of everything else, the fog and Martha and the deepening rain.

He was a soldier, after all.

Half smiling, Lieutenant Jimmy Cross took out his maps. He shook his head hard, as if to clear it, then bent forward and began planning the day's march. In ten minutes, or maybe twenty, he would rouse the men and they would pack up and head west, where the maps showed the country to be green and inviting. They would do what they had always done. The rain might add some weight, but otherwise it would be one more day layered upon all the other days.

He was realistic about it. There was that new hardness in his stomach. He loved her but he hated her.

No more fantasies, he told himself.

Henceforth, when he thought about Martha, it would be only to think that she belonged elsewhere. He would shut down the daydreams. This was not Mount Sebastian, it was another world, where there were no pretty poems or midterm exams, a place where men died because of carelessness and gross stupidity. Kiowa was right. Boom-down, and you were dead, never partly dead.

Briefly, in the rain, Lieutenant Cross saw Martha's gray eyes gazing back at him.

He understood.

It was very sad, he thought. The things men carried inside. The things men did or felt they had to do.

He almost nodded at her, but didn't.

Instead he went back to his maps. He was now determined to perform his duties firmly and without negligence. It wouldn't help Lavender, he knew that, but from this point on he would comport himself as an officer. He would dispose of his good-luck pebble. Swallow it, maybe, or use Lee Strunk's slingshot, or just drop it along the trail. On the march he would impose strict field discipline. He would be careful to send out flank security, to prevent straggling or bunching up, to keep his troops moving at the proper pace and at the proper interval. He would insist on clean weapons. He would confiscate the remainder of Lavender's dope. Later in the day, perhaps, he would call the men together and speak to them plainly. He would accept the blame for what had happened to Ted Lavender. He would be a man about it. He would look them in the eyes, keeping his chin level, and he would issue the new SOPs in a calm, impersonal tone of voice, a lieutenant's voice, leaving no room for argument or discussion. Commencing immediately, he'd tell them, they would no longer abandon equipment along the route of march. They would police up their acts. They would get their shit together, and keep it together, and maintain it neatly and in good working order.

He would not tolerate laxity. He would show strength, distancing himself.

Among the men there would be grumbling, of course, and maybe worse, because their days would seem longer and their loads heavier, but Lieutenant Jimmy Cross reminded himself that his obligation was not to be loved but to lead. He would dispense with love; it was not now a factor. And if anyone quarreled or complained, he would simply tighten his lips and arrange his shoulders in the correct command posture. He might give a curt little nod. Or he might not. He might just shrug and say, Carry on, then they would saddle up and form into a column and move out toward the villages west of Than Khe.

A Good Man Is Hard to Find

by Flannery O'Connor

Introduced by Sue Miller

IT'S DAUNTING TO TRY TO SAY ANYTHING NEW ABOUT "A GOOD MAN Is Hard to Find," Flannery O'Connor's astonishing short story. Certainly it must be one of the most widely collected pieces of American fiction. On the long shelf of anthologies my husband and I have assembled in our years of teaching, anyway, it appears in at least two-thirds. I have, then, eight or nine versions of it, many with questions or commentary appended, among these O'Connor's own comments by way of an introduction she gave before reading it once—none of which (try as some seemingly do) can detract from the bracing quality of the experience of reading the story itself. Bracing even after many rereadings, but unquestionably bracing the first time. Shocking even. And funny too.

But I think the feeling I had most clearly on reading it first was of having confronted something quite mysterious and strange: of something's having happened in the story which required further thought, further reading, further exploration. But in a most jolting and insistent way, a way that made me turn back then, at that moment, to the beginning of the story to start over. A kind of "What *was* that?" sensation.

Some of this, of course, was the violence in the story. Or rather, what initially seemed the random descent of violence into what initially seemed an amusing tale of human vanity and frailty. It was as though the story turned from being one *kind* of thing to another at this point, and it was a disorienting experience for me, one that seemed to ask me to try to integrate the moods of the two sections. And of course there was the sense at this point, too, of confronting the language of spiritual discovery, the feeling that however the two pieces came together, it had to do with this.

And so on rereading I understood that implicit in this story is the idea of an active, seeking God, following the grandmother and her family on their various crazy detours, even down the wrong dirt road in the wrong state. The very tortuousness of the road, the very complication in the details which set the accident in motion—the manipulativeness of the grandmother in getting Bailey to turn off, the embarrassment which causes her to jerk her legs, the presence of the cat—all these bits of humor and unlikely turns become emblematic of the mystery possible if not inherent in O'Connor's version of grace: the lengths to which God will go to find you! And the acts of violence which bring the grandmother to her receptiveness to the moment of grace convey the notion of God as a muscular, powerful force in her life—in *our* lives, as O'Connor sees them—a God whose beneficence can take the cruelest, most unlikely forms.

On reading more widely in O'Connor, I understood that she often works with this juxtaposition of the humorous and the violent and the spiritual. I think, in fact, that she counts on the disorientation this produces in her reader—as other writers count on psychological identification with the characters, say, or a grand sweep of language—whatever it takes, whatever the gift is that makes the reader wish to penetrate to another level of the writer's work. But O'Connor's method is an extraordinarily unusual and courageous one, never more amazing than when encountered the first time but always amazing. It is as though Jesus had told the parable of the prodigal son from the stay-at-home jealous brother's point of view and made him, what's more, a smug yokel, with all the prejudices and rituals of self-satisfaction inherent in that. And then yanked him to his revelation through a violent act that undercut all the humor that had gone before—but connected to it too, oh, yes!

And this brings me to the other aspect of my initial delight in the story. I didn't read O'Connor until I was in my late thirties, and I'm grateful for that—partly because I think I was by then more interested in the questions her fiction raises than I was earlier in my life, more likely to be jolted into rereading her, but also because I was writing seriously by then, and her fiction was an astonishment to me simply for the way it works. O'Connor herself talks in her collected letters and essays about the various levels at which fiction makes meaning. But the experience of her stories is a visceral acquaintanceship with those levels. And "A Good Man Is Hard to Find" is one of the stories with the fewest narrative connections made *for* the reader to the deepest level. Compare it to "The Artificial Nigger," for example, with its explanation of the motion of grace as it arrives to touch Mr. Head. Here all we have is the grandmother's gesture, which emerges from all those other claims that The Misfit, like herself, has good blood and therefore ought not to kill her; but also stands away from them enough to be remarked on because of elements O'Connor offers both here and earlier—the grandmother's deep sense of recognition of The Misfit, the fact that her head "cleared" at this moment, the fact that this is the first time she reaches to touch him, the fact that the blood bond she claims now is maternal, loving, rather than social and exculpatory, the fact that The Misfit recoils "as if a snake had bitten him," in O'Connor's deliberate echoing of the Fall which is the bond that unites these two and all people. The gesture becomes the embodiment of the moment of mercy, of grace, of triumph in the story, and it happens just in time.

Part of what stunned me as a *writing* reader, then, was the sense of the story's working at so many levels simultaneously—and of its being so satisfying simultaneously on all of them, as closer and closer examination bore out. You can exult, for instance, in the knowing humor, the perfection of syntax in the grandmother's exchange with Red Sammy, how perfectly balanced and amusing their mutual bowing and scraping to each other is, their joint project in self-congratulation over their exemption from the general mire of humanity. But their discussion is also theological; it is about what goodness consists in, and it feeds the deepest meaning of the story. It reveals the great distance the grandmother is from acknowledging the sinfulness of what it means to be human, and therefore the distance she has to come—and does, all down that road and into the ditch, by God's mercy—to embrace it.

You can enjoy the way the narrative consciousness replicates the grandmother's (why should the guns be the *last* thing described about the outlaws as they step forward? Well, why on earth would anyone *want* to notice such a thing?), and also how it occasionally slyly moves outside that perspective, so that we get, for instance, the monkey picking fleas off itself and delicately devouring them as a commentary on the nature of the conversation between Red Sammy and the grandmother.

The notion of fiction as parable, as story which makes sense at several levels at once, is a thrilling model for a fiction writer and defines for me a kind of fiction to aspire to. O'Connor has made just that kind of fiction here: the story of a defeat which is a tale of triumph, the story of a death which is a revelation of spiritual birth. And it's also, by the way, genuinely funny and truly riveting.

A Good Man Is Hard to Find

Flannery O'Connor

The grandmother didn't want to go to Florida. She wanted to visit some of her connections in east Tennessee and she was seizing at every chance to change Bailey's mind. Bailey was the son she lived with, her only boy. He was sitting on the edge of his chair at the table, bent over the orange sports section of the *Journal*. "Now look here, Bailey," she said, "see here, read this," and she stood with one hand on her thin hip and the other rattling the newspaper at his bald head. "Here this fellow that calls himself The Misfit is aloose from the Federal Pen and headed toward Florida and you read here what it says he did to these people. Just you read it. I wouldn't take my children in any direction with a criminal like that aloose in it. I couldn't answer to my conscience if I did."

Bailey didn't look up from his reading so she wheeled around then and faced the children's mother, a young woman in slacks, whose face was as broad and innocent as a cabbage and was tied around with a green head-kerchief that had two points on the top like a rabbit's ears. She was sitting on the sofa, feeding the baby his apricots out of a jar. "The children have been to Florida before," the old lady said. "You all ought to take them somewhere else for a change so they would see different parts of the world and be broad. They never have been to east Tennessee."

The children's mother didn't seem to hear her but the eight-year-old boy, John Wesley, a stocky child with glasses, said, "If you don't want to go to Florida, why dontcha stay at home?" He and the little girl, June Star, were reading the funny papers on the floor.

"She wouldn't stay at home to be queen for a day," June Star said without raising her yellow head.

"Yes and what would you do if this fellow, The Misfit, caught you?" the grandmother asked.

"I'd smack his face," John Wesley said.

"She wouldn't stay at home for a million bucks," June Star said. "Afraid she'd miss something. She has to go everywhere we go."

"All right, Miss," the grandmother said. "Just remember that the next time you want me to curl your hair."

June Star said her hair was naturally curly.

The next morning the grandmother was the first one in the car, ready to go. She had her big black valise that looked like the head of a hippopotamus in one corner, and underneath it she was hiding a basket with Pitty Sing, the cat, in it. She didn't intend for the cat to be left alone in the house for three days because he would miss her too much and she was afraid he might brush against one of the gas burners and accidentally asphyxiate himself. Her son, Bailey, didn't like to arrive at a motel with a cat.

She sat in the middle of the back seat with John Wesley and June Star on either side of her. Bailey and the children's mother and the baby sat in front and they left Atlanta at eight forty-five with the mileage on the car at 55890. The grandmother wrote this down because she thought it would be interesting to say how many miles they had been when they got back. It took them twenty minutes to reach the outskirts of the city.

The old lady settled herself comfortably, removing her white cotton gloves and putting them up with her purse on the shelf in front of the back window. The children's mother still had on slacks and still had her head tied up in a green kerchief, but the grandmother had on a navy blue straw sailor hat with a bunch of white violets on the brim and a navy blue dress with a small white dot in the print. Her collars and cuffs were white organdy trimmed with lace and at her neckline she had pinned a purple spray of cloth violets containing a sachet. In case of an accident, anyone seeing her dead on the highway would know at once that she was a lady.

She said she thought it was going to be a good day for driving, neither too hot nor too cold, and she cautioned Bailey that the speed limit was fifty-five miles an hour and that the patrolmen hid themselves behind billboards and small clumps of trees and sped out after you before you had a chance to slow down. She pointed out interesting details of the scenery: Stone Mountain; the blue granite that in some places came up to both sides of the highway; the brilliant red clay banks slightly streaked with purple; and the various crops that made rows of green lace-work on the ground. The trees were full of silver-white sunlight and the meanest of them sparkled. The children were reading comic magazines and their mother had gone back to sleep.

"Let's go through Georgia fast so we won't have to look at it much," John Wesley said.

"If I were a little boy," said the grandmother, "I wouldn't talk about my native state that way. Tennessee has the mountains and Georgia has the hills."

"Tennessee is just a hillbilly dumping ground," John Wesley said, "and Georgia is a lousy state too."

"You said it," June Star said.

"In my time," said the grandmother, folding her thin veined fingers, "children were more respectful of their native states and their parents and everything else. People did right then. Oh look at the cute little pickaninny!" she said and pointed to a Negro child standing in the door of a shack.

"Wouldn't that make a picture, now?" she asked and they all turned and looked at the little Negro out of the back window. He waved.

"He didn't have any britches on," June Star said.

"He probably didn't have any," the grandmother explained. "Little niggers in the country don't have things like we do. If I could paint, I'd paint that picture," she said.

The children exchanged comic books.

The grandmother offered to hold the baby and the children's mother passed him over the front seat to her. She set him on her knee and bounced him and told him about the things they were passing. She rolled her eyes and screwed up her mouth and stuck her leathery thin face into his smooth bland one. Occasionally he gave her a faraway smile. They passed a large cotton field with five or six graves fenced in the middle of it, like a small island. "Look at the graveyard!" the grandmother said, pointing it out. "That was the old family burying ground. That belonged to the plantation."

"Where's the plantation?" John Wesley asked.

"Gone With the Wind," said the grandmother. "Ha. Ha."

When the children finished all the comic books they had brought, they opened the lunch and ate it. The grandmother ate a peanut butter sandwich and an olive and would not let the children throw the box and the paper napkins out the window. When there was nothing else to do they played a game by choosing a cloud and making the other two guess what shape it suggested. John Wesley took one the shape of a cow and June Star guessed a cow and John Wesley said, no, an automobile, and June Star said he didn't play fair, and they began to slap each other over the grandmother.

The grandmother said she would tell them a story if they would keep quiet. When she told a story, she rolled her eyes and waved her head and was very dramatic. She said once when she was a maiden lady she had been courted by a Mr. Edgar Atkins Teagarden from Jasper, Georgia. She said he was a very good-looking man and a gentleman and that he brought her a watermelon every Saturday afternoon with his initials cut in it, E. A. T. Well, one Saturday, she said, Mr. Teagarden brought the watermelon and there was nobody at home and he left it on the front porch and returned in his buggy to Jasper, but she never got the watermelon, she said, because a nigger boy ate it when he saw the initials, E. A. T.! This story tickled John Wesley's funny bone and he giggled and giggled but June Star didn't think it was any good. She said she wouldn't marry a man that just brought her a watermelon on Saturday. The grandmother said she would have done well to marry Mr. Teagarden because he was a gentleman and had bought Coca-Cola stock when it first came out and that he had died only a few years ago, a very wealthy man.

They stopped at The Tower for barbecued sandwiches. The Tower was a part stucco and part wood filling station and dance hall set in a clearing outside of Timothy. A fat man named Red Sammy Butts ran it and there were signs stuck here and there on the building and for miles up and down the highway saying TRY RED SAMMY'S FAMOUS BARBECUE. NONE LIKE FAMOUS RED SAMMY'S! RED SAM! THE FAT BOY WITH THE HAPPY LAUGH! A VETERAN! RED SAMMY'S YOUR MAN!

Red Sammy was lying on the bare ground outside The Tower with his head under a truck while a gray monkey about a foot high, chained to a small chinaberry tree, chattered nearby. The monkey sprang back into the tree and got on the highest limb as soon as he saw the children jump out of the car and run toward him.

Inside, The Tower was a long dark room with a counter at one end and tables at the other and dancing space in the middle. They all sat down at a board table next to the nickelodeon and Red Sam's wife, a tall burnt-brown woman with hair and eyes lighter than her skin, came and took their order. The children's mother put a dime in the machine and played "The Tennessee Waltz," and the grandmother said that tune always made her want to dance. She asked Bailey if he would like to dance but he only glared at her. He didn't have a naturally sunny disposition like she did and trips made him nervous. The grandmother's brown eyes were very bright. She swayed her head from side to side and pretended she was dancing in her chair. June Star said play something she could tap to so the children's mother put in another dime and played a fast number and June Star stepped out onto the dance floor and did her tap routine.

"Ain't she cute?" Red Sam's wife said, leaning over the counter. "Would you like to come be my little girl?"

"No I certainly wouldn't," June Star said. "I wouldn't live in a broken-down place like this for a million bucks!" and she ran back to the table.

"Ain't she cute?" the woman repeated, stretching her mouth politely.

"Aren't you ashamed?" hissed the grandmother.

Red Sam came in and told his wife to quit lounging on the counter and hurry up with these people's order. His khaki trousers reached just to his hip bones and his stomach hung over them like a sack of meal swaying under his shirt. He came over and sat down at a table nearby and let out a combination sigh and yodel. "You can't win," he said. "You can't win," and he wiped his sweating red face off with a gray handkerchief. "These days you don't know who to trust," he said. "Ain't that the truth?"

"People are certainly not nice like they used to be," said the grandmother.

"Two fellers come in here last week," Red Sammy said, "driving a Chrysler. It was a old beat-up car but it was a good one and these boys looked all right to me. Said they worked at the mill and you know I let them fellers charge the gas they bought? Now why did I do that?"

"Because you're a good man!" the grandmother said at once.

"Yes'm, I suppose so," Red Sam said as if he were struck with this answer.

His wife brought the orders, carrying the five plates all at once without a tray, two in each hand and one balanced on her arm. "It isn't a soul in this green world of God's that you can trust," she said. "And I don't count nobody out of that, not nobody," she repeated, looking at Red Sammy.

"Did you read about that criminal, The Misfit, that's escaped?" asked the grandmother.

"I wouldn't be a bit surprised if he didn't attact this place right here," said the woman. "If he hears about it being here, I wouldn't be none surprised to see him. If he hears it's two cent in the cash register, I wouldn't be a tall surprised if he . . . "

"That'll do," Red Sam said. "Go bring these people their Co'-Colas," and the woman went off to get the rest of the order.

"A good man is hard to find," Red Sammy said. "Everything is getting terrible. I remember the day you could go off and leave your screen door unlatched. Not no more."

He and the grandmother discussed better times. The old lady said that in her opinion Europe was entirely to blame for the way things were now. She said the way Europe acted you would think we were made of money and Red Sam said it was no use talking about it, she was exactly right. The children ran outside into the white sunlight and looked at the monkey in the lacy chinaberry tree. He was busy catching fleas on himself and biting each one carefully between his teeth as if it were a delicacy.

They drove off again into the hot afternoon. The grandmother took cat naps and woke up every few minutes with her own snoring. Outside of Toombsboro she woke up and recalled an old plantation that she had visited in this neighborhood once when she was a young lady. She said the house had six white columns across the front and that there was an avenue of oaks leading up to it and two little wooden trellis arbors on either side in front where you sat down with your suitor after a stroll in the garden. She recalled exactly which road to turn off to get to it. She knew that Bailey would not be willing to lose any time looking at an old house, but the more she talked about it, the more she wanted to see it once again and find out if the little twin arbors were still standing. "There was a secret panel in this house," she said craftily, not telling the truth but wishing that she were, "and the story went that all the family silver was hidden in it when Sherman came through but it was never found. . . ."

"Hey!" John Wesley said. "Let's go see it! We'll find it! We'll poke all the woodwork and find it! Who lives there? Where do you turn off at? Hey Pop, can't we turn off there?"

"We never have seen a house with a secret panel!" June Star shrieked. "Let's go to the house with the secret panel! Hey Pop, can't we go see the house with the secret panel!"

"It's not far from here, I know," the grandmother said. "It wouldn't take over twenty minutes."

Bailey was looking straight ahead. His jaw was as rigid as a horseshoe. "No," he said.

The children began to yell and scream that they wanted to see the house with the secret panel. John Wesley kicked the back of the front seat and June Star hung over her mother's shoulder and whined desperately into her ear that they never had any fun even on their vacation, that they could never do what THEY wanted to do. The baby began to scream and John Wesley kicked the back of the seat so hard that his father could feel the blows in his kidney.

"All right!" he shouted and drew the car to a stop at the side of the road. "Will you all shut up? Will you all just shut up for one second? If you don't shut up, we won't go anywhere."

"It would be very educational for them," the grandmother murmured.

"All right," Bailey said, "but get this: this is the only time we're going to stop for anything like this. This is the one and only time."

"The dirt road that you have to turn down is about a mile back," the grandmother directed. "I marked it when we passed."

"A dirt road," Bailey groaned.

After they had turned around and were headed toward the dirt road, the grandmother recalled other points about the house, the beautiful glass over the front doorway and the candle-lamp in the hall. John Wesley said that the secret panel was probably in the fireplace.

"You can't go inside this house," Bailey said. "You don't know who lives there."

"While you all talk to the people in front, I'll run around behind and get in a window," John Wesley suggested.

"We'll all stay in the car," his mother said.

They turned onto the dirt road and the car raced roughly along in a swirl of pink dust. The grandmother recalled the times when there were no paved roads and thirty miles was a day's journey. The dirt road was hilly and there were sudden washes in it and sharp curves on dangerous embankments. All at once they would be on a hill, looking down over the blue tops of trees for miles around, then the next minute, they would be in a red depression with the dust-coated trees looking down on them.

"This place had better turn up in a minute," Bailey said, "or I'm going to turn around."

The road looked as if no one had traveled on it in months.

"It's not much farther," the grandmother said and just as she said it, a horrible thought came to her. The thought was so embarrassing that she turned red in the face and her eyes dilated and her feet jumped up, upsetting her valise in the corner. The instant the valise moved, the newspaper top she had over the basket under it rose with a snarl and Pitty Sing, the cat, sprang onto Bailey's shoulder.

The children were thrown to the floor and their mother, clutching the baby, was thrown out the door onto the ground; the old lady was thrown into the front seat. The car turned over once and landed right-side-up in a gulch off the side of the road. Bailey remained in the driver's seat with the cat—gray-striped with a broad white face and an orange nose—clinging to his neck like a caterpillar.

As soon as the children saw they could move their arms and legs, they scrambled out of the car, shouting, "We've had an ACCIDENT!" The grandmother was curled up under the dashboard, hoping she was injured so that Bailey's wrath would not come down on her all at once. The horrible thought she had had before the accident was that the house she had remembered so vividly was not in Georgia but in Tennessee.

Bailey removed the cat from his neck with both hands and flung it out the window against the side of a pine tree. Then he got out of the car and started looking for the children's mother. She was sitting against the side of the red gutted ditch, holding the screaming baby, but she only had a cut down her face and a broken shoulder. "We've had an ACCIDENT!" the children screamed in a frenzy of delight.

"But nobody's killed," June Star said with disappointment as the grandmother limped out of the car, her hat still pinned to her head but the broken front brim standing up at a jaunty angle and the violet spray hanging off the side. They all sat down in the ditch, except the children, to recover from the shock. They were all shaking.

"Maybe a car will come along," said the children's mother hoarsely.

"I believe I have injured an organ," said the grandmother, pressing her side, but no one answered her. Bailey's teeth were clattering. He had on a yellow sport shirt with bright blue parrots designed in it and his face was as yellow as the shirt. The grandmother decided that she would not mention that the house was in Tennessee.

The road was about ten feet above and they could see only the tops of the trees on the other side of it. Behind the ditch they were sitting in there were more woods, tall and dark and deep. In a few minutes they saw a car some distance away on top of a hill, coming slowly as if the occupants were watching them. The grandmother stood up and waved both arms dramatically to attract their attention. The car continued to come on slowly, disappeared around a bend and appeared again, moving even slower, on top of the hill they had gone over. It was a big black battered hearselike automobile. There were three men in it.

It came to a stop just over them, and for some minutes the driver looked down with a steady expressionless gaze to where they were sitting, and didn't speak. Then he turned his head and muttered something to the other two and they got out. One was a fat boy in black trousers and a red sweat shirt with a silver stallion embossed on the front of it. He moved around on the right side of them and stood staring, his mouth partly open in a kind of loose grin. The other had on khaki pants and a blue striped coat and a gray hat pulled down very low, hiding most of his face. He came around slowly on the left side. Neither spoke.

The driver got out of the car and stood by the side of it, looking down at them. He was an older man than the other two. His hair was just beginning to gray and he wore silver-rimmed spectacles that gave him a scholarly look. He had a long creased face and didn't have on any shirt or undershirt. He had on blue jeans that were too tight for him and was holding a black hat and a gun. The two boys also had guns.

"We've had an ACCIDENT!" the children screamed.

The grandmother had the peculiar feeling that the bespectacled man was someone she knew. His face was as familiar to her as if she had known him all her life but she could not recall who he was. He moved away from the car and began to come down the embankment, placing his feet carefully so that he wouldn't slip. He had on tan and white shoes and no socks, and his ankles were red and thin. "Good afternoon," he said. "I see you all had you a little spill."

"We turned over twice!" said the grandmother.

"Oncet," he corrected. "We seen it happen. Try their car and see will it run, Hiram," he said quietly to the boy with the gray hat.

"What you got that gun for?" John Wesley asked. "Whatcha gonna do with that gun?"

"Lady," the man said to the children's mother, "would you mind calling them children to sit down by you? Children make me nervous. I want all you all to sit down right together there where you're at."

"What are you telling US what to do for?" June Star asked.

Behind them the line of woods gaped like a dark open mouth. "Come here," said their mother.

"Look here now," Bailey began suddenly, "we're in a predicament! We're in . . . "

The grandmother shrieked. She scrambled to her feet and stood staring. "You're The Misfit!" she said. "I recognized you at once!"

"Yes'm," the man said, smiling slightly as if he were pleased in spite of himself to be known, "but it would have been better for all of you, lady, if you hadn't of reckernized me."

Bailey turned his head sharply and said something to his mother that shocked even the children. The old lady began to cry and The Misfit reddened.

"Lady," he said, "don't you get upset. Sometimes a man says things he don't mean. I don't reckon he meant to talk to you thataway."

"You wouldn't shoot a lady, would you?" the grandmother said and removed a clean handkerchief from her cuff and began to slap at her eyes with it.

The Misfit pointed the toe of his shoe into the ground and made a little hole and then covered it up again. "I would hate to have to," he said.

"Listen," the grandmother almost screamed, "I know you're a good man. You don't look a bit like you have common blood. I know you must come from nice people!"

"Yes mam," he said, "finest people in the world." When he smiled he showed a row of strong white teeth. "God never made a finer woman than my mother and my daddy's heart was pure gold," he said. The boy with the red sweat shirt had come around behind them and was standing with his gun at his hip. The Misfit squatted down on the ground. "Watch them children, Bobby Lee," he said. "You know they make me nervous." He looked at the six of them huddled together in front of him and he seemed to be embarrassed as if he couldn't think of anything to say. "Ain't a cloud in the sky," he remarked, looking up at it. "Don't see no sun but don't see no cloud neither."

"Yes, it's a beautiful day," said the grandmother. "Listen," she said, "you shouldn't call yourself The Misfit because I know you're a good man at heart. I can just look at you and tell."

"Hush!" Bailey yelled. "Hush! Everybody shut up and let me handle this!" He was squatting in the position of a runner about to sprint forward but he didn't move.

"I pre-chate that, lady," The Misfit said and drew a little circle in the ground with the butt of his gun.

"It'll take a half a hour to fix this here car," Hiram called, looking over the raised hood of it.

"Well, first you and Bobby Lee get him and that little boy to step over yonder with you," The Misfit said, pointing to Bailey and John Wesley. "The boys want to ast you something," he said to Bailey. "Would you mind stepping back in them woods there with them?"

"Listen," Bailey began, "we're in a terrible predicament! Nobody realizes what this is," and his voice cracked. His eyes were as blue and intense as the parrots in his shirt and he remained perfectly still.

The grandmother reached up to adjust her hat brim as if she were going to the woods with him but it came off in her hand. She stood staring at it and after a second she let it fall on the ground. Hiram pulled Bailey up by the arm as if he were assisting an old man. John Wesley caught hold of his father's hand and Bobby Lee followed. They went off toward the woods and just as they reached the dark edge, Bailey turned and supporting himself against a gray naked pine trunk, he shouted, "I'll be back in a minute, Mamma, wait on me!"

"Come back this instant!" his mother shrilled but they all disappeared into the woods.

"Bailey Boy!" the grandmother called in a tragic voice but she found she was looking at The Misfit squatting on the ground in front of her. "I just know you're a good man," she said desperately. "You're not a bit common!"

"Nome, I ain't a good man," The Misfit said after a second as if he had considered her statement carefully, "but I ain't the worst in the world neither. My daddy said I was a different breed of dog from my brothers and sisters. 'You know,' Daddy said, 'it's some that can live their whole life out without asking about it and it's others has to know why it is, and this boy is one of the latters. He's going to be into everything!' " He put on his black hat and looked up suddenly and then away deep into the woods as if he were embarrassed again. "I'm sorry I don't have on a shirt before you ladies," he said, hunching his shoulders slightly. "We buried our clothes that we had on when we escaped and we're just making do until we can get better. We borrowed these from some folks we met," he explained.

"That's perfectly all right," the grandmother said. "Maybe Bailey has an extra shirt in his suitcase."

"I'll look and see terrectly," The Misfit said.

"Where are they taking him?" the children's mother screamed.

"Daddy was a card himself," The Misfit said. "You couldn't put anything over on him. He never got in trouble with the Authorities though. Just had the knack of handling them."

"You could be honest too if you'd only try," said the grandmother. "Think how wonderful it would be to settle down and live a comfortable life and not have to think about somebody chasing you all the time."

The Misfit kept scratching in the ground with the butt of his gun as if he were thinking about it. "Yes'm, somebody is always after you," he murmured.

The grandmother noticed how thin his shoulder blades were just behind his hat because she was standing up looking down on him. "Do you ever pray?" she asked.

He shook his head. All she saw was the black hat wiggle between his shoulder blades. "Nome," he said.

There was a pistol shot from the woods, followed closely by another. Then silence. The old lady's head jerked around. She could hear the wind move through the tree tops like a long satisfied insuck of breath. "Bailey Boy!" she called.

"I was a gospel singer for a while," The Misfit said. "I been most everything. Been in the arm service, both land and sea, at home and abroad, been twict married, been an undertaker, been with the railroads, plowed Mother Earth, been in a tornado, seen a man burnt alive oncet," and looked up at the children's mother and the little girl who were sitting close together, their faces white and their eyes glassy; "I even seen a woman flogged," he said.

"Pray, pray," the grandmother began, "pray, pray . . . "

"I never was a bad boy that I remember of," The Misfit said in an almost dreamy voice, "but somewheres along the line I done something wrong and got sent to the penitentiary. I was buried alive," and he looked up and held her attention to him by a steady stare.

"That's when you should have started to pray," she said. "What did you do to get sent to the penitentiary that first time?"

"Turn to the right, it was a wall," The Misfit said, looking up again at the cloudless sky. "Turn to the left, it was a wall. Look up it was a ceiling, look down it was a floor. I forget what I done, lady. I set there and set there, trying to remember what it was I done and I ain't recalled it to this day. Oncet in a while, I would think it was coming to me, but it never come."

"Maybe they put you in by mistake," the old lady said vaguely.

"Nome," he said. "It wasn't no mistake. They had the papers on me."

"You must have stolen something," she said.

The Misfit sneered slightly. "Nobody had nothing I wanted," he said. "It was a head-doctor at the penitentiary said what I had done was kill my daddy but I known that for a lie. My daddy died in nineteen ought nineteen of the epidemic flu and I never had a thing to do with it. He was buried in the Mount Hopewell Baptist churchyard and you can go there and see for yourself."

"If you would pray," the old lady said, "Jesus would help you."

"That's right," The Misfit said.

"Well then, why don't you pray?" she asked, trembling with delight suddenly.

"I don't want no hep," he said. "I'm doing all right by myself."

Bobby Lee and Hiram came ambling back from the woods. Bobby Lee was dragging a yellow shirt with bright blue parrots in it.

"Thow me that shirt, Bobby Lee," The Misfit said. The shirt came flying at him and landed on his shoulder and he put it on. The grandmother couldn't name what the shirt reminded her of. "No, lady," The Misfit said while he was buttoning it up, "I found out the crime don't matter. You can do one thing or you can do another, kill a man or take a tire off his car, because sooner or later you're going to forget what it was you done and just be punished for it."

The children's mother had begun to make heaving noises as if she couldn't get her breath. "Lady," he asked, "would you and that little girl like to step off yonder with Bobby Lee and Hiram and join your husband?"

"Yes, thank you," the mother said faintly. Her left arm dangled helplessly and she was holding the baby, who had gone to sleep, in the other. "Hep that lady up, Hiram," The Misfit said as she struggled to climb out of the ditch, "and Bobby Lee, you hold onto that little girl's hand."

"I don't want to hold hands with him," June Star said. "He reminds me of a pig."

The fat boy blushed and laughed and caught her by the arm and pulled her off into the woods after Hiram and her mother.

Alone with The Misfit, the grandmother found that she had lost her voice. There was not a cloud in the sky nor any sun. There was nothing around her but woods. She wanted to tell him that he must pray. She opened and closed her mouth several times before anything came out. Finally she found herself saying, "Jesus, Jesus," meaning, Jesus will help you, but the way she was saying it, it sounded as if she might be cursing.

"Yes'm," The Misfit said as if he agreed. "Jesus thrown everything off balance. It was the same case with Him as with me except He hadn't committed any crime and they could prove I had committed one because they had the papers on me. Of course," he said, "they never shown me my papers. That's why I sign myself now. I said long ago, you get a signature and sign everything you do and keep a copy of it. Then you'll know what you done and you can hold up the crime to the punishment and see do they match and in the end you'll have something to prove you ain't been treated right. I call myself The Misfit," he said, "because I can't make what all I done wrong fit what all I gone through in punishment."

There was a piercing scream from the woods, followed closely by a pistol report. "Does it seem right to you, lady, that one is punished a heap and another ain't punished at all?"

"Jesus!" the old lady cried. "You've got good blood! I know you wouldn't shoot a lady! I know you come from nice people! Pray! Jesus, you ought not to shoot a lady. I'll give you all the money I've got!"

"Lady," The Misfit said, looking beyond her far into the woods, "there never was a body that give the undertaker a tip."

There were two more pistol reports and the grandmother raised her head like a parched old turkey hen crying for water and called, "Bailey Boy, Bailey Boy!" as if her heart would break.

"Jesus was the only One that ever raised the dead." The Misfit continued, "and He shouldn't have done it. He thrown everything off balance. If He did what He said, then it's nothing for you to do but throw away everything and follow Him, and if He didn't, then it's nothing for you to do but enjoy the few minutes you got left the best way you can—by killing somebody or burning down his house or doing some other meanness to him. No pleasure but meanness," he said and his voice had become almost a snarl.

"Maybe He didn't raise the dead," the old lady mumbled, not knowing what she was saying and feeling so dizzy that she sank down in the ditch with her legs twisted under her.

"I wasn't there so I can't say He didn't," The Misfit said. "I wisht I had of been there," he said, hitting the ground with his fist. "It ain't right I wasn't there because if I had of been there I would of known. Listen, lady," he said in a high voice, "if I had of been there I would of known and I wouldn't be like I am now." His voice seemed about to crack and the grandmother's head cleared for an instant. She saw the man's face twisted close to her own as if he were going to cry and she murmured, "Why you're one of my babies. You're one of my own children!" She reached out and touched him on the shoulder. The Misfit sprang back as if a snake had bitten him and shot her three times through the chest. Then he put his gun down on the ground and took off his glasses and began to clean them.

Hiram and Bobby Lee returned from the woods and stood over the ditch, looking down at the grandmother, who half sat and half lay in a puddle of blood with her legs crossed under her like a child's and her face smiling up at the cloudless sky.

Without his glasses, The Misfit's eyes were red-rimmed and pale and defenseless-looking. "Take her off and throw her where you thrown the others," he said, picking up the cat that was rubbing itself against his leg.

"She was a talker, wasn't she?" Bobby Lee said, sliding down the ditch with a yodel.

"She would of been a good woman," The Misfit said, "if it had been somebody there to shoot her every minute of her life."

"Some fun!" Bobby Lee said.

"Shut up, Bobby Lee," The Misfit said. "It's no real pleasure in life."

I Stand Here Ironing

by Tillie Olsen

Introduced by Amy Hempel

IN *SILENCES,* TILLIE OLSEN'S BOOK ABOUT THE THINGS THAT CONSPIRE to keep a writer from writing, she says, "In the twenty years I bore and reared my children, usually had to work on a paid job as well, the simplest circumstances for creation did not exist." She says that when the youngest of her four was in school, she could finally begin to carry her writing around in her head, and "the beginnings struggled toward endings."

> Time on the bus, even when I had to stand, was enough; the stolen moments at work, enough; the deep night hours for as long as I could stay awake, after the kids were in bed, after the household tasks were done, sometimes during. It is no accident that the first work I considered publishable began, "I stand here ironing, and what you asked me moves tormented back and forth with the iron."

While that line, in conjunction with the last line of the story, always opens the cisterns for me, there is something that follows the last line that moves me enormously in a different way. At the end of what is, in the small paperback edition of *Tell Me a Riddle* that I carry, a twelve-page story, there is a notation we associate with the ending of a *novel*—the time it took the author to complete it, in this case: "1953–1954" ("It is distraction, not meditation, that becomes habitual; interruption, not continuity"—*Silences*).

Of the stories I go back to "when"—as Barry Hannah writes in his exquisite "Water Liars"—"I am run down and flocked around by the world," of the handful of restorative stories by which I set a course, the touchstone is that raw elegy "I Stand Here Ironing," a woman's lament for her daughter, her first child who "has much to her and probably little will come of it." The story is a litany of "what should have been and what cannot be helped," from a young mother, deserted by her husband, compromised by poverty, whose "wisdom came too late."

I have read this story several times a year since I first read it twenty years ago, and my response has always been a visceral one, though the story is also a *technical* feat and can be admired for the ways in which, without ever moving her attention from the girl, Emily, Olsen gives us the life of a family and of a generation, of the country during the Depression. The course she sets herself is one that goes deeper and deeper down into harder and harder truths. Olsen never hides from feeling behind irony; as a result, the story is, at times, almost embarrassing in its naked declarations and never less than wrenching, as when the mother comes home to find the front door open, opened by her little girl so that the mother could come home faster.

And speaking tactically, what if Olsen had cast this story in the daughter's voice? If the story had been a catalog of all the ways the *daughter* believed her mother had failed her? We'd have had no patience with the whining. Or if the mother's concern were for herself, for all the things *she* missed out on? The story's dignity comes from the mother recounting the things she was unable to do *for her daughter.* "So all that is in her will not bloom": the mother who knows this would not be comforted by British psychoanalyst D. W. Winnicott's notion of "the good *enough* mother." What she feels is not guilt but grief.

"I Stand Here Ironing" is a story that readers will have read before. I am not here to signal a discovery; I am here to say, Read it again. Especially if you are a writer, for among this story's merits is what it calls for in return. I am grateful to stories that make other stories possible. I was able to write "Today Will Be a Quiet Day" because Mary Robison had first written "Widower." And I am at work on a story now that came about, in large part, because Tillie Olsen stood there ironing.

I Stand Here Ironing

Tillie Olsen

I stand here ironing, and what you asked me moves tormented back and forth with the iron.

"I wish you would manage the time to come in and talk with me about your daughter. I'm sure you can help me understand her. She's a youngster who needs help and whom I'm deeply interested in helping."

"Who needs help." . . . Even if I came, what good would it do? You think because I am her mother I have a key, or that in some way you could use me as a key? She has lived for nineteen years. There is all that life that has happened outside of me, beyond me.

And when is there time to remember, to sift, to weigh, to estimate, to total? I will start and there will be an interruption and I will have to gather it all together again. Or I will become engulfed with all I did or did not do, with what should have been and what cannot be helped.

She was a beautiful baby. The first and only one of our five that was beautiful at birth. You do not guess how new and uneasy her tenancy in her now-loveliness. You did not know her all those years she was thought homely, or see her poring over her baby pictures, making me tell her over and over how beautiful she had been—and would be, I would tell her—and was now, to the seeing eye. But the seeing eyes were few or nonexistent. Including mine.

I nursed her. They feel that's important nowadays. I nursed all the children, but with her, with all the fierce rigidity of first motherhood, I did like the books then said. Though her cries battered me to trembling and my breasts ached with swollenness, I waited till the clock decreed.

Why do I put that first? I do not even know if it matters, or if it explains anything.

She was a beautiful baby. She blew shining bubbles of sound. She loved motion, loved light, loved color and music and textures. She would lie on the floor in her blue overalls patting the surface so hard in ecstasy her hands and feet would blur. She was a miracle to me, but when she was eight months old I had to leave her daytimes with the woman downstairs to whom she was no miracle at all, for I worked or looked for work and for Emily's father, who "could no longer endure" (he wrote in his good-bye note) "sharing want with us."

I was nineteen. It was the pre-relief, pre-WPA world of the depression. I would start running as soon as I got off the streetcar, running up the stairs, the place smelling sour, and awake or asleep to startle awake, when she saw me she would break into a clogged weeping that could not be comforted, a weeping I can hear yet.

After a while I found a job hashing at night so I could be with her days, and it was better. But it came to where I had to bring her to his family and leave her.

It took a long time to raise the money for her fare back. Then she got chicken pox and I had to wait longer. When she finally came, I hardly knew her, walking quick and nervous like her father, looking like her father, thin, and dressed in a shoddy red that yellowed her skin and glared at the pockmarks. All the baby loveliness gone.

She was two. Old enough for nursery school they said, and I did not know then what I know now—the fatigue of the long day, and the lacerations of group life in the kinds of nurseries that are only parking places for children.

Except that it would have made no difference if I had known. It was the only place there was. It was the only way we could be together, the only way I could hold a job.

And even without knowing, I knew. I knew the teacher that was evil because all these years it has curdled into my memory, the little boy hunched in the corner, her rasp, "why aren't you outside, because Alvin hits you? that's no reason, go out, scaredy." I knew Emily hated it even if she did not clutch and implore "don't go Mommy" like the other children, mornings.

She always had a reason why we should stay home. Momma, you look sick. Momma, I feel sick. Momma, the teachers aren't there today, they're sick. Momma, we can't go, there was a fire there last night. Momma, it's a holiday today, no school, they told me.

But never a direct protest, never rebellion. I think of our others in their three-, four-year-oldness—the explosions, the tempers, the denunciations, the demands—and I feel suddenly ill. I put the iron down. What in me demanded that goodness in her? And what was the cost, the cost to her of such goodness?

The old man living in the back once said in his gentle way: "You should smile at Emily more when you look at her." What *was* in my face when I looked at her? I loved her. There were all the acts of love.

It was only with the others I remembered what he said, and it was the face of joy, and not of care or tightness or worry I turned to them—too late for Emily. She does not smile easily, let alone almost always as her brothers and sisters do. Her face is closed and sombre, but when she wants, how fluid. You must have seen it in her pantomimes, you spoke of her rare gift for comedy on the stage that rouses a laughter out of the audience so dear they applaud and applaud and do not want to let her go.

Where does it come from, that comedy? There was none of it in her when she came back to me that second time, after I had had to send her away again. She had a new daddy now to learn to love, and I think perhaps it was a better time.

Except when we left her alone nights, telling ourselves she was old enough.

"Can't you go some other time, Mommy, like tomorrow?" she would ask. "Will it be just a little while you'll be gone? Do you promise?"

The time we came back, the front door open, the clock on the floor in the hall. She rigid awake. "It wasn't just a little while. I didn't cry. Three times I called you, just three times, and then I ran downstairs to open the door so you could come faster. The clock talked loud. I threw it away, it scared me what it talked."

She said the clock talked loud again that night I went to the hospital to have Susan. She was delirious with the fever that comes before red measles, but she was fully conscious all the week I was gone and the week after we were home when she could not come near the new baby or me.

She did not get well. She stayed skeleton thin, not wanting to eat, and night after night she had nightmares. She would call for me, and I would rouse from exhaustion to sleepily call back: "You're all right, darling, go to sleep, it's just a dream," and if she still called, in a sterner voice, "Now go to sleep, Emily, there's nothing to hurt you." Twice, only twice, when I had to get up for Susan anyhow, I went in to sit with her.

Now when it is too late (as if she would let me hold and comfort her like I do the others) I get up and go to her at once at her moan or restless stirring. "Are you awake, Emily? Can I get you something?" And the answer is always the same: "No, I'm all right, go back to sleep, Mother."

They persuaded me at the clinic to send her away to a convalescent home in the country where "she can have the kind of food and care you can't manage for her, and you'll be free to concentrate on the new baby." They still send children to that place. I see pictures on the society page of sleek young women planning affairs to raise money for it, or dancing at the affairs, or decorating Easter eggs or filling Christmas stockings for the children.

They never have a picture of the children so I do not know if the girls still wear those gigantic red bows and the ravaged looks on the every other Sunday when parents can come to visit "unless otherwise notified"—as we were notified the first six weeks.

Oh it is a handsome place, green lawns and tall trees and fluted flower beds. High up on the balconies of each cottage the children stand, the girls in their red bows and white dresses, the boys in white suits and giant red ties. The parents stand below shrieking up to be heard and the children shriek down to be heard, and between them the invisible wall "Not To Be Contaminated by Parental Germs or Physical Affection."

There was a tiny girl who always stood hand in hand with Emily. Her parents never came. One visit she was gone. "They moved her to Rose Cottage" Emily shouted in explanation. "They don't like you to love anybody here."

She wrote once a week, the labored writing of a seven-year-old. "I am fine. How is the baby. If I write my leter nicly I will have a star. Love." There never was a star. We wrote every other day, letters she could never hold or keep but only hear read—once. "We simply do not have room for children to keep any personal possessions," they patiently explained when we pieced one Sunday's shrieking together to plead how much it would mean to Emily, who loved so to keep things, to be allowed to keep her letters and cards.

Each visit she looked frailer. "She isn't eating," they told us.

(They had runny eggs for breakfast or mush with lumps, Emily said later, I'd hold it in my mouth and not swallow. Nothing ever tasted good, just when they had chicken.)

It took us eight months to get her released home, and only the fact that she gained back so little of her seven lost pounds convinced the social worker.

I used to try to hold and love her after she came back, but her body would stay stiff, and after a while she'd push away. She ate little. Food sickened her, and I think much of life too. Oh she had physical lightness and brightness, twinkling by on skates, bouncing like a ball up and down up and down over the jump rope, skimming over the hill; but these were momentary.

She fretted about her appearance, thin and dark and foreign-looking at a time when every little girl was supposed to look or thought she should look a chubby blond replica of Shirley Temple. The doorbell sometimes rang for her, but no one seemed to come and play in the house or be a best friend. Maybe because we moved so much.

There was a boy she loved painfully through two school semesters. Months later she told me how she had taken pennies from my purse to buy him candy. "Licorice was his favorite and I brought him some every day, but he still liked Jennifer better'n me. Why, Mommy?" The kind of question for which there is no answer.

School was a worry to her. She was not glib or quick in a world where glibness and quickness were easily confused with ability to learn. To her overworked and exasperated teachers she was an overconscientious "slow learner" who kept trying to catch up and was absent entirely too often.

I let her be absent, though sometimes the illness was imaginary. How different from my now-strictness about attendance with the others. I wasn't working. We had a new baby, I was home anyhow. Sometimes, after Susan grew old enough, I would keep her home from school, too, to have them all together.

Mostly Emily had asthma, and her breathing, harsh and labored, would fill the house with a curiously tranquil sound. I would bring the two old dresser mirrors and her boxes of collections to her bed. She would select beads and single earrings, bottle tops and shells, dried flowers and pebbles, old postcards and scraps, all sorts of oddments; then she and Susan would play Kingdom, setting up landscapes and furniture, peopling them with action.

Those were the only times of peaceful companionship between her and Susan. I have edged away from it, that poisonous feeling between them, that terrible balancing of hurts and needs I had to do between the two, and did so badly, those earlier years.

Oh there are conflicts between the others too, each one human, needing, demanding, hurting, taking—but only between Emily and Susan, no, Emily toward Susan that corroding resentment. It seems so obvious on the surface, yet it is not obvious. Susan, the second child, Susan, golden- and curly-haired and chubby, quick and articulate and assured, everything in appearance and manner Emily was not; Susan, not able to resist Emily's precious things, losing or sometimes clumsily breaking them; Susan telling jokes and riddles to company for applause while Emily sat silent (to say to me later: that was *my* riddle, Mother, I told it to Susan); Susan, who for all the five years' difference in age was just a year behind Emily in developing physically.

I am glad for that slow physical development that widened the difference between her and her contemporaries, though she suffered over it. She was too vulnerable for that terrible world of youthful competition, of preening and parading, of constant measuring of yourself against every other, of envy, "If I had that copper hair," "If I had that skin. . . ." She tormented herself enough about not looking like the others, there was enough of the unsureness, the having to be conscious of words before you speak, the constant caring—what are they thinking of me? without having it all magnified by the merciless physical drives.

Ronnie is calling. He is wet and I change him. It is rare there is such a cry now. That time of motherhood is almost behind me when the ear is not one's own but must always be racked and listening for the child cry, the child call. We sit for a while and I hold him, looking out over the city spread in charcoal with its soft aisles of light. "*Shoogily,*" he breathes and curls closer. I carry him back to bed, asleep. *Shoogily*. A funny word, a family word, inherited from Emily, invented by her to say: *comfort*.

In this and other ways she leaves her seal, I say aloud. And startle at my saying it. What do I mean? What did I start to gather together, to try and make coherent? I was at the terrible, growing years. War years. I do not remember them well. I was working, there were four smaller ones now, there was not time for her. She had to help be a mother, and housekeeper, and shopper. She had to set her seal. Mornings of crisis and near hysteria trying to get lunches packed, hair combed, coats and shoes found, everyone to school or Child Care on time, the baby ready for transportation. And always the paper scribbled on by a smaller one, the book looked at by Susan then mislaid, the homework not done. Running out to that huge school where she was one, she was lost, she was a drop; suffering over her unpreparedness, stammering and unsure in her classes.

There was so little time left at night after the kids were bedded down. She would struggle over books, always eating (it was in those years she developed her enormous appetite that is legendary in our family) and I would be ironing, or preparing food for the next day, or writing V-mail to Bill, or tending the baby. Sometimes, to make me laugh, or out of her despair, she would imitate happenings or types at school.

I think I said once: "Why don't you do something like this in the school amateur show?" One morning she phoned me at work, hardly understandable through the weeping: "Mother, I did it. I won, I won; they gave me first prize; they clapped and clapped and wouldn't let me go."

Now suddenly she was Somebody, and as imprisoned in her difference as she had been in her anonymity.

She began to be asked to perform at other high schools, even in colleges, then at city and statewide affairs. The first one we went to, I only recognized her that first moment when thin, shy, she almost drowned herself into the curtains. Then: Was this Emily? The control, the command, the convulsing and deadly clowning, the spell, then the roaring, stamping audience, unwilling to let this rare and precious laughter out of their lives.

Afterwards: You ought to do something about her with a gift like that—but without money or knowing how, what does one do? We have left it all to her, and the gift has as often eddied inside, clogged and clotted, as been used and growing.

She is coming. She runs up the stairs two at a time with her light graceful step, and I know she is happy tonight. Whatever it was that occasioned your call did not happen today.

"Aren't you ever going to finish the ironing, Mother? Whistler painted his mother in a rocker. I'd have to paint mine standing over an ironing board." This is one of her communicative nights and she tells me everything and nothing as she fixes herself a plate of food out of the icebox.

She is so lovely. Why did you want me to come in at all? Why were you concerned? She will find her way.

She starts up the stairs to bed. "Don't get *me* up with the rest in the morning." "But I thought you were having midterms." "Oh, those," she comes back in, kisses me, and says quite lightly, "in a couple of years when we'll all be atom-dead they won't matter a bit."

She has said it before. She *believes* it. But because I have been dredging the past, and all that compounds a human being is so heavy and meaningful in me, I cannot endure it tonight.

I will never total it all. I will never come in to say: She was a child seldom smiled at. Her father left me before she was a year old. I had to work her first six years when there was work, or I sent her home and to his relatives. There were years she had care she hated. She was dark and thin and foreign-looking in a world where the prestige went to blondness and curly hair and dimples; she was slow where glibness was prized. She was a child of anxious, not proud, love. We were poor and could not afford for her the soil of easy growth. I was a young mother, I was a distracted mother. There were the other children pushing up, demanding. Her younger sister seemed all that she was not. There were years she did not let me touch her. She kept too much in herself, her life was such she had to keep too much in herself. My wisdom came too late. She has much to her and probably little will come of it. She is a child of her age, of depression, of war, of fear.

Let her be. So all that is in her will not bloom—but in how many does it? There is still enough left to live by. Only help her to know—help make it so there is cause for her to know—that she is more than this dress on the ironing board, helpless before the iron.

Wants

by Grace Paley

Introduced by Janet Kauffman

THE WOMAN WHO SITS ON THE LIBRARY STEPS AT THE BEGINNING OF Grace Paley's short story "Wants" doesn't want anything—that's her problem, according to her ex-husband. And she doesn't want things, purchases, that's true. Her wants are political, so deeply political they can look whimsical in these United States. She wants to be "the effective citizen" in "this dear urban center." Well, when I first read this story, in 1980, I just plain cheered. I was writing fiction for the first time then, and it wasn't only the narrator's political mindfulness that made me happy but also Paley's writing of the story that encouraged me: the way it begins on the steps of the library and doesn't go farther than through the door, returning books; the nerve and confidence of the sentences, straightforward, talky, a woman's voice that made me think the simple thought—Here is a person.

Before reading this story—it's the opening one in *Enormous Changes at the Last Minute*—I'd never run across, or noticed, writing like Paley's spare, free-wheeling sentences and the play of story from here to there, with the meander I recognized as the way things really go along. The "plumber's snake" sentence in this story is a sentence, along with the two sentences after it, I still often read to students. The paragraph sounds simple; it just goes along and yaks. But for me, it's wild and drastic writing—the way it keeps going "through the ear down the throat." The paragraph twists and turns, easy and painful, comic and devastating. It's a knowing paragraph, comprehending more than it claims, embodying things we think of as personal or political or cultural in the plain tones of a speaking voice, the shaped air out of that woman's mouth.

In this story, Grace Paley clearly doesn't want a fancy narrative or anything "choking with equipment." She's one of the writers whose work, early on, convinced me I don't want much in a story either. Not the big purchases, the fine finishes. "I'm short of requests and absolute requirements," as the woman says. Paley's story opens up and pares down a woman's voice to the bare bones of her politics and imagination. It's a story that convinced me then, and still convinces me, that fiction doesn't need, even if it wants, large events or epiphanies or dramatic turns. At least, some of us don't want them, don't require them, don't trust them. These are political issues as well as writing issues, and Paley's match of these matters in "Wants" made me want to shake her hand, kiss her hair. "Take some appropriate action"—in words, finally, here.

Wants

Grace Paley

I saw my ex-husband in the street. I was sitting on the steps of the new library.

Hello, my life, I said. We had once been married for twenty-seven years, so I felt justified.

He said, What? What life? No life of mine.

I said, O.K. I don't argue when there's real disagreement. I got up and went into the library to see how much I owed them.

The librarian said $32 even and you've owed it for eighteen years. I didn't deny anything. Because I don't understand how time passes. I have had those books. I have often thought of them. The library is only two blocks away.

My ex-husband followed me to the Books Returned desk. He interrupted the librarian, who had more to tell. In many ways, he said, as I look back, I attribute the dissolution of our marriage to the fact that you never invited the Bertrams to dinner.

That's possible, I said. But really, if you remember: first, my father was sick that Friday, then the children were born, then I had those Tuesday-night meetings, then the war began. Then we didn't seem to know them any more. But you're right. I should have had them to dinner.

I gave the librarian a check for $32. Immediately she trusted me, put my past behind her, wiped the record clean, which is just what most other municipal and/or state bureaucracies will *not* do.

I checked out the two Edith Wharton books I had just returned because I'd read them so long ago and they are more apropos now than ever. They were *The House of Mirth* and *The Children,* which is about how life in the United States in New York changed in twenty-seven years fifty years ago.

A nice thing I do remember is breakfast, my ex-husband said. I was surprised. All we ever had was coffee. Then I remembered there was a hole in the back of the kitchen closet which opened into the apartment next door. There, they always ate sugar-cured smoked bacon. It gave us a very grand feeling about breakfast, but we never got stuffed and sluggish.

That was when we were poor, I said.

When were we ever rich? he asked.

Oh, as time went on, as our responsibilities increased, we didn't go in need. You took adequate financial care, I reminded him. The children went to camp four weeks a year and in decent ponchos with sleeping bags and boots, just like everyone else. They looked very nice. Our place was warm in winter, and we had nice red pillows and things.

I wanted a sailboat, he said. But you didn't want anything.

Don't be bitter, I said. It's never too late.

No, he said with a great deal of bitterness. I may get a sailboat. As a matter of fact I have money down on an eighteen-foot two-rigger. I'm doing well this year and can look forward to better. But as for you, it's too late. You'll always want nothing.

He had had a habit throughout the twenty-seven years of making a narrow remark which, like a plumber's snake, could work its way through the ear down the throat, halfway to my heart. He would then disappear, leaving me choking with equipment. What I mean is, I sat down on the library steps and he went away.

I looked through *The House of Mirth,* but lost interest. I felt extremely accused. Now, it's true, I'm short of requests and absolute requirements. But I do want *something.*

I want, for instance, to be a different person. I want to be the woman who brings these two books back in two weeks. I want to be the effective citizen who changes the school system and addresses the Board of Estimate on the troubles of this dear urban center.

I *had* promised my children to end the war before they grew up.

I wanted to have been married forever to one person, my ex-husband or my present one. Either has enough character for a whole life, which as it turns out is really not such a long time. You couldn't exhaust either man's qualities or get under the rock of his reasons in one short life.

Just this morning I looked out the window to watch the street for a while and saw that the little sycamores the city had dreamily planted a couple of years before the kids were born had come that day to the prime of their lives.

Well! I decided to bring those two books back to the library. Which proves that when a person or an event comes along to jolt or appraise me I *can* take some appropriate action, although I am better known for my hospitable remarks.

In Dreams Begin Responsibilities

by Delmore Schwartz

Introduced by Tim O'Brien

I'VE TRIED AND TRIED TO THINK UP SMART THINGS TO SAY ABOUT this wonderful story by Delmore Schwartz. But the story is so much better than anything I can tell you about it. Irving Howe, who was also asked to say smart things about the story, came up with some very good ones for his foreword to my copy of *In Dreams Begin Responsibilities and Other Stories.* Howe explains that the title story is "distinctively urban," that it has "tragic force," that it is a "protest against life itself," that it appeals to Howe's "deepest feelings." I agree wholeheartedly with each of these insights. The story appealed to my own deepest feelings. (I might add that, by way of contrast, *Moby Dick* strikes me as distinctively marine. Otherwise, Melville's novel and Schwartz's story share a great deal, especially when it comes to tragic force.) Howe also does a fine job of describing the plot of "In Dreams Begin Responsibilities." In fact, in Howe's foreword, the story gets pretty much told in its entirety; the most memorable and beautiful and inventive lines are helpfully quoted in advance; the story's conclusion receives special detailed attention, which is a smart idea, since readers might experience unnecessary shivers and shock when they get there for themselves.

After much thought, I did finally arrive at three smart things to tell you about "In Dreams Begin Responsibilities." The first smart thing is this. Dreams are real. The second smart thing is even smarter. If you don't love this story, I'm not responsible. The third smart thing is fabulous. If you do love it, I'm not responsible. Your dreams are.

In Dreams Begin Responsibilities

Delmore Schwartz

I

I think it is the year 1909. I feel as if I were in a moving-picture theatre, the long arm of light crossing the darkness and spinning, my eyes fixed upon the screen. It is a silent picture, as if an old Biograph one, in which the actors are dressed in ridiculously old-fashioned clothes, and one flash succeeds another with sudden jumps, and the actors, too, seem to jump about, walking too fast. The shots are full of rays and dots, as if it had been raining when the picture was photographed. The light is bad.

It is Sunday afternoon, June 12th, 1909, and my father is walking down the quiet streets of Brooklyn on his way to visit my mother. His clothes are newly pressed, and his tie is too tight in his high collar. He jingles the coins in his pocket, thinking of the witty things he will say. I feel as if I had by now relaxed entirely in the soft darkness of the theatre; the organist peals out the obvious approximate emotions on which the audience rocks unknowingly. I am anonymous. I have forgotten myself: it is always so when one goes to a movie; it is, as they say, a drug.

My father walks from street to street of trees, lawns and houses, once in a while coming to an avenue on which a street-car skates and gnaws, progressing slowly. The motorman, who has a handle-bar mustache, helps a young lady wearing a hat like a feathered bowl onto the car. He leisurely makes change and rings his bell as the passengers mount the car. It is obviously Sunday, for everyone is wearing Sunday clothes and the street-car's noises emphasize the quiet of the holiday (Brooklyn is said to be the city of churches). The shops are closed and their shades drawn but for an occasional stationery store or drugstore with great green balls in the window.

My father has chosen to take this long walk because he likes to walk and think. He thinks about himself in the future and so arrives at the place he is to visit in a mild state of exaltation. He pays no attention to the houses he is passing, in which the Sunday dinner is being eaten, nor to the many trees which line each street, now coming to their full green and the time when they will enclose the whole street in leafy shadow. An occasional carriage passes, the horses' hooves falling like stones in the quiet afternoon, and once in a while an automobile, looking like an enormous upholstered sofa, puffs and passes.

My father thinks of my mother, of how lady-like she is, and of the pride which will be his when he introduces her to his family. They are not yet engaged and he is not yet sure that he loves my mother, so that, once in a while, he becomes panicky about the bond already established. But then he reassures himself by thinking of the big men he admires who are married: William Randolph Hearst and William Howard Taft, who has just become the President of the United States.

My father arrives at my mother's house. He has come too early and so is suddenly embarrassed. My aunt, my mother's younger sister, answers the loud bell with her napkin in her hand, for the family is still at dinner. As my father enters, my grandfather rises from the table and shakes hands with him. My mother has run upstairs to tidy herself. My grandmother asks my father if he has had dinner and tells him that my mother will be down soon. My grandfather opens the conversation by remarking about the mild June weather. My father sits uncomfortably near the table, holding his hat in his hand. My grandmother tells my aunt to take my father's hat. My uncle, twelve years old, runs into the house, his hair tousled. He shouts a greeting to my father, who has often given him nickels, and then runs upstairs, as my grandmother shouts after him. It is evident that the respect in which my father is held in this house is tempered by a good deal of mirth. He is impressive, but also very awkward.

II

Finally my mother comes downstairs and my father, being at the moment engaged in conversation with my grandfather, is made uneasy by her entrance, for he does not know whether to greet my mother or to continue the conversation. He gets up from his chair clumsily and says "Hello" gruffly. My grandfather watches this, examining their congruence, such as it is, with a critical eye, and meanwhile rubbing his bearded cheek roughly, as he always does when he reasons. He is worried; he is afraid that my father will not make a good husband for his oldest daughter. At this point something happens to the film, just as my father says something funny to my mother: I am awakened to myself and my unhappiness just as my interest has become most intense. The audience begins to clap impatiently. Then the trouble is attended to, but the film has been returned to a portion just shown, and once more I see my grandfather rubbing his bearded cheek, pondering my father's character. It is difficult to get back into the picture once more and forget myself, but as my mother giggles at my father's words, the darkness drowns me.

My father and mother depart from the house, my father shaking hands with my grandfather once more, out of some unknown uneasiness. I stir uneasily also, slouched in the hard chair of the theatre. Where is the older uncle, my mother's older brother? He is studying in his bedroom upstairs, studying for his final examinations at the College of the City of New York, having been dead of double pneumonia for the last twenty-one years. My mother and father walk down the same quiet streets once more. My mother is holding my father's arm and telling him of the novel she has been reading and my father utters judgments of the characters as the plot is made clear to him. This is a habit which he very much enjoys, for he feels the utmost superiority and confidence when he is approving or condemning the behavior of other people. At times he feels moved to utter a brief "Ugh," whenever the story becomes what he would call sugary. This tribute is the assertion of his manliness. My mother feels satisfied by the interest she has awakened; and she is showing my father how intelligent she is and how interesting.

They reach the avenue, and the street-car leisurely arrives. They are going to Coney Island this afternoon, although my mother really considers such pleasures inferior. She has made up her mind to indulge only in a walk on the boardwalk and a pleasant dinner, avoiding the riotous amusements as being beneath the dignity of so dignified a couple.

My father tells my mother how much money he has made in the week just past, exaggerating an amount which need not have been exaggerated. But my father has always felt that actualities somehow fall short, no matter how fine they are. Suddenly I begin to weep. The determined old lady who sits next to me in the theatre is annoyed and looks at me with an angry face, and being intimidated, I stop. I drag out my handkerchief and dry my face, licking the drop which has fallen near my lips. Meanwhile I have missed something, for here are my father and mother alighting from the street-car at the last stop, Coney Island.

III

They walk toward the boardwalk and my mother commands my father to inhale the pungent air from the sea. They both breathe in deeply, both of them laughing as they do so. They have in common a great interest in health, although my father is strong and husky, and my mother is frail. They are both full of theories about what is good to eat and not good to eat, and sometimes have heated discussions about it, the whole matter ending in my father's announcement, made with a scornful bluster, that you have to die sooner or later anyway. On the boardwalk's flagpole, the American flag is pulsing in an intermittent wind from the sea.

My father and mother go to the rail of the boardwalk and look down on the beach where a good many bathers are casually walking about. A few are in the surf. A peanut whistle pierces the air with its pleasant and active whine, and my father goes to buy peanuts. My mother remains at the rail and stares at the ocean. The ocean seems merry to her; it pointedly sparkles and again and again the pony waves are released. She notices the children digging in the wet sand, and the bathing costumes of the girls who are her own age. My father returns with the peanuts. Overhead the sun's lightning strikes and strikes, but neither of them are at all aware of it. The boardwalk is full of people dressed in their Sunday clothes and casually strolling. The tide does not reach as far as the boardwalk, and the strollers would feel no danger if it did. My father and mother lean on the rail of the boardwalk and absently stare at the ocean. The ocean is becoming rough; the waves come in slowly, tugging strength from far back. The moment before they somersault, the moment when they arch their backs so beautifully, showing white veins in the green and black, that moment is intolerable. They finally crack, dashing fiercely upon the sand, actually driving, full force downward, against it, bouncing upward and forward, and at last petering out into a small stream of bubbles which slides up the beach and then is recalled. The sun overhead does not disturb my father and my mother. They gaze idly at the ocean, scarcely interested in its harshness. But I stare at the terrible sun which breaks up sight, and the fatal merciless passionate ocean. I forget my parents. I stare fascinated, and finally, shocked by their indifference, I burst out weeping once more. The old lady next to me pats my shoulder and says "There, there, young man, all of this is only a movie, only a movie," but I look up once more at the terrifying sun and the terrifying ocean, and being unable to control my tears I get up and go to the men's room, stumbling over the feet of the other people seated in my row.

IV

When I return, feeling as if I had just awakened in the morning sick for lack of sleep, several hours have apparently passed and my parents are riding on the merry-go-round. My father is on a black horse, my mother on a white one, and they seem to be making an eternal circuit for the single purpose of snatching the nickel rings which are attached to an arm of one of the posts. A hand organ is playing; it is inseparable from the ceaseless circling of the merry-go-round.

For a moment it seems that they will never get off the carousel, for it will never stop, and I feel as if I were looking down from the fiftieth story of a building. But at length they do get off; even the hand-organ has ceased for a moment. There is a sudden and sweet stillness, as if the achievement of so much motion. My mother has acquired only two rings, my father, however, ten of them, although it was my mother who really wanted them.

They walk on along the boardwalk as the afternoon descends by imperceptible degrees into the incredible violet of dusk. Everything fades into a relaxed glow, even the ceaseless murmuring from the beach. They look for a place to have dinner. My father suggests the best restaurant on the boardwalk and my mother demurs, according to her principles of economy and housewifeliness.

However they do go to the best place, asking for a table near the window so that they can look out upon the boardwalk and the mobile ocean. My father feels omnipotent as he places a quarter in the waiter's hand in asking for a table. The place is crowded and here too there is music, this time from a kind of string trio. My father orders with a fine confidence.

As their dinner goes on, my father tells of his plans for the future and my mother shows with expressive face how interested she is, and how impressed. My father becomes exultant, lifted up by the waltz that is being played, and his own future begins to intoxicate him. My father tells my mother that he is going to expand his business, for there is a great deal of money to be made. He wants to settle down. After all, he is twenty-nine, he has lived by himself since his thirteenth year, he is making more and more money, and he is envious of his friends when he visits them in the security of their homes, surrounded, it seems, by the calm domestic pleasures, and by delightful children, and then as the waltz reaches the moment when the dancers all swing madly, then, then with awful daring, then he asks my mother to marry him, although awkwardly enough and puzzled as to how he had arrived at the question, and she, to make the whole business worse, begins to cry, and my father looks nervously about, not knowing at all what to do now, and my mother says: "It's all I've wanted from the first moment I saw you," sobbing, and he finds all of this very difficult, scarcely to his taste, scarcely as he thought it would be, on his long walks over Brooklyn Bridge in the revery of a fine cigar, and it was then, at that point, that I stood up in the theatre and shouted: "Don't do it! It's not too late to change your minds, both of you. Nothing good will come of it, only remorse, hatred, scandal, and two children whose characters are monstrous." The whole audience turned to look at me, annoyed, the usher came hurrying down the aisle flashing his searchlight, and the old lady next to me tugged me down into my seat, saying: "Be quiet. You'll be put out, and you paid thirty-five cents to come in." And so I shut my eyes because I could not bear to see what was happening. I sat there quietly.

V

But after a while I begin to take brief glimpses and at length I watch again with thirsty interest, like a child who tries to maintain his sulk when he is offered the bribe of candy. My parents are now having their picture taken in a photographer's booth along the boardwalk. The place is shadowed in the mauve light which is apparently necessary. The camera is set to the side on its tripod and looks like a Martian man. The photographer is instructing my parents in how to pose. My father has his arm over my mother's shoulder, and both of them smile emphatically. The photographer brings my mother a bouquet of flowers to hold in her hand, but she holds it at the wrong angle. Then the photographer covers himself with the black cloth which drapes the camera and all that one sees of him is one protruding arm and his hand with which he holds tightly to the rubber ball which he squeezes when the picture is taken. But he is not satisfied with their appearance. He feels that somehow there is something wrong in their pose. Again and again he comes out from his hiding place with new directions. Each suggestion merely makes matters worse. My father is becoming impatient. They try a seated pose. The photographer explains that he has his pride, he wants to make beautiful pictures, he is not merely interested in all of this for the money. My father says: "Hurry up, will you? We haven't got all night." But the photographer only scurries about apologetically, issuing new directions. The photographer charms me, and I approve of him with all my heart, for I know exactly how he feels, and as he criticizes each revised pose according to some obscure idea of rightness, I become quite hopeful. But then my father says angrily: "Come on, you've had enough time, we're not going to wait any longer." And the photographer, sighing unhappily, goes back into the black covering, and holds out his hand, saying: "One, two, three, Now!," and the picture is taken, with my father's smile turned to a grimace and my mother's bright and false. It takes a few minutes for the picture to be developed and as my parents sit in the curious light they become depressed.

VI

They have passed a fortune-teller's booth and my mother wishes to go in, but my father does not. They begin to argue about it. My mother becomes stubborn, my father once more impatient. What my father would like to do now is walk off and leave my mother there, but he knows that that would never do. My mother refuses to budge. She is near tears, but she feels an uncontrollable desire to hear what the palm reader will say. My father consents angrily and they both go into the booth which is, in a way, like the photographer's, since it is draped in black cloth and its light is colored and shadowed. The place is too warm, and my father keeps saying that this is all nonsense, pointing to the crystal ball on the table. The fortune-teller, a short, fat woman garbed in robes supposedly exotic, comes into the room and greets them, speaking with an accent. But suddenly my father feels that the whole thing is intolerable; he tugs at my mother's arm but my mother refuses to budge. And then, in terrible anger, my father lets go of my mother's arm and strides out, leaving my mother stunned. She makes a movement as if to go after him, but the fortune-teller holds her and begs her not to do so, and I in my seat in the darkness am shocked and horrified. I feel as if I were walking a tightrope one hundred feet over a circus audience and suddenly the rope is showing signs of breaking, and I get up from my seat and begin to shout once more the first words I can think of to communicate my terrible fear, and once more the usher comes hurrying down the aisle flashing his searchlight, and the old lady pleads with me, and the shocked audience has turned to stare at me, and I keep shouting: "What are they doing? Don't they know what they are doing? Why doesn't my mother go after my father and beg him not to be angry? If she does not do that, what will she do? Doesn't my father know what he is doing?" But the usher has seized my arm, and is dragging me away, and as he does so, he says: "What are *you* doing? Don't you know you can't do things like this, you can't do whatever you want to do, even if other people aren't about? You will be sorry if you do not do what you should do. You can't carry on like this, it is not right, you will find that out soon enough, everything you do matters too much," and as he said that, dragging me through the lobby of the theatre, into the cold light, I woke up into the bleak winter morning of my twenty-first birthday, the window-sill shining with its lip of snow, and the morning already begun.

The Man to Send Rain Clouds

by Leslie Marmon Silko

Introduced by Louis Owens

THE FIRST TIME I READ "THE MAN TO SEND RAIN CLOUDS," I WAS UNDER a canvas tarp in Arizona's White Mountains, listening to a thunderstorm that seemed to be walking right up the river canyon. The flashes of lightning and sound came simultaneously, and the thunder had the almost painful metallic crack that meant it was directly overhead. The summer monsoon season was strangely late and hitting the San Carlos Apache Reservation pretty hard. I'd backpacked in alone to do some reservation fly-fishing, and each day a thunderstorm had rumbled in at about one o'clock in the afternoon and stayed for three hours before clearing out. In three days I had seen elk, deer, black bear, ospreys, bighorn sheep, golden eagles, beavers, wild turkeys, quail, rattlesnakes, and much more, but as far as people went there wasn't even a footprint. I had the river to myself. I had sat on top of a bluff and watched a black bear fishing for crawdads and seen an osprey come in low over my head to take a trout a hundred feet upstream. I had watched a large male coyote take a new fawn away from its desperate mother, almost hating the coyote for the laughing ease with which he succeeded. And each day I had caught big heavy rainbows, one after the other.

For two afternoons I had sat out the storms by hunching into myself and going into a kind of rain sleep, a trancelike musing upon the meaning of life, the morning's fishing and the late-afternoon fishing to come, but on the third day I was restless. That was when I pulled out the book I'd brought along, a collection by the Laguna Pueblo writer Leslie Silko. I'd talked—probably too much—about how I admired Silko's novel *Ceremony,* so a friend in Flagstaff had shown up on the eve of my fishing trip with a book called *Storyteller,* insisting that it was the perfect backpacking companion. I'd accepted with proper gratitude but looked at the volume with disgust. It was too big, oddly shaped, at least two pounds, and while I lied to my friend, I knew *Storyteller* would never make it into my backpack. I'd stopped taking books backpacking years before after realizing that reading is the last god-damned thing I want to do when I'm alone in the mountains.

But at the last second—out of guilt, no doubt—I stuck the ungainly book in the top of my pack, and it was there when I set up camp seven miles down the river. Waiting for the storm to pass, I read "The Man to Send Rain Clouds." And then I immediately read it again.

The second time through I realized what a superb piece of writing it was. There is a wonderful beauty about the story, as clean and sparse as the New Mexico landscape where it's set. Like Hemingway at his best, Silko leaves almost everything out. Maria Chona, a wise Papago woman, once said, "The song is very short, because we understand so much." Silko communicates this in "The Man to Send Rain Clouds." She presents a Pueblo world with simple and profound clarity—no sentimental posturing, no romantic lens filter, no explanation. She expects us to enter the terrain of the Pueblo world the same way the priest in the story does, through an accommodation made with understanding and, above all, respect. We know we are outsiders, but we are drawn into that space between Catholic priest and Pueblo family, bridging the distance and, like the priest, allowing feeling to displace the need for empirical knowledge. Silko makes us, above all, *feel* this world.

"The Man to Send Rain Clouds" is a story about our common humanity and our common bonds with the natural world. It doesn't lecture us about the syncretic strength of the Pueblo world, that dynamic which allowed the Indian people of the Southwest to subsume Catholicism so easily into their own traditions. Instead, it shows us.

Narrated in the third person, primarily from the point of view of a family going about the business of burying their dead grandfather, the story speaks to us as though our understanding is a given. As the old man is found and prepared for burial, nothing is explained. Told with precision and care, the story deals with the dead grandfather in a loving, matter-of-fact manner. A man of obvious dignity and significance in life—he is tending sheep alone when death comes—the grandfather remains significant in death. He still has an important role to play in the life of the pueblo, for it is the responsibility of the dead to bring the rain.

Just as the Indian people in the story allow the priest to have a place in their world, the story allows us to participate, no questions asked. But it never panders to us the way weaker fiction does, trying to attract or entice us. Everything is conducted with an attitude of dignity and tact. And that, I realized finally, is where the amazing power of this story comes from. It is, in a diffidently Indian way, a supremely tactful story. Like a well-cast dry fly, it insists upon nothing, but graciously presents itself in a matter-of-fact, superbly understated manner. We rise to the level of the story and are eased into another world, knowing the rain will be back tomorrow. The artifice is dazzling.

For traditional Native Americans, however, words have real power. Words bring-into-being and compel the real world to order and significance. The storyteller bears enormous responsibility. In every line of "The Man to Send Rain Clouds," we feel the narrative's consciousness of such power and responsibility. As Silko showed us in *Ceremony,* a story is more than artifice; each story is a ceremony, and every ceremony changes the world.

The Man to Send Rain Clouds

Leslie Marmon Silko

They found him under a big cottonwood tree. His Levi jacket and pants were faded light blue so that he had been easy to find. The big cottonwood tree stood apart from a small grove of winterbare cottonwoods which grew in the wide, sandy arroyo. He had been dead for a day or more, and the sheep had wandered and scattered up and down the arroyo. Leon and his brother-in-law, Ken, gathered the sheep and left them in the pen at the sheep camp before they returned to the cottonwood tree. Leon waited under the tree while Ken drove the truck through the deep sand to the edge of the arroyo. He squinted up at the sun and unzipped his jacket—it sure was hot for this time of year. But high and northwest the blue mountains were still in snow. Ken came sliding down the low, crumbling bank about fifty yards down, and he was bringing the red blanket.

Before they wrapped the old man, Leon took a piece of string out of his pocket and tied a small gray feather in the old man's long white hair. Ken gave him the paint. Across the brown wrinkled forehead he drew a streak of white and along the high cheekbones he drew a strip of blue paint. He paused and watched Ken throw pinches of corn meal and pollen into the wind that fluttered the small gray feather. Then Leon painted with yellow under the old man's broad nose, and finally, when he had painted green across the chin, he smiled.

"Send us rain clouds, Grandfather." They laid the bundle in the back of the pickup and covered it with a heavy tarp before they started back to the pueblo.

They turned off the highway onto the sandy pueblo road. Not long after they passed the store and post office they saw Father Paul's car coming toward them. When he recognized their faces he slowed his car and waved for them to stop. The young priest rolled down the car window.

"Did you find old Teofilo?" he asked loudly.

Leon stopped the truck. "Good morning, Father. We were just out to the sheep camp. Everything is O.K. now."

"Thank God for that. Teofilo is a very old man. You really shouldn't allow him to stay at the sheep camp alone."

"No, he won't do that any more now."

"Well, I'm glad you understand. I hope I'll be seeing you at Mass this week—we missed you last Sunday. See if you can get old Teofilo to come with you." The priest smiled and waved at them as they drove away.

* * *

Louise and Teresa were waiting. The table was set for lunch, and the coffee was boiling on the black iron stove. Leon looked at Louise and then at Teresa.

"We found him under a cottonwood tree in the big arroyo near sheep camp. I guess he sat down to rest in the shade and never got up again." Leon walked toward the old man's bed. The red plaid shawl had been shaken and spread carefully over the bed, and a new brown flannel shirt and pair of stiff new Levi's were arranged neatly beside the pillow. Louise held the screen door open while Leon and Ken carried in the red blanket. He looked small and shriveled, and after they dressed him in the new shirt and pants he seemed more shrunken.

It was noontime now because the church bells rang the Angelus. They ate the beans with hot bread, and nobody said anything until after Teresa poured the coffee.

Ken stood up and put on his jacket. "I'll see about the gravediggers. Only the top layer of soil is frozen. I think it can be ready before dark."

Leon nodded his head and finished his coffee. After Ken had been gone for a while, the neighbors and clanspeople came quietly to embrace Teofilo's family and to leave food on the table because the gravediggers would come to eat when they were finished.

The sky in the west was full of pale yellow light. Louise stood outside with her hands in the pockets of Leon's green army jacket that was too big for her. The funeral was over, and the old men had taken their candles and medicine bags and were gone. She waited until the body was laid into the pickup before she said anything to Leon. She touched his arm, and he noticed that her hands were still dusty from the corn meal that she had sprinkled around the old man. When she spoke, Leon could not hear her.

"What did you say? I didn't hear you."

"I said that I had been thinking about something."

"About what?"

"About the priest sprinkling holy water for Grandpa. So he won't be thirsty."

Leon stared at the new moccasins that Teofilo had made for the ceremonial dances in the summer. They were nearly hidden by the red blanket. It was getting colder, and the wind pushed gray dust down the narrow pueblo road. The sun was approaching the long mesa where it disappeared during the winter. Louise stood there shivering and watching his face. Then he zipped up his jacket and opened the truck door. "I'll see if he's there."

Ken stopped the pickup at the church, and Leon got out; and then Ken drove down the hill to the graveyard where people were waiting. Leon knocked at the old carved door with its symbols of the Lamb. While he waited he looked up at the twin bells from the king of Spain with the last sunlight pouring around them in their tower.

The priest opened the door and smiled when he saw who it was. "Come in! What brings you here this evening?"

The priest walked toward the kitchen, and Leon stood with his cap in his hand, playing with the earflaps and examining the living room—the brown sofa, the green armchair, and the brass lamp that hung down from the ceiling by links of chain. The priest dragged a chair out of the kitchen and offered it to Leon.

"No thank you, Father. I only came to ask you if you would bring your holy water to the graveyard."

The priest turned away from Leon and looked out the window at the patio full of shadows and the dining-room windows of the nuns' cloister across the patio. The curtains were heavy, and the light from within faintly penetrated; it was impossible to see the nuns inside eating supper. "Why didn't you tell me he was dead? I could have brought the Last Rites anyway."

Leon smiled. "It wasn't necessary, Father."

The priest stared down at his scuffed brown loafers and the worn hem of his cassock. "For a Christian burial it was necessary."

His voice was distant, and Leon thought that his blue eyes looked tired.

"It's O.K., Father, we just want him to have plenty of water."

The priest sank down into the green chair and picked up a glossy missionary magazine. He turned the colored pages full of lepers and pagans without looking at them.

"You know I can't do that, Leon. There should have been the Last Rites and a funeral Mass at the very least."

Leon put on his green cap and pulled the flaps down over his ears. "It's getting late, Father. I've got to go."

When Leon opened the door Father Paul stood up and said, "Wait." He left the room and came back wearing a long brown overcoat. He followed Leon out the door and across the dim churchyard to the adobe steps in front of the church. They both stooped to fit through the low adobe entrance. And when they started down the hill to the graveyard only half of the sun was visible above the mesa.

The priest approached the grave slowly, wondering how they had managed to dig into the frozen ground; and then he remembered that this was New Mexico, and saw the pile of cold loose sand beside the hole. The people stood close to each other with little clouds of steam puffing from their faces. The priest looked at them and saw a pile of jackets, gloves, and scarves in the yellow, dry tumbleweeds that grew in the graveyard. He looked at the red blanket, not sure that Teofilo was so small, wondering if it wasn't some perverse Indian trick—something they did in March to ensure a good harvest—wondering if maybe old Teofilo was actually at sheep camp corralling the sheep for the night. But there he was, facing into a cold dry wind and squinting at the last sunlight, ready to bury a red wool blanket while the faces of his parishioners were in shadow with the last warmth of the sun on their backs.

His fingers were stiff, and it took him a long time to twist the lid off the holy water. Drops of water fell on the red blanket and soaked into dark icy spots. He sprinkled the grave and the water disappeared almost before it touched the dim, cold sand; it reminded him of something—he tried to remember what it was, because he thought if he could remember he might understand this. He sprinkled more water; he shook the container until it was empty, and the water fell through the light from sundown like August rain that fell while the sun was still shining, almost evaporating before it touched the wilted squash flowers.

The wind pulled at the priest's brown Franciscan robe and swirled away the corn meal and pollen that had been sprinkled on the blanket. They lowered the bundle into the ground, and they didn't bother to untie the stiff pieces of new rope that were tied around the ends of the blanket. The sun was gone, and over on the highway the eastbound lane was full of headlights. The priest walked away slowly. Leon watched him climb the hill, and when he had disappeared within the tall, thick walls, Leon turned to look up at the high blue mountains in the deep snow that reflected a faint red light from the west. He felt good because it was finished, and he was happy about the sprinkling of the holy water; now the old man could send them big thunderclouds for sure.

Helping

by Robert Stone

Introduced by Louise Erdrich

WHEN WE STAND BEFORE ANOTHER HUMAN, WE STAND BEFORE THE gates of hell," wrote Franz Kafka. In other words, I suppose, even the most obnoxious of us suffers. At the very least, one must allow for the possibility. In "Helping," the despair that a veteran's counselor, Elliot, undergoes is brought on by his terror at identifying and connecting a dream told by his unsavory client. His annoyance with the man ripens to rage and deepens to depression in skillfully written scenes and is finally acted out with the "help" of that most tedious and desperate of anodynes, liquor. Elliot is a recovering alcoholic. He takes the first drink, and from then on, as the saying goes, the drinks take him. His portrait enlarges to include his wife, Grace, a social worker, and then, in one of the most extraordinarily piteous and moving conversations in literature, these two people talk and fight about the enormously complex task of staying together.

Long marriages are beyond anyone's explanation, perhaps most especially those who live within the bonds. People feel the range of emotions in the course of a relationship—and hatred in this case is the flip side of an affection that the reader is left to infer. These two people depend most upon the same qualities that they despise in one another—her savior's complex, for she is a born rescuer, and his wretched and occasional losses of control that end in self-disgust. It is a painful conversation, but to me the true center of this story is within their exchange. This woman's stubborn refusal to leave this man is an everyday miracle and an act of sacrifice and grace, as her name implies. Is it love? That, the reader must answer. Some people roll the stone of their commitments up the hill, day after day, year in and year out; there is no explanation for it. Is it love, or neurotic need, or is there any way to distinguish between the two? A contained and violent weariness rules the exchange between Elliot and Grace—the symptom of a relationship that finds its groove and most honest rhythm when one of the partners cannot turn from the other in the deepest extremity of need.

"Helping" is about need, and surely about anger, frustration, and the demons of perfect despair, but it is also about whatever the reader brings to it—compassion and even a certain hope. Embarked on a predictable binge, having taken cheap satisfaction in frightening a neighbor, Elliot finds himself emerging, almost reborn, into a dreadful clarity. Perhaps his lows are necessary, the shading to the fragile moment that follows in a winter-pure world of snow and sky. The end of the story leaves a question frozen in the long space that follows Elliot's wave from a field, outside, to his wife standing in the window of their house. Does her own hand, in return, rise against the darkness?

Helping

Robert Stone

One gray November day, Elliot went to Boston for the afternoon. The wet streets seemed cold and lonely. He sensed a broken promise in the city's elegance and verve. Old hopes tormented him like phantom limbs, but he did not drink. He had joined Alcoholics Anonymous fifteen months before.

Christmas came, childless, a festival of regret. His wife went to Mass and cooked a turkey. Sober, Elliot walked in the woods.

In January, blizzards swept down from the Arctic until the weather became too cold for snow. The Shawmut Valley grew quiet and crystalline. In the white silences, Elliot could hear the boards of his house contract and feel a shrinking in his bones. Each dusk, starveling deer came out of the wooded swamp behind the house to graze his orchard for whatever raccoons had uncovered and left behind. At night he lay beside his sleeping wife listening to the baying of dog packs running them down in the deep moon-shadowed snow.

Day in, day out, he was sober. At times it was almost stimulating. But he could not shake off the sensations he had felt in Boston. In his mind's eye he could see dead leaves rattling along brick gutters and savor that day's desperation. The brief outing had undermined him.

Sober, however, he remained, until the day a man named Blankenship came into his office at the state hospital for counseling. Blankenship had red hair, a brutal face, and a sneaking manner. He was a sponger and petty thief whom Elliot had seen a number of times before.

"I been having this dream," Blankenship announced loudly. His voice was not pleasant. His skin was unwholesome. Every time he got arrested the court sent him to the psychiatrists and the psychiatrists, who spoke little English, sent him to Elliot.

Blankenship had joined the Army after his first burglary but had never served east of the Rhine. After a few months in Wiesbaden, he had been discharged for reasons of unsuitability, but he told everyone he was a veteran of the Vietnam War. He went about in a tiger suit. Elliot had had enough of him.

"Dreams are boring," Elliot told him.

Blankenship was outraged. "Whaddaya mean?" he demanded.

During counseling sessions Elliot usually moved his chair into the middle of the room in order to seem accessible to his clients. Now he stayed securely behind his desk. He did not care to seem accessible to Blankenship. "What I said, Mr. Blankenship. Other people's dreams are boring. Didn't you ever hear that?"

"Boring?" Blankenship frowned. He seemed unable to imagine a meaning for the word.

Elliot picked up a pencil and set its point quivering on his desk-top blotter. He gazed into his client's slack-jawed face. The Blankenship family made their way through life as strolling litigants, and young Blankenship's specialty was slipping on ice cubes. Hauled off the pavement, he would hassle the doctors in Emergency for pain pills and hurry to a law clinic. The Blankenships had threatened suit against half the property owners in the southern part of the state. What they could not extort at law they stole. But even the Blankenship family had abandoned Blankenship. His last visit to the hospital had been subsequent to an arrest for lifting a case of hot-dog rolls from Woolworth's. He lived in a Goodwill depository bin in Wyndham.

"Now I suppose you want to tell me your dream? Is that right, Mr. Blankenship?"

Blankenship looked left and right like a dog surrendering eye contact. "Don't you want to hear it?" he asked humbly.

Elliot was unmoved. "Tell me something, Blankenship. Was your dream about Vietnam?"

At the mention of the word "Vietnam," Blankenship customarily broke into a broad smile. Now he looked guilty and guarded. He shrugged. "Ya."

"How come you have dreams about that place, Blankenship? You were never there."

"Whaddaya mean?" Blankenship began to say, but Elliot cut him off.

"You were never there, my man. You never saw the goddamn place. You have no business dreaming about it! You better cut it out!"

He had raised his voice to the extent that the secretary outside his open door paused at her word processor.

"Lemme alone," Blankenship said fearfully. "Some doctor you are."

"It's all right," Elliot assured him. "I'm not a doctor."

"Everybody's on my case," Blankenship said. His moods were volatile. He began to weep.

Elliot watched the tears roll down Blankenship's chapped, pitted cheeks. He cleared his throat. "Look, fella . . . " he began. He felt at a loss. He felt like telling Blankenship that things were tough all over.

Blankenship sniffed and telescoped his neck and after a moment looked at Elliot. His look was disconcertingly trustful; he was used to being counseled.

"Really, you know, it's ridiculous for you to tell me your problems have to do with Nam. You were never over there. It was me over there, Blankenship. Not you."

Blankenship leaned forward and put his forehead on his knees.

"Your troubles have to do with here and now," Elliot told his client. "Fantasies aren't helpful."

His voice sounded overripe and hypocritical in his own ears. What a dreadful business, he thought. What an awful job this is. Anger was driving him crazy.

Blankenship straightened up and spoke through his tears. "This dream . . ." he said. "I'm scared."

Elliot felt ready to endure a great deal in order not to hear Blankenship's dream.

"I'm not the one you see about that," he said. In the end he knew his duty. He sighed. "O.K. All right. Tell me about it."

"Yeah?" Blankenship asked with leaden sarcasm. "Yeah? You think dreams are friggin' boring!"

"No, no," Elliot said. He offered Blankenship a tissue and Blankenship took one. "That was sort of off the top of my head. I didn't really mean it."

Blankenship fixed his eyes on dreaming distance. "There's a feeling that goes with it. With the dream." Then he shook his head in revulsion and looked at Elliot as though he had only just awakened. "So what do you think? You think it's boring?"

"Of course not," Elliot said. "A physical feeling?"

"Ya. It's like I'm floating in rubber."

He watched Elliot stealthily, aware of quickened attention. Elliot had caught dengue in Vietnam and during his weeks of delirium had felt vaguely as though he were floating in rubber.

"What are you seeing in this dream?"

Blankenship only shook his head. Elliot suffered a brief but intense attack of rage.

"Hey, Blankenship," he said equably, "here I am, man. You can see I'm listening."

"What I saw was black," Blankenship said. He spoke in an odd tremolo. His behavior was quite different from anything Elliot had come to expect from him.

"Black? What was it?"

"Smoke. The sky maybe."

"The sky?" Elliot asked.

"It was all black. I was scared."

In a waking dream of his own, Elliot felt the muscles on his neck distend. He was looking up at a sky that was black, filled with smoke-swollen clouds, lit with fires, damped with blood and rain.

"What were you scared of?" he asked Blankenship.

"I don't know," Blankenship said.

Elliot could not drive the black sky from his inward eye. It was as though Blankenship's dream had infected his own mind.

"You don't know? You don't know what you were scared of?"

Blankenship's posture was rigid. Elliot, who knew the aspect of true fear, recognized it there in front of him.

"The Nam," Blankenship said.

"You're not even old enough," Elliot told him.

Blankenship sat trembling with joined palms between his thighs. His face was flushed and not in the least ennobled by pain. He had trouble with alcohol and drugs. He had trouble with everything.

"So wherever your black sky is, it isn't Vietnam."

Things were so unfair, Elliot thought. It was unfair of Blankenship to appropriate the condition of a Vietnam veteran. The trauma inducing his post-traumatic stress had been nothing more serious than his own birth, a routine procedure. Now, in addition to the poverty, anxiety, and confusion that would always be his life's lot, he had been visited with irony. It was all arbitrary and some people simply got elected. Everyone knew that who had been where Blankenship had not.

"Because, I assure you, Mr. Blankenship, you were never there."

"Whaddaya mean?" Blankenship asked.

When Blankenship was gone Elliot leafed through his file and saw that the psychiatrists had passed him upstairs without recording a diagnosis. Disproportionately angry, he went out to the secretary's desk.

"Nobody wrote up that last patient," he said. "I'm not supposed to see people without a diagnosis. The shrinks are just passing the buck."

The secretary was a tall, solemn redhead with prominent front teeth and a slight speech disorder. "Dr. Sayyid will have kittens if he hears you call him a shrink, Chas. He's already complained. He hates being called a shrink."

"Then he came to the wrong country," Elliot said. "He can go back to his own."

The woman giggled. "He *is* the doctor, Chas."

"Hates being called a shrink!" He threw the file on the secretary's table and stormed back toward his office. "That fucking little zip couldn't give you a decent haircut. He's a prescription clerk."

The secretary looked about her guiltily and shook her head. She was used to him.

Elliot succeeded in calming himself down after a while, but the image of the black sky remained with him. At first he thought he would be able to simply shrug the whole thing off. After a few minutes, he picked up his phone and dialed Blankenship's probation officer.

"The Vietnam thing is all he has," the probation officer explained. "I guess he picked it up around."

"His descriptions are vivid," Elliot said.

"You mean they sound authentic?"

"I mean he had me going today. He was ringing my bells."

"Good for Blanky. Think he believes it himself?"

"Yes," Elliot said. "He believes it himself now."

Elliot told the probation officer about Blankenship's current arrest, which was for showering illegally at midnight in the Wyndham Regional High School. He asked what probation knew about Blankenship's present relationship with his family.

"You kiddin'?" the P.O. asked. "They're all locked down. The whole family's inside. The old man's in Bridgewater. Little Donny's in San Quentin or somewhere. Their dog's in the pound."

Elliot had lunch alone in the hospital staff cafeteria. On the far side of the double-glazed windows, the day was darkening as an expected snowstorm gathered. Along Route 7, ancient elms stood frozen against the gray sky. When he had finished his sandwich and coffee, he sat staring out at the winter afternoon. His anger had given way to an insistent anxiety.

On the way back to his office, he stopped at the hospital gift shop for a copy of *Sports Illustrated* and a candy bar. When he was inside again, he closed the door and put his feet up. It was Friday and he had no appointments for the remainder of the day, nothing to do but write a few letters and read the office mail.

Elliot's cubicle in the social services department was windowless and lined with bookshelves. When he found himself unable to concentrate on the magazine and without any heart for his paperwork, he ran his eye over the row of books beside his chair. There were volumes by Heinrich Muller and Carlos Casteneda, Jones's life of Freud, and *The Golden Bough*. The books aroused a revulsion in Elliot. Their present uselessness repelled him.

Over and over again, detail by detail, he tried to recall his conversation with Blankenship.

"You were never there," he heard himself explaining. He was trying to get the whole incident straightened out after the fact. Something was wrong. Dread crept over him like a paralysis. He ate his candy bar without tasting it. He knew that the craving for sweets was itself a bad sign.

Blankenship had misappropriated someone else's dream and made it his own. It made no difference whether you had been there, after all. The dreams had crossed the ocean. They were in the air.

He took his glasses off and put them on his desk and sat with his arms folded, looking into the well of light from his desk lamp. There seemed to be nothing but whirl inside him. Unwelcome things came and went in his mind's eye. His heart beat faster. He could not control the headlong promiscuity of his thoughts.

It was possible to imagine larval dreams traveling in suspended animation undetectable in a host brain. They could be divided and regenerate like flatworms, hide in seams and bedding, in war stories, laughter, snapshots. They could rot your socks and turn your memory into a black-and-green blister. Green for the hills, black for the sky above. At daybreak they hung themselves up in rows like bats. At dusk they went out to look for dreamers.

Elliot put his jacket on and went into the outer office, where the secretary sat frowning into the measured sound and light of her machine. She must enjoy its sleekness and order, he thought. She was divorced. Four redheaded kids between ten and seventeen lived with her in an unpainted house across from Stop & Shop. Elliot liked her and had come to find her attractive. He managed a smile for her.

"Ethel, I think I'm going to pack it in," he declared. It seemed awkward to be leaving early without a reason.

"Jack wants to talk to you before you go, Chas."

Elliot looked at her blankly.

Then his colleague, Jack Sprague, having heard his voice, called from the adjoining cubicle. "Chas, what about Sunday's games? Shall I call you with the spread?"

"I don't know," Elliot said. "I'll phone you tomorrow."

"This is a big decision for him," Jack Sprague told the secretary. "He might lose twenty-five bucks."

At present, Elliot drew a slightly higher salary than Jack Sprague, although Jack had a Ph.D. and Elliot was simply an M.S.W. Different branches of the state government employed them.

"Twenty-five bucks," said the woman. "If you guys have no better use for twenty-five bucks, give it to me."

"Where are you off to, by the way?" Sprague asked.

Elliot began to answer, but for a moment no reply occurred to him. He shrugged. "I have to get back," he finally stammered. "I promised Grace."

"Was that Blankenship I saw leaving?"

Elliot nodded.

"It's February," Jack said. "How come he's not in Florida?"

"I don't know," Elliot said. He put on his coat and walked to the door. "I'll see you."

"Have a nice weekend," the secretary said. She and Sprague looked after him indulgently as he walked toward the main corridor.

"Are Chas and Grace going out on the town?" she said to Sprague. "What do you think?"

"That would be the day," Sprague said. "Tomorrow he'll come back over here and read all day. He spends every weekend holed up in this goddamn office while she does something or other at the church." He shook his head. "Every night he's at A.A. and she's home alone."

Ethel savored her overbite. "Jack," she said teasingly, "are you thinking what I think you're thinking? Shame on you."

"I'm thinking I'm glad I'm not him, that's what I'm thinking. That's as much as I'll say."

"Yeah, well, I don't care," Ethel said. "Two salaries and no kids, that's the way to go, boy."

* * *

Elliot went out through the automatic doors of the emergency bay and the cold closed over him. He walked across the hospital parking lot with his eyes on the pavement, his hands thrust deep in his overcoat pockets, skirting patches of shattered ice. There was no wind, but the motionless air stung; the metal frames of his glasses burned his skin. Curlicues of mud-brown ice coated the soiled snowbanks along the street. Although it was still afternoon, the street lights had come on.

The lock on his car door had frozen and he had to breathe on the keyhole to fit the key. When the engine turned over, Jussi Björling's recording of the Handel Largo filled the car interior. He snapped it off at once.

Halted at the first stoplight, he began to feel the want of a destination. The fear and impulse to flight that had got him out of the office faded, and he had no desire to go home. He was troubled by a peculiar impatience that might have been with time itself. It was as though he were waiting for something. The sensation made him feel anxious; it was unfamiliar but not altogether unpleasant. When the light changed he drove on, past the Gulf station and the firehouse and between the greens of Ilford Common. At the far end of the common he swung into the parking lot of the Packard Conway Library and stopped with the engine running. What he was experiencing, he thought, was the principle of possibility.

He turned off the engine and went out again into the cold. Behind the leaded library windows he could see the librarian pouring coffee in her tiny private office. The librarian was a Quaker of socialist principles named Candace Music, who was Elliot's cousin.

The Conway Library was all dark wood and etched mirrors, a Gothic saloon. Years before, out of work and booze-whipped, Elliot had gone to hide there. Because Candace was a classicist's widow and knew some Greek, she was one of the few people in the valley with whom Elliot had cared to speak in those days. Eventually, it had seemed to him that all their conversations tended toward Vietnam, so he had gone less and less often. Elliot was the only Vietnam veteran Candace knew well enough to chat with, and he had come to suspect that he was being probed for the edification of the East Ilford Friends Meeting. At that time he had still pretended to talk easily about his war and had prepared little discourses and picaresque anecdotes to recite on demand. Earnest seekers like Candace had caused him great secret distress.

Candace came out of her office to find him at the checkout desk. He watched her brow furrow with concern as she composed a smile. "Chas, what a surprise. You haven't been in for an age."

"Sure I have, Candace. I went to all the Wednesday films last fall. I work just across the road."

"I know, dear," Candace said. "I always seem to miss you."

A cozy fire burned in the hearth, an antique brass clock ticked along on the marble mantel above it. On a couch near the fireplace an old man sat upright, his mouth open, asleep among half a dozen soiled plastic bags. Two teenage girls whispered over their homework at a table under the largest window.

"Now that I'm here," he said, laughing, "I can't remember what I came to get."

"Stay and get warm," Candace told him. "Got a minute? Have a cup of coffee."

Elliot had nothing but time, but he quickly realized that he did not want to stay and pass it with Candace. He had no clear idea of why he had come to the library. Standing at the checkout desk, he accepted coffee. She attended him with an air of benign supervision, as though he were a Chinese peasant and she a medical missionary, like her father. Candace was tall and plain, more handsome in her middle sixties than she had ever been.

"Why don't we sit down?"

He allowed her to gentle him into a chair by the fire. They made a threesome with the sleeping old man.

"Have you given up translating, Chas? I hope not."

"Not at all," he said. Together they had once rendered a few fragments of Sophocles into verse. She was good at clever rhymes.

"You come in so rarely, Chas. Ted's books go to waste."

After her husband's death, Candace had donated his books to the Conway, where they reposed in a reading room inscribed to his memory, untouched among foreign-language volumes, local genealogies, and books in large type for the elderly.

"I have a study in the barn," he told Candace. "I work there. When I have time." The lie was absurd, but he felt the need of it.

"And you're working with Vietnam veterans," Candace declared.

"Supposedly," Elliot said. He was growing impatient with her nodding solicitude.

"Actually," he said, "I came in for the new Oxford *Classical World*. I thought you'd get it for the library and I could have a look before I spent my hard-earned cash."

Candace beamed. "You've come to the right place, Chas, I'm happy to say." He thought she looked disproportionately happy. "I have it."

"Good," Elliot said, standing. "I'll just take it, then. I can't really stay."

Candace took his cup and saucer and stood as he did. When the library telephone rang, she ignored it, reluctant to let him go. "How's Grace?" she asked.

"Fine," Elliot said. "Grace is well."

At the third ring she went to the desk. When her back was turned, he hesitated for a moment and then went outside.

The gray afternoon had softened into night, and it was snowing. The falling snow whirled like a furious mist in the headlight beams on Route 7 and settled implacably on Elliot's cheeks and eyelids. His heart, for no good reason, leaped up in childlike expectation. He had run away from a dream and encountered possibility. He felt in possession of a promise. He began to walk toward the roadside lights.

Only gradually did he begin to understand what had brought him there and what the happy anticipation was that fluttered in his breast. Drinking, he had started his evening from the Conway Library. He would arrive hung over in the early afternoon to browse and read. When the old pain rolled in with dusk, he would walk down to the Midway Tavern for a remedy. Standing in the snow outside the library, he realized that he had contrived to promise himself a drink.

Ahead, through the storm, he could see the beer signs in the Midway's window warm and welcoming. Snowflakes spun around his head like an excitement.

Outside the Midway's package store, he paused with his hand on the doorknob. There was an old man behind the counter whom Elliot remembered from his drinking days. When he was inside, he realized that the old man neither knew nor cared who he was. The package store was thick with dust; it was on the counter, the shelves, the bottles themselves. The old counterman looked dusty. Elliot bought a bottle of King William Scotch and put it in the inside pocket of his overcoat.

Passing the windows of the Midway Tavern, Elliot could see the ranks of bottles aglow behind the bar. The place was crowded with men leaving the afternoon shifts at the shoe and felt factories. No one turned to note him when he passed inside. There was a single stool vacant at the bar and he took it. His heart beat faster. Bruce Springsteen was on the jukebox.

The bartender was a club fighter from Pittsfield called Jackie G., with whom Elliot had often gossiped. Jackie G. greeted him as though he had been in the previous evening. "Say, babe?"

"How do," Elliot said.

A couple of men at the bar eyed his shirt and tie. Confronted with the bartender, he felt impelled to explain his presence. "Just thought I'd stop by," he told Jackie G. "Just thought I'd have one. Saw the light. The snow. . . ." He chuckled expansively.

"Good move," the bartender said. "Scotch?"

"Double," Elliot said.

When he shoved two dollars forward along the bar, Jackie G. pushed one of the bills back to him. "Happy hour, babe."

"Ah," Elliot said. He watched Jackie pour the double. "Not a moment too soon."

For five minutes or so, Elliot sat in his car in the barn with the engine running and his Handel tape on full volume. He had driven over from East Ilford in a baroque ecstasy, swinging and swaying and singing along. When the tape ended, he turned off the engine and poured some Scotch into an apple juice container to store providentially beneath the car seat. Then he took the tape and the Scotch into the house with him. He was lying on the sofa in the dark living room, listening to the Largo, when he heard his wife's car in the driveway. By the time Grace had made her way up the icy back-porch steps, he was able to hide the Scotch and rinse his glass clean in the kitchen sink. The drinking life, he thought, was lived moment by moment.

Soon she was in the tiny cloakroom struggling off with her overcoat. In the process she knocked over a cross-country ski, which stood propped against the cloakroom wall. It had been more than a year since Elliot had used the skis.

She came into the kitchen and sat down at the table to take off her boots. Her lean, freckled face was flushed with the cold, but her eyes looked weary. "I wish you'd put those skis down in the barn," she told him. "You never use them."

"I always like to think," Elliot said, "that I'll start the morning off skiing."

"Well, you never do," she said. "How long have you been home?"

"Practically just walked in," he said. Her pointing out that he no longer skied in the morning enraged him. "I stopped at the Conway Library to get the new Oxford *Classical World*. Candace ordered it."

Her look grew troubled. She had caught something in his voice. With dread and bitter satisfaction, Elliot watched his wife detect the smell of whiskey.

"Oh, God," she said. "I don't believe it."

Let's get it over with, he thought. Let's have the song and dance.

She sat up straight in her chair and looked at him in fear.

"Oh, Chas," she said, "how could you?"

For a moment he was tempted to try to explain it all.

"The fact is," Elliot told his wife, "I hate people who start the day cross-country skiing."

She shook her head in denial and leaned her forehead on her palm and cried.

He looked into the kitchen window and saw his own distorted image. "The fact is I think I'll start tomorrow morning by stringing head-high razor wire across Anderson's trail."

The Andersons were the Elliots' nearest neighbors. Loyall Anderson was a full professor of government at the state university, thirty miles away. Anderson and his wife were blond and both of them were over six feet tall. They had two blond children, who qualified for the gifted class in the local school but attended regular classes in token of the Andersons' opposition to elitism.

"Sure," Elliot said. "Stringing wire's good exercise. It's life-affirming in its own way."

The Andersons started each and every day with a brisk morning glide along a trail that they partly maintained. They skied well and presented a pleasing, wholesome sight. If, in the course of their adventure, they encountered a snowmobile, Darlene Anderson would affect to choke and cough, indicating her displeasure. If the snowmobile approached them from behind and the trail was narrow, the Andersons would decline to let it pass, asserting their statutory right-of-way.

"I don't want to hear your violent fantasies," Grace said.

Elliot was picturing razor wire, the Army kind. He was picturing the decapitated Andersons, their blood and jaunty ski caps bright on the white trail. He was picturing their severed heads, their earnest blue eyes and large white teeth reflecting the virginal morning snow. Although Elliot hated snowmobiles, he hated the Andersons far more.

He looked at his wife and saw that she had stopped crying. Her long, elegant face was rigid and lipless.

"Know what I mean? One string at Mommy and Daddy level for Loyall and Darlene. And a bitty wee string at kiddie level for Skippy and Samantha, those cunning little whizzes."

"Stop it," she said to him.

"Sorry," Elliot told her.

Stiff with shame, he went and took his bottle out of the cabinet into which he had thrust it and poured a drink. He was aware of her eyes on him. As he drank, a fragment from old Music's translation of *Medea* came into his mind. "Old friend, I have to weep. The gods and I went mad together and made things as they are." It was such a waste; eighteen months of struggle thrown away. But there was no way to get the stuff back in the bottle.

"I'm very sorry," he said. "You know I'm very sorry, don't you, Grace?"

The delectable Handel arias spun on in the next room.

"You must stop," she said. "You must make yourself stop before it takes over."

"It's out of my hands," Elliot said. He showed her his empty hands. "It's beyond me."

"You'll lose your job, Chas." She stood up at the table and leaned on it, staring wide-eyed at him. Drunk as he was, the panic in her voice frightened him. "You'll end up in jail again."

"One engages," Elliot said, "and then one sees."

"How can you have done it?" she demanded. "You promised me."

"First the promises," Elliot said, "and then the rest."

"Last time was supposed to be the last time," she said.

"Yes," he said, "I remember."

"I can't stand it," she said. "You reduce me to hysterics." She wrung her hands for him to see. "See? Here I am, I'm in hysterics."

"What can I say?" Elliot asked. He went to the bottle and refilled his glass. "Maybe you shouldn't watch."

"You want me to be forbearing, Chas? I'm not going to be."

"The last thing I want," Elliot said, "is an argument."

"I'll give you a fucking argument. You didn't have to drink. All you had to do was come home."

"That must have been the problem," he said.

Then he ducked, alert at the last possible second to the missile that came for him at hairline level. Covering up, he heard the shattering of glass, and a fine rain of crystals enveloped him. She had sailed the sugar bowl at him; it had smashed against the wall above his head and there was sugar and glass in his hair.

"You bastard!" she screamed. "You are undermining me!"

"You ought not to throw things at me," Elliot said. "I don't throw things at you."

He left her frozen into her follow-through and went into the living room to turn the music off. When he returned she was leaning back against the wall, rubbing her right elbow with her left hand. Her eyes were bright. She had picked up one of her boots from the middle of the kitchen floor and stood holding it.

"What the hell do you mean, that must have been the problem?"

He set his glass on the edge of the sink with an unsteady hand and turned to her. "What do I mean? I mean that most of the time I'm putting one foot in front of the other like a good soldier and I'm out of it from the neck up. But there are times when I don't think I will ever be dead enough—or dead long enough—to get the taste of this life off my teeth. That's what I mean!"

She looked at him dry-eyed. "Poor fella," she said.

"What you have to understand, Grace, is that this drink I'm having"—he raised the glass toward her in a gesture of salute—"is the only worthwhile thing I've done in the last year and a half. It's the only thing in my life that means jack shit, the closest thing to satisfaction I've had. Now how can you begrudge me that? It's the best I'm capable of."

"You'll go too far," she said to him. "You'll see."

"What's that, Grace? A threat to walk?" He was grinding his teeth. "Don't make me laugh. You, walk? You, the friend of the unfortunate?"

"Don't you hit me," she said when she looked at his face. "Don't you dare."

"You, the Christian Queen of Calvary, walk? Why, I don't believe that for a minute."

She ran a hand through her hair and bit her lip. "No, we stay," she said. Anger and distraction made her look young. Her cheeks blazed rosy against the general pallor of her skin. "In my family we stay until the fella dies. That's the tradition. We stay and pour it for them and they die."

He put his drink down and shook his head.

"I thought we'd come through," Grace said. "I was sure."

"No," Elliot said. "Not altogether."

They stood in silence for a minute. Elliot sat down at the oilcloth-covered table. Grace walked around it and poured herself a whiskey.

"You are undermining me, Chas. You are making things impossible for me and I just don't know." She drank and winced. "I'm not going to stay through another drunk. I'm telling you right now. I haven't got it in me. I'll die."

He did not want to look at her. He watched the flakes settle against the glass of the kitchen door. "Do what you feel the need of," he said.

"I just can't take it," she said. Her voice was not scolding but measured and reasonable. "It's February. And I went to court this morning and lost Vopotik."

Once again, he thought, my troubles are going to be obviated by those of the deserving poor. He said, "Which one was that?"

"Don't you remember them? The three-year-old with the broken fingers?"

He shrugged. Grace sipped her whiskey.

"I told you. I said I had a three-year-old with broken fingers, and you said, 'Maybe he owed somebody money.'"

"Yes," he said, "I remember now."

"You ought to see the Vopotiks, Chas. The woman is young and obese. She's so young that for a while I thought I could get to her as a juvenile. The guy is a biker. They believe the kid came from another planet to control their lives. They believe this literally, both of them."

"You shouldn't get involved that way," Elliot said. "You should leave it to the caseworkers."

"They scared their first caseworker all the way to California. They were following me to work."

"You didn't tell me."

"Are you kidding?" she asked. "Of course I didn't." To Elliot's surprise, his wife poured herself a second whiskey. "You know how they address the child? As 'dude.' She says to it, 'Hey, dude.'" Grace shuddered with loathing. "You can't imagine! The woman munching Twinkies. The kid smelling of shit. They're high morning, noon, and night, but you can't get anybody for that these days."

"People must really hate it," Elliot said, "when somebody tells them they're not treating their kids right."

"They definitely don't want to hear it," Grace said. "You're right." She sat stirring her drink, frowning into the glass. "The Vopotik child will die, I think."

"Surely not," Elliot said.

"This one I think will die," Grace said. She took a deep breath and puffed out her cheeks and looked at him forlornly. "The situation's extreme. Of course, sometimes you wonder whether it makes any difference. That's the big question, isn't it?"

"I would think," Elliot said, "that would be the one question you didn't ask."

"But you do," she said. "You wonder: Ought they to live at all? To continue the cycle?" She put a hand to her hair and shook her head as if in confusion. "Some of these folks, my God, the poor things cannot put Wednesday on top of Tuesday to save their lives."

"It's a trick," Elliot agreed, "a lot of them can't manage."

"And kids are small, they're handy and underfoot. They make noise. They can't hurt you back."

"I suppose child abuse is something people can do together," Elliot said.

"Some kids are obnoxious. No question about it."

"I wouldn't know," Elliot said.

"Maybe you should stop complaining. Maybe you're better off. Maybe your kids are better off unborn."

"Better off or not," Elliot said, "it looks like they'll stay that way."

"I mean our kids, of course," Grace said. "I'm not blaming you, understand? It's just that here we are with you drunk again and me losing Vopotik, so I thought why not get into the big unaskable questions." She got up and folded her arms and began to pace up and down the kitchen. "Oh," she said when her eye fell upon the bottle, "that's good stuff, Chas. You won't mind if I have another? I'll leave you enough to get loaded on."

Elliot watched her pour. So much pain, he thought; such anger and confusion. He was tired of pain, anger, and confusion; they were what had got him in trouble that very morning.

The liquor seemed to be giving him a perverse lucidity when all he now required was oblivion. His rage, especially, was intact in its salting of alcohol. Its contours were palpable and bleeding at the borders. Booze was good for rage. Booze could keep it burning through the darkest night.

"What happened in court?" he asked his wife.

She was leaning on one arm against the wall, her long, strong body flexed at the hip. Holding her glass, she stared angrily toward the invisible fields outside. "I lost the child," she said.

Elliot thought that a peculiar way of putting it. He said nothing.

"The court convened in an atmosphere of high hilarity. It may be Hate Month around here but it was buddy-buddy over at Ilford Courthouse. The room was full of bikers and bikers' lawyers. A colorful crowd. There was a lot of bonding." She drank and shivered. "They didn't think too well of me. They don't think too well of broads as lawyers. Neither does the judge. The judge has the common touch. He's one of the boys."

"Which judge?" Elliot asked.

"Buckley. A man of about sixty. Know him? Lots of veins on his nose?"

Elliot shrugged.

"I thought I had done my homework," Grace told him. "But suddenly I had nothing but paper. No witnesses. It was Margolis at Valley Hospital who spotted the radiator burns. He called us in the first place. Suddenly he's got to keep his reservation for a campsite in St. John. So Buckley threw his deposition out." She began to chew on a fingernail. "The caseworkers have vanished—one's in L.A., the other's in Nepal. I went in there and got run over. I lost the child."

"It happens all the time," Elliot said. "Doesn't it?"

"This one shouldn't have been lost, Chas. These people aren't simply confused. They're weird. They stink."

"You go messing into anybody's life," Elliot said, "that's what you'll find."

"If the child stays in that house," she said, "he's going to die."

"You did your best," he told his wife. "Forget it."

She pushed the bottle away. She was holding a water glass that was almost a third full of whiskey.

"That's what the commissioner said."

Elliot was thinking of how she must have looked in court to the cherry-faced judge and the bikers and their lawyers. Like the schoolteachers who had tormented their childhoods, earnest and tight-assed, humorless and self-righteous. It was not surprising that things had gone against her.

He walked over to the window and faced his reflection again. "Your optimism always surprises me."

"My optimism? Where I grew up our principal cultural expression was the funeral. Whatever keeps me going, it isn't optimism."

"No?" he asked. "What is it?"

"I forget," she said.

"Maybe it's your religious perspective. Your sense of the divine plan."

She sighed in exasperation. "Look, I don't think I want to fight anymore. I'm sorry I threw the sugar at you. I'm not your keeper. Pick on someone your own size."

"Sometimes," Elliot said, "I try to imagine what it's like to believe that the sky is full of care and concern."

"You want to take everything from me, do you?" She stood leaning against the back of her chair. "That you can't take. It's the only part of my life you can't mess up."

He was thinking that if it had not been for her he might not have survived. There could be no forgiveness for that. "Your life? You've got all this piety strung out between Monadnock and Central America. And look at yourself. Look at your life."

"Yes," she said, "look at it."

"You should have been a nun. You don't know how to live."

"I know that," she said. "That's why I stopped doing counseling. Because I'd rather talk the law than life." She turned to him. "You got everything I had, Chas. What's left I absolutely require."

"I swear I would rather be a drunk," Elliot said, "than force myself to believe such trivial horseshit."

"Well, you're going to have to do it without a straight man," she said, "because this time I'm not going to be here for you. Believe it or not."

"I don't believe it," Elliot said. "Not my Grace."

"You're really good at this," she told him. "You make me feel ashamed of my own name."

"I love your name," he said.

The telephone rang. They let it ring three times, and then Elliot went over and answered it.

"Hey, who's that?" a good-humored voice on the phone demanded.

Elliot recited their phone number.

"Hey, I want to talk to your woman, man. Put her on."

"I'll give her a message," Elliot said.

"You put your woman on, man. Run and get her."

Elliot looked at the receiver. He shook his head. "Mr. Vopotik?"

"Never you fuckin' mind, man. I don't want to talk to you. I want to talk to the skinny bitch."

Elliot hung up.

"Is it him?" she asked.

"I guess so."

They waited for the phone to ring again and it shortly did.

"I'll talk to him," Grace said. But Elliot already had the phone.

"Who are you, asshole?" the voice inquired. "What's your fuckin' name, man?"

"Elliot," Elliot said.

"Hey, don't hang up on me, Elliot. I won't put up with that. I told you go get that skinny bitch, man. You go do it."

There were sounds of festivity in the background on the other end of the line—a stereo and drunken voices.

"Hey," the voice declared. "Hey, don't keep me waiting, man."

"What do you want to say to her?" Elliot asked.

"That's none of your fucking business, fool. Do what I told you."

"My wife is resting," Elliot said. "I'm taking her calls."

He was answered by a shout of rage. He put the phone aside for a moment and finished his glass of whiskey. When he picked it up again the man on the line was screaming at him. "That bitch tried to break up my family, man! She almost got away with it. You know what kind of pain my wife went through?"

"What kind?" Elliot asked.

For a few seconds he heard only the noise of the party. "Hey, you're not drunk, are you, fella?"

"Certainly not," Elliot insisted.

"You tell that skinny bitch she's gonna pay for what she did to my family, man. You tell her she can run but she can't hide. I don't care where you go—California, anywhere—I'll get to you."

"Now that I have you on the phone," Elliot said, "I'd like to ask you a couple of questions. Promise you won't get mad?"

"Stop it!" Grace said to him. She tried to wrench the phone from his grasp, but he clutched it to his chest.

"Do you keep a journal?" Elliot asked the man on the phone. "What's your hat size?"

"Maybe you think I can't get to you," the man said. "But I can get to you, man. I don't care who you are, I'll get to you. The brothers will get to you."

"Well, there's no need to go to California. You know where we live."

"For God's sake," Grace said.

"Fuckin' right," the man on the telephone said. "Fuckin' right I know."

"Come on over," Elliot said.

"How's that?" the man on the phone asked.

"I said come on over. We'll talk about space travel. Comets and stuff. We'll talk astral projection. The moons of Jupiter."

"You're making a mistake, fucker."

"Come on over," Elliot insisted. "Bring your fat wife and your beat-up kid. Don't be embarrassed if your head's a little small."

The telephone was full of music and shouting. Elliot held it away from his ear.

"Good work," Grace said to him when he had replaced the receiver.

"I hope he comes," Elliot said. "I'll pop him."

He went carefully down the cellar stairs, switched on the overhead light, and began searching among the spiderwebbed shadows and fouled fishing line for his shotgun. It took him fifteen minutes to find it and his cleaning case. While he was still downstairs, he heard the telephone ring again and his wife answer it. He came upstairs and spread his shooting gear across the kitchen table. "Was that him?"

She nodded wearily. "He called back to play us the chain saw."

"I've heard that melody before," Elliot said.

He assembled his cleaning rod and swabbed out the shotgun barrel. Grace watched him, a hand to her forehead. "God," she said. "What have I done? I'm so drunk."

"Most of the time," Elliot said, sighting down the barrel, "I'm helpless in the face of human misery. Tonight I'm ready to reach out."

"I'm finished," Grace said. "I'm through, Chas. I mean it."

Elliot rammed three red shells into the shotgun and pumped one forward into the breech with a satisfying report. "Me, I'm ready for some radical problem solving. I'm going to spray that no-neck Slovak all over the yard."

"He isn't a Slovak," Grace said. She stood in the middle of the kitchen with her eyes closed. Her face was chalk white.

"What do you mean?" Elliot demanded. "Certainly he's a Slovak."

"No he's not," Grace said.

"Fuck him anyway. I don't care what he is. I'll grease his ass."

He took a handful of deer shells from the box and stuffed them in his jacket pockets.

"I'm not going to stay with you. Chas. Do you understand me?"

Elliot walked to the window and peered out at his driveway. "He won't be alone. They travel in packs."

"For God's sake!" Grace cried, and in the next instant bolted for the downstairs bathroom. Elliot went out, turned off the porch light and switched on a spotlight over the barn door. Back inside, he could hear Grace in the toilet being sick. He turned off the light in the kitchen.

He was still standing by the window when she came up behind him. It seemed strange and fateful to be standing in the dark near her, holding the shotgun. He felt ready for anything.

"I can't leave you alone down here drunk with a loaded shotgun," she said. "How can I?"

"Go upstairs," he said.

"If I went upstairs it would mean I didn't care what happened. Do you understand? If I go it means I don't care anymore. Understand?"

"Stop asking me if I understand," Elliot said. "I understand fine."

"I can't think," she said in a sick voice. "Maybe I don't care. I don't know. I'm going upstairs."

"Good," Elliot said.

When she was upstairs, Elliot took his shotgun and the whiskey into the dark living room and sat down in an armchair beside one of the lace-curtained windows. The powerful barn light illuminated the length of his driveway and the whole of the back yard. From the window at which he sat, he commanded a view of several miles in the direction of East Ilford. The two-lane blacktop road that ran there was the only one along which an enemy could pass.

He drank and watched the snow, toying with the safety of his 12-gauge Remington. He felt neither anxious nor angry now but only impatient to be done with whatever the night would bring. Drunkenness and the silent rhythm of the falling snow combined to make him feel outside of time and syntax.

Sitting in the dark room, he found himself confronting Blankenship's dream. He saw the bunkers and wire of some long-lost perimeter. The rank smell of night came back to him, the dread evening and quick dusk, the mysteries of outer darkness: fear, combat, and death. Enervated by liquor, he began to cry. Elliot was sympathetic with other people's tears but ashamed of his own. He thought of his own tears as childish and excremental. He stifled whatever it was that had started them.

Now his whiskey tasted thin as water. Beyond the lightly frosted glass, illuminated snowflakes spun and settled sleepily on weighted pine boughs. He had found a life beyond the war after all, but in it he was still sitting in darkness, armed, enraged, waiting.

His eyes grew heavy as the snow came down. He felt as though he could be drawn up into the storm and he began to imagine that. He imagined his life with all its artifacts and appetites easing up the spout into white oblivion, everything obviated and foreclosed. He thought maybe he could go for that.

When he awakened, his left hand had gone numb against the trigger guard of his shotgun. The living room was full of pale, delicate light. He looked outside and saw that the storm was done with and the sky radiant and cloudless. The sun was still below the horizon.

Slowly Elliot got to his feet. The throbbing poison in his limbs served to remind him of the state of things. He finished the glass of whiskey on the windowsill beside his easy chair. Then he went to the hall closet to get a ski jacket, shouldered his shotgun, and went outside.

There were two cleared acres behind his house; beyond them a trail descended into a hollow of pine forest and frozen swamp. Across the hollow, white pastures stretched to the ridge line, lambent under the lightening sky. A line of skeletal elms weighed with snow marked the course of frozen Shawmut Brook.

He found a pair of ski goggles in a jacket pocket and put them on and set out toward the tree line, gripping the shotgun, step by careful step in the knee-deep snow. Two raucous crows wheeled high overhead, their cries exploding the morning's silence. When the sun came over the ridge, he stood where he was and took in a deep breath. The risen sun warmed his face and he closed his eyes. It was windless and very cold.

Only after he had stood there for a while did he realize how tired he had become. The weight of the gun taxed him. It seemed infinitely wearying to contemplate another single step in the snow. He opened his eyes and closed them again. With sunup the world had gone blazing blue and white, and even with his tinted goggles its whiteness dazzled him and made his head ache. Behind his eyes, the hypnagogic patterns formed a monsoon-heavy tropical sky. He yawned. More than anything, he wanted to lie down in the soft, pure snow. If he could do that, he was certain he could go to sleep at once.

He stood in the middle of the field and listened to the crows. Fear, anger, and sleep were the three primary conditions of life. He had learned that over there. Once he had thought fear the worst, but he had learned that the worst was anger. Nothing could fix it; neither alcohol nor medicine. It was a worm. It left him no peace. Sleep was the best.

He opened his eyes and pushed on until he came to the brow that overlooked the swamp. Just below, gliding along among the frozen cattails and bare scrub maple, was a man on skis. Elliot stopped to watch the man approach.

The skier's face was concealed by a red-and-blue ski mask. He wore snow goggles, a blue jumpsuit, and a red woolen Norwegian hat. As he came, he leaned into the turns of the trail, moving silently and gracefully along. At the foot of the slope on which Elliot stood, the man looked up, saw him, and slid to a halt. The man stood staring at him for a moment and then began to herringbone up the slope. In no time at all the skier stood no more than ten feet away, removing his goggles, and inside the woolen mask Elliot recognized the clear blue eyes of his neighbor, Professor Loyall Anderson. The shotgun Elliot was carrying seemed to grow heavier. He yawned and shook his head, trying unsuccessfully to clear it. The sight of Anderson's eyes gave him a little thrill of revulsion.

"What are you after?" the young professor asked him, nodding toward the shotgun Elliot was cradling.

"Whatever there is," Elliot said.

Anderson took a quick look at the distant pasture behind him and then turned back to Elliot. The mouth hole of the professor's mask filled with teeth. Elliot thought that Anderson's teeth were quite as he had imagined them earlier. "Well, Polonski's cows are locked up," the professor said. "So they at least are safe."

Elliot realized that the professor had made a joke and was smiling. "Yes," he agreed.

Professor Anderson and his wife had been the moving force behind an initiative to outlaw the discharge of firearms within the boundaries of East Ilford Township. The initiative had been defeated, because East Ilford was not that kind of town.

"I think I'll go over by the river," Elliot said. He said it only to have something to say, to fill the silence before Anderson spoke again. He was afraid of what Anderson might say to him and of what might happen.

"You know," Anderson said, "that's all bird sanctuary over there now."

"Sure," Elliot agreed.

Outfitted as he was, the professor attracted Elliot's anger in an elemental manner. The mask made him appear a kind of doll, a kachina figure or a marionette. His eyes and mouth, all on their own, were disagreeable.

Elliott began to wonder if Anderson could smell the whiskey on his breath. He pushed the little red bull's-eye safety button on his gun to Off.

"Seriously," Anderson said, "I'm always having to run hunters out of there. Some people don't understand the word 'posted.'"

"I would never do that," Elliot said, "I would be afraid."

Anderson nodded his head. He seemed to be laughing. "Would you?" he asked Elliot merrily.

In imagination, Elliot rested the tip of his shotgun barrel against Anderson's smiling teeth. If he fired a load of deer shot into them, he thought, they might make a noise like broken china. "Yes," Elliot said. "I wouldn't know who they were or where they'd been. They might resent my being alive. Telling them where they could shoot and where not."

Anderson's teeth remained in place. "That's pretty strange," he said. "I mean, to talk about resenting someone for being alive."

"It's all relative," Elliot said. "They might think, 'Why should he be alive when some brother of mine isn't?' Or they might think, 'Why should he be alive when I'm not?'"

"Oh," Anderson said.

"You see?" Elliot said. Facing Anderson, he took a long step backward. "All relative."

"Yes," Anderson said.

"That's so often true, isn't it?" Elliot asked. "Values are often relative."

"Yes," Anderson said. Elliot was relieved to see that he had stopped smiling.

"I've hardly slept, you know," Elliot told Professor Anderson. "Hardly at all. All night. I've been drinking."

"Oh," Anderson said. He licked his lips in the mouth of the mask. "You should get some rest."

"You're right," Elliot said.

"Well," Anderson said, "got to go now."

Elliot thought he sounded a little thick in the tongue. A little slow in the jaw.

"It's a nice day," Elliot said, wanting now to be agreeable.

"It's great," Anderson said, shuffling on his skis.

"Have a nice day," Elliot said.

"Yes," Anderson said, and pushed off.

Elliot rested the shotgun across his shoulders and watched Anderson withdraw through the frozen swamp. It was in fact a nice day, but Elliot took no comfort in the weather. He missed night and the falling snow.

As he walked back toward his house, he realized that now there would be whole days to get through, running before the antic energy of whiskey. The whiskey would drive him until he dropped. He shook his head in regret. "It's a revolution," he said aloud. He imagined himself talking to his wife.

Getting drunk was an insurrection, a revolution—a bad one. There would be outsize bogus emotions. There would be petty moral blackmail and cheap remorse. He had said dreadful things to his wife. He had bullied Anderson with his violence and unhappiness, and Anderson would not forgive him. There would be damn little justice and no mercy.

Nearly to the house, he was startled by the desperate feathered drumming of a pheasant's rush. He froze, and out of instinct brought the gun up in the direction of the sound. When he saw the bird break from its cover and take wing, he tracked it, took a breath, and fired once. The bird was a little flash of opulent color against the bright-blue sky. Elliot felt himself flying for a moment. The shot missed.

Lowering the gun, he remembered the deer shells he had loaded. A hit with the concentrated shot would have pulverized the bird, and he was glad he had missed. He wished no harm to any creature. Then he thought of himself wishing no harm to any creature and began to feel fond and sorry for himself. As soon as he grew aware of the emotion he was indulging, he suppressed it. Pissing and moaning, mourning and weeping, that was the nature of the drug.

The shot echoed from the distant hills. Smoke hung in the air. He turned and looked behind him and saw, far away across the pasture, the tiny blue-and-red figure of Professor Anderson motionless against the snow. Then Elliot turned again toward his house and took a few labored steps and looked up to see his wife at the bedroom window. She stood perfectly still, and the morning sun lit her nakedness. He stopped where he was. She had heard the shot and run to the window. What had she thought to see? Burnt rags and blood on the snow. How relieved was she now? How disappointed?

Elliot thought he could feel his wife trembling at the window. She was hugging herself. Her hands clasped her shoulders. Elliot took his snow goggles off and shaded his eyes with his hand. He stood in the field staring.

The length of the gun was between them, he thought. Somehow she had got out in front of it, to the wrong side of the wire. If he looked long enough he would find everything out there. He would find himself down the sight.

How beautiful she is, he thought. The effect was striking. The window was so clear because he had washed it himself, with vinegar. At the best of times he was a difficult, fussy man.

Elliot began to hope for forgiveness. He leaned the shotgun on his forearm and raised his left hand and waved to her. Show a hand, he thought. Please just show a hand.

He was cold, but it had got light. He wanted no more than the gesture. It seemed to him that he could build another day on it. Another day was all you needed. He raised his hand higher and waited.

Master and Man

by Leo Tolstoy

Introduced by Ron Hansen

WITH *WAR AND PEACE, ANNA KARENINA,* AND "THE DEATH OF IVAN Ilych," "Master and Man" is generally considered one of Leo Tolstoy's masterpieces, though one would never guess that from his diary entries about it. "I have now written the rough draft of a not very interesting story," he initially noted, "but it helped me to while away the time." Weeks later while further revising it he wrote, "Don't know whether it is good. Very insignificant." Still later he was concerned that the content was "feeble" and that "it is no good. No character—neither the one nor the other." Even after a favorite editor accepted "Master and Man," Tolstoy was so pained about his failure with it that he wrote a friend, "I have sinned with the story I sent off to *The Northern Messenger.* I write 'I have sinned' because I am ashamed to have wasted my time on such stuff."

Written in the fall of 1894 and fully revised thirteen times before he finally surrendered it to publication in 1895, the story is set some twenty years earlier in order to give it the flavor of a legend or folk tale. "*Khozyain i rabotnik,*" its Russian title, could be translated literally as "Householder and Laborer" but for the story's Christian underpinnings, which insist on the terms of the Gospels, where Jesus is often referred to as Master and humanity in general is the subject of his parables. And a parable "Master and Man" surely is, a highly metaphoric but accessible tale of common life whose purpose is the spiritual conversion of its audience.

We miss, in our English translations, the high-flown historical tone of the first pages gradually giving way to a plainer ingenuous style and the urgency of the present tense. We miss, too, the significance of the names. The second guild merchant Vassili Brekhunoff's last name is from the Russian term for a braggart or liar, his village is Kresti, the Crosses, and Nikita, of course, must have been christened in honor of Saint Nicholas, the fourth-century Turkish bishop and wonderworker whose cult provided the basis for our Santa Claus. Like Charles Dickens's "A Christmas Carol," with which Tolstoy was familiar, "Master and Man" features a haughty employer who feels only contempt for his lowly hired hand but finally has his worldview upset as he learns how to live and to love.

When Leo Tolstoy was first famous at twenty-nine, Ivan Turgenev characterized him as a "poet, Calvinist, fanatic, aristocrat." At age sixty-six, when he wrote "Master and Man," Count Tolstoy was changed only in having given up Calvinism for a fanatical Christian religion wholly his own and having forfeited a great deal of his wealth and prestige in order to live, to his mind, the holy life of a *muzhik,* or peasant.

At fifty-five he'd written, in *What I Believe,* that he'd been from the age of fifteen to fifty a Nihilist, one who has no religious beliefs.

> Five years ago I began to believe in the teaching of Jesus Christ, and my life was suddenly changed. I ceased to care for all that I had formerly desired, and began to long for what I had once cared nothing for. What had before seemed good, seemed bad, and what had seemed bad, now seemed good. That happened to me which might happen to a man, who, having left his home on business, should suddenly realize that the business was unnecessary and should go home again.

Adopting a metaphor that he would take up again in his great short story, Tolstoy wrote still later in *What I Believe* of the conflicting urges in his own psychology at the time of his religious conversion:

> I am lost in a snowstorm. One of my companions assures me that he sees lights in the distance and that there is a village. But it is only a delusion, which we believe because we wish to do so. We have searched for those lights and cannot find them. Another comrade goes looking about in the snow, and at last he reaches the road, and cries to us, "Do not go on, the lights you see are in your own fancy; you will but wander about and perish. Here is the road, I am standing on it, and it will lead us to safety." It is very little. While we believed in the lights that shone only in our bewildered eyes we foresaw ourselves in the village, in a warm hut, safe and at rest. Now we have nothing but the hard road. But if we follow the false lights we must surely perish: if we follow the road, we shall surely be saved.

"Master and Man" can be read as a fictional elaboration of that metaphor, positing, in Brekhunoff, Tolstoy's self-portrait of pride, independence, waywardness, and death and, in Nikita, his hoped-for future self of simplicity, participation, certitude, and the firm road to life everlasting. Brekhunoff fancies himself formidable and self-sufficient, but in crisis he's hapless, selfish, and lost, a church elder whose religious feelings have been a sham, a scheming businessman whose intrigues are useless in the wilds. Nikita has no illusions about himself. Wholly lacking in possessions, importance, or aspirations, scorned as an "old fool," a drunkard, and cuckold, Nikita is free to be affectionate, genuine, humble, in harmony with nature, faithful to God, and unafraid of death. Tolstoy's own fierce struggle for human integrity and religious consolation is given form in these hugely different men who ultimately find and heed the same life force.

The plot is wonderfully simple. Merchant and hired man head off for a village but so often get lost in a harrowing snowstorm that they have to wait out the night in their sledge. Brekhunoff selfishly tries to flee on the horse, but fate brings him back to the freezing Nikita. Brekhunoff's first impulse is to protect Nikita from the cold as he would any of his properties, but when he offers his heated body to the old peasant and feels Nikita reviving beneath him, Brekhunoff is gradually changed. "Then he began to think about his money, his store, his house, his sales and purchases, and

Mironoff's millions. He could not understand how that man whom men called Vassili Brekhunoff could bear to interest himself in such things as he did." Earlier he'd felt "to live" (*zhit'*) was "to acquire" (*nazhit'*), but as Brekhunoff selflessly sacrifices himself for Nikita, he is fulfilled by Christ's gospel message that " 'Greater love has no man than this, that a man lay down his life for his friends.' "

Tolstoy annihilated a great deal of fiction for me with "Master and Man." Everything I'd been reading up till then seemed petty and unimportant. Like Brekhunoff I could not understand how I could bear to interest myself in such things as I did. It was in the seventies, in winter; I was a first-year graduate student at the University of Iowa's Writers Workshop, and fat flakes of snow were softly falling as I hiked the two miles to Vance Bourjaily's afternoon class on Tolstoy's masterpieces. And as I hunched forward in a Russian cold with Tolstoy's story in my head, I felt challenged to be the kind of writer he was but also haunted by the fear that my standard was now too high.

And so it was for Tolstoy, too. Except for a handful of fables and the flawed novel *Resurrection,* "Master and Man" was the last fictional work Leo Tolstoy would publish. Two years after the story appeared, he argued in *What Is Art?* that the highest form of art was religious and, under that aesthetic, condemned his own great works of fiction up to that point as failures. He feuded with his wife, Sofya, and his family of thirteen children over their life of ease on his grand estate at Yasnaya Polyana and in accordance with the faith he professed tried to give away all he owned and to be more and more like a peasant. At last, in late October 1910, Tolstoy took flight from his estate hoping to find refuge and religious consolation in an eastern monastery, and he was on his way there when he died of pneumonia in the railroad station in Astapovo, Riazan, at the age of eighty-two.

Tolstoy's dying must have seemed to him a good deal like Nikita's—not at home, but with *ikons* and candles, his wife left behind but forgiven, his focus wholly on "that other life which had been growing more and more familiar and alluring." Whether Tolstoy was disillusioned or found what he expected, we shall all soon know.

Master and Man

Leo Tolstoy

Translated by Constance Garnett and C. I. Hogarth

1

It was in the seventies, the day after the feast of Saint Nicholas in the winter. There had been a festival in the parish, and the church sexton, Vassili Andreitch Brekhunoff (who was also a merchant of the second guild), had been forced to remain at home, since not only was his presence necessary at the church, but he had been receiving and entertaining some of his friends and relations. Now, however, the last of his guests had departed, and he was able to get himself ready to visit a neighbouring landowner, for the purpose of buying some timber for which he had long been in treaty. He was in a hurry to be off, lest rival buyers from the town should deprive him of this eligible bargain. The only reason why the young landowner had asked ten thousand roubles for the timber was that Vassili Andreitch had offered him seven—and seven represented about a third of its value. Perhaps Vassili might have gone on haggling still further (for the wood was in his own district, and there was a recognized agreement between the local merchants and himself that one merchant should not bid against another in the same district), were it not that he had heard that the Government forest contractors were also thinking of coming to treat for the Goviatchkinsky timber, and therefore he had better make up his mind to go at once and clinch the matter. So, as soon as ever the festival was over, he took seven hundred roubles of his own out of the strong-box, added to them two thousand three hundred more out of the church funds which he had by him (making three thousand in all), and counted them carefully. Then he placed them in his pocket-book and got ready to go.

Nikita—the only one of Vassili's workmen who was not drunk that day—ran to put the horse in. Nikita was not drunk that day for the reason that he had formerly been a toper, but, after pawning his jacket and leather boots for drink during the flesh-eating days, had suddenly foresworn liquor altogether, and drunk nothing during the second month. Even on the present occasion he had kept his vow, in spite of the temptation of the liquor which had flowed in all directions during the first two days of the festival.

He was a *muzhik* of about fifty, and hailed from a neighbouring village—where, however, it was said that he was not a householder, but had lived most of his life among strangers. Everywhere he was valued for his handiness, industry and strength, as well as, still more, for his kindly, cheerful disposition. Yet he had never remained long in any one place, since twice a year, or more, he had been accustomed to get drunk, and at those times would not only pawn everything he possessed, but grow uproarious and quarrelsome as well. Vassili himself had dismissed him more than once, yet had always taken him on again because of the store which he set by his honesty, care for animals, and (most important of all) cheapness. In fact, Vassili allowed Nikita a wage, not of eighty roubles a year—the true market value of such a workman—but of forty only. Moreover, this wage was doled out irregularly and in driblets, as well as, for the most part, not in cash at all, but in the form of goods purchased at a high price from Vassili's own store.

Nikita's wife, Martha—a rugged dame who had once been good-looking—lived at home with their little lad and two girls, but never invited her husband to come and see her; since, in the first place, she had lived for the last twenty years with a cooper (originally a *muzhik* from a distant village who had come to lodge in the hut), and, in the second, because, although she could do what she liked with her husband when he was sober, she dreaded him like fire when he was drunk. Once, for instance, when drunk at home he had seized the occasion to avenge himself upon his wife for all his submissiveness to her when sober by breaking into her private box, possessing himself of her best clothes, laying all the gowns and other gewgaws upon the wood-block, and chopping them into shreds with an axe. Yet all his earnings were handed over to Martha. Never once had he disputed this arrangement. In fact, only a couple of days before the festival she had driven over to Vassili's store, and been supplied by him with white meal, tea, sugar, and a pint of vodka, to the value of three roubles, as well as with five roubles in cash—for all of which she had thanked Vassili as for a particular favour, although, as a matter of fact, Vassili was in Nikita's debt to the extent of at least twenty roubles.

"What agreement need you and I make together?" Vassili had said to Nikita. "Take what you need as you earn it. I don't do business as other folks do—keep my creditors waiting, and go in for detailed accounts and deductions and so on. You and I can trust one another. Only serve me well, and I shall never fail you."

In saying this, Vassili really had believed that he was being good to Nikita, for he could speak so persuasively and had always been so entirely supported in his decisions by his dependents, from Nikita upwards, that even he himself had come to feel comfortably persuaded that he was not cheating them, but actually benefiting them.

"Yes, yes, I understand you, Vassili Andreitch," Nikita had replied. "I understand you perfectly well, and will serve and work for you as for my own father."

Nevertheless Nikita had not been ignorant that Vassili was cheating him. He had only felt that it would be no use his trying to get a detailed account out of his master, and that, in default of another place to go to, he had better grin and bear it and take what he could get.

So, when ordered to harness the horse, Nikita proceeded to the stable in his usual cheerful, good-natured manner, and with the usual easy stride of his rather waddling legs. There he took down from a peg the heavy headstall, with its straps and tassels, and, rattling the bit against the side-pieces, proceeded to the stall where the horse was standing which he was to get ready.

"Oh ho, so you find time long, do you, my little beauty?" he said in reply to the low whinny of welcome which greeted him from the shapely, middle-sized, low-rumped, dark-brown stallion cob* which was the sole occupant of the loose-box.

"Nay, nay," he went on. "You are in a hurry to be off, I daresay, but I must water you first" (he always spoke to the animal as one might speak to a being capable of understanding human speech). Then, having wiped the sleek, though dusty and harness-galled, back of the cob with a cloth, he adjusted the headstall to the handsome young head, pulled the ears and forehead-tuft through, let down the halter, and led the animal out to drink. As soon as Brownie had picked his way gingerly out of the dung-heaped stall he grew lively and threw up his heels, pretending that he wanted to kick Nikita as the latter trotted beside him to the water-trough.

"Quiet then, quiet then, you little rascal!" exclaimed Nikita, though well aware that Brownie was taking good care to throw out his hind leg in such a manner as only to graze Nikita's greasy fur coat, not strike it direct—a trick which Nikita always admired. Having drunk his fill of cold water, the animal snorted as he stood twitching his strong, wet lips, from the hairs of which the bright, transparent drops kept dripping back into the trough. Then he stood motionless for an instant or two, as though engaged in thought, and then suddenly gave a loud neigh.

"You don't want any more. You wouldn't get it even if you did, so you needn't ask for it," said Nikita, explaining his conduct to Brownie with absolute gravity and precision. Then he set off running back to the stable, holding the spirited young cob by the halter as the animal kicked and snorted all across the yard. None of the other workmen were about—only the cook's husband, who had come over for the festival from another village.

"Go in, will you, my boy," said Nikita to this man, "and ask which sledge I am to get ready—the big one or the little one?"

The man disappeared into the house (which was iron-roofed and stood upon a raised foundation), and returned in a moment with a message that it

* Thick-set, short-legged horse.

was the little sledge which was to be used. Meanwhile Nikita had slipped the collar over the cob's head and adjusted the brass-studded saddle-piece, and was now walking, with the light-painted *douga** in one hand and the end of the cob's halter in the other, towards the two sledges standing beneath the shed.

"If the little sledge, then the little sledge," he remarked, and proceeded to back the clever little animal into the shafts (it pretending meanwhile to bite him) and, with the other man's assistance, to harness it to the vehicle. When all was ready and there remained only the reins to be put on, Nikita sent his assistant to the stable for some straw, and then to the storehouse for a sack.

"There now, that will do," said Nikita as he stuffed into the sledge the freshly cut oaten straw which the man had brought. "But nay, nay" (to Brownie). "You need not prick your ears like that!—Well, suppose we put the straw so, and the sack on the top of it. Then it will be comfortable to sit upon"—and he suited the action to the words by tucking the edges of the sack under the straw disposed around the seat.

"Thank you, my boy," he added to the cook's husband. "Two pairs of hands work quicker than one." After that he buckled the loose ends of the reins together, mounted the splashboard, and drove the good little steed, all impatient to be off, across the frozen dung of the yard to the entrance-gates.

"Uncle Mikit, Uncle Mikit!" came the shrill little voice of a seven-year-old boy from behind him, as the youngster ran hastily out of the porch into the yard—a youngster who was dressed in a short jacket of black fur, new white bast shoes, and a cosy cap. "Let *me* get up too," he implored, fastening his jacket as he ran.

"Well, well! Come here then, my dear," said Nikita, pulling up. Then, seating his master's pale, thin little son behind him, he drove the boy, beaming with pleasure, out into the street.

It was now three o'clock in the afternoon and freezing hard, the thermometer registering only ten degrees; yet the weather was dull and gusty, and fully half the sky was covered by a low, dark bank of cloud. In the courtyard the air was still, but directly one stepped into the street outside the wind became more noticeable and the snow could be seen twirling itself about in wreaths as it was swept from the roof of a neighbouring outbuilding into the corner near the bath-house. Hardly had Nikita returned through the gates and turned the cob's head towards the steps when Vassili Andreitch—a cigarette between his lips, and a sheepskin coat upon his shoulders, fastened tightly and low down with a belt—came out of the house-door upon the high, snow-trampled flight of steps, making them creak loudly under his felt boots as he did so.

Drawing the last whiff from his cigarette, he threw down the fag end

* The curved frame, fitted with bells, which surmounts the collar in a Russian harness.

and stamped it out. Then, puffing the smoke out of his moustache, he glanced at the cob as it re-entered the gates, and began to turn out the corners of his coat-collar in such a way that the fur should be next his face on either side (his face was clean-shaven, except for a moustache), and yet not liable to be fouled with his breath.

"So you have managed it, you little monkey?" he exclaimed as he caught sight of his little boy seated in the sledge. Vassili was a little animated with the wine which he had been drinking with his guests, and therefore the more ready to approve of all that belonged to him and all that he had done in life. The aspect of his little son at that moment—of the little boy whom he intended to be his heir—afforded him the greatest satisfaction as he stood blinking at him and grinning with his long teeth. In the porch behind Vassili stood his pale, thin wife, Vassilia Andreitcha. She was *enceinte,** and had her head and shoulders muffled up in a woollen shawl, so that only her eyes were visible.

"Had not you better take Nikita with you?" she said, stepping timidly forward from the porch. Vassili returned her no answer, but merely frowned angrily as though somehow displeased at her words, and spat upon the ground.

"You see, you will be travelling with money on you," she continued in the same anxious tone. "Besides, the weather might grow worse."

"Don't I know the road, then, that I must needs have a guide with me?" burst out Vassili with that unnatural stiffening of his lips which marked his intercourse with buyers and sellers when he was particularly desirous of enunciating each syllable distinctly.

"Yes, do take him, for heaven's sake, I implore you," repeated his wife as she shifted her shawl to protect the other side of her face.

"Goodness! Why, you stick to me like a bathing towel!" cried Vassili. "Where can I find room for him on the sledge?"

"I am quite ready to go," put in Nikita, cheerfully. "Only, someone else must feed the other horses while I am away" (this last to his mistress).

"Yes, yes, I will see to that, Nikita," she replied. "I will tell Simon to do it."

"Then I am to go with you, Vassili Andreitch?" said Nikita, expectantly.

"Well, I suppose I must humour the good lady," answered Vassili. "Only, if you go, you had better put on a rather better, not to say warmer, diplomatist's uniform than that"—and he smiled and winked one eye at Nikita's fur jacket, which, truth to tell, had holes under its two arms, down the back, and round the sides, besides being greasy, matted, shorn of hooks, and torn into strips round the edges.

"Here, my good fellow! Come and hold the cob, will you?" shouted Nikita across the yard to the cook's husband.

* Pregnant.

"No, no, let *me* do it," cried the little boy, drawing his small, red, frozen hands out of his pockets and catching hold of the chilly reins.

"Don't be too long over your new uniform, please," said Vassili to Nikita with a grin.

"No, no, Vassili Andreitch—I shan't be a moment," protested Nikita as he went shuffling hurriedly off in his old felt boots towards the servants' quarters across the yard.

"Now then, my good Arininshka, give me my *khalat** from the stove! I am going with master!" shouted Nikita as he burst into the hut and seized his belt from a peg. The cook, who had been enjoying a good sleep after dinner and was now getting tea ready for her husband, greeted Nikita cheerfully, and, catching the infection of his haste, began to bustle about as briskly as he himself. First she took from near the stove a shabby, but well-aired, cloth *khalat,* and set about shaking and smoothing it out with all possible speed.

"*You* are far more fit to go with the master than I am," he said to the cook, in accordance with his usual habit of saying something civil to everyone with whom he came in contact. Then, twisting about him the shabby, well-worn belt, he succeeded first in compressing his not over-prominent stomach, and then in drawing the belt with a great effort over his fur coat.

"There you are!" he said (not to the cook but to the belt) as he tucked its ends in. "You can't very well burst apart like that." Then, with a hoist and much heaving of the shoulders, he drew the cloth *khalat* over all (stretching its back well, to give looseness in the arms), and patted it into place under the arm-pits. Finally he took his mittens from a shelf.

"Now," said he, "I am all right."

"But you have forgotten about your feet," cried the cook. "Those boots are awful."

Nikita stopped as if struck by this.

"Yes, perhaps I ought to ch—" he began, but changed his mind, and exclaiming, "No, he might go without me if I did—I have not far to walk," bolted off into the yard.

"But won't you be cold in that *khalat* only, Nikita?" said his mistress when he reached the sledge.

"No indeed! How should I? It is *very* warm," answered Nikita as he disposed the straw over the forepart of the sledge in such a manner as would conceal his feet after he had mounted, and thrust the whip (not needed for so willing a steed) under the straw.

Vassili had already taken his seat, his broad back, with its double covering of furs, filling almost the entire rear part of the sledge. Then, taking up the reins, he flicked the cob with them, while Nikita jumped into the

* A kind of frock-coat.

forepart of the sledge just as it started, and sat leaning forward to the left and sticking out one leg.

II

The good little cob moved the sledge rapidly along with a light creaking of the runners as he trotted at a round pace over the well-beaten, frozen piece of road leading to the village.

"Hullo! What have *you* jumped up for?" cried Vassili, suddenly, clearly enjoying the fact that an unauthorized passenger was trying to perch himself upon the runners behind. ("Give me the whip, Nikita!" he interjected.) "*I'll* thrash you, you young rascal! Run along home to your mother!"

The boy jumped off. Brownie broke into a gallop, but soon changed to a trot again.

Kresti, where Vassili lived, was a hamlet of six houses only, and when they had got beyond the blacksmith's hut at the end they at once perceived that the wind was much stronger than they had thought it to be, and that the road ahead was almost invisible. The track of the sledge became snowed over almost as fast as made, and only the fact that the road was a little higher than the ground on either side of it rendered it at all distinguishable. The snow was whirling over the whole country-side and blotting out the horizon, while the Teliatinsky forest—generally clearly visible—now showed only as a dark mass looming at intervals through the snow-dust. The wind was blowing from the left, and kept turning Brownie's mane over his thick, fat neck and blowing his feathery tail—bound at the top in a plain knot—across his flank. Owing to the wind, too, Nikita's tall coat-collar, where he sat on the weather side of the sledge, kept pressing itself tightly against his cheeks and nose.

"The cob can't get up much of a pace to-day; there's too much snow on the ground," said Vassili, who prided himself on the excellence of his steed. "Once I drove him to Pashutino in half an hour."

"What did you say?" asked Nikita, whose tall coat-collar had prevented him from hearing what was said.

"I said that I have driven to Pashutino in half an hour," bawled Vassili.

"That's something to boast of indeed! He's a good animal if ever there was one!" commented Nikita, after which they kept silence for a while. Vassili, however, was inclined to be talkative.

"What do you think? I told your wife the other day not to let her cooper drink all the tea," he bawled once more, in the firm conviction that Nikita must be feeling flattered at being talked to by such an important and highly educated man as himself, as well as so greatly taken with his own joke about the cooper that it never entered into his head that the topic might be distasteful to Nikita. However, the latter had once more failed to catch his master's words for the violence of the wind, so Vassili repeated his pleasantry at the very top of his "educated" voice.

"God be with her, Vassili Andreitch!" returned Nikita when he understood. "I never interfere with their affairs. She has given me little cause for blame, and, so long as she treats the lad well, I merely say, 'God be with her!' "

"Well, well," said Vassili, and changed the subject. "Are you going to buy a horse in the spring?" he continued.

"I only wish I could," replied Nikita as he turned his coat-collar back a little and leant over towards his master. The new topic interested him, and he wanted to catch every word. "My little lad is fast growing up and ought to learn to plough, but I have squandered all my money."

"Well, if you'll take the low-rumped nag off my hands I won't ask you much for it," said Vassili, whose spirits were rising, and who therefore recurred instinctively to his ruling passion—the passion which absorbed his whole faculties—namely, the pursuit of bargains.

"I would rather you lent me fifteen roubles and let me go and buy one in the horse-market," answered Nikita, knowing full well that the low-rumped nag which Vassili was asking him to buy was worth no more than seven roubles at the outside, but that as soon as ever Vassili had handed him over the animal he would swear that it was worth at least twenty-five, and therefore retain about half a year's wages to cover the amount.

"The horse is a splendid one," went on Vassili in his precise, businesslike tones. "I want to do you a service as well as myself. Honestly, now. Brekhunoff would never do *any* man a bad turn. I would rather be out of pocket myself than see others so. Yes, on my honour. The horse is a magnificent one."

"I am sure of it," said Nikita with a sigh. Then, finding it useless to try and listen further, he turned up his coat-collar again, and his face and ear became covered in a twinkling. For about half an hour they drove in silence. The wind kept getting down Nikita's legs and through a hole in his mitten, but he hunched his shoulders and breathed into the coat-collar muffled over his mouth, so that he did not feel the cold very much after all.

"What do you think? Shall we go round by Karamishevo or straight on?" asked Vassili presently. The road by way of Karamishevo was the longer and the rougher one, yet, on the other hand, it was clearly defined by posts on either side. The road straight on was a good deal nearer, but used by few travellers, as well as either altogether devoid of posts or marked only by small ones which would now be almost drifted over. Nikita debated matters for a moment.

"The road by Karamishevo is longer than the other one, but a good deal the easier to drive over," he decided at length.

"Yet, if we go straight on," pursued Vassili, who was inclined towards the route he named, "we have only to get into the hollow, and then we can't possibly lose our way. It will be splendid going through the forest."

"As you wish," said Nikita, and turned up his coat-collar again.

Accordingly Vassili had his way, and after driving about half a verst* further on, turned to the left where a tall young oak tree stood. Its branches and the few dead leaves which still clung to them were being madly dashed about by the wind, which, after the turning, met the travellers almost full in the face. Light snow began to fall, and Vassili tightened the reins, puffed out his cheeks, and let the breath escape slowly from under his moustache, while Nikita dozed. They had driven like this in silence for about ten minutes when Vassili gave an exclamation.

"What is it?" asked Nikita, opening his eyes.

Vassili returned no answer, but twisted himself round to look back. Then he gazed ahead. The cob was still trotting along, his flanks steaming with sweat.

"What is it?" asked Nikita again.

"What is it, do you say?" cried Vassili in angry mimicry of the question. "Why, only that I can't see any posts now. We must be off the road."

"Wait a minute, then, while I go and look for it," said Nikita as he leapt lightly from the sledge and, taking the whip from beneath the straw, went ahead and towards the left—the side on which he had been sitting. The snow had not been very deep that year, so that, as yet, the road had been easily passable the whole way along; but here there were patches where it reached knee-high and smothered Nikita's boot-tops. He kept on trying the ground, both with his feet and the whip, as he walked along; yet the road had vanished.

"Well?" said Vassili when Nikita returned to the sledge.

"No road on this side," answered Nikita. "I must try the other."

"There seems to be something dark showing ahead," remarked Vassili. "Go and see what it is."

Nikita did so, and found it to be only a spot where the naked sprouts of some winter corn sown on a piece of black earth were making a dark patch on the snow as they waved before the wind. Nikita circled round to the right, and then returned to the sledge again, beat the snow from his *khalat* and boots, and remounted.

"We must go to the right," he said with decision. "The wind was on our left a moment ago, but now it is straight in our faces. Yes, to the right," he concluded with an air of conviction.

Vassili just managed to catch what he said, and turned the cob in the direction indicated; yet no road revealed itself there, although they went on for a considerable time. Meanwhile the wind showed no signs of dropping, and the snow continued.

"Well, we are altogether lost now, Vassili Andreitch," observed Nikita, suddenly, and half as though he were pleased at the fact. "What is this,

* The verst is about two-thirds of a mile.

though?" he went on, pointing to a blackened potato-top which was projecting above the snow. Vassili at once stopped the cob, which was now sweating heavily and moving its stout flanks with difficulty.

"Yes, what is it?" he echoed.

"It means that we are on the Zakharovek estate. That is where we have got to."

"Surely not?" exclaimed Vassili.

"Yes, it is as I say," insisted Nikita. "You can tell, too, by the sound of the sledge-runners that we are driving over a potato-field. Look at the bits of potato-tops which they have dragged off. Yes, these are the Zakharovek market-gardens."

"A fine place to get landed in!" said Vassili. "Well, what is to be done now?"

"We must keep on going to the right, and we shall be sure to come out somewhere or other," answered Nikita. "If we don't actually strike Zakharovek we shall at all events come across some tenant's farm."

Vassili assented, and drove the cob forward in the direction Nikita had advised. They proceeded thus for a considerable time, now coming upon bare grass, now upon rough patches of frozen ground, over which the sledge went grating loudly. Then, again, they would find themselves passing over stubble of winter or spring corn, with the dead straw or sticks of weeds projecting above the snow and waving madly before the wind. More than once they found themselves labouring through deep, level, pure-white drifts, with nothing whatever showing above the top. All the while the snow-fall continued and the snow-dust whirled about the ground. The cob was evidently failing now, for his flanks were white and steaming with sweat, and he proceeded only at a foot's pace. Suddenly he stumbled, and then plunged forward into some ditch or gully. Vassili was for pulling up, but Nikita shouted to him:

"Why stop? Go on, go on! We must get him out of this. Now then, my beauty! Now then, my pet!" he went on to the cob encouragingly as he leapt from the sledge—only to stick fast in the ditch himself. However, the cob extricated himself presently, and scrambled back onto the frozen ridge which lined the bank. Evidently it was a ditch dug out by hand.

"Where are we now?" queried Vassili.

"We must find that out," answered Nikita. "Let us push on a bit, and we shall arrive somewhere."

"Isn't that the Goviatchkinsky forest, surely?" said his master presently, pointing to something black looming through the snow ahead.

"It may be. We had better push on and find out," rejoined Nikita. As a matter of fact, he had already distinguished the oblong patches of some withered vine-leaves showing against the blackness of the object in question, and knew, therefore, that it was more likely to be a habitation of some kind than a forest; yet he hesitated to speak before he knew for certain. Sure enough, they had not proceeded more than twenty yards beyond the ditch when trees showed up clearly before them and some melancholy sound became audible. Nikita had guessed rightly. It was not a forest they had come to, but a row of tall vines, with a few withered leaves still quivering upon them. Evidently they marked the trench of a threshing-floor. Just as the travellers had almost reached these vines and could tell that the melancholy sound arose from the wind sweeping through their rustling leaves, the cob took a sudden plunge upwards with his fore hoofs, pulled up his hindquarters after them, turned to the left, and went on with the snow no longer reaching to his knees. It was the road again!

"Now we have reached it!" exclaimed Nikita, "but the Lord only knows where!"

The cob, however, never faltered, but went straight ahead along the snow-swept road; until, just as they had covered about a hundred yards, there uprose before them the rectangular outlines of a wattled barn, with its roof piled with snow and the snow-dust blowing from it in clouds. Passing the barn, the road wound back into the wind a little, and they found themselves in a snowdrift. A short way further on could be seen an opening between two buildings, so that it was clear that the road lay through the snowdrift, and that the latter must be surmounted. Sure enough, they had no sooner accomplished this than they found themselves in a village street, in the nearest courtyard of which some frozen linen was hanging from a line and rustling distractedly in the wind. It comprised two shirts (one of them white and the other one red), a pair of drawers, some leggings, and a petticoat, of which the white shirt was particularly abandoned in its antics as it waved its sleeves before the wind.

"Ugh, the lazy woman—though I am sorry to have to say it of her!" said Nikita with a glance at the waving shirts. "To think of not getting one's linen ready for the festival!"

III

The wind was as strong at the entrance to the street as it had been in the open country, and the roadway piled with snow, but in the middle of the hamlet everything seemed warm and quiet and cheerful. A dog came barking out of a yard, while in another yard an old woman came running from somewhere, with her head swathed in a handkerchief, but stopped as she was making for the door of the hut and stood for a moment on the threshold to gaze at the new arrivals. From the middle of the village came the sound of girls singing, and altogether there seemed to be less wind and cold and snow here than outside.

"Why, this must be Grishkino," said Vassili.

"It is," replied Nikita: and Grishkino it was.

It turned out afterwards that they had left the road upon their right, and travelled some eight versts at a tangent to their former direction—though still more or less in the direction of their proper goal. Yet Goviatchkina was fully five versts from Grishkino.

Halfway up the street they encountered a tall man walking in the centre of the roadway.

"Who are you?" he cried as he stopped. Then, recognizing Vassili, he caught hold of one of the shafts, rested his hands upon it, and climbed to the seat of the sledge. It was a friend of Vassili's named Isai, known as the worst horse-thief in the district.

"Well, and whither is God taking you now?" said Isai, suffusing Nikita with the smell of the vodka which he had been drinking.

"We have been trying to get to Goviatchkina."

"What a way to take, then! You should have gone by Malakhovo."

"It's no good saying what we *should* have done when we didn't do it," retorted Vassili as he pulled up the cob.

"That is a good animal," remarked Isai, looking the cob over, and passing his hand under the now drooping stump of its stout, knotted tail in his usual horsey manner. "Are you going to stay the night here?"

"No, my friend. We have further to go yet."

"You had much better stay. But who is this? Why, if it isn't Nikita Stepanitch!"

"Yes, no one else," replied Nikita. "But pray tell us, brother, how to avoid losing our way again."

"How to avoid losing your way again? Why, turn back, go right along the street, and the road is straight in front of you. Don't turn to the left, but keep on until you come nearly to a large village, and then—to the right."

"But whereabouts is the turning near that village?" asked Nikita again. "Is it on the summer or the winter road?"

"The winter. You will come to a copse there, and exactly opposite the copse there stands a tall, ragged oaken post. That is where you are to turn off."

Accordingly Vassili turned the cob's head round, and drove off down the street again.

"You had better have stayed the night here," shouted Isai after them, but Vassili shook up the cob and returned no answer. To cover five versts of level road, of which two would run through forest, seemed an easy enough prospect, especially in view of the fact that the snow now seemed to them to have ceased and the wind to have dropped.

Passing from the street again, with its roadway trampled hard and showing black here and there with patches of fresh dung, they drove past the yard where the linen was hanging out to dry (the white shirt had now partly torn away from the line and was dangling by one frozen sleeve only), and went on until they came to the vine-stocks with their quaintly murmuring leaves. Here they were in the open country again—only to discover that the blizzard had in no way abated, but rather, on the contrary, increased. The road was drifted over ahead, and nothing but the posts alongside could keep them from leaving it. These posts, too, were difficult to distinguish, since the wind was head on.

Vassili knit his brows as he bent forward to watch for the posts, but gave the cob more rein than before, and trusted to its sagacity. Sure enough, the cob never faltered, but went on turning to the left or right, according to the windings of the road, and feeling for it with his hoofs; so that, despite the fact that the wind kept rising and the snow falling ever thicker and thicker, the posts remained plainly visible on either side.

They had been driving like this for about ten minutes when there suddenly loomed up something black in front of the cob—something which was moving along in a tangled whirl of wind-driven snow. It was a party of fellow-travellers whom Brownie had outpaced, and the back of whose sledge he had actually struck into with his fore-hoofs.

"Pull out! Hi! Look out in front of you!" came in a chorus of shouts from this vehicle, and Vassili pulled out accordingly. In the sledge were seated three *muzhiks* and an old woman. Evidently they were guests returning from the village festival. One of the men was lashing the snow-covered flanks of their pony with a dry branch, his two comrades were shouting and gesticulating at one another in the forepart of the sledge, and the old woman—muffled up and white over with snow—was seated motionless at the back.

"Whose men are you?" shouted Vassili.

"A-a-a-skie!" was all that could be heard in answer.

"Eh?"

"A-a-a-skie!" repeated one of the *muzhiks* at the top of his voice, but it was impossible to distinguish precisely what he said.

"Lay on! Don't give way to them!" shouted another to the one belabouring the pony with the branch.

"You are returning from the festival, I suppose?"

"They are gaining, they are gaining! Lay on, Semka! Pull out, you! Lay on!"

The sledges kept bumping against each other, almost interlocking, and then parting again, until finally the *muzhik's* sledge began to be overhauled. Their shaggy, fat-bellied, snow-covered pony, blowing heavily under its low *douga,** and evidently frantic (though in vain) to escape from the flagellation of the dry branch, kept shuffling along on its stumpy legs through the deep snow, although at times they almost gave way beneath it. Its muzzle—that, apparently, of a young animal, with its lower lip projecting like a fish's, the nostrils distended, and the ears laid back in terror—kept level with Nikita's shoulder for a few seconds, and then began to drop behind.

"That's what drink will make men do," observed Nikita. "The pony will be ruined by treatment like that. What Asiatic brutes the fellows are!"

For several minutes the sobbing of the distressed pony's nostrils could be heard behind them, as well as the drunken shouts of the *muzhiks*. Then the first sound died away, and presently the second also. Nothing whatever was to be heard now except the whistling of the wind in the travellers' ears

* Shaft bow.

and an occasional faint scrape of the runners over patches which the wind had swept bare.

This contest with the rival sledge had cheered and enlivened Vassili, so that he drove the cob with greater assurance than ever, and without watching for the posts at all—leaving matters, in fact, to the cob entirely. Nikita also had nothing to do, so that, as usual with him when thus situated, he fell into a doze, in order to make up for arrears of sleep at other times. Suddenly the cob stopped short, almost pitching Nikita forward out of the sledge.

"We have gone wrong again," said Vassili.

"How do you know?"

"Because there are no posts to be seen. We must have left the road."

"Well, if we have, I must look for it again," remarked Nikita abruptly as he got out and began to trudge about the snow, stepping as lightly as possible on the balls of his splayed-out feet. He kept this up for a long time—now disappearing from view, now reappearing, now vanishing again—and then returned.

"No road there," he remarked as he mounted the sledge. "It must be somewhere ahead."

The dusk was now coming on, and although the blizzard had not increased it also had not lessened.

"If only we could hear those *muzhiks!*" sighed Vassili.

"They won't overtake us now," replied Nikita, "for we must have left the road a long way back. Perhaps they have done the same," he added, as an afterthought.

"Well, which way now?" inquired Vassili.

"Give the cob his head," advised Nikita, "and perhaps he will take us right. Here, give me the reins."

Vassili relinquished them none the less readily because his hands were half frozen in their warm mittens. Nikita took the reins, but let them lie quite passively in his fingers, endeavouring not to give them the slightest twitch. In fact, he took keen pleasure in thus trying the intelligence of his favourite. Sure enough, after pricking his ears first to the one side and then to the other, the clever animal started to turn round.

"He can almost speak!" cried Nikita. "My word, how well he knows what to do! On you go, then! On with you! Tchk, tchk!"

The wind was now at their backs again, and it seemed warmer.

"Ah, what a knowing fellow he is!" went on Nikita, delighted with his pet. "Kirghizenok is strong enough, of course, but an absolute fool; whereas this fellow—well, see what he found out with his ears alone! No need of telegraphs for him, when he can smell out a road a verst away!"

And, indeed, less than half an hour later a black object—either a wood or a village—began to loom ahead, while the posts reappeared on their right, placing it beyond doubt that the travellers had hit the road once more.

"If this isn't Grishkino again!" exclaimed Nikita suddenly.

And Grishkino it was. On their left showed the barn with the snow-dust blowing from its roof, while further on could be seen the clothes-line, with its burden of shirts and drawers still fluttering in the wind. Once again they drove up the street and found everything grown suddenly quiet and warm and cheerful. Once again the miry roadway appeared, voices and singing became audible, and the dog barked as before. The dusk, however, was now so far advanced that lights could be seen gleaming in some of the windows.

Half-way up the street Vassili turned the cob's head towards a large hut with a double coping of bricks, and pulled up at the steps. Nikita approached the gleaming, snow-encrusted window, in the light of which the dancing snowflakes glittered brightly, and knocked at a pane with the butt-end of his whip.

"Who is there?" cried a voice in answer to Nikita's summons.

"The Brekhunoffs from Kresti, brother," replied Nikita. "Please let us in."

Someone could be heard moving away from the window, and in another two minutes the sound of the inner door opening with a wrench. Then the latch of the outer door rattled, and there came out a tall old white-bearded *muzhik,* holding the door half closed behind him to keep the wind from blowing into the hut. He was clad in a fur coat, hastily thrown over a white holiday shirt, while behind him stood a young fellow in a red shirt and tall boots.

"How is it with you, Andreitch?" inquired the old man.

"We have lost our way, my friend," replied Vassili. "We tried to get to Goviatchkina, but landed here. Then we set off again, and have just missed the road for the second time."

"But how came you to go wrong?" asked the old man. "Here, Petrushka"—and he turned to the young fellow in the red shirt—"go and open the yard-gates."

"Certainly," responded the youngster cheerfully, and ran forward out of the porch.

"No, no. We must not stop the night," interposed Vassili.

"But where can you be going now? It is nearly dark. You had much better stay here."

"I should have been only too glad to do so, but I simply cannot. Business, you see, my friend—and business won't wait."

"Then at least come in and warm yourselves with some tea," said the old man.

"Yes, we might do that," replied Vassili. "The night won't grow any darker than it is now, for the moon will soon be rising. Shall we go in and warm ourselves, Nikita?"

"Yes, I could do with something to warm me," replied Nikita, who was desperately cold, and only too eager to thaw his frozen limbs before a stove.

Vassili thereupon entered the hut with the old man, while Nikita drove the sledge through the yard-gates, duly opened for him by Petrushka. Under the latter's guidance he then led the cob under the roof of a shed. The shed was heaped high with dung, so that the cob's lofty *douga* caught upon a beam; whereupon the cock and hens which were roosting there were moved to uneasy flutterings and scratchings of their claws, some sheep darted away in terror, with much pattering of their hoofs over the frozen dung, and a dog whined loudly, then growled in angry alarm, and finally barked at the intruder in puppy fashion.

Nikita had a word for them all. He begged the hens' pardon, and quieted them by saying that he would not disturb them further; chided the sheep for their unreasoning nervousness; and never ceased to make overtures to the dog as he tied up his steed.

"We shall be all right now," he said as he beat the snow from his clothes. "Hush, then, how he growls!" he added to the dog. "It is all right now. Quiet, then, stupid! Be quiet! You are only disturbing yourself for nothing. We are not thieves."

"They are what we might call our three domestic councillors," remarked Petrushka as he drew the sledge under the shed with his powerful hands.

"Why 'councillors'?" asked Nikita.

"Because," said Petrushka, with a smile, "you will find it written in Paulson's book: 'When a thief is sneaking up to a house the dog barks out in his own language—Wake up! the cock sings out—Get up! and the cat starts washing herself—meaning thereby to say: A guest is at hand, so let us be ready to receive him!' "

Petrushka, it seemed, was of a literary turn, and knew by heart the only book which he possessed—some book or other by Paulson. He was particularly fond of it when he had had a little to drink—as now—and would quote such extracts from it as might seem to him to fit the occasion.

"That is just right," observed Nikita.

"Yes, isn't it?" answered Petrushka. "But you are simply frozen. Shall I take you in to tea now, my boy?"

"Yes, by all means," replied Nikita, and they crossed the yard to the hut door.

IV

The homestead where Vassili had pulled up was one of the richest in the village, for the family held no less than five lots of land, as well as rented some, while in the stables stood six horses, three cows, two draught-bullocks, and a flock of twenty sheep. In all, there lived around the courtyard of the homestead twenty-two souls—namely, four married sons, six grandchildren (of whom one—Petrushka—was married), two great-grandchildren, three orphans, and four daughters-in-law, with their children. In addition to these there were two sons employed as water carriers in Moscow, while a third was in the army. At the present moment there were at home only the old man, his wife, the second of the married sons, the elder of the two sons who worked at Moscow (come over for the festival), the various wives and children, and a neighbouring gossip.

It was one of those rare households which are still to be found undivided, yet one in which there were already at work those deep-rooted internal dissensions which generally originate among the women of a family, and which would break up this family also in time.

Over the table in the hut there hung a shaded lamp, throwing a clear light upon the crockery below, upon a bottle of vodka, and upon sundry viands, as well as over the clay walls of the room. In one corner—the "corner beautiful"—there hung some *ikons,* with pictures on either side of them. In the place of honour at the table sat Vassili, stripped now to his black under-jacket, and chewing his frozen moustache as he gazed round the hut and at those about him with his prominent, hawklike eyes. Next to him sat the bald, white-bearded head of the family (dressed in a white shirt of home manufacture), while, further on, were the son who had come over from Moscow for the festival (straight-backed, square-shouldered, and wearing a similar shirt to his father's, but of finer material), a second square-shouldered son (the eldest of those living at home), and, lastly, the neighbour—a red-haired, lanky *muzhik.*

These *muzhiks* had had their supper and vodka, and were just about to drink tea when the travellers arrived. Consequently, the *samovar* on the floor by the stove was already boiling. Near the stove, also, and in shelf-bunks could be seen various children, while the old woman—her face covered in every direction with fine wrinkles, furrowing even her lips—bustled about behind Vassili. As Nikita entered the hut she was just taking her guest some vodka, which she had poured out into a tumbler of thick glass.

"You must not refuse it, Vassili Andreitch," she said. "No, you really must not. You need something to refresh you. Drink it down, my dear sir."

Nikita found himself greatly excited by the smell of the vodka—especially now that he was so cold and hungry. He knit his brows and, shaking the snow from his hat and *khalat,* halted for a moment before the *ikons,* with his eyes turned away from the company. He crossed himself three times and made a genuflexion, after which he turned first to his host and saluted him, then to those present at the table, and then to the women standing by the stove. Finally, with a general greeting of "A merry festival to you all!" he started to take off his *khalat*—though still without looking at the table.

"But you are frozen all over, my brother!" cried the eldest brother as he stared at Nikita's snow-caked eyes, beard and face. For answer, Nikita divested himself of his *khalat,* shook it out, and hung it over the stove; after which he at length approached the table. Offered vodka, he had almost taken the glass and tilted the fragrant, shining liquor into his mouth, when he glanced at Vassili and remembered the pawned boots, as well as the cooper and the young son for whom he had promised to buy a horse in the spring. So he ended by declining the vodka with a sigh.

"I would rather not drink it, I thank you humbly," he said with knitted brows, and seated himself on a bench by the window.

"But why?" asked the eldest brother.

"Because I would rather not, I would rather not," Nikita replied without raising his eyes as he squinted down at his short beard and moustache and thawed the icicles out of them.

"It does not suit him," put in Vassili, smacking his lips over a cracknel washed down with vodka.

"Well, give me the tea-pot, then," said the kindly old woman. "I will get you some tea, for you must be frozen. Why are you so long with the *samovar,* my good women?"

"It is quite ready," retorted one of the younger ones as she wiped the covered *samovar* with a napkin. Then, raising it with some difficulty, she came and plumped it down on the table.

Meanwhile, Vassili had been relating how he and his companion had missed their way, wandered about, fallen in with the drunken *muzhiks,* and twice returned to the village. His hosts marvelled at the story, and then went on to explain how and where they had gone wrong, who the drunken *muzhiks* had been, and the route which Vassili and Nikita must take when they set off again.

"Why, even a child could find the way as far as Moltchanovka," said the neighbour; "and, once there, you only have to hit the turning near the village. You will see a copse there. To think that you never got so far!"

"But hadn't you better stay the night here?" put in the old woman, persuasively. "The women shall get you a bed ready."

"Yes, do so, for if you were to get lost again it might be a terrible business," added her husband.

"No, no, I really cannot, my good friend," replied Vassili. "Business is business. Delay an hour, and you lose a year," he added, remembering the timber and the rival buyers who might forestall him. "Shall we go now?" (this last to Nikita).

Nikita returned no answer for a moment, and seemed absorbed in the task of thawing out his beard and moustache. At length he muttered gruffly:

"It would hardly do to get lost again, would it?"

As a matter of fact, he was gruff because he wanted the vodka so badly, and the only thing which would assuage that yearning of his was tea—which he had not yet been offered.

"But we need only to reach that turning," protested Vassili, "and we simply *can't* lose our way afterwards. From there onwards it will be all forest road."

"Well, it is for you to say, Vassili Andreitch," said Nikita as he took the tumbler of tea now proffered him. "If we must go, we must, that's all."

"Drink up the tea, then, and quick march."

Nikita said no more (although he shook his head disapprovingly), but poured the tea out carefully into the saucer and began to warm his work-swollen fingers in the steam. Then, having bitten off a crumb from his lump of sugar, he bowed to his hosts, said "A good health to you all!" and poured the grateful liquid down his throat.

"If only we had someone to guide us to the turning!" sighed Vassili.

"That could be managed," said the eldest brother. "Petrushka could harness a horse and go with you as far as that."

"Harness up, then, brother, and my best thanks to you," exclaimed Vassili.

"And to you also, good sir," said the hospitable old woman. "We have been only too pleased to see you."

"Petrushka, off you go and harness the mare," ordered the eldest brother.

"Very well," replied Petrushka smilingly as he seized his cap from a peg and departed.

Whilst the horses were being got ready the conversation passed to the subject which had been interrupted when Vassili drove up to the window. It seemed that the old man had been complaining to the neighbour (who was also the local *starosta**) about his third son, who had sent him no gift for the festival but had given his wife a French shawl.

"The young people are getting out of hand nowadays," said the old man.

"Indeed they are!" agreed the neighbour. "There is no living with them. They are growing much too clever. Look at Demotchkin, who broke his father's arm the other day—all through his being too clever, of course!"

Nikita kept listening and looking from one to the other of the speakers' faces with an evident desire to join in the conversation, but he was too full of tea to do so, and therefore merely nodded his head approvingly at intervals. He had drunk tumbler after tumbler of tea, until he had grown warmer and warmer and more and more good-humoured. The conversation lasted for quite a long time on this subject—on the evil of dividing up families—and proved too absorbing to be successfully diverted, so that in time it passed to the dissensions in this particular household—to the separation which the second son (who had been sitting by meanwhile and maintaining a sullen silence) was demanding. Evidently it was a moot point, and the question above all others which was exercising the household, yet politeness had hitherto prevented the family from discussing such a private affair before strangers. At length, however, the old man could not forbear, and with tears in his voice went on to say that, so long as he lived, he would never permit the separation; that he maintained his household to the glory of God; and that, once it were divided, it would become scattered all over the world.

"Yes, that is what happened to the Matvieffs," observed the neighbour.

* The village headman.

"They were a comfortable household once, but separated—and now not a single one of them has anything left."

"That is what you desire for *us,* I suppose?" said the old man, turning to his son.

The son returned no answer, and an awkward silence ensued until interrupted by Petrushka, who had duly harnessed his horse and been back in the hut for some minutes past, smiling the whole time.

"It reminds me of a fable in Paulson," he said. "A father gave his son a broom to tear across. None of them could tear it: but, twig by twig—well, that was easy enough. So also it will be in our case," he added with a broad smile. "But I am quite ready to start now."

"Then, if you are ready, let us be off," said Vassili. "About that separation, good grandfather—do not give in. It is *you* who have made the household, and therefore it should be *you* who are master of it. If necessary, refer the matter to the *mirovoi.** He would settle it for you."

"But to behave like this, to behave like this!" cried the old man, with unrestrained grief. "There is no living with them. It is the Devil's doing entirely."

Meanwhile Nikita, his fifth tumbler of tea swallowed, had placed the empty glass by his side instead of returning it, in the hope that he would be given a sixth. But there was no more water left in the *samovar,* and so the hostess brewed no more tea, while Vassili was already putting his fur coat on. Accordingly, there being nothing else for it, Nikita rose, replaced his lump of sugar (which he had nibbled on every side) in the sugar-basin, wiped his perspiring face with the lappet of his jacket, and went to put on his *khalat.* This done, he sighed heavily. Then he thanked and took leave of his hosts, and left the warm, bright living-room for the cold, dark porch, which was rattling with the wind which hurtled through it and which had drifted the snow through the chinks of the quaking outer door until it lay in heaps upon the floor. Thence he passed into the dark courtyard.

Petrushka, clad in a sheepskin jacket, was standing by his horse in the middle of the yard and smilingly quoting some verses from Paulson:

"The lowering tempest hides the sky,
The whirlwind brings the driving snow;
Now like a wild beast it doth cry,
Now like a child it whimpers low."

Nikita nodded his head approvingly and unhooked the reins, while the old man brought a lantern into the porch to guide Vassili to the sledge. He tried to light him with it, but it was blown out in a twinkling. Even in the yard it was easy to tell that the storm was worse than ever.

* The local magistrate.

"What fearful weather!" thought Vassili to himself. "Perhaps we shall never get there. However, there is business to be thought of. Besides, I have got myself ready now, and my host's horse has been put in. God send we get there, though!"

The old man likewise was thinking that it would be better for them not to set out, but he had already tried to dissuade them, and they had not listened to him. It would be no use asking them again.

"Perhaps, too, it is only old age which makes me so nervous, and they will arrive safely," he thought. "Let us ourselves at least go to bed in the meanwhile. Enough of talking for to-night."

Petrushka, at all events, had no thought of danger. He knew the road and the whole neighbourhood too well for that. Moreover, he had been greatly put upon his mettle by the couplet about the whirlwind and the snow, which seemed to him to describe with extraordinary exactness what was to be seen in the yard. As for Nikita, he had no wish to go at all, but he had been too long accustomed not to have his own way and to serve others; so that in the end there was no one to prevent them from setting out.

V

Vassili walked through the porch, peered about in the darkness till he discerned where the sledge was, took the reins, and climbed in.

"All right in front!" he cried. Petrushka, kneeling in his own sledge, started his horse, and Brownie, with a loud neigh as he scented the mare in front of him, dashed away after her. They issued thus into the village street, passed the outskirts, and took the same road as before—the road which ran past the yard with the frozen linen (although the linen was quite invisible now), past the barn heaped with snow, and from the gables of which a cloud of snow-dust kept blowing, and past the bending vines with their mysterious murmurings and pipings. Then once more the travellers were launched upon a sea of snow, which raged both above and below them. The wind was so strong that when it was upon their flank and their wrappings filled before it, it actually careened the sledge to one side and threw the cob out of his stride. Petrushka kept shouting encouragement as he drove his stout mare ahead of them, while the cob followed her closely.

After about ten minutes' driving, Petrushka turned aside and shouted something, but neither Vassili nor Nikita could tell what he said for the sound of the wind. They guessed, however, that they had reached the turning. Sure enough, Petrushka had wheeled to the right, and the wind, which had hitherto been chiefly on their flank, now met them full in the face, whilst something could be seen showing black through the snow on their right hand. It was the copse which marked the turning.

"God go with you!" cried Petrushka.

"Thank you, thank you, Petrushka!"

"The lowering tempest hides the sky," shouted the lad once more, and vanished.

"Goodness, what a poetry-spouter!" remarked Vassili as he started the cob again.

"Yes, he is a fine young fellow, a real honest *muzhik,*" returned Nikita, and they went on. In order not to squander the warmth engendered by the tea which he had drunk in the hut, Nikita wrapped himself up well, hunched his shoulders until his short beard covered his throat, and sat perfectly silent. In front of him he could see the two dark lines of the shafts forever cheating his eye, and looking to him like the ruts of a beaten road; the cob's tossing flank and knotted, wind-blown tail; and, further ahead, the animal's lofty *douga,* nodding head and neck, and dishevelled mane. At intervals posts would leap into sight, and he would know that the sledge was still keeping the road and that there was nothing for him to do. Vassili held the reins loosely, leaving it to the cob to guide himself. Nevertheless, although Brownie had had a long rest in the village, he went unwillingly, and as though he would like to turn aside at any moment, so that Vassili frequently had to straighten him again.

"There goes a post on the right—two—three," counted Vassili. "And there is the forest in front," he went on to himself as he gazed at something showing dark ahead of them. However, what had seemed to him a forest proved to be only a bush. This they passed, and had covered another fifty yards or so—when, behold! there was neither forest nor a fourth post to be seen!

"Never mind; we shall be at the forest in a moment," thought Vassili as, excited by the vodka and tea, he jerked the reins again instead of pulling up. The willing, docile animal obeyed and, now at an amble and now at a moderate trot, went whither he was driven, although he knew that it was in the wrong direction. Another ten minutes passed, and still there was no forest.

"We have missed the road again!" exclaimed Vassili, at last pulling up. Without speaking, Nikita descended from the sledge, and, after tucking up his *khalat,* which sometimes clung to him and sometimes flapped up and down, according to the strength of the gusts of wind, began to flounder about over the snow. First he tried the one side, and then the other, and thrice vanished altogether. At last, however, he returned, and took the reins from Vassili's hands.

"We must go towards the right," he said brusquely and decisively as he turned the cob in that direction.

"Very well; if to the right, to the right," agreed Vassili as he surrendered the reins and thrust his numbed hands up his sleeves. Nikita said nothing more beyond crying, "Now do your best, my pet!" to the cob. Nevertheless, the animal moved forward only at a foot's pace, in spite of all Nikita's shaking of the reins. The snow was knee-deep in places, and the sledge moved through it in jerks with each stride of the animal. Presently Nikita took up the whip, which had been hanging over the splash-board, and used it once; whereupon the good cob, unused to its lash, plunged forward and broke into a trot—only, however, to subside again into an alternative amble and walk. They proceeded thus for about five minutes. It was so dark, and there was such a swirl of snow both around them and on the ground, that it was scarcely possible for them even to see the cob's *douga*. Sometimes, indeed, it was almost as though the sledge were standing still and the ground gliding backwards from it.

Suddenly the cob stopped short, as though he had scented something in front of him. Nikita threw down the reins and leapt lightly out, in order to go to the cob's head and see what he was jibbing at; but hardly had he taken a single stride ahead of the animal when his legs shot up and he rolled down some steep declivity.

"Phew, phew, phew!" he kept exclaiming all the time he was descending and trying in vain to stop himself, but his course was only arrested when his legs ploughed their way into a deep snowdrift at the bottom, while, shaken by his struggles, the drift overhanging the bank above him descended upon his head and crammed a large portion of its mass down the back of his neck.

"What a one you are, then!" said Nikita, reproachfully, both to the snowdrift and to the ravine, as he attempted to shake the snow out of his coat-collar.

"Nikita, Nikita!" came in a shout from Vassili above, but Nikita sent no answering call. He was too busy for that, for he was employing all his energies in shaking himself and searching for the whip, which had rolled away somewhere while he was shooting down the declivity. Having found it at last, he tried to reascend at the spot where he had come down, but found it impossible to do so, since he merely slid back with each successive attempt; so that finally he was forced to proceed along the bottom to find a way out. Nevertheless, only a few yards from the point where he had descended he found a place where he managed to creep up on all fours, after which he began to walk along the edge towards the spot where he judged the cob to be. Both cob and sledge were wholly invisible, but inasmuch as he was walking against the wind, he could hear Vassili's shouts and Brownie's welcoming neigh some moments before he actually caught sight of them.

"I am coming, I am coming," he exclaimed. "Why make such a fuss about it?"

It was not until he was almost upon the sledge that he was able to distinguish the cob, with Vassili standing beside it—the latter looming very large in the obscurity.

"How the devil did you manage to lose yourself?" began his master, angrily. "We must turn back and at least try to return to Grishkino."

"I should be only too glad," retorted Nikita. "But which way are we to go? If we fall into this ravine we might never get out of it again. I myself have just found it pretty hard to do so."

"Yet we cannot stay here, can we? We *must* go *some*where," retorted Vassili.

Nikita said nothing, but sat down on the rim of the sledge, pulled off his boots, and shook out the snow which had collected in them. That done, he gathered up a handful of straw and carefully plugged a hole in the left one.

Vassili also said nothing, as though he meant now to leave everything to Nikita. When the latter had finished pulling on his boots again, he tucked his legs onto the sledge, put on his mittens, took up the reins, and turned the cob parallel to the ravine. They had not gone more than a hundred yards, however, before the animal pulled up short. In front of them lay the ravine again!

Once more Nikita got out and went probing about over the snow. He was absent for some time, but at length reappeared on the opposite side of the sledge to that which he had started from.

"Are you there, Andreitch?" he shouted.

"Yes," replied Vassili. "Well, what now?"

"There is no getting out this way; it is too dark, and there are too many ravines about. We must try driving back against the wind."

After doing so for a little while they stopped, and Nikita once more alighted and went creeping about over the snow. Then he remounted, but only to alight again almost immediately; until at length he came to a halt by the sledge in a perfectly breathless condition.

"Well, what?" inquired Vassili.

"Only that I am fairly done, and the cob nearly so too."

"What are we to do, then?"

"Wait a minute." Nikita departed again, but returned in a moment or two.

"Keep close behind me," he cried as he walked on before the cob. Vassili had now ceased to give orders, but humbly obeyed Nikita's directions.

"This way—after me," cried the latter again as he turned sharply to the right and, taking Brownie by the head, led him downwards towards a snowdrift. The cob held back at first, and then made a plunge forward as though to leap the snowdrift. Failing in the attempt, he sank in up to the collar.

"Get out of the sledge," cried Nikita to Vassili, who had retained his seat meanwhile. Then, grasping one of the shafts, he exerted all his strength to help the cob to drag the sledge out of the drift.

"Pull, my pet!" he cried to Brownie. "One good pull and the thing is done. Now, now! Just one good pull!"

The cob made a brave effort, and yet another, but, failing to extricate himself, settled down as though to reflect upon the situation.

"Come, come, my pet; this won't do," Nikita adjured Brownie. "Now then, once again!" and he tugged at the shaft on his side, while Vassili tugged at the other. The cob shook his head for a moment, and then plunged forward suddenly in another attempt.

"That's it! You're not going to be buried this time, eh?" cried Nikita, encouragingly.

Another plunge—a second—a third—and the cob had cleared the drift and stopped short, shaking himself all over and breathing heavily. Nikita was for dragging the sledge a little further yet, but Vassili was so exhausted with the weight of his two heavy coats that he gave up and climbed in again.

"Let me rest a minute," he said, as he loosened the handkerchief which he had wound round his coat-collar before leaving the village.

"Very well; there is no great hurry," returned Nikita. "Sit still, and I will lead the cob."

Accordingly Vassili remained in the sledge, while Nikita led the animal forward for about ten yards, down a slope, then up again a little way, and finally came to a halt.

The spot where he had done so was not actually in the ravine itself, where the snow blowing off the hillocks and accumulating might have buried them entirely, but in a spot partly sheltered by the lee side of the ravine. Occasionally the wind seemed to drop a little, but it was not for long; whilst, as if to make up for such lulls, the blizzard would increase tenfold after they were over, and tear and swirl around the travellers more cruelly than ever. One of these violent gusts struck the sledge just as Vassili was descending from it to go and take counsel with Nikita as to what they should do next, with the result that they could only cower down without speaking until the fury of the squall was spent. As for Brownie, he flattened his ears and shook his head in disgust. When the squall had abated a little, Nikita took off his mittens, tucked them into his belt, blew upon his hands, and set to work to unfasten the bow-rein from the *douga*.

"Why are you doing that?" asked Vassili.

"Because there is nothing else to be done," replied Nikita, though half-apologetically. "I am absolutely tired out now."

"Then aren't we going to try and get any further?"

"No, for we are only exhausting the cob for nothing," said Nikita, pointing to the animal where it stood patiently waiting for what might be required of it, yet scarcely able to hold itself upright on its stout, sweat-belathered flanks. "Brownie is willing enough, but he can hardly stand on his legs. There is nothing for it but to spend the night here."

Nikita said this as if he were proposing to put up in an inn-yard, and went on unfastening the collar-thong until the two clasps of the collar fell apart.

"But we shall freeze to death here!" cried Vassili.

"Well? What if we do? It cannot be helped," was all that Nikita vouchsafed to reply.

VI

Vassili was warm enough in his two heavy coats, especially after his exertions in the snowdrift. Yet, for all that, the frost seemed to breathe down his back when he understood that they had to spend the night there. To calm his apprehensions, he sat down in the sledge and pulled out his matches and cigarettes.

Meanwhile Nikita unharnessed the cob. He undid the belly-band and saddle-piece, ran the reins out, unfastened the traces, and took off the *douga,* talking cheerily to the animal the while.

"Out you come, out you come," he said as he led it out of the shafts. "Let me take off your bit and tie you up here, and then you shall have some straw." He suited the action to the word. "Eat away, and you will feel all the better for it."

Nevertheless, Brownie did not seem to grow easier under Nikita's touch, but kept fidgeting about as he stood tail onwards to the wind. Every moment he would shift his legs, press up to the sledge, and rub his head against Nikita's sleeve. However, as if unwilling to seem churlish about the meal of straw which Nikita had strewn before his nose, he took an occasional straw from the sledge, but appeared at once to come to the conclusion that straw did not meet the case, and threw it down again; whereupon the wind caught it in a twinkling, whirled it away, and buried it in the snow.

"Suppose we make a signal of distress," said Nikita, presently. He turned the sledge a little towards the wind, tied the shafts together with the belly-band, turned them up, and rested them against the splashboard.

"Now, if anyone passes this way they will be able to see us by the shafts, and come and dig us out. I learnt that trick from the old people," and he clapped his mittens together and put them on.

Meanwhile Vassili had unhooked his fur coat and made a shelter of its skirts. Then he struck match after match against the steel match-box, but his hands were shaking so violently with the cold that each successive match either failed to light at all or was blown out by the wind as he was in the act of lifting it to his cigarette. At length a match did flare up properly, illuminating for a brief second the pelt of his fur coat, his hand with the gold ring on its curved index finger, and the snow-covered straw which projected from under the sacking. The cigarette lighted, he drew a couple of greedy whiffs, swallowed the smoke, and puffed it out again through his moustache. Then he was about to take a third whiff, when the wind caught the lighted end of the cigarette and carried it away to join the wisps of straw!

Nevertheless, even these meagre mouthfuls of smoke had exercised a cheering effect upon him. "If we *must* spend the night here, well, we must, that's all," he said undauntedly. "Wait a moment and I will rig up a flag."

Picking up the handkerchief which he had unwound from his neck and thrown down upon the floor of the sledge, he took off his mittens, climbed onto the splashboard, stretched himself on tiptoe to reach the belly-band, and tied the handkerchief round one end of it and of the shaft in a stout knot. The handkerchief at once began to wave wildly—now clinging to the shaft, now suddenly filling out again and straining at the knot as its folds cracked in the wind.

"Is not that clever of me?" said Vassili as he stepped down again, much pleased with his handiwork. "Now, if we could lie together, that would be the warmest way, but I'm afraid that there isn't room for both of us."

"Never mind; I will find a place for myself," answered Nikita. "Only, I must cover the cob over first, for he has been sweating a lot and is tired out. Wait a minute"—and, diving into the sledge, he dragged the sacking from under Vassili. Possessed of this, he folded it double, and, removing the saddle-piece and crupper from Brownie's back, covered him over.

"You will be warmer like this, little fool," he said as he replaced the saddle-piece and crupper. "And now," he added to Vassili, "I will take the apron if you don't want it to-night. Give me some straw, too," and, thus taking one thing and another from beneath Vassili, he went to the back of the sledge, dug a hole in the snow there, and lined it with straw. Then he pulled his cap over his eyes, wrapped his *khalat* about him, with the apron over all, and squatted down upon the straw with his back resting against the bark tail-board of the sledge, that it might protect him from the wind and snow.

Vassili shook his head in disapproval of Nikita's proceedings (it was contrary to his habit to encourage the peasantry in their rude, uncouth ways), and then set about making his own preparations for the night. First of all, he smoothed out what straw was left in the sledge, padding it a little thicker where his thighbone was to rest. Then he pulled on his mittens and lay down with his head in one of the corners near the splashboard, that the latter might protect him from the wind.

Somehow he did not feel sleepy, but lay thinking. He thought chiefly of the one thing which constituted his whole pride, ideal, aim and joy in life—namely, the making of money, and yet more money. He thought of the means by which certain acquaintances of his had made their money, how they were using it, and the means by which he, like they, might make a great deal more than he already possessed. The purchase of the Goviatchkinsky forest seemed to him a matter of vast importance, since out of this forest he hoped to make, at one stroke, a sum, possibly, of ten thousand roubles. He mentally reckoned up the value of the timber which he had viewed in the autumn, and on the basis of the two *dessiatins** he had then inspected went on to calculate the whole.

"The oak-wood will do for sledge-runners if cut up, and for beams as they stand," he said to himself. "And after they are felled there should be left about 30 *sazhens*† of firewood to the *dessiatin*." Thus calculating, he could see that the total value of the forest worked out at about 12,000 roubles, but could not reckon to an exact figure in the absence of tables. "All the same," he went on, "I am not going to give even so much as 10,000 for it—only 8000—and that subject to deductions for open spaces. I will grease the sur-

* The dessiatin = 2⅘ acres.

† The sazhen = 7 feet.

veyor's palm with a hundred roubles, or perhaps a hundred and fifty, and he will measure me off the clearings at at least five *dessiatins*. Yes, the owner will be glad to let the forest go at 8000 roubles. I have 3000 ready for him here," thought Vassili as he felt for his pocket-book with the inside of his fore-arm; "and that should melt him. How on earth we came to miss that turning God only knows. There must be a forest and a forest-keeper somewhere about there. His dog ought to have heard us. The cursed brutes never bark when they're wanted to."

He turned back his coat-collar from his ear and listened. Nothing was to be heard but the whistling of the wind, the rustling and cracking of the handkerchief on the shafts, and the swish of the snow as it lashed the bark sides of the sledge. He covered his ear over again.

"If only I had known that we should have to spend the night here!" he thought. "Well, we shall get there to-morrow, all the same. It will only mean one day lost. Besides, those other fellows wouldn't come either—not in such weather."

Suddenly he remembered that on the 9th of the month he was to be paid some money for wethers by the butcher.

"I ought to be back by then to receive it. He couldn't take me in over the price, whereas my wife doesn't in the least know how to bargain. In fact, she doesn't understand how to talk to *anyone,*" he went on as he remembered her failure to make conversation to the *stanovoi,* who had been one of their guests of yesterday for the festival. "She is a *woman*—that is the long and the short of it. Moreover, what had she ever seen before I married her? Her father was only a well-to-do *muzhik.* A shabby little farm—that was all his property. But what have I not acquired in fifteen years? A store, two taverns, a mill, a granary, two rented holdings, and an iron-roofed villa and warehouse combined." He swelled with pride. "Rather different to her father, I think! In fact, who is the chief man in the district to-day? Why, Vassili Brekhunoff, of course!"

"And why so?" he continued presently. "Because I devote my whole attention to business and work hard—not like some people who lie abed and play the fool. *I* don't sleep whole nights away. No. Blizzard or no blizzard, out I go if necessary, and my business gets done. They think me a fool, and laugh at my money-making: but never mind, Vassili—go on working hard, even if it makes your head ache. If necessary, spend a night in the open like this rather than lose time. Never mind if you cannot sleep, either. To be able to think such thoughts is a pillow in itself," he concluded proudly.

"Some people seem to think that riches come to one by chance. Pooh! There is only one Mironoff in a million. No. Work hard, and God will give you the rest. If only He give you health and strength, that alone should be sufficient."

And the mere thought that he might one day become such a millionaire as Mironoff, who had risen from nothing, so fired Vassili with ecstasy that he yearned to have someone to speak to. Yet there was no one. Ah, but, once he could win to Goviatchkina, he would have a landowner to speak to—and to bamboozle as well!

"Good heavens, how it blows!" he continued as he listened to a squall of wind which was beating against the splashboard and bending it inwards as it lashed the bark planking with snow. "It is drifting the snow so much that perhaps we shall never get out in the morning."

Nothing could be seen in the white swirl of obscurity but Brownie's dark head and tail and the sack covering his back. At intervals the wind would toss the corners of the sack aloft, while in front and behind and on either side of the sledge whirled the same uniform mass of whiteness—now lightening a little, now suddenly becoming denser.

"I was a fool ever to have listened to Nikita," he thought. "We ought to have gone on again, and we should have landed somewhere. We might have reached Grishkino again, and been able to put up at Tarass's place after all. Yet here we have to stick all night! What is the good of that? God gives to those who help themselves, but not to loafers, sluggards and fools. I must try smoking again."

He sat up, got out a cigarette, and then rolled over on his stomach to shield the flame of the match from the wind with the flap of his coat. Yet the wind found an entry somehow, and blew out the matches, one by one. At length he contrived to keep one alight, and started smoking. He felt greatly pleased with his success, and although the wind got more of the smoke than he did, he managed to draw three whiffs, and was much cheered by them. He rolled himself back into a sitting posture, wrapped himself up again, and started once more to think over and consider matters; until suddenly, and without warning, he lost consciousness and went off into a doze.

All at once something seemed to jostle him, and he awoke. It might have been Brownie pulling away straw from beneath him, or it might have been the result of some internal disturbance, but at all events he awoke—and with his heart beating so fast and so furiously that the very sledge seemed to be shaking under him. He opened his eyes. The scene around him appeared exactly the same, except that it seemed lighter.

"It must be the dawn." he thought to himself. "It will soon be morning now."

Then all at once he remembered that the fact of its getting lighter could only mean that the moon was rising. He raised himself again, and looked at the cob. Brownie was standing with his hindquarters to the wind, and shaking all over. The snow-heaped sacking was turned up over his back on the windward side, and the crupper was slipping down over his flank, while his snow-powdered head and wind-tossed mane and forehead-tuft were more clearly visible than before. As for Nikita, he was still squatting in the same position as when he had first sat down, with his feet and the apron with which he had covered his head all piled with snow.

"A *muzhik* never freezes," thought Vassili as he bent over the back of the sledge and looked at him. "No, not for all his poor clothes. He can be trusted for that. Yet the *muzhiks* are a stupid lot—a mere welter of ignorance."

For a moment he thought of taking the sacking off the cob's back and covering Nikita over with it, but it was too cold to get up and make the effort. Moreover, he was afraid of the cob starving if he did.

"What on earth did I take Nikita for?" he reflected. "I have *her* stupidity to thank for it all" (he was thinking of his wife). Then he rolled back into his former position by the splashboard. "My uncle spent a night in the snow like this," he went on, "yet he took no harm. Sebastian, too, once had to be dug out," he continued as another instance occurred to him. "Sebastian died, though, for he was frozen stiff as a carcase. If only we had stayed at Grishkino!"

Wrapping his coat more carefully about him, so that the protection of the fur should not be wasted at any point, but keep him warm from head to heels, he closed his eyes and tried to sleep again. Yet, for all his efforts, he could not succeed, but, on the contrary, continued absolutely alert and wakeful. Once more he began to make business calculations and to run over his outstanding debts. Once more, too, he began to appraise himself and to congratulate himself on his position in the world.

None the less, his every thought seemed to be broken in upon by a sort of haunting fear, as well as by a feeling of vexation that they had not stayed at Grishkino.

"To think of it!" he murmured. "Why, at this moment I might have been lying in a warm bed!"

More than once he turned himself over and resettled himself, in a vain endeavour to find an easier position and one more protected from the wind, but each new posture proved more uncomfortable than the last. At length he raised himself again, changed his position altogether, wrapped his legs up carefully, closed his eyes, and tried to lie perfectly still. Yet, either his feet, squeezed into their stiff top-boots, had begun to ache, or the wind was catching him somewhere, but at all events he had not been lying long in this position before he found himself angrily remembering that at this very moment he might have been lying in a warm hut at Grishkino. Again he raised himself, again he wrapped his coat about him, and resettled himself. Once he thought he heard the far-off sound of cocks crowing, whereupon he turned down the collar of his coat in a tremor of joy and listened attentively; yet, for all his straining of his ears, he could hear nothing but the whistling of the wind through the shafts, the flapping of the handkerchief, and the lashing of the snow against the bark sides of the sledge.

As for Nikita, he remained squatting as he had done since the previous evening. Never once had he stirred, nor returned any answer to Vassili's shouts, although the latter had called to him more than once.

"*He* seems to have no difficulty in sleeping," thought Vassili with irritation as he leant over the back of the sledge and looked at the snow-covered Nikita.

In all, Vassili must have got up and lain down again at least twenty times. It seemed to him as if the night would never end.

"Surely it must be nearly morning now?" he thought once as he raised himself and glanced about him. "How would it be to look at my watch? But no; I might get frozen if I unhooked my coat. Yet, once I knew that it was drawing towards morning, things would seem better, and we would set about harnessing the cob."

In the depths of his soul, however, Vassili knew quite well that it could not be near morning yet. The truth was that his nervous panic was increasing to such an extent that he wished both to verify his supposition and to deceive himself. In the end he finished by carefully unhooking his fur coat, thrusting his hand in, and groping about till he dug down to his waistcoat. A further series of efforts enabled him to draw out his silver watch, with its enamelled chasing of flowers. Then he tried to look at it, but nothing could be seen without a light. Once more he lay down upon his elbows and stomach (as he had done when getting ready to smoke), pulled out his matches, and set about striking one. By this time he had grown more expert at the business, and, feeling for the match with the largest head of sulphur, he contrived to light it at the first attempt. Then, thrusting the dial of the watch under the light, he looked at it, and could hardly believe his eyes! It was only ten minutes past one! The whole night lay before him!

"Oh, the long, long night!" he groaned, feeling as though the frost were striking down his back already. Then, hooking his coat up again and wrapping it about him, he sat back in the corner of the sledge, and prepared to wait with what patience he might.

Suddenly, above the monotonous wail of the wind he heard a new sound—a sound made by some living creature. It grew steadily louder, attained its maximum, and began as steadily to die away again. There could be no doubt what it was. It was a wolf. Nor was the beast so far off that the wind could drown the gradations of tone in its howl as it moved its jaws from side to side. Vassili put back his coat-collar from his ear and listened strainedly. Brownie was doing the same, his ears sharply pricked, and when the howl ceased he changed his legs and snorted uneasily. After this Vassili found it more than ever impossible to sleep—found it impossible to steady his nerves for a moment. The more he tried to think of his business affairs and accounts, his reputation, dignity and wealth, the more did terror begin to master him; while, above all other thoughts, and yet mixed up with them, floated the persistent question—"Why did we not stop the night at Grishkino?"

"God be with that landowner and his forest," he thought to himself, "yet I wish I had never come across either of them. To have to spend the night here! They say that men who have been drinking always freeze readily, and *I* have been drinking to-night."

Listening thus to his own suggestions, he could feel himself beginning to tremble, though he hardly knew why—whether from cold, that is to say, or from fear. He tried to cover himself up and lie down as before, but found this impossible. He could not remain still, even for a second, but felt as if he must be up and doing something to stifle the terror which was rising in him, and against which he felt himself powerless. He got out his matches and cigarettes once more, but of the former there remained but three, and they of the sorriest kind. Indeed, all of them fizzled out without lighting when struck.

"The devil take you, you cursed bit of rubbish! Go and be hanged to you!" he burst out (though hardly knowing what it was he was swearing at) as he hurled the battered cigarette away. The matchbox was about to follow it, when he stayed his hand, and thrust the box into his pocket. Such a fit of restlessness now seized upon him that he could stay no longer where he was. Leaping from the sledge, and standing with his back to the wind, he began lowering and tightening up his belt again.

"Why should we lie here, waiting for death to come?" he exclaimed as a new idea suddenly struck him. "Why not mount the cob and ride away? With only a man on his back he would never stick fast." Then he thought of Nikita. "Oh, but it would be nothing to him to die," he went on. "What can his life matter to him? He has nothing much to lose with it, whereas I have much to gain with mine."

So he untied the cob, threw the halter over its neck, and tried to mount, but his fur coat and boots weighed him down, and he slipped back every time. Then he climbed onto the sledge and tried to mount from there, but the sledge kept rocking under his weight, and he failed again. At length, and for the third time, he drew the cob close to the sledge, balanced himself cautiously on the rim, and succeeded so far as to find himself stretched face downwards athwart the animal's back. Lying thus, he wriggled himself forward once or twice until he had got his leg over and seated himself, his toes resting in the trace-loops of the saddle-piece. But the jolting of the sledge as it shook under Vassili's weight had awakened Nikita, who now raised himself and seemed to Vassili to be saying something.

"Look here, you fool," shouted Vassili. "It's all through you that we have got into this plight—got into it for nothing, too," and, tucking the flapping skirts of his greatcoat beneath his knees, he turned the cob round, and rode away from the sledge in the direction where he thought the forest and the forest-keeper's lodge must be.

VII

Up to this moment Nikita had never once stirred since he first squatted down behind the sledge and covered himself over with the apron. Like all people who live in close contact with nature and are familiar with hardship, he was patient, and could sit waiting for hours, or even for days, without growing restless or losing his temper. He had heard his master call out to him twice, yet had returned no answer, for the sole reason that he did not feel inclined to stir or to go to the trouble of raising his voice. Although he was warm enough at the time he had sat down, both with the tea which he had drunk and with the exertion of plunging through snowdrifts, he knew that that would not last long, and that he would be powerless to restore the warmth by exercising himself, since he felt as utterly worn out as a horse feels when he stops and can go no further, despite the severest whipping, and his master sees that no further work can be got out of him until he has been rested and fed. Moreover, one of his feet had got frost-bitten through its ragged boot, so that the big toe had lost all sensation and his whole body was becoming steadily colder and colder. Consequently, in time, the thought began to enter his head that he might have to die that night. Yet the thought was neither particularly unwelcome nor particularly awe-inspiring. It was not particularly unwelcome, for the reason that his life had not been exactly an uninterrupted holiday, but, on the contrary, a life of ceaseless servitude, of which he was beginning to grow weary. Nor did the thought seem to him particularly awe-inspiring, for the reason that, over and above the masters whom he had served on earth—masters such as Vassili Andreitch—he had always felt himself dependent upon the Great Master who had sent him into this life, and knew that, in dying, he would still remain that Master's servant, and that that Master would be good to him.

"Should I be sorry to leave the life in which I am settled and which I am accustomed to?" he thought. "Well, even if I have to go, I cannot help myself, and it were best to prepare for the new one."

"My sins?" he went on presently as he remembered his drunken orgies, the money squandered on drink, his insults to his wife, his frequent oaths, his neglect of church-going, his non-observance of fast-days, and all the many things for which the priest had reproved him at confession time. "Well, of course they were sins—I have never denied that; but it was God who made me what I am. Yet, what terrible sins they have been! What will become of me for such sins?"

Then, from thinking of what might be in store for him that night he passed, without recurring to that thought, to memories which came into his head at random. He thought of Martha's arrival, of the workmen's carouse, of his refusal to share their liquor, of the present expedition, of Tarass's hut, of the talk about family separations, of his little lad, of Brownie (now, doubtless, growing warm under his sacking), and of the master who was making the sledge creak above him as he tossed and turned.

"Well, I had plenty of tea to drink there and was tired," he thought. "*I* had no wish to start out again. *I* had no wish to leave such good living to come and die in this hole. Yet *he* wished otherwise."

Then all these memories swam together and jumbled themselves up in his head, and he went off into a doze.

From this doze he was awakened by Vassili shaking the sledge as he mounted the cob—shaking it so violently that it slewed right round and struck Nikita in the back with one of its runners, forcing him, willy-nilly, to shift his position. Stretching out his legs with some difficulty and sweeping the snow off them, he raised himself a little, and at once felt a pang shoot through his body. Understanding at the first glance what Vassili intended to do, he begged him to leave the sacking behind, since the cob no longer needed it and it would make an additional covering for himself. He shouted to Vassili to that effect, but the latter disappeared in the snow-dust without heeding him. Left alone, Nikita considered what he had better do. He felt that he had not sufficient strength also to go off in search of a human habitation, while it was impossible for him to resume his old seat, since the snow had filled up the hole already. Even if he got into the sledge, things would not mend, for he had no extra covering, and his *khalat* and fur jacket no longer kept him warm. He could not have felt colder if he had been clad only in a shirt.

The situation was becoming one of positive agony.

"Little Father—our Little Father in Heaven!" he cried aloud; and the knowledge that he was not alone, but that there was One who could hear him and would never abandon him, brought him comfort. He drew a deep sigh and, with the apron still covering his head, crept into the sledge and lay down where his master had been. Even there, however, he could not grow warm. At first he kept shivering all over. Then the shivering fit passed away, and he began to lose consciousness. He might have been dead or asleep, for all he could tell, yet felt prepared for either eventuality.

VIII

Meanwhile Vassili was using his heels and the spare end of the halter to urge the cob in the direction where, for some reason or another, he supposed the forest and the forest-keeper to be. The snow blinded his eyes and the wind seemed as if it were struggling to stop him, but, bending forward at times to double the skirts of his coat and tuck them between his knees and the icy saddle-piece which made his seat such an uncomfortable one, he pressed the cob onwards unceasingly. The animal moved with difficulty, yet proceeded whither it was directed in its usual docile manner.

For what seemed to him some five minutes Vassili rode straight ahead, seeing nothing in front of him but the cob's head and ears and a sea of whiteness, and hearing nothing but the whistling of the wind over the cob's ears and round the collar of his fur coat. Suddenly, however, something black showed up before him. His heart began to beat hopefully, and he rode towards the object, imagining that he already discerned in its outlines the walls of the houses forming a village. The object did not keep still, however, but was forever waving from side to side. In fact, it turned out to be, not a village, but a tall piece of wormwood, which, growing out of a boundary ridge and projecting above the snow, bent violently over to one side each time that the wind struck it and went whistling through its stems. Somehow the sight of this wormwood thus tortured by the cruel wind caused Vassili to shudder, and he re-started the cob in haste, without noticing that, in turning aside to the wormwood, he had deviated from his former direction, and was now riding at a tangent to it. None the less, he imagined himself still to be bearing in the fancied direction of the forest-keeper's hut, and, although the cob kept trying to swerve to the right, he as often straightened it again to the left.

For the second time a dark object loomed up before him, filling his heart with joy, since he felt certain this time that here was a village at last: yet it proved to be only another boundary ridge topped with wormwood. As in the case of the first one, the sound of the wind wailing through the dried stems seemed to fill Vassili with fear. This piece of wormwood was exactly similar to the other piece in all respects save one—namely, that beside this second piece ran the track of a horse's hoofs, slightly powdered over with snow. Vassili pulled up, leaned forward, and looked at the track carefully. It was the track of a small-sized hoof, and the covering of snow upon it was, as yet, a mere sprinkling. In short, it was the track of his own cob! He had described a complete circle, and that not a large one.

"So this is how I am to perish!" he thought. Then, lest he should yield to his terror, he started forward again, and urged on the cob even more strenuously than before. At every moment, as he strained his eyes into the swirl of whiteness before him, he seemed to see dark points stand out for a second and then vanish as soon as he looked at them. Once he thought he heard what might have been either the barking of a dog or the howl of a wolf, but the sound was so faint and uncertain that he could not be sure whether he had really heard anything or whether it had been only his fancy. He stopped and listened attentively.

Suddenly a weird, startling cry sounded in his very ears, and everything beneath him seemed to heave and tremble. He clutched the cob's mane, yet found that that too was quivering, while the cry grew ever more and more piercing. For some seconds Vassili could not frame a thought or understand in the least what was happening. Yet all that had happened was that the cob had been seized with the idea either of inspiriting himself or of calling for help, and had neighed loudly in his raucous, guttural tones.

"How the beast frightened me, be hanged to it!" gasped Vassili to himself. Yet, although he understood now the cause of his terror, he could not shake himself free from it.

"I must consider things a moment and steady myself," he thought. Yet it was all to no purpose, for he could not master himself—could not keep from urging the cob on; taking no heed the while that he was now riding before the wind instead of against it. His body was chilled and aching all over, but especially in the lower part, next the saddle-piece, where his coat was unhooked, whilst his hands and feet were shaking violently and his breath came in gasps. He felt sure now that he was to perish in the midst of this fearful waste of snow, and that nothing could save him.

Suddenly the cob gave a groan as it stuck fast in a snowdrift, and, struggling violently, began to sink sideways onto its flank. Vassili leapt off, displacing as he did so the trace-loops in which his feet had been resting, and so also the saddle-piece on which he had been seated. Yet he had no sooner dismounted than the cob righted himself, lurched forward, took a couple of plunges, and disappeared with a loud neigh, trailing behind him the sacking and harness, and leaving Vassili stranded in the snowdrift. Vassili made a rush to catch him, but the snow was so deep, and his fur coat so heavy, that he sank knee-deep at every step, and had taken no more than twenty strides when his breath failed him, and he had to stop.

"The timber, the wethers for the butcher, the rent-hold land, the store, the taverns, the iron-roofed villa and warehouse, my little heir—am I to leave them all?" he thought. "Is it to end like this? No, no, it cannot be!"

For some reason or another there came into his mind at that moment a picture of the wormwood waving in the wind, and of himself twice riding up to it. Such terror seized upon him that he could hardly believe in the reality of what was happening. "I must be dreaming it all," he thought, and tried, as it were, to awake from his dream: yet there was no awakening for him. It was real snow that was lashing his face, heaping his form over, and chilling his right hand, which had lost its mitten. It was a real desert, too, in which he was now left lonely—as lonely as the wormwood—and in which he must await an imminent, a swift, and an unthinkable death.

"O Queen of Heaven! O Holy Father Saint Nicholas who teachest us abstinence!" he began, with a dim recollection of the thanksgiving service of yesterday, of the *ikon* with its blackened face and golden vestment, and of the candles for that *ikon* which he had sold, and which, returned to him straightway, he had replaced in his locker after lighting them for a brief moment. Again and again he besought the wonder-working Saint Nicholas to save him from his fate, promising in return a thanksgiving and many candles. Yet all the time he knew beyond the possibility of doubt that, although that blackened face and golden vestment, as well as the candles, the priest, and the thanksgivings, were all of them very important and necessary there in the church, they could do nothing for him here, and that between those candles and thanksgivings on the one hand, and his present forlorn plight on the other, there could be no real connection whatever.

"Still, I must not despair," he thought. "I have only to follow the cob's track before it gets snowed over, and it will bring me out somewhere. Only, I must not hurry too much, or I might plunge into another snowdrift and be worse off than ever."

Nevertheless, for all his determination to go quietly, he could not help quickening his pace, breaking into a run, tumbling down continually, picking himself up again, and once more falling. Moreover, the cob's track was almost invisible where the snow was not deep.

"I am done for!" he said at last. "I am not following the cob's track at all, but only losing myself."

Just as he said this, however, he happened to glance ahead, and caught sight of something dark there. It was Brownie! And not Brownie alone, but also the shafts and the handkerchief! The cob was standing beside the sledge, with the harness and sacking still dangling down his flank—but standing in a different position to before, since he was just under the shafts, and had his head (which he kept shaking at intervals) drawn close to the ground by the halter, which had caught round his pastern. It seemed that Vassili had stuck fast in the same ravine as that into which Nikita and he had previously blundered—that, as a matter of fact, the cob had been carrying him straight back to the sledge, and that, at the moment when he jumped off, he had only been fifty paces from it!

IX

Staggering up to the sledge, Vassili grasped hold of it and stood for a long time without moving as he endeavoured to steady himself and regain his breath. There was nothing to be seen of Nikita in his old position, but in the sledge there lay something heaped with snow, which Vassili guessed to be his servant. Vassili's terrors had now vanished—or, if any were left, it was merely lest he should have a return of the horrible panic which he had experienced on the cob's back, and, still more, when he found himself left in the snowdrift. At all costs he must not give way to that panic again; and if he would avoid that, he must be up and doing something—must be occupying his thoughts with something. First of all he planted himself with his back to the wind, and unfastened his fur coat to cool himself. Then, when he had regained his breath a little, he shook the snow off his boots and left-hand mitten (the other one was hopelessly lost, and probably lying somewhere a couple of inches below the snow), and refastened his belt tightly—much as he was accustomed to do when he was about to step out of his store to buy cartloads of grain which the *muzhiks* had brought. This done, he set about exerting himself. The first thing which it occurred to him to do was to disentangle the cob's leg, and, the halter thus freed, he tied Brownie up to the rim of the splashboard where he had been tied before. Next, he had just gone behind the cob to straighten the crupper, sacking and saddle-piece on his back, when he saw something stir in the sledge, and then the head of Nikita emerge from beneath the snow which covered it. The frozen man raised himself a little—though evidently with a great effort—and made a strange gesture with his hand in front of his face, as though he were brushing away a fly. As he did this he seemed to Vassili to be saying something—probably Vassili's name—so the latter left the sacking unstraightened and stepped up to the sledge.

"How is it with you now?" he asked, "and what are you trying to say?"

"Only that I—I am dying," answered Nikita with difficulty and in gasps. "Give my wages to the little lad or to the wife—it does not matter which."

"Are you frozen, then?" said Vassili.

"Yes—and dying; I know it quite well," replied Nikita in a choking voice, and still fluttering his hand before his face as though to brush away a fly. "Pardon me, for Christ's sake."

For about half a minute Vassili stood without moving and in silence.

Then all at once, and with the same air of decision as marked him when he had struck hands over a good bargain, he took a step backwards, tucked up the sleeves of his coat, and began with both hands to rake the snow off Nikita and out of the sledge. This done, he unhooked his belt, opened his fur coat, pushed Nikita hastily into a straight posture, and lay down upon him in such a way that the latter should be covered, not only with the coat, but with Vassili's own warm, overheated body. With one skirt of the coat tucked between Nikita's form and the side of the sledge, and the tail of it grasped between his ankles, Vassili remained lying prone, with his head resting upon the splashboard and his ears deaf either to the movements of the cob or to the howling of the wind, but intent only on listening to Nikita's breathing. For a long time Nikita lay without moving. Then he gave a deep sigh, and stirred faintly.

"There you are, you see, and yet you talk of dying!" began Vassili. "Just you lie still and grow warm, and we—"

To his great surprise Vassili found that he could say no more, for tears were welling from his eyes and his lower jaw was working. He broke off short, and swallowed a lump in his throat.

"How absurdly weak and nervous I have made myself," he thought. Yet not only did he find this weakness far from unpleasant, but it actually gave him a sensation of joy such as he had never yet experienced.

"Yes, we shall manage it all right like this," he said to himself, conscious of a rapturous feeling of emotion. After this he lay for a long time in silence, merely wiping his eyes against the fur of the coat, and tucking back its right-hand skirt as the wind blew it up at intervals; but at length he felt as though he must communicate his joy to a fellow-creature.

"Nikita," he said.

"That is better. I am getting warm now," came from underneath him.

"Nikita, my old friend, I thought we were done for. You would have been frozen, and I—"

Once more Vassili's cheeks started quivering and his eyes filled with tears, so that he could say no more.

"No, it is no good," he said to himself. "Yet I know what I know," and he remained silent. Still he lay there. Warmth seemed to be passing into his body from Nikita below and from the fur coat above. Only the hands with which he held the skirts of the coat against Nikita's sides, and his feet, from between which the wind kept blowing the skirts away, were beginning to feel frozen. His mittenless right hand in particular felt numbed. Yet he never thought of his hands or feet—only of how he could best warm the peasant who was lying beneath him.

More than once he glanced at the cob and saw that its back was uncovered, since the sacking had now slipped off altogether and was lying on the snow. He felt as if he ought to go and cover the animal over again, yet could not make up his mind to leave Nikita, even for a moment, and thus break the spell of that rapturous joy which now possessed him. As for his terrors, they had long since fled away.

"By heavens, I am not going to be beaten!" he said to himself with reference to his efforts to warm Nikita—speaking, indeed, in just the same boastful tone in which he had been accustomed to speak of his sales or purchases.

He lay for an hour—for two—for three, but took no heed of the passing of time. At first there danced before his vision dim pictures of the storm, of the shafts, and of the cob under its high *douga*. Then these pictures became exchanged for jumbled memories of the festival, of his wife, of the *stanovoi,* and of the candle-locker—but beneath the picture of the candle-locker lay Nikita. Then again he saw the *muzhiks* trading with him, and the white, iron-roofed walls of his house—but beneath the picture of those walls again lay Nikita. Then everything became confused. One thing ran into another, until at last these various scattered impressions came together as the colours of a rainbow merge into a beam of white light, and he fell asleep. For long he slept without dreaming, but, just before the dawn came there came also some sleep-visions. He seemed to be standing by the candle-locker, while old mother Tikhonova was asking him for a five-copeck candle for the festival. He tried to take the candle out and give it to her, but his hands remained glued in his pockets. Then he tried to walk round the locker, but his legs refused to move, and his new, clean shoes stuck fast to the stone floor, so that he could not even raise his feet to take the shoes off.

Then suddenly the locker was not a locker at all, but a bed, and on that bed Vassili could see himself lying, face downwards—lying on his own bed at home. He was lying on the bed, and could not rise, although it was necessary for him to do so, seeing that Ivan Matveitch, the *stanovoi,* was coming to see him presently, and he must go with Ivan either to buy some timber or to put the crupper straight on the cob's back—he could not be sure which. He kept asking his wife, "Has he not come yet, Mikolovna?" and she kept answering him, "No, not yet." Then he could hear someone driving up to the steps outside. Surely it must be he? But no—the vehicle had driven past. "Is he not come yet, Mikolovna?" he asked his wife once more, and once more she replied, "No, not yet." Thus he lay and lay upon the bed, unable to rise, and ever waiting—waiting: and the waiting was at once painful and joyous. Suddenly the joy of it was filled to the full! He for whose coming he had been waiting, was now at hand and it was not Ivan Matveitch nor anyone else. Yet still it was the Man for whom he had been waiting. He entered—did that Man—and called him: and this Man who had called him cried out to him again and bade him go and lie down upon Nikita. And Vassili was glad that this Someone had come. "Yes, I will go!" he cried in his joy, and with that cry Vassili awoke.

Yes, he awoke—but awoke a very different man to what he had been when he fell asleep. He tried to rise, and could not. He tried to move his hand, and could not. He tried to move his leg, and could not. Then he tried to turn his head, but that also he could not do. This surprised him, yet in no way troubled him. Then he remembered that Nikita was lying beneath him, and that Nikita was growing warm and was coming back to life. It seemed to him that he was Nikita, and Nikita he, and that his life was no longer within himself, but within Nikita. He strained his ears till he caught the sound of breathing—yes, the faint, deep breathing of Nikita. "Nikita is alive!" he cried to himself in triumph. "and therefore so also am I!"

Then he began to think about his money, his store, his house, his sales and purchases, and Mironoff's millions. He could not understand how that man whom men called Vassili Brekhunoff could bear to interest himself in such things as he did. "That man can never have known what is the greatest thing of all," he thought of this Vassili Brekhunoff. "He can never have known what I know. Yes, I know it for certain now. At last—I KNOW!"

Once again he heard the Man calling him who had called to him before, and his whole being seemed to respond in joy and loving-kindness as he replied: "I am coming, I am coming!" For he felt that he was free at last, and that nothing could hold him further.

And, indeed, nothing further than that did Vassili Andreitch see or hear or feel in this world.

Around him the tempest still kept on. The same swirls of snow kept circling in eddies and covering the coats of the dead Vassili Andreitch and the trembling Brownie, the sledge (now almost invisible) and, stretched out upon its floor, the now reviving Nikita as he lay prone beneath the body of his dead master.

X

Just before morning Nikita awoke. It was the frost making its way down his back which aroused him. He had just been dreaming that he was driving from the mill with a load of his master's flour, and that, instead of taking the bridge over the stream, he went by the ford, and stuck fast. He could see himself getting under the load and trying to lift it as he straightened his back. Yet, strange to say, the load would not move, but clung always to his back, so that he could neither move the cart nor withdraw himself from beneath it. It seemed to be breaking his very loins. And how cold it felt! At all costs he must get away from beneath it. "Hold on," he found himself saying to the someone who was causing the load to break his back. "Take off some of the sacks." Yet the load kept growing colder and colder, and pressing more and more heavily upon him. Then suddenly something gave a loud bang, and he became fully awake and remembered all that had happened. That chilly load—it was his dead frozen master. That loud bang—it had been caused by Brownie striking his hoofs against the sledge.

"Andreitch, Andreitch!" he cried cautiously to his master (though he half guessed the truth already) as he raised his back stiffly. But Andreitch returned no answer, while his body and legs were cold and stiff and heavy as weights.

"There is no doubt that he is dead," thought Nikita. He turned his head round, pushed the snow away from in front of his face, and opened his eyes. It was quite light now. The wind was still humming through the shafts and the snow streaming down—but with this difference, that the snow was no longer dashing itself against the sides of the sledge, but piling itself up in silence over sledge and cob—from the latter of which not even the sound of breathing was now to be heard.

"Brownie too must be frozen," thought Nikita. And, indeed, those two loud hoof-strokes upon the sledge which had awakened him had been the last efforts of the now dead and frozen animal to keep upon his legs.

'O God, Little Father of ours, surely thou wilt call me also?" said Nikita. "If so, Thy will be done. It would be hard that two of us should be taken and the other left. Let death come when it will," and he drew his hand in again, closed his eyes and fell asleep, firmly convinced that this time he was really and truly dead.

It was about the time of the midday meal next day when some *muzhiks* dug out Vassili and Nikita—seventy yards only from the road, and half a verst from the village.

The snow had drifted completely over the sledge, but the shafts, with the handkerchief on them, were still visible. Brownie, belly-deep in the snow, stood a white frozen mass, his dead muzzle pressed tightly inwards against his rigid neck, his nostrils fringed with icicles, and his eyes coated over and glazed with ice as with frozen tears. Moreover, he had so wasted away in that one night that there remained of him but skin and bones. As for Vassili, he too was as stiff as a frozen carcase, and when his legs were pulled aside the corpse rolled off Nikita in a solid lump. His prominent, hawk-like eyes were frozen hard, and his mouth (open a little under his cropped moustache) filled with snow. Nikita only was alive, though frostbitten all over. Yet, when brought to himself, he could not be persuaded that he was not dead, and that all that was now happening to him was not taking place in the next world instead of in this. Indeed, his first feeling when he heard the *muzhiks* shouting above him as they dug out the sledge and then rolled the stiffened Vassili off him was one of surprise that *muzhiks* shouted in the next world even as they had shouted in this, and had similar bodies! When at length he understood that he was really here—here in this present world—he felt vexed rather than pleased, especially as he could feel that the fingers of both his hands were frostbitten.

For about two months he lay in hospital. Three of his fingers had to be amputated, but the others healed, so that he was able to go to work again and to live twenty years longer—first as a labourer, and then, in his old age, as a watchman. Indeed, he died only this year—at home and under the *ikons,* with a lighted wax candle in his hands, just as he had always wished.

Before his death he took leave of his old wife, and pardoned her for the cooper. He took leave also of his son and grandchildren, and died thoroughly happy to think that his death left his son and daughter-in-law freed from the burden of having a supernumerary mouth to feed, and that this time he himself would really pass from a life which had grown wearisome to him to that other life which had been growing more and more familiar and alluring to him each year and hour. Is he better or worse off now where he has awakened after his death—the death which really came that time? Is he disillusioned, or has he really found what he expected? Soon we shall all know.

Packed Dirt, Churchgoing, a Dying Cat, a Traded Car

by John Updike

Introduced by Lorrie Moore

AS I FINISHED READING THIS STORY FOR THE FIRST TIME, YEARS AGO, I had the kind of welling, poetic encounter often described by others (including Emily Dickinson) with such violent terms as "blown away" or "knocked off" (usually socks, tops of heads, other writers, or texts somehow lying about submerged in water).

I was stunned, held paralyzed by the story's beauty, as if by some genius Doberman pinscher. I could not move to read anything else. Surely I would never read anything else, ever, only this. I held the book so long I got a paper cut and bled on the page.

Structurally, the story is a masterpiece. Cobbled and hinged, it takes as its form a faux essay. It is composed of seemingly discrete pieces—Dirt, Church, Cat, Car—and the commas of the title find expression in the story proper as eloquent spaces, yearning leaps of a kind of symphonic carpentry. One can marvel at the way the story's *built,* its order and design, its searching segues, its surprise reprise at the end like a brilliant move in chess.

But looked at in more emotional ways, the story opens up ceaselessly. It's rich with reminiscence, haunted by emotional stillbirth, nagged by death peering in at the windows. In the main the story is a valedictory to the narrator's father, but it is also a story about writing. In sequence, there is a paean to churchgoing (father worship) bookended in warnings, an experience of first fatherhood supplanted by the death of a cat, and finally the narrator's father's dying—for which the narrator neither stays nor finds the proper bedside words. This last is the kind of human failure a writer heads for, writes into, worries with language, and attempts to illumine with story. Partaking of a ceremony of correction and enriched farewell, Updike seems to say here, the writer writes into absences. What's the point of writing? a character asks the protagonist. "We in America need ceremonies," replies the latter, though too late to have it serve as a reply. Life, as most of us experience it, suggests Updike, is perhaps not fully life—not without the opportunity to redress and reformulate, to re-court events through narrative, that unruly tool. It is a writer's dictum.

Updike's fictional world has typically involved the unending self-parody of heterosexuality: its psychic pratfalls replayed through the decades if not the ages. Heterosexuality is Updike's metaphor of human uneasiness in the world. "The world is our bride," says the narrator here, "given to us to love, and the terror and joy of the marriage is that we bring to it a nature not our bride's." Lives begin and occur *in* the world, and, like the sexual *in,* the preposition is freighted and fraught. The domestic drama is the existential one; the lover's quarrel, the marital spat are our local tropes. "The earth is our playmate," Updike writes. And the very pebbles on the ground are "like the confetti aftermath of a wedding."

No frayed pen or casual mind could have written such a magnificent story as this one, with its poetic rigor and generosity and poise. "Different things move us," the story begins, perhaps already sensing its own difference. It has moved me, always; almost unutterably. It demands the heart. It slashes the hands.

Packed Dirt, Churchgoing, a Dying Cat, a Traded Car

John Updike

Different things move us. I, David Kern, am always affected—reassured, nostalgically pleased, even, as a member of my animal species, made proud—by the sight of bare earth that has been smoothed and packed firm by the passage of human feet. Such spots abound in small towns: the furtive break in the playground fence dignified into a thoroughfare, the trough of dust underneath each swing, the blurred path worn across a wedge of grass, the anonymous little mound or embankment polished by play and strewn with pebbles like the confetti aftermath of a wedding. Such unconsciously humanized intervals of clay, too humble and common even to have a name, remind me of my childhood, when one communes with dirt down among the legs, as it were, of presiding fatherly presences. The earth is our playmate then, and the call to supper has a piercingly sweet eschatological ring.

The corner where I now live was recently widened so that the cars going back and forth to the summer colony on the Point would not be troubled to slow down. My neighbor's house was sold to the town and wrecked and picked clean by salvagers and finally burned in a great bonfire of old notched beams and splintered clapboards that leaped tree-high throughout one whole winter day's cold drizzle. Then bulldozers, huge and yellow and loud, appeared on the street and began to gnaw, it seemed, at the corner of our house. My third child, a boy not yet two, came running from the window in tearful panic. After I tried to soothe him with an explanation, he followed me through the house sobbing and wailing "'Sheen! 'Sheen!" while the machines made our rooms shake with the curses of their labor. They mashed my neighbor's foundation stones into the earth and trimmed the levelled lot just as my grandmother used to trim the excess dough from the edge of the pieplate. They brought the curve of the road right to the corner of my property, and the beaten path that does for a sidewalk in front of my home was sheared diagonally by a foot-high cliff.

Last night I was coming back from across the street, fresh from an impromptu civic lamentation with a neighbor at how unsightly, now that the snow was melted, the awkward-shaped vacant lot the bulldozers had left looked, with its high raw embankment gouged by rivulets and littered with old chimney bricks. And soon, we concluded, now that spring was here, it would be bristling with weeds. Crossing from this conversation, I noticed that where my path had been looped the cliff no longer existed; feet—children's feet, mostly, for mostly children walk in our town—had worn the sharpness away and molded a little ramp by which ascent was easier.

This small modification, this modest work of human erosion, seemed precious to me not only because it recalled, in the slope and set of the dirt, a part of the path that long ago had led down from my parents' back yard to the high-school softball field. It seemed precious because it had been achieved accidentally, and had about it that repose of grace that is beyond willing. We in America have from the beginning been cleaving and baring the earth, attacking, reforming the enormity of nature we were given, which we took to be hostile. We have explored, on behalf of all mankind, this paradox: the more matter is outwardly mastered, the more it overwhelms us in our hearts. Evidence—gaping right-of-ways, acres mercilessly scraped, bleeding mountains of muddy fill—surrounds us of a war that is incapable of ceasing, and it is good to know that now there are enough of us to exert a counter-force. If craters were to appear in our landscape tomorrow, the next day there would be usable paths threading down the blasted sides. As our sense of God's forested legacy to us dwindles, there grows, in these worn, rubbed, and patted patches, a sense of human legacy—like those feet of statues of saints which have lost their toes to centuries of kisses. One thinks of John Dewey's definition of God as the union of the actual and the ideal.

There was a time when I wondered why more people did not go to church. Taken purely as a human recreation, what could be more delightful, more unexpected than to enter a venerable and lavishly scaled building kept warm and clean for use one or two hours a week and to sit and stand in unison and sing and recite creeds and petitions that are like paths worn smooth in the raw terrain of our hearts? To listen, or not listen, as a poorly paid but resplendently robed man strives to console us with scraps of ancient epistles and halting accounts, hopelessly compromised by words, of those intimations of divine joy that are like pain in that, their instant gone, the mind cannot remember or believe them; to witness the windows donated by departed patrons and the altar flowers arranged by withdrawn hands and the whole considered spectacle lustrous beneath its patina of inheritance; to pay, for all this, no more than we are moved to give—surely in all democracy there is nothing like it. Indeed, it is the most available democratic experience. We vote less than once a year. Only in church and at the polls are we actually given our supposed value, the soul-unit of one, with its noumenal arithmetic of equality: one equals one equals one.

My preaching fouls the words and corrupts me. Belief builds itself unconsciously and in consciousness is spent. Throughout my childhood I felt nothing in church but boredom and an oppressive futility. For reasons my father never explained, he was a dutiful churchman; my mother, who could use her senses, who had read Santayana and Wells, stayed home Sunday mornings, and I was all on her side, on the side of phenomena, in those years, though I went, with the other children, to Sunday school. It was not until we moved from the town and joined a country church that I, an adolescent of fifteen, my head a hotbed of girls and literature, felt a pleasant emotion in church. During Lent—that dull season, those forty suspended days during which Spring is gathering the mineral energy to make the resurrection that the church calendar seizes upon as conveniently emblematic—I ushered with my father at the Wednesday-night services. We would arrive in our old car—I think it was the Chevrolet then—on those raw March nights and it pleasantly surprised me to find the building warm, the stoked furnace already humming its devotions in the basement. The nave was dimly lit, the congregation small, the sermon short, and the wind howled a nihilistic counterpoint beyond the black windows blotted with garbled apostles; the empty pews, making the minister seem remote and small and emblematic, intensified our sensation of huddling. There was a strong sepia flavor of early Christianity: a minority flock furtively gathered within the hostile enormity of a dying, sobbing empire. From the rear, the broad back and baked neck of the occasional dutiful son loomed bullishly above the black straw hats of the mischievous-looking old ladies, gnarled by farmwork, who sat in their rows like withered apples on the shelves of a sweet-smelling cellar. My father would cross and uncross and recross his legs and stare at his thoughts, which seemed distant. It was pleasant to sit beside him in the rear pew. He was not much of a man for sitting still. When my parents and I went to the movies, he insisted on having the aisle seat, supposedly to give his legs room. After about twenty minutes he would leap up and spend the rest of the show walking around in the back of the theatre drinking water and talking to the manager while my mother and I, abandoned, consoled ourselves with the flickering giants of make-believe. He had nothing of the passive in him; a church always became, for him, something he helped run. It was pleasant, and even momentous, when the moment for action came, to walk by his side up the aisle, the thump of our feet the only sound in the church, and to take the wooden, felt-floored plates from a shy blur of white robes and to administer the submission of alms. Coins and envelopes sought to cover the felt. I condescended, stooping gallantly into each pew. The congregation seemed The Others, reaching, with quarters glittering in their crippled fingers, toward mysteries in which I was snugly involved. Even to usher at a church mixes us with the angels, and is a dangerous thing.

The churches of the Village had this Second Century quality. In Manhattan, Christianity is so feeble its future seems before it. One walks to church past clattering cafeterias and ravaged newsies in winter weather that is always a shade of Lent, on pavements spangled with last night's vomit. The expectantly hushed shelter of the church is like one of those spots worn bare by a softball game in a weed-filled vacant lot. The presence of the city beats like wind at the glowing windows. One hastens home afterward, head down, hurrying to assume the disguise—sweaters and suntans—of a non-churchgoer. I tried not to go, but it was not in me not to go. I never attended the same church two Sundays in succession, for fear I would become known, and be expected. To be known by face and name and financial weight robs us of our unitary soul, enrolls us against those Others. Devil's work. We are the others. It is of the essence to be a stranger in church.

On the island the very color of my skin made me strange. This island had been abandoned to the descendants of its slaves. Their church was on a hill; it has since been demolished, I have learned from letters, by a hurricane. To reach it one climbed a steep path made treacherous by the loose rubble of coral rock, jagged gray clinkers that bore no visible relation to the pastel branches that could be plucked, still pliant, from the shallows by Maid's Beach. Dull-colored goats were tethered along the path; their forelegs were tangled in their ropes so tightly that whenever they nodded the bush anchoring them nodded in answer. For windows the church possessed tall arched apertures filled not with stained glass but with air and outward vision; one could see the goats stirring the low foliage and the brightly dressed little girls who had escaped the service playing on the packed dirt around the church. The service was fatiguingly long. There were exhaustive petitionary prayers (for the Queen, the Prime Minister, Parliament) and many eight-versed hymns sung with a penetrating, lingering joy and accompanied by a hand-pumped organ. The organ breathed in and out, loud and soft, and the congregation, largely female, followed its ebb and flow at a brief but noticeable distance; their lips moved behind the singing, so I seemed immersed in an imperfectly synchronized movie. Musical stress, the British accent, and Negro elision worked upon the words a triple harmony of distortion. "Lait eth's waadsa *cull* raio-ind . . . " Vainly seeking my place in the hymn—for without a visual key I was lost—I felt lifted within a sweet, soughing milk, an aspiring chant as patient as the nodding of the goats.

Throughout the service, restless deacons slipped in and out of the windows. Bored myself—for we grow sated even with consolation—I discovered that without moving from my pew I too could escape through those tall portals built to admit the breeze. I rested my eyes on earth's wide circle round. From this height the horizon of the sea was lifted halfway up the sky. The Caribbean seemed a steeply tilted blue plane to which the few fishing boats in the bay below had been attached like magnetized toys. God made the world, Aquinas says, in play.

Matter has its radiance and its darkness; it lifts and it buries. Things compete; a life demands a life. On another English island, in Oxford—it is a strange fact about Americans, that we tend to receive our supernatural mail on foreign soil—I helped a cat die. The incident had the signature: decisive but illegible. For six years I did not tell my wife about it, for fear it would frighten her. Some hours before, I had left her at the hospital in the early stages of labor. Wearing a sterilized gown and mask, I had visited her in a white-tiled room along whose walls gleaming gutters stood ready to drain torrents of blood. Her face, scrubbed and polished, was fervent like a child's, and she seemed, lying there swathed in white, ready for nothing so much as a graduation ceremony. She would break off talking, and listen as if to the distant voice of a schoolmistress, and her face would grow rapt, and when the contraction had passed she would sigh and say, "That was a good one," and chatter some more to me of how I would feed myself alone and who I would send the telegrams to.

Shooed from the room, stripped of my mask, I tried to wait, and was told, the comical husband of the American cartoons, to run on home; it would be a time. I went outside and took a bus home. It was the last day of March. I had been born in March, and I had looked forward to welcoming my child to the month; but she was late. We lived on Iffley Road, and around midnight, for some reason—I think to mail a letter, but what letter could have been that important?—I was out walking a few blocks from our flat. The night was cold enough for gloves. The sensations of turning into a father—or, rather, the lack of sensations; the failure of sympathetic pain, the hesitation of dread, the postponement of pride—made the street seem insubstantial. There was not that swishing company of headlights that along an American road throws us into repeated relief. The brick homes, save for an occasional introverted glow in an upstairs window, were dark in the vehement shadows of privacy behind the dry hedges and spiked walls. The streetlamps—wintry, reserved—drained color from everything. Myself a shadow, I noticed another in the center of the road. A puddle of black, as I watched, it curled on itself; its ends lifted from the macadam and seemed to stretch in a yawn. Then it became inert again. I was horrified; the shape was about the size of a baby. When it curled the second time, I went to it, my footsteps the only sound in the street.

It was a cat that had been struck by a car. Struck but not quite killed: a testament to the modest speed and sensible size of English automobiles. By the impersonal witness of the lamps burning in the trees I couldn't be sure what color its fur was—it seemed orange-yellow, tabbied with stripes of dark ginger. The cat was plump and wore a collar. Someone had loved it. Blackness from one ear obscured one side of its head and when I touched here it was like a cup. For the third time, the cat stretched, the tips of its hind feet quivering luxuriously in that way cats have. With a great spastic effort it flipped over onto its other side, but made no cry. The only sound between us was my crooning as I carried it to the side of the street and laid it behind the nearest hedge.

A sallow upstairs light in this home was glowing. I wondered if the cat was theirs. Was it their love invested in my hands? Were they watching as I pushed, crouching, with my burden through their hedge? I wondered if I would be taken for a trespasser, a "poacher"; as an American, I was nervous of English tabus. In my own brutal country it was a not uncommon insult to kill a cat and throw the body into an enemy's yard, and I was afraid that this would be taken that way. I thought of writing a note to explain everything, but I had no paper and pen. I explained to the cat, how I was taking her (I felt it was female) out of the street so no more cars would hit her, how I would put her here in the nice safe dirt behind the hedge, where she could rest and get well. I did not believe she would get well; I think she was dead already. Her weight had felt dead in my hands and when I laid her down she did not stretch or twitch again.

Back in my flat, I discovered that one glove was smeared with blood. Most of the palm and three of the fingers were dyed wine-brown. I hadn't realized there was so much blood. I took off my gloves and carefully wrote a note, explaining that I had found this cat in the middle of the street, still alive, and that I had put it behind this hedge to be safe. If, as I thought, the cat was dead, I hoped that the finders would bury it. After some deliberation, I signed my name and address. I walked back and tucked the note under the cat's body, which seemed at home behind the hedge; it suffered my intrusion a trifle stiffly. It suggested I was making too much fuss, and seemed to say to me, *Run on home.*

Back in my flat once more, I felt abruptly tired, though my heart was pounding hugely. I went to bed and set the alarm for three and read a book. I remember the title, it was Chesterton's *The Everlasting Man*. I turned off the light and prayed for my wife and, though I did not believe myself capable of it, fell asleep. The alarm at three came crashing into some innocent walk of a dream and my frail head felt like a hollow cup. I dressed and went out to the public phone booth a block away and called the hospital. A chirping voice, after some rummaging in the records, told me that several hours ago, in the first hour of April (in the United States it was still March), a perfect female infant had been born. To me.

The next morning, after all the telegrams had been managed, I went back to the hedge, and the cat and my note were gone. Though I had left my address, I never received a letter.

When we returned from England, we bought a car. We had ordered it through my parents from folders they had sent us, and, though its shade of blue was more naïve, more like a robin's egg, than we had expected, this '55 Ford proved an excellent buy. Whether being shuffled from side to side of West Eighty-fifth Street every morning or being rammed in second gear up a washed-out mountain road in Vermont, it never complained. In New York, hot tar from a roof-patching job rained onto its innocent paint, and in Vermont its muffler was racked and rent on a shelf of rock, and in Massachusetts it wallowed, its hot clutch stinking, up from repeated graves of snow. Not only sand and candy wrappers accumulate in a car's interior, but heroisms and instants of communion. We in America make love in our cars, and listen to ball games, and plot our wooing of the dollar: small wonder the landscape is sacrificed to these dreaming vehicles of our ideal and onrushing manhood.

In the beginning, my wife and I would lovingly lave with soap and warm water the unflecked skin of the hood as if it were the thorax of a broad blue baby, and toward the end we let the gallant old heap rust where it would. Its eggshell finish grew grizzled with the stains of dropped maple seeds. Its doors balked at closing; its windows refused to roll down. But I somehow never believed we would ever trade it in, though the little girl born across the ocean in the ominous turning of April, now a vocal and status-conscious democrat of nearly six, applied more and more petulant pressure. The deal was consummated while my soul had its face turned, and Detroit the merciless mother contracted to devour her child. But before the new car arrived, there was a month's grace, and in this grace I enjoyed a final fling with my car, my first, my only—for all the others will be substitutes. It happened this way:

Dancing at a party with a woman not my wife, it seemed opportune to turn her hand in mine and kiss her palm. For some time her thighs had been slithering against mine, and, between dances, she developed a nervous clumsy trick of lurching against me, on tiptoe, and rubbing her breasts against my forearm, which was braced across my chest as I held a cigarette. My first thought was that I might burn her; my second, that Nature in her gruff maternal way had arranged one of her opportunities—as my mother, when I was a child, would unpredictably determine to give me a birthday or Hallowe'en party. Obediently I bowed my head and kissed my friend's moist palm. As it withdrew from the advance, her fingertips caressed my chin in the absent-minded manner of one fingering the muzzle of an importunate dog. The exchange transposed us into a higher key; I could hardly hear my own voice, and our dancing lost all connection with the music, and my hand explored her spine from a great aerial distance. Her back seemed mysteriously taut and hard; the body of a strange woman retains more of its mineral content, not being transmuted, through familiarity, into pure emotion. In a sheltered corner of the room we stopped dancing altogether and talked, and what I distinctly remember is how her hands, beneath the steady and opaque appraisal of her eyes, in nervous slurred agitation blindly sought mine and seized and softly gripped, with infantile instinct, my thumbs. Just my thumbs she held, and as we talked she moved them this way and that as if she were steering me. When I closed my eyes, the red darkness inside my lids was trembling, and when I rejoined my wife, and held her to dance, she asked, "Why are you panting?"

After we got home, and surveyed our four children, and in bed read a few pages made unbearably brilliant by their patina of martinis, and turned out the light, she surprised me by not turning her back. Alcohol, with its loosening effect, touches women more deeply than men in this respect; or perhaps, like a matched pair of tuning forks, I had set her vibrating. Irritated by whatever illicit stimulations, we took it out on each other.

To my regret, I survived the natural bliss of satiety—when each muscle is like a petal snugly curved in a corolla of benediction—and was projected onto the wrinkled, azoic territory of insomnia. That feathery anxious embrace of my erect thumbs tormented me in twenty postures. My stomach turned in love of that woman; I feared I would be physically sick and lay on my back gingerly and tried to soothe myself with the caress of headlights as they evolved from bright slits on the wall into parabolically accelerating fans on the ceiling that then vanished: this phenomenon, with its intimations of a life beyond me, had comforted wakeful nights in my earliest childhood. In Sunday school I had been struck by the passage in which Jesus says that to lust after a woman in thought is the same as committing adultery. Now I found myself helplessly containing the conviction that souls, not deeds, are judged. To feel a sin was to commit it; to touch the brink was to be on the floor of the chasm. The universe that so easily permitted me to commit adultery became, by logical steps each one of which went more steeply down than the one above it, a universe that would easily permit me to die. The enormities of cosmic space, the maddening distension of time, history's forgotten slaughters, the child smothered in the dumped icebox, the recent breakdown of the molecular life-spiral, the proven physiological roots of the mind, the presence in our midst of idiots, Eichmanns, animals, and bacteria—all this evidence piled on, and I seemed already eternally forgotten. The dark vibrating air of my bedroom seemed the dust of my grave; the dust went up and up and I prayed upward into it, prayed, prayed for a sign, any glimmer at all, any microscopic loophole or chink in the chain of evidence, and saw none. I remembered a movie I had seen as a child in which a young criminal, moaning insanely, is dragged on rubber legs down the long corridor to the electric chair. I became that criminal. My brain in its calcium vault shouted about injustice, thundered accusations into the lustreless and tranquil homogeneity of the air. Each second my agony went unanswered justified it more certainly: the God who permitted me this fear was unworthy of existence. Each instant my horror was extended amplified God's non-existence, so, as the graph of certain equations fluctuates more and more widely as it moves along the lateral coördinate, or as the magnetic motive-power in atom-smashers accelerates itself, I was caught in a gathering vortex whose unbearably shrill pitch moved me at last to drop my weight on my wife's body and beg, "Wake up. Elaine. I'm so frightened."

I told her of the centuries coming when our names would be forgotten, of the millennia when our nation would be a myth and our continent an ocean, of the aeons when our earth would be vanished and the stars themselves diffused into a uniform and irreversible tepidity. As, an hour before, I had transferred my lust to her, so now I tried to pass my fear into her. It seemed to offend her sense of good taste that I was jealous of future aeons and frantic because I couldn't live through them; she asked me if I had never been so sick I gave up caring whether I lived or died. This contemptible answer—the decrepit Stoic response—acquired a curious corroboration: eventually, just as I had during the strenuous birth of my fatherhood, I fell asleep, and dreamt of innocent and charming scenes.

The next day, a Saturday, was my birthday. It passed like any day except that underneath the camouflage of furniture and voices and habitual actions I felt death like a wide army invisibly advancing. The newspaper told of nothing but atrocities. My children, wounded and appalled in their competition, came to me to be comforted and I was dismayed to see myself, a gutted shell, appearing to them as the embodiment and pledge of a safe universe. Friends visited, and for the first time truly in my life I realized that each face is suppressing knowledge of an immense catastrophe; our faces are dams that wrinkle under the strain. Around six the telephone rang. It was my mother calling from Pennsylvania; I assumed she had called because of my birthday, so I chattered humorously about the discomforts of growing old for a minute before she could tell me, her voice growing faint, the news. My father was in the hospital. He had been walking around with chest pains for two weeks and suffered shortness of breath at night. She had finally seduced him into a doctor's office; the doctor had taken a cardiogram and driven him to the hospital. He was a seriously sick man.

Instantly I was relieved. The weight on me rolled away. All day death had been advancing under cover and now it had struck, declared its position. My father had engaged the enemy and it would be defeated.

I was restored to crisp health in the play-world of action. That night we had a few friends in for my birthday party and the next day I took the two older children to Sunday school and went myself to church. The faintly lavender lozenge-panes of the white-mullioned windows glowed and dimmed fitfully. It was a spottily overcast day, spitting a little snow. While I was at church my wife had cooked a lamb dinner and as I drank the coffee it became clear that I must drive to Pennsylvania. My mother and I had agreed I would fly down and visit him in a few days; I would have to see about renting a car at the Philadelphia end. This was potentially awkward because, self-employed, I had no credit card. The awkwardness suddenly seemed easy to surmount. I would drive. The car would be traded in a few days, it had just been greased; I had a vision of escaping our foul New England spring by driving south. In half an hour my bag was packed and in my churchgoing suit I abandoned my family. *Run on home.*

Along Route 128 I picked up a young sailor who rode with me all the way to New York and, for two hours through Connecticut, drove my car. I trusted him. He had the full body, the frank and fleshy blue-eyed face of the docile Titans—guileless, competent, mildly earnest—that we have fattened, an ocean removed from the slimming Latin passions and Nordic anxieties of Europe, on our unprecedented abundance of milk and honey, vitamins and protein. He had that instinctive optimism of the young animal that in America is the only generatrix of hope we have allowed ourselves; until recently, it seemed enough. He was incongruously—and somehow reassuringly—tanned. He had got the tan in Key West, where he had spent twenty-four hours, hitching the rides to and from on Navy jets. He had spent the twenty-four hours sleeping on the beach and selecting souvenirs to send back to his parents and girl friend. His parents lived in Salem, his girl friend in Peabody. He wanted to marry her, but his parents had old-fashioned ideas, they thought he was too young. And a lot of these guys in the service say, Don't get married, don't ever get married. But she was a nice girl, not so pretty or anything, but really nice: he really wanted to marry her.

I asked him how old he was. He was twenty-two, and was being trained as an airplane mechanic. He wanted at the end of his hitch to come back to Salem and live. He figured an airplane mechanic could find some sort of job. I told him, with a paternal firmness that amazed my ears, to marry her; absolutely; his parents would get used to it. The thing about parents, I told him, was that secretly, no matter what you did, they liked you anyway. I told him I had married at the age of twenty-one and had never for a minute been sorry.

He asked me, "What do you do? Teach?"

This impressed me. My grandfather had been a teacher, and my father was a teacher, and from my childhood up it had been assumed by the people of our neighborhood that I in turn would become a teacher.

"No," I said. "I'm a writer."

He seemed less offended than puzzled. "What do you write?"

"Oh—whatever comes into my head."

"What's the point?"

"I don't know," I told him. "I wish I did."

We talked less freely after that. At his request I left him off in wet twilight at a Texaco station near the entrance of the New Jersey Turnpike. He hoped to get a ride from there all the way to Washington. Other sailors were clustered out of the rain in the doorways of the station. They hailed him as if they had been waiting for him, and as he went to them he became, from the back, just one more sailor, anonymous, at sea. He did not turn and wave goodbye. I felt I had frightened him, which I regretted, because he had driven for me very well and I wanted him to marry his girl. In the dark I drove down the pike alone. In the first years of my car, when we lived in Manhattan, it would ease up to seventy-five on this wide black stretch without our noticing; now the needle found its natural level at sixty. The windshield wipers beat, and the wonderland lights of the Newark refineries were swollen and broken like bubbles by the raindrops on the side windows. For a dozen seconds a solemn cross of colored stars was suspended stiffly in the upper part of the windshield: an airplane above me was coming in to land.

I did not eat until I was on Pennsylvania soil. The Howard Johnsons in Pennsylvania are cleaner, less crowded, more homelike in their furnishings. The decorative plants seem to be honestly growing, and the waitresses have just a day ago removed the Mennonite cap from their hair, which is still pulled into a smooth bun flattering to their pallid, sly faces. They served me with that swift grace that comes in a country where food is still one of the pleasures. The familiar and subtle irony of their smiles wakened in me that old sense, of Pennsylvania knowingness—of knowing, that is, that the truth is good. They were the innkeeper's daughters, God had given us crops, and my wagon was hitched outside.

When I returned to the car, the music on the radio had changed color. The ersatz hiccup and gravel of Atlantic Seaboard hillbilly had turned, inland, backwards into something younger. As I passed the Valley Forge intersection the radio relived a Benny Goodman quintet that used to make my scalp freeze in high school. The speedometer went up to seventy without effort.

I left the toll road for our local highway and, turning into our dirt road, I was nearly rammed from behind by a pair of headlights that had been pushing, Pennsylvania style, six feet behind me. I parked beside my father's car in front of the barn. My mother came unseen into the yard, and, two voices calling in the opaque drizzle, while the dogs yapped deliriously in their pen, we debated whether I should move my car further off the road. "Out of harm's way," my grandfather would have said. Complaining, I obeyed her. My mother turned as I carried my suitcase down the path of sandstone steppingstones, and led me to the back door as if I would not know the way. So it was not until we were inside the house that I could kiss her in greeting. She poured us two glasses of wine. Wine had a ceremonial significance in our family; we drank it seldom. My mother seemed cheerful, even silly, and it took an hour for the willed impetus of gaiety to ebb away. She turned her head and looked delicately at the rug and the side of her neck blushed as she told me, "Daddy says he's lost all his faith."

Since I had also lost mine, I could find nothing to say. I remembered, in the silence, a conversation I had had with my father during a vacation from college. With the habitual simplicity of his eagerness to know, he had asked me, "Have you ever had any doubts of the existence of a Divine Being?"

"Sure," I had answered.

"I never have," he said. "It's beyond my ability to imagine it. The divinity of Jesus, yes; but the existence of a Divine Being, never." He stated this not as an attempt to influence me, but as a moderately curious fact he had that moment discovered about himself.

"He never was much one for faith," my mother added, hurt by my failure to speak. "He was strictly a works man."

I slept badly; I missed my wife's body, that weight of pure emotion, beside me. I was enough of a father to feel lost out of my nest of little rustling souls. I kept looking out of the windows. The three red lights of the chimneys of the plant that had been built some miles away, to mine low-grade iron ore, seemed to be advancing over our neighbor's ridged field toward our farm. My mother had mistaken me for a stoic like my father and had not put enough blankets on the bed. I found an old overcoat of his and arranged it over me; its collar scratched my chin. I tipped into sleep and awoke. The morning was sharply sunny; sheep hustled, heads toppling, through the gauzy blue sky. It was authentic spring in Pennsylvania. Some of the grass in the lawn had already grown shiny and lank. A yellow crocus had popped up beside the BEWARE OF THE DOG sign my father had had a child at school make for him.

I insisted we drive to Alton in my car, and then was sorry, for it seemed to insult their own. Just a few months ago my father had traded in on yet one more second-hand car: now he owned a '53 Plymouth. But while growing up I had been ambushed by so many mishaps in my father's cars that I insisted we take the car I could trust. Or perhaps it was that I did not wish to take my father's place behind the wheel of his car. My father's place was between me and Heaven; I was afraid of being placed adjacent to that far sky. First we visited his doctor. Our old doctor, a man who believed that people simply "wore out" and nothing could be done about it, had several years ago himself worn out and died. The new doctor's office, in the center of the city, was furnished with a certain raw sophistication. Rippling music leaked from the walls, which were hung with semi-professional oils. He himself was a wiry and firm-tongued young man not much older than myself but venerable with competence and witnessed pain. Such are the brisk shepherds who hop us over the final stile. He brought down from the top of a filing cabinet a plaster model of the human heart. "Your own heart," he told me, "is nice and thin like this; but your dad's heart is enlarged. We believe the obstruction is here, in one of these little vessels on the outside, luckily for your dad."

Outside, in the streets of Alton, my own heart felt enlarged. A white sun warmed the neat façades of painted brick; chimneys like peony shoots thrust through budding treetops. Having grown accustomed to the cramped, improvised cities of New England, I was patriotically thrilled by Alton's straight broad streets and superb equipment of institutions. While my mother went off to buy my daughter a birthday present, I returned a book she had borrowed to the Alton Public Library. I had forgotten the deep aroma of that place, mixed of fust and cleaning fluid and binder's glue and sweet pastry baking in the shop next door. I revisited the shelf of P. G. Wodehouse that in one summer I had read straight through. I took down *Mulliner Nights* and looked in the back for the stamped date, in '47 or '48, that would be me. I never thought to look for the section of the shelves where my own few books would be placed. They were not me. They were my children, mysterious and self-willed.

In driving to the hospital on Alton's outskirts, we passed the museum grounds, where every tree and flower-bed wore a name-tag and black swans drifted through flotillas of crumbled bread. As a child I had believed literally that bread cast upon the waters came back doubled. I remembered that within the museum there were mummies with astonished shattered faces; a tiny gilt chair for a baby Pharaoh; an elephant tusk carved into thousands of tiny Chinamen and pagodas and squat leafy trees; miniature Eskimo villages that you lit up with a switch and peeped into like an Easter egg; cases of arrowheads; rooms of stuffed birds; and, upstairs, wooden chests decorated with hearts and pelicans and tulips by the pious "plain people" and iridescent glassware from the kilns of Baron von Stiegel and slashing paintings of Pennsylvania woodland by the Shearers and bronze statuettes of wrestling Indians that stirred my first erotic dreams and, in the round skylit room at the head of the marble stairs, a black-rimmed pool in whose center a naked green lady held to her pursed lips a shell whose lucent contents forever spilled from the other side, filling this whole vast upstairs—from whose Palladian windows the swans in their bready pond could be seen trailing fan-shaped wakes—with the music and chill romance of falling water. The world then seemed an intricate wonder displayed for my delight with no price asked. Above the trees across the pond one saw rose glints of the hospital, an orderly multitude of tall brick rectangles set among levelled and lovingly tended grounds, an ideal city of the ill.

I had forgotten how grand the Alton hospital was. I had not seen its stately entrance, approached down a grassy mall bright with the first flush of green, since, at the age of seven, I had left the hospital unburdened of my tonsils. Then, too, it had been spring, and my mother was with me. I recalled it to her, and she said, "I felt so guilty. You were so sick."

"Really? I remember it as so pleasant." They had put a cup of pink rubber over my nose and there had been a thunderous flood of the smell of cotton candy and I opened my eyes and my mother was reading a magazine beside my bed.

"You were such a hopeful boy," my mother said, and I did not look at her face for fear of seeing her crying.

I wondered aloud if a certain girl in my high school class were still a nurse here.

"Oh, dear," my mother said. "Here I thought you came all this way to see your poor old father and all you care about is seeing—" And she used the girl's maiden name, though the girl had been married as long as I had.

Within the hospital, she surprised me by knowing the way. Usually, wherever we went, it was my father or I who knew the way. As I followed her through the linoleum maze, my mother's shoulders seemed already to have received the responsible shawl of widowhood. Like the halls of a palace, the hospital corridors were lined with patient petitioners. Negro girls electrically dramatic in their starched white uniforms folded bales of cotton sheets; gray men pushed wrung mops. We went through an Exit sign, down a stairway, into a realm where gaunt convalescents in bathrobes shuffled in and out of doorways. I saw my father diagonally through a doorway before we entered his room. He was sitting up in bed, supported sultanlike by a wealth of pillows and clad in red-striped pajamas.

I had never seen him in pajamas before; a great man for the shortest distance between two points, he slept in his underclothes. But, having been at last captured in pajamas, like a big-hearted lion he did not try to minimize his humiliation, but lay fully exposed, without a sheet covering even his feet. Bare, they looked pale, gentle, and oddly unused.

Except for a sullen lymphatic glow under his cheeks, his face was totally familiar. I had been afraid that his loss of faith would show, like the altered shape of his mouth after he had had all his teeth pulled. With grins we exchanged the shy handshake that my going off to college had forced upon us. I sat on the window sill by his bed, my mother took the chair at the foot of the bed, and my father's roommate, a tanned and fortyish man flat on his back with a crushed vertebra, sighed and blew smoke toward the ceiling and tried, I suppose, not to hear us. Our conversation, though things were radically changed, followed old patterns. Quite quickly the talk shifted from him to me. "I don't know how you do it, David," he said. "I couldn't do what you're doing if you paid me a million dollars a day." Embarrassed and flattered, as usual, I tried to shush him, and he disobediently turned to his roommate and called loudly, "I don't know where the kid gets his ideas. Not from his old man, I know that. I never gave that poor kid an idea in my life."

"Sure you did," I said softly, trying to take pressure off the man with the painful back. "You taught me two things. Always butter bread toward the edges because enough gets in the middle anyway, and No matter what happens to you, it'll be a new experience."

To my dismay, this seemed to make him melancholy. "That's right, David," he said. "No matter what happens to you, it'll be a new experience. The only thing that worries me is that *she*"—he pointed at my mother—"will crack up the car. I don't want anything to happen to your mother."

"The car, you mean," my mother said, and to me she added, "It's a sin, the way he worships that car."

My father didn't deny it. "Jesus I love that car," he said. "It's the first car I've ever owned that didn't go bad on me. Remember all those heaps we used to ride back and forth in?"

The old Chevy was always getting dirt in the fuel pump and refusing to start at awkward hours. Once, going down Fire Hill, the left front wheel had broken off the axle; my father wrestled with the steering wheel while the tires screamed and the white posts of the guard fence floated calmly toward my eyes. When the car slid sideways to a stop just short of the embankment my father's face was stunned and the corners of his mouth dribbled saliva. I was surprised; it had not occurred to me to be frightened. The '36 Buick had drunk oil, a quart every fifty miles, and loved to have flat tires after midnight, when I would be gliding home with a scrubbed brain and the smell of lipstick in my nose. Once, when we had both gone into town and I had dropped him off and taken the car, I had absent-mindedly driven home alone. I came in the door and my mother said, "Why, where's your father?"

My stomach sank. "My Lord," I said, "I forgot I had him!"

As, smiling, I took in breath and prepared to dip with him into reminiscence of these adventures, my father, staring stonily into the air above his pale and motionless toes, said, "I love this place. There are a lot of wonderful gentlemen in here. The only thing that worries me is that mother will crack up the car."

To my horror I saw that my mother, leaning forward red-faced in the chair at the foot of the bed, was silently crying. He glanced at her and said to me, "It's a funny feeling. The night before we went to see the doctor I woke up and couldn't get my breath and realized I wasn't ready to die. I had always thought I would be. It's a funny feeling."

"Luckily for your dad," "all his faith," "wonderful gentlemen": these phrases were borne in on me with a dreadful weight and my tongue seemed pressed flat on the floor of its grave. The pajama stripes under my eyes stirred and streamed, real blood. I wanted to speak, to say how I needed him and to beg him not to leave me, but there were no words, no form of words available in our tradition. A pillar of smoke poured upward from the sighing man in the other bed.

Into this pit hesitantly walked a plain, painfully clean girl with a pad and pencil. She had yellow hair, thick lips, and, behind pink-rimmed glasses, large eyes that looked as if they had been corrected from being crossed. They flicked across our faces and focussed straight ahead in that tunnel-vision gaze of those who know perfectly well they are figures of fun. The Jehovah's Witnesses who come to the door wear that funnelled expression. She approached the bed where my father lay barefoot and, suppressing a stammer, explained that she was from Lutheran Home Missions and that they kept accounts of all hospitalized Lutherans and notified the appropriate pastors to make visitations. Clearly she had measured my father for a rebuff; perhaps her eyes, more practiced in this respect than mine, spotted the external sign of loss of faith that I had missed. At any rate my father was a Lutheran by adoption; he had been born and raised a Presbyterian and still looked like one.

"That's *aw*fully nice of you," he told the girl. "I don't see how you people do it on the little money we give you."

Puzzled, she dimpled and moved ahead with her routine. "Your church is—?"

He told her, pronouncing every syllable meticulously and consulting my mother and me as to whether the word "Evangelical" figured in the official title.

"That would make your pastor Reverend—"

"Yeah. He'll be in, don't worry about it. Wild horses couldn't keep him away. Nothing he likes better than to get out of the sticks and drive into Alton. I didn't mean to confuse you a minute ago; what I meant was, just last week in church council we were talking about you people. We couldn't figure out how you do anything on the little money we give you. After we've got done feeding the furnace and converting the benighted Hindoo there isn't anything left over for you people that are trying to help the poor devils in our own back yard."

The grinning girl was lost in this onslaught of praise and clung to the shreds of her routine. "In the meantime," she recited, "here is a pamphlet you might like to read."

My father took it from her with a swooping gesture so expansive I got down from the window sill to restrain him physically, if necessary. That he must lie still was my one lever, my one certainty about his situation. "That's awfully nice of you," he told the girl. "I don't know where the hell you get the money to print these things."

"We hope your stay in the hospital is pleasant and would like to wish you a speedy recovery to full health."

"Thank you; I know you're sincere when you say it. As I was telling my son David here, if I can do what the doctors tell me I'll be all right. First time in my life I've ever tried to do what anybody ever told me to do. The kid was just telling me, 'No matter what happens to you, Pop, it'll be a new experience.' "

"Now if you will excuse me I have other calls to pay."

"Of course. You go right ahead, sick Lutherans are a dime a dozen. You're a wonderful woman to be doing what you're doing."

And she left the room transformed into just that. As a star shines in our heaven though it has vanished from the universe, so my father continued to shed faith upon others. For the remainder of my visit with him his simple presence so reassured me, filled me with such a buoyant humor, that my mother surprised me, when we had left the hospital, by remarking that we had tired him.

"I hadn't noticed," I said.

"And it worries me," she went on, "the way he talks about the movies all the time. You know he never liked them." When I had offered to stay another night so I could visit him again, he had said, "No, instead of that why don't you take your mother to the movies?" Rather than do that, I said, I would drive home. It took him a moment, it seemed, to realize that by my home I meant a far place, where I had a wife and children; though at the time I was impatient to have his consent, it has since occurred to me and grieved me that during that instant his face was blank he was swallowing the realization that he was no longer the center of even his son's universe. Having swallowed, he told me how good I had been to come all this way to see him. He told me I was a good son and a good father; he clasped my hand. I felt I would ascend straight north from his touch.

I drove my mother back to her farm and got my bag and said goodbye on the lawn. The little sandstone house was pink in the declining sunlight; the lawn was a tinkling clutter of shy rivulets. Standing beside the BEWARE OF THE DOG sign with its companion of a crocus, she smiled and said, "This is like when you were born. Your father drove through a snowstorm all the way from Wheeling in our old Ford." He had been working with the telephone company then; the story of his all-night ride was the first myth in which I was a character.

Darkness did not fall until New Jersey. The hour of countryside I saw from the Pennsylvania Turnpike looked enchanted—the branches of the trees underpainted with budding russet, the meadows nubbled like new carpets, the bronze sun slanting on Valley Forge and Levittown alike. I do not know what it is that is so welcome to me in the Pennsylvania landscape, but it is the same quality—perhaps of reposing in the certainty that the truth is good—that is in Pennsylvania faces. It seemed to me for this sunset hour that the world is our bride, given to us to love, and the terror and joy of the marriage is that we bring to it a nature not our bride's.

There was no sailor to help me drive the nine hours back. New Jersey began in twilight and ended in darkness, and Manhattan made its gossamer splash at its favorite hour, eight o'clock. The rest of the trip was more and more steeply uphill. The Merritt Turnpike seemed meaninglessly coquettish, the light-controlled stretch below Hartford maddeningly obstinate, and the hour above that frighteningly empty. Distance grew thicker and thicker; the intricate and effortful mechanics of the engine, the stellar infinity of explosive sparks needed to drive it, passed into my body, and wearied me. Repeatedly I stopped for coffee and the hallucinatory comfort of human faces, and after every stop, my waiting car, companion and warm home and willing steed, responded to my pressure. It began to seem a miracle that the car could gather speed from my numb foot; the very music on the radio seemed a drag on our effort, and I turned it off, obliterating time. We climbed through a space fretted by scattered brilliance and bathed in a monotonous wind. I had been driving forever; furniture, earth, churches, women, were all things I had innocently dreamed. And through those aeons my car, beginning as a mechanical spiral of molecules, evolved into something soft and organic and consciously brave. I lost, first, heart, then head, and finally any sense of my body. In the last hour of the trip I ceased to care or feel or in any real sense see, but the car, though its soul the driver had died, maintained steady forward motion, and completed the endless journey safely. Above my back yard the stars were frozen in place, and the shapes of my neighbors' houses wore the wonder that children induce by whirling.

Any day now we will trade it in; we are just waiting for the phone to ring. I know how it will be. My father traded in many cars. It happens so cleanly, before you expect it. He would drive off in the old car up the dirt road exactly as usual and when he returned the car would be new, and the old was gone, gone, utterly dissolved back into the mineral world from which it was conjured, dismissed without a blessing, a kiss, a testament, or any ceremony of farewell. We in America need ceremonies, is I suppose, sailor, the point of what I have written.

The Flowers

by Alice Walker

Introduced by Edward P. Jones

ALICE WALKER'S CAREER HAS BEEN BUILT ON THE STRENGTH AND HONesty of her novels, but long before she became more widely known with *The Color Purple,* she published a book of short stories titled *In Love & Trouble.* I don't wish to take anything from her novels, but I have believed for a long while that *In Love & Trouble* is one of her best works and one of the best collections of stories I've ever read. And that feeling remains even some twenty years after *In Love & Trouble* was first published, even after several more Walker novels and another collection of stories have appeared since *The Color Purple* to wide approval and acclaim.

There is a story in *In Love & Trouble,* "The Flowers," that is not only wonderful but exquisite in its simplicity and brevity. I sometimes use "The Flowers"—along with Frank O'Connor's "Guests of the Nation"—to try to show students the essence of what I believe a short story should be. There are a number of reasons for my liking "The Flowers," but the fact that I can point to it and tell students, especially students new to writing, to use it as a kind of road map when they're hacking their way through the thicket of their own work makes it especially precious. In the end, I say simply, a story should be about some change, large or small, in the universe of a person or people in a story. Generally, there is no story for me if all there is is another day in the life of a character, a day like all the others. To use a simple example, the whole point of something like "Humpty Dumpty" is that one day he falls off that wall and falls to pieces, after perhaps days or months or years of sitting there with nothing happening except time passing. He falls and all the powers of the king and his kingdom cannot put the thing together again.

"The Flowers" is only two pages and begins with a summer day in the life of ten-year-old Myop. The day is full of child's play, no more or less than all the others when "nothing existed for her but her song." But this *particular* day she sets off on "her own path," a path different from the ones she and her mother have taken before. She picks flowers. Finally, just before she is ready to "circle back . . . to the peacefulness of the morning," she comes upon a skeleton and lets out a "little" yelp of surprise when she steps into the skull. For some writers, I suppose, a ten-year-old girl with an armful of flowers stepping into the eyeless eyes of a skull in the woods on a summer day would have been enough of a story. "Child Meets Death, Which Kills Innocence." But Walker takes things a step further. Myop is different, and she gazes at the whole scene "with interest"; she even picks the wild pink rose growing near the skull.

It is here that Walker takes a leap and the story becomes not just that of a black girl, and one day in her life, but a story about a race and the oppression of that race. Around the rose's root is the raised mound of the remains of a noose. Walker's lines are few; no judgment is made by the author; Myop speaks no words. The noose is rotted, and there is the implication that the dead man has lain there longer than Myop has been alive, perhaps even longer than her mother, who might have warned her daughter of such a place, has been alive. The noose makes all the difference in Myop's universe, where lynchings of black men were as common as coming-out parties, and seeing the noose changes her universe. She lays down the flowers, as if on a grave. The story ends, "And the summer was over." And by implication, of course, the girl's childhood.

There are, to be sure, hundreds of stories that create a believable universe and that teach the simple lesson that a story should be about something: stuff of the heart, as Faulkner said, not of the glands. Walker's story is among the hundreds, and it does its job with an economy of words. We ask a lot of a literary work that is supposed to endure, not least of which is that it stay in the mind and the heart for months and years. "The Flowers," those two pages, does that for me, more than twenty years after I first read it.

The Flowers

Alice Walker

It seemed to Myop as she skipped lightly from hen house to pigpen to smokehouse that the days had never been as beautiful as these. The air held a keenness that made her nose twitch. The harvesting of the corn and cotton, peanuts and squash, made each day a golden surprise that caused excited little tremors to run up her jaws.

Myop carried a short, knobby stick. She struck out at random at chickens she liked, and worked out the beat of a song on the fence around the pigpen. She felt light and good in the warm sun. She was ten, and nothing existed for her but her song, the stick clutched in her dark brown hand, and the tat-de-ta-ta-ta of accompaniment.

Turning her back on the rusty boards of her family's sharecropper cabin, Myop walked along the fence till it ran into the stream made by the spring. Around the spring, where the family got drinking water, silver ferns and wildflowers grew. Along the shallow banks pigs rooted. Myop watched the tiny white bubbles disrupt the thin black scale of soil and the water that silently rose and slid away down the stream.

She had explored the woods behind the house many times. Often, in late autumn, her mother took her to gather nuts among the fallen leaves. Today she made her own path, bouncing this way and that way, vaguely keeping an eye out for snakes. She found, in addition to various common but pretty ferns and leaves, an armful of strange blue flowers with velvety ridges and a sweetsuds bush full of the brown, fragrant buds.

By twelve o'clock, her arms laden with sprigs of her findings, she was a mile or more from home. She had often been as far before, but the strangeness of the land made it not as pleasant as her usual haunts. It seemed gloomy in the little cove in which she found herself. The air was damp, the silence close and deep.

Myop began to circle back to the house, back to the peacefulness of the morning. It was then she stepped smack into his eyes. Her heel became lodged in the broken ridge between brow and nose, and she reached down quickly, unafraid, to free herself. It was only when she saw his naked grin that she gave a little yelp of surprise.

He had been a tall man. From feet to neck covered a long space. His head lay beside him. When she pushed back the leaves and layers of earth and debris Myop saw that he'd had large white teeth, all of them cracked or broken, long fingers, and very big bones. All his clothes had rotted away except some threads of blue denim from his overalls. The buckles of the overalls had turned green.

Myop gazed around the spot with interest. Very near where she'd stepped into the head was a wild pink rose. As she picked it to add to her bundle she noticed a raised mound, a ring, around the rose's root. It was the rotted remains of a noose, a bit of shredding plowline, now blending benignly into the soil. Around an overhanging limb of a great spreading oak clung another piece. Frayed, rotted, bleached, and frazzled—barely there—but spinning restlessly in the breeze. Myop laid down her flowers.

And the summer was over.

No Place for You, My Love

by Eudora Welty

Introduced by Russell Banks

MAYBE ONE HAS TO BE OVER FORTY BEFORE ONE CAN APPRECIATE this story properly. Or, more to the point, maybe *I* had to be over forty before *I* was capable of getting it. Had I come upon it earlier, I would probably have reacted as most of my students do on those rare occasions when I fly in the face of my better judgment and try to teach it. Excuse me? You're saying this story left you breathless the first time you read it, made your heart pound, your legs weak, caused your hands to sweat—you say it left you spellbound? Middle-aged married man meets thirtyish woman at a civic luncheon, man and woman ride around in his rented car for a while, man and woman dance in a roadhouse, they come back to the city, man drops woman off at her hotel. That's *it?* The man and woman don't even *say* anything to each other, except for the dozen or so opaque, curiously deflective sentences which they use mostly for kicking the other person away, moving him or her to the far corner of the car seat, and then, just as opaquely, drawing him or her back.

> "It looks to me like your road can't go much further," she remarked cheerfully. "Just over there, it's all water."
>
> "Time out," he said, and with that he turned the car into a sudden road of white shells that rushed at them narrowly out of the left.

My student doesn't get it. She wants to know, How come you guys over forty get so excited and *moved* by this story? She thinks it must have something to do with *aging*.

Well, yes. It does have a lot to do with the passage of time, with the "too late" of so much of one's life after a certain age—"he thought that here was a woman who was having an affair. . . . With a married man, most likely . . . he was long married. . . . He guessed her age . . . thirty-two. He himself was further along"—and thus it surely must have to do with all our lost chances for love and with the imminence of death. Aging, the end of youth, at least, can bring you up against those twinned subjects with a certain undeniable ferocity, can shove them in your face and say, Son (or Daughter), deal. And most of us would prefer not to deal, thank you, until we happen onto a story like this and find ourselves brought face-to-face, heart-to-heart, with the painful, inexplicable beauty of the transience of human consciousness.

I happened onto it in 1986 in an anthology called *The Art of the Tale,* edited by Daniel Halpern. It's an atypical and little-known Welty story from her 1952 collection, *The Bride of Innisfallen and Other Stories.* I have never seen it anthologized anywhere else. The story is told from an omniscient point of view that refuses to privilege one character over the other. It keeps both the man and the woman on a shifting plane that switches with disorienting swiftness from a distant, detached objectivity to a wise, all-knowing, Jamesian intimacy. The man and the woman, both Northerners, both unnamed, are described in their immediate present as they drive down from New Orleans through a dark geography that's "south of South," where they pass below the city and head out across the delta into the gulf.

The story has the symmetry of a folk tale. It's a journey outside time through a highly symbolic landscape laid down with the precision and mystery of the Stations of the Cross—a road, a bridge, a levee, a ferry, a cemetery, on to the very edge of the continent, where they stop and dance and then reluctantly return to their respective hotels. The action, such as there is, arises from the alternating currents of aggression and flight in the relations between the two individuals, as they shuck and exchange roles of predator and quarry. First the man pursues the woman, until suddenly, unexpectedly, she turns on him and sends him backing, converting him to prey and herself to predator. They'll play these roles until the next stop on their journey, when they will switch again, and then yet again. (Like all dance, it's sexual, of course, but, like good sex, it's profoundly metaphysical too.)

At last they run out of road and can go no further south of South. The chase has ended. Out of a tolerable solitude they have reluctantly come forward and after great resistance permitted themselves to pass through a flashpoint of communion. They seem for an instant to have become a single person, merged into an entity that a moment later will be compelled to split into two discrete, isolated parts—leaving them just as they were before, only different.

Following fusion, inevitably, fission occurs. For having sought and fought and then accepted that one moment—that brief slow dance with a stranger in a roadhouse on a night south of New Orleans—a man and a woman have been subtly, significantly, changed. And the ideal reader of this incantatory story (a person over forty, probably) has been changed also, and very likely in the same way as has Welty's mysterious couple: the reader's knowledge of them and their strangely ordered yet utterly unfamiliar landscape is an exact replication of the couple's knowledge of each other and the world they have briefly entered together. It's a meticulously structured encounter, theirs with each other and ours with them. We have entered and passed through the mystery with them: our communion with them, the tear in our habitual solitude, that has been provided by the story is precisely the intrusion and resultant communion that Eudora Welty's man and woman on this random summer night have provided for each other. Thus, for a few moments, a story has restored our lives to us filled with "the lilt and expectation of love." No wonder that we are left spellbound by it.

No Place for You, My Love

Eudora Welty

They were strangers to each other, both fairly well strangers to the place, now seated side by side at luncheon—a party combined in a free-and-easy way when the friends he and she were with recognized each other across Galatoire's. The time was a Sunday in summer—those hours of afternoon that seem Time Out in New Orleans.

The moment he saw her little blunt, fair face, he thought that here was a woman who was having an affair. It was one of those odd meetings when such an impact is felt that it has to be translated at once into some sort of speculation.

With a married man, most likely, he supposed, slipping quickly into a groove—he was long married—and feeling more conventional, then, in his curiosity as she sat there, leaning her cheek on her hand, looking no further before her than the flowers on the table, and wearing that hat.

He did not like her hat, any more than he liked tropical flowers. It was the wrong hat for her, thought this Eastern businessman who had no interest whatever in women's clothes and no eye for them; he thought the unaccustomed thing crossly.

It must stick out all over me, she thought, so people think they can love me or hate me just by looking at me. How did it leave us—the old, safe, slow way people used to know of learning how one another feels, and the privilege that went with it of shying away if it seemed best? People in love like me, I suppose, give away the short cuts to everybody's secrets.

Something, though, he decided, had been settled about her predicament—for the time being, anyway; the parties to it were all still alive, no doubt. Nevertheless, her predicament was the only one he felt so sure of here, like the only recognizable shadow in that restaurant, where mirrors and fans were busy agitating the light, as the very local talk drawled across and agitated the peace. The shadow lay between her fingers, between her little square hand and her cheek, like something always best carried about the person. Then suddenly, as she took her hand down, the secret fact was still there—it lighted her. It was a bold and full light, shot up under the brim of that hat, as close to them all as the flowers in the center of the table.

Did he dream of making her disloyal to that hopelessness that he saw very well she'd been cultivating down here? He knew very well that he did not. What they amounted to was two Northerners keeping each other company. She glanced up at the big gold clock on the wall and smiled. He didn't smile back. She had that naïve face that he associated, for no good reason, with the Middle West—because it said "Show me," perhaps. It was a serious, now-watch-out-everybody face, which orphaned her entirely in the company of these Southerners. He guessed her age, as he could not guess theirs: thirty-two. He himself was further along.

Of all human moods, deliberate imperviousness may be the most quickly communicated—it may be the most successful, most fatal signal of all. And two people can indulge in imperviousness as well as in anything else. "You're not very hungry either," he said.

The blades of fan shadows came down over their two heads, as he saw inadvertently in the mirror, with himself smiling at her now like a villain. His remark sounded dominant and rude enough for everybody present to listen back a moment; it even sounded like an answer to a question she might have just asked him. The other women glanced at him. The Southern look—Southern mask—of life-is-a-dream irony, which could turn to pure challenge at the drop of a hat, he could wish well away. He liked naïveté better.

"I find the heat down here depressing," she said, with the heart of Ohio in her voice.

"Well—I'm in somewhat of a temper about it, too," he said.

They looked with grateful dignity at each other.

"I have a car here, just down the street," he said to her as the luncheon party was rising to leave, all the others wanting to get back to their houses and sleep. "If it's all right with—Have you ever driven down south of here?"

Out on Bourbon Street, in the bath of July, she asked at his shoulder, "South of New Orleans? I didn't know there was any south to *here*. Does it just go on and on?" She laughed, and adjusted the exasperating hat to her head in a different way. It was more than frivolous, it was conspicuous, with some sort of glitter or flitter tied in a band around the straw and hanging down.

"That's what I'm going to show you."

"Oh—you've been there?"

"No!"

His voice rang out over the uneven, narrow sidewalk and dropped back from the walls. The flaked-off, colored houses were spotted like the hides of beasts faded and shy, and were hot as a wall of growth that seemed to breathe flowerlike down onto them as they walked to the car parked there.

"It's just that it couldn't be any worse—we'll see."

"All right, then," she said. "We will."

So, their actions reduced to amiability, they settled into the car—a faded-red Ford convertible with a rather threadbare canvas top, which had been standing in the sun for all those lunch hours.

"It's rented," he explained. "I asked to have the top put down, and was told I'd lost my mind."

"It's out of this world. *Degrading* heat," she said and added, "Doesn't matter."

The stranger in New Orleans always sets out to leave it as though following the clue in a maze. They were threading through the narrow and one-way streets, past the pale-violet bloom of tired squares, the brown steeples and statues, the balcony with the live and probably famous black monkey dipping along the railing as over a ballroom floor, past the grille-work and the lattice-work to all the iron swans painted flesh color on the front steps of bungalows outlying.

Driving, he spread his new map and put his finger down on it. At the intersection marked Arabi, where their road led out of the tangle and he took it, a small Negro seated beneath a black umbrella astride a box chalked "Shou Shine" lifted his pink-and-black hand and waved them languidly good-by. She didn't miss it, and waved back.

Below New Orleans there was a raging of insects from both sides of the concrete highway, not quite together, like the playing of separated marching bands. The river and the levee were still on her side, waste and jungle and some occasional settlements on his—poor houses. Families bigger than housefuls thronged the yards. His nodding, driving head would veer from side to side, looking and almost lowering. As time passed and the distance from New Orleans grew, girls ever darker and younger were disposing themselves over the porches and the porch steps, with jet-black hair pulled high, and ragged palm-leaf fans rising and falling like rafts of butterflies. The children running forth were nearly always naked ones.

She watched the road. Crayfish constantly crossed in front of the wheels, looking grim and bonneted, in a great hurry.

"How the Old Woman Got Home," she murmured to herself.

He pointed, as it flew by, at a saucepan full of cut zinnias which stood waiting on the open lid of a mailbox at the roadside, with a little note tied onto the handle.

They rode mostly in silence. The sun bore down. They met fishermen and other men bent on some local pursuits, some in sulphur-colored pants, walking and riding; met wagons, trucks, boats in trucks, autos, boats on top of autos—all coming to meet them, as though something of high moment were doing back where the car came from, and he and she were determined to miss it. There was nearly always a man lying with his shoes off in the bed of any truck otherwise empty—with the raw, red look of a man sleeping in the daytime, being jolted about as he slept. Then there was a sort of dead man's land, where nobody came. He loosened his collar and tie. By rushing through the heat at high speed, they brought themselves the effect of fans turned onto their cheeks. Clearing alternated with jungle and canebrake like something tried, tried again. Little shell roads led off on both sides; now and then a road of planks led into the yellow-green.

"Like a dance floor in there." She pointed.

He informed her, "In there's your oil, I think."

There were thousands, millions of mosquitoes and gnats—a universe of them, and on the increase.

A family of eight or nine people on foot strung along the road in the same direction the car was going, beating themselves with the wild palmettos. Heels, shoulders, knees, breasts, back of the heads, elbows, hands, were touched in turn—like some game, each playing it with himself.

He struck himself on the forehead, and increased their speed. (His wife would not be at her most charitable if he came bringing malaria home to the family.)

More and more crayfish and other shell creatures littered their path, scuttling or dragging. These little samples, little jokes of creation, persisted and sometimes perished, the more of them the deeper down the road went. Terrapins and turtles came up steadily over the horizons of the ditches.

Back there in the margins were worse—crawling hides you could not penetrate with bullets or quite believe, grins that had come down from the primeval mud.

"Wake up." Her Northern nudge was very timely on his arm. They had veered toward the side of the road. Still driving fast, he spread his map.

Like a misplaced sunrise, the light of the river flowed up; they were mounting the levee on a little shell road.

"Shall we cross here?" he asked politely.

He might have been keeping track over years and miles of how long they could keep that tiny ferry waiting. Now skidding down the levee's flank, they were the last-minute car, the last possible car that could squeeze on. Under the sparse shade of one willow tree, the small, amateurish-looking boat slapped the water, as, expertly, he wedged on board.

"Tell him we put him on hub cap!" shouted one of the numerous olive-skinned, dark-eyed young boys standing dressed up in bright shirts at the railing, hugging each other with delight that that last straw was on board. Another boy drew his affectionate initials in the dust of the door on her side.

She opened the door and stepped out, and, after only a moment's standing at bay, started up a little iron stairway. She appeared above the car, on the tiny bridge beneath the captain's window and the whistle.

From there, while the boat still delayed in what seemed a trance—as if it were too full to attempt the start—she could see the panlike deck below, separated by its rusty rim from the tilting, polished water.

The passengers walking and jostling about there appeared oddly amateurish, too—amateur travelers. They were having such a good time. They all knew each other. Beer was being passed around in cans, bets were being loudly settled and new bets made, about local and special subjects on which they all doted. One red-haired man in a burst of wildness even tried to give away his truckload of shrimp to a man on the other side of the boat—nearly all the trucks were full of shrimp—causing taunts and then protests of "They good! They good!" from the giver. The young boys leaned on each other thinking of what next, rolling their eyes absently.

A radio pricked the air behind her. Looking like a great tomcat just above her head, the captain was digesting the news of a fine stolen automobile.

At last a tremendous explosion burst—the whistle. Everything shuddered in outline from the sound, everybody said something—everybody else.

They started with no perceptible motion, but her hat blew off. It went spiralling to the deck below, where he, thank heaven, sprang out of the car and picked it up. Everybody looked frankly up at her now, holding her hands to her head.

The little willow tree receded as its shade was taken away. The heat was like something falling on her head. She held the hot rail before her. It was like riding a stove. Her shoulders dropping, her hair flying, her skirt buffeted by the sudden strong wind, she stood there, thinking they all must see that with her entire self all she did was wait. Her set hands, with the bag that hung from her wrist and rocked back and forth—all three seemed objects bleaching there, belonging to no one; she could not feel a thing in the skin of her face; perhaps she was crying, and not knowing it. She could look down and see him just below her, his black shadow, her hat, and his black hair. His hair in the wind looked unreasonably long and rippling. Little did he know that from here it had a red undergleam like an animal's. When she looked up and outward, a vortex of light drove through and over the brown waves like a star in the water.

He did after all bring the retrieved hat up the stairs to her. She took it back—useless—and held it to her skirt. What they were saying below was more polite than their searchlight faces.

"Where you think he come from, that man?"

"I bet he come from Lafitte."

"Lafitte? What you bet, eh?"—all crouched in the shade of trucks, squatting and laughing.

Now his shadow fell partly across her; the boat had jolted into some other strand of current. Her shaded arm and shaded hand felt pulled out from the blaze of light and water, and she hoped humbly for more shade for her head. It had seemed so natural to climb up and stand in the sun.

The boys had a surprise—an alligator on board. One of them pulled it by a chain around the deck, between the cars and trucks, like a toy—a hide that could walk. He thought, Well they had to catch one sometime. It's Sunday afternoon. So they have him on board now, riding him across the Mississippi River. . . . The playfulness of it beset everybody on the ferry. The hoarseness of the boat whistle, commenting briefly, seemed part of the general appreciation.

"Who want to rassle him? Who want to, eh?" two boys cried, looking up. A boy with shrimp-colored arms capered from side to side, pretending to have been bitten.

What was there so hilarious about jaws that could bite? And what danger was there once in this repulsiveness—so that the last worldly evidence of some old heroic horror of the dragon had to be paraded in capture before the eyes of country clowns?

He noticed that she looked at the alligator without flinching at all. Her distance was set—the number of feet and inches between herself and it mattered to her.

Perhaps her measuring coolness was to him what his bodily shade was to her, while they stood pat up there riding the river, which felt like the sea and looked like the earth under them—full of the red-brown earth, charged with it. Ahead of the boat it was like an exposed vein of ore. The river seemed to swell in the vast middle with the curve of the earth. The sun rolled under them. As if in memory of the size of things, uprooted trees were drawn across their path, sawing at the air and tumbling one over the other.

When they reached the other side, they felt that they had been racing around an arena in their chariot, among lions. The whistle took and shook the stairs as they went down. The young boys, looking taller, had taken out colored combs and were combing their wet hair back in solemn pompadour above their radiant foreheads. They had been bathing in the river themselves not long before.

The cars and trucks, then the foot passengers and the alligator, waddling like a child to school, all disembarked and wound up the weed-sprung levee.

Both respectable and merciful, their hides, she thought, forcing herself to dwell on the alligator as she looked back. Deliver us all from the naked in heart. (As she had been told.)

When they regained their paved road, he heard her give a little sigh and saw her turn her straw-colored head to look back once more. Now that she rode with her hat in her lap, her earrings were conspicuous too. A little metal ball set with small pale stones danced beside each square, faintly downy cheek.

Had she felt a wish for someone else to be riding with them? He thought it was more likely that she would wish for her husband if she had one (his wife's voice) than for the lover in whom he believed. Whatever people liked to think, situations (if not scenes) were usually three-way—there was somebody else always. The one who didn't—couldn't—understand the two made the formidable third.

He glanced down at the map flapping on the seat between them, up at his wristwatch, out at the road. Out there was the incredible brightness of four o'clock.

On this side of the river, the road ran beneath the brow of the levee and followed it. Here was a heat that ran deeper and brighter and more intense than all the rest—its nerve. The road grew one with the heat as it was one with the unseen river. Dead snakes stretched across the concrete like markers—inlaid mosaic bands, dry as feathers, which their tires licked at intervals that began to seem clocklike.

No, the heat faced them—it was ahead. They could see it waving at them, shaken in the air above the white of the road, always at a certain distance ahead, shimmering finely as a cloth, with running edges of green and gold, fire and azure.

"It's never anything like this in Syracuse," he said.

"Or in Toledo, either," she replied with dry lips.

They were driving through greater waste down here, through fewer and even more insignificant towns. There was water under everything. Even where a screen of jungle had been left to stand, splashes could be heard from under the trees. In the vast open, sometimes boats moved inch by inch through what appeared endless meadows of rubbery flowers.

Her eyes overcome with brightness and size, she felt a panic rise, as sudden as nausea. Just how far below questions and answers, concealment and revelation, they were running now—that was still a new question, with a power of its own, waiting. How dear—how costly—could this ride be?

"It looks to me like your road can't go much further," she remarked cheerfully. "Just over there, it's all water."

"Time out," he said, and with that he turned the car into a sudden road of white shells that rushed at them narrowly out of the left.

They bolted over a cattle guard, where some rayed and crested purple flowers burst out of the vines in the ditch, and rolled onto a long, narrow, green, mowed clearing: a churchyard. A paved track ran between two short rows of raised tombs, all neatly white-washed and now brilliant as faces against the vast flushed sky.

The track was the width of the car with a few inches to spare. He passed between the tombs slowly but in the manner of a feat. Names took their places on the walls slowly at a level with the eye, names as near as the eyes of a person stopping in conversation, and as far away in origin, and in all their music and dead longing, as Spain. At intervals were set packed bouquets of zinnias, oleanders, and some kind of purple flowers, all quite fresh, in fruit jars, like nice welcomes on bureaus.

They moved on into an open plot beyond, of violent-green grass, spread before the green-and-white frame church with worked flower beds around it, flowerless poinsettias growing up to the windowsills. Beyond was a house, and left on the doorstep of the house a fresh-caught catfish the size of a baby—a fish wearing whiskers and bleeding. On a clothesline in the yard, a priest's black gown on a hanger hung airing, swaying at man's height, in a vague, trainlike, ladylike sweep along an evening breath that might otherwise have seemed imaginary from the unseen, felt river.

With the motor cut off, with the raging of the insects about them, they sat looking out at the green and white and black and red and pink as they leaned against the sides of the car.

"What is your wife like?" she asked. His right hand came up and spread—iron, wooden, manicured. She lifted her eyes to his face. He looked at her like that hand.

Then he lit a cigarette, and the portrait, and the right-hand testimonial it made, were blown away. She smiled, herself as unaffected as by some stage performance; and he was annoyed in the cemetery. They did not risk going on to her husband—if she had one.

Under the supporting posts of the priest's house, where a boat was, solid ground ended and palmettos and water hyacinths could not wait to begin; suddenly the rays of the sun, from behind the car, reached that lowness and struck the flowers. The priest came out onto the porch in his underwear, stared at the car a moment as if he wondered what time it was, then collected his robe off the line and his fish off the doorstep and returned inside. Vespers was next, for him.

After backing out between the tombs he drove on still south, in the sunset. They caught up with an old man walking in a sprightly way in their direction, all by himself, wearing a clean bright shirt printed with a pair of palm trees fanning green over his chest. It might better be a big colored woman's shirt, but she didn't have it. He flagged the car with gestures like hoops.

"You're coming to the end of the road," the old man told them. He pointed ahead, tipped his hat to the lady, and pointed again. "End of the road." They didn't understand that he meant, "Take me."

They drove on. "If we do go any further, it'll have to be by water—is that it?" he asked her, hesitating at this odd point.

"You know better than I do," she replied politely.

The road had for some time ceased to be paved; it was made of shells. It was leading into a small, sparse settlement like the others a few miles back, but with even more of the camp about it. On the lip of the clearing, directly before a green willow blaze with the sunset gone behind it, the row of houses and shacks faced out on broad, colored, moving water that stretched to reach the horizon and looked like an arm of the sea. The houses on their shaggy posts, patchily built, some with plank runways instead of steps, were flimsy and alike, and not much bigger than the boats tied up at the landing.

"Venice," she heard him announce, and he dropped the crackling map in her lap.

They coasted down the brief remainder. The end of the road—she could not remember ever seeing a road simply end—was a spoon shape, with a tree stump in the bowl to turn around by.

Around it, he stopped the car, and they stepped out, feeling put down in the midst of a sudden vast pause or subduement that was like a yawn. They made their way on foot toward the water, where at an idle-looking landing men in twos and threes stood with their backs to them.

The nearness of darkness, the still uncut trees, bright water partly under a sheet of flowers, shacks, silence, dark shapes of boats tied up, then the first sounds of people just on the other side of thin walls—all this reached them. Mounds of shells like day-old snow, pink-tinted, lay around a central shack with a beer sign on it. An old man up on the porch there sat holding an open newspaper, with a fat white goose sitting opposite him on the floor. Below, in the now shadowless and sunless open, another old man, with a colored pencil bright under his hat brim, was late mending a sail.

When she looked clear around, thinking they had a fire burning somewhere now, out of the heat had risen the full moon. Just beyond the trees, enormous, tangerine-colored, it was going solidly up. Other lights just striking into view, looking farther distant, showed moss shapes hanging, or slipped and broke matchlike on the water that so encroached upon the rim of ground they were standing on.

There was a touch at her arm—his, accidental.

"We're at the jumping-off place," he said.

She laughed, having thought his hand was a bat, while her eyes rushed downward toward a great pale drift of water hyacinths—still partly open, flushed and yet moonlit, level with her feet—through which paths of water for the boats had been hacked. She drew her hands up to her face under the brim of her hat; her own cheeks felt like the hyacinths to her, all her skin full of too much light and sky, exposed. The harsh vesper bell was ringing.

"I believe there must be something wrong with me, that I came on this excursion to begin with," she said, as if he had already said this and she were merely in hopeful, willing, maddening agreement with him.

He took hold of her arm, and said, "Oh, come on—I see we can get something to drink here, at least."

But there was a beating, muffled sound from over the darkening water. One more boat was coming in, making its way through the tenacious, tough, dark flower traps, by the shaken light of what first appeared to be torches. He and she waited for the boat, as if on each other's patience. As if borne in on a mist of twilight or a breath, a horde of mosquitoes and gnats came singing and striking at them first. The boat bumped, men laughed. Somebody was offering somebody else some shrimp.

Then he might have cocked his dark city head down at her; she did not look up at him, only turned when he did. Now the shell mounds, like the shacks and trees, were solid purple. Lights had appeared in the not-quite-true window squares. A narrow neon sign, the lone sign, had come out in bright blush on the beer shack's roof: "Baba's Place." A light was on on the porch.

The barnlike interior was brightly lit and unpainted, looking not quite finished, with a partition dividing this room from what lay behind. One of the four cardplayers at a table in the middle of the floor was the newspaper reader; the paper was in his pants pocket. Midway along the partition was a bar, in the form of a pass-through to the other room, with a varnished, second-hand fretwork overhang. They crossed the floor and sat, alone there, on wooden stools. An eruption of humorous signs, newspaper cutouts and cartoons, razor-blade cards, and personal messages of significance to the owner or his friends decorated the overhang, framing where Baba should have been but wasn't.

Through there came a smell of garlic and cloves and red pepper, a blast of hot cloud escaped from a cauldron they could see now on a stove at the back of the other room. A massive back, presumably female, with a twist of gray hair on top, stood with a ladle akimbo. A young man joined her and with his fingers stole something out of the pot and ate it. At Baba's they were boiling shrimp.

When he got ready to wait on them, Baba strolled out to the counter, young, black-headed, and in very good humor.

"Coldest beer you've got. And food—What will you have?"

"Nothing for me, thank you," she said. "I'm not sure I could eat, after all."

"Well, I could," he said, shoving his jaw out. Baba smiled. "I want a good solid ham sandwich."

"I could have asked him for some water," she said, after he had gone.

While they sat waiting, it seemed very quiet. The bubbling of the shrimp, the distant laughing of Baba, and the slap of cards, like the beating of moths on the screens, seemed to come in fits and starts. The steady breathing they heard came from a big rough dog asleep in the corner. But it was bright. Electric lights were strung riotously over the room from a kind of spider web of old wires in the rafters. One of the written messages tacked before them read, "Joe! At the boyy!!" It looked very yellow, older than Baba's Place. Outside, the world was pure dark.

Two little boys, almost alike, almost the same size, and just cleaned up, dived into the room with a double bang of the screen door, and circled around the card game. They ran their hands into the men's pockets.

"Nickel for some pop!"

"Nickel for some pop!"

"Go 'way and let me play, you!"

They circled around and shrieked at the dog, ran under the lid of the counter and raced through the kitchen and back, and hung over the stools at the bar. One child had a live lizard on his shirt, clinging like a breast pin—like lapis lazuli.

Bringing in a strong odor of geranium talcum, some men had come in now—all in bright shirts. They drew near the counter, or stood and watched the game.

When Baba came out bringing the beer and sandwich, "Could I have some water?" she greeted him.

Baba laughed at everybody. She decided the woman back there must be Baba's mother.

Beside her, he was drinking his beer and eating his sandwich—ham, cheese, tomato, pickle, and mustard. Before he finished, one of the men who had come in beckoned from across the room. It was the old man in the palm-tree shirt.

She lifted her head to watch him leave her, and was looked at, from all over the room. As a minute passed, no cards were laid down. In a far-off way, like accepting the light from Arcturus, she accepted it that she was more beautiful or perhaps more fragile than the women they saw every day of their lives. It was just this thought coming into a woman's face, and at this hour, that seemed familiar to them.

Baba was smiling. He had set an opened, frosted brown bottle before her on the counter, and a thick sandwich, and stood looking at her. Baba made her eat some supper, for what she was.

"What the old fellow wanted," said he when he came back at last, "was to have a friend of his apologize. Seems church is just out. Seems the friend made a remark coming in just now. His pals told him there was a lady present."

"I see you bought him a beer," she said.

"Well, the old man looked like he wanted *something*."

All at once the juke box interrupted from back in the corner, with the same old song as anywhere. The half-dozen slot machines along the wall were suddenly all run to like Maypoles, and thrown into action—taken over by further battalions of little boys.

There were three little boys to each slot machine. The local custom appeared to be that one pulled the lever for the friend he was holding up to put the nickel in, while the third covered the pictures with the flat of his hand as they fell into place, so as to surprise them all if anything happened.

The dog lay sleeping on in front of the raging juke box, his ribs working fast as a concertina's. At the side of the room a man with a cap on his white thatch was trying his best to open a side screen door, but it was stuck fast. It was he who had come in with the remark considered ribald; now he was trying to get out the other way. Moths as thick as ingots were trying to get in. The cardplayers broke into shouts of derision, then joy, then tired derision among themselves; they might have been here all afternoon—they were the only ones not cleaned up and shaved. The original pair of little boys ran in once more, with the hyphenated bang. They got nickels this time, then were brushed away from the table like mosquitoes, and they rushed under the counter and on to the cauldron behind, clinging to Baba's mother there. The evening was at the threshold.

They were quite unnoticed now. He was eating another sandwich, and she, having finished part of hers, was fanning her face with her hat. Baba had lifted the flap of the counter and come out into the room. Behind his head there was a sign lettered in orange crayon: "Shrimp Dance Sun. PM." That was tonight, still to be.

And suddenly she made a move to slide down from her stool, maybe wishing to walk out into that nowhere down the front steps to be cool a moment. But he had hold of her hand. He got down from his stool, and, patiently, reversing her hand in his own—just as she had had the look of being about to give up, faint—began moving her, leading her. They were dancing.

"I get to thinking this is what we get—what you and I deserve," she whispered, looking past his shoulder into the room. "And all the time, it's real. It's a real place—away off down here. . . ."

They danced gratefully, formally, to some song carried on in what must be the local patios, while no one paid any attention as long as they were together, and the children poured the family nickels steadily into the slot machines, walloping the handles down with regular crashes and troubling nobody with winning.

She said rapidly, as they began moving together too well, "One of those clippings was an account of a shooting right here. I guess they're proud of it. And that awful knife Baba was carrying . . . I wonder what he called me," she whispered in his ear.

"Who?"

"The one who apologized to you."

If they had ever been going to overstep themselves, it would be now as he held her closer and turned her, when she became aware that he could not help but see the bruise at her temple. It would not be six inches from his eyes. She felt it come out like an evil star. (Let it pay him back, then, for the hand he had stuck in her face when she'd tried once to be sympathetic, when she'd asked about his wife.) They danced on still as the record changed, after standing wordless and motionless, linked together in the middle of the room, for the moment between.

Then, they were like a matched team—like professional Spanish dancers wearing masks—while the slow piece was playing.

Surely even those immune from the world, for the time being, need the touch of one another, or all is lost. Their arms encircling each other, their bodies circling the odorous, just-nailed-down floor, they were, at last, imperviousness in motion. They had found it, and had almost missed it: they had had to dance. They were what their separate hearts desired that day, for themselves and each other.

They were so good together that once she looked up and half smiled. "For whose benefit did we have to show off?"

Like people in love, they had a superstition about themselves almost as soon as they came out on the floor, and dared not think the words "happy" or "unhappy," which might strike them, one or the other, like lightning.

In the thickening heat they danced on while Baba himself sang with the mosquito-voiced singer in the chorus of *"Moi pas l'aimez ça,"* enumerating the *ça*'s with a hot shrimp between his fingers. He was counting over the platters the old woman now set out on the counter, each heaped with shrimp in their shells boiled to iridescence, like mounds of honeysuckle flowers.

The goose wandered in from the back room under the lid of the counter and hitched itself around the floor among the table legs and people's legs, never seeing that it was neatly avoided by two dancers—who nevertheless vaguely thought of this goose as learned, having earlier heard an old man read to it. The children called it Mimi, and lured it away. The old thatched man was again drunkenly trying to get out by the stuck side door; now he gave it a kick, but was prevailed on to remain. The sleeping dog shuddered and snored.

It was left up to the dancers to provide nickels for the juke box; Baba kept a drawerful for every use. They had grown fond of all the selections by now. This was the music you heard out of the distance at night—out of the roadside taverns you fled past, around the late corners in cities half asleep, drifting up from the carnival over the hill, with one odd little strain always managing to repeat itself. This seemed a homey place.

Bathed in sweat, and feeling the false coolness that brings, they stood finally on the porch in the lapping night air for a moment before leaving. The first arrivals of the girls were coming up the steps under the porch light—all flowered fronts, their black pompadours giving out breathlike feelers from sheer abundance. Where they'd resprinkled it since church, the talcum shone like mica on their downy arms. Smelling solidly of geranium, they filed across the porch with short steps and fingers joined, just timed to turn their smiles loose inside the room. He held the door open for them.

"Ready to go?" he asked her.

Going back, the ride was wordless, quiet except for the motor and the insects driving themselves against the car. The windshield was soon blinded. The headlights pulled in two other spinning storms, cones of flying things that, it seemed, might ignite at the last minute. He stopped the car and got out to clean the windshield thoroughly with his brisk, angry motions of driving. Dust lay thick and cratered on the roadside scrub. Under the now ash-white moon, the world traveled through very faint stars—very many slow stars, very high, very low.

It was a strange land, amphibious—and whether water-covered or grown with jungle or robbed entirely of water and trees, as now, it had the same loneliness. He regarded the great sweep—like steppes, like moors, like deserts (all of which were imaginary to him); but more than it was like any likeness, it was South. The vast, thin, wide-thrown, pale, unfocused star-sky, with its veils of lightning adrift, hung over this land as it hung over the open sea. Standing out in the night alone, he was struck as powerfully with recognition of the extremity of this place as if all other bearings had vanished—as if snow had suddenly started to fall.

He climbed back inside and drove. When he moved to slap furiously at his shirtsleeves, she shivered in the hot, licking night wind that their speed was making. Once the car lights picked out two people—a Negro couple, sitting on two facing chairs in the yard outside their lonely cabin—half undressed, each battling for self against the hot night, with long white rags in endless, scarflike motions.

In peopleless open places there were lakes of dust, smudge fires burning at their hearts. Cows stood in untended rings around them, motionless in the heat, in the night—their horns standing up sharp against that glow.

At length, he stopped the car again, and this time he put his arm under her shoulder and kissed her—not knowing ever whether gently or harshly. It was the loss of that distinction that told him this was now. Then their faces touched unkissing, unmoving, dark, for a length of time. The heat came inside the car and wrapped them still, and the mosquitoes had begun to coat their arms and even their eyelids.

Later, crossing a large open distance, he saw at the same time two fires. He had the feeling that they had been riding for a long time across a face—great, wide, and upturned. In its eyes and open mouth were those fires they had had glimpses of, where the cattle had drawn together: a face, a head, far down here in the South—south of South, below it. A whole giant body sprawled downward then, on and on, always, constant as a constellation or an angel. Flaming and perhaps falling, he thought.

She appeared to be sound asleep, lying back flat as a child, with her hat in her lap. He drove on with her profile beside his, behind his, for he bent forward to drive faster. The earrings she wore twinkled with their rushing motion in an almost regular beat. They might have spoken like tongues. He looked straight before him and drove on, at a speed that, for the rented, overheated, not at all new Ford car, was demoniac.

It seemed often now that a barnlike shape flashed by, roof and all outlined in lonely neon—a movie house at a crossroads. The long white flat road itself, since they had followed it to the end and turned around to come back, seemed able, this far up, to pull them home.

A thing is incredible, if ever, only after it is told—returned to the world it came out of. For their different reasons, he thought, neither of them would tell this (unless something was dragged out of them): that, strangers, they had ridden down into a strange land together and were getting safely back—by a slight margin, perhaps, but margin enough. Over the levee wall now, like an aurora borealis, the sky of New Orleans, across the river, was flickering gently. This time they crossed by bridge, high above everything, merging into a long light-stream of cars turned cityward.

For a time afterward he was lost in the streets, turning almost at random with the noisy traffic until he found his bearings. When he stopped the car at the next sign and leaned forward frowning to make it out, she sat up straight on her side. It was Arabi. He turned the car right around.

"We're all right now," he muttered, allowing himself a cigarette.

Something that must have been with them all along suddenly, then, was not. In a moment, tall as panic, it rose, cried like a human, and dropped back.

"I never got my water," she said.

She gave him the name of her hotel, he drove her there, and he said good night on the sidewalk. They shook hands.

"Forgive . . . " For, just in time, he saw she expected it of him.

And that was just what she did, forgive him. Indeed, had she waked in time from a deep sleep, she would have told him her story. She disappeared through the revolving door, with a gesture of smoothing her hair, and he thought a figure in the lobby strolled to meet her. He got back in the car and sat there.

He was not leaving for Syracuse until early in the morning. At length, he recalled the reason; his wife had recommended that he stay where he was this extra day so that she could entertain some old, unmarried college friends without him underfoot.

As he started up the car, he recognized in the smell of exhausted, body-warm air in the streets, in which the flow of drink was an inextricable part, the signal that the New Orleans evening was just beginning. In Dickie Grogan's, as he passed, the well-known Josefina at her organ was charging up and down with *Clair de Lune*. As he drove the little Ford safely to its garage, he remembered for the first time in years when he was young and brash, a student in New York, and the shriek and horror and unholy smother of the subway had its original meaning for him as the lilt and expectation of love.

Paper Garden

by Jerome Wilson

Introduced by Al Young

JUST BEFORE I LEFT CALIFORNIA TO SPEND THE FALL OF 1992 AS A VISiting writer at the University of Michigan, Ann Arbor, where I myself had been a Spanish major during the Cold War fifties, *Ploughshares,* the influential American literary quarterly published by Emerson College, Boston, invited me to guest-edit its Spring 1993 issue. Like a good freelancer, I accepted.

As always, being back in Ann Arbor affected me in profound and sometimes unexpected ways. Not only had I done a lot of growing up there, but it was at Michigan that I had decided to follow my heart and write fiction and poetry for the rest of my life. I had turned twenty-one in Ann Arbor and now, past fifty, I often felt as though I were crisscrossing my way simultaneously through museumized time and the good old ever-blooming present.

By December, my hundred-year-old grandmother was dying. A lifelong Mississippi farm girl transplanted quite late in life to Detroit, she was hospitalized and barely holding on. Once when I visited her, this dying woman, supposedly out of it, began to whisper and giggle and talk to me of events that had taken place more than eighty-five years ago. Mama spoke the names of people I had never heard of, even though she and my long-gone grandfather had helped raise and care for me much of my first decade at the family farm. Her smiling, half-muttered remarks about an early boyfriend made me think of the family-surrounded dying matriarch at the center of Katherine Anne Porter's amazing story "The Jilting of Granny Weatherall."

One lightless December afternoon, sorting through my mail and papers at the English office in Haven Hall, I struck up a conversation with Carolyn Stone, one of the older graduate students enrolled at the time in the MFA Writing Program at Michigan. When Carolyn asked me what I was up to, I told her I was editing a forthcoming *Ploughshares.*

"What will the theme be?" she asked knowingly.

"I want to call it Celebration, but I doubt that's going to work out."

"Why?"

"Because the literary scene is anything but celebratory."

"Oh," she said, "I know a beautiful young writer back in Memphis. And his work certainly qualifies as celebratory."

"Oh, yeah?"

"Yes," said Carolyn. "He's black, too, and he's only twenty-two or twenty-three. But he's having a hard time.

"He works nights bagging Fritos at the Frito-Lay factory, and it's affecting his studies. The department is getting ready to flunk him out, and he still gets a lot of writing done."

"Carolyn, are you in touch with him?"

"I sure am."

"Then have him send me something to look at for the issue."

"I will."

And Carolyn Stone did just that.

My grandmother died in Detroit just before Christmas, and that was still very much with me when I got back to the Bay Area. I withdrew to my apartment and spent the next several weeks reading through stacks of manuscripts that were still arriving for the issue. One chilly January morning I opened the manila envelope containing Jerome Wilson's "Paper Garden." The moment I connected with his lead character William's opening lines, I knew I was in the hands of an exciting, new, warranted, bona fide writer:

> Back in the days when life was easy and you could walk down the street at night and not worry about anybody knocking you over the head with some blunt object and taking all of your pocket change, Miss Mamie Jamison, the neighborhood kids' godmother who gave us money and candy and let us hide in her parlor when the big boys chased us from the playground, took seriously ill one summer and had to be put to bed.

"Paper Garden" celebrates everything I hold dear about storytelling. Not only does the story take place in an imaginable community, where there are actual families and kin and community concerns, but here was a voice telling us about the time an arty woman from New York City suddenly turned up in Tennessee to teach Shakespeare and give elocution lessons to somewhat countrified school kids. Everything about it felt and sounded just right. I probably bored a couple of workshop-buried, deadline-driven writer friends by thoughtlessly telephoning them to share my enthusiasm. Nevertheless, they registered more than polite enthusiasm when I read them passages aloud from Wilson's story.

Why did I fall in love with "Paper Garden"? Obviously, it must have reminded me of southern communities I remembered. But that wasn't enough. For me stories work best when they work at the level of magic; that is, when they somehow alchemize what you yourself have been through or think you know by turning that experience and knowledge into something golden. To quote novelist Joseph Heller, something happened. That is, something changed in me after I read about how Miss Marion, New York City actress and drama teacher, hits that little town of Harper and turns Little League football hopeful William "Sonny Buck" Jackson all the way around—and a number of other townspeople as well. No one gets stabbed or murdered. There's no suicide, no rape, no incest, no sexual abuse. And neither is there there any trivialization of grand emotions; no, no minimalist or debilitating racialist posturing. Jerome Wilson stands back, gets out of the way, and lets William tell us the story. And before it reaches its bittersweet, blues-suffused conclusion, the story tells us yet again what all the best stories have always confirmed. In his 1842 poem "The Spanish Student," Henry Wadsworth Longfellow put it this way: "There's nothing in this world so sweet as love, /And next to love the sweetest thing is hate."

Paper Garden

Jerome Wilson

Back in the days when life was easy and you could walk down the street at night and not worry about anybody knocking you over the head with some blunt object and taking all of your pocket change, Miss Mamie Jamison, the neighborhood kids' godmother who gave us money and candy and let us hide in her parlor when the big boys chased us from the playground, took seriously ill one summer and had to be put to bed. Her daughter, the one all the way from New York, moved in with her, dressed in nothing but what looked like black bodysuits and tall fruit-basket hats like that Chiquita woman wears on banana peels. If it wasn't black bodysuits, she was wearing a pair of men's trousers and shirt along with a mighty fine pair of work boots. But despite her icky clothes, she looked like a movie star from the silent screens: deep, dark black hair, thin red lips, and that pale, powdery skin color, like she was waiting for some invisible director to yell "Action!" and give her the go-ahead to say her lines like that was the only thing God created her for.

Of course, the only reason the Chiquita woman, Miss Marion, wasn't talked about like a dog too much by the other ladies in the neighborhood was because she *was* from New York. Meaning, Miss Marion obviously knew what the latest fashions were, and knew much more about fads and styles than these country women, including my own mama, would ever know in their whole lifetime. Which was also why she was called "Miss" Marion, even by the old folks—the way she spoke, calling everybody "darling" and "sweetie" and always saying how much she loved somebody, even complete strangers she met walking down the street. You would have thought they were blood relatives.

My mama was the main gofer over Miss Marion; she would come home just about every other day with some catchy word or phrase that she had heard Miss Marion say, or what someone else had heard her say. Once, while leaving out the door to go to a Daughters of the Confederate Army meeting, Mama said to Papa and me, "I'll be back in about an hour. Chow." And when she closed the door, Papa, with a puzzled look on his face, looked up from his evening paper and asked me, "What dog?"

Something was happening to the town of Harper. All the women wanted to be Miss Marion, ordering just about every dress and hat and scarf and shoe that the Sears, Roebuck catalog had to offer. Even the men, down to the youngest and up to the oldest, watched Miss Marion out of the corner of their eyes. We watched how she swished her way through town knowing full well everybody was looking at her in a skirt that was at least ten inches too short and ten years ahead of Harper's time. Eddie T., who claimed he was blind, sat on that old tree stump at the end of the main street playing his harmonica, wrote and sang a song about her that teetered on the edge of vulgarity, sometimes drawing a good crowd if it was a Saturday and a nice pile of spending money in his ragged hat that he kept between his feet.

Even Papa, whenever he saw Miss Marion coming up on our side of the sidewalk, all of a sudden had to go check the oil in the car, or he had to go clip the hedges, or the grass was too tall and he had to go cut it. I think Mama knew what Papa was up to, but it was summer and it was hot and the price of ground beef had dropped and life was just too wonderful so Mama didn't say anything. "At least he's away from that paper," she said. It was true: Papa had about three weeks' worth of *Harper's Sentinel*s piled up on the coffee table. Most times now, he spent looking out the big picture window.

It wasn't long before Miss Marion had announced that she would start giving acting lessons down at the community center, since she had some acting degree from NYU and saw that it was not only a good deed but "an absolute duty"—another one of her catchy phrases that she almost wore out—that she bring some of her "expertise" back home to those who weren't as fortunate as her.

So, to be honest, I wasn't in the least bit surprised when I came home from playing kickball with Terry and Kicky, and Mama asked me if I was planning to take any acting lessons from Miss Marion—as if we had already discussed it before.

"I thought you were going to play football this summer, Sonny Buck?" Papa asked me, not even giving my head the chance to let the first question sink in good.

"And what's wrong with acting lessons?" Mama asked Papa in that tone of voice that said you best watch what you say.

And Papa caught the hint, so he shuffled around in his favorite chair, the one that sits in front of the television set, then he lowered his newspaper just enough so we could see his eyes. "There's nothing wrong with taking acting lessons if that's what Sonny Buck wants to do. I just thought maybe he wanted to play football since he's been playing for the last three summers."

"Well, missing football this year is not going to kill him none. I think it will do you some good to expand your culture, Sonny Buck. I'll give you ten dollars." Then she gave Papa that look that told him that he had better not bid against her. And when he didn't, she said, "Good. Now that's settled. The class starts Monday."

I looked over at Papa, but he was already behind his paper again. So there I was.

But it wasn't bad. Come to find out, all the mothers in the neighborhood—except for Kicky's mama—made their kids go see Miss Marion for acting lessons, which consisted mainly of remembering some line from a Shakespeare play and reciting it while she shouted how you should be standing, or lecturing you on the proper facial expression, or having fits on when you should be breathing. And if you weren't doing it just right, she would just get all undone: flapping her arms, twisting her face, then sometimes dropping to her knees and saying: "Lord, please help me educate these ignorant people." That ignorant part was something we didn't feature too well and Debra Ann told her so, being since Debra Ann was brought up that way; that is, brought up to cuss grown folks out and not think twice about it.

But Miss Marion took an interest in me. She didn't yell when I read, but watched me with her mouth hanging open, telling everybody to knock off the noise back there—mainly Terry and another boy we called Scootie who could make funny noises with his armpits. Miss Marion said that I was talented.

What she say that for? I recited Shakespeare for Mama and Papa almost every evening before, during, and after dinner. Papa said that I was real good. Mama said I was a born actor. A genius was the word Miss Robbins—the school's English teacher who doubled as the drama coach in the springtime—used one night when she came over just to hear me read a few lines from *A Midsummer Night's Dream*. I was good. No lie. I imagined myself going to Hollywood, or to New York like Miss Marion, and becoming a real actor like James Cagney or Humphrey Bogart and star in films where I get to shoot the bad guy and run off with his dame because he's nothing but a big gorilla and she had been giving me the eye all along at the bar between sippings of tequilas and straight shots of brandy. I was Othello hanging upside down from a big tree in our front yard; I was Romeo on the football field. At the groceries: Puck. At the gas station with Papa: Macbeth. Then Henry VIII, then Hamlet, then King Lear, and I couldn't stop. Terry and Kicky couldn't keep up and came close to hating me, something I couldn't blame them for. I was crazy. I figured if I didn't make it in pro football, at least I had my acting talents to fall back on.

But the gist of this story really didn't kick in until about a month later, a July evening. Terry and Kicky were over my house for dinner: Terry was fat and would eat anything that couldn't get up and run; but Mama was always inviting Kicky over because she said Kicky was from a dysfunctioning family on account of his daddy been to jail about ten times and his mama was always hooking up with somebody who was going to Memphis for a couple of days. So, sometimes, if Kicky didn't eat with us, he didn't eat.

"So, how's the acting coming along?" Papa asked Terry and me.

Terry, between mouthfuls of some hot meatball dish—a recipe Mama got from Miss Marion: "It's okay. We studying *Romeo and Juliet*. Can I have some water?"

"Oh, that's nice," Mama said. "I remember in the springtime the senior class would always put on *Romeo and Juliet* out on the front lawn of the school. That's how we paid for the prom every year. I was Juliet. We decorated the whole stage with honeysuckles and white clovers and I wore a crown of white roses." Mama smiled. "I was beautiful then."

Papa said, "What do you mean? You're still beautiful."

Mama looked up at Papa, just like everybody else at the table did. I remember one time he was telling everybody down at the lodge how his boy was going to make the football team and go on to play for some Ivy League school. But I remember getting cut the first week of tryouts, so I hid out over Kicky's house all day long. It didn't do any good, Papa knew exactly where I was because Debra Ann told him out of spite on account of me not wanting to carry her books after school. When he found me, he said, "Let's go home, Sonny Buck," and the way he said it I knew I had let him down. At home Papa got on the phone and called an emergency meeting being since he was sort of like the vice-president of the lodge. He told me to come with him. When we got there all the men were fussing and wondering what was so important. Then Papa said, "This is my son, William 'Sonny Buck' Jackson, and he didn't make the Little League football team. If he never makes any other team in his life, he's still my boy and I love him. And if any of you say anything out of pocket I'll bust your damn noses." Then we went down to Olive Branch and he bought me a beer at Tang's. Papa said not to say anything about the nose busting or the beer drinking, being since he was sort of like a deacon at church. That was the only time I ever remember Papa saying or doing something profound and not being behind his paper.

At the table, Mama put her napkin up to her face and dabbed at the corner of her eyes. "Frank, you're so kind. I love you. I love you all." Then she got up and went around the table kissing everybody. Just like Miss Marion, except Mama wasn't performing. Even Kicky probably wanted to cry; I don't think he had ever been kissed by his mother.

And right then and there I made a vow that if ever the moon and the sun and all the constellations ever decided to twist, switch up, collide, or explode in the heavens and cause me to lose my mind and want to run away from home, I was going to take these two beloved people with me.

After dinner, Mama told me to take a plate of rum muffins over to Miss Marion. She told Kicky and Terry to go with me, but they suddenly claimed to hear their mothers calling them. So I had to go by myself. I picked up the plate and said "Chow" to everybody.

When I got to the house, I was standing in an open doorway. "Miss Marion?" I peeped in, looking into a dark living room full of bulky antique furniture, the stench of Vicks Vapo Rub and the confined, wet, musty smell, like after a long, hot summer rain—and it crept out on the porch with me and tingled my nose. "Miss Marion?" I repeated.

"William, is that you?"

I peeped farther into the room and saw a figure move in a chair over there in a corner. "Yes, this is me."

"Well, why you out there? Come in here."

I walked in, bumped into something, and she clicked on a table lamp.

She had been drinking. She wasn't wearing a hat. Her hair was down and she was more white than usual except for her eyes: bloodshot and veiny red-like.

"You okay, Miss Marion?"

"I couldn't be better," she said slowly, then she brought a glass up to her mouth and sipped.

I stood there watching, not knowing what to do, but then I remembered why I had come. "My mama sent you these." I held the plate out in front of me. "She made rum muffins."

She laughed. "That's all I need." She downed the rest of her drink. Then she frowned up at me like I was something awful. "Do you know how evil the world is?"

"Excuse me?" I asked, steady holding onto the plate of muffins because I was too nervous to do anything else.

"The world is full of evil. You knew that, didn't you?"

"Ahh . . . yes, I knew that."

"But you know, I don't think anybody else knows about this world but me and you." She burped. "I don't think most folks know they're mean. If they don't know any better, how do you expect them to act good? You see what I'm saying, William?"

"Yes, I think so."

"You know what bad thing I did one time? I made this fat girl cry. When I was up in New York, I went to this restaurant with this friend of mine and he brought his girlfriend with him. She was as big as a house. I don't know what Judd saw in her. She must've pissed Jack Daniels. I don't know. Anyway, I think I was drinking, I can't remember, but I remember telling this girl that I bet she eats a lot. Then Judd tells me that she's a vegetarian. A vegetarian. Can you believe that, William? A three-hundred-pound vegetarian?"

I shook my head no.

"I couldn't believe it either. So I ask him what in the hell has his vegetarian been snacking on? A damn California redwood? I thought it was funny but she started crying and Judd was trying to hush her up because everybody was looking at us. The more she cried, the louder I got, until they put all of us out of the restaurant. They didn't have good food anyway. But now I feel so bad about what I said. I got to tell everybody what I've done. That's my punishment." She grabbed some tissues from a roll of toilet paper and dabbed at her eyes and blew her nose. "You know, I think this world would be a lot better place to live if everyone would just do as I say. Know what I'm talking about, William?"

"Miss Marion," I hesitated, "are you drunk?"

"Not yet, but I have the potential of becoming an outstanding alcoholic. You just give me time."

I didn't say a word. I picked up the roll of toilet paper and tore some off, and out of nervousness started playing with it as Miss Marion was steady talking—mainly about how much money her mama had spent on her education and now she can't even find an acting job off-Broadway. I twisted the paper—tucking it here, pulling it there, twisting the bottom—until finally, I had created a little flower, something between a carnation or a rose, but a nice-looking flower just the same. We both looked down at the object in my hand; I think I was more surprised.

She took the flower from me and started crying. "You know what this is, William?"

"A paper flower?"

"No," between sobs, "this is beauty. Painful beauty. You're just like me. You can look right through pain and see the beauty of it. This is painful beauty. Thank you, William."

I was ready to go home. I tried to throw a hint by moving closer to the door and shuffling my feet like I suddenly heard someone calling my name.

"Sit down, William," she said, handing me the roll of paper. She refilled her glass, then leaned back on the couch. "You got it, William."

"Got what, Miss Marion?" I asked, steady making the paper flowers.

"It! You got that third eye right here"—she tapped her forehead—"and you can see right down that narrow line. I can't see that line as clearly as I want to. I never seen anybody read Shakespeare like you can. How do you do it? You ain't got to answer that. Most folks who are good at something usually don't know how they do it."

Since it wasn't a big roll, I had quickly made about twenty flowers and they were on the floor around my feet.

Miss Marion dropped to her knees and ran her fingers through the flowers like they were gold coins. "These are beautiful." Then, like a sudden afterthought: "I'll be back. I got to go check on Mama."

She disappeared down the dark hallway, leaving me alone in the parlor. I was trying to decide whether to leave, figuring that she was too drunk to remember whether I was here or not, but that wouldn't be a proper thing to do. By the time I had made up my mind to make a break for the door, Miss Marion came back with a flashlight and two new rolls of toilet paper.

"Mama's doing just fine. Let's go."

"Where we going?"

Miss Marion looked at me like I had a hole in my head. "Outside. We're going to plant these beautiful flowers in the garden. You don't actually think that I'm going to let all these flowers just multiply inside my house, do you?"

Though it was late, about eight or nine, it was still hot. Miss Marion started digging small holes in the empty garden with her fingers. She placed a flower in the hole and then she mashed the soft dirt around the paper stem.

She was quiet, working quickly, stopping every once in a while to take a sip from the bottle that she had brought out here, or to grab some more paper flowers from me, or to tell me where to shine the flashlight. This went on for about an hour until we had the whole flower bed in the front yard covered in paper flowers.

Miss Marion started crying again. "This is just damn lovely!"

We stood there in the night looking at the paper garden. It really did look nice.

"You know, William, some things are just too good for this world." Then she looked up at me like she was expecting me to add to what she had just said. But I kept my eyes on the garden.

Fortunately, I heard Papa calling me and I told Miss Marion that I had to go. I started running down the street, pushing what she had said off to the side somewhere.

She yelled, "Goodbye, William! Come back in the morning and we can see how beautiful this garden looks in the daylight!"

"Okay," I yelled, running wildly in the middle of the street like I had just been set free out of a cage, looking back only once just in time to see her wave at me and take another sip.

But the next day it rained, a thunderstorm so terrible that even Mama said, "Maybe you shouldn't go to class today, Sonny Buck. Miss Marion will understand." I sat in the house all day until the rain stopped about early evening.

Later I walked down to Miss Marion's house and stood in front of the paper garden. The rain had melted the flowers and the only thing that was left was soggy toilet paper all over the yard. I stared at the garden for a long time.

I knocked on the door, but there wasn't an answer. I peeped through the windows into the parlor, but I didn't see anything. Once, I thought I saw Miss Marion ducking down the dark hallway, but I wasn't sure. I knocked on the door and yelled her name, but there was no answer. I went home.

Suddenly, everything changed. Not a change back, not a change forward, but a change like the closing scene of a play when the curtain comes down and you wonder were you really there. Like the melting of the paper garden was an omen of what was to happen next: Miss Mamie Jamison died toward the end of the summer. She was buried the next day, then the next day after that Miss Marion packed up everything in the middle of the night and left, and not too long after that the house was boarded up. Just like that. Then slowly Harper went back to the way it was: boring. Like a rubberband, Harper had stretched to accommodate one of its own, then quickly snapped back into place—nothing different, but the same. My mother went back to her meatloaf on Mondays, spaghetti on Tuesdays, and pork chops, chicken, roast, noodles, and stew on the other days. I went back to my football practices, and Papa slipped back behind his paper.

Once, I wondered if Miss Marion was a real person, or if she was one of those fallen angels who comes to earth to earn her wings. You would wonder about anybody who steps into your life and charms and dazzles you, forces your imagination to soar higher than the heavens, then for no reason, quietly disappears, never realizing that someone has been left behind whose love for life is now running on an uncontrollable high. Though it didn't last long, but for one brief moment in my life, I wasn't William "Sonny Buck" Jackson, the junior varsity football player. Instead, I was William "Sonny Buck" Jackson, the Broadway star, the Hollywood actor—the whole town not the town, but a stage; the townspeople not the townspeople, but the audience. Maybe Miss Marion knew what she was doing and was just giving me a taste of what could be, letting me know that there's a different world outside the four walls of Harper.

I wondered what had become of Miss Marion. I imagined myself traveling from town to town, city to city, looking for a Miss Marion. Stories would spring up about me, about some kid looking for a friend that he met one summer. Toothless old men with guitars will be moaning some sad song about lost friendship and loneliness and how cruel the world can get without a good friend or a faithful dog. I will become a legend. Of course, some folks will say I never existed, but just somebody's crazy imagination gone wild. But that wouldn't get me down, since worrying about that kind of stuff doesn't bother me none anyway.

About the Authors

James Agee was born in Knoxville, Tennessee, in 1909. Educated at Phillips Exeter Academy and Harvard College, he published a book of poems, *Permit Me Voyage,* and worked for *Fortune* magazine in the 1930s, investigating the plight of tenant farmers in Alabama, a five-year project that became *Let Us Now Praise Famous Men*. Later a film critic for *Time* and *The Nation,* Mr. Agee also wrote the screenplays for *The African Queen, The Night of the Hunter,* and *Noa Noa*. His sole novel, *A Death in the Family,* appeared after his death in New York City in 1955 and was awarded the 1958 Pulitzer Prize. Married three times, he was the father of four children.

Julia Alvarez was born in the Dominican Republic and came to the United States when she was ten years old. Her writings include the poetry collection *Homecoming* and *How the Garcia Girls Lost Their Accents,* a novel-in-stories. *In the Time of the Butterflies,* a novel, is her latest work. She was educated at Middlebury College, where she now teaches. She lives with her husband in Vermont.

Isaac Babel was born in 1894 to Jewish merchants in Odessa. He served on the Romanian Front in World War I and worked as a press correspondent attached to the Soviet cavalry, the Cossacks. The anomaly of a Jew serving with a Cossack regiment formed a tension at the heart of perhaps his greatest work, *Red Cavalry*. The previous year he published *The Story of My Dove-Cote,* another collection. Though he published stories in magazines for the next thirteen years, only one more book, *Tales of Odessa,* appeared. First hailed in his native country as a master stylist, he was by the time of Stalin's purges in the 1930s attacked for his ideological ambiguity. In 1937 he was arrested, for reasons that were never made clear. He died in a concentration camp in either 1939 or 1940.

James Baldwin was born in 1924 and grew up in Harlem, the eldest of nine children. The son of an evangelical minister and an after-school preacher himself, he wrote of his religious experience in his first novel, *Go Tell It on the Mountain,* and in his play, *The Amen Corner.* His other published works include the novels *Giovanni's Room, Another Country, Tell Me How Long the Train's Been Gone,* and *If Beale Street Could Talk;* another play, *Blues for Mister Charlie;* and three books of essays, *Notes of a Native Son, Nobody Knows My Name,* and *The Fire Next Time*. His short stories were collected in *Going to Meet the Man*. On December 1, 1987, he died in St. Paul de Vence in southern France.

Russell Banks was born in Newton, Massachusetts, in 1940. He attended Colgate University for eight weeks in 1958 before dropping out with the intention, never carried out, of visiting Cuba in support of Castro. He got his B.A. nearly ten years later from the University of North Carolina. He published his first collection of stories, *Trailerpark,* in 1981. His works since include *Continental Drift* and *Affliction,* both novels. He lives in New Hampshire.

Donald Barthelme was born in 1931 in Philadelphia and raised in Houston. As a young man he wrote film criticism for the *Houston Post* and at thirty became director of the Contemporary Arts Museum. In 1962 he began spending half his year in New York City. He became a frequent and long-term contributor to *The New Yorker.* He published three novels, including *The Dead Father,* and eight collections of short fiction, including *Come Back, Dr. Caligari* and *Unspeakable Practices, Unnatural Acts.* He died in 1989 from cancer.

Charles Baxter was born in Minneapolis, Minnesota, in 1947. He attended Macalester College and received his Ph.D. from the State University of New York at Buffalo. He worked as a high school teacher in Pinconning, Michigan, before teaching at Wayne State University and then at the University of Michigan. His first published book was a collection of poetry, *Chameleon,* in 1970. He published his first book of fiction, *Harmony of the World,* in 1984. Since then he has published five more books, including *Through the Safety Net,* a collection of stories, and *Shadow Play,* a novel. He lives in Ann Arbor, Michigan.

Jorge Luis Borges was born in 1899 in Buenos Aires and educated in Europe. He returned to Argentina as a young man and worked in the National Library, rising to direct it before being forced out by dictator Juan Perón. He was active for sixty years as an essayist, critic, and editor, and published four collections of fiction, including *Labyrinths* and *The Aleph and Other Stories.* In his later years, a progressive blindness increasingly circumscribed his activities until his death in 1986.

Jane Bowles was born in New York City in 1917. Educated at Stoneleigh and by French tutors in Switzerland, where she was hospitalized for tuberculosis, she married the composer Paul Bowles in 1938 and traveled widely with him in Europe and Africa before settling in Tangier in 1952. Collected in *My Sister's Hand in Mine* are her sole novel, *Two Serious Ladies,* her play, *In the Summer House,* and her book of stories, *Plain Pleasures.* She died in a Spanish convent near Tangier in 1973.

Paul Bowles was born in New York City in 1910. He studied musical composition under Aaron Copland and Virgil Thompson, was a music critic for the *New York Herald-Tribune,* and wrote the scores for Broadway shows in the thirties and forties. Gertrude Stein met him in Paris in 1931 and urged him to go to Morocco, where she thought his composing skills would flourish, and he explored all of North Africa before finally settling in Tangier. Inspired to take fiction writing seriously by the example of his wife, Mr. Bowles published his first novel, *The Sheltering Sky,* to great critical acclaim and followed it with *Let It Come Down, The Spider's House,* and *Up Above the World*. His *Collected Stories* appeared in 1976. He is also the translator of the Moroccan storyteller Mohammed Mrabet.

T. Coraghessan Boyle was born in 1948 and raised in New York's Hudson Valley. After undergraduate studies and high school teaching, he was educated at the University of Iowa's Writers Workshop, where he earned both an M.F.A. and a Ph.D. His first book of stories, *Descent of Man,* was published in 1979 and was followed by *Greasy Lake* and *If the River Was Whiskey* and by the novels *Water Music, Budding Prospects, East Is East,* and *The Road to Wellville.* His novel *World's End* was given the 1988 PEN/Faulkner Award for Fiction. He is currently a professor of English at the University of Southern California.

Mary Caponegro was born in Brooklyn, New York, in 1956. She studied writing at Bard College and Brown University. Her first collection of stories, *The Star Café,* was published in 1990. She teaches at Hobart and William Smith Colleges and lives in Geneva, New York.

Angela Carter was born in London in 1940. She studied English literature at the University of Bristol and worked as a journalist, editor, and teacher. She was the author of eleven novels, eight children's books, *The Company of Wolves* and other film and radio scripts, and the story collections *Fireworks* and *The Bloody Chamber,* as well as the critical study *The Sadeian Woman and the Ideology of Pornography.* She died of cancer in 1992.

Raymond Carver was born in Clatskanie, Oregon, in 1939 and educated at Chico State College, where he studied writing under John Gardner; Humboldt State College; the University of Iowa's Writers Workshop; and Stanford University, where he held a Wallace Stegner Creative Writing Fellowship. He was the author of five books of poetry and five collections of short stories, including his selection *Where I'm Calling From.* In 1983 he was given the prestigious Mildred and Harold Strauss Living Award and resigned his professorship at Syracuse University. In 1988 he was elected to the American Academy and Institute of Arts and Letters, but on August 2 of that year he died of lung cancer at his home in Port Angeles, Washington.

John Cheever was born in Quincy, Massachusetts, in 1912 and went to school at South Braintree's Thayer Academy, from which he was expelled in his senior year for intractability. A frequent contributor to *The New Yorker,* he was the author of five novels, including *The Wapshot Chronicle* and *Oh, What a Paradise It Seems,* and seven volumes of short stories, which were collected in 1978 in *The Stories of John Cheever* and for which he won the National Book Critics Circle Award and the Pulitzer Prize. Mr. Cheever was also a recipient of the National Book Award and the American Academy of Arts and Letters Howells Medal for Fiction. In June 1982 he died of cancer in his home in Ossining, New York. He is survived by his wife and three children.

Anton Chekhov was born in 1860 and wrote his first stories while a medical student at Moscow University, to help his family pay off debts. His grandfather had been a serf, his father an unsuccessful grocer. In 1886 his comic stories were collected in book form, and by 1887 his first play, *Ivanov,* had been produced. In 1890 he published *Sakhalin Island,* an investigation of convict life in Siberia that helped catalyze widespread prison reforms instituted two years later. In his working life he wrote over fifty short stories; between 1895 and 1904, his plays included *The Seagull, Uncle Vanya, The Three Sisters,* and *The Cherry Orchard.* Consumption forced him to divide his later years between the south coast of the Crimea and French and German health resorts. He died in 1904 in Badenweiler.

Robert Coover was born in Charles City, Iowa, in 1932. After receiving a B.A. from Indiana University, he served in the U.S. Navy for four years, attaining the rank of lieutenant. He then earned an M.A. from the University of Chicago and began teaching literature and creative writing at such universities as Princeton, Iowa, and Brown. *The Origins of the Brunists* won a William Faulkner Award for the best first novel of 1966 and was followed by *The Universal Baseball Association Inc., J. Henry Waugh, Prop., The Public Burning, Spanking the Maid, Gerald's Party,* and *Pinocchio in Venice,* as well as the story collections *Pricksongs and Descants* and *A Night at the Movies.* Among his honors are the Brandeis Citation for Fiction, an American Academy of Arts and Letters award, and the Rea Award for the Short Story. He is married and the father of three children.

Charles Dickens was born in Portsmouth, England, in 1812 but spent his happiest childhood years in Chatham. His father's financial embarrassments forced Charles to perform hard labor at a blacking factory as a boy while his father served time in a debtor's prison, and those experiences would influence much of his later fiction. His formal schooling ended at age fifteen. He thereafter worked as a clerk in a solicitor's office, as a shorthand reporter in the London courts, and as a parliamentary journalist before finding literary success in 1836 with his *Sketches by "Boz"* and the hugely popular comic narrative *The Pickwick Papers.* His fourteen novels include *Oliver Twist, Nicholas Nickleby, Martin Chuzzlewit, David Copperfield, Bleak House,* and *Great Expectations;* he was also an indefatigable editor of newspapers and magazines and the author of histories, plays, essays, and Christmas books—a form he invented. The father of nine children, he died suddenly on June 9, 1870, and was buried in Westminster Abbey.

Annie Dillard was born in Pittsburgh, Pennsylvania, in 1945. Educated at Hollins College, she has been a contributing editor to *Harper's* and a columnist for *Living Wilderness.* Her books include the poetry collection *Tickets for a Prayer Wheel,* the memoir *An American Childhood,* a historical novel *The Living,* and *Pilgrim at Tinker Creek, Living by Fiction, Holy the Firm, Teaching a Stone to Talk,* and *The Writing Life.* She lives in Connecticut.

Deborah Eisenberg was born in Winnetka, Illinois, in 1945. She attended Marlboro College and The New School for Social Research, and in 1982 had her play *Pastorale* produced by Second Stage in New York. Her first collection of stories, *Transactions in a Foreign Currency,* was published in 1986, and her second, *Under the 82nd Airborne,* in 1992.

Louise Erdrich was born in Little Falls, Minnesota, in 1954. Her father, a teacher, and her mother, a Chippewa Indian, were both affiliated with the Bureau of Indian Affairs. Educated at Dartmouth College and Johns Hopkins University, she worked as a beet weeder, waitress, psychiatric aide, poetry teacher in prisons, lifeguard, and construction flag signaler. *Love Medicine,* a novel, and *Jacklight,* a book of poems, were published in 1984, and were followed by the poetry collection *Baptism of Desire* and the novels *The Beet Queen, Tracks, The Crown of Columbus,* and, most recently, *The Bingo Palace.* She lives with her husband and seven children in Minnesota.

Molly Giles was born in California in 1940. She was educated at the University of California at Berkeley and San Francisco State University, where she now teaches in the creative writing department. Her stories have appeared in *Shenandoah, Redbook, North American Review, Ascent,* and *McCall's* and were collected in *Rough Translations,* winner of the 1985 Flannery O'Connor Award for Short Fiction. She is the mother of three daughters.

Mary Gordon was born on Long Island, New York, in 1949. She studied writing with Elizabeth Hardwick at Barnard College and received her M.A. from Syracuse University. Her first novel, *Final Payments,* was published in 1978. Her other works include *The Company of Women,* another novel, and *Temporary Shelter,* a collection of stories. She lives in New York City.

Allan Gurganus was born in Rocky Mount, North Carolina, in 1947. He studied painting at the University of Pennsylvania and the Pennsylvania Academy of Fine Arts, served in the U.S. Navy during the Vietnam War, and enrolled at Sarah Lawrence College to study writing with Grace Paley. He attended the University of Iowa's Writers Workshop on a Danforth fellowship, studying with Stanley Elkin and John Cheever, and Stanford University on a Wallace Stegner Creative Writing Fellowship, staying on to teach there as a Jones Lecturer. Mr. Gurganus has subsequently taught at Duke, Iowa, and Sarah Lawrence. His first novel, *Oldest Living Confederate Widow Tells All,* was named winner of the Sue Kaufman prize, given by the American Academy of Arts and Letters, for the best first work of fiction published in 1989. *White People* collected stories and novellas previously published in *Harper's, The New Yorker, The Paris Review,* and elsewhere. He lives in Chapel Hill, North Carolina.

Lars Gustafsson was born in 1936 in Västerås, Sweden, and studied philosophy at Uppsala University, receiving a Ph.D. in 1978. He edited the influential *Bonniers Litterära Magasin* from 1961 to 1972. His early reputation was mainly that of a lyric poet, but he has since received acclaim in nearly all genres: short fiction, novels, nonfiction, drama. Perhaps his greatest achievement is considered to be five novels given the overall title *The Cracks in the Wall: Mr. Gustafsson Himself, Wool, The Family Party, Sigismund,* and *The Death of a Beekeeper.* Other works include his collection

Sonnets, Stories of Happy People, and the novel *Bernard Foy's Third Castling*. He continues to be one of the most productive and versatile of writers.

Ron Hansen was born in Omaha, Nebraska, in December 1947. Educated in English literature at Creighton University, he served as a lieutenant in the U.S. Army, then studied under John Irving and John Cheever at the University of Iowa's Writers Workshop, where his classmates included T. Coraghessan Boyle and Allan Gurganus, and under John L'Heureux at Stanford University, where he held a Wallace Stegner Creative Writing Fellowship. His first novel, *Desperadoes,* was published in 1979 and was followed by *The Assassination of Jesse James by the Coward Robert Ford,* a children's book, *The Shadowmaker,* a book of stories, *Nebraska,* and the novel *Mariette in Ecstasy*. He lives in California.

John Hawkes was born in Stamford, Connecticut, in 1925 and served in World War II. He graduated from Harvard in 1947 and has produced a book of short plays, two collections of short fiction, and thirteen novels, including *The Blood Oranges, The Lime Twig, Death, Sleep, and the Traveler,* and *Whistlejacket*. He is a member of both the American Academy of Arts and Sciences and the American Academy and Institute of Arts and Letters. He lives in Providence, Rhode Island, with his wife, Sophie.

Amy Hempel was born in Chicago in 1951 but spent much of her life in California. Educated in a nonlinear way at five different universities, she has been widely published in both fiction and nonfiction, appearing in *Esquire, Harper's, Vanity Fair, Vogue,* and other magazines. Author of the story collections *Reasons to Live* and *At the Gates of the Animal Kingdom,* she lives with her husband in New York City.

Oscar Hijuelos was born in New York City in 1951. He received his B.A. and M.A. from City College and in 1983 published his first novel, *Our House in the Last World*. Since then he has published two more novels, *The Mambo Kings Play Songs of Love* and *Fourteen Sisters of Emilio Montez O'Brien*. He lives in New York City.

John Irving was born in Exeter, New Hampshire, in 1942. He attended the University of Pittsburgh on a wrestling scholarship, studied comparative literature at the University of Vienna and the University of New Hampshire, and received an M.F.A. from the University of Iowa's Writers Workshop, where he studied with Kurt Vonnegut, Jr. The author of eight novels including *Setting Free the Bears, The Water-Method Man, The World According to Garp, A Prayer for Owen Meany,* and, most recently, *A Son of the Circus,* Mr. Irving is married and the father of three sons. He lives in Vermont.

Ruth Prawer Jhabvala was born to Polish-Jewish parents in Cologne, Germany, in 1927. In 1939 her parents fled to England, where she became a British citizen and earned a degree in literature in 1951. She married a Parsee architect and lived in India from 1951 to 1975. Her work includes her first novel, *To Whom She Will, A Backward Place,* and *Heat and Dust*. She lives in New York City, collaborating on screenplays and television scripts as well as continuing to write fiction.

Edward P. Jones was born and raised in Washington, D.C. He was educated at Holy Cross College and the University of Virginia. *Lost in the City,* his first collection of stories, appeared in 1992. He lives in Arlington, Virginia.

James Joyce was born in 1882 in a suburb of Dublin and was educated at both the best Jesuit schools and at home, depending upon the state of his parents' financial decline. After taking his bachelor's degree from University College, Dublin, he moved to Paris in 1904 and never again lived in Ireland, settling in Trieste, Zurich, and Paris again. His collection of stories, *Dubliners,* was finished in 1905 but only published in 1916 after a bitter struggle with Irish publishers. His first novel, *A Portrait of the Artist as a Young Man,* was published the same year. He produced two more novels, *Ulysses* and *Finnegan's Wake*. He died in 1941.

Franz Kafka was born in 1883 in Prague. In 1906 he received a doctorate in jurisprudence and began work as a civil service lawyer. He never married and lived most of his life with his parents. His collections of stories included *Meditation, The Stoker: A Fragment, The Metamorphosis, The Judgement, In the Penal Colony,* and *A Country Doctor*. He died of tuberculosis in 1924. Three novels—*Amerika, The Trial,* and *The Castle*—were published posthumously, against his expressed wishes.

Janet Kauffman was born in Lancaster, Pennsylvania, in 1945. She attended Juniata College and received her Ph.D. from the University of Chicago. She published her first book of poems, *The Weather Book,* in 1981, and her first book of fiction, *Places in the World a Woman Could Walk,* in 1984. She has since published a novel, *Collaborators,* and another collection of stories, *Obscene Gestures for Women*. She lives in Hudson, Michigan.

Jamaica Kincaid was born in St. Johns, Antigua, in the West Indies in 1949. After high school she left Antigua to study in the United States but considered college "a dismal failure" and so educated herself. She published stories in various places, including *The New Yorker,* where she became a staff writer in 1978. She published her first collection of stories, *At the Bottom of the River,* six years later, and her second, *Annie John,* a year after that. She lives in Vermont and New York City.

David Leavitt was born in Palo Alto, California, in 1961 and graduated from Yale University in 1983. He moved to New York and began publishing stories and articles. His first collection of stories, *Family Dancing,* appeared a year later. He has since published a second collection, *A Place I've Never Been,* and three novels, *The Lost Language of Cranes, Equal Affections,* and *While England Sleeps*. He lives in East Hampton, Long Island, and spends much of his time in Florence, Italy.

John L'Heureux was born in South Hadley, Massachusetts, in 1934. Educated at the National Academy of Theater Arts, the College of the Holy Cross, Boston College, and Harvard University, he has been a staff editor and contributing editor to *The Atlantic* and for many years was Director of the Creative Writing Program at Stanford University. He has published four books of poetry, a memoir *Picnic in Babylon,* the story collections *Family Affairs, Desires,* and *Comedians,* and six novels, including *A Woman Run*

Mad, An Honorable Profession, and *The Shrine at Altamira.* He lives with his wife in California.

Clarice Lispector was born in the Ukraine in 1925 and was raised in Brazil. As a young woman she studied European literature and became one of Brazil's first women journalists. In 1944 she published her first novel, *Close to the Savage Heart.* For the next thirty-three years she published many novels and collections of short fiction, including *Family Ties, An Apprenticeship, or the Book of Delights,* and *The Hour of the Star.* She died in 1977 from cancer.

Katherine Mansfield was born in New Zealand in 1888 to wealthy parents. She studied, and settled, in London, and in 1911 produced her first book of stories, *In a German Pension.* She married the critic John Middleton Murry in 1918. She published two other collections, *Bliss and Other Stories* and *The Garden Party*—and a total of more than seventy stories—before her death from tuberculosis in 1923.

Bobbie Ann Mason was born in Mayfield, Kentucky, in 1942. After attending the University of Kentucky she worked in New York City, writing articles for movie magazines, and then received her Ph.D. from the University of Connecticut with a dissertation on Nabokov's *Ada.* She published *The Girl Sleuth: A Feminist Guide to the Bobbsey Twins, Nancy Drew, and Their Sisters* in 1975, and her first collection, *Shiloh and Other Stories,* in 1981. She has since published two novels, *In Country* and *Feather Crowns,* and another collection of stories, *Love Life.* She lives in Lawrenceburg, Kentucky.

Kenneth A. McClane, Jr., was born in New York City in 1951, the son of a family physician in Harlem, and received his B.A., M.A., and M.F.A. degrees from Cornell University, where he is now a professor of English. He is the author of seven poetry collections, including *Take Five,* and of autobiographical essays collected in *Walls.*

Sue Miller was born in 1943 and attended Radcliffe College. She published her first novel, *The Good Mother,* in 1986, and followed that with a collection of stories, *Inventing the Abbotts and Other Stories,* and two more novels, *Family Pictures* and *For Love.* She lives in Boston with her husband, the writer Douglas Bauer, and one son.

Lorrie Moore was born in Glens Falls, New York, in 1957. She attended St. Lawrence University and Cornell University and published her first collection of stories, *Self-Help,* in 1985. She has since produced a novel, *Anagrams,* another collection, *Like Life,* and a book for children, *The Forgotten Helper.* She lives in Madison, Wisconsin.

Alice Munro was born near Lake Huron in Ontario, Canada, in 1931. After attending the University of Western Ontario for two years, she married and moved to British Columbia. She published her first collection of stories, *Dance of the Happy Shades,* in 1968 to great acclaim. Other collections have included *Lives of Girls and Women, Something I've Been Meaning to Tell You, The Moons of Jupiter,* and *The Progress of Love.* She lives in southern Ontario.

Vladimir Nabokov was born in St. Petersburg, Russia, in 1899 and fled with his family to Germany during the Russian revolution. He was educated at Cambridge University and spent his subsequent years in Berlin and Paris, leaving France with his family in 1940 in the midst of the German invasion. He settled in America, where he wrote *Lolita,* the success of which allowed him to devote his full time to writing. He produced over forty volumes of fiction, criticism, and poetry, including *Invitation to a Beheading, Speak, Memory, Pnin, Nabokov's Dozen,* and *Pale Fire.* He died in Montreux, Switzerland, in 1977.

Joyce Carol Oates was born in Lockport, New York, in 1938. She remembers creating stories in pictures even before she could write. She received her B.A. from Syracuse University and her M.A from the University of Wisconsin. Since her first collection of stories *By the North Gate* appeared in 1963, she has been one of America's most widely anthologized and prolific authors, publishing over a hundred short stories and over forty books, including the novels *them, Expensive People,* and *Black Water.* She lives in Princeton, New Jersey.

Tim O'Brien was born in 1946 in Austin, Minnesota. After graduating *summa cum laude* from Macalester College, he served in the U.S. Army in Vietnam, where he was awarded a Purple Heart and achieved the rank of sergeant. O'Brien studied for a doctorate in political science at Harvard before becoming a national affairs reporter for *The Washington Post.* His first book was *If I Die in a Combat Zone, Box Me Up and Ship Me Home,* and was followed by the novels *Northern Lights, Going After Cacciato,* for which he won the National Book Award, and *The Nuclear Age.* His most recent book is *The Things They Carried.* He lives in Massachusetts.

Flannery O'Connor was born in Savannah, Georgia, in 1925 and was raised in Milledgeville. She graduated from Women's College of Georgia and got an M.F.A. from the University of Iowa's Writers Workshop. Her first novel, *Wise Blood,* was published in 1952 and was followed by *The Violent Bear It Away* as well as the story collections *A Good Man Is Hard to Find* and *Everything That Rises Must Converge.* She received three O. Henry First Prizes for her short fiction, and *The Complete Stories* was given a National Book Award posthumously in 1971. She died of lupus on August 3, 1964.

Tillie Olsen was born in Omaha, Nebraska, in 1913, the second of six children of Jewish immigrants. She joined the Young Communist League in the early 1930s, then moved to California, where she married and worked as a union organizer, waitress, laundress, and secretary before enrolling in creative writing classes at San Francisco State University. She was awarded a Wallace Stegner Creative Writing Fellowship at Stanford University based on stories that finally would be published in *Tell Me a Riddle.* She's also written *Yonnondio,* a novel from the thirties, and *Silences,* a collection of essays. She is the mother of three daughters.

Louis Owens was born in Lompoc, California, in 1948. Of Choctaw, Cherokee, and Irish descent, he is the author of the critical studies *Other Des-*

tinies: Understanding the American Indian Novel and *American Indian Novelists: An Annotated Critical Bibliography.* Educated in English literature at the University of California, Santa Barbara, and with a Ph.D. from the University of California, Davis, he is also author of the novels *The Sharpest Sight, Wolfsong,* and, most recently, *Bone Game.* Mr. Owens lives outside Albuquerque with his wife and two daughters and is Director of Creative Writing at the University of New Mexico.

Grace Paley was born in New York City in 1922. She studied at Hunter College and New York University and published her first book of stories, *The Little Disturbances of Man,* in 1959. During the next two decades she was prominent as an activist against the Vietnam War. She has since published two more collections, *Enormous Changes at the Last Minute* and *Later the Same Day.* She lives in New York and Vermont.

Francine Prose was born in Brooklyn, New York, in 1947 to parents who were both physicians. She attended Radcliffe College and Harvard University and published her first novel, *Judah the Pious,* in 1973. She has since continued to publish novels and collections of short fiction, including *Household Saints* and *Women and Children First.* She lives in Krumville, New York.

Delmore Schwartz was born in Brooklyn, New York, to Jewish immigrant parents in 1913. He studied philosophy at several universities and received his degree in 1935. In 1937 his short story "In Dreams Begin Responsibilities" appeared in the inaugural issue of *The Partisan Review* and was immediately hailed as a masterpiece. A first collection of poetry and prose appeared with the same title a year later. The critical reception for his next two major works, *Shenandoah; or, The Naming of the Child,* a surrealistic verse play, and *Genesis: Book One,* an epic poem, bitterly disappointed him. He went on to publish three more collections of poetry and fiction, including *The World Is a Wedding,* and was active as a critic and essayist until his death in 1966.

Jim Shepard was born in Stratford, Connecticut, in 1956 and graduated from Trinity College and from Brown University, where he studied fiction writing with John Hawkes. His short stories have appeared in *The Atlantic, Esquire, Harper's, The New Yorker,* and *Triquarterly.* His first novel, *Flights,* published in 1983, was followed by *Paper Doll, Lights Out in the Reptile House,* and *Kiss of the Wolf.* He teaches fiction writing and film at Williams College in Massachusetts.

Leslie Marmon Silko was born in 1948 to Laguna Pueblo Indian parents in New Mexico, and was educated at the University of New Mexico. She has produced two novels, *Ceremony* and *The Almanac of the Dead,* and a personal anthology of the Laguna Pueblo culture, *Storyteller.* She lives in Tucson.

Jane Smiley was born in Los Angeles, California, in 1949 to a father who was an army officer and a mother who was a writer. She received her B.A. from Vassar College and her M.A., M.F.A., and Ph.D. from the University of Iowa. She published her first novel, *Barn Blind,* in 1980; since then she has published seven more books, including two collections of novellas,

The Age of Grief and *Ordinary Love & Good Will,* and the novel *A Thousand Acres,* for which she won both the National Book Critics Circle Award and the Pultizer Prize. She lives in Ames, Iowa.

Robert Stone was born in Brooklyn in 1937 to a father he never knew and a mother who was institutionalized for schizophrenia. Educated in Catholic schools on the West Side of Manhattan, he joined the U.S. Navy at seventeen and served as a journalist, attaining the rank of petty officer third class. After that he worked for the New York *Daily News* and attended New York University and then Stanford on a Wallace Stegner Creative Writing Fellowship. His first novel, *A Hall of Mirrors,* won a William Faulkner Foundation Award; his second, *Dog Soldiers,* received a National Book Award; and his third, *A Flag for Sunrise,* the PEN/Faulkner Award. His most recent novels are *Children of Light* and *Outerbridge Reach*. The father of two children, Mr. Stone lives with his wife in Connecticut.

Amy Tan was born in Oakland, California, in 1952. Her parents emigrated from Beijing, China, in 1949. After her father's death, she attended high school in Switzerland and college in Oregon; she visited China with her mother for the first time in 1984. Her first novel, *The Joy Luck Club,* was published in 1989; her second, *The Kitchen God's Wife,* a few years later. She lives in San Francisco.

Leo Tolstoy was born in 1828 in Yasnaya Polyana, about one hundred miles south of Moscow. Orphaned at nine, he was brought up by an elderly aunt, educated at Kazan University, and served as a junior officer in the Russian army before retiring from his commission in 1856. His first books, *Childhood, Boyhood,* and *Youth,* were fictions based on his diaries, and the sketches in *Sevastopol* on his firsthand experience of the Crimean War. Count Tolstoy married Sofya Behrs in 1862 and fathered thirteen children while managing his country estate and creating his two greatest masterpieces, *War and Peace* and *Anna Karenina*. Educational, religious, and social reform preoccupied him throughout his life, particularly after 1880, but it was in this period, too, that he produced "The Death of Ivan Ilych," "The Kreutzer Sonata," and "Master and Man." His last novel was *Resurrection*. In November, 1910, Tolstoy died of pneumonia at a railway station in Astapovo.

John Updike was born in Shillington, Pennsylvania, in 1932 and graduated *summa cum laude* in English literature from Harvard College in 1954. After a year in England on the Knox Fellowship at Oxford University, he spent two years on the staff of *The New Yorker,* to which he has continued to contribute short stories, poems, essays, and book reviews. He is the author of nine collections of stories, including *The Same Door, Pigeon Feathers, The Music School, Museums and Women, Problems,* and *Trust Me,* and of sixteen novels, four collections of nonfictional prose, a memoir, *Self-Consciousness,* and children's books and poetry collections, for which he has received the Pulitzer Prize, the National Book Award, the American Book Award, and the National Book Critics Circle Award. He is the father of four children and lives in Massachusetts.

Stephanie Vaughn was born in Millersburg, Ohio, in 1945, and she grew up on military installations in Ohio, New York, Oklahoma, Texas, the Philippine Islands, and Italy. She was educated at Ohio State University, the University of Iowa, and Stanford University, where she held a Wallace Stegner Creative Writing Fellowship. Her short stories have appeared in *Antaeus, The New Yorker,* and *Redbook,* and in the O. Henry and Pushcart Prize collections. She is the author of *Sweet Talk* and teaches fiction writing and literature at Cornell University.

Alice Walker was born in 1944 to sharecroppers in Eatonton, Georgia. She attended Spelman College in Atlanta, and Sarah Lawrence, and published her first book of poetry, *Once,* in 1968. Since then she has published collections of poetry, short stories, and essays, and four novels, including *The Color Purple,* winner of the American Book Award and the Pulitzer Prize.

Eudora Welty was born in 1909 in Jackson, Mississippi, where she still lives in a house built by her family. She graduated from the University of Wisconsin and attended the Columbia University Graduate School of Business. She is the author of a memoir, *One Writer's Beginnings;* a book of essays, *The Eye of the Story;* five novels, *The Robber Bridegroom, Delta Wedding, The Ponder Heart, Losing Battles,* and *The Optimist's Daughter;* and five volumes of short stories, most recently *The Collected Stories of Eudora Welty.* She has been honored with the Pulitzer Prize, the National Medal for literature, the American Academy and Institute of Arts and Letters Howells Medal for Fiction, the National Institute of Arts and Letters Gold Medal for the Novel, and the Presidential Medal of Freedom.

Joy Williams was born in Chelmsford, Massachusetts, in 1944. She received an M.A. from Marietta College and an M.F.A. from the University of Iowa's Writers Workshop. She worked as a marine researcher and data analyst in the Florida Keys before studying at Stanford University on a Wallace Stegner Creative Writing Fellowship. She's published the novels *State of Grace, The Changeling,* and *Escapes,* and the short story collections *Taking Care* and *Breaking & Entering.* She is married and the mother of one daughter.

Jerome Wilson was born in 1969 in Memphis, Tennessee. He's currently studying English literature at Memphis State and has worked as a restaurant busboy, a shipping clerk in a potato chip company, and a librarian's assistant. "Paper Garden" is his first published story.

Tobias Wolff was born in Alabama in 1945 and was raised in Concrete, Washington, the location of his memoir *This Boy's Life.* He served as a lieutenant with the U.S. Army in Vietnam, then attended Oxford University, where he earned a First in English literature. After teaching high school in San Francisco, he studied at Stanford University on a Wallace Stegner Creative Writing Fellowship. He is now a professor of English at Syracuse University. His two collections of stories are *In the Garden of the North American Martyrs* and *Back in the World.* His short novel *The Barracks Thief* won the PEN/Faulkner Award and he is the recipient of a Lila Wallace–Reader's Digest Writers' Award. Mr. Wolff is married and the father of three children.

Al Young was born in Ocean Springs, Mississippi, in 1939, the son of a professional musician and autoworker. He studied Spanish at the University of Michigan and was a Wallace Stegner Creative Writing Fellow at Stanford. He's been a jazz and blues singer and musician, an FM station disk jockey, and an instructor and lecturer at numerous universities. His books include the poetry collections *Dancing, The Song Turning Back on Itself, Geography of the Near Past,* and *Heaven: Collected Poems 1956–1990,* as well as the novels *Snakes, Sitting Pretty,* and *Seduction by Light.* He lives in Palo Alto, California.

Grateful acknowledgment is made for permission to reprint the following copyrighted material:

"A Mother's Tale," by James Agee. Reprinted by permission of the James Agee Trust.

"Guy de Maupassant," by Isaac Babel. Reprinted by permission of S. G. Phillips, Inc., from *The Collected Stories of Isaac Babel*, Copyright © 1955 by S. G. Phillips, Inc.

"Sonny's Blues" from *Going to Meet the Man* by James Baldwin. Copyright © 1957 by James Baldwin. Copyright renewed. "Sonny's Blues" was originally published in *Partisan Review*. Reprinted with permission of the James Baldwin Estate.

"The School" from *60 Stories* by Donald Barthelme. Reprinted with the permission of Wylie, Aitken & Stone, Inc.

"The Aleph" by Jorge Luis Borges, translated by Anthony Kerrigan, from *A Personal Anthology*, copyright © 1969 by Grove Press Inc. Used by permission of Grove/Atlantic Inc.

"A Day in the Open" from *The Collected Works of Jane Bowles*. Copyright © 1966 by Jane Bowles. Reprinted by permission of Farrar, Straus & Giroux, Inc. Reprinted in Canada by permission of Peter Owen Publishers.

"A Distant Episode," © 1945, 1946, 1947, 1948, 1949, 1950 by Paul Bowles. From *The Delicate Prey: And Other Stories*. First printed by the Ecco Press in 1972. Reprinted with permission.

"The Star Café," reprinted with the permission of Charles Scribner's Sons, an imprint of Macmillan Publishing Company, from *The Star Café* by Mary Caponegro. Copyright © 1990 by Mary Caponegro.

"Reflections" from *Fireworks* by Angela Carter. Copyright © 1974 by Angela Carter. Reprinted by permission of HarperCollins Publishers, Inc. Reprinted in Canada by permission of Rogers, Coleridge & White Ltd.

"Cathedral" from *Cathedral* by Raymond Carver. Copyright © 1981 by Raymond Carver. Reprinted by permission of Alfred A. Knopf, Inc.

"Goodbye, My Brother" from *The Stories of John Cheever* by John Cheever. Copyright 1951 by John Cheever. Reprinted by permission of Alfred A. Knopf, Inc.

"Pie Dance" from *Rough Translations* by Molly Giles. Copyright © 1985 by Molly Giles. Reprinted by permission of the publisher, the University of Georgia Press, Athens, Georgia.

"Greatness Strikes Where It Pleases," by Lars Gustafsson: *Stories of Happy People*. Copyright © 1981 by Lars Gustafsson. Reprinted by permission of New Directions Publishing Corp.

"The Interview," by Ruth Prawer Jhabvala. Originally appeared in *The New Yorker*. Copyright © 1957, 1985 Ruth Prawer Jhabvala. Reprinted by permission of Harriet Wasserman Literary Agency, Inc., as agents for the author.

"In the Penal Colony" from *Franz Kafka: Complete Stories* by Franz Kafka, ed. N. Glatzer. Copyright © 1946, 1947, 1948, 1949, 1954, 1958, 1971 by Schocken Books, Inc. Reprinted by permission of Schocken Books, published by Pantheon Books, a Division of Random House, Inc.

"Girl" from *At the Bottom of the River* by Jamaica Kincaid. Copyright © 1978, 1983 by Jamaica Kincaid. Reprinted by permission of Farrar, Straus & Giroux, Inc.

Elizabeth Bishop's translation of "The Smallest Woman in the World" by Clarice

Lispector first appeared in *The Kenyon Review*, Summer 1964, OS Volume XXVI, Number 3. Copyright 1964 by Kenyon College. Translation copyright © 1964 by Elizabeth Bishop. Reprinted by permission of Farrar, Straus & Giroux, Inc. The story first appeared in book form in Clarice Lispector's collection *Laços de Família*, copyright © 1960, which was published in the translation by Giovanni Pontiero under the title *Family Ties*, copyright © 1970, by the University of Texas Press.

"The Daughters of the Late Colonel" from *The Short Stories of Katherine Mansfield* by Katherine Mansfield. Copyright 1922 by Alfred A. Knopf, Inc., and renewed 1950 by John Middleton Murry. Reprinted by permission of the publisher.

"Labor Day Dinner" from *The Moons of Jupiter and Other Stories* by Alice Munro. Copyright © 1982 by Alice Munro. Reprinted by permission of Alfred A. Knopf, Inc. Reprinted in Canada by permission of Macmillan Canada.

"Spring in Fialta" from *Nabokov's Dozen* by Vladimir Nabokov. Copyright © 1958 by Vladimir Nabokov. Reprinted by permission of Vintage Books, a Division of Random House, Inc.

"The Things They Carried" from *The Things They Carried* by Tim O'Brien. Copyright © 1990 by Tim O'Brien. Reprinted by permission of Houghton Mifflin Co./Seymour Lawrence. All rights reserved.

"A Good Man Is Hard to Find" from *A Good Man Is Hard to Find and Other Stories*, copyright 1953 by Flannery O'Connor and renewed 1981 by Regina O'Connor, reprinted by permission of Harcourt Brace and Company.

"I Stand Here Ironing" from *Tell Me a Riddle* by Tillie Olsen. Copyright © 1956, 1957, 1960, 1961 by Tillie Olsen. Used by permission of Delacorte Press/Seymour Lawrence, a division of Bantam Doubleday Dell Publishing Group, Inc.

"Wants" from *Enormous Changes at the Last Minute* by Grace Paley. Copyright © 1974 by Grace Paley. Reprinted by permission of Farrar, Straus & Giroux, Inc.

"In Dreams Begin Responsibilities," Delmore Schwartz: *In Dreams Begin Responsibilities.* Copyright © 1978 by New Directions Publishing Corporation. Reprinted by permission of New Directions Publishing Corp.

"The Man to Send Rain Clouds" by Leslie Marmon Silko. Reprinted by permission of the author.

"Helping," by Robert Stone. Copyright 1987 by Robert Stone. Originally published in *The New Yorker*, 6/8/87. Reprinted by permission of Donadio & Ashworth, Inc.

"Packed Dirt, Churchgoing, a Dying Cat, a Traded Car" from *Pigeon Feathers and Other Stories* by John Updike. Copyright © 1962 by John Updike. Reprinted by permission of Alfred A. Knopf, Inc.

"The Flowers" from *In Love and Trouble: Stories of Black Women*, copyright © 1973 by Alice Walker, reprinted by permission of Harcourt Brace & Company.

"No Place for You, My Love" from *The Bride of the Innisfallen and Other Stories*, copyright 1952 and renewed 1980 by Eudora Welty, reprinted by permission of Harcourt Brace & Company.

(Introduction to Chekhov's "Gooseberries") from *The Eye of the Story: Selected Essays & Reviews* by Eudora Welty. Copyright © 1978 by Eudora Welty. Reprinted by permission of Random House, Inc.

"Paper Garden" by Jerome Wilson. Reprinted by permission of the author.